DATE			

APR   1995

BAKER & TAYLOR

LORDS OF THE SKY

ALSO BY ANGUS WELLS

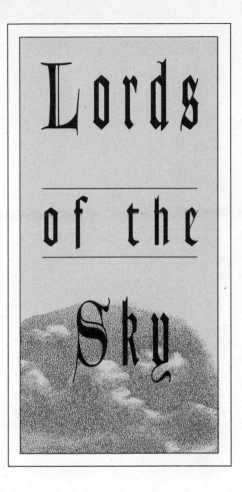

Lords of the Sky

Angus Wells

BANTAM BOOKS
NEW YORK • TORONTO • LONDON • SYDNEY • AUCKLAND

LORDS OF THE SKY

A Bantam Spectra Book / October 1994

SPECTRA and the portrayal of a boxed "s" are trademarks
of Bantam Books, a division of Bantam Doubleday Dell
Publishing Group, Inc.

Book design by Richard Oriolo
Map designed by Laura Hartman Maestro

Library of Congress Cataloging-in-Publication Data

Wells, Angus.
Lords of the sky / by Angus Wells.
p.   cm.
ISBN 0-553-37395-1
I. Title.
PR6073.E386L67   1994
823'.914—dc20   94-15260
CIP

Published simultaneously in the United States and Canada

Bantam Books are published by Bantam Books, a division of Bantam Doubleday Dell Publishing Group, Inc.
Its trademark, consisting of the words "Bantam Books"
and the portrayal of a rooster, is Registered in U.S. Pa-
tent and Trademark Office and in other countries. Marca
Registrada. Bantam Books, 1540 Broadway, New York,
New York 10036.

PRINTED IN THE UNITED STATES OF AMERICA

0 9 8 7 6 5 4 3 2 1

For John Stewart,
with thanks for all the good music.

Mnēmonikos: Greek, from *mnēmōn* mindful, from *mnasthai* to remember.

Mnemonics: noun. 1. the art or practice of improving or of aiding the memory. 2. a system of rules to aid the memory.

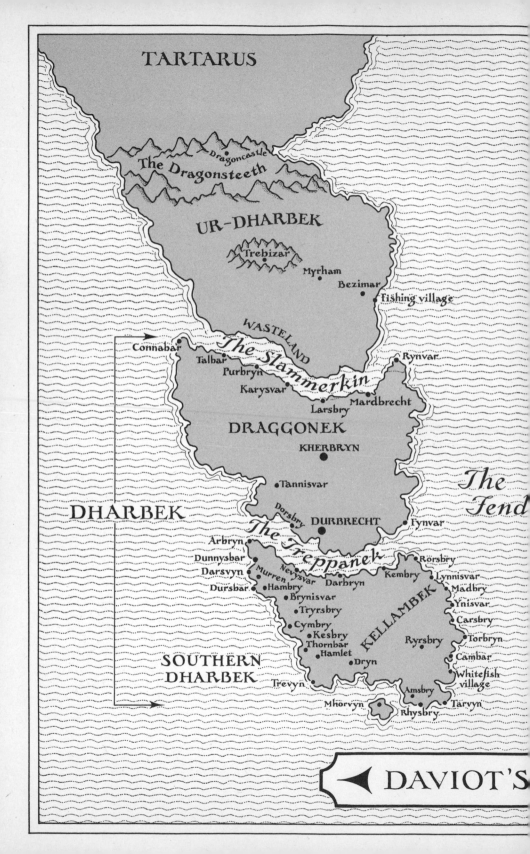

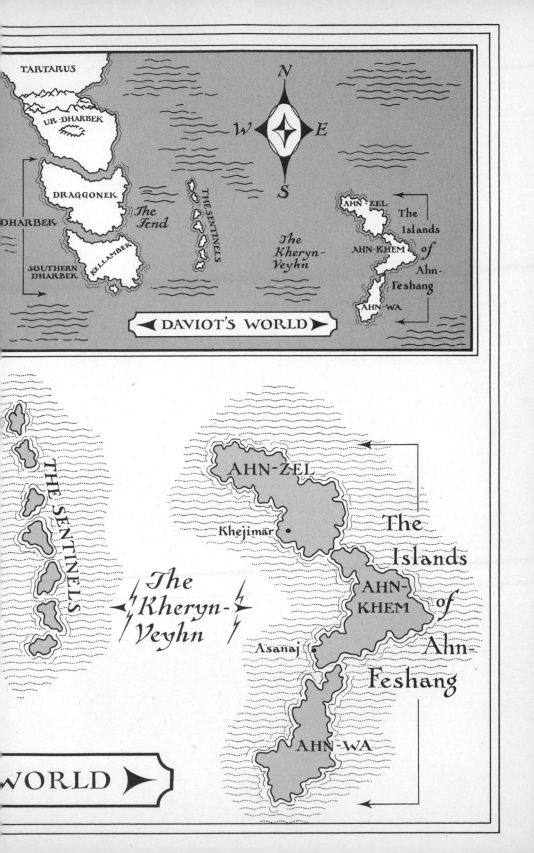

Part I

The Gathering Storm

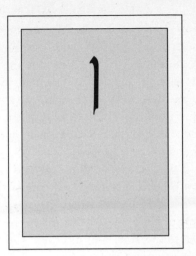

hen I was in my twelfth year, I saw the Sky Lords.

I was born in Kellambek, in a village named Whitefish, for its chief source of food and revenue. It lay some seven leagues south of the river Cambar, on a cove shaded by cliffs where black pines grew and the wind blew warm off the Fend through all the long hot summers. Through childhood's eyes I see the sky forever blue, the sea like rippled silk torn by the fishing boats, the hearthfire in winter merry, the shutters secure against the cold. Through those eyes taught in Durbrecht, I know this was not so: in summer, the air stank of fish and tar and sweat; in winter, draughts blew and the sea roared angry. Both memories are mine, and I think perhaps both are true.

My parents were fisherfolk. My father was named Aditus and owned a boat crewed by himself and two others, one my uncle, Battus, wed to my father's sister, Lyrta; the other a taciturn man named

4 / ANGUS WELLS

Thorus, a widower, who seemed never to smile save when he held a
cup or spoke with me. My mother was named Donia and, like my
father, smiled a great deal, though I think that between the netting
and the gutting of the fish and the tending of we children they had
little enough, in reality, in which to find such good humor. But they
did, and I suppose that is the way of simple folk who accept what is
unquestioningly and lack that spark (or curse?) that looks for change.
I had one brother, Tonium, and one sister, Delia, both younger by a
descending year apiece.

I was a fisher-child. I played on the sand, amongst the beached
boats or amongst the black pines. I hoarded shells and bird's eggs.
When the brille swarmed, I waded in, knee-deep, to haul the nets. I
swung a sling and pulled girls' hair; fought with other boys and listened to the stories of old men. On the cliff above the village I had a
secret camp: a fortress great as the Lord Protector's keep, from which
I and Tellurin and Corum and all the rest defended Whitefish village
against the Kho'rabi. Sometimes I *was* a Kho'rabi knight and with my
bark-peeled blade wrought slaughter on my friends, though I always
liked it better when I had the part of a Dhar warrior—a commur, or a
jennym, even a pyke—for then I felt, with all the intensity of childhood's fierce emotions, that I fought for Kellambek, to hold off those
invaders the Sentinels could not prevent from crossing the waters of
the Fend. Those were carefree days when, in the ignorance of childhood, I knew only that the dawn be sunny and I should go to play
again.

What did I know then of the Comings?

Little enough: to me, the Kho'rabi knights, the kingdom of Ahn-
feshang, they were legends. When I was very young—too young to
laugh at the threat—my mother used to tell me that should I disobey
her, a Kho'rabi knight should come and take my head. I spent some
small time cowering beneath my blanket at that, but as I grew older,
sneered. Kho'rabi knights—what were they to me? Creatures of legend, of no more account than the fabled dragons of the Forgotten
Country, who had gone away before even my grandfather was born.

But then I saw the Sky Lords.

It was the end of summer, when the winds off the Fend shift and
blow westward. The sky was a cloudless cobalt blue, hot and hard, the
sun a sullen eye that challenged observation. The sea was still, unrip-
pled. I was on the sand, passing my father the tools he needed to sew
gashes in his nets. Battus and Thorus worked with him on the skein:
they had decided to forgo the evening tide and spend the dusktime in
repairing.

Thorus was the first to see the skyboat, dropping his needle as he sprang to his feet, shouting. My father and my uncle were no slower upright, the net forgotten on the warm sand. I followed them, staring to where they pointed, not sure what it was they pointed at or what set such fear in their eyes. I knew only that my father, who was afraid of *nothing*, was indeed afraid. I felt the fear, like the waft of sour sweat, or a drunkard's breath. Battus shouted and ran from the beach toward the mantis's cella.

I remember that Thorus said, "They come again," and my father answered, "It is not the time," and then told me to run homeward, to tell my mother that the Sky Lords came, and she would know what to do.

As all the men not at sea gathered, staring skyward, I lingered a moment, wondering what held them so, what set them so rigid, like the old, time-carved statues that guarded the entrance to the cella.

Against the knife-sharp brilliance of the sky, I saw a shape. It seemed in that moment like a maggot, a bloated grub taken up by the hot late-summer wind, a speck against the eye-watering azure, that drifted steadily toward me. I felt my skin grow chill with apprehension.

Then my father, knowing me, shouted again, and I ran to our cottage and yelled at my mother that the Sky Lords came.

I think that then, for the first time, I truly knew what terror they induced.

Tonium and Delia fashioned castles from the dirt of our yard, grubby in a manner I—the older—was too adult to entertain. My mother screamed at them, bringing them tearful to her arms, she so distraught she found only brief, hurried words to calm their wailing as she gathered them up. The bell that hung above the cella began to sound, sonorous in the late-afternoon air, its clanging soon augmented by a great shouting from all the women, and the old men, and the howling of confused and frightened children who, like me, knew only that something unfamiliar occurred to induce fear and near-panic in our parents. My mother snatched Delia's and Tonium's hands in hers, shouted at me to follow, and drew my siblings, trotting, away from the house toward the cella. The mantis stood atop the dome. The sinews in his fat arms stood out like cords from the effort of his bell-ringing, and his plump face, usually set in a smile, was grim, his head craned around to peer at the shape approaching across the sky. All around me I heard the single word *Kho'rabi*, said in tones of awe and terror, but for all the panic, I was fascinated. I watched as the mantis gathered up the skirts of his robe and slid ungainly down the sloping side of the dome. Robus, who owned the only horse in Whitefish village—

a venerable gelding sometimes used to haul stricken boats from the winter surf, but more usually to drag a cart up the coast to Cambar town with catches of fish to sell—waited nervously. He had belted an ancient sword to his waist. All the men, and not a few of the women, carried weapons of one kind or another: fish knives, axes, mattocks. The mantis spoke urgently with Robus, and though I could not hear what was said, I perceived it had a great effect on Robus, for he dragged himself astride the old horse and slapped the gray flanks with his rusty blade, sending the animal into a startled, lumbering trot out of the village in the direction of the Cambar road. Then the mantis shouted that all should follow him and led the way to the cliff path, up through the pines to the fields beyond, where a track wound by dry-stone walls to a wood where caves ran down into the earth.

In the confusion I became separated from my mother, and as I watched the worried faces of those who passed me, I succumbed to childhood's temptation.

I was afraid—how should I not be?—but I was also intrigued, fascinated to know the *why* of it. I felt a stone grind my foot, between my sole and my sandal, and I ducked clear of the throng to dislodge the annoyance. As I unlaced my sandal and shook out the pebble, I saw the last of the villagers go by, five grandfathers in rear guard, clutching old swords and flensing poles. They were so anxious, they failed to spot me where I crouched beside a wall, and in moments a cloud of dust raised by hurried feet hung betwixt me and them. I laced my sandal and, with the unthinking valiance of innocent youth, turned back toward Whitefish village.

I knew my mother would be angry when she found me gone, but I soon enough dismissed that concern and ran back to the cliff path.

I halted amongst the pines, where they edged and then fell down over the slope, looking first at the village and then at the sky. The village was empty; the beach was lined with men. The sky was still that steel-hot blue; the shape of the Sky Lords' boat was larger.

I could discern its outline clearer now: a cylinder of red, the color of blood; the carrier beneath was a shadow, like a remora suckered to a shark's belly, sparkling with glints of silver as the sun struck the blades of the warriors there. I wondered how it had come up so fast. I watched it awhile, my eyes watering in the sun glare, picking out the strange sigils daubed over bearer and basket, fear and fascination mingling in equal measure. I looked back and thought perhaps I should have done better to go after my mother and find the safety of the wood, where the ancient crypts ran down into the earth.

Instead, I ran down to the village, through the emptied houses, to the beach, to my father.

He did not see me at first, for his face was locked on the sky, etched over with shadows of disbelief. He stood with a flensing pole held across his chest, high, the curved blade striking brilliance from the sun. Thorus stood beside him, and in his hand was a sword, not rusted like Robus's old blade but bright with oil, darker along the edges, where the whetstone had shaped cutting grooves. It was a blade such as soldiers carried, and for a moment I stared and lusted after such a weapon.

I suppose I must have made a sound for my father turned and saw me, Thorus with him, though their faces bore very different expressions. My father's was angry; Thorus's amused. I felt a fear greater than anything a Kho'rabi knight might induce at the one; pleasure at the other.

My father said, "What in the God's name are you doing here?"

I would likely have run away then, back through the village and up the cliff path, across the fields to the wood, far more afraid of the look gouged over my father's face than of any Kho'rabi knight. But Thorus said, "Blood runs true, friend," to my father; and to me, "Best find yourself a blade if you stand with us, Daviot."

My father said, "God's name, man, he's only a boy," but I was swelled with pride and honor and found a discarded net hook that I picked up for want of better weapon and strode to stand between them. Thorus laughed and clapped me on the shoulder hard enough that I tottered, and said, "Blood to blood, Aditus."

My father's face remained dark, but then he grunted and nodded and said, "Likely they'll pass over. So, you can stay, boy. But on my word, you run for the caves. *Yes?*"

I nodded, without any intention whatsoever of keeping my word: if the enlarging shape of the Sky Lords' boat dropped fylie of the Kho'rabi knights upon us, I planned to stand shoulder-to-shoulder with my fellow warriors. I planned to die gloriously in defense of Whitefish village, in defense of Kellambek.

I watched the ship grow larger, my hands tight on my hook. It came up faster than any natural wind might propel it. It seemed like a great, bloody wound on the face of the sky. I saw the glimmer of the magic that drove it, trailing back from the pointed tail like the shifting translucence of witchfire's glow. It seemed to move the faster for its proximity with our coastline, as though propulsion were augmented with attraction, speeding as it drew nearer. The sea gulls that were a constant punctuation of the sky fled before it, and I suddenly realized that the cats that prowled the shoreline were also gone; likewise the handful of dogs our village boasted. That seemed very strange to me —the absence of such familiar things—and I glanced around, my valor threatened. I saw that my father's knuckles bulged white from his tanned hands, and that Thorus's lips were spread back from clenched teeth in a kind of snarl. I realized then that a terrible silence had fallen, as if this unexpected Coming drove stillness before it, or the presence of the Sky Lords absorbed sound. No one moved; there was no shuffling of feet on sand; even the waves that lapped the beach went unheard. I stared in shared dread, feeling the shadow of the boat fall over me, which it should not have done, for the sun westered and that shadow should not—nor could—have reached us yet. I trembled, for all my youthful bravery, in its cold. It felt as though a hand reached out from the grave to pluck at my heart, at my courage. I shivered and saw that my father did the same, though he sought to hide it from me, looking down at me and smiling. I thought his smile was like the grin I had seen on the faces of drowned men.

Then the great shape was directly above us, and I thought that this must be how a lamb feels, when it *feels* the shadow of an eagle darken its vision. I craned my head back, shivering, seeing that the airboat hung high above us, and where it rode the sky, strange prancing shapes showed through the blue, as if elementals sported there.

I looked to my father and saw his face grim; at Thorus, who raised his sword above his head like a talisman. I looked up, nearly overbalancing, as the Sky Lords' ship floated, serene and ghastly, over my home.

Some arrows fell, unflighted by the height, and fired, I think, in amusement; a fisherman named Vadim even caught one in his hand, that feat producing a shout of encouragement from all the rest.

And then the ship was gone, passed beyond the cliff and out of sight.

It was both disappointment and relief to me: I had anticipated glorious battle; I was also glad that horrible weight had passed. I enjoyed the way my father held my one shoulder, Thorus my other, and both told me I had played my part, even as men went running to the cliff to follow the ship's passage.

I went running with them, still clutching my hook, for they all still held their weapons. I was suddenly possessed of a dreadful fear that the ship had gone past the village to land in the fields—the wood —beyond and disgorge the Kho'rabi knights to massacre my mother and my siblings and all the others hiding in the caves. But Thorus hauled me back and shouted at my father that the wind was wrong, and whatever magic the sorcerers of Ahn-feshang commanded, it was not enough to ground the boat to disembark the fylie.

Even so, I was not satisfied, nor my father, until we topped the path and saw the ship drifting on over the wood, disappearing into the haze of the afternoon sun, like blood drying on a wound.

Several of the younger fishermen ran to the wood then, to tell the mantis and his charges that the danger was gone by. They emerged, laughing and praising the God for his mercy. Then I basked in the admiring gaze of my friends, for they had all obeyed and hidden, and I alone, of all the children in the village, had remained. I swung my hook in vivid demonstration of how I should have fought, coming close to harming more than one innocent onlooker until my father took the tool from me, his face stern.

My mother's, when she found me, was haggard and she raised a hand to strike me, but my father halted her, speaking softly, and she sighed, shaking her head, her expression one I did not then understand. Tonium and Delia stared at me in awe.

We went back to the village, and Thorym, who owned what passed for the village tavern, announced that he would broach a keg in celebration of deliverance, promising a mug to every man who had stood his ground on the beach. My mother returned to our cottage, like all the other women, to prepare the evening meal, for by now the day grew old and the sun stood close to setting, but I succeeded in avoiding her and insinuated myself amongst the men. After all, had I not stood with them?

Thorym paused when he saw me in his taproom, unsure—it was not our custom to allow children ale until they reached their fourteenth year and were deemed young men. But Thorus shouted that I was a warrior born and had sided him and so earned my sup. The rest shouted laughter at that, and my father first frowned and then smiled, torn between disapproval and pride, but then he said I might take a sip or two, for it was true that I had stood my place like a man.

I had never held a mug of ale before, and it was all I could do to stretch my hands around the cup and lift it to my mouth, but I was aware that all there watched me and I raised the mug and drank deep. And immediately choked, spitting out the sour-tasting brew and spilling half the cup over my feet, blushing furiously.

My father took it from me, glancing angrily at Thorus as he urged me to try again, and suggested that I go make peace with my mother. My reluctance must have shown, for he allowed me one more sip before finally retrieving the mug and sending me from the tavern. I went outside, but no farther, skirting around the wall to where a window allowed me to spy on the men and listen to their conversation. It told me little enough, being mostly concerned with the unlikely Coming of the airboat, which they agreed was out of time, its appearance unseasonal. I gathered, from what they said, that none had anticipated sighting the Sky Lords for years yet, when the Worldwinds were due once more to shift. Not even the mantis could offer explanation, save that the sorcerers of Ahn-feshang had developed new usage of their occult powers.

That set them all to arguing and muttering, some perplexed, some fearful; some to suggesting that this was but a single event, a foray attempted and failed, that the boat had somehow succeeded in defeating the winds and the emanations of the Sentinels; some to forecasting a strengthening of Ahn-feshang's magic and a new Coming.

Then, though, I had more immediate concerns—to wit, my mother, who sent Tonium looking for me with word that did I fail to appear at home on the instant, I might anticipate punishment of a magnitude that should render a Kho'rabi attack the merest prickling.

I hurried back, ignoring my smug and envious brother, and found myself—the grossest ignominy, I thought, given my new-proven valor—ordered to scrub cooking pots before I was allowed to eat. She did not cuff me, which at the time I failed to realize was token of her thanks for my survival, but neither would she speak to me; nor much to my father when he returned, holding him in some measure responsible for my disobedience.

I ate and sulked my way to an early bed, only a little mollified by the open admiration of Delia who, as we lay on our pallets, insisted on a whispered retelling of all that had happened. I admit to embroidering the tale: for my little sister's ears the Kho'rabi arrows fell in swarms about me, their boat so close above, I saw the grimacing faces of the fanatic death-warriors, felt (this not entirely untrue) the horrible strength of their magical sigils, the malign power of the sorcerer-steersmen.

In time, even my adoring sister was sated with the tale, and her snores joined those of my brother. I lay longer awake, reliving the day and vowing that when I reached my manhood I should quit Whitefish village to be a soldier in Cambar Keep and defend Kellambek against our ancient enemies.

The next dawn, I saw my first real soldiers.

Robus, mounted on his old slow horse, had reached the aeldor's holding during the night. The watchmen had brought him before the lord, who had immediately ordered three squadrons to patrol the coast road, one to ride instanter for Whitefish village.

They arrived a few hours after sun's rise, dirty, tired, and irritable. To me, then, they looked splendid. They wore shirts of leather and mail, draped across with Cambar's plaid, cinched in with wide belts from which hung sheathed swords and long-hafted axes, and every one carried a lance from which the colors of Kellambek fluttered in the morning breeze; round shields hung from their saddles. There was a commur-mage with them, clad all in black sewn with the silver markings of her station, a short-sword on her hip. Her hair was swept back in a tail, like our mantis's, but was bound with a silver fillet, and unlike her men, she seemed untired. She raised a hand as the squadron reached the village square, halting the horsemen, waiting as the mantis approached and made obeisance, gesturing him up with a splendid languid hand.

I and all the children—and most of our parents, no less impressed—gathered about to watch.

The soldiers climbed down from their horses, and I smelled the sweat that bled from their leather tunics as they waited on the mage. She, too, dismounted, conferring with the mantis, and then followed our plump and friendly priest to the cella, calling back over her shoulder that the men with her might find breakfast where they could, and ale if they so desired, for it seemed the danger was gone.

I felt a measure of disappointment at that: I had become, after all, a warrior, and was reluctant to find my new-won status so quickly lost. I compensated by taking the bridle of a horse and leading the animal to where Robus kept his fodder. I had never seen so large an animal before, save the sharks that sometimes followed our boat, and I was—I admit—more than a little frightened by the way it tossed its head and stamped its feet and snorted. The man who rode it chuckled and spoke to it and told me to hold it firm; and then he set a hand on my shoulder, as Thorus had done, and I straightened my back and reminded myself I was a man and brought it to Robus's little barn, where it became docile as his old nag when I fed it oats and hay and filled the water trough.

The soldier grinned at that and checked the beast for himself, taking off the high-cantled cavalry saddle, resting his shield and lance against the wall of the pen. I touched the metaled face of the shield with reverent fingers and studied his sword and axe. He turned to me and asked where he might find food and ale, and I told him, "Thorym's tavern," and asked, "Shall you fight the Kho'rabi?"

He said, "I think they're likely gone, praise the God," and I wondered why a soldier would be thankful his enemy was not there.

I brought him to the tavern and fetched him a pot of ale as his fellows gathered, and Thorym, delighted at the prospect of such profit, set fish to grilling and bread to toasting. His name was Andyrt, and as luck would have it, he was jennym to the commur-mage, a life-sworn member of the warband and, I realized, fond of children. He let me crouch by his side and even passed me his helm to hold, bidding the rest be silent when they looked at me askance and wondered what a child did there, amongst men.

I bristled at that and told them I had stood upon the sand with hook in hand, ready to fight, as the Sky Lords passed over. Some laughed then, and some called me liar, but Andyrt bade them silent and said that he believed me, and that his belief was theirs, else they chose to challenge him. None did, and I saw that they feared him somewhat, or respected him, and I studied him anew.

He was, I surmised, of around my father's age (though any man, then, of more than twenty years was old to me) and traces of gray were spun into his brown hair. His face was paler than a fisherman's, but still quite dark, except across his forehead, where his helm sat. A thin cut bisected his left cheek, and several of his teeth were missing, though the rest were white—the mark of a sound lord's man's diet— and his eyes were a light blue, webbed round with tiny wrinkles. His hands were brown and callused in a manner different from a fisherman's, marked by reins and sword's hilt and lance. To me, he was exotic; glamorous and admirable.

I ventured to pluck at his sleeve and ask him what it took to be a warrior and find a place in the warband.

"Well," he said, and chuckled, "first you must be strong enough to wield a blade and skilled enough in its wielding. Save you prefer to slog out your life as a pyke, you must ride a horse."

At that, several of his companions laughed and raised their buttocks from Thorym's crude chairs, moaning and rubbing themselves as if in pain.

"Often for long leagues," said Andyrt, himself chuckling. "You must be ready to spend long hours bored, and more drinking. To hold your drink. And you must be ready to kill men; and to be yourself killed."

"I am," I said, thinking of the beach and the skyboat; and Andyrt said, "It is not so easy to put a blade into a man. Harder still to take his in you."

"I'd kill Kho'rabi," I told him firmly. "I'd give my life to defend Kellambek."

He touched my cheek then, gently, as sometimes my father did, and said, "That's an easy thing to say, boy. The doing of it is far harder. Better you pray our God grants strength to the Sentinels, and there's no Coming in your lifetime."

"I'd slay them," I answered defiantly, thinking I was patronized. "How dare they come against Kellambek?"

"Readily enough," he told me, "for they lay claim to this land."

"You fight them," I said. "You're a warrior."

He nodded at that. A shadow passed across his face, like the cold penumbra of the Sky Lords' boat. He said, "I'm life-sworn, boy; I know no other way."

I opened my mouth to question him further, to argue, but just then the commur-mage entered the tavern, our mantis on her heels like a plump and fussing hen, and a silence fell.

Andyrt began to rise, sinking back on the sorcerer's gesture. The black-clad woman approached our table, and two of the warband sprang to their feet, relinquishing their places. I found myself crouched between Andyrt and the commur-mage, who asked mildly, "Who's this?"

Andyrt said, grinning, "A young warrior, by all accounts. He stood firm when the skyboat came."

The mantis said, "His name is Daviot, elder son of Aditus and Donia. I understand he did, indeed, run back to join his father on the beach."

The commur-mage raised blue-black brows at that, and her fine lips curved in a smile. I stood upright, shoulders squared, and looked her in the eye. Had I not, after all, proved myself? Was I not, after all, intent on becoming a warrior?

"So," she said, her voice soft and not at all mocking, "Whitefish village breeds its share of men."

That was fine as Thorus's praise; as good as my father's hand on my shoulder. I nodded modestly. The commur-mage continued to study me, not even turning when Thorym passed her a mug of ale and set a fresh plate of fried fish and bread before her, bowing and ducking. She waved regal thanks and Thorym withdrew; her eyes did not leave my face, as if she saw there things I did not know about myself.

"You stood upon the beach?" she said, her voice gentle, speculative as her gaze. "Were you not afraid?"

I began to shake my head, but there was a power in her eyes that compelled truth, that brought back memory. I set Andyrt's helm carefully down on the cleanest patch of dirt between the chairs and nodded.

"Tell me," she said.

I looked awhile at her face. It was dark as Andyrt's, which is to say lighter than any in the village, but unmarked by scars. I thought her beautiful; nor was she very old. Her eyes were green, and as I looked into them, they seemed to obscure the men around her, to send the confines of the tavern into shadow, to absorb the morning light. It was like staring into the sun at its rising, or its setting, when only that utter brilliant absorption—green now, not gold or red—fills up all the world.

I told her everything, and when I was done, she nodded and said, "You saw that the cats and dogs—the gulls, even—were gone?"

"Then," I told her, and frowned as an unrecognized memory came back. "But this morning the dogs were awake again, and the cats were on the beach. And the gulls"—I pointed seaward, at the shapes wheeling and squalling against the new-formed blue—"they're back."

"Think you they fled the Coming?" she asked.

"They were not there then," I said. "The sky was empty, save for the boat. I think they must have."

"Why?" she asked me, and I said, "I suppose they were frightened. Or they felt the power of the Sky Lords. But they *were* gone, then."

She sipped a mouthful of ale, chewed a mouthful of fish and bread, still staring at me. I watched her face, wondering what she made of me, what she wanted of me. I felt I was tested and judged. I tried to find Andyrt's eyes, but could not; it was as though the mage's compelling gaze sunk fishhooks in my mind, in my attention, locking me to her as soundly as the lures of the surf-trollers locked the autumnal grylle to their barbed baits.

"Your father," she said, surprising me. "What did he hold?"

"A flensing pole," I answered. "Thorus held a sword. I told you that."

She nodded, wiped her mouth, and asked, "Who caught the arrow?"

"Vadim," I said. "But it was an easy catch: it was fired from so high."

She turned then to the mantis, and my attention was unlocked as if I were a fish burst free of the hook. I looked to Andyrt, who smiled reassuringly and shrugged, motioning for me to be silent and wait. I did, nervous and impatient. The commur-mage said to the mantis, "He's talents, think you?"

The mantis favored me with a look I could not interpret and ducked his head. "He's a memory," he agreed—though then I was unaware of what exactly he meant—and added, "Of all my pupils he's the best-schooled in the liturgics: he can repeat them back, word for word."

"As he did this Coming," said the commur-mage, and turned to me again.

"You brought Andyrt's horse to stable, no? Tell me about his horse and his kit."

"It was brown," I said, confused. "A light brown with golden hair in its mane and tail. Its hooves were black, but the right foreleg was patched with white, and the hoof there was shaded pale. The saddle was dark with sweat and the bucket where the lance rests was stitched with black. The stirrups were leather, with dull metal inside. There were two bags behind the saddle, brown, with golden buckles. When he took it off, the horse's hide was pale and sweaty. It was glad to be rid of the weight. It was a gelding, and it snorted when he took off the bridle, and flicked its tail as it began to eat the oats I brought it."

The commur-mage clapped a hand across my eyes then, the other behind my head, so that I could not move, startling me, and said, "What weapons does Andyrt carry?"

"A lance," I told her, for all I was suddenly terrified. "That he left in Robus's stable. Twice a man's height, of black wood, with a long, soft-curved blade. Not like a fishing hook. Also, a sword, an axe, and a small knife."

"Where, exactly, on his body?" asked the mage.

Her hands were still about my face, blinding me; frightening me, for all they rested gentle there. I said: "His sword is sheathed on his left side, from a wide, brown belt of metal-studded leather with a big, gold buckle that is a little tarnished. The axe is hung to his right, in a bucket of plain leather. The knife is in the small of his back."

The hands went away from my face and I saw the commur-mage smiling, Andyrt grinning approvingly. The mantis looked nervous. The others seated around the table seemed wonderstruck; I wondered why, for it seemed entirely natural to me to recall such simple things in their entirety.

"He's the knack, I think," the commur-mage said. "Not my talent, but that of memory."

And the mantis nodded. "I'd wondered. I'd thought of sending word to Cambar."

"You should have," said the commur-mage.

I preened, aware that I was somehow special, that I had passed a test of some kind.

"Are his parents agreeable, he should go to Durbrecht," the commur-mage said. "This one is a natural."

A natural *what*, I did not know, nor what or where Durbrecht was. I frowned and said, "I'd be a soldier."

"There are other callings," said the commur-mage, and smiled a small apology to Andyrt. "Some higher than the warband."

"Like yours?" I asked, emboldened by her friendly manner. "Do I have magic in me, then?"

She chuckled at that, though not in an unkind way, and shook her head. "Not mine," she advised me. "And I am only a lowly commur-mage, who rides on my lord's word. No, Daviot, you've not my kind of magic in you; you've the magic of your memory."

I frowned anew at that: what magic was there in memory? I remembered things—was that unusual? I always had. Everyone in Whitefish village knew that. Folk came to me asking dates, confirmation of things said, and I told them: it was entirely natural to me, and not at all magical.

"He's but twelve years old," I heard the mantis say, and saw the commur-mage nod, and heard her answer, "Then on his manhood. I'd speak with his parents now, however."

The mantis rose, like a plump soldier attending an order, and went bustling from the tavern. I shifted awhile from foot to foot, more than a little disconcerted, and finally asked, "What's Durbrecht?"

"A place," the commur-mage said. "A city and a college, the two the same. Do you know what a Storyman is?"

"Yes," I told her, and could not resist demonstrating my powers of recall, boasting. "One came to the village a year ago. He was old— his hair was white and he wore a beard—he rode a mule. He told stories of Gahan's coronation, and of the Comings. His name was"—I paused an instant, the old man's face vivid in the eye of my mind; I smelled again the garlic that edged his breath, and the faint odor of sweat that soured his grubby white shirt—"Edran. He stayed here only two days, with the widow Rya, then went on south."

The commur-mage ducked her head solemnly, her face grave now, and said, "Edran learned to use his art in Durbrecht. He memorized the old tales there, under the Mnemonikos."

"Nuh . . . moni . . . kos?" I struggled to fit my tongue around the unfamiliar word.

"The Mnemonikos." The commur-mage nodded. "The Rememberers; those who keep all our history in their heads. Without them, our past should be forgotten; without them, we should have no history."

"Is that important?" I wondered, sensing that my soldierly ambitions were somehow, subtly, defeated.

"If we cannot remember the past," the commur-mage said, "then we must forever repeat our mistakes. If we forget what we were, and what we have done, then we go blind into our future."

I thought awhile on that, scarcely aware that she spoke to me as to a man, struggling as hard with the concept as I had struggled to pronounce the word *Mnemonikos*. At last I nodded with all the gravity of my single decade and said, "Yes, I think I see it. If my grandfather's father had not told him about the tides and the seasons of the fish, then he could not have told my father, and then he should have needed to learn all that for himself."

"And if *he* did not remember, then he could not pass on that knowledge to you," said the commur-mage.

"No," I allowed, "but I want to be a soldier."

"But," said the commur-mage, gently, "you see the importance of remembering."

I agreed a trifle reluctantly, for I felt that she steered our conversation toward a harbor that should render me swordless, bereft of my recently found ambition. I looked to Andyrt for support, but his scarred face was bland and he hid it behind his cup.

"The Mnemonikos hold all our history in their heads," the commur-mage said softly. "All the tales of the Comings; all the tales of the land. They know of the Kho'rabi; of the Sky Lords and the Dragonmasters: all of it. Without them, we should have no past. The swords they bear never rust or break or blunt—"

"They bear swords?" I interrupted eagerly, finding these mysterious Rememberers suddenly more interesting. "They're warriors, then?"

The commur-mage smiled and chuckled and shook her head. She said, "Not swords as you mean, Daviot, though some carry arms to protect themselves, and all are versed in the martial arts. I mean the blade that finds its scabbard here"—she tapped her forehead—"in the mind. And that—my word on it!—is the sharpest blade of all. Think you this"—she tapped the short-sword on her hip now—"is a greater weapon than what I wear here?" She tapped her head again. "No! The blade is for carving flesh, when needs must. The knowledge here" —again she touched her skull—"is what can defeat the magic of the Sky Lords. How say you, Andyrt?"

The jennym appeared no less surprised than I by this abrupt question. He set down his mug, brows lifted, and wiped a moustache of foam from his mouth.

"I'll face a Kho'rabi knight," he said, "and trade him blow for blow. I'd not assume to trust steel against their wizards, though— that's a fight for your kind, Rekyn: magic against magic."

It was the first time I had heard the commur-mage referred to by name. I watched her nod and smile and heard her say, "Aye, to each his own talent. Do you understand, Daviot? When warrior faces warrior, with blade or lance or bow or axe, I'd wager my money on Andyrt. But a sorcerer of Ahn-feshang could slay Andyrt with a spell."

"But I've no magic," I protested. "But I'm strong enough, and when I attain my manhood, I want to be a warrior."

"You've the strength of memory," Rekyn said. "All I've heard from you this day tells me that—and that's a terrible strength, my friend. It's the strength of things past, recalled; it's the strength of time, of history. It's the strength of *knowing*, of knowledge. It's the strength that binds the land, the people. Listen to me! In four years you become a man, and when you do, I'd ask that you go to Durbrecht and hone that blade you carry in your head."

So intense was her voice, her expression—though she used no magic on me then—that I heard proud clarions, a summons to battle; and still confusion.

"Is Durbrecht far?" I asked.

"Leagues distant," she answered. "On the north shore of the Treppanek, where Kellambek and Draggonek divide. You should have to quit this village, your parents."

"How should I live?" I asked. I was a fisherman's child: I had acquired a measure of practicality.

And she laughed and said, "Be you accepted by the college, all will be paid for you. You'd have board and lodging, and a stipend for pleasure while you learn."

A stipend for pleasure—that had a distinct appeal.

There was little real coin in Whitefish village, our transactions being mostly by barter, and the only coin I had ever held was an ancient penny piece I had found on the beach, worn so smooth by time and wave that the face of the Lord Protector whose image marked it was blunted, indiscernible, which I had dutifully given to my father. The thought of a *stipend*, of coin of my own, to spend as I pleased, was mightily attractive. Nonetheless, I was not entirely convinced: it seemed too easy. That I should be paid to learn? In Whitefish village we learned to survive. To know the tides and the seasons of the fish, to caulk a boat, to ride the storms, to bait a hook and cast a net; for that learning, the payment was food in our bellies and blankets on our beds. We expected no more.

"But how," I wondered, "should I earn all that?"

"By learning to use that memory of yours," she said, solemnly and urgently, "and by learning our history."

"Not work?" I asked, not quite understanding.

"Only at learning," she replied.

I pondered awhile, more than a little confused. I looked to where

Andyrt's helm lay, observing the dented steel, the sweaty stains on the leather straps, the sheen of oil that overlay the beginnings of rust, pitting the metal like the marks I saw on the cheeks of boys—men!— older than me. I looked at the jennym's sword hilt, leather-wrapped and indented with the familiar pressure of his fingers. I looked at his face and found no answer there. I said, "And I'd learn the martial arts, too?"

Rekyn nodded: "You'd learn to survive."

"Is Durbrecht very big?" I asked, and she answered, "Bigger than Cambar."

"Have you been there?" I demanded.

"I was trained there," she said. "I was sent by my village mantis when I came of age. There is a Sorcerous College there, too, besides that of the Mnemonikos. I learned to use my talent there, and then was sent to Cambar."

I scuffed my feet awhile in the dirt of Thorym's tavern, aware that I contemplated my future. Then I looked her in the eye again and asked, "If I do not like it, may I come back?"

"If you do not like it," she said, "or they do not like you, then you come back. In the first year they test you, and then—be you unfit, or they for you—you come back to Whitefish village."

"Or to Cambar Keep," said Andyrt. "To be a soldier, if you still so wish."

That seemed to me a reasonable enough compromise. What was a year? A spring, a summer, an autumn, and a winter: not much time, then. But sufficient that I might see something of the world beyond Whitefish village. It seemed an opportunity no boy could, in his right mind, refuse.

"Yes," I said, and added after a moment's thought, "do my parents agree."

"We'll ask them," said Rekyn.

I followed her gaze and saw my mother and my father coming with the mantis toward the tavern. They both seemed disturbed, though in different ways. My mother's face was set in a pattern I recognized from those times I, or my siblings, had been hurt more seriously than was our habit; my father's was stern and confused at the same time. I had seen that look when he balanced the chance of a good catch against the advent of an approaching storm.

I waited, all my pride dissolved.

My mother curtsied and my father bent his knee, which added to my confusion, for such formality was unlike them and told me that they regarded this woman to whom I spoke as an equal as their superior. I felt embarrassed for them and, by extension, for myself.

But Rekyn smiled and rose, greeting them courteously as if they were some lord and lady come avisiting the keep, and motioned soldiers away to clear places, holding back a chair for my mother and thanking them both for granting her their valuable time. I shuffled my feet, studying the dirt, and only when I looked up did I see that all the soldiers save Andyrt were gone, and only Rekyn and the mantis and my parents remained. I paced a sideways step closer to my father, who set a hand on my shoulder and said, "I thought to find you at the boat. We've a net to mend, remember."

I mumbled an apology, immensely grateful for Rekyn's intervention: she said, "The blame is mine, friend Aditus. I kept him here to speak of his talent."

"My lady?" my father said, and I saw that he held the commurmage in some awe.

Rekyn said, "Not *lady*, friend. That title's for greater than I. I am called Rekyn. I'd speak with you of your son's talent, of his future. But first, ale?"

My parents exchanged glances, awkward and embarrassed as I; they looked to the mantis for guidance, and he beamed and ducked his head, impressing chins one upon the other. Rekyn beckoned Thorym —himself awed by such attention—over to our table and asked that mugs be brought.

"Your son has a great talent," she said when they were served and Thorym gone, though not far enough he could not overhear such tasty gossip, "and I'd speak with you of that."

I thought then that my mother looked frightened. My father's face stayed stolid. I had seen it thus when he rode a boat into the teeth of the wind and the waves howled up over the gunwales: it frightened me, so that I heard little of the conversation that followed.

I know only that, at its ending, Rekyn and my parents were friends, and that it was agreed that on my attaining manhood I should be allowed to decide my own future: to go to Durbrecht, or seek a place in the Cambar warband, or remain in Whitefish village.

That agreement was sealed with more ale than either of my parents was accustomed to drink at that early hour, and neither was entirely steady on their feet as they quit the tavern. I rose from where I had squatted, idly stroking the dust from Andyrt's helmet, to join them—this I remember clearly—and my father looked a question at my mother, who nodded, and then my father said to me, "I go to mend the net. Do you come with me, or remain here with Rekyn?"

I think that sometimes there comes a precise moment, a fragment of time, crystallized, trapped forever in the alembic of our internal eye, that tells us all when and where we chose our path through life.

Mine was then: I said, "I'll remain."

That was the moment, the instant, that I opted to be a Rememberer.

I was a celebrity for a few short weeks—the lad who had stood with the men on the beach when the Sky Lords came, the lad singled out by the commur-mage. But the fish still swam in the Fend, and the boats still put out, and I still had duties to attend, favored or not. Fisherfolk are above all practical, and until I quit the village for greater things I remained a fisherman's son.

Then, for a while, my new-won prominence grew irksome. The mantis found a fresh interest in me, perceiving it to his advantage I suspect that he school me above and beyond my fellows. Consequently I found myself expected to undertake additional lessons that, given those duties I owed my parents, left me little enough time to myself. I am grateful to him now, but then, during those four years, I came close to hating him at times. What boy would not, when his friends went to gaming in the sunshine whilst he must sit indoors at his lessons, prisoner of his own elevation? I sulked, I think, but the mantis pressed on, blithely oblivious of the imaginative fates I dreamed of inflicting on him, and in time I found myself enjoying his pedagogy. History, I discovered, was fascinating, for all the mantis's grasp of Dharbek's past was at best tenuous, circumscribed by his religious training. Even so, what he told me through those long hours put flesh on the bones of legend so that by the time I left for Cambar Keep, I knew more of this land of ours than any other child in the village.

He spoke to me primarily of the Dhar, hardly at all of the Ahn, who were, in his narrow opinion, no more than demons, banished by the will of the God to Ahn-feshang, from whence they sought to return to spread their evil. Having then no other knowledge with which to balance this hereditary view, I accepted it: I had, after all, spent my life hearing tales of the Sky Lords' atrocities. But the stories of the Dhar—oh, those thrilled me, and I lapped them up, binding them to me with the ropes of my memory.

Of the Dawntime he spoke, when the Wanderer Kings came down out of the unknown north into the Forgotten Country and there encountered the dragons. He told me of the Dragonmasters and their magic that bent the ferocious flying creatures to their will. The which, he carefully explained, was the first gift of the God. The second was that magic that enabled the creation of the Changed, and when I questioned—innocently enough—the morality of such action, the mantis bade me still my heretical tongue on fear of losing that favor I had won whilst earning in its place a cuffing. I obeyed, for I knew I might push only so far and no farther, and besides there was sufficient else to occupy me without risking a beating on behalf of creatures I had never seen and knew of only as vague legends. So I held my tongue and listened to the old tales of the crossing of the Slammerkin and the conquest of Draggonek, where Emeric, first of the Lords Protector, built Kherbryn; the bridging of the Treppanek, when the people entered Kellambek and met the Ahn; the exodus of those folk to their unknown land; of great Tuwyan, who ordered the construction of Durbrecht; and Canovar, who founded the Sentinels on the seven islands that ward our eastern shores; of the gift of peace that brought all Dharbek to worship of the God.

This latter, I comprehended, was to the cost of the Ahn, who had, after all, been first come to Kellambek, but as the Dark Folk were enemies of the God and become the Sky Lords, I accepted what the mantis told me quite unthinking, save for one question.

"Why," I asked him one winter's evening as we sat before the fire in his little cottage beside the cella, "does the God allow the Comings? If we Dhar are his chosen people, and the Ahn are his enemies, why does he not destroy them?"

Had I been already precocious, I was worse now, and my question clearly took the good mantis aback. He delivered a sound blow to my head and then murmured a prayer that the God forgive me my ignorant heresy. Then, as I rubbed at my stinging ear and bit back tears, he thought to offer an explanation.

In the Dawntime, he told me—a trifle nervously I thought, as if this were a matter he had rather not discussed—the Dhar had worshipped false gods, the Three Deciders, and for that sin had earned the displeasure of the one true God. Even now, albeit we had come to the true faith, we must suffer for that sin, the memory of the deity being, naturally, prodigious. Until such time as this original sin should be forgiven, we must suffer the depredations of the Sky Lords in penance for our transgression.

That seemed to me harsh. I had not, before that evening, even heard of the Three Deciders—so why should I, or Whitefish village, pay for a sin not of our commitment? I wondered, albeit briefly then, being not much used to wrestling with such theological mysteries, if it had not been better had we Dhar made peace with the Ahn, so that they should never have fled to become our enemies. My ear still burned, however, and I held my tongue. That church of which our village mantis was a lowly representative was a power in the land, an authority unquestioned, versed in the God's mysteries and invested with the temporal interpretation of his will. I elected to accept the ritual explanation.

Before I attained my manhood, I saw the Sky Lords' boats again.

The first was too far out to sea and too far south to present any threat to the village, and after a while it passed out of sight.

The second time I was at sea. It was midsummer, a little after the Sastaine festival, the days long and gentle as the Fend's soft swell. Dusk approached, the sea a match to the sky's transparent blue, glinting bright where the westering sun laid bands of gold across the water. We were bringing in a filled net when Battus loosed his hold, eliciting a curse from my father that became a gasp as he followed my uncle's gaze to where the sky was marred by a distant shape. I recognized it on the instant and saw that it must pass north of our position, save it change direction. Still, it rode very low and I felt a mixture of excitement and dread.

My father said, "In the God's name, are the Sentinels asleep?"

And Thorus replied, "I think perhaps the Sky Lords own new magicks," which set a chill on my spine, for I heard a great doubt in his voice and found myself reminded of the priest's talk of ancient sin.

Then my father said, "Best we bring this net in and turn for home, I think."

We had our catch aboard and the boat turned about before the Sky Lords had advanced more than three fingers' width across the blue. There was no wind to speak of, and so Battus and Thorus manned the oars, my father the tiller, leaving me free to watch. Or act as valiant lookout, I chose to think.

So it was I saw for the first time what the magic of the Sentinels could do.

I saw the darkening sky grow brighter above the closest island. It was akin to the jack-o'-lantern fires that would sometimes dance over the marshier fields above the village, pale and pink as a wound at first, then stronger, like a kindling flame. Then it became a column of searing red that sprang skyward to envelop the airboat, wrapping about the cylinder. For a moment that seemed to me a very long time, it bathed the vessel, then came an eruption of light and I saw the airboat broken like a spine-snapped beast, falling down in a great ball of flame, mundane now, trailers of smoke dragging behind it. There was a sound, as of distant thunder, and the Sky Lords' craft went down to meet the sea. In a little while there was only a single plume of smoke that drifted leisurely shoreward, merging with the sky.

Thorus said, "I believe they are awake," and my father chuckled, nodding, and we turned again for home.

The third airboat I saw was an anticlimax after that.

It was sighted late in the year before I left for Durbrecht, when the season hung undecided between autumn and winter, the winds contrary and the Fend choppy. It was clear from the first that the airboat must pass south of Kellambek's farthest shores, and I wondered to where. Later I questioned the mantis, but he professed ignorance, pointing out to me that argument still continued as to whether the world be flat or round, and if the one, then the Sky Lords must pass over the edge; if the other, then they should likely perish for want of food and water. Either fate suited him.

I was then fifteen, my manhood now in sight, the past three years flown as years do, unnoticed save in their remembrance. I had come to realize the mantis had little more to teach me, that his knowledge was boundaried by his calling, limited by that dogma I yet accepted whilst sensing larger truths beyond its narrow borders. I had learned —courtesy of sore ears and more than one flogging—either to hold back my less orthodox questions or to put them circumspect. The matter of the Sky Lords' fate I left to destiny.

I had also discovered another interest. For some time now I had grown increasingly aware that I was not alone in my approach to adulthood. It was obvious, from the blemished skin and fluctuating voices of myself and my friends, that we grew. It was equally obvious, from other, far more appealing signs, that those girls with whom we had roughly played as children matched us.

I was intrigued by this new aspect life revealed, and there were (this in all modesty) not a few daughters who flirted with me, for all I passed the next year sporting a ferocious crop of pimples and was seldom sure whether my voice should come out squeaking or gruff.

But as the spring approached the days lengthened, and in direct proportion the time left before I should depart shortened.

When the time came, it was very hard. Nor is it a time on which I care to dwell overlong, and so I tell it brief.

The ceremonies celebrating the coming of age of both Tellurin and Corum preceded mine, and both were followed within days by their betrothals.

My own ceremony approached, midway through that spring. I waited on word from Rekyn. I grew somewhat surly when none came, wondering if the commur-mage had forgotten her promise. The day dawned bright, and I rose early, before my parents even, walking out alone through the village to the Cambar road, where I climbed a tree to peer nervously northward. Tonium found me there, sent by my mother to bring me back for the ritual preparations, and took great delight in my discomfort until I reminded him that did Rekyn fail to come and I remain in the village, his own hopes of advancement must be dashed. That was small satisfaction as I trudged homeward to bathe and dress in the breeks and tunic my mother had lovingly stitched for this propitious day.

Dressed, I went at my father's side to the cella, where the mantis waited, clad in his ceremonial robe, no longer my plump tutor, but the representative of the God. As was customary on such days, no boats put out, but all the villagers stood watching outside the cella. Alone, I followed the mantis inside. There he spoke to me of manhood, of its responsibilities and duties, of the God and our debt to him. I gave the ritual responses and drank the sacred wine, ate the bread and the salt, he drew back my hair and tied it in manhood's tail; and all the while my ears were pricked for the sound of hoofbeats, the jangle of harness.

Then, the ceremony completed, the mantis led me out and cried, "Welcome, Daviot, who is now a man." I followed into the cool spring sunlight, blinking a moment as all shouted in answer, "Welcome, Daviot, who is now a man."

I felt not at all like smiling, for I feared Rekyn had forgotten me, forgotten her promise. I saw my father, an arm about my mother's shoulders, his face proud, hers a struggling admixture of pride and grief. Delia was beaming, waving enthusiastically, and even Tonium managed a grin. Battus and Lyrta stood beside them, and grave-faced Thorus; Tellurin and Corum with their betrothed; all Whitefish village. Then I saw her, Andyrt at her side, both smiling, and I shouted for joy and in that instant entirely forgot my fear.

My parents approached to embrace me. I saw tears on my mother's cheeks. I hugged them, hugged Delia, and looked to Rekyn. Commur-mage and jennym both came close, and Rekyn said, "Did you think I had forgotten?"

I blushed and toed the dirt a moment with my new-polished boots, then shrugged and answered, "I was afraid you had."

She smiled. The sun struck blue-black sparks from her hair as she shook her head. I studied her face and asked her bluntly, "When do we depart?"

Andyrt laughed at that and said, "Are you in such a hurry, Daviot? May we not sample the feast before we go?"

I looked at him—there was a little more gray in his hair now, and a recent scar on his chin—and past his shoulder saw my parents. Almost, I said that I had sooner go on the instant: it would have been easier. Instead I smiled and shook my head in turn and answered him, "Of course, and welcome."

The crowd was a boon then, surrounding me as I walked from the cella to the village square, where Thorym's tables were augmented by an array of planks and trestles, all set with food and barrels of ale and wine. I thought that, despite the contributions all made to such festivities, this must have cost my father dear. I went to the head of the appointed table—places set there for my family and the mantis, two more for our honored guests—and faced the crowd, and cried, "I bid you welcome and ask you join me."

That was as much formality as Whitefish village countenanced: the tables were rapidly occupied, the feasting soon begun. I was intent on Rekyn and Andyrt, on the myriad questions that filled my mind.

"You're in a mighty hurry," the commur-mage remarked when I again asked when we should depart. I could only shrug, embarrassed, as Rekyn's finely arched brows rose in mute inquiry.

Then she added gravely, "Do you change your mind, Daviot?"

"No!" I shook my head vigorously, embarrassed afresh as my answer sent crumbs of new-baked bread spilling across the table. "No! I'd go with you to Durbrecht still."

Rekyn ducked her head once and smiled. "We take you only so

far as Cambar Keep," she said, "to present you to the aeldor. From Cambar you go on alone to Durbrecht."

That took me a little aback: I had not thought to make so great a journey alone, but in company of my sponsors. Rekyn must have read my expression, for she added gently, "We'll see you safe aboard a vessel, and you'll carry an introduction from the aeldor. You'll be met in Durbrecht." Then, after a moment's pause, "We've duties of our own in Cambar."

"The more with these new Comings," Andyrt muttered, "the God condemn the Kho'rabi."

"What does it mean?" my father asked.

"I cannot say," Rekyn told him honestly. "Only that the Sky Lords come unseasonal. Seven of their craft have passed north of Cambar this year alone; more up the coast. Two grounded last year in Draggonek. The Kho'rabi were slain, but the fighting was fierce."

My father nodded, digesting this. My mother gasped, her eyes finding my face, fearful, as if to the sadness she knew at loss of her son was added the fear he might fall to a Sky Lord's blade. Rekyn said, "None close to Durbrecht, Donia. Nor likely to come there—the Sorcerous College lies there, remember."

My mother nodded and essayed a wan smile, her eyes finding mine, troubled.

I had not thought overmuch of my parents' feelings in the matter of my advancement, being far more enwrapped in my own. Now, in that single instant, I recognized the pain I gave them. Oh, they were proud that I should be so singled out, and pleased for me, but still they saw a son lost to them. We had not spoken of it much—that was not our way—but we knew that at least one year must pass before we might meet again, and—should I remain in Durbrecht—we could not know how many more. Perhaps this would be our last time together.

But I was young, and now a man, and set that burden aside. I drank ale to which I was not accustomed and asked again, "When do we depart?" wishing it might be on the instant, without sad farewells, and at the same time that it might be never.

I believe Rekyn understood, for she chuckled and said, "Certainly you *are* in a mighty hurry," making a jest of it. "But in your honor we came by sea, and the return shall not take long."

I nodded and emptied my mug, and after a while pipes and a gittern were brought out and the dancing began. I drank more ale as Tellurin and Corum, all my friends, came to shake my hand and bid me farewell.

Then, as melancholy threatened (much aided by the ale), Rekyn suggested we depart. My mother presented me with a change of clothing bundled in an oilskin and the admonishment I look after myself, and she held me so close I feared my ribs should break. My father shook my hand, man to man, then himself embraced me and gave me a purse that jingled with the few coins he could afford. Delia flung her arms about my neck and wet my face with kisses and tears in equal measure. Tonium, unusually subdued, clutched my hand. The mantis called the God's blessing on me. Battus and Lyrta said their good-byes, and taciturn Thorus presented me with a knife held in a leather sheath he had decorated himself. I thanked him and gravely set the scabbard on my belt. I was close to tears myself and grateful for Andyrt's touch on my shoulder, his calm reminder that the day aged and we had best catch the tide lest we need row our way to Cambar.

We went down to the beach, where a little single-masted cutter waited. I slung my bundle on board and turned to survey Whitefish village.

It seemed now the day had passed in the blinking of an eye, that the last four years had flown by. The feasting had lasted well into the afternoon, and the sun now stood above the headland. The pines there were stark and black, limned in sunlight. The roof of the cella shone white, its bell gleaming. The village looked very small; the world be-yond seemed infinitely large. I clambered into the boat after Rekyn. Andyrt took the tiller; I went to the mast, raising the sail to catch the offshore breeze. I stood there as Andyrt took us out, all the time looking back to where everyone and everything I knew, all that was familiar to me, lay, growing steadily smaller as I went away.

We came to the mouth of the river Cambar as dusk gave way to night. It was not a long journey; but then it was the farthest I had ever been from home, and it felt to me a very long way indeed. The half-filled moon stood pale at our backs, flinging shards of silver light over the quickening swell that marked the river's mouth, where fresh water met the salt sea between two headlands topped with windblown pines. Andyrt swung the tiller over, and I sprang unthinking to the sail. It did not occur to me that Rekyn must have taken this duty before, and she said nothing, leaving me to my task. I believe it was a kindness on her part, that I might begin these steps along the new path of my life with some sense of usefulness, not merely as a passenger. I caught the sail before it luffed, and we rode the last of the wind a little way upriver. Then it was oarwork, and that, too, Rekyn left to me, so that I faced Andyrt's shadowed form as we proceeded up the Cambar. In consequence I did not see the keep until we docked.

There was no beach here, but a stone-walled anchorage, fishing craft bobbing on the tide, moored neat along the harbor. Nimbly (my racing blood and the wind had dispelled the effects of the ale) I sprang to the stone, tying the painter to a metal ring. Then I stood, staring inland.

The cliffs that flanked the river were low, and about the harbor there was a wide cleft, gently sloped and covered at the foot with cottages akin to those I had left behind. Higher, I saw what seemed to me very grand houses, with tiled roofs that glittered in the moonlight, some even sporting balconies about their upper stories. They were set about either side of a broad avenue that ran up to the clifftop, ending at a structure that trapped and held my eyes.

The keep, from this low angle, seemed a single vast column rising atop the ridge, a great stone cylinder set all around with bright-lit windows, a beacon blazing in the night. I stood gape-mouthed, a country bumpkin confronted with a dream. The houses along the avenue were dwarfed, dismissed into insignificance by this wondrous tower. This was the home hold of the aeldor Bardan: this was the gateway to my future.

I started as Andyrt thrust my bundle at me and clapped a cheerful hand to my shoulder. "Save you'd spend the night here, do we go on?" he chuckled. "The sea edges my appetite, and all well dinner will be served soon."

I nodded, still staring upward, and fell into step, Rekyn on my left. She said mildly, "This is not so great a hold, Daviot. Wait until you see the towers of Durbrecht."

I nodded again, lost for words; it seemed to me no place could possibly be grander than this. I shouldered my bundle and went with them across the cobbles of the harbor to the avenue. Now I tore my eyes from the great keep and stared instead at the marvelous houses, their windows paned with clear glass, not the yellow membrane of sheepgut, their woodwork carved and painted for no reason other than decoration. Robus and the mantis had sometimes been persuaded to speak of Cambar—as best I knew then, they were the only men in our village who ever came here—and I had wondered at their tales, but they did nothing to prepare me for this fabulous place, and I walked with eyes and mouth wide, dumbstruck.

And then the avenue ended at a wall, and I saw that the keep was not a single column but was surrounded by this dry-stone barrier, and through the open wooden gate that lesser buildings huddled about its foot.

I thought there should be guards there, but I was wrong. The only sentries were three enormous gray hounds, all shaggy hair and flashing fangs, they seemed to me, that came barking up, to be re-buffed by Andyrt with a shouted command that sent them trotting back to the shelter of a stable where horses nickered and stamped. I took my hand from my knife's hilt and pretended I had not been afraid as my two companions brought me across the yard to the keep's entrance. Rekyn motioned me forward, but I hesitated, struck sud-denly by a new concern: "Do I meet the aeldor now? How should I address him?"

" 'My lord' will do," she told me, "and you've no reason to fear him. Bardan's no ogre, and you come as welcome guest to this hold."

I swallowed, took a deep breath, and nodded; we entered the keep. I saw how thick were the walls, marveling at the builder's skill, then frowned as I realized we did not stand in the great hall I had expected but in a kind of cellar, a huge, circular chamber, dim and stacked all about with casks and barrels, firewood, sacks, haunches of meat hung from hooks set in the wooden roof. Rekyn touched me gently, indicating a broad stairway that rose around the curve of the wall. She moved ahead of me then, and Andyrt fell in behind, and we climbed toward another open door, light bright there, and noise.

On Rekyn's heels I went in and gaped anew despite myself. This chamber was as large as the one below but set with deep-cut embra-sures and circled by sconces in which candles burned, augmenting the blaze of the fire in the massive hearth and the lanterns that hung from the beams overhead. The floor was wood, scattered with rushes, long tables and benches occupied by more men than women, the latter sex emerging from doorways, carrying platters of meat, bread, steaming vegetables, pitchers of ale. Off to one side a minstrel—I had neither seen nor heard one before, but I knew from the kithara he plucked that was his calling—fought the roar of the diners. He stood behind a table set a little apart from the others, three men and two women seated there.

"The aeldor," Rekyn murmured in my ear. "The Lady Andolyne is to his right; the other woman is Gwennet, wife of Sarun, who is heir. The other man is Bardan's second son, Thadwyn."

I nodded in thanks and acknowledgment, committing the names to my memory, eager to make as good an impression as I might, and walked with the commur-mage and Andyrt to stand before the table.

Andyrt sketched a casual bow; Rekyn ducked her head and said, "Lord Bardan, this is Daviot of Whitefish village."

I bowed, my eyes fixed on the floor. I saw a bone there, and then another of the great gray hounds snatch it up. The room grew silent save for the soft strumming of the kithara, and then a deep voice said,

"In the God's name, Daviot of Whitefish village, will you stand up and look me in the eye, or are you bent-backed?"

I felt my cheeks grow warm. I stood, mumbling, "My lord aeldor, Lady Andolyne . . . No, I am not . . . I—"

Bardan laughed, the sound rumbling from his broad chest, and I met his gaze. I saw a rotund face, ale-flushed and dense-bearded, streaks of white in the russet, the eyes large and brown, twinkling with amusement. He was a heavy-set man, past his prime, but yet muscular. The sleeves of his tunic were rolled back, revealing fore-arms corded thick. He smiled at me, beckoning me forward.

"So you're the one," he said. "Rekyn speaks well of you— Andyrt, too—and I trust their judgment. You'd be a Mnemonikos, eh?"

"Does it serve you," I said, and thought to add, "my lord aeldor."

"Me," said Bardan, "the Lord Protector, Dharbek. Aye, have you the makings of a Rememberer, then you shall serve us all."

"And does that not work out," said Andyrt, with what I then thought was massive presumption, "I'll have him for the warband."

Bardan laughed again, not at all put out, and shouted for places to be set at his table, ale to be brought us.

As we waited I took the opportunity to study his kinfolk. His wife, the Lady Andolyne, was of an age with him, which is to say old in my eyes, but like the aeldor she seemed hale, if not so beautiful as I had thought so elevated a personage should be. Her hair was not yet touched with gray, but its brown was somewhat faded, and though her eyes shone bright, they nested amongst lines. Gwennet's hair was a soft gold, and she was pretty in a vague way. She was clearly some few years younger than her husband, and the smile she bestowed on me was friendly. Indeed, they were all friendly, even Sarun, who was a hawk to his father's bear, lean of feature, with the same brown eyes but those more piercing—appraising me, I thought. Thadwyn was not much older than I and favored his mother. Much to my surprise, it was he who pushed a filled tankard to me when we sat.

After the ale I had already drunk, I had poor appetite for more, but I deemed it ungracious to refuse and so smiled my thanks and sipped. Bardan saw my caution and exaggerated a frown. "What's this?" he demanded. "A would-be Mnemonikos who's no taste for ale? In the God's name, young Daviot, that's a thing unknown."

"Perhaps," said Andolyne with a smile, "Daviot shall set a new standard, and introduce sobriety to his calling."

"Unlikely," said Sarun. "Have you ever met a Storyman without a taste for ale?"

"Or wine," said Thadwyn.

"Or mead," said Gwennet.

"Or fire-wine," said Sarun, and studied me with hooded eyes a moment before grinning as if we were old friends. "I suspect you'll learn in time, Daviot. The Storymen have a certain reputation, you know."

"In your own time," Andolyne said kindly. "And as I say—do you choose to introduce new ways . . ."

Then, basking in their ready friendship, I felt only put at my ease, grateful to them, and to Rekyn, Andyrt, that I, a plain fisherman's son, should sit so welcome at their table.

And so, as my confidence grew, I ate, and drank more ale, and found my tongue. And as I talked, my mouth grew dry and I supped more, until I swayed in my chair and their faces began to blur, and I found the words become harder of finding, and harder still to speak.

Andyrt, I discovered, carried me to my bed, and Rekyn had the keep's herbalist prepare a decoction for which I was later mightily grateful, though it tasted bitter and I fought it at the time. Thanks to that I passed the night in sound sleep, waking to the sounds of the rising hold, unaware at first of where I lay. This was the first morning of my life I had not woke in my parents' home, and I experienced a moment of wild panic as I opened my eyes and wondered where I was. Then I remembered and sprang from my bed, only to totter, my head spinning, needles seeming to pierce my skull and eyes. I groaned and sat back, pressing hands to my throbbing temples until I succeeded in focusing my eyes, and examined my chamber.

It was all stone, but with a faded carpet on the flags underfoot. I had never set foot on a carpet before. A lantern hung from the center of the ceiling, and opposite the narrow bed there was a washstand, beneath the window an ottoman. I went to the washstand, wondering who had removed my clothes and where they were, and drank deep of the wondrously cold water, then applied a liberal quantity to my face and head—carefully, for the needles were not yet gone from my skull. I found my clothes in the ottoman and quickly dressed, belted on my dagger, and belatedly remembered to tie back my hair. I felt simultaneously hungry and nauseated by the thought of food, nor sure whether I should remain or quit the chamber. I knelt on the ottoman as I pondered, marveling that the window be paned and thus allow me clear sight of the yard below.

I was on the west side of the keep. Beyond the encircling wall I could see planted fields and grazing sheep, woodland in the distance, hazy at this early hour. Within the confines of the wall I recognized a smithy, the farrier's hammer already clanging, a small building I thought must be a fane, and others I could not define. The yard was busy, soldiers in their plaid striding to and fro, women, children, dogs, a few cats. I was entranced and might well have spent the entire morning observing all this unfamiliar activity had Rekyn not come for me.

She knocked at my door, which was unusual enough, and it was a moment before I thought to bid her enter. In place of her black riding gear she wore breeks of dark leather and a belted tunic, a long dagger sheathed there. She smiled, holding out a beaker of horn, and said, "Day's greetings, Daviot. I suspect you'll welcome this. Perhaps without a fight today."

For an instant I found no memory at all of the previous night's closing and frowned, then blushed as she explained and I remembered. I took the draught and drank it down, wincing at the taste and my embarrassment.

Rekyn settled on the bed, her gray eyes on my face. "Now tell me of last night," she said. "All that you remember."

I guessed this was a test of some kind. I composed my thoughts, much aided by the herbalist's skill, and recited all I could recall.

When I was done, Rekyn nodded in satisfaction and I felt my discomfort evaporate as she said, "Excellent. The ale does not fuddle your memory."

"Thanks to you." I gestured with the beaker. "And this."

"That helped." Her face grew solemn. "Most men forget what they do when in their cups."

I frowned and said, "But last night Sarun, the others, all spoke of the Storymen as drinkers. Does drink obliterate memory, how can they? Why do they?"

"Sarun and his kin spoke mostly in jest," she told me, "albeit in jest there's often truth. Aye, the Storymen *do* drink. Indeed, they've something of a reputation for their capacity, and often enough it's the only payment offered for their tales. But also, they are not as most men. I suspect that whatever accident of blood gifts them with memory gifts them, too, with the ability to drink and still remember. I've not the *how* of it, but I believe that must be the way. Now, do we see if any breakfast's left us?"

I found, to my surprise, that my appetite was returned: I nodded, and we quit the room.

●　　●　　●

As we ate, Rekyn told me that a trade ship was anticipated within the next few days and that it would take me north, save—an ominous reminder and grim portent of the future—the Sky Lords come again to delay the sailing.

I digested this thoughtfully, vaguely aware of the women who now began to clear away the detritus of the morning meal, and when Rekyn suggested we investigate the environs of the keep, I agreed eagerly.

It felt odd to me to venture abroad so late in the day, and I thought fleetingly that my father would be long asea, with Tonium in my place. A moment's nostalgia then, rapidly replaced with wonder as we crossed the court to where Andyrt and others of the warband exercised. Sarun was with them, greeting me with a brief wave before returning to his swordwork. Andyrt hailed me, but no more than that, and with Rekyn I stood watching the flash of light on darting blades, listening to the clangor of steel on steel.

They wore helms and thick-padded jerkins, sewn with plates and nets of metal, but even so I thought surely men must be sore hurt at this practicing. I was right and before long saw a man miss his defensive stroke and take a blow that sent him reeling, his face gone abruptly pale. Andyrt caught the mistake and halted his own combat to roughly curse the luckless fellow for his carelessness before sending him off to a thin, bald man in a green tunic who stood behind a table spread with sundry pots and bandages and bottles.

Rekyn said, "That's Garat, our herbalist and chirurgeon. You've him to thank your head's not hurting."

We went to watch, seeing Garat remove the soldier's jerkin and examine his shoulder—which was dislocated—with fingers as gentle as his curses were ferocious. I had never heard a man so foul-mouthed, nor seen one so tender in his ministrations. His mouth was thin and seemed angry until he smiled and asked me how my head felt. I told him it was entirely cured and offered my thanks, at which he shrugged angular shoulders and cursed me for a fool that I drank with more excess than experience. Laughing, Rekyn declared that she had best remove me from his company ere I become as corrupted of language as he, and we wandered randomly about the yard. It was, in effect, a small village, self-contained and easily defended. Save, I thought, from aerial attack: I ventured to make the point.

" 'Tis true," Rekyn agreed. "Indeed, at the time of the last Coming the Kho'rabi wizards sent their magicks against the keep. See?" She pointed at the ramparts of the great turret, and I saw blocks there paler than their elder kin, the surrounding stones blackened as if with fire. "Two airboats there were, and both grounded inland. There was a great battle."

I said nothing, but she must have read the enthusiasm on my face, for she smiled a little and went on: "The boats grounded to the west, and the fylie marched on Cambar. You noticed the wood there? That was the place of battle. It was a mere copse then, but so many brave men died there that Ramach, who was Lord Bardan's father, decreed it should be left uncut, a monument."

I promised myself I would, had I the time, go there. I asked, "Dhar and Sky Lords lie there together?"

Rekyn nodded. "Aye. For Ramach deemed the Kho'rabi valiant foes."

"And you?" I asked. "What do you say?"

She hesitated a moment, then shrugged. "I am neither philosopher nor theologian, Daviot, but I agree with Ramach. This was once their land, and they surely came a very long way to meet their fate. Why not accord them that poor solace? Bardan, too, decrees the wood sacred."

I felt my question was not entirely answered and frowned, fearing I went too far, as I said, "Are they not then evil?"

"I have never met one in the flesh," she answered, turning toward me as we strolled, "and so cannot say for sure. The priests will tell you so, and perhaps they are right. Perhaps the Sky Lords *are* the God's punishment for the sins of our fathers; perhaps they are only warriors sent into battle by their own priests. I'll not judge them until I've spoken with one and learned more of their ways."

This seemed to me sensible and I ducked my head in agreement. "Has anyone?" I asked. "Spoken with a Sky Lord?"

"No." Rekyn shook her head, the loose black tail of her hair flying. "No Sky Lord was ever taken alive. Do they not fall in battle, they fall on their own blades. It seems they count it a great dishonor to be taken captive."

"They kill themselves?" I asked, aghast, for this ran utterly contrary to our own teachings.

"Rather than be taken alive," Rekyn confirmed.

I swallowed, digesting this as we completed our perambulation and went out through the gates. As we ambled leisurely down the avenue, my mind was only half on the grandeur of the houses; the other half wrestled with the notion of a folk so savage as to take their own lives. It was a thing too strange, too enormous, for my young mind to properly encompass. I wondered what manner of men were the Sky Lords, that they did this.

"So, shall we eat?"

Rekyn's question brought me from my musing, and I saw that we had come to a building I now recognized as a tavern. I nodded dumbly: my experience of such establishments was limited to Thorym's humble aleshop, and I did my best to assume an air of sophistication, a pace behind Rekyn as she found a table by the inner wall and settled casually on the bench there.

As we ate, Rekyn spoke to me of Cambar, of its trade and commerce and people, opening my eyes still wider to the world beyond Whitefish village, which even in the short time since I had left dwindled in my sight. It was strange that the place that only two days before had been the whole compass of my existence could so swiftly become so small a thing. It felt that betwixt sleeping and waking my narrow world was being replaced with another, larger place, and my excitement mounted as the commur-mage spoke. I listened rapt until she drained the last of her ale and suggested we find our way to the harbor.

I felt far more at home there, amongst familiar sights and sounds and smells. Even so, it was very different to Whitefish village. Many of the boats were larger, and to the north of the anchorage I saw two galleasses nodding on the tide's ebb, their lateen sails furled, their oars stowed. Near where they rode at anchor there was a squat stone building I did not think was a warehouse, a throng of large, impressively muscled men lounging about the doors. Rekyn saw where I looked and told me, "Lord Bardan commands two warships."

She paid the men scant attention, but they fascinated me. I had never seen shoulders so massive, nor chests so deep; I thought they must be powerful warriors. And yet there was something about them I could not quite define, a difference—something in the shape of their skulls, their broad foreheads and deep-set eyes—that set them apart from the men of Andyrt's warband. As I watched a man in Cambar's plaid emerged from the building and called some order that sent four of the giants down to the harbor's edge. Two barrels stood there, huge casks I assumed they would shift on rollers or a cart, and even then only with difficulty. Instead, they took each cask, one man to either end, tilted it, and lifted it as if it weighed nothing, carrying both back to the building easily as if they bore no more than panniers of fish. I gasped, hardly able to believe men could be so strong.

Rekyn noticed the object of my amazement and said, "Each galleass is rowed by Changed. Those are bull-bred."

Her tone was casual, as though such prodigious strength were entirely natural; as though the presence of Changed were entirely normal. To her it was; to me it was yet another thing of wonder.

"I have never seen Changed before," I said.

"You have." Rekyn smiled at my disbelieving frown. "Bardan keeps several bull-bred about the hold, for the heavier work. And not a few as servants. Those are cat- or dog-bred, of course. In Durbrecht you'll see far more. Likely, do you elect to remain beyond your first year, you'll have one for a body-servant."

A servant? *My* servant? My jaw fell, and Rekyn laughed anew.

"It is felt," she advised me, "that those training to become Mnemonikos are better employed in study than in such trivial matters as the cleaning of their quarters."

"Did you have one?" I asked her. "When you attended the Sorcerous College?"

"A cat-bred female," she answered, a hint of fond nostalgia in her voice. "Mell was her name." Her tone changed, and it seemed to me a door closed behind her eyes. "When I left, she fled across the Slammerkin into Ur-Dharbek. I'd not thought Mell would go to the wild ones."

I feared, from Rekyn's expression, from her colder tone, that I trespassed on forbidden ground. But I was to become a Storyman, and how should I pursue that following save I asked questions? "Wild ones?" I queried.

The commur-mage nodded absently, yet a little lost in some private past. "The lands of the Truemen end at the Slammerkin," she murmured, "and beyond lay those lands given over to the wild Changed. The Lord Protector Philedon decreed it so—that the dragons have prey to hunt and need not venture south."

I did not properly understand her reticence—she had evinced little enough on most other subjects—but I felt it sure enough. I said, in what I hoped was an easy way, "The mantis spoke somewhat to me of the dragons. He said they are dead now, or gone away into the Forgotten Country."

I thought for a moment Rekyn had not heard me, but then she nodded again and said, "Perhaps they are. Certainly, they prey no more on Truemen; and men do not venture into Ur-Dharbek."

"Nor the Changed—the wild Changed—come south across the Slammerkin?" I ventured.

"No," was all the answer I got, and I set my wealth of questions aside for some later time.

But I approached the hold with better-opened eyes, surveying the folk I saw, assessing who was Trueman and who Changed. The smith, I guessed, for he possessed the massive frame of the men (I could not think of them as beasts) I had seen at the harbor, and when I watched the serving folk, I thought I discerned aspects of the feline in several of the women, canine in more than one man. Rekyn was clearly indisposed to discuss them further, and I wondered if some taboo existed; I deemed it wise to hold my tongue. Besides, we found Andyrt in the hall and he called us over, so that we were soon embroiled in conversation with jennym and soldiers, and I found myself quaffing yet more ale.

Thus we passed what little remained of the afternoon, and in a while the candles and lanterns were lit against the burgeoning dark, and servants came out to set the tables for the evening meal. The aeldor and the Lady Andolyne appeared with Sarun and Gwennet, greeting me as friendly as before. Thadwyn, I learned, was gone north to Torbryn Keep in amorous pursuit of Lydea, daughter of the aeldor Keryn. Bardan questioned me concerning my day and I, emboldened by his easy manner, expressed my wish to see the site of his father's battle with the Kho'rabi.

He and Andolyne exchanged a glance at that, and then he tugged his beard and said quietly, "Are the woods gone from Whitefish village, then?"

"No," I said, "but no battle was ever fought there."

"It's naught but trees, Daviot," he told me, serious now. "There's no fine monument, nor trace of the fight. Only trees."

I suppose my disappointment showed on my face, for he chuckled then and said, "But if you must, so be it. Andyrt, do you take the time on the morrow? I've matters to discuss with Rekyn anyway."

I thought the jennym's face clouded a moment; surely his response was delayed. From the corner of my eye I saw Bardan nod, and then Andyrt favored me with a wicked smile. "We'll ride out there, eh?" he suggested.

I voiced enthusiastic agreement, picturing myself astride one of Cambar's great warhorses, Thorus's gift-dagger become a sword, myself in Cambar's plaid.

The reality, I discovered the next day, was somewhat different.

Andyrt sat proud on the warhorse whilst I was brought a pony. A pretty enough beast: a gray-dappled mare with gentle eyes and, I was assured, a no less gentle gait. An ostler I suspected was horse-bred led her out and helped me mount. I climbed astride and felt myself raised a disconcerting distance from the ground, warily clutching the reins and then the saddle as the placid animal shifted under me.

Over his shoulder Andyrt called, "Ware the cobbles, Daviot. Do you fall, they're somewhat hard."

Fortunately for me, his humor did not extend to leading me into a fall. He held his own mount to a walk as we circled the wall and turned westward across the pasture land, and as we rode he instructed me in the basics of horsemanship. I was far more concerned with the simple act of staying in the saddle, but I filed his comments in my memory, albeit I could barely comprehend how the shifting of leather against the animal's neck, or the touch of a heel to its ribs, should steer it in one direction or another did it choose to ignore those hints. A boat I could understand; this swaying, undulating beast was a mystery. Still, I did not tumble, and felt I regained some measure of dignity. One day, I thought, I should become as confident a rider as my companion.

We went on at a slow pace, past grazing sheep, a herdsman who waved a greeting, over a little brook, more grass. The wood spread before us, all green and shadowy in the early morning sun. It was a plantation of oak, the tall trees rustling in the wind off the Fend. Andyrt reined in a little distance off, my pony halting less in obedience to my urgings than in parody of his stallion, innocently threatening to dislodge me as she lowered her head to crop.

"The wood," Andyrt said needlessly, gesturing at the timber. "There's little enough to it."

"Can we enter it?" I asked.

"If you wish."

I felt he hesitated an instant, and as he swung limber from the saddle I saw him make the sign of warding. I did not, for as I strove to climb down I felt my legs and buttocks shafted with pain and become as straws, quite inadequate to the task of supporting me. I clutched at the saddle, leaning for support against the pony, which stirred, threatening to topple me. I heard Andyrt chuckle and gritted my teeth, pushing gingerly clear of my equine prop as I forced my back straight and turned on unsteady legs toward the wood.

"The first time always hurts," Andyrt said. "Folk think you need only climb astride a horse and sit there, but there's more to it than that. I'll ask Garat potion a bath for you when we return."

"My thanks," I said, and then: "I've much to learn."

Andyrt said, "Aye," and cheered me by adding, "but I'll wager you make a good enough horseman in time."

I smiled and hobbled closer to the wood.

Andyrt surprised me then, setting a hand on my shoulder to halt me as he dropped to one knee, hands crossed against his chest in attitude of prayer. Confused, I waited for him to rise with a question on my lips that I bit off as I saw his face. I was not sure what expression sat there; not fear, but an emotion not entirely divorced. Awe, perhaps; and something of disquiet. I looked to the wood and wondered why.

It seemed no more than a plain oak hurst, the massy branches verdant with spring's new growth. The closer trees were mostly young as oaks go, though toward the center I could espy vast, majestic trunks that must have been ancient when Ramach faced the Kho'rabi. I turned to Andyrt and asked him, "Were you here then?"

"No." He shook his head, favoring me with a brief smile. "Think you I'm so old? Bardan himself was a babe in arms when this battle was fought."

I mumbled an apology he seemed not hear, intent on the holt. I had never set foot in a place of worship larger than the village cella, but it came to me that his must be the attitude of a man entering some sacred precinct, a cathedral . . . or a sepulchre. I fell silent as we walked slowly through the edge timber, moving deeper into the wood. It dawned on me that I heard no birdsong, that no squirrels chattered from the branches, nor were there the usual sounds of the small animals amongst the roots and fallen leaves. Indeed, nothing other than the oaks grew here: there was no undergrowth, nor even moss on the gnarled trunks. It was unnaturally quiet, the only sound the faint susurration of the wind-stirred leaves, as if the oaks murmured amongst themselves; as if they discussed our presence.

I felt suddenly uncomfortable. The dull aching of my thighs and buttocks was forgotten, replaced with a prickling sensation that prompted me to turn to and fro, convinced eyes watched me from hidden places.

"You feel it." Andyrt did not ask a question, and I nodded, whispering, "Yes."

"It was a terrible battle." His voice was low as if he made confession. "Two full warbands met the fylie of two airboats. Steel met steel, and more—the sorcerers of Cambar and Torbryn fought with the Kho'rabi wizards. Hundreds died here—it was five years and more before the warbands regained their full strength. Ramach declared this wood should be their monument, that it be left grow unchecked. It does, and it remembers, I think. Nothing lives here save the oaks and the spirits of the dead."

I looked about, at a wood no longer merely that. It seemed that for an instant I saw the fight. The sunlight slanting through the latticed overlay of branches glinted on bloody swords, armored men clashed, bolts of occult power exploded. Men roared, battle-shouts and dying screams. I realized I was very cold as the momentary vision faded. I shivered, my mouth gone too dry to speak.

"Enough?" asked Andyrt.

I nodded and we turned about, our departure swifter than our entrance.

Outside the wood, the sight of the placidly cropping horses, the fields beyond, a restoration of normality, we halted and looked back. "It was the height of summer," Andyrt said slowly. "Two days short of the Sastaine festival, it began; it ended two days after. None come near on those nights."

I thought of my vision and asked, "It's haunted?"

"I've not come to find out." Andyrt shrugged and grinned with some small resumption of his customary good humor. "Those who've been in sight—shepherds, late-traveling peddlers—say they've heard the sounds of battle, or even seen warriors fighting amongst the trees, but none have lingered to see more. Sometimes, from the keep you can see lights . . . like witchfire."

"I thought I saw . . ." I shook my head and grinned shame-faced.

"Some do, if they've the gift." Andyrt ran absent fingers through the stallion's mane. The big horse tossed its head and snorted. "Perhaps that talent that shall make you a Storyman grants you the sight. Now do we return?"

We rode back at funereal pace, and I am sure my face was a red-lit beacon as I was aided down and hobbled stiff-legged across the yard. Andyrt helped me climb the stairs to my room, our progress met with amiable derision by the soldiers lounging in the hall, and summoned servants to draw a bath. Promising to find Garat for me, he left me alone. I waited standing.

A Changed servant brought in the tub, and others filled it with steaming water. The herbalist came, cursing my idiocy and Andyrt's sadism in equal measure, spilling a selection of aromatic liquids into the bath, then leaving me with instructions to apply a salve to my tender parts and the observation that for all his efforts I should likely take my next few meals on my feet and sleep on my belly. I thanked him and sank hopefully into the water.

In a while hope became gratitude, and I blessed Garat's skill as my aches abated. I rose and dried myself, carefully applied Garat's salve, and made my way down to the hall.

Rekyn met me there, to advise me the merchantman on which I should travel north would dock on the morrow. I asked her how she knew, and she smiled and said, "Magic, Daviot. How else? The galley comes down the coast, and we sorcerers send word from keep to keep."

I thought I should not sleep that night, but I did, and soundly, thanks to Garat's potions.

4

I was awake early the next morning, roused from dreamless sleep
by anticipation. I hurried to the hall, my appetite somehow
sharpened by excitement: I had consumed a full platter of cold
meat and half a loaf when Rekyn and Andyrt came in. They
smiled at the sight of me and wished me the day's greetings. I asked
when I should leave, at which Andyrt chuckled and drew out a chair
for Rekyn, hooking one close for himself. "Two days, and already he
tires of our company," he said.

I began to protest, and laughing, Rekyn motioned me to silence.
"The boat's not likely to arrive until late morning," she advised me.
"Bardan would see you ere then, to give you token of introduction.
Can you curb your impatience?"

I nodded, mumbling further apologies lest I offend my benefac-
tors.

Rekyn said, "Does the galley arrive as promised, she'll catch the afternoon tide. Save the weather turns, you'll sight Durbrecht soon after Ennas Day."

I suspected she looked to ease my going and smiled my gratitude, asking, "What should I do when I arrive?"

"You'll be met," she answered. "A representative of the College will be at the harbor to meet you all."

"There are others?" I asked.

"Two," she said. "One from Ynisvar; one from Madbry. I've not their names, but the boat will collect them farther up the coast."

I nodded sagely, for all I had no sure idea where Ynisvar or Madbry lay. Save I was aware the waters of the Treppanek divided Kellambek from Draggonek, and those of the Slammerkin that latter from Ur-Dharbek, I had little better knowledge of my homeland's geography.

I'd have had a lesson there and then, but a Changed servant came with word Lord Bardan would see me now, and I followed him to the tower's higher levels, to the aeldor's private quarters. The chamber was not especially large, but very comfortable. A single window admitted light, and against one wall a fire burned in a low hearth. Bardan sat behind a desk of dark wood, in a high-backed chair matched by a second facing him. He bade me take that and I lowered myself, marveling at the softness of the cushioned seat. He set me at my ease with a cheerful inquiry as to the condition of my lower body, and I, greatly surprised he should show such interest, answered that thanks to Garat I was largely unafflicted.

"He's a fine herbsman," said the aeldor absently. "Now, Rekyn's told you the galley's on its way? You're ready?"

I nodded and thanked him for his hospitality. He waved a dismissive hand and took a wax disk from the desk, tossed it to me. "Now, do you take this and guard it well," he advised. "When you dock in Durbrecht, pass it to the College's man who'll meet you there."

I ducked my head, securing the token beneath my shirt.

"So, enough," Bardan said. "The God go with you, Daviot. May he make you the finest Rememberer Dharbek's known."

I smiled and nodded and rose, recognizing dismissal.

Rekyn and Andyrt remained where I had left them, engaged in a game of kells, and I studied the board with poorly contained impatience until word came that the galley was arrived. Andyrt chuckled as I sprang to my feet. "There's cargo to be offloaded," he told me, "and the master'll not leave without you."

"Even so," said Rekyn, more sympathetic to my nervous impatience, "we might find our way to the harbor, no? We can acquaint

Daviot with the captain and, if there's time, take a pot of ale in fare-well."

We quit the hall, and I must curb the impulse to run as we tra-versed the avenue, down toward the harbor, toward my future.

I had seen galleys before, but only at a distance, watching from the shoreline or my father's boat as they ran sleek and swift, like hunting dogs coursing the waves. This was the first time I had seen one at close quarters, and I appraised her lines with all the experience of my sixteen years. I thought she looked swift, for all the belly-spread of her hold, and kept well. Rekyn pointed to the angled prow and told me her name was the *Seahorse*.

I was agog to board her, but my friends held me back, and I acknowledged that this was not the time: a double row of hulking Changed were unloading cargo, slinging bales and crates and casks from hand to hand as easily as children might toss a ball. They were supervised by a man I took to be the master, and I asked his name, which Rekyn told me was Kerym. I had been content to wait and watch until the offloading was done and whatever trade goods Cambar returned stowed on board, but Andyrt declared himself thirsty and we repaired to a tavern redolent of fish and spilled beer. The occupants were instantly recognizable as sailors or longshoremen. Off to one side sat a group of Changed. We took a table by the door, and Andyrt called for ale and platters of the fish I could smell grilling. Through the open doorway I could see the galley: I ate and drank watching her.

I started halfway from my chair as the line of Changed broke up, dispersing toward the taverns, but Rekyn put a hand on my arm, urging me be still, and said, "There's business yet to be concluded, Daviot, and likely the captain's hungry, too. He'll not sail without you."

I sank back, mumbling an apology. It seemed an age before Kerym returned, although the sun was only a little way past zenith and the tide only just on its turn. I drained the last of my ale in a gulp and reached for my bag as I saw the captain cross the wharf. He fetched a whistle from his tunic and blew a single note that brought his Changed crew striding obediently toward the galley. I heard Andyrt chuckle and murmur something to Rekyn, but my attention was focused entirely on the *Seahorse* and her master. I quit the tavern ahead of my companions, resisting the temptation to run.

The crew filed on board and Kerym turned toward us, a hand raised in salute. He seemed small beside his massive crew, but he was of average height for a Trueman and not very old. Younger than my father, I thought, his hair a brown streaked pale by sun and sea, a close-trimmed beard bordering his jaw.

"Day's greetings." His voice was surprisingly deep. "This is my passenger?"

Eyes narrowed from long hours staring into the sun studied me dispassionately. I felt somehow judged and found wanting. I said, "I am. My name is Daviot."

Kerym nodded absently and said, "Then let's be aboard, lad. I'll not waste the tide."

I did not much like his air, but still he was the master: I turned to my companions. Now I felt a pang at thought of bidding them farewell.

Rekyn smiled and took my hand. "Fare you well, Daviot. The God go with you; and may your road return here someday."

I was taken a little aback by the abruptness of her good-bye. But in her eyes I saw only kindness and realized that she would cut short a potentially sad parting. I said, "Fare you well, Rekyn; and you, Andyrt. You've both my eternal gratitude."

The jennym grinned and clasped my wrist in the warrior's manner. "May Durbrecht find favor in your eyes," he said.

I nodded, seeking some grand words of farewell, but finding none turned about, following the captain over the gangplank onto the deck of the galley.

Kerym pointed me to the stern, where the deck was raised to a small poop dominated by the tiller. Two Changed cast off the mooring lines and sprang agile aboard as the plank was hauled in. I saw there were six oarsmen to the side, two others stationed by the mast. The oars came down, pushing the craft clear of the harbor wall. Kerym called an order and the sweeps dipped. The prow swung around, and the *Seahorse* moved toward the open ocean.

I looked back, raising a hand in last farewell. Rekyn and Andyrt answered, then turned away.

"You've sea legs," Kerym observed as I braced myself against the tilt and sway of the deck.

"I was born in Whitefish village," I told him.

He nodded, one arm hung over the tiller, steering the galley with the same casual expertise as Andyrt sat a horse. He did not speak again until we had cleared the anchorage and rode the ebb tide of the river. Then he shouted for the oarsmen to cease their rowing and the sail be lowered, a triangle of pale blue canvas that caught the shifted wind, carrying us out to sea.

"You'll sleep on deck," he told me. "There's but one cabin, and that's mine. The God willing, we'll make Durbrecht ere Ennas Day dawns."

As I have said, my knowledge of Dharbek's geography was scanty then, but even so it seemed to me his confidence was overweening, and I said, "That seems a very swift passage. Are you so sure of favorable winds?"

"I believe the wind will hold," he said, "but does it not . . ." He gestured with his chin at the patient oarsmen. "Why, then these bonny boys will man their sweeps and we'll go on regardless."

The massive men seated on the rowing benches hardly seemed to me "bonny boys," but I saw his point. Still, I resented his somewhat condescending manner and so demanded, "All the way to Durbrecht?"

"If needs be," he answered with a composure I found tremendously irritating. "You've not known Changed before, eh?"

"I saw them in Cambar," I replied, defensive now.

Kerym chuckled again, and said, "Around the harbor? Hauling crates and the like?"

I began to perceive he had the habit of asking such questions as were designed to lead me into admissions of ignorance, but all I could do, in honesty, was nod and allow it was so.

"You've not seen them at work until you've seen them rowing into the teeth of a storm," he declared. "These are hand-picked, every one. Bred from fine, strong stock, they are. Needs be, they'll row all the way to Durbrecht, night and day without stopping."

I had no idea whether he spoke the truth or merely boasted. Certainly, the oarsmen were huge, and hugely muscled. Even so, it seemed unlikely even these giants could row so long without halt—I looked Kerym in the eye and let my expression answer.

He had the grace to smile at that, and shrugged, and said, "Perhaps I exaggerate a trifle. Perhaps not *all* the way, but I've known them go a day and a night without surcease."

I could hear the note of pride in his voice. It was such as a man might use when speaking of some prized animal: a fine hunting dog or a valuable horse. I realized that I thought of the Changed oarsmen as men not unlike myself—save in size and strength—whilst Kerym saw them as possessions, as carefully selected beasts whose prowess reflected credit on him. "Do they not object?" I asked.

His eyes widened at that, fixing on me as if confronted with rank insanity. For a moment he was silent. Then he shook his head, chuckling, and murmured to himself, "Whitefish village! Fishermen!" so that I flushed, less in embarrassment than in anger. I think he saw my vexation, for he moderated his tone and said, "No, they do not. They are Changed, Daviot. Changed do not object, only obey and do their duty."

I scowled and asked, "Have they any choice in that? I mean—do they choose their duty?"

Kerym sighed wearily and answered me, "They are *Changed*," as if that were all the response necessary. I suppose my expression prompted his amplification, for he shook his head again in an insulting manner and explained, "They are *bred* to the task. In the God's name, do you ask a horse if it wants to be ridden? An ox if it welcomes the plow harness?"

"I saw Changed drinking in the tavern," I said, "and for that they need coin, but no one pays a horse or an ox."

I felt it was a sophisticated argument—that I scored a point—but Kerym only shrugged and returned me, "A beast needs fodder, no? And water. Save I keep these fellows fed and allow them a tot now and again, they'll weaken." He repeated his exasperating chuckle. "I'd not have the finest oarsmen on either coast flag."

"They receive no other pay?" I asked, thinking of the stipend I was promised merely for studying.

"I feed them; and well," said Kerym grandly. "Three meals a day and a tankard of good ale with every one. When we've the time and they've no other work, I give them small coin for the taverns. What more should they want?"

I had no idea. Indeed, when I thought about it, that was as much as I received for working with my father on our boat. Save, it occurred to me, I had anticipated owning my own boat someday, and a cottage, a wife. I frowned and asked him, "Shall they always be oarsmen? May they quit your employ? What happens when they get old? Or are hurt?" The questions came in a rush, compelled as much by my desire to best the man as to learn the answers.

"So many questions." He favored me with a smile I found patronizing. "Still, you hope to be a Rememberer, eh? Well—no, they shall not always be oarsmen, for they *will* get old, or damaged, and then they'll be little use on the *Seahorse*. When that happens, they'll be given other, less arduous employment—about the harbor, or in a warehouse. May they quit my employ? Of course not—I *own* them."

He seemed to me smugly satisfied with the correctitude of his answer. I pressed my point: "And when they're too old for even that? What happens to them then?"

Kerym flipped a dismissive wrist. "Do they choose, they are allowed to cross the Slammerkin," he said. "Or they rely on the charity of their fellows, whatever they've managed to save."

I thought they should not be able to save much, and that the charity of the Changed must of necessity be a precarious living. But his mention of the Slammerkin reminded me of Rekyn's words, and I said, "They go into Ur-Dharbek to join the wild Changed?"

"Yes," said Kerym, his tone so different I stared at him, hearing something in his voice I did not understand. I felt as I had with Rekyn —that I ventured into some area that was not . . . I was not sure . . . *proper*, or polite to mention. His smile was gone, his face cold: I sensed I had gone too far, though I did not understand why or how. He said, "Enough questions."

We stood in silence awhile, and then I asked if I might go forrard, to observe our progress from the bow. Kerym responded with a nod, and I quit his company feeling distinctly uncomfortable.

I made my way along the central deck, surreptitiously observing the crew. Save for their great size and their vaguely taurine physiognomy, they seemed to me quite human. They chattered quietly amongst themselves and several smiled at me as I passed. Some, I saw, played the simpler version of kells known as catch-dice, and for some reason that more than anything else rendered them sympathetic. I decided that, did the opportunity arise, I would speak with them.

I had no chance then, however, for no sooner had I reached the foredeck than the wind shifted and Kerym blew his whistle, the piercing note bringing out the sweeps as the oarsmen bent to their duty. I thought then that Kerym's boasting might contain some element of truth, for the galley swept forward and I tottered an instant as the deck lurched under me. I wondered if the master looked to humble me, clutching at the gunwale as white water foamed around the bow. The foremost rower called, "Take care, master," in a gruff, kindly voice, and I smiled and waved, regaining my sea legs. I might not have sailed on a galley before, but I was a fisherman's son and would not grant Kerym the amusement of seeing me fall.

We continued thus until the wind once more picked up and the sail bellied again. Kerym gave some order then, and the two crewmen not engaged on the sweeps set to preparing food. It was plain fare, but filling: fish and rice and hard bread, and everyone on board was passed a tankard brimming with good Cambar ale. I took my ration on the foredeck, not much wanting to rejoin our captain at the stern. Perhaps I sulked, but also I pondered on all he had said; and what he refused to discuss.

When the meal was done, the sweeps came out again and we rowed through the afternoon. I watched the coastline pass, seeing villages the twin to my own, once the high column of a keep I thought must be Torbryn, coves and inlets where houses clustered about the shore. There were fishing boats out, but we rode beyond the catch grounds and soon left them behind. The sun westered, the sky to the east a purple pricked through with stars, the moon a butter-yellow crescent. Soon the coast was a shadow, marked by the phosphorescent wash of breaking surf. We ate again (the same fare), and I wondered if Kerym would put in for the night and ride out the dark hours at anchor, but he showed no sign of slowing and after a while sent a crewman to where I stood to advise me I might make my bed at fore- or poopdeck.

I went back astern then and found Kerym in better humor.

"I'm sworn to make Ynisvar no later than the morrow's noon," he told me, "so we go on through the night. I'll find my bed now; do you sleep where you will. But stay out of the way, eh?"

I nodded and he passed the tiller to a Changed, disappearing into his little cabin. The night grew chill, and I broke out my cloak. The crew fetched an array of motley garments from beneath their benches, and I saw that three to each side stretched out asleep. Running lights were hung at prow and stern, and in their light I studied the tillerman. He was older than the rest, with hints of gray in the sleek black hair hanging straight about his weathered face. A small clay pipe was clasped between his teeth, the bowl glowing red in the darkness, smoke drifting from between his heavy lips. I thought this an excellent opportunity to satisfy my curiosity and lounged against the taffrail.

"Have you sailed with Kerym long?" I asked.

"Yes, master," he said.

"How long?" I asked.

He shrugged, the movement like tree trunks shifting, and said, "Since I was old enough, master."

"I've sailed all my life," I told him. "I'm a fisherman's son."

He only nodded, unspeaking. I asked his name, and he answered, "Bors, master."

"I'm Daviot," I returned, to which he nodded again.

He seemed, to say the least, disinclined to converse with me, but I refused to be put off. "Where are you from?" I asked.

"Durbrecht, master," he said.

"I go there," I said. "To the College of the Rememberers."

He nodded. Whether he was unimpressed or uninterested or intent on his duty, I could not tell: his features remained impassive. I am ashamed to admit I thought him distinctly bovine in his placid acceptance. I thought of a cow chewing the cud, instinctively flicking its tail at the swarming flies represented by my attempts to engage him in conversation. "I love the sea," I declared. "Do you?"

He offered no response, as if the question were without meaning. I asked, "Do you enjoy life on the *Seahorse*?"

His wide eyes narrowed a fraction, as though he struggled to comprehend the inquiry, as though enjoyment were a concept beyond his understanding. Finally he shrugged, still silent.

I opted for bold measures. "What do you know of Ur-Dharbek?" I demanded. "Your people live free there, I'm told."

That did produce a reaction, albeit fleetingly, for he hid it swift. I saw his eyes widen, then narrow again, and his teeth clenched tighter on his pipe, the tobacco glowing fierce a moment as he sucked in a sharp breath.

"Nothing, master," he said.

There was a finality in his tone that denied all opportunity for further questions on that particular subject, and for all my curiosity I could not but recognize it was closed—which of course fueled my interest the more.

"Nothing at all?" I asked, unwilling yet to give up.

"No, master," he said. And added, "Nothing at all."

I sighed and tried another tack: "Why do you call me master? I'm not your master."

"You're a Trueman," he said.

"And all Truemen are called master?" I asked.

"Yes, master," he said.

"Are there many of your people in Durbrecht?" I asked.

He said, "Yes, master."

I saw that I should not get far with Bors; certainly not find answers to my many questions. I wondered if that was a trait of his taurine kind, or of the Changed in general; or if he hid things. Surely he knew more of Ur-Dharbek than he admitted, and no less surely refused to speak of it. I gave up: it seemed a fruitless exercise to question him further. I said, "I think I'll sleep now," and he said, "Yes, master," so I gathered up my bag and carried it to the foredeck, where I rolled myself in my cloak, the bag for a pillow, and fell asleep to the slap of water against the bow. I dreamed of sailing forever on a galley manned by silent Changed, whose only answer, whenever I spoke, was "Yes, master."

We sighted Ynisvar before noon. It was a place larger than Cambar, which made it the largest place I had ever seen, spread in a semicircle around a gentle bay. Shallow headlands like the lowered horns of a bull ran down to a wide sand beach on which fishing boats were grounded; beyond, houses climbed the slopes, clustering about the keep that dominated the heights. Kerym brought the *Seahorse* in through the shallows to a jetty, and we moored.

I thought I should go ashore, but Kerym told me he would halt only long enough to take his new passenger on board, and so I waited on the foredeck as the midday meal was prepared and passed out. Kerym, it appeared, ate on shore, for it was some time before he reappeared, accompanied by a small crowd that gathered on the jetty as a young man of about my own age said his farewells. He was a little smaller than me, and reddish-haired, with a dramatically freckled face that looked torn between excitement and trepidation. His clothes, I noticed, were similar to my own, though he wore no dagger. When he came on board, I saw instantly that he was no sailor.

Kerym introduced us. The newcomer's name was Pyrdon. I took him forrard as we cast off, watching his ruddy face turn pale as the galley backed and swung about.

"I've not much experience of boats," he announced.

I nodded sagely, feeling immediately superior, and told him, "You'll find your sea legs soon enough."

The Fend was calm, only a gentle swell running, but as we rowed from the bay Pyrdon's face grew so ashen, it seemed every freckle glowed red as a pox sore. He clutched the gunwale, his knuckles white, and I felt amused until he groaned, "Oh, in the God's name, why could I not go horseback?"

I remembered my own equestrian experience then and felt abashed. I asked if he could ride, and he nodded and mumbled an affirmative as if such accomplishment were as natural as my own familiarity with the sea. Then he gasped and emptied his belly overboard. I felt immediately sorry for him and brought him a cup of water. "Perhaps Kerym has some remedy," I said, and left the unfortunate Pyrdon draped over the forecastle as I made my way to the stern. In any event, Kerym had no such nostrum and expressed only a supercilious amusement at Pyrdon's plight, advising me to warn him that he had best avoid fouling the *Seahorse*'s deck. His attitude did nothing to improve my opinion of him, and I returned to the bow wearing an irritated scowl.

"Perhaps we'll have time to find a herbalist in Madbry," I suggested, to which Pyrdon answered mournfully, "Madbry's a day or more distant."

I was impressed that he owned such knowledge and set to questioning him about his origins, which served to distract his mind somewhat from the—to me—smooth motion of the galley.

His recitation was punctuated with groans and frequent pauses as he hung his head over the side, but I gathered that he was a season older than me, the second son of a tanner, from a town some leagues inland called Sterbek. He took his familiarity with horses as casually as I took mine with boats, and assured me that had he known what a sea voyage was like, he would have endeavored to persuade his father to gift him a horse and made his own way to Durbrecht. That his family could afford so generous a gift suggested he enjoyed a wealth unknown to my parents, and I forbore to elaborate on my humbler background. Pyrdon scarcely noticed, being far more concerned with his misery, but despite his discomfort I thought him a cheerful enough fellow, whose company I should likely enjoy when his seasickness was passed.

Sadly, it did not. Indeed, for the remainder of the voyage to Madbry he continued unwell, swearing that once we reached our destination he would never again set foot on a boat of any kind. I did what I could to ease his suffering, but that was not much, and by the time we sighted Madbry he was gaunt for lack of sustenance and bringing up a clear bile from his empty stomach.

Madbry hove in sight early on the morning of our third day at sea. It was large as Ynisvar, but lay on the jut of a headland, the buildings climbing the steep flanks of the promontory to the aeldor's tower. The keep was outlined stark by the new-risen sun, like a finger pointing accusingly at the sky. The wind was brisk, slapping waves against the mole we rounded to find the calmer waters of the harbor, and as we approached I went to Kerym.

"Shall there be chance to find a herbalist?" I asked. "Pyrdon's in some need of a cure."

"I'll not delay." Kerym's eyes remained fixed on the harbor wall, gauging our speed against the run of the tide. I did not like him, but I had to admit he was a skilled captain. "And Cleton comes now."

I had not realized he knew the names of his passengers in advance. I looked toward the town and saw a veritable procession descending from the keep. I gasped and said, "He lives in the keep?"

"Thought you all Rememberers were fishermen or tanners?" he returned, and chuckled. "Cleton's third son to the aeldor Brython."

It had not occurred to me an aeldor's son might become Mnemonikos, and I wondered briefly how one so elevated would find my company. But that was not my immediate concern. I said, "Still, save Pyrdon's found a remedy, he'll likely vomit his way to Durbrecht."

Kerym shrugged as if this was a matter of no concern; I refused to leave it. I said, "Surely we might wait so long as it takes to find a herbman."

Kerym shouted an order that reversed the sweeps, slowing us as he brought the tiller over, the *Seahorse* drifting neat to the wharf. Bors and the other older Changed leaped ashore with the mooring lines. Kerym nodded his satisfaction and answered me, "Durbrecht by Ennas Day, I swore. I've a sizable wager riding on it."

That seemed to me a piss-poor reason for Pyrdon's continued suffering, and I had to restrain myself from expressing my opinion of our captain. I mastered my anger, however, and instead said, as calmly as I was able, "He's eaten nothing since he came aboard. He's heaving dry now, and ere long he'll bring up blood. He could die. How shall they take that in Durbrecht? And when word gets back to Sterbek?"

Kerym's face darkened at that and he tugged at his short beard, his dark eyes fixing me with a furious glare. I would not be quelled but met his gaze until he looked away and muttered, "Very well. Do you go find a herbalist, then. But quick, mark you! And do I lose my wager—"

If he completed his threat I did not hear it, for I was already gone from the poop and running for the gangplank, calling over my shoulder to Pyrdon that I went to find him a cure.

I sprang to the wharf and studied the buildings that faced the harbor. I saw warehouses and taverns, but no sign to indicate a herbalist, so I began to run toward the closest alehouse, thinking to secure directions there. It stood on the corner of the avenue leading up to the keep, and as I drew close, the procession I had seen emerged from between the buildings. There were about a score of riders, led by a black-bearded man whose fine clothes told me he was the aeldor Brython. On his right, the side on which the tavern lay, rode a young man with yellow hair wearing tunic and breeks not unlike my own, but of better cut and finer material. My headlong passage brought me almost into collision with his startled horse, and he mouthed a curse as the animal skittered, ears flattened. Instantly two riders, their plaid and the swords they carried marking them for members of the warband, urged their mounts forward, straight at me. I thought them likely to ride me down, or beat me with the flats of their blades, and veered away, seeking refuge, an arm raised in defense.

Brython called them to a halt, reining in. "He came off the galley," he said, and fastened eyes of a startlingly pale blue on my face. "What's about, lad, that you come in such haste?"

"Forgive me, my lord." I shaped a sketchy bow. "I've a friend sick on board, and I'd find a herbman."

"A seasick sailor?" It was the yellow-haired young man who spoke. "What manner of vessel am I committed to?"

This, I realized, must be Cleton. I said, "Not a sailor," and wondered if I should add "my lord." I decided not: we should, after all, be fellow students soon enough. "His name is Pyrdon," I explained, "and he's Durbrecht-bound, like me."

"Ah, a kindred Mnemonikos-elect." I saw that Cleton's eyes were the same pale hue as his father's, which made them seem cold and distant until he smiled. "Then best a remedy be found instanter. Mathyn, do you go swift to the keep and have Naern prepare a nostrum. Bring it to us on the boat, if you will."

A soldier swung his horse around and galloped back the way they had come. Cleton returned his eyes to me and said, "So . . ."

He frowned an inquiry, and I said, "Daviot."

"So, Daviot, do you come introduce me to our captain? I, by the way, am Cleton."

He reached down from his saddle, and we clasped hands. I fell into step beside him as the column walked on toward the *Seahorse*. Kerym stood fidgeting by the gangplank, but neither Cleton nor his father appeared in any great hurry, reining in and dismounting as Kerym flourished a deep bow and bade them the day's greetings.

Brython returned the salutation and said, "A man's gone to bring a remedy for your sick passenger, captain, so you're delayed awhile."

Kerym nodded, glancing irritably at me. Cleton caught his look and said calmly, "You'd not deliver a sick man to Durbrecht, would you, captain?"

Kerym reddened somewhat and shook his head vigorously, mouthing unctuous denial. I enjoyed his discomfort, and decided that I should like Cleton, did he continue in this manner. I saw that although his clothes were grander, he carried no more baggage than I, and that himself, waving away Kerym's offer of a crewman for porter with the pronouncement that he was now merely one more Mnemonikos-elect, no different to his companions Daviot and Pyrdon.

The statement seemed to me designed to put Kerym in his place and simultaneously elevate me. I grinned, and then caught Cleton's eye as he winked and grinned the wider.

We waited there, Brython engaging Kerym in conversation as Cleton questioned me, much as I had interrogated Pyrdon. He was an easy fellow to talk with, putting me at my ease so that I soon felt there was no barrier between us, despite the very different circumstances of our births.

Before long Mathyn returned with the herbman's potion and his instructions as to its use. Brython insisted, politely but with no argument brooked, that Kerym wait while Pyrdon swallow the vile-smelling concoction, and our hasty captain was forced to curb his impatience as Cleton and I tended our unfortunate companion. Cleton himself administered the draught, wondering aloud if he should not require a measure before we reached our destination. In point of fact, he was an excellent sailor, as at home on the waves as I, and I realized he pretended for Pyrdon's sake. I liked him better by the moment.

In a while Pyrdon declared himself somewhat recovered. Certainly he regained a measure of his color and took a few mouthfuls of ale, and Cleton said his final farewells, and Kerym was at last permitted to depart.

We three young men stood together on the foredeck, watching Madbry dwindle behind us. Ahead lay Durbrecht and a future none of us anticipated, I the least of all.

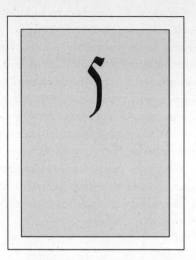

The journey was the pleasanter for the company of Cleton and Pyrdon, whose recovered health revealed him to be as I had guessed: a cheerful, good-natured fellow, if a trifle timid. He was clearly in some awe of the aeldor's son, even though Cleton took pains to assure us we were all equal, and his easy manner contained no hint of pride or superiority. Still, both Pyrdon and Kerym tended to deference, whilst I took him at face value. I suspect that was because both our captain and the tanner's son had dealings with the aristocracy, and some sense of rank, whereas I had no experience other than of Bardan and his kin, and they had shown me only kindness. So I accepted Cleton for what he declared himself to be: only another student.

Nonetheless, I remained somewhat intrigued that he should forgo his life in Madbry's keep for that of a humble catechumen. It seemed to me he gave up more than he would gain, and one fine evening as we watched dolphins sport about the bow, I asked him why.

"What's the third son of an aeldor to look forward to?" he asked in reply. Then answered himself: "My oldest brother will inherit the title, and Decan stands to make a better marriage than I. Did I stay, it should be as a hanger-on, reliant on Mordan's charity. That, or find myself wedded off to some hold-daughter too homely to win herself a first or second son. I'd sooner stand on my own feet."

He paused, grinning, and lowered his voice to a conspiratorial whisper, looking melodramatically about. "And I'm none too good a soldier, Daviot, for I've little taste for taking orders and a thirst for knowledge. I'd learn all I can about this land of ours. And how better do that than as a Mnemonikos?"

I considered a moment, then said, "I think we shall have to take orders in the College, Cleton."

"Then I think," he said, his voice and handsome face so solemn, I at first took him seriously, "that I shall likely find myself in trouble." I laughed with him as the gravity quit his features.

Of the remainder of that voyage there's little enough of import, save that as we closed on the eastern ingress of the Treppanek, airboats were sighted.

It was late in the afternoon of the fifth day. Kerym had the sail up to catch the breeze and the oarsmen bent to their sweeps, driving the *Seahorse* swift over the darkening blue of the ocean—our captain looked to win his wager. Mare's-tails streamered white overhead, and the coastline to port stood shadowy as the sun went westward. The moon was not yet up, but the sky to the east grew gentian. I lounged on the foredeck, rolling dice with Cleton and Pyrdon. We rose as a Changed—Bors, I saw as I sprang up—vented a bellow that suggested his taurine origins. I stared to where he pointed, hearing Kerym's voluble cursing echo Bors's shout. The wind that drove the clouds across the heavens also drove more solid objects that I recognized instantly as the Sky Lords' great airborne vessels.

There were three, coming swift toward us, a little to the north, on a course that would carry them above the line of the Treppanek. They hung lower in the sky than any I had seen before, so that the sigils decorating the vast tubes supporting the baskets were clear; or would have been, had they not seemed to burn and writhe like living things, as if the magic imbued in the arcane forms clawed at the air like the arms of swimmers. The sky about the cylinders was itself distorted by the sorcery of the Kho'rabi wizards, roiling and boiling, tinged with red, as if the Sky Lords trailed fire in their wake. As with that first I had seen, I thought I saw nebulous creatures, elemental beings, dancing about the bloodred craft, speeding their passage faster than any natural wind might drive them. The sun was to our west, but shadow raced ahead of the airboats to encompass our galley, bringing with it a dreadful chill, a numbing stillness to the air. I shivered, hating that malign aura. At my side I heard Pyrdon mouth a prayer that the God defend us, Cleton utter a string of oaths. I saw that in moments their path and ours must coincide. I clutched the hilt of my dagger, a useless gesture, but somehow comforting.

The airboats closed on the coast. They came so low, I saw the pale blurs of faces looking down from the black baskets. I heard Cleton say, "They make for Durbrecht," his voice leached of its usual humor. I felt as if some occult hand reached down into my belly, squeezing tight and horribly cold. I felt afraid and knew that it was more than any natural fear—that was to be expected, faced so close with the terrible Kho'rabi knights. This was far greater; it was as if the shadow that darkened the galley, the sea itself, robbed me of hope, as if the magic of the Sky Lords pierced my soul. I felt paralyzed, my feet rooted to the deck, my hand frozen about my dagger's hilt. All I could do was watch, gape-mouthed and trembling. Had a Kho'rabi dropped down then, I think I should have stood still and silent as he slew me. I do not think I *could* have moved.

In moments the three airboats were directly overhead. It was as if an icy winter's night fell. I did move then, for my teeth began to chatter uncontrollably, clattering in my mouth like madly beaten tabors. I felt my body begin to shudder helplessly. It seemed my eyes were connected by some occult thread to the airboats and I could only follow their progress, robbed of volition. They filled all the sky, and I thought I heard spirits howling, imps and malicious sprites delivered from Ahn-feshang to torment Dharbek. My head craned around; my neck ached with the pressure, but I could not shift my body. I saw nothing but the Sky Lords' vessels. Cleton, Pyrdon, the *Seahorse* disappeared into some insubstantial occult shadow land. All that existed were those three vast airboats and myself. I had never before felt so utterly helpless; nor so dreadfully afraid. It seemed they hung an eternity overhead, but it could only have been moments, for as swiftly as they had come, they were moving inland, following the wide Treppanek westward toward Durbrecht.

For a while the sky behind them continued to roil, and there drifted down a faint, sulphurous smell. Then they were hidden beyond the line of the coast, and I found I could move again. I spat: it seemed a foul taste filled my mouth. I saw Pyrdon vomit. Cleton stood pale and silent, a hand running slowly over his yellow hair. We stared at one another. His face was set in lines of rigid horror; I suppose mine was the same. Then I realized something of which I had been aware throughout that horrid interlude, but on a subconscious level that only now impressed itself upon my conscious mind: The passage of the *Seahorse* had not slowed.

I turned to observe the oarsmen. They manned their sweeps as before, their rhythm unbroken. It was as though the ghastly magic of the Sky Lords had no effect on them. I saw Bors standing by the mast. His wide face was turned westward, to where the airboats had gone, and it seemed to me he wore a smile. I shook my head, blinking, and when I looked at him again his features were returned to their customary blandness. I decided I was wrong: that what I had taken for a smile was the residue of fear.

I turned back to Cleton and said, "They seem not at all afraid."

He did not understand me at first and I said, "The crew—they went on rowing. The Sky Lords' magic seemed not to affect them."

"Perhaps it does not," he said. His voice was hoarse. "Perhaps they've not the sensibility." He forced a laugh. "I'd name them lucky."

I licked my lips and wiped hands I suddenly felt were slick with sweat against my tunic. "Still," I said, "it seems strange to me."

"They're Changed," he said. "You're a Trueman."

"And yet, when I saw a boat before, when I was young"—I frowned, recalling that evening on the shore when I had stood with my father watching that first airboat pass over us—"then all the animals in Whitefish village fled. Even the gulls quit the sky."

"What do you say?" Cleton asked.

"I'm not sure." I felt the furrowing of my brow. "Only that it seems . . . odd."

"That the Changed do not feel what Truemen feel?" he asked, and chuckled. "Daviot, they're lesser beings than you or I; not really that much more than the animals from which they come."

"But that's my point," I said. "That even the animals sense the danger. These seemed . . . unaware . . . or not at all afraid."

Cleton's shoulders rose in a dismissive shrug. "Kerym's trained them well," he said. "No order was given to cease their rowing, so they continued at their duty."

"Perhaps."

He was an aeldor's son—he had far more experience of the Changed than I: I allowed him the point, but I was not convinced. I did not understand why, but I felt sure there was more to it. I could not explain my conviction. Indeed, I could not truly name it *conviction;* rather, it was an amalgam of what I had observed, or thought I observed, and inchoate suspicion. I could put it in no better words, and for then I bowed to Cleton's judgment. Besides, we had much else to concern us, as Pyrdon reminded us.

His face was gone again pale, and he wiped at his mouth, his breath sour with his puking as he stared to the west and said in a soft, horrified voice, "There were three. In the God's name, there were *three*! And they're headed for Durbrecht."

"I think they'll not damage the College." Cleton made a joke of it for Pyrdon's sake, I thought.

"But it's not the *time.*" Pyrdon was too shocked to allow the jest. "The last Coming was but—what?—thirty years ago. It's not the *time.*"

"It was a little over twenty-nine," said Cleton, no longer laughing. "But still I think they'll not harm Durbrecht."

Pyrdon tore his gaze from the sky and faced us. "How can you be so sure?" he demanded.

His eyes asked Cleton for reassurance. I found his mood communicated to me and realized I hung on Cleton's answer. He said confidently, "There's powerful magic in Durbrecht. Remember the Sorcerous College is there, too."

"And the Sentinels there." Pyrdon flung an arm to the east. "And they did not halt the Sky Lords."

"Aye, there's that." Cleton faltered a moment, less assured, then said, "But still, the greatest of our mages reside in the College of Durbrecht, and they'll know by now the airboats approach. Likely the Sentinels were taken by surprise—Durbrecht shall not be."

Pyrdon mulled this over. I could see that he wanted to accept it. No less did I, and when he nodded I felt relieved, as if his agreement took some weight from me. Then Cleton murmured, "And we'll find out soon enough. All well, another day should see us there," and I realized he was far less convinced by his own arguments than he pretended.

I could think of nothing to say.

I was roused from a dream in which I stood immobile on a becalmed galley as the sky above me filled with the Sky Lords' airboats and a crew of Changed applauded the arrows that rained about me. It was a moment or two before I shook off the sensation of impotent horror and recognized Pyrdon. He said, "Come; look," and there was such awe in his voice, I sprang immediately to my feet and followed him to the port side of the *Seahorse.* Cleton was already there, staring intently into the gray-white mist that hung above the water. It was not yet dawn, and the world was lit with the opalescent glow that presages the arrival of the sun. The forward running light cast a red illumination that reminded me of the Kho'rabi balloons. Pyrdon pointed and said, "There."

I followed the direction of his outflung arm and gasped, for only a short distant off it seemed the skeleton of some vast primordial beast thrust from the channel.

Massive ribs curved upward, thick and black against the glow of the false dawn. The mist was damp and deadened smell, but even so I caught the aftermath of burning, as though a tremendous fire had been not long ago doused. Amongst the ribs I saw dark, solid objects that I did not at first recognize as the bodies of dead men.

Cleton said, "One airboat at least failed to reach Durbrecht."

His voice was hushed by the enormity of the monolithic wreckage, and I said nothing, only nodded, staring. I wondered how many Kho'rabi knights had that boat carried, most sunk under the weight of their armor, those I could see caught amongst the burning spars of their vessel.

Pyrdon said, "The God be praised."

I watched the wreckage go by, calculating the length of the airboat against that of the *Seahorse*. The Sky Lords' craft was four times, or more, our length.

Cleton said, "I wonder how the others fared."

"Destroyed like this, the God willing," said Pyrdon.

I turned to observe the skeleton as it slipped away astern. It was soon lost in the mist, and then the zodiacal light faded and I fetched my cloak from the deck as the morning grew chill.

We none of us felt able to sleep after that awesome sight and stood on the foredeck wrapped in our cloaks as the sky behind us brightened. The sun rose, and before long we came in sight of Durbrecht. I felt my jaw drop.

The Treppanek curved slightly north here, a low headland sheltering a wide bay. Atop the higher ground stood a wall that ran inland to sweep westward in a vast semicircle before returning to the shore. It encompassed all the sprawling city, and at each end there stood a pharos, like an aeldor's keep in miniature. Penned within these ramparts there stood such a multitude of buildings as dwarfed all the towns I had seen on our journey. Madbry, Ynisvar, and Cambar might all have been set down here and gone unnoticed, so large was this marvelous place. On the riverside there was a harbor, jetties extending out from the long line of the wharf, myriad craft rocking at anchor, the dockside abustle. Farther back, past the docks and warehouses, splendid structures glittered in the early morning sun. I saw wide avenues, the greenery of parks, and spread across the rising flank of the hinterland, three enormous complexes of buildings. One I felt sure must be the College of the Mnemonikos, the others that of the sorcerers and the palace of the city's commander, the koryphon.

I started as Cleton nudged me and said, "Close your mouth, Daviot. Or would you swallow it all?"

I nodded and smiled, and went on staring. To my left I heard Pyrdon say softly, "In the God's name, I have never seen its like."

"Save for Kherbryn, it has no like," said Cleton, and grinned hugely. "I believe we shall enjoy ourselves here, my friends."

I nodded again, lost for words, watching rapt as Kerym brought the *Seahorse* into the wharf and the mooring lines were made fast.

Cleton needed nudge me again before I shifted from my observation, reminded that I had best secure my gear, which did not take long, so that by the time the gangplank was run out, we all three stood waiting, eager to go ashore.

I halted on the wharf, unsure what we should do next, thinking I should say something to our captain. For all I did not like him, he had surely brought us here safe and swift, even were it less for our sake than the winning of his wager. He resolved that problem readily enough, for he came after us down the gangplank and said, "Well, you're here and my duty done. I bid you farewell."

He ducked his head and turned to go, halted by Cleton, who demanded, "What do we do now, captain?"

Kerym frowned with ill grace and said, "Someone from the College will be here soon enough. Wait for him."

He delayed no longer but waved and walked away, soon lost in the bustling throng. Cleton said, "Doubtless he's anxious to collect his winnings. Well, no matter, save I'd not stand here like some lost sheep."

"What else should we do?" asked Pyrdon.

Cleton's eyes roved over the anchorage, settling on a tavern. "We could find ourselves breakfast," he suggested.

"Is that a good idea?" Pyrdon shifted nervously from foot to foot. "What if the College sends for us and we're not here?"

"I imagine we can find our own way to the College," Cleton said. "Likely we're early, and not yet expected."

Pyrdon frowned, clearly ill at ease. Cleton grinned at me and asked, "How say you, Daviot? Do we stand here like goggling bumpkins, or eat and quench our thirst?"

I was tempted, though I was quite happy to study the activity around us, and thought Pyrdon correct in his caution. I mused a moment, then said, "Perhaps it were wiser we remain, Cleton. Likely the College knows of our arrival."

"I shall stay here," said Pyrdon firmly.

"Then does someone come for us," said Cleton, "you can tell them Daviot and I may be found in yon alehouse. Eh, Daviot?"

He grinned a challenge. I looked a moment at the earnest Pyrdon, then at the smiling Cleton, torn between sensible caution and the promise of adventure. Cleton's cheerful disregard of authority was infectious. I shrugged and said, "I *am* hungry."

"Then come on," Cleton said, and waved an expansive arm, "and I shall buy you breakfast."

I hesitated only a moment longer, then shouldered my bag and went with Cleton to the tavern.

The sign outside depicted a lusciously breasted woman clad in nothing more than her long golden hair, her lower body a sweeping fishtail. I gazed, wondering if such a creature might truly exist. There were letters inscribed across the bottom of the board that Cleton translated: "The Mermaid."

"Can you read?" I asked.

He nodded and said, "A little," but his attention was focused on the alehouse.

It was early yet, but the place was busy, loud with voices and the clinking of tankards, redolent of ale and tobacco and cooking food. We found a space at the long serving counter and ordered beer, then Cleton asked what fare was on offer. I let him choose and found myself soon confronted with a platter of sausages still spitting fat and warm bread. I had never tasted a sausage before, and I ate with gusto, studying the other customers.

They were an exotic bunch: as many Changed as Truemen, though the Changed occupied tables to one side of the smoky room, the central aisle apparently a tacit demarcation line. I saw sailors and longshoremen, soldiers wearing Durbrecht's plaid, traders and merchants, women both serving and sitting with the men. I drank it all in as thirstily as I swallowed my ale, thinking all the time: *I am in Durbrecht!* The enormity of it widened my eyes, and I think I must then have looked a true bumpkin, goggling at the marvels of the city.

And Cleton, for all he was son of an aeldor, was little better, staring around with a huge smile, not speaking, but like me simply watching and listening.

It was impossible in the din to hear more than fragments of conversation, but what I could make out was entirely concerned with the Sky Lords' attack. I gathered that the three airboats had perished, but some small amount of damage been done. I listened as avidly as I watched and so did not see Pyrdon come pushing through the throng until he arrived before us, his freckled face flushed, his eyes anxious.

"You're to come immediately," he declared. "The warden's waiting."

I snatched up my bag; Cleton drained the last of his mug. We followed Pyrdon out to find a tall man, his sandy hair plaited, standing tapping a short caduceus impatiently against his thigh. He was very thin, his tunic seeming overlarge on his narrow shoulders, and his face was cadaverous, the eyes that fixed us deep-sunk. I was minded of small burrowing animals peering from their lairs.

"I am Ardyon," he announced without preamble, "warden of the College. You may address me as Warden or by my name. You are . . . ?"

We identified ourselves, and he nodded, extending a hand. I thought for a moment he would greet us formally, but Cleton offered his token of introduction, and I dug mine from beneath my shirt. Ardyon studied the seals on each disc, then nodded his skull-like head in silent confirmation and said, "Why did you not wait as your companion did?"

His voice was cold as his stare, and I fidgeted awkwardly, lost for words. Cleton smiled cheerfully and answered, "Kerym offered us no breakfast, and we deemed it as well we acquaint ourselves with something of Durbrecht. We left Pyrdon on watch."

"Whilst you drank ale," said Ardyon.

"And broke our fast," said Cleton.

Ardyon sniffed. It was impossible to read his expression, but I thought it likely disapproving. In the same toneless voice he said, "Amongst my duties is the meeting of newcomers. That is but one task to which I must attend. There are others, as you'll learn, but foremost is the maintenance of discipline amongst the Mnemonikos-elect. This" —he flourished the caduceus—"is the badge of my office. You will obey any Trueman bearing this emblem. Do you understand?"

We nodded and assured him it was so.

"Good," he said. "Now understand this. When you are sent for, you attend. You do not go exploring the alehouses of Durbrecht, or any other of the city's many pleasures. You wait. You do as you are bid and no more; nor any less. Remember that, and your sojourn here shall not be too unpleasant. Now follow me."

He spun about, spindleshanks propelling him swiftly away: we hastened to follow. Cleton and I exchanged a glance, my friend exaggerating an expression of remorse. I felt abashed, and even Pyrdon, though he had not been included in the reprimand, looked distinctly nervous. I thought it an inauspicious beginning.

But my doubts faded as we traversed the streets of the city, overwhelmed by the wonders all about me. Ardyon led us from the harbor through a maze of warehouses that filled the air with exotic perfumes, onto a wide avenue faced on both sides by emporiums offering such a wealth of produce as widened my eyes and set my nostrils to twitching like a questing hound's. We saw arcades and bazaars, whole squares filled with canopied stalls, grand taverns and eating houses, plazas where fountains played and trees grew, protected by ornate fences. And people—more people than I had thought the whole world could hold, merchants and their customers, folk who did no more than stroll leisurely as if they had no work to call them, but only time in which to wander this cornucopia of wonders.

We hurried after the briskly striding warden down streets over-hung with balconies that trailed bright flowers, past walls painted with a kaleidoscope of colors, or tiled; up stairways narrow and wide; across squares where statues stood proud. I saw loaded carts driven by Changed and carriages holding Truemen, horses ridden by men and women both. I gaped and goggled my way to a great white wall where Ardyon halted and gestured with his staff.

"This is the College of the Mnemonikos," he announced. "Save you are dismissed early, this shall be your home for the next year at least."

I was too excited to allow his reminder of possible failure to dampen my spirits. I stared, wondering if the wall was to keep us in or the city out. There was a gate, tall and wide, stained a pale blue, standing open. Ardyon led us through into a courtyard paved with great stone slabs, shrubs and fledgling trees growing in stone basins, benches set along the inner face of the wall occupied by men old and young. A few Changed went about menial tasks. Ardyon continued his march without breaking pace, across the courtyard to a high build-ing with windows set like watching eyes and an arch at its center that granted entry to the cloistered quadrangle beyond. We turned off there, following our guide up a stairway to a door of black wood, where he motioned us to halt, tapping three times with his caduceus. A muffled voice bade us enter, and Ardyon swung the door open.

A small man, the light from the window at his back shining on his pate, sat behind a desk. He did not rise, but I could see he was not tall and that his face was unlined and amiable as his welcome.

"The day's greetings," he said pleasantly. "Welcome to Dur-brecht."

Pyrdon and I mumbled a response, Cleton replying more firmly. Ardyon named us one by one, tapping us each on the chest with his staff, and handed over our tokens. The bald man glanced at the disks and set them aside. "I am Decius," he said, "master of the College. Your journey here was comfortable, I trust?"

Pyrdon nodded.

I said, "We saw the skyboats that attacked the city."

Cleton said, "And the wreck of one; along the Treppanek."

Decius smiled and said, "Do you tell me what you saw?"

He motioned for me to begin. I know not why, for I was not entirely at ease, whilst Cleton seemed quite confident, as if an interview with so elevated a personage was to him an everyday event.

I swallowed, cleared my throat, and commenced to tell him all I remembered. I was speaking of the elementals I believed I had seen sporting about the Sky Lords' craft when he raised a hand to halt me and bade Cleton continue. Cleton took up the tale and was in his turn halted, Pyrdon finishing with an account of the wrecked airboat.

"How many bodies did you see?" asked Decius, when Pyrdon fell silent.

Pyrdon frowned and shrugged and said, "I am not sure, master."

Decius smiled and raised inquiring brows at Cleton, who said, "I think there were thirteen."

I found those mild eyes fastened on me then, and I closed my own an instant, conjuring the image. I said, "There were fifteen, master."

"You're sure?" asked Decius.

I hesitated a moment and then said, "Not absolutely. They were amid the wreckage, like bodies in the belly of a dead beast. But I think there were fifteen."

Decius nodded, and I wondered if I had done well or badly in what I took to be a test. I was not told, for he turned his face to the warden then and said, "Do you show them to their dormitory, Ardyon? And I'd suppose they'll want to eat. After, do you bring them to Martus."

Ardyon offered a brief bow in response and motioned for us to follow him again. We quit the room, trailing after the warden back down the stairs, across the quadrangle to a separate building that he advised us held the dormitories of the Mnemonikos-elect.

Ours was a long, high-windowed room containing twenty beds, each with a cupboard beside that Ardyon explained was for our sole use. There were, he told us in his toneless voice, only fifteen candidates in residence, and no more were expected. He took our daggers into safekeeping, promising their return at the year's end, waited as we chose our beds and stowed our gear, and then brought us to the dining hall, which lay on the far side of the quadrangle. He was meticulous in the dispensation of his duties, and even though neither Cleton nor I had appetite left, we were settled at a table with Pyrdon, watching as porridge, bread, and tea were brought him by a servant I recognized as Changed. As he ate, Ardyon outlined the timetable of our days.

Cleton caught my eye as we quit the dining hall, and on his face I saw the promise of disobedience to come.

He remained dutifully silent, however, as Ardyon led us through gardens to a walled enclosure, where a man of middle years sat with the fifteen candidates already in residence. We were introduced, and the warden left us. The man studied us a moment, then said, "I am Martus, your tutor for the next year. Do you tell me something of yourselves?"

We each in turn recited our brief histories, and Martus named our fellow candidates. I studied him and them. He seemed a pleasant enough man of no especial distinction. He was of average height and build, shaven clean, with an abundant head of light brown hair and eyes that seemed somewhat sleepy, though I soon learned they missed nothing. He was clad in well-worn breeks and tunic, with a sash of vivid red. The other students were a disparate lot, as might be expected, given they came from all over Dharbek. There were fishermen like me, another tanner's son, two blacksmiths, several merchants' offspring, three from taverns; Cleton was the only student of noble descent. Nor, Martus explained, were there female Mnemonikos, our itinerant lives being deemed unsuitable for the supposedly gentler sex.

That first day passed swift, and it seemed not long at all before a gong summoned us to the dining hall for the evening meal. The hall was filled with students of all ages and loud with the buzz of conversation. I was marveling at the richness of our fare when one of the farriers' sons, a hulking fellow from the west coast whose name was Raede, fixed Cleton with his small eyes and said, "So you're an aeldor's son, eh?"

Cleton nodded, smiled amiably, and answered, "That I am. Brython of Madbry is my father."

Raede snorted. Like one of the horses he helped his father shoe, I thought. Certainly he was built for the work, or the work had built him. I was no weakling—rowing a boat and hauling nets had put muscle on my frame—but next to Raede I was nothing. He was huge, with bulging forearms and a neck thick as a bull's: I had seen no one bigger save Kerym's Changed crewmen. He studied Cleton awhile, then said, "I suppose you think yourself better than us."

A hamhock hand gestured at the others. Cleton, still smiling, said, "No. Why should I?"

Raede paused a moment, frowning, and said, "You're an aeldor's son." It appeared he found that sufficient explanation and cause for resentment.

Cleton nodded again and said, "Here we are all students, equal."

"I'm stronger," said Raede.

"I can see that," said Cleton.

I suppose I had, in a way, led a sheltered life. There had been no bullies in Whitefish village, and it was a while before I recognized that Raede was less concerned with Cleton's antecedents than with establishing his own authority. I stared at his blunt features and wondered why he sought to provoke this argument, simultaneously realizing that Cleton's mild responses served only to irritate him the more.

"I could break you," he said.

"Perhaps," said Cleton.

I thought there was no *perhaps* about it. I thought Raede could likely break us both. I thought it a pity Ardyon had confiscated our weapons. I heard Raede say, "The aeldor of Kesbry had a son; a snotty creature he was."

"Some are," Cleton said.

"Like you," said Raede.

"You make swift judgments, friend Raede," Cleton said, still mild, as if they conducted an entirely friendly conversation. "You've known me but a single afternoon and already you mark me one with a man I've never set eyes on. Think you you're perhaps a trifle hasty?"

Raede said, "No. I think you're a popinjay. I think you're a pampered keep-son. And I don't like you."

To his right and left two students sniggered. Their names were Leon and Tyras. I thought that did this come to the fight Raede appeared intent on provoking, they would take his side. I thought that singly I could defeat either one, but together . . . I glanced sidelong at Pyrdon, wondering if he would aid us, and saw his eyes shifting nervously between Cleton and Raede. I thought he would not.

Cleton said equably, "That's your right, my friend. Indeed, I must admit I've not much fondness for you." Then his eyes flashed and his voice dropped, though his words came clear: "But still I'll warn you—do you continue this, you'll regret it."

Raede was a moment taken aback, then he snorted laughter and said, "I'll regret it, eh? And how shall you make me regret it, popinjay?"

Cleton's voice was mild again, but his eyes were pale and hard. "I'll thrash you," he said confidently.

Raede's eyes narrowed until they were tiny slits: I thought no longer of a bull, but of a wild boar brought to bay and ready to attack. He said, "We'll see. After dinner."

"As you wish," said Cleton.

After we had eaten we left the hall and waited outside for the tutors to disperse. As is the way of such things, word had gone around the students, and a crowd was gathered in the quadrangle, eager for the promised diversion. Raede announced that the enclosure where we had taken our first lessons was a suitable place, and we made our way there, as stealthily as any group of bloodthirsty young men. It was foolish of us to think we should go unnoticed, but we believed ourselves unobserved as we filled the space, the spectators spreading along the walls, Cleton and I facing Raede and his two acolytes at the center. The night was starry, and sufficient light came from the College buildings and the streets of Durbrecht that we could see well enough. I saw that Raede was smiling hugely.

"I trust this is between we two alone," Cleton said, intending insult, "and your friends shall not aid you."

"I'll not need aid," Raede answered.

"Then do we begin?" said Cleton.

Raede grunted and took a long step forward, swinging a clublike fist at Cleton's head. He was not yet seventeen years old, but that blow could have downed a full-grown man. Cleton, however, was not there for the fist to strike: I saw him dance clear, ducking, and then rise to grasp Raede's wrist in both his hands. I am not sure what happened next—there was a swift shifting of feet, sudden movement, and Raede lay on his back. I laughed. Cleton stood waiting, smiling. Raede climbed to his feet and attacked again. And once more was toppled, landing this time on his face in a flowerbed. He pushed up, shaking his head, dirt smeared over his cheeks and mouth. Then he snarled and stood, staring at Cleton with furious eyes. He was not hurt, but he was humiliated, and perhaps aware for the first time that this might not be the easy victory of his anticipation. He advanced more cautiously, his head down and his hands extended from his sides. Cleton stood waiting for him, that easy smile still on his lips. Raede came on slowly, then sprang, faster than I had thought his size should allow, his great hands reaching for Cleton's throat. Had they landed, I think he would have choked my friend, or broken his neck. Instead, they found only empty air as Cleton again ducked under his opponent's reach, took hold of his tunic, and fell backward, crashing down with Raede into a bush. This time Raede cried out, and when he extricated himself, I saw his face was scratched, thin lines scored across his forehead and cheeks. He wiped a dirtied hand over his wounds and muttered a foul oath, then lowered his head and charged, caution forgotten.

It was a foolish move: Cleton simply stepped a pace sideways and in an eye's blink pivoted and kicked out, knocking Raede's legs from under him. For the fourth time the bully went down, skidding help-lessly over the flagstones. When he rose, his nose was bloodied and his lips puffed, his tunic filthy. I became aware of the audience mut-tering, that wagers had been placed. I grinned, sure now that Cleton must win.

Raede, too, had that thought, for he swung his heavy head and made some sign to Leon and Tyras. I saw it, and then that Raede maneuvered to turn Cleton's back to his supporters, advancing slowly again, his arms spread wide, driving Cleton across the opened space. I moved from my position, making my way along the edge of the crowd until I stood behind Leon and Tyras. I watched as Raede came on-ward, Cleton sensing some subterfuge, so that he risked a glance over his shoulder. He saw the two, and me behind, and nodded once as I waved, trusting me. Then he turned to face Raede again, feinting to one side and then the other, the larger man blocking his escape each time. I saw Leon and Tyras exchange a look and their shoulders tense in preparation. As Cleton was driven back, they readied to grab him. Raede smiled now, which was an ugly sight, and darted at Cleton, intending to force him back against Leon and Tyras.

They raised their arms, and I set a hand against each of their temples and slammed their heads together. I was, as I have said, no weakling, and I put all my strength into my effort. There was a dull sound, like two blocks of wood banged, and both gasped and went limp, falling bonelessly to the stones.

Cleton said, "I thought you needed no aid; I see you've no honor," and I heard both anger and contempt in his voice.

Raede grunted and continued his advance. Cleton stood his ground, and I feared he would be caught in Raede's terrible embrace. Then I winced, instinctively sympathetic, as he kicked Raede between the legs.

Raede squealed like a pig at gelding and clasped both hands to his assaulted manhood, knees and waist bending as he curled over the source of his pain. His eyes were closed and his mouth wide open. Cleton performed a kind of pirouette that spun him full around and lifted his other leg in a sweeping kick to Raede's chest. It was again so swift, I was not quite sure what my friend had done, but I saw Raede lifted onto his toes and toppled sideways. A choking moan burst from his open mouth, and he made no effort to rise, instead twisting in a fetal ball. Even in the yard's wan light I could see his face was horribly pale. I wondered if he was dying.

Cleton stood watching him, his expression dispassionate. There was a murmur from the onlookers, and someone called for Cleton to finish the fight. My friend said, "It is finished."

And then a toneless voice said, "Indeed it is, and now the price shall be paid."

I turned, startled, to find Ardyon at my back, behind him two Changed. He glanced at the two students lying unconscious at my feet and raised his brows in silent inquiry. I nodded, silent myself, my heart beating very fast. He touched me on the shoulder with his caduceus and said, "Come with me." The staff jutted in Cleton's direction and the warden said, "And you."

The crowd parted, opening a path to the gate, and we followed Ardyon to our punishment.

I learned a great deal about stables in the days that followed. Ardyon decreed that we should relieve the Changed whose task it usually was to tend the horse pens, and so for three weeks Cleton and I spent our evenings shoveling dung. It was tedious, but not especially hard labor; the worst thing about it was the smell that permeated our clothes. I grew accustomed to it soon enough, but for all we found we had won a new respect amongst our fellow students, still we must suffer their teasing—the ostentatiously pinched nostrils, the elaborate offers of pomanders and scented soaps. We grinned and bore it: at least we were not expelled.

I was intrigued by the expertise with which Cleton had dispatched Raede (who lay recovering in the infirmary with Leon and Tyras for company) and was about to question him the first evening when a small man with the fair hair and pale skin of northern Draggonek came into the stable. He had very bright eyes, set close together, and wore the black sash of an instructor in the martial arts.

"I am called Keran," he said, and preempted my inquiry. "Where did you learn to fight?"

"With the warband," Cleton answered, leaning on his shovel.

Keran nodded and settled atop a stall watching us. "Don't let me halt your labors," he said, "else Ardyon shall find you more."

We returned to the task in hand. Keran said, "Did you not think it unfair? Raede is, after all, without skill in the art." His voice was soft, with a slight northern burr, giving no hint whether he criticized or merely questioned.

Cleton deposited a pile of steaming dung in the cart and shrugged. "I warned him against baiting me," he said, "and he'd the advantage of his size and strength."

Keran's face was impassive as he returned, "But you well know that size and strength are no match for skill."

"Raede is stupid," said Cleton calmly. "He took offense at the accident of my birth. I sought no fight, but he forced it on me—because I am an aeldor's son, which should have warned him I'd have the advantage of training."

I thought Keran might have smiled then, but his tone remained dispassionate as he said, "You might have killed him."

"I might," Cleton agreed, "but I did not. Only taught him a lesson when he called his friends to help him."

Keran grunted and looked to me. I read a question in his eyes and said, "I saw Raede signal them, and then they readied to grab Cleton. That was unfair."

"So you tapped their heads," said Keran.

"I've not Cleton's skill," I said, "so I did what I could. Should I have stood by?"

"No," said Keran, and he did smile then. "Not whilst a comrade faced unfair odds."

I felt both vindicated and relieved. "They're not bad hurt?" I asked.

"They'll wake with aching heads," he told me. "And Raede will ache in other parts, but they'll survive. Likely they've learned a lesson, too. But you two—here not a full day and already fighting?"

"They left us little choice," said Cleton. "What else could we do?"

Keran nodded as if thinking about that, then murmured, "We've rules here, and one is that disputes be settled under the eyes of a tutor. I suspect it's unlikely you'll receive another challenge, but does it come, you'll meet it with me watching. Do you understand?"

We nodded dutifully, and I ventured to ask, "When shall the lessons begin?"

Keran chuckled then and said, "Are you so bloodthirsty, Daviot?"

I was somewhat surprised he knew my name, and shook my head, blushing. "No," I assured him, "but I'd learn to defend myself. Like Cleton."

"In time you shall," he promised. "But not for this year. The Mnemonikos-elect receive no training in the martial arts until they are formally accepted. Do you remain, then next year you'll start to learn."

This was not what Andyrt had led me to believe, and once I should have been disappointed, but now I only nodded, accepting.

"Patience is one of the virtues cultivated here," said Keran. "Do you study on that."

Again we nodded, and he sprang limber from his perch, waving a casual farewell as he sauntered away.

When he was gone out the door, Cleton said, "I'll tutor you, if you wish. But it had best be in secret."

So it was that I received clandestine instruction in the art of unarmed combat. It was not easy, for our sudden fame brought us a following and we must escape our admiring friends to practice, but we managed as best we could, and Cleton taught me well.

Martus was our sole official tutor for that year. He seemed to me a fount of knowledge, his memory prodigious, his ability to impart his erudition astounding. History and the basic mnemonic techniques were his subjects—what he casually named "the tricks of our trade"—and from him I learned to refine my natural talent. It was not, I came to realize, simply a matter of remembering: there was too much to remember, and to hold and recall all of it, we must learn to use those mental devices that enable us to fix things in our minds as if in storage, to be called up by means of specific images or key words. I remember well Martus's first explanation of the technique.

He brought us to a study chamber where there stood a cabinet set with numerous drawers, a piece of simple carpentry. Martus set a hand on its polished surface and said, "This is your mind. Each drawer holds a memory." He tapped a drawer. "Label each one, and when you need it"—he took a rosewood knob and drew out the drawer—"you may simply open it."

Behind me I heard someone—Raede, I think—mutter, "Are we then woodenheads?" Martus only smiled, easygoing man that he was, and said, "This is the simplest explanation—one even a woodenhead can understand," which elicited laughter and ended the muttering. He was a fine tutor: he made our lessons enjoyable, and so we learned them the better.

He taught us to observe and memorize, to listen and recall with total accuracy, devoid of embellishment. He would take us about the College and have us study rooms, or the sundry walled gardens, then ask us, singly and alone, to describe them; sometimes we would go into the city, and after recount all we had seen, retrace our routes. Thus did we learn something of Durbrecht's geography—and its taverns, for Martus was fond of good ale and saw no reason why our lessons should not be conducted in taprooms. I excelled at this, and I drank in the history he taught us, finding soon that I need not think consciously of his analogy with the cabinet, but employed it automatically. Thus I learned of our past and came to understand better the age-old enmity of Dhar and Ahn. And, though I knew it not, the seed of an idea was planted.

In the Dawntime the people were nomads, wandering the cold northern plains far beyond the Dragonsteeth Mountains. There were no Rememberers then, and so little is known of those ancient times, save that the wanderers came south into what then was named Tartarus and now is called the Forgotten Country.

There they met the dragons.

The land was mountainous, the slopes and valleys thickly wooded, and no men lived there, only the dragons and the game on which the dragons preyed.

They were great, the dragons, vast and ferocious, terrible hunters whose wings would darken the sky, their teeth and talons like sword blades. They were the Lords of the Sky then, living in their great Dragoncastles, lofty on the highest peaks, descending into the valleys to hunt. And to them the Dhar were no more than prey: they hunted men as they did the animals of the woods and fields. The people feared them, but the people had traveled far in their wanderings and found a land rich in game, where they might linger and—were they not taken by the dragons—grow sleek on the land's bounty. So it was they settled in Tartarus, finding ways in which they might defeat the great sky-hunters.

They built strong holds and tamed the wild beasts, raising herds of meat animals for themselves, but also for the dragons, to whom they offered sacrifice from their herds, that the winged ones not slaughter men. Thus did cunning overcome strength, and the people spread through the valleys and forests. But none ventured, ever, into the high country, which was the domain of the dragons.

And then the Dhar found the beginnings of magic.

There were some amongst them, they discovered, able to converse with the dragons. This was a thing of great wonder, for the people had thought the dragons like wolves, or the mountain cats—all fury and hunger. But they were not; they were, in their alien fashion, more akin to men than the beasts, for they spoke amongst themselves, and gathered in squadrons, and were loyal one to another. It was a very great wonder, and those men able to understand the sky-hunters' tongue were named Dragonmasters and hailed as saviors, for they interceded betwixt the Dhar and the dragons, oftentimes persuading the great predators to take their kills from the offered herds, not the people.

Then there was a time of peace and the Dhar grew in numbers, until the Dragonmasters warned that they were become so many, the dragons felt their ancestral land was overrun and spoke of culling the invaders.

Some scoffed at this, and the chiefs told the Dragonmasters that their duty it was to dissuade the dragons and protect their fellow men, and the warnings went unheeded. And in time the dragons came against the people in a terrible slaughter, seeking to drive them from Tartarus. Then did many turn against the Dragonmasters, blaming them, but the more sensible of the chieftains saw that they could not defeat such dreadful foes and looked once more southward. And so the Dhar became wanderers again, going down from the mountains into Ur-Dharbek, and those who remained behind were never heard of again and were supposed dead, slain by the dragons.

It was a hard land, Ur-Dharbek, a place of bleak moors and poor hunting, but still the people had their herds and thought to make a life there, free of the dragons.

They were wrong. The dragons followed, for they had found a taste for the sport of it, and for human flesh. They quested southward over Ur-Dharbek, and none were safe save the Dragonmasters, whom the sky-beasts would not touch, perceiving a kind of kinship. Then the Dragonmasters were hated, for they could not—or perhaps, would not—dissuade the dragons from their killing, and many were slain in rage and others chose to go away from the people, back north to the Forgotten Country. They were lost to the Dhar, and if they still live, there is no one knows it.

That was a time of suffering for the people, for it seemed they must forever be hunted and never find a peaceful land. But then it seemed the Three Deciders, or the One God, took pity on the Dhar, for that magic that had enabled the Dragonmasters to converse with the beasts grew stronger, albeit along different roads.

There were born ever-increasing numbers of children gifted with the occult talent, such that they were able to send their magicks against the dragons and destroy them. But even so they were not enough, and for every dragon slain it seemed the fury of its kin waxed the greater, until the mages turned their powers to other means of defense. They found ways in which to transform animals into semblance of men, and they named these creations the Changed, and sent them out to be the dragons' prey while the people, the Truemen, went on southward across the Slammerkin into the land they called Draggonek.

This was a country far richer than bleak Ur-Dharbek, and the sorcerers bent all their powers to making Changed that they sent back across the Slammerkin into Ur-Dharbek, that the dragons hunt them and not Truemen. Then the sorcerers, like the Dragonmasters before them, were hailed as saviors, and the aeldors of the Dhar joined together in the building of the Border Cities, along the south bank of the Slammerkin. Seven cities they built, each with a band of sorcerers whose task it was to create Changed and send them north and deny them return, or the dragons passage over the dividing gulf. Thus did Ur-Dharbek become the province of the Changed, where they might live free, and Truemen be safe. No Trueman goes there, but any Changed who so elects, if his or her duty be done, may cross the Slammerkin to join the wild Changed.

The Dhar prospered then and spread across all Draggonek to the gulf of the Treppanek, and across that into Kellambek, where they found a new tribulation.

There was a folk already there, who named themselves the Ahn. They were hunters and fishermen, and few in numbers, but very fierce, and they opposed the people's coming into Kellambek. But the Dhar were strong and would not give up this new land, and in time the Ahn were defeated, made slaves or banished renegade to the lonely places, where they lived as the beasts.

The people owned all the land now and named it Dharbek. The dragons and the Dragonmasters were gone into legend and the Ahn made subject folk: the Dhar prospered. And as is the way of these matters, the petty chieftains fell to warring one with the other, vying over borders and fishing rights, hunting lands, and farm country. Those years are named the Red, and they were ended by Emeric, the first Lord Protector.

He was but an aeldor then, his keep that of Kherbryn, but he was wiser than his fellows and saw that save peace be imposed on the people, they must destroy themselves.

Kherbryn was a strong keep even then, and through all the Red years it was never taken, nor Emeric defeated in battle, this in part due to his skill in war, and also because he was aided by the sorcerer, Caradon. He gathered about him other mages and made alliance with such aeldors as shared his views, or could be persuaded to them, until he commanded an army, which he sent out in battle, himself at its head, conquering keep after keep until all Dharbek was his. Then did he name himself Lord Protector and vow that never again should Dhar go awarring with Dhar. Thus were the Red years ended and the land given peace.

And in peace as in war, Emeric was a wise leader. Of Kherbryn he made a great city, and when he died his son, Tuwyan, decreed that Durbrecht be built, no lesser but devoted to the arts of peace, establishing here the Sorcerous College and this of the Mnemonikos. And that all the people be further bound, Tuwyan embraced the worship of the One God, renouncing the Three, and built the Seminary of the Church in Durbrecht.

But while the Dhar came to worship of the God, the Ahn clung to the old ways. Their deities stood triumvirate—Vachyn of the Sky, Byr of the Earth, and Dach of the Waters. This was frowned on by the Church and the shrines of the Ahn torn down, but they were a defeated people and none paid overmuch attention to their furtive ways. Thus were they able to effect their great exodus.

Kellambek was not then much populated, and as the sorcerers created ever more Changed to perform the menial tasks, there was less need of Ahn slaves. They were, anyway, a surly and secretive folk, given to resentment and sly escape, and so were not much missed when they slipped away. They built their boats and murdered any who found them or endeavored to halt them, and they sailed from Dharbek eastward across the Fend, which then was only the eastern sea, and for long years were never seen again. Indeed, they were forgotten like the dragons.

Then, when Laocar was Lord Protector and the Dhar grown used to peace, they returned.

Great skyboats were seen, propelled by magic, a fleet that bore beneath them huge carts filled with fylie of Kho'rabi warriors. They grounded across Dharbek, and there was a dreadful slaughter, for the Kho'rabi were terrible in battle and would sooner die than admit defeat. This was the first Coming, and the dead were numbered in the thousands. Keeps were razed, villages and whole towns laid waste. That word—*Kho'rabi*—became a dread thing, a curse. Laocar readied for war then, but when the last Sky Lord was slain there were no more, nor another Coming in his lifetime.

For fifty years there was not another Coming. Then once more a fleet, and fighting, and after that the airboats were sometimes seen, but not often until the century turned and the Kho'rabi attacked again. And so it went, fifty years by fifty years did the Ahn send their warriors against Dharbek to take back the land, their Comings like a plague that visits death and destruction. The people learned to fear these cycles, when the Sky Lords' great boats would fill the sky, and Theodus, who was Lord Protector after Laocar, and Canovar after him, looked to the sorcerers for explanation, for it was clearly magic that governed the Comings.

And the mages decided that it was, indeed, sorcery that drove the airboats, but also the worldwinds, that each half century turn and blow from the east, that allowed the Ahn wizards to send the Kho'rabi knights against us. They looked then for a means to defeat the attacks and told Canovar that just as the Border Cities defend the Slammerkin shore, so he must construct fortresses on those islands we now call the Sentinels to destroy the airboats ere they reach our coast.

At this point in Martus's narration a student called Braen said, "Not always," and our tutor sighed and nodded and said, "The wizardry of the Ahn grows stronger, I think."

Another said, "But surely not so strong as to overcome the Sentinels," and our history lesson became a debate, which Martus seemed not to mind. At least, he made no attempt to return us to our original course, but did his best to answer the questions that were flung at him.

"There were three skyboats come but recently," cried a fellow named Nevvid, "but this is not the time. How could they pass the Sentinels?"

Martus shrugged and spread helpless hands. "I am no mage," he told us. "I can only think the Ahn have found new powers."

"They've come unseasonal these past few years," said Tyras. And Leon echoed him with: "Do they overcome the worldwinds now?"

I said nothing. I could see that Martus lacked the answers; I wondered if any save the Ahn themselves could explain. And I was intrigued by all our tutor had said. Whilst my fellow students fired their barrage of questions, I thought of dragons and Dragonmasters, and of a land filled with Changed. I sat silent through the babble until Martus roused me from my musings, asking if I had nothing to say.

My head was aswim with unshaped notions that I could not articulate, and so I asked, "When is the next Coming?"

"Be it as before," Martus said, "in twenty years."

"Shall we be ready?" I asked.

Cleton said, "The keeps are ready," and Martus nodded and amplified: "As is the Lord Protector, so are the koryphons and the aeldors of Dharbek sworn to defend the land. For that reason they maintain the warbands, even in peaceful times, that the Sky Lords never find us unready."

I thought on things Andyrt had told me and said, "But our soldiers are not enough." I smiled an apology to my friend and went on, "Save the Sentinels be strengthened, how shall we defeat them?"

"The Sentinels *are* strengthened," said Martus. "Even now the strongest of the young sorcerers are sent, to lend their untrained power to the adepts."

I frowned and said, "But still—the three boats that came . . ."

Martus smiled somewhat grimly, nodded, and said, "They overcame the Sentinels, aye; but the strengthening goes on now, and soon, I think, shall be unpassable."

That raw young sorcerers were taken from their College was indeed true—but that the Sentinels should soon be unpassable? I must wonder at that: we Dhar knew nothing of the Ahn, save we had once defeated them and they had fled. We knew they returned out of the east, but not from where. We knew they commanded powerful magicks and that their warriors came to slay us, but nothing of their ultimate goals. Perhaps they were bent on our destruction, dedicated to the reconquest of the land that was once theirs; perhaps purposed only to revenge.

I could only nod, accepting, and hold to myself the thought that save we could destroy the Sky Lords in the air, before they reached our shores, we must forever live in dread of the Comings. An image entered my mind then of the Sky Lords locked in combat with the dragons of legend. It was an exciting thought, but fleeting and I set it aside as Cleton spoke.

He was ever more practical than I, and son of an aeldor, his thinking shaped by familiarity with his father's warband. Pragmatically he said to Martus, "We saw those airboats as we entered the Treppanek—all three, unharmed. They had passed the Sentinels, then, and were not brought down until they closed on Durbrecht. How was that?"

"The Sorcerous College," said our tutor. "Save for the Border Cities and the Sentinels, Durbrecht's the greatest concentration of mages, and some of the most powerful: their work, it was. They sent their magic against the Sky Lords and slew them ere they could ground."

He paused, and I could see from his expression he was concerned that the more timid amongst us might find cause for fear. He set a confident smile on his mouth and added, "I think we could not be in a safer place. We've the Sorcerous College and the koryphon Trevid's warband, both, to protect us."

Cleton nodded, satisfied, and I heard a murmur of relief from the timorous.

Our lessons with Martus were like that: an account of a Lord Protector's life was likely to become a debate, a discussion of *why* and *how*, questions asked and answered before we returned, often as not days later, to the original topic. He instilled in most of us, beyond the basics of our technique and the history he taught us, a *desire* to learn, a curiosity that prompted us to investigate, seeking ever more information with which to fill the drawers of our memories.

For that year we knew mostly peace. We heard of airboats burned over the Fend, and twice saw the great ships erupt in explosions of terrible fire within a league of Durbrecht. Once there was a great alarum, when an airboat grounded east of the city and Trevid sent his warband out in full force to confront the Kho'rabi. The city was loud that night, and Cleton persuaded me to an adventure.

Word had come from the Sentinels that a ship had eluded them, passed from mage to mage along the line of keeps down the Treppanek. We were told the warband rode, but even had we not received that information we should have known something was afoot, for the streets outside the College rang with the nervous cries of the populace and we could hear the thunder of urgent hooves, the clatter of armor and bridle bits. It was evening, our lessons were done, and we had eaten. Cleton and I had repaired to a secluded part of the College grounds, a storage area close by the north wall, where he continued my secret instruction in the martial arts. Since dusk, when word first came, our conversation had been of the landing and the koryphon's response, and we were agog with curiosity.

It was late summer then, the days long and the nights light. I remember a full moon, pale yellow, hung in a cloudless sky. Our practice was interrupted by the sounds from beyond the wall, for we would halt, trying to discern what was shouted or what the latest passage of horsemen meant, and then fall to discussing what we would do, were we in Trevid's shoes. Finally we left our exercises altogether and only listened.

Cleton eyed the wall, and in the moonlight I saw a smile curve his lips. He turned it on me, and it was like a challenge.

"We could climb that," he said.

It was as if he made only a casual observation, but I knew him well by then. I said, "We are forbidden. Would you spend the rest of the year shoveling dung?"

He gave no answer except that smile and crossed to stand beneath the wall. After a while he said, "My father keeps his walls smooth. This is rich in handholds."

As if experimenting, he probed a crack, found another, and was soon perched like a fly above me. "We might gain the top and watch," he called. "No more than that."

I knew him and he knew me: well enough that he was confident I would follow. He clambered higher; I went after him.

We gained the vertex and lay flat across the width. We were on a level with the upper windows of a repository. My fingers stung where the sharp-edged niches had inflicted small cuts, and I had torn one nail. I sucked the wound as a half-squadron galloped past below us. They were mounted archers.

"They go east," said Cleton.

"The Sky Lords grounded to the east," I said. "They're going to the east gate."

Cleton nodded absently and turned his face in that direction. Durbrecht was encircled by a protective ridge, and atop that was the city wall. I could see beacons there, and a multitude of individual torches shifting and flickering in the night.

Cleton said, "It would be interesting, eh?"

I said, "Is dung interesting?"

Cleton said, "We've come this far."

I said, "Yes," and my friend was promptly sprawled across the wall with his feet probing the outer surface for holds. I sighed as he slipped over, still smiling.

The descent was harder than the climb, but we reached the street safely and huddled a moment in the wall's shadow. A full squadron of lancers went by without a glance in our direction.

The warband was long gone by the time we reached the gate. Above us on the wall beacons burned, and we could see soldiers moving there. A squad of halbediers approached, and Cleton asked the jennym what went on. The officer returned him the suggestion we go home, leave what fighting there might be to those trained for such duty. We hung about a while, but nothing exciting arose to capture our attention, and before long we agreed we should return.

This time I thought the College wall looked higher. The moon certainly was higher, and I thought we had been longer gone than we had anticipated. I was correct.

We climbed the wall and worked our way back down the inner side. The College was ominously quiet, light showing at only a few windows. There was none at all in our dormitory as we slunk like thieves in the night along the edges of the quadrangle. We reached the door, and I was indulging in a measure of self-congratulation (and relief) when a familiar voice spoke our names.

I was convinced then that Ardyon possessed a sixth sense in addition to keen eyesight, excellent hearing, and an ability to conceal himself. I suppose they are qualities desirable in a warden. He emerged from the shadows silent as a ghost, tapping his caduceus in a most threatening manner against one narrow shoulder. Cleton and I stood rigid, like rabbits frozen by a fox's gaze.

Ardyon stepped close, bending forward a little with his nostrils flaring. I realized he sought the smell of liquor on our breath. When he found none, he nodded and took a pace back. "Where?" he asked.

Cleton it was who answered. "We went to the east gate," he said. "We thought it an excellent opportunity to observe the deployment of Trevid's warband. We hoped to learn from it."

I was impressed by his quick wits and sheer audacity. If Ardyon shared my admiration, he gave no sign. He only said, "You knew it forbidden."

Cleton nodded and said, "I persuaded Daviot we should go."

"No," I said. "There was no persuasion. I went of my own will."

Ardyon sniffed. He had a way of sniffing that could chill the blood. "At least you're honest," he said. "What did you see?"

"Not much," I said. "The warband was gone and the gate closed."

Ardyon nodded again. Then he said, "Find me when your morning's lesson is done," and turned away, fading back into the shadows.

So it was I learned something of the culinary arts, for our punishment this time—in addition to stable duties—was that we help in the kitchens. Being unskilled, we were set to peeling and paring, washing and scrubbing, with barely time left to snatch a mouthful of the food we readied; and in the evenings, after, we must return to the horses and their voluminous output. I thought it unfair we had earned such a sentence in return for no more than a shut gate and a few soldiers.

However, our adventure and its outcome were not without some harvest of knowledge.

Primarily, that Ardyon was inescapable; ubiquitous, it seemed to me. But also that whilst the College would mete out punishment for such infringement of its rules, it tacitly applauded the initiative demonstrated. A Mnemonikos-elect who showed such independence was safe from expulsion. Not from punishment—most assuredly not!—but he would not lose his place in the College. Indeed, there were only three expelled during my time there—one for theft, one for the rape of a younger student, and one for a knifing.

And I came to know the Changed better.

As was the way throughout Durbrecht, the menial tasks about the College were performed by them. They cooked our food, tended the horses and the gardens, cleaned the rooms and courtyards. They were a mostly silent, always subservient, presence we scarcely noticed —they were simply *there*, and we accepted them as we did the statuary or the birds that left their droppings on the stone for the Changed to scrub away. Working with them in the kitchens I came into greater contact with them and began to perceive them not as faceless menials but as individuals, with quirks and characteristics as personal as any Trueman's.

Oh, there was an undoubted degree of anonymity to their features and physique did I only glance unthinking, as most Truemen did —just as dogs of a particular breed are indistinguishable one from the other to the eye of the inexperienced, or as one ox looks much like another. But to the kennelmaster and the farmer, each is different. And I saw that these biddable creatures were each different. There was a cook—Ard was his name—who sang softly as he worked; a kitchenmaid, Dala, was always smiling; Taz, who could lift and carry two full sacks of potatoes with ease, told jokes (not usually funny, but he always laughed hugely). I came to know their names, and them, and I think the power that lies in names edged my awareness keener: I began to see them as people.

Cleton would have none of it. To him, accustomed in his father's hold to the presence of Changed, they remained faceless. It was one of the few things we disagreed on, and we chose, for the sake of our friendship, to leave it undiscussed. But just as Martus's tales of the dragons and the Dragonmasters had sown a seed, so did this experience, and after I was thought somewhat an eccentric because I called the Changed by name and gave them greeting when I met them.

So did my first year in Durbrecht pass. Not very different from any student's, save Cleton and I perhaps found more than our share of trouble. We learned, we listened, we observed, we memorized. Whitefish village became, consciously, my past: I could not imagine returning there, save as a Storyman. Nor did I any longer contemplate joining Bardan's warband. Martus, the College, had opened my eyes wider than had Rekyn, and I saw ahead the full breadth of the world I might explore as a journeyman Mnemonikos. It lay before me like a lure before a hungry fish: I was avid to take it and swallow it.

Summer faded into autumn, and that season into winter; the spring came. I was seventeen when Decius summoned me and questioned me and told me I might remain, did I wish.

My answer was a heartfelt *Aye!*

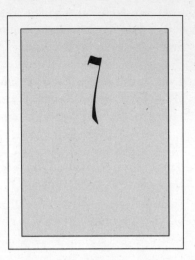

My second year in Durbrecht began with a winnowing of we newcomers. Of the students with whom I had shared the dormitory, three were deemed unfit to continue and five elected to return home. I was not sorry to see Raede and Tyras counted amongst that number; delighted that Cleton remained. Martus was no longer our tutor, his place taken by Clydd, who lectured us on history and the art of storytelling, and Bael, whose duty it was to hone our mnemonic skills. Keran made good his promise to teach us the martial arts, and I at last learned to ride, thanks to Padryn; from Telek we learned something of herbal lore and the chirurgeon's art. It was a busy year, the pace much quickened. I was mightily occupied, rushing from the chambers where Clydd spoke to the gymnasium where Keran waited; hurrying, sweaty, from there to Telek's herb garden, or his surgery; on to the stables and Padryn, thence to Bael, lesson after lesson. Sometimes it seemed that even we, gifted with the talent of memory, dedicated to its practice, should not be able to store so much information.

I learned a great deal: History, of course, and the recounting of a good story, but also those more practical things that would enable us to live easier as Storymen. I learned to recognize the medicinal herbs and to prepare such decoctions as could ease pain, clear drink-fuddled heads, and such like. I learned to set broken bones and how to stitch a wound. I learned, as I have said, to ride (and employed Telek's lessons in the learning!) and came at last to sit a horse without discomfort. From Cleton I had already acquired a basic knowledge of the martial arts, but now Keran refined that, and I became a proficient fighter, learning how to defend myself with my hands and feet alone, or with a quarterstaff, also with a sword, a knife, and a bow. It was a round that seemed sometimes endless, we students like sponges soaking up information, scurrying like busy ants from one tutor to another.

But we enjoyed greater privileges and, in fact, were granted more time to ourselves. We no longer slept in the dormitory, but had rooms of our own. Cleton and I (somewhat to our surprise, for we had thought our escapades might prompt the College to separate us) were assigned a chamber together. It was a plain room, with a curtained alcove that held a privy and a washstand, but there were two comfortable beds, a shared wardrobe, a stove, and a window that looked onto a garden. To me it was the utmost luxury. And to that prodigality of comforts was added a thing undreamed of: we had a servant.

Urt was his name, and we were advised he should tend us so long as we remained in Durbrecht. Cleton took this in his stride—he had grown with servants about him—but to me it was a thing of wonder, and I was ofttimes chided by my friend for performing those tasks he deemed properly belonged to Urt. I was not used to servants and found it difficult to leave my bed unmade, or my clothes unfolded, despite Urt's quiet presence. No less did Cleton wonder at my interest in the Changed, for whilst he was always kind, as a man is to his horse or hound, he could not understand my desire to speak with Urt.

Indeed, Urt himself found it at first disconcerting and met my attempts at conversation with the same bland subservience I had discerned in Bors. But I persevered, and as the days went by I won his confidence and learned something of his life. He held much back but still I garnered knowledge that few Truemen bothered to investigate.

He was of canine stock, a few years older than I and unwed himself. His parents were owned by a merchant dwelling in the Border City of Rynvar, and he had been sold at the age of ten to the College, where he had been a servant since. He dwelt with the other

Changed in the College and was as proud as I of the small chamber given him when he was promoted to the rank of body-servant. This, he told me, was a post much prized by his kind, for it conferred a certain status and was, besides, far easier than the drudgery of stables or kitchens. Such duties were the province of the duller species, those of equine stock or bull-bred, from which announcement I realized there was a hierarchy amongst the Changed. I had not thought on that before, but from Urt I learned the canine- and feline-bred considered themselves somewhat superior to all save those of porcine stock.

He told me much, for I was intrigued and very patient and bent myself to drawing him out. It was then no more than a somewhat vicarious interest, a fascination with a life of which I had no experience, with which I had only recently come into contact. That I was the son of simple fisherfolk, still an innocent, made it easier, and in time he spoke more freely. Save when I asked of Ur-Dharbek and the wild Changed: then he faltered and denied all knowledge, and fell silent.

"But surely you must know something," I insisted.

I sat perched on the sill of our window, awaiting Cleton's arrival. It was a festival day, Sastaine, at the height of summer, and we were granted freedom from our lessons. We planned to spend it wandering the city—which we were now allowed to do unsupervised. Urt was sweeping the bare boards of the floor and shook his head without meeting my eyes. I watched him, thinking it very difficult to tell him from a Trueman. He was a little shorter than I, and slender, his features somewhat angular but not unhandsome, and in his plain breeks and tunic he looked entirely human. It was only when I studied his coarse gray hair and looked into his eyes, which showed no white, that I might clearly perceive him for Changed.

He shrugged: his only reply. I sought to employ those maieutic techniques Bael was teaching us and said, "Aren't those of your folk who so wish allowed to go there?"

Urt said, "Is their service done."

I wondered if I heard resentment in his voice, but when I sought to see his face, it was turned away, intent on some invisible dust.

"You mean when they are too old to work?" I asked.

He nodded and said, "Or does the master grant permission."

"Why should he do that?" I inquired.

Urt shrugged again and said, "Sometimes . . . as a reward."

"Is it a reward?" I asked. "To leave the civilized lands for such a wilderness?"

"Some deem it freedom," he muttered, then busied himself, as if he regretted that admission.

"Would you go there?" I asked.

"I cannot," he said.

"But when you're older," I said. "Then?"

He said nothing, setting aside his broom in favor of a cloth, which he commenced to apply industriously. Bael had taught us something of body language and its interpretation, and I read Urt's clear: he was uncomfortable with my questions. Even so, I pressed on.

"On the galley that brought me here," I said, "the captain told me when your folk are old, they may remain in Dharbek, dependent on the charity of their fellows; or they may cross the Slammerkin. Which would you choose?"

Urt's answer came muffled from beneath my bed: "I'm not old yet."

That was equivocation, and I asked, "But when you are?"

His head emerged, nose twitching, and he sneezed prodigiously. I thought it subterfuge and was about to continue my interrogation when a thought abruptly struck me and killed the question on my tongue. None spoke much of Ur-Dharbek, save in terms of the past, and whenever I had heard the wild Changed mentioned, the speaker had soon after fallen silent or changed the subject. Even my tutors, who surely must know as much as any, avoided the topic; or, when I had pressed them, claimed to know only that wild Changed dwelt there, and nothing more. It seemed some unspoken taboo existed. Urt was obviously loath to answer my queries. I felt convinced he knew more than he admitted; and feared that did I continue, I might lose the trust established between us. I opted for tactful withdrawal and said, "Forgive me. I'd not pry, save I'd learn all I may of the world."

He looked at me then and I saw surprise on his face. I could not at first understand why—perhaps he had grown so accustomed to my interrogations he found it startling I should give up so easily. Then he smiled, and in his expression there was genuine fondness. I shrugged myself and said, "I apologize for pestering you."

He stared straight at me. His eyes were very dark and set with pupils of a singular blue. They were difficult to read, but his smile was broad, a most human expression for all that it revealed sharp teeth.

I frowned, confused, and said, "What? What is it?"

He said, "No Trueman has ever apologized to me."

That simple statement robbed me of words. It was such a little thing; and an enormity. It summed up the status of the Changed and the attitude of Truemen. I had apologized unthinking, in part for fear I gave offense, and also, I had to admit, for fear I should dam the flow of information I got from him. But even so—that none should deliver so simple a courtesy? All I could find to say was, "Never?"

Urt shook his head, still staring at me, still smiling. "Never," he said. I could not then read his expressions well, but I felt that in his gaze, in those whiteless eyes, I saw gratitude, and something else I could not define. Speculation perhaps, or hope. I could not be sure, but I felt our relationship was changed in some subtle fashion. I grinned and shrugged, uncertain what to say and curiously embarrassed, and before we had chance to speak again, Cleton entered the room.

He came flinging in with his usual enthusiasm, greeting me with a smile, barely noticing Urt.

"So, are you ready? We've the rest of the day to ourselves. Come on!"

At that moment I had sooner remained with Urt, that we might continue our conversation, but when I glanced at the Changed, I saw that moment of intimacy was lost. He had returned to his cleaning: returned to his lowly status. Cleton ignored him, impatiently beckoning me. I said, "Urt," and he looked up, his expression bland, and asked, "Master?" In Cleton's presence he always used the honorific term. Only when we were alone did he show that truer side, and even then kept a part of himself hid. I smiled and said, "Nothing. We'll speak again later."

"Yes, master."

He ducked his head, turning away. I checked my purse for coin as Cleton fidgeted by the door, and we left him.

That past year had been grim. The great bloodred vessels of the Sky Lords had fouled our air too often. Rumors had spread of a new, untimely Coming; the koryphon had recruited ever greater numbers to his warband; there had been talk of conscripting squadrons of Changed, even. Fifteen nights Cleton and I had climbed to the rooftops of the College to watch the terrible pyrotechnics of opposing sorceries light the sky. On several others Ardyon had confined us to our quarters under threat of a twelvemonth of punishment. Word had come of sightings and groundings throughout Dharbek. The Lord Protector Gahan had led his own warband against twelve fylie of Kho'rabi knights whose airboats had come down close to Kherbryn. Throughout the year itinerant Storymen had brought the College tales of battle, of victories and defeats, and whilst none of the Kho'rabi had survived, still keeps and villages had suffered horribly.

Then, with winter's advent, the Comings had ceased. It was as though the gray skies with their skirling snowfall denied the Sky Lords crossing of the Fend. We had heard from the Sentinels that no airboats were seen, and Dharbek breathed a little easier, tending her wounds. But seasons turn, and as the snow gave way to rain and the air warmed, folk began again to speak of attack. Trevid had been busy that winter, constructing great war-engines that now sat atop Durbrecht's walls in augmentation of the mages' sorcery. Cleton and I had —of course—inspected them, marveling at the cunning that allowed machinery to hurl great bolts skyward, like vast bows. It was said that Kherbryn, too, was defended by such engines, and that the Lord Protector promised to see every keep in the land equipped as well. But still, as the rain gave way to the blue skies of spring, it was feared the Sky Lords should return, and folk doubted even those impressive engines could stand against the magic of the Ahn. If the Sky Lords could defeat the sorcerers of the Sentinels, they said, how should mere man-made engines halt them? It was the chief topic of conversation in every tavern and aleshop, and as spring advanced it seemed that Durbrecht held its breath in horrid anticipation.

It was a palpable mood, but there was no Coming, neither against Durbrecht nor any other place, and as spring became summer, the city relaxed. The Church, which these past months had offered prayers that the God defend us, now held services of thanksgiving. This Sastaine was to be a great celebration, for Gahan and the Primate both had decreed the Sky Lords defeated. The Ahn, so the official word had it, had mustered all their forces to attempt invasion and had failed. Their threat was done, said Kherbryn and the Church, and for that give thanks to the God and the stout hearts of Dharbek.

We of the College doubted this was so. We studied history: we knew more of the Ahn than did our fellow Dhar, and we believed it unlikely the Sky Lords should forsake an ambition held so long, so avidly. We held our peace and spoke not at all of our beliefs save amongst ourselves. Better, Decius advised us, that the people have hope, that their confidence be allowed to grow. Should we find ourselves questioned, he told us, then we should speak of victories, of past glories, not of gloomy matters. I saw then, for the first time, that the task of we Mnemonikos was more than the recording and recounting of history; that it was as much our work to firm the people's hearts, to instill in them a faith, a loyalty to Dharbek, that they be better able to withstand the depredations of the Sky Lords.

It was a perfect summer's day: the sky was blue and cloudless, the sun benign. The streets were bright with flowers, and pennants fluttered overhead. Bells carilloned from the towers of the churches, vying for attention with the musicians who strummed and blew and beat in the plazas. Stalls with vivid awnings sold trinkets and tidbits, favors of blossoms or ribbons in Durbrecht's colors, skewers of grilled meat, sugary confections, votive offerings.

We fell into a portentous discussion of the various merits of our favorite taverns as we proceeded on our pleasure-bent way. We had done our best to sample them all, a program much aided by the coin Cleton had from his father. The small sum my own had given me, and the stipend we got from the College, did not stretch far in this metropolis, and I was somewhat dependent on my friend's generosity when we went adrinking, or to the house of Allya. That had embarrassed me at first, and as I saw my hoarded wealth depleted, I had made excuses that Cleton cheerfully refused to countenance. He had persuaded me, or I had allowed him to, and so we drank and whored by courtesy of Madbry's aeldor. Our faces were by now well known in numerous of Durbrecht's alehouses.

No less by our favorite cyprians. I had at first balked at the notion of purchasing a woman's favors, but I had met no one to satisfy the natural longings of a healthy young man, nor any desire to take that path some of our fellow students chose, and consequently spent long months frustrated. I had thought to meet some city girl, but when we were allowed to roam free, I had discovered few willing to engage themselves with a man destined to depart ere long. We Rememberers, I found, had a reputation for unfaithfulness—it was a hazard of our calling that we must go awandering as Storymen; it rendered us poor prospects for respectable young women, who turned cold faces to our blandishments and whose parents ofttimes threatened a hotter reception. So Cleton had told me of Allya's house, recommended him by no less an authority than his father, and we had made ourselves known there. Thais was my chosen companion; Vaera, Cleton's. They were both our senior by several years (which rendered them all the more attractive in our estimation, and we the more sophisticated) and skilled in their chosen calling.

So it was in a mood of cheerful optimism that we made our way into the city. We were not required to return to the College until dawn, a concession to the Sastaine festival and the apparent cessation of the Kho'rabi attacks, and we were determined to make the most of such freedom.

We had decided to investigate the fair set up in the central plaza. There was dancing, we understood, and gaming stalls, acrobats, and jugglers, even a dancing bear from the highlands of Kellambek. That, we felt, should carry us through to dusk, when we would eat and afterward visit our cyprian mistresses. It was a satisfying prospect, and after quenching our thirst we strolled link-armed to the plaza.

That errant gift of our talent that enabled us to drink close to excess without suffering the consequences afflicting ordinary folk served us well that day. We were neither of us drunkards (as some Rememberers become), but we soon enough found a beer stall where we drank some more. We were happy, somewhat heady, and bent on taking our fill of pleasure: we emptied our cups and joined the dancers. We tried our luck at toss-penny and won as much we lost. At skittles we each won tokens in Durbrecht's colors that we pinned with mock solemnity to one another's tunics, delivering proud accolades to our undoubted skill. We ate skewers of charcoal-roasted meat of indeterminate origin and washed it down with more ale. We listened to a balladeer, accompanied by a dwarf who played the kithara rather well, sing songs of love thwarted and requited.

Finally, as dusk turned into night, we wandered away, our bellies pleasantly awash with ale and now in need of more solid sustenance.

There was an eating house not far distant that was a favorite of we students. The fare was plain, but good, and not expensive: we went there.

The streets were still crowded when we emerged. I remember the moon stood huge overhead, like a great round of butter, and stars spangled the velvet blue of the sky. Moonlight and lanterns rendered the streets bright. They were loud with laughter and music. It seemed all Durbrecht was abroad this night.

As we walked toward Allya's, I espied a woman I took at first to be a cyprian, but then, as she came within the compass of a tavern's light, I saw she wore the blue gown of the sorcerers. I halted in my tracks, staring, for I had never seen so beautiful a being. This, I know, was a personal reaction, some individual chemistry sparking within me so that my mouth gaped open and I clutched at Cleton's sleeve, pointing dumbstruck. I was rooted where I stood. My friend did not see her through my eyes, for he only shrugged and said, "Not bad, but Thais awaits you, and you'll have little luck with that one."

Indeed, it did seem she hurried. Likely she took this road for a shortcut. I said, "Cleton, I am in love."

I jested, then. I held no hope it should go further; none that I might effect a meeting. Thais did, indeed, await me.

But . . . as she passed into brighter light, I saw the long spillage of her hair burn like molten metal, red and gold, and that her face was a pale oval, her mouth wide, her lips full and very red, as if the blood ran hot there. I thought of cooling that heat with my kisses. I saw that her figure was slim, yet deliciously rounded, and that her eyes were huge and as green as the sea at that moment just before the sun climbs above the horizon. I saw that she was blind and used her talent for sight. I cursed myself for a clumsy, tongue-tied oaf as I struggled for some excuse to approach her, some words that should persuade her to linger awhile, to agree to an assignation.

All I found was, again, "I am in love."

I did not then know I spoke the truth. I gaped; I stood as Cleton laughed and clapped my shoulder and said, "Come on. There's surer target for your love not far."

I grunted, or moaned, and allowed him to push me a faltering step onward, he still laughing, I still staring.

Then the God, or fate, or whatever powers command our destinies, took a hand. Three mariners—westcoasters by their look, come trading down the Treppanek, and rough as all their kind—emerged from a tavern ahead of my desire's quarry. They were in their cups.

They spied her and called for her to join them. She answered mildly that she could not, for she went about the business of her College and must not delay. They took this for no answer at all and surrounded her, blocking her path, and their comments grew bawdy. They would not let her pass. She asked they leave her be, and they refused. I took a step toward them and looked to Cleton for support. He shrugged and said that she was a mage and so quite capable of defending herself, and that we were forbidden—on pain of Ardyon's wrath—to brawl. I thought that likely she was under some similar stricture; certainly I believed that I sensed in her a reluctance to use her magic against men. I stood a moment longer. The westcoasters were plucking at her gown now. One touched her magnificent hair.

That was enough for me: I strode toward them.

The sailors were big men and wore long knives sheathed on their belts. Their eyes were reddened and their faces flushed with ale. Their breath smelled. I suppose mine did, but theirs was offensive. I suggested—politely—that they find some more amenable woman, indicating the green lanterns strung all along the street. They laughed and cursed and told me I should find my own doxy; that this beauty was theirs.

I ignored their taunts and offered her my arm. I said, "Shall I escort you to your College?"

She turned her face toward me and smiled, but before she had opportunity to speak, a sailor set a rough hand on my shoulder and said, "Go your way, boy. Find your own whore."

He pushed me back. That was too much: I took hold of his wrist and spun around, driving an elbow into his ribs. It was as Keran had taught me—but those lessons were in the gymnasium, and our blows were halted short of harm there. I was angry now. No: I was incensed. I felt bone break and heard the man yelp. I turned more, twisting his arm so that he fell unbalanced, the limb I clutched dislocating at the shoulder. He screamed, and I experienced a savage satisfaction. I let him go, seeing his swarthy face paled, his mouth hung open in surprise and discomfort. His companions drew their knives.

They were experienced: they crouched, the blades thrust forward, edges uppermost. One said, "You pay for that, boy." The other, "I'll have your heart for a purse." They moved apart, intent on attacking me from both sides.

I heard Cleton say, "Best take your friend and go. Else we must hurt you."

Both sailors laughed, an ugly sound. Cleton moved to my side, confronting one of them. His eyes were pale and cold, the blue of a winter moon. He was smiling.

The woman said, "For the God's sake, stop!"

A sailor answered, "When this is done, I'll stopper you, my lovely."

He lunged at me as the sentence ended. I took a pace back, letting the blade slice air a finger's width before my belly, and then a pace forward. I set a hand about his wrist and drove my other, flat-palmed, against his elbow. At the same time I kicked him hard in the knee. I felt his elbow tear as he fell. His scream was shrill; the knife dropped from his grasp. I kicked him again before he could rise, hard, just below the buckle of his wide belt. He made a choking sound and began to vomit.

I turned to see Cleton dispatch the other with a hand's edge delivered sharp against the westcoaster's neck. The man's eyes bulged, his mouth springing wide. Then both eyes and mouth closed as his chin struck the cobbles. A thread of blood dribbled from between his lips.

The man I had first struck was staring at us. His right arm hung loose, his left was pressed against his broken rib. I asked, "You'd have more?" He shook his head, eyes wide.

Cleton said, "Keran would be proud of us."

I thought he might; and that Ardyon would be only angry. I glanced about, but saw no one from the College, nor any watchmen. There were only drinkers and doormen, staring admiringly. Someone called, "Well done, lads."

A serving woman said, "That was bravely fought."

I looked at the woman I had sought to defend and said, "My name is Daviot. I am a student in the College of the Mnemonikos."

She said, "My thanks for your gallantry, Daviot."

Her voice was musical, almost husky. I stared at her. I suppose I preened; certainly I basked in what I thought must be her admiration. I asked, "And your name?"

She said, "Rwyan," and touched her gown. "I am with the Sorcerous College, as you can see."

I said, softly, "Rwyan."

I had jested before, but I fell truly in love at that moment.

We looked at one another. I thought her sightless eyes fathomless as the ocean. I wanted to drown in them. I willed her to share my feelings. She said, "I had best be on my way."

I gasped. She could not go now! Surely not. I said, "Shall I escort you?"

Rwyan shook her head and smiled. "I think I shall be safe enough now," she said, and gestured at the green lanterns. "And you've doubtless business here."

I blushed then and began to deny the obvious. Then halted, for I had no wish to lie to her. There seemed such a purity to her blind gaze, I knew she would recognize dissemblance. There seemed to me no disapproval in her words, or face, or stance; instead, a great understanding. I thought her likely wiser than me. I shrugged and grinned.

"I've duties to attend," she said.

Hopefully, I asked, "You'll not take wine with me?" Gestured at the now-impatient Cleton and added, "With us?"

I wanted her to know I should sooner spend time in her company than go on to my destination.

She said, "Again, my thanks—but, no. I must not linger."

I said, "I'll take you to the street's end, at least. Lest you be molested again."

She indicated the street with a toss of her head that set lantern light to dancing in her hair like witchfire, entrancing. It was not so far, her smile said. Aloud she said, "I think your friend grows impatient. And after so brave a show, I think I shall be safe. Fare you well."

She moved a step away, and I aped the mariners: I touched her sleeve, not wanting her to go.

"When?" I mumbled, disconcerted.

"When what?" she asked.

"Shall I see you again?"

She smiled and said, "I do not know."

I gathered up my disordered thoughts as best I could; forced my tongue to some semblance of coherence. "I must," I said. "See you again, I mean. I cannot lose you now."

"Lose me?" She laughed. No bells, no kithara, no harp could sound so wondrous. "How shall you lose me? Do you own me, then?"

"No," I said swiftly, lest she think me no better than some amorous street brawler. "But to know you are here, in Durbrecht, and never see you again—that should be torture."

"A true Storyman," she murmured. "Your tongue drips silver."

There was such humor in her voice, I could not help but smile. I shook my head and said, "Words are too poor a coin to pay you tribute, Rwyan, but all I have. *May* I see you again?"

She paused, her face become a moment pensive, then ducked her head. I think the Sky Lords might have landed on the city then and I not noticed. I think had a fallen foe arisen to put his knife in my back, I should not have noticed.

"My College allows me no more time than does yours you," she said, "but when we've such freedom . . . Do you know a tavern called the Golden Apple?"

I said, "No, but I shall find it. When?"

"When next we're allowed," she said. "I can offer you no more."

"It's enough," I said. "I shall be in the Golden Apple when next I may. I shall haunt it. They shall think me an alehound. I'll take a room there."

"Then perhaps I shall find you there," she said. "But now, truly, farewell."

Her smile lit the street bright as that Sastaine day's sun. I bowed extravagantly and heard her laugh again. I stood watching until she had reached the end of the street and was lost to my enraptured sight. She did not look back, but I thought perhaps her sorcerous talent told her I gazed after her. I hoped it did.

"By the God," said Cleton, "I've seen puppies with that same expression."

"I'm in love," I said. "Truly."

"She was pretty enough, I suppose," he said, "but gone now. And none too easy to find again. So—shall you stand here until the watchmen come to take us in disgrace back to the College? Or find shelter with a more available mistress?"

I had forgotten the sailors. When I looked, they were huddled against the wall of a tavern, drunkenly attempting to mend their injuries. A doorman followed my glance and called, "No need to fear the watchmen, lads. These sots will not lay complaint against you."

He emphasized his assurance with a menacing swing of his cudgel and a fierce leer in the direction of the wounded men. The westcoasters took the hint and shook their heads. Cleton and I called thanks and went to Allya's house.

I felt somewhat guilty as we entered and our cyprians flew into our arms. I thought of Rwyan, but then Thais pressed her lips to mine and promised unmentionable delights in honor of the day. I was but eighteen, and the fight had warmed my blood: I set unspoken promise aside and looked to the reality of the woman in my arms.

But all the time I lay with Thais, I saw Rwyan's face.

I had not thought ever to see my friendship with Cleton weakened, but in the months that followed my first meeting with
Rwyan it was tested. That it did not break was a mark of its
depth, of the regard we felt for one another. Of the two of us, I
was the milder, the more malleable—save in those matters I felt instinctively demanded greater investigation. It was Cleton, more often
than not, who led me into our escapades, but I who earned the reputation of rebel. Indeed, had I not demonstrated such talent for our art—
so Decius once advised me—I should have been expelled. I could not
blindly accept: I found a need to question that ofttimes drove my
tutors close to distraction.

I argued that we had driven the Ahn from their ancestral homeland and thus must surely accept some measure of blame for the Sky
Lords. I wondered if we might not reach some accommodation with
them, and thus end their attacks. These arguments I lost, for I could
not say *how* we might discourse with them or, did it by some miracle
become possible, what treaties might be made.

It became a small bone of contention betwixt Cleton and I, one that we gnawed on in our chamber, and over ale. An aeldor's son, he was raised to his father's code, taught from infancy that the Sky Lords were our implacable enemies, that we or they must one day stand victorious. I could not see how we might hope to defeat them, or they to conquer us, and began to perceive both Dhar and Ahn as locked in an endless cycle of bloody war. Such arguments we customarily agreed were drawn, and left them. I believe Cleton knew himself close to losing his temper at such times and held himself back for fear of friendship's destruction. He was a good man.

Of my burgeoning fascination with the Changed, we spoke not at all. Cleton disapproved and elected to remain silent on that matter, whilst I spent longer and longer in conversation with Urt, which Cleton could simply not understand. He saw me—so he admitted in an unguarded moment—akin to a man overly fond of a pet hound, pointlessly discoursing with the beast, which had nothing of interest to offer in return save its mindless devotion. I knew him to be wrong, for Urt, albeit descended from canine stock, was no mindless creature but, I came to learn, as intelligent as most men. From him (even though he still held much back) I gleaned much knowledge of the Changed. I came to see that just as Durbrecht was underpinned with cellars and catacombs, so there existed beneath the society of we Truemen one of the Changed. There were more of them in the city than there were Truemen, but they were like ghosts—they existed side-by-side with us, but unseen, unnoticed, ignored. I hesitated to ask Urt the questions that sprang to my lips when I realized that: *If you are so many, why do you serve us? Why do you not rise up and make yourselves the masters?*

I thought on that, and on how many centuries had passed since first the sorcerers made animals into the semblance of men, and how those progenitors had bred, until whole lineages of Changed existed, and then I would wonder if sufficient time had not passed that the Changed were become a people in their own right. And if so, whether we Truemen still had the right to use them as we did. But I could not find an answer.

Nor could I learn much more of Ur-Dharbek than that it was there, across the Slammerkin, and that none went there save the Changed. It was grown akin, it seemed, to the Forgotten Country, Tartarus of old, and save in terms of legend, none spoke of it or were interested in it. Urt would speak of it not at all.

I applied myself to the problem and came away frustrated, and intrigued by another.

Just as the wild Changed were relegated to myth, so were the dragons and the Dragonmasters. Oh, we students heard tales of their exploits, stripped of that disapprobation that had attached since their efforts failed and sorcery became our bulwark against the great flying beasts. We were told (somewhat vaguely, for we delved here into a past so long ago, it was misty even to the Masters of the College) how they had come to truce with the dragons. How some had even mounted on the beasts and flown—like gods! I thought—borne aloft by the great wings to climb the sky. How some had fallen into such communion that they forsook the company of men and chose to live amongst the dragons.

"What if," I asked both Clydd and Bael, "the dragons live still? And the Dragonmasters? What if they joined with us in combat against the Sky Lords? Might they not defeat the Kho'rabi?"

Bael answered me, "And were all the legends true, we might send virgins out to capture unicorns and ride them against our enemy."

And Clydd told me, "Likely the dragons are all dead, and the Dragonmasters with them. And are they not, our past teaches us they've little love of men. Surely, we've none now might commune with the creatures, so how should we persuade them—do they live— to aid us?"

I responded, "But if the dragons are gone, what point to the Border Cities?"

He answered with a question: "Would you empty them?"

Doggedly, I said, "No. But what's their *point* now? They were built to hold Dharbek safe from dragons, but if there are no more dragons, what's their *point*? Save to contain the wild Changed? Are they such a danger, then?"

Clydd fixed me with a look I could not interpret. It reminded me somewhat, somehow, of Urt's expression when I ventured onto this ground. He said, "A city is its own point, Daviot. It exists because people live there; its reason shifts with time."

I saw that he hoped this was answer enough, and I denied him that hope: "And the wild Changed?"

Someone sighed dramatically. A voice I could not identify whispered, "Daviot rides his hobbyhorse again."

Clydd shrugged and said, "If they are a danger, the Border Cities protect us from them. No Truemen go there, so I cannot answer you with any great authority, but I think they are not."

It seemed to me an unsatisfactory answer. It seemed to me a gap in our knowledge, as if even the Mnemonikos chose to forget or to ignore Ur-Dharbek and the mysterious wild Changed. It seemed to me our duty to investigate. But before I had opportunity to pursue that line of thought, Clydd changed the subject and led the class into a discussion of Kherbryn's founding, and I was left momentarily defeated.

I could raise far more questions than I was able to answer; nor could my tutors satisfy me, save to pass down that learning they had had from their instructors, which was again, as with Cleton, much to do with dogma. I determined to explore these avenues for myself. I gained a reputation as an eccentric.

And there was Rwyan.

I could not forget her. Even were I not gifted with that talent that would soon make me Mnemonikos, but solely with the memory of mortal men, I should not—could not!—have forgotten her. It was as if her presence had blazed so fierce in that moonlit street, she was branded on my mind. Gifted with my talent, I could conjure her image precise. I could define the contours of her cheek and forehead, the angle of her nose, the shape of her lips. I could see, imprinted on the screen of my closed eyes, her hair, her eyes; and did, often, as I lay upon my bed or gazed from the window of our chamber. I knew myself in love with Rwyan and could not be with her. I think that sometimes our eyes may alight on one particular person and a spark be struck that kindles an undying fire that knows not the boundaries of distance or time, but burns unquenchable. Such is, I sometimes think, the curse of Truemen, or the gift, I know not which, only that I loved Rwyan in a manner incredible and unsuspected. I wondered if it were not easier to be as the Changed, governed not by the alchemical processes of love but by those simpler biological imperatives they inherit from their animal forebears.

I visited Thais still, but less often, and in the way that a man visits the gymnasium—to stretch and test his muscles. She knew it and said nothing, even when, at the height of our passion, I would sometimes cry out Rwyan's name. I thought of Rwyan. I *wanted* Rwyan. I spoke of Rwyan.

Cleton was the recipient of my longings, for both ours and the Sorcerous College frowned on such liaisons, deeming them impractical, a hazard to concentration and future duty. Had Rwyan been a cyprian or some city lass, there would have been no difficulties, for it would have been understood that such a relationship was foredoomed, save the woman follow me down my Storyman's road. But future Mnemonikos and future sorcerer—no: both were callings that demanded a single-minded concentration. Such couplings were not expressly forbidden, but I knew that if the College learned of my intention—which was to pursue Rwyan, no matter the consequences, no matter the disapprobation—ways would be found to thwart me. Consequently, Cleton was sworn to secrecy.

It irked him, who saw it as infatuation and nothing more, a needless threat to my chosen future.

"In the God's name," he would cry, torn between frustration and irritation and amusement, "you've seen her but the once. How can you think yourself in love with her?"

And I would answer simply, "I am. I cannot explain it or help it, but I am."

And he would tell me, "Daviot, heed me—ere long you'll be a Storyman and she a mage. You'll go your separate ways and likely never meet again. Forget her!"

And I would return him, "I cannot. Even be it hopeless, I cannot."

And he would sigh, or groan, and clench his fist, mocking a blow, and mutter, "The God grant you come to your senses, for there's no reason in you. She's bewitched you."

And I would tell him cheerfully, "She has."

Even so, for all his argument, he would come with me to the Golden Apple, where we became as well known as at any of our favorite alehouses.

I saw her not at all for the remainder of that summer and came close to despairing as the season turned and the rains of autumn began. But that flame still burned, and I still clung to my hope as winter spread its cold cloak over the land.

Then, on the feast day of Machan, when the sky was a sullen gray and the wind blew knife-edged from the north, skirling the first flakes of winter's snow, I encountered her again. Cleton and I sat by the hearth, our cloaks drying on chairbacks, tankards of mulled ale in our hands. The day was already dark, and we must soon return to the College; I had thought it another fruitless venture. Then she entered the tavern, and it was as if the sun descended to walk the earth. She was with several of the Sorcerous College, both male and female, but I saw only her. She wore a cloak of dark brown wool, with a hood she threw back as she came in. Her hair was bound up. Her neck was pale and long and slender. I thought of how it should feel, did I press my lips to that intoxicating flesh. I rose to my feet and called her name. Her companions—none of them were blind—looked toward me. She turned her face and I saw her smile, and though she said my name but softly, it sounded to me a clarion. I quit my place and went to her, taking her hands.

I said, "It has been so long."

She blushed and nodded. I wondered why she looked surprised; embarrassed, even. Had she thought I would not wait? At her side a fair-haired woman smiled and said, "So this is the Mnemonikos, eh?"

Rwyan said, "Daviot, this is Chiara."

I mumbled some acknowledgment, but my eyes were firm upon her face. No boat was ever anchored surer. I said, "Shall you sit with me?"

She nodded again and called some apology to her companions. I was at first disappointed that she asked Chiara to accompany us, but then remembered Cleton and bade the woman a warmer welcome. We went to the hearth, and I called for mulled ale.

I had rehearsed this often enough: I had so many pretty speeches prepared, so many reasons we should be alone, so many stratagems. All fled me as I gazed at her face, and had she not introduced her friend to Cleton, I think I should have sat unspeaking, content to stare, to drink in her beauty. As it was—as is the way of these matters —our conversation was largely of the commonplace. How did our studies go? How hers? What news of the Sentinels? Did her college believe the Sky Lords were defeated? Too soon she was reminded she must return, and we were parted, with no better a promise of another assignation than before.

I saw her only once more that winter and in much the same circumstances, though I did then succeed, thanks to the aid of Cleton and Chiara, in steering her a little distance away, to the poor privacy of a corner, where I told her I loved her.

She frowned then and asked, "How can that be? You scarce know me, even."

"But still," I said, "I do," and took her hand in both of mine.

I was terribly afraid she would loose my grip; afraid she would laugh or name me foolish. But she did none of that, only faced me with her lovely sightless eyes and pursed her lips as if she struggled with some doubt, or sought words she could not find.

I saw hope in her expression and gathered up my courage and whispered, "I love you, Rwyan. From that first moment I saw you, I have loved you. Shall you tell me you feel nothing for me?"

There are things I have done since that day I suppose men would name brave, but I think that was the bravest thing I have ever done. I felt in those moments I awaited her reply that all my life, all my future, hung suspended from the unspoken thread of her answer. It seemed to me there was no sound within the tavern save the drumbeat pounding of my heart, the tidal wash of my blood as I waited. It seemed a very long time, but I suppose it was only a little while before she lowered her face, gravely, and said softly, "No, I cannot tell you that."

"You love me!" I fought the urge to shout as I said it. "You love me!"

She said, "Daviot, I cannot, either, tell you that."

As a bird soaring aloft, free and triumphant, is felled by the hunter's arrow, so my heart went down in ruin.

She could not see my face, save through the gift of her magic, but she heard my groan, felt the stiffening of my fingers where they rested about her hand. She said, "I do not tell you it is not so . . . or cannot be. But . . . Daviot, I've met you but these three times. You know nothing of me, nor I of you. And our Colleges . . . what should they say?"

Fierce, desperate, I answered her, "I care not what they say. I know only that I love you."

She asked me, "How can you be so sure?"

"I am," I said. "How, I know not; but I am."

"Perhaps." She smiled, and my spirits halted their descending arc. "And perhaps I am, too. But I'll not tell you so certainly. Not till I know you better."

So sensible: I did not know whether I loved her the more for it, or cursed her prudence. I knew I'd not relinquish my hope easily. I said, endeavoring a calm I felt not at all, "And how shall that be?"

I felt her fingers stroke my hand then. She answered me, "Not easily, but do we put our minds to it . . ."

"And all my heart," I told her.

It was no easy matter, and had I not won Urt's confidence it should have proven impossible. He it was, hearing me bemoan the difficulties of my thwarted affair to Cleton, who sought me out when I was alone to suggest a means of correspondence at the least, and trysts did the fates smile on us, thanks to that society of his kindred.

As with we of the Mnemonikos, so did the Sorcerous College employ Changed servants. Urt made it his business to seek them out, to learn their names and win their friendship. Rwyan and Chiara were tended by a Changed woman of canine stock whose name was Lyr. Urt made her acquaintance (she was not, he told me, unattractive) and persuaded her to join him as a go-between. Thus were Rwyan and I able to pass messages between us, to better organize those days we were permitted the freedom of the city, that we might meet more frequently—and, with the connivance of our chambermates, more privately.

I was joyous then, for all it dug that rift with Cleton deeper. He aided us because he was my friend and his loyalty was unquestioning, but I quite lost my taste for Thais and during my fourth year in Durbrecht refused to join Cleton on his visits to Allya's house. I was determined to remain faithful to my love, which Cleton could not at all comprehend. Also, at every opportunity I was in Rwyan's company, leaving Cleton either alone or with Chiara. I knew we drifted apart, but could not help it: I was in love.

The coin faced about, I was more in Urt's company, for he was often my guide, bringing me to some clandestine trysting place where Rwyan waited with Lyr. The two Changed would go about whatever business they pursued, leaving Rwyan and I some few precious hours together.

It was our secret, a little portion of time stolen from duty and expectancies, and the sweeter for that. Perhaps, in our youth and innocence, we perceived ourselves as characters in some drama, tragic lovers. I do not know, for then we were too concerned with discovery to speak of the future, too busy with the exploration of one another to think beyond the present. We made the most of what we stole, and in the spring of that year, in a rooming house on the edge of a quarter given over to the Changed and the poor, we became, truly, lovers. I will not speak of that, for it was a wondrous private thing (as doubtless it is for all who find their desires met and answered), and it told us in ways beyond words that for us there could be no others.

I was happy then as I had never been; but there hung above us that ignored shadow: I was Mnemonikos, she a mage. Soon—just as Cleton had warned—we should be sent out to pursue our callings. I should soon be a Storyman, itinerant, and she delivered to occult duties. We spoke not at all of that, but it lent our lovemaking an urgency that was edged with the poignant knowledge of impending parting.

And with the new year's advent our meetings were made the harder for the renewal of the Sky Lords' attacks.

They had not been defeated, as so many chose to believe. Rather, it seemed that twelvemonth respite had been for them a gathering of strength, for they came in terrible numbers, as if the calendar of the years were speeded forward and the Coming begun.

Skyboats were sighted early in the spring, few in numbers at first and destroyed before they reached our shores, but then in greater quantity, progressing deeper inland. We saw them again close to Durbrecht, and though none breached our defenses, the city fell once more into a mood of presentiment. Then, early in the summer, word came from the Sentinels of an armada. The Fend lay dark beneath the shadow of the massed airboats. They were too many even the augmented strength of our magical guardians might hope to defeat them. Durbrecht girded for the onslaught. The koryphon had not allowed his vigilance to slacken, and our walls were soon manned by his soldiers and the levies of the militia. The sorcerers readied. I wondered if Rwyan stood amongst them, within her College or on the city walls, but only briefly, for we of the Mnemonikos College were called to the fight.

I was in class with Telek when the message came, and I saw the herbalist pale as the news was whispered. He nodded and turned to us. "The Sky Lords come in strength," he said, "and we must fight. Go to your chambers and find your sturdiest gear. Have you weapons, fetch them. You'll assemble in the quadrangle."

We hurried to obey. I found myself both excited and afraid as Cleton and I swiftly tugged on sound boots and leather tunics, which were, I thought, poor defense against Kho'rabi steel.

"By the God," Cleton declared, "but they must come in force are we summoned."

He seemed not at all afraid, only enthusiastic. I nodded, thinking that my mouth was gone very dry, and therefore wondering why I felt such a desire to spit. I hoped I should not disgrace myself. Urt was there, fussing about us, and I caught his eye. He smiled, which I took for encouragement, and I said, "Do you take care, Urt."

"I've no fear," he said calmly, at which Cleton chuckled sourly and said, "With the Kho'rabi wizards overhead, I think you should."

I said, "Likely you'll be safe enough here. The cellars are sound."

I think I spoke less to reassure Urt than for want of calming my own pounding heart. He seemed very little disturbed, and had I not been so engaged with my own trepidation, I think I should have wondered at his tranquillity. He said, "Ward yourself well, Daviot," which prompted a sharp, shocked look from Cleton, for it was the first time he had heard my Changed friend address me by my given name. Urt added, "And you, Master Cleton."

I essayed an unconfident smile and said, "We shall, fear not."

Then I went out with Cleton into the crowded corridor, jostling my fellow students as we ran to answer our call to arms.

Of all the folk in Durbrecht not of the warband, we were the best trained in combat. Even the militias, for all they were equipped with armor and the uniforms of war, were largely untrained citizens or aging soldiers, reinforced with officers from Trevid's squadrons. There was neither sufficient time nor gear to armor us, but we were given what weapons were available—bows, swords, axes, even knives from the kitchens. Keran was our commander, his motley troops divided into squads, each ordered by one of the younger tutors. We numbered no more than a century and one half, but we were avid for our duty. I forgot all my musings, all my talk of parleys and cycles of war, as Keran gathered us in the quadrangle. I was a child of my times. The blood of my Dhar ancestors ran in my veins (and should, I hoped, remain there), and it was that called me now. The Sky Lords came! They threatened my homeland! Against that weight of time's and blood's memory, my philosophical musings faded.

Keran sprang to the plinth of a statue that he might look down on us. He wore black leather that shone dull in the sun, as if it had seen much service. It reminded me of Andyrt's gear. He wore a long sword and his face was grave as he addressed us.

"The Sky Lords approach," he cried, shouting over the tumult that rose from the streets outside. "They come in numbers greater than any since the last Coming, and Durbrecht's need of us. We are called to fight for our city and all Dharbek. How shall we answer?"

"We fight!" we roared.

Swords were flourished, bows waved aloft; sunlight glinted off axeheads and spears. We were patriotic, vigorous in our courage, our outrage hot. Keran told us off into companies, and I found myself under Martus's command. He carried a long-hafted axe and from somewhere had found a dented helmet. His pleasant face was grim as we formed a ragged column and made for the gates.

Keran led us at a trot to the south wall. The streets were emptying as the inhabitants sought the refuge of their homes or took up weapons and straggled after officers of the militia. The bazaars, all the emporiums, were closed, save for those of the herbalists, the apothecaries, and the chirurgeons. I thought they would likely have work enough before too long.

We reached the wall and found ourselves deployed along a length between two of the bolt-throwing engines. It was early in the afternoon and the stone was warm from the sun's caress. The sky was blue, streaked with high cloud blown out like the manes of running horses. It was a day when larks and swallows should have darted about the ramparts and the fields beyond, but there were none. I looked to the east, where farmland stretched away from the city, and saw folk hurrying for the safety of Durbrecht. To my right, the wide expanse of the Treppanek glittered silvery blue, empty of vessels. I licked my lips and spat; fingered my borrowed sword. I thought of those days—ages past, it seemed now—when I had voiced childhood's bravery to Andyrt and thought there could be no better life than to be a soldier. He had told me that was largely waiting, and that the waiting was the hardest part. He had been right. I felt a great desire to relieve myself; and a greater fear of embarrassment. I looked to Cleton, who grinned as if he had not a care in the world. Past him, I saw Pyrdon. His freckled face was pale and his eyes were narrowed as he stared at the empty sky.

Then it was empty no longer.

It was as though a storm swept toward us from the east. The horizon was dark, as if a great bank of nimbus advanced. I heard Pyrdon muttering and turned my eyes briefly sideways, seeing him make the God's sign as he prayed. He was not alone. I heard Keran shout, "Courage! Stand firm!" I thought Cleton's tan a shade lighter. I forgot my need to urinate.

The darkness came on, and through it I saw the spark and flash of magic as the keeps along the Treppanek flung sorcery at the airboats that were the fundament of the shadow.

Someone cried, "So many! How can we defeat them?"

Martus answered, loud so that all his troop should hear it, "With courage. We've magic of our own, and stout hearts."

Darkness and light approached in unison. I saw airboats fall flaming from the solidity of the armada, great balls of awful fire that drifted almost leisurely to the land, or the water. Along the wall, from by a war-engine, a jennym shouted, "They're not so many. See? They use the darkness like night-come thieves!"

Surely they used the darkness, or it was manifestation of Kho'rabi wizardry, for it came as always before them, and where it fell there was a numbing cold, a horrid sensation of dread that crept into our souls and slowed our blood. I could see now that the jennym spoke true—what had first seemed to be a fleet that filled all the sky was, in fact, only a wave of airboats, perhaps twenty of them. But twenty, their magic said, was ample. How should we stand against so many? Twenty was too many. The sky-borne craft would land their fylie of Kho'rabi knights and those warriors would slaughter us. I stared, a rabbit transfixed by a stoat's rabid gaze.

Once again I discerned those half-seen elemental things that sported about the airboats, thought I heard their weird, wild singing. I realized abruptly the skycraft were almost on us. There was a ghastly familiarity to the scene as the shifting sigils that decorated the blood-red cylinders grew clear, the black baskets that hung beneath began to show the pale blurs of faces. I stared, paralyzed, convinced of our defeat.

Then hope sprang bright and burning from where a group of sorcerers stood. It flew, magic's unleashed arrow, into the sky—a searing blast of light that struck the foremost airboat as spark to tinder. The darkness was exiled, replaced with honest fire. The airboat did not burn and drift to earth, but exploded, incandescent, thunder roiling above the ramparts, echoed by a great surging cheer as ragged, flaming fragments of vessel and men dropped all helter-skelter down onto the fields.

To right and left I heard a deep twanging sound and saw vast bolts of wood tipped with sharp metal hurtle upward. The war-engines had loosed their shafts! I cheered as those missiles struck, tearing through baskets that broke apart to spill Kho'rabi like dark-armored raindrops. I saw a bolt pierce the supporting cylinder, which emitted a shrieking whistle, expelling fetid gas, its structure collaps-ing. It deflated like a drained wineskin, crumpling, losing height. A second missile and then a third drove in, and the airboat, like a bro-ken-winged bird, began a rapid descent.

I waved my sword, defying the Sky Lords, challenging them to set foot in *my* city, my spirits risen anew. I cheered as the airboat fell —then staggered as it struck the wall directly below my position.

The stone shuddered beneath me, the impact greater than any structure so flimsy as that emptying sack should impart. There was a gout of sulphurous flame in which it seemed weirdling creatures were borne aloft, their ethereal features contorted in rage, their mouths loosing a horrid howling. I could not be sure. I was flung against the ramparts and felt heat sear my face. Cleton snatched me back. His fair hair was dark with soot, dirt streaked his face, and he was smiling ferociously. He stooped to retrieve my sword, which I had not known I dropped, and set my hand about the hilt. I found no comfort there; I was afraid. I thought it should perhaps be easier to face a Kho'rabi in honest fight than suffer this onslaught of untouchable magic. I real-ized we stood in shadow that was no longer that nimbus produced by the Ahn wizards but the physical penumbra of a sky occluded by their vessels.

Whatever occult wind transported them from their distant land to ours had ceased: they hung as if at anchor above us. Arrows, javelins, balls of spiked metal rained down. Then worse—shining glass globes fell, and where they struck, they splashed liquid fire that ran and flamed and could not be doused. A commur of the warband came running down our line, bellowing over the tumult that all save those wearing armor should quit the wall for the surer refuge of the avenue below. Martus shouted for us to go, and we darted for the stairs.

I felt a plucking at my sleeve and saw a black-fletched arrow driven through the leather. I snapped it off and flung it from me as if it were a serpent. Cleton was at my back as we reached the stair, and I saw Pyrdon ahead. He waited for the crowded steps to clear, and as he did, I glanced up. Whether I saw the globe that fell, or somehow sensed it, I cannot say, only that I shouted and flung myself back against Cleton, knocking him into the men behind so that we all fell down and thus were saved.

The globe struck Pyrdon's left shoulder, and he became on the instant a column of flame. I am not sure he screamed, even, so swift was it. I scrabbled back, horrified, as his clothing and then the skin beneath blackened and was devoured. The spear he held was a brand that dropped to the street below, soon followed by Pyrdon himself, a human torch. Where he had stood, flames licked as if in search of some fresh victim. I clambered to my feet, staring aghast at that unholy fire. Then Martus's hand was on my shoulder, and he urged me forward. I held my breath and lunged through the flames, plunging down to the street. I saw Pyrdon there, or what was left of him, and promptly emptied my stomach.

Keran appeared, rallying us, advising us that we were to be a flying squad, to go where commanded. I thought that we should not be enough, that all the city's warband, all the levies of militia, should not be enough. Yet there were now only some dozen of the Sky Lords' craft left above us, the rest downed by magic and war-engines, and of those remaining some burned and fell even as I stared.

And yet, as I crouched in the poor safety of the ravaged wall, I felt neither comfort nor confidence. I knew fear; oh, yes, in full measure. I knew, also, anger—that this city I now thought of as my own should be so threatened, that friends and fellow-soldiers should die, that the Sky Lords should dare this affront. For all my fear I knew that did a target for my rage present itself, I should attack.

Meanwhile, however, I saw the sky dark with the foul shapes of the Sky Lords' boats, the flash and blast of magicks. I saw a war-engine consumed and topple, blazing, into the street. I saw airboats fall in flames over Durbrecht. I wondered if the city should survive.

Then orders came, and half our number was sent racing through the streets. I saw the object of our pursuit some time before we reached it: a stricken airboat descended toward the center of the city. It was pierced with bolts, tongues of flame darting about its flanks, brighter and cleaner than the bloody red of its canopy. The carrier basket beneath had been struck—I could make out the holes—but still it held its lethal cargo and would deliver those Kho'rabi knights into the very streets of Durbrecht.

It was lost to sight after a while, but the reeking smoke it trailed served for a marker and we ran toward that. A company of foot soldiers joined us, led by a commur to whom Keran deferred, and a troop of militia. I hoped there would be more. Then we emerged on a plaza filled with the wreckage of the burning airboat. Some thirty Kho'rabi had survived the landing and now stood ready to fight. At the head of our column, Keran raised his sword, halting us. The commur roared orders—that we should avoid close combat if possible, use bows and spears, that if we faced the Kho'rabi knights it should be only in numbers, that we should better employ cunning than courage. Then he waved us to attack.

I had never seen a Kho'rabi knight before. They were the stuff of nightmares, of a mother's threat. Now they stood before me, dread given flesh. They were armored all in black so that they seemed like great beetles, carapaced and armed with sharp steel. There seemed not a soft part on them, nothing vulnerable, but all—chests and legs and arms and heads—encompassed in that glossy armor. They had no faces, for they had locked chin- and cheek-pieces in place, so that only savage eyes glared out at us. And somehow worse, they shouted no battle cries but faced us in silence, which gave them an air of dreadful implacability, as if they were not human but automatons, killing machines.

I feared my courage would fail me then and threw myself forward before I should turn and flee. Cleton was at my side, Martus a pace ahead. I heard Cleton shout, "For Madbry! For Dharbek!" I do not know if I shouted. It is quite likely I whimpered.

Confusion reigned as we students, the foot soldiers, and the militiamen joined in battle with the invaders. Those students given bows loosed a volley, and I saw the black armor was not impenetrable. Several of the Kho'rabi fell. Better, they screamed, which rendered them more human in my eyes—and therefore capable of defeat. I saw one stagger, three arrows jutting from his chest, two from his swordarm. A spearman thrust at his midriff, and Martus delivered him a blow that cracked his helmet and split the skull beneath. I vaulted the body and found myself suddenly confronted with a warrior whose eyes blazed furiously from within the shadow of his helm. I ducked, flinging myself clear as his long blade swung like a scythe intent on cropping my head. Martus brought his axe hard against the Kho'rabi's side; Cleton parried the returning stroke; a soldier hammered at the jet helm. I saw that the black armor was not all of one piece, but segmented over the thighs and groin, joined to the cuirass with rings of black metal. I thrust my blade in there, trusting to Cleton and Martus to hold off the warrior's riposte as I drove all my weight forward.

It is a strange and ugly sensation to feel your steel pierce flesh. A memory of gutted fish flashed brief across my mind. I turned my blade as Keran had taught me and saw the angry eyes flicker wide, the light within them going out, so that even though the orbs still reflected sunlight and flame, they grew abruptly dull as the life fled. I dragged my sword back as Martus sent his axe thudding against the dead man's helmet. I did not know how I felt in that instant when I first slew a man, only that I wanted very badly to live.

I turned, finding chaos all about me. The archers had ceased firing for fear of hitting friends. Close by four students armed with spears drove a silent Kho'rabi slowly back toward the wreckage of the airboat. I saw men fall; heard shouts; the screaming of wounded men. The air stank of sweat and blood and sulphur; there was the sharp reek of urine. I swung my blade double-handed against a black-armored back. Martus hacked the legs. Cleton thrust his sword under the sweeping wings of the helmet, into the neck. He shouted, "Madbry!" as he did it, and his eyes were very cold, his lips spread wide in a terrible smile.

I saw a figure come at Martus from the side and screamed, "Martus! Beware!"

He turned, axe rising, using the haft to block the descending blade. From behind the Kho'rabi a spear thrust out, the blow too weak to pierce his armor, but enough that he staggered, momentarily unbalanced. Martus lifted his axe, and as he did, another beetlelike warrior sliced a sword across his belly. I saw his face go pale. The axe fell from his hands. He moaned, clutching at his wound as if pained by a belly ache. The first Kho'rabi stabbed him in the ribs. I aimed a blow at the warrior's helm; Cleton cut at his legs. Leon—for it was his spear—stepped close and rammed the lance between the Kho'rabi's shoulders.

The fighting surged about us, and for a while I only ducked and parried, standing shoulder-to-shoulder with Cleton. Leon disappeared. I caught a glimpse of Martus. He lay on his side, his beard all bloodied, wounds gaping.

There was a parting then, embattled men drifting from us, and I saw Keran dancing backward, desperately parrying the onslaught of two Kho'rabi. Cleton and I sprang to his aid. I hammered my blade against black pauldrons. The Kho'rabi seemed unaware of my attack: I sprang at his back, left hand clawing at his helm as I sought to slice my sword across his throat. Keran stabbed him in the groin, and he made a strange, high-pitched yelping sound. I cut his windpipe and found myself tumbled down with him. I felt boots trample me and thought a blade must surely find me ere I gained my feet, or that I should be stamped to death in the press. Then a hand grasped my arm and I was hauled upright. I was surprised to find myself looking into Ardyon's eyes. One was reddened, blood oozing from a cut on the brow. He said, "Can you not fight longer, find safety," and I shook my head, unable to speak, but not yet willing to flee.

He nodded, and we turned in search of fresh foemen.

There were fewer now, as the sheer weight of our numbers over-came the Kho'rabi. They fought savagely and with a terrible skill, but there were not enough and in time there were none at all.

When it was done I found I was wounded. My arms and chest were cut, and a deep gash painted my breeks red. It was hard to stand on that leg. Cleton was cut about the ribs, and his left arm was broken. We tended one another's hurts as best we could and limped together to hear our commander's orders.

Night had fallen, albeit the darkness was colored with flame from the burning buildings. Folk came out to fight the fires, and the city was still loud with the clamor of battle. Keran surveyed us grimly and told the worst hurt to make their way back to the College. I rested my weight on Cleton and he on me, and we both swore we were fit. I said, "Martus is slain," and Keran ducked his head and commanded we return with the wounded.

We obeyed, joining the sorry column that made its way slowly through a city ravaged by this unprecedented attack. None spoke, but many turned their faces skyward, and all flinched as magic flashed and thundered, or blazing buildings collapsed. I could see no more of the Sky Lords' craft overhead and thought the worst of the fighting likely over. I felt horribly weary.

It was past midnight before we reached the College and gave ourselves up to Telek's ministrations. We were not the worst hurt— five students died that night—and we waited for him to sew my thigh and set Cleton's arm. He was aided by the Changed servants, and I saw Urt tending wounds and applying bandages with a silent efficiency. I thought then of Rwyan, and a terrible fear gripped me—that I knew not whether she lived or died. As soon I might, I beckoned Urt over.

He studied the stained bandage wrapping my thigh. "I am glad you live," he said.

I smiled my thanks, far more concerned then with Rwyan's welfare than my own. "Do you find the opportunity," I asked, albeit without overmuch hope, "I'd know how Rwyan fared."

"I do not think I can slip away," he replied.

I grimaced, as much in disappointment as in pain, though my wound throbbed horribly and I felt, as the rush of battle's excitement left me, very weak. "No," I said, "I suppose not. But when you can . . . if you can . . . I'd be mightily grateful."

Urt nodded and smiled briefly. "When I can," he promised.

I said, "My thanks," and he clasped my shoulder, squeezing a moment, which was a most unusual thing, for the Changed did not usually touch Truemen so familiar. I noticed for the first time that his nails were blunt and very dark. There was dried blood on his hand.

He left me then, and I did not see him again for some time. My weakness grew, and I found myself becoming sleepy, resting against Cleton. Telek attended me around dawn, stitching the gash and declaring me weak from blood loss. He had Changed servants carry me to our chamber, Cleton supervising them, his arm splinted and bound tight against his chest. His temper was not improved by such disability, and he spent a while cursing before declaring his intention of returning to the infirmary to offer what aid he might. I told him I should be safe enough alone. Indeed, I began to find his impatience annoying, for it distracted me when what I wanted most—besides hearing that Rwyan was unharmed—was to sleep.

When he had gone I closed my eyes. Images of Rwyan swam across the screen of my mind. I saw her blasted by the Sky Lords' wizardry, riven by a Kho'rabi blade, consumed by flames. I sweated, feverish, turning on my bed, so that I cried out as my wound was twisted. In time I slept.

I woke to find Urt squatted at my side. He held a bowl from which savory steam rose. I ignored it. I said, "Rwyan?" My mouth was dry, and it seemed my lips were gummed.

Urt shook his head and said, "Not yet. I've no word."

I cursed and began to rise. The room wavered, and from a long way away I heard Urt say, "Lie still, Daviot. Master Telek says you've lost much blood. You're not to use that leg, but rest."

I remember that I tried to answer, to argue, but it seemed that waves of light and distant sound washed over me, and I was turned around, like a piece of flotsam caught in the eddies of the tide. I found it very difficult to focus my eyes. I thought of netted fish drawn struggling from their ocean home; and then of gutted fish.

I lay three days in fever (so Urt and Cleton later advised me), bathed and fed by my friends, and through those days the Sky Lords came again and again, delivering such damage to Durbrecht as none had thought to see, none thought possible.

When the fever broke I was newborn weak, and had it not been for Telek's potions and the care of my friends, I think I should have died. As it was, I recovered enough that I lay abed frustrated and frightened, hearing the sounds of battle in the sky and the streets, unable to do more than grind my teeth and clutch at the sheets. The fighting continued for two more days and then silence fell. There was still no word of Rwyan.

Five more days passed before Telek deemed me fit to rise and I was able to hobble, leaning heavily on a crutch, about the College. It had not gone unscathed: walls and towers had been blasted by the Sky Lords' wizardry, statues lay toppled, windows bared teeth of jagged glass, gardens were seared. The city, I was told (I was as yet too weak to venture beyond our ravaged walls), had fared worse. Fires had raged, sunk boats clogged the harbor, hundreds were dead.

I mourned them, but I longed more for news of Rwyan.

Urt brought it me on the twelfth day. He had been much occupied—as were all the able-bodied, both Changed and Truemen—but nonetheless had contrived to contact Lyr through that mysterious network of his kind. He found me alone in our chamber late that afternoon. I was staring from the window, impatient now as Cleton had been, watching the rubble cleared, the masons begin the work of repair. It had been a sunny day, the sky clear of both clouds and airboats. I turned as he entered, not needing to speak, for my question was writ clear on my face.

He closed the door and said, "I've spoken with Lyr."

His tone, his expression, induced an awful foreboding. I felt suddenly chilled. It seemed a pit opened, black, before me, or inside me. I felt hollow. I took a deep breath and voiced words I did not want to utter: "She's dead?"

"No." Urt shook his head. "Not dead."

Desolation was replaced with a new fear. "Hurt, then?" I asked. "She was wounded. Badly?"

He came deeper into the room, standing before me. His body told me he bore bad news. I tried to read his eyes, but they were only compassionate. He shook his head again, a brief movement of negation, and said, "She's unhurt. She was not wounded."

Hope flared. "What then?" I asked.

He said, "She's gone."

"Gone?" I shook my head helplessly. "How mean you, gone? Gone where?"

He stepped a pace forward, and I thought he was about to touch me again, as if the word he brought were such as should require he comfort me again. Instead, he raised both hands and let them fall to his sides. He said, "To the Sentinels."

"What?"

I started from my seat. I know not what I thought in that moment—to hobble my way to the harbor, perhaps. To find and halt her boat. I cried out as pain lanced my wound, and fell back, staring at his face, gesturing that he continue.

He said, "As soon as the fighting ended, it was decided the Sentinels must be strengthened. Kherbryn itself was attacked, and the

Lord Protector sent word the Sorcerous College must send as many near-adepts as might be spared. Your Rwyan was one." He closed the gap between us now and did touch me, pushing me gently back as I sought to rise again. "Her boat sailed two days ago. I have only just gotten word from Lyr."

I said, "Two days ago."

My voice was harsh. The pit I had sensed earlier gaped wide, beckoning me. Urt crossed the room to where Cleton and I kept a keg of ale. He filled a mug and gave it me. I drank automatically. The ale tasted sour; or my mouth was filled with despair's ash.

Urt looked a moment out the window, and then at me again. "She left a message with Lyr," he said.

Dully, I asked, "What is it?"

He paused an instant, as if summoning up a memory, then said, " 'Tell Daviot that I love him. Tell him that I shall always love him, but I cannot refuse my duty. I must go where I am bid, as must he in time. Tell him I pray he recovers. Tell him I shall never forget.' "

He fell silent, and I asked, "Was that all?"

He said, "Yes, that was all."

I nodded. My eyes were open but I saw nothing, for they filled with tears. That I had known this must eventually happen, that we should be someday parted by our callings, meant nothing. It was no comfort: the day had come too soon—would always have come too soon—and I knew only grief.

I cursed my calling then, for as I sat there my memory conjured her face in precise detail, and I knew it should always be there, re-minder of my loss. I drained the mug and held it blindly out to Urt to refill. And I cursed my calling anew, for it denied me even the tempo-rary oblivion of drunkenness. Even did I wish it, I could not forget her. She would always be with me. I heard Urt say, "I am sorry, Daviot," but I gave no reply. I could not.

I had never felt so alone as I did then.

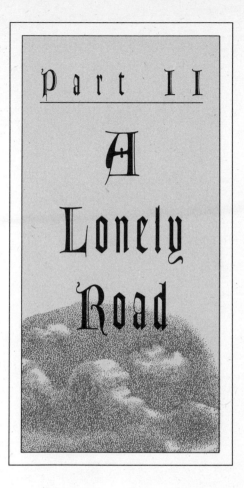

Part II

A Lonely Road

Despite the immense fatigue that gripped her, Rwyan remained on deck, her face turned resolutely back toward Durbrecht. It was an effort to focus those senses that replaced her sight, harder for the draining of her occult energies during the fighting and after, but somewhere within the ravaged walls Daviot lay wounded and she could not allow herself to succumb to the temptation to sleep. She could not, she knew, "see" him, nor would he be aware of her observation, but it seemed to her a kind of farewell. It seemed to her she left a piece of her heart there.

The city stood battle-scarred in the early-morning light, like a warrior resting on his bloodied sword, hurt but undefeated. Gaps showed in the ramparts, and in the harbor scorched hulks lay half-sunk, masts thrust from the Treppanek like skeletal fingers clutching at the sky. In the fields beyond the walls great columns of black smoke rose from the pyres of the Sky Lords' dead. Durbrecht's slain would find resting places in the mausoleums—for the Kho'rabi there were only the bonfires, like obscene celebrations of hard-won victory. Few enough celebrated, she thought. Rather, there was a licking of wounds, a fearful anticipation of the next attack, the horrid certainty that it *would* come. And would Daviot be still there, she wondered; and would he survive again? She felt her eyes grow moist, slow tears roll down her cheeks, trailing in their wake a resentment of the duty that tore her from the man she loved.

She thought, *It is not fair.* And then upbraided herself for that weakness, that traitorous thought, and sternly told herself, *I am a sorcerer, he a Mnemonikos, and we both of us knew this must come to pass. We both of us have a duty we cannot forgo.*

But still the pain lingered, and she wiped a hand across her tears, watching until the steady sweep of the oars had carried the galleass far enough along the Treppanek that Durbrecht was lost, its position marked only by the black funerary columns.

She felt a hand upon her shoulder then and turned to find Chiara at her side. The blond woman said gently, "It cannot be helped; and you knew it should happen."

"You sound like Cleton," Rwyan said. "Daviot told me he held the same opinion."

"How else could it be?" Chiara shrugged. "Best that you forget him."

"I know." Rwyan dried the last of her tears and endeavored to smile. "But I cannot."

"In time you will." Chiara stroked her friend's hair. "Perhaps on the Sentinels you'll meet another. One of our kind."

"No!" Rwyan shook her head.

Chiara sighed. "Are you so certain?" she asked. "Shall you give your heart to a man you'll likely never see again?"

Rwyan said, "Yes," and felt Chiara's hand drop from her hair, heard the small intake of frustrated breath.

"At least rest," Chiara suggested. "The God knows you must be weary enough."

Rwyan nodded and turned from her observation, going with her friend to the cabin assigned them.

It was already crowded, littered with bodies and baggage, the bunks taken by those sisters gone earlier to rest, all weary as Rwyan. There was little enough space left even on the floor, but they found a place and stretched out. Chiara was soon aslumber, but for all Rwyan's weariness, sleep was hard to find. The cabin was warm with the press of bodies, redolent of skin and breath and the unfamiliar odors of a ship. The small square window was open, but what ventilation it allowed was poor, the breeze coming from the east, heated by advancing summer. The brothers of the Sorcerous College slept on deck and should until the galleass reached its destination, and she wished she might join them. That, however, was deemed immodest, and so the females must fit themselves as best they might into the ship's scanty private accommodations. If she could not sleep, she decided, she would meditate.

Even that was difficult, for all that had passed this year ran pell-mell through her mind, defying the disciplines of meditation like a runaway horse careless of bit and bridle, one event piling upon another, and all the time Daviot's face imposing itself between.

At least Urt had been able to bring word, and she able to send back a message via Lyr, so she knew Daviot lived and that his wound was not unduly serious. He would limp awhile, Urt had said, but in other ways was entire. That, Rwyan told herself, was a comfort, though she would have loved him had he been crippled or scarred, and found herself conjuring the image of his face. She was pleased that had not been marked, for it was a pleasant visage. Not handsome like his friend Cleton, but neither homely. It was, she supposed, a face typical of Kellambek: wide of brow and mouth, the jaw square, the nose straight, the eyes a blue that was almost gray. She thought then of the way those eyes studied her—as if they marveled, intent on some wondrous discovery—and of the feel of his thick black hair between her fingers; and that prompted memories of other things—of flesh smooth over hard muscle, of embraces—and she groaned with the sense of loss.

Beside her, Chiara turned drowsily, mumbling an inquiry, and Rwyan murmured an apology and willed herself to silence, seeking to banish that intrusive image. She willed herself to think instead of her duty. That had greater call on her loyalties than mere personal desire: it was the belief of the Sorcerous College that the Sky Lords planned a full-scale invasion.

Rwyan stirred on her hard bed, not much pleased with her contemplation. Her talent was not yet so well defined, nor yet so well tutored, that she could direct her magicks against the invaders—that would be taught her on the islands—but she possessed, like all her companions on this voyage, the innate ability. The power lay within her, and when the airboats had crowded the sky over Durbrecht, and when the Kho'rabi had roamed the streets, the adepts had drawn on that power, taking it like draining blood from her veins. That she had given freely—it was her duty and her desire—could not erase the image of vampiric leaching. She thought it must have been like that in the earliest days. Daviot had told her tales, as they lay together, of folk taken for witches, for wizards, for vampires, blamed and burned for wasting deaths. They had likely been, he had said, sorcerers whose power was unrecognized, who had drawn from others with the talent, unthinking. Did the Sky Lords come again, as she felt sure they must, before she was fully versed in the usage of her talent, then the adepts of the Sentinels would require that leaching of her again. And when she became adept, then likely she must play the vampire.

It was not a thought Rwyan welcomed. For all it was necessary, she found it distasteful. She wished there were some other way to overcome the Ahn wizards. Which brought her mind back to Daviot, for he had spoken of another way.

He had smiled as he told her—she thought how white and strong his teeth were—but behind his laughter she had heard a wondering, an echo of a scarce-shaped dream. Suppose, he had said, that the great dragons still live. Suppose there are still Dragonmasters, hidden in the Forgotten Country. Suppose they could be persuaded to fly against the Sky Lords. We could defeat them then, surely. Think on it, Rwyan! The dragons battling with the Sky Lords! Surely, did the dragons patrol the skies there should be peace.

He had laughed then and shaken his head, dismissing an impossible dream. She thought how boyish he had looked as embarrassment overtook his enthusiasm, and how she had agreed and put her arms about him and drawn him close again in that little room above the inn. She could recall it so precisely. . . .

In the God's name! Rwyan ground her teeth, her eyes screwed tight closed against the threat of tears. *Do I remember so well, what is it like for Daviot? To remember as he is able must be a curse.*

She pushed the shared hurt away as best she could, ordering her mind to contemplation of more practical matters. To end the endless cycle of the Comings was a noble dream, but the dragons were not—could not be—the answer. They were dead, the Dragonmasters with them. And even did they survive, it must be in the wastes of the Forgotten Country, in Tartarus, which none could reach save they cross Ur-Dharbek, and that none did. That was the domain of the wild Changed—no Trueman ventured there.

Fleetingly, she wished she had been sent to the Border Cities. When Daviot was sent out as Storyman, he might go there. Might even be assigned a residency in some aeldor's keep. And did the God, or whatever powers wove the strands of both their destinies, look on them with favor, then she would be mage of that keep, and they be together again.

But the God was not so kind. She was bound for the Sentinels, and Storymen did not go there. Those islands were the domain of the sorcerers alone, and whilst she must remain there, likely Daviot should be sent awandering Draggonek's west coast, or Kellambek's, so that all the Fend and the mass of Dharbek stand between them. Or —an awful thought!—the Sky Lords would come again over Durbrecht and he fall to their wizardry, or a Kho'rabi blade.

Rwyan pressed her face against her pillow that her cry not disturb her companions. There were some amongst them, she knew, had taken lovers not of their own calling and left them without tears. She wondered, briefly, if they were the more fortunate, and told herself, *No, they cannot be. If they can part so easily, they cannot have loved as I do.*

An errant, hurtful thought then: *Shall Daviot forget me?*

And the answer: *No. How can he?*

And then: *But shall he find another love? Shall he meet someone to take my place?*

And the answer: *It may be so, but it shall not affect what I feel. I love him, and I shall always love him.*

It was little enough comfort, near as much pain, but Rwyan clutched it to her as sheer exhaustion finally lulled her troubled mind and granted her the respite of sleep.

And the galleass, propelled by its Changed oarsmen, moved steadily along the Treppanek, past the wreckage of fallen airboats and the ravaged keeps that marked their passage. Eastward, toward the gulf's meeting with the Fend, toward the Sentinels: Rwyan's future.

She woke in a cabin stifled by summer's heat. The air was thick, and her head, for all she was rested and felt no further need of sleep, ached. She sat up, finding only a few sisters remaining, Chiara gone. Her mouth tasted gritty, her blind eyes sore from weeping. She sighed and clambered to her feet, going out into the fresher air of the deck.

Dusk approached, and she realized she had slept away the day. She found the water barrel and scooped out a pannikin, slaking her thirst and freshening her face. Along the deck a brazier glowed red, the smell of charcoal and grilling meat reminding her of hunger. Chiara stood by the port rail, and Rwyan went to join her friend, hoping she would not suffer another lecture on the pointlessness of love.

Thankfully, Chiara was more occupied with the novelty of sailing and only smiled and gestured at the expanse of water, at the deck of the galleass, saying, "Is this not marvelous?"

Rwyan turned slowly around, taking proper notice of their surroundings for the first time. "Yes," she answered. "Yes, it is."

She had traveled over water only once before, Chiara never. The blond sorcerer came from Kherbryn itself, where her family was prominent amongst the city's merchants, which sometimes gave her airs, and she had come overland to Durbrecht. Rwyan had spent her childhood in Hambry, which lay inland of Kellambek's west coast, a village devoted to sheep and farming. When her talent was recognized by the village mantis (who perceived that despite her obvious blindness, she could "see" as well as any sighted child) she had been dispatched to Murren Keep, to an interview with the commur-mage of that hold, whose examination confirmed the suspicions of the mantis. When she came of age, she had gone back to Murren, and thence by cart to Nevysvar on the Treppanek. She had crossed the gulf on a ferryboat, finding the experience mildly terrifying, and been glad to set foot once more on solid ground. Now it occurred to her that she was not at all afraid—the galleass seemed safe.

She turned her sight from the ship to the water. It sparkled blue and silver, gold where the rays of the descending sun struck the wavelets radiating from the bow. The evening was still, the light translucent, clear enough she could make out the dark shadow of the north bank. Overhead a flight of geese passed raucous to their roosting grounds; over the shimmering water an osprey hung, dived, and emerged with a fish. It was an idyllic scene. The galleass creaked in a companionable way, the dip of the oars was rhythmic, the sway of the deck was gentle. To the east, the moon hung pale in a sky still blue, unsullied by the obscene intrusion of the Sky Lords' vessels.

She said, "I was frightened the first time I was on a boat."

"This is a ship," Chiara replied authoritatively. "A ship is large enough to carry a boat."

Rwyan nodded, allowing her friend that superior knowledge as loss once more impinged: boats and ships and water were things with which Daviot was familiar. She struggled to control herself, to fight down the fresh flood of memories. Her fingers threatened to gouge splinters from the rail.

If Chiara was aware of her discomfort, she gave no sign, continuing in cheerful spate. "I spoke with the captain while you slept. By the God, I thought you'd never wake! His name's Lyakan. He's from the west coast of Draggonek, and he owns this ship and a crew of thirty bull-bred oarsmen. He's employed by the College to supply the Sentinels."

Perhaps she spoke to cheer Rwyan, to occupy her. Rwyan neither knew nor cared but let the softly accented voice wash over her, content to leave Chiara to her dissertation as she fought her internal battle. It would never be as Chiara suggested, that time should blunt her love, but she hoped the passage of the days would allow her to control that awful sense of loss, to accommodate it within her daily round.

She had never thought to feel like this, had not known it was possible; until now the worst hurt she had known had been parting from her family, from parents and siblings, the friends of childhood in Hambry. But that had been assuaged by the great adventure before her. To be chosen as candidate to the Sorcerous College, to go to Durbrecht, that had been so exciting a prospect, she had felt guilty she was so glad to depart.

She had been a virgin then, when she left Hambry, and a virgin when she met Daviot—*In the God's name, it was impossible not to think of him!*—in that street of pleasure houses. She smiled at the memory of his expression, that first time they had met. No man had ever looked at her in that way, nor so assiduously sought her out.

She had not truly thought to meet him again. After all, it was but a casual encounter, and her mention of the Golden Apple had been less promise than desire to be about her business unhindered by some casual suitor. She had been much surprised to find him there; more that his presence afforded her such pleasure. But even then she had thought he would resign himself and it prove only a casual flirtation. She had known it was more, on his side at least, when she learned he frequented the tavern, and then recognized her own feelings, at first unwilling—surely unwilled—as she found herself drawn back. His love, he had told her, was immediate: he had known from the first moment. Hers came more slowly, kindled by his own, enhanced by the sense of intrigue that accompanied their meetings. And then it had blazed, and she was no longer a virgin and could no more forget him than she could forsake her talent. Or the duty that drove them apart.

"You're thinking of him again."

Chiara's voice, admonishing, interrupted Rwyan's thoughts and she nodded defiantly.

"You'll forget him," Chiara said, echo of so many other conversations.

And Rwyan answered, "No. Perhaps I shall learn to live without him, but I shall never forget him."

There was such certainty in her tone, and such pain, that Chiara forgot her disapproval and was only friend. She took Rwyan's hand gently in her own and said no more. Instead, they stood in silence as the twilight deepened and the surface of the Treppanek was no longer painted with the sun's red gold but became as blue velvet, a softly whispering cushion to the moon's silvered reflection.

Then a bell summoned them to their dinner, and they went, still hand-in-hand, along the deck to where their fellow sorcerers clustered eagerly about a brazier on which meat grilled.

It was easier in company. Conversation made demands on her

attention that enabled her to concentrate on what was said and how she would respond, and none there, save Chiara, knew of Daviot. So she spoke of the Sentinels and the recent attack, and of the expectations of the College, and for a while felt not at all sad. And Lyakan passed the tiller to a Changed and joined them, broaching a keg of good ale, which he cheerfully declared must be consumed before they reached the islands, which announcement was met with enthusiastic agreement.

Rwyan drank somewhat more than was her wont, and joined in the singing that ensued, and that night slept quite soundly, for all her last thoughts were of Daviot.

There were no more attacks as the galleass sailed east, nor as she ventured onto the Fend. The weather remained mild, Lyakan setting his three lateen sails as the tower of Rorsbry Keep hove in view, Fynvar a distant thimble shape to the north. He tacked eastward, supplying remedies to those who found the ocean's chop distressing. Rwyan was pleased she suffered no discomfort; a little guilty that Chiara's violent illness did not trouble her more.

A day, a night, and the morning of another day they sailed, and then the closest of the seven Sentinels were in sight.

Rwyan found herself a place at the prow, her senses focused on the islands. She held her place as they came closer, until only one was visible, the rest lost to the dip and bob of the galleass. Lyakan ordered the sails furled, and the oarsmen bent once again to their sweeps, propelling the ship onward. The wind blew colder out here, and soon she heard the murmur of surf, the beat of the rollers that swept across all the width of the ocean, perhaps from the distant lands of the Sky Lords even, to break on these isolate stones. She wondered if the anchorage would be dangerous.

Then danger was forgotten as her talent revealed the island in all its rugged splendor.

She had been told of the Sentinels, but to be *told* was not the same as seeing, and the descriptions had been delivered by sorcerers. It would take a Storyman to do this place justice. It was a vast slab of rock, as if a single, inconceivably massive boulder had been dropped into the Fend. Waves broke against the feet of sheer cliffs, smooth and high: unscalable. White spume crashed against blue-black stone, a foaming line of demarcation broken only where an impossibly narrow gap showed in the rock. It was not, Rwyan "saw," an inlet but a cave's mouth, barely high enough the galleass's masts might enter unharmed. She held her breath as Lyakan put his tiller over and the vessel raced, driven by sweeps and tide, for the opening. The glittering tower was lost, the cliffs loomed above, surf's roar drowned the apprehensive murmurs of her companions. Then Lyakan bellowed and the oars were brought inboard, and the galleass slid between the sea-gates guarding the dark ingress.

Rwyan felt the magic that drew the craft in, defying the tug of the sea, the Fend's currents as nothing to that power. At her side, Chiara cried out, clutching her arm as darkness fell like sudden night, only a glimmer of day behind, and even that lost as the sea-gates closed. For Rwyan darkness held little meaning, and so she "saw" the proximity of the cliffs to either side, the roof frighteningly low above. She might have reached out to touch the stone, so close was it. Then daylight returned, blinding natural sight after the stygian depths of the entrance, and the galleass floated gently to a harbor cut by magic's might from the heart of the rock.

From seaward, the island had appeared entirely forbidding; now it appeared entirely paradisal.

The inlet was circular, a beach of pale yellow sand interrupted only by the blue granite pile of a quay and the hulls of fishing boats sweeping in a great calm arc around the saltwater lake. There were buildings constructed of wood and stone, pale blue, white, or rose petal pink, along the water line. More scattered randomly amongst stands of cedar and pine and myrtle, where little streamlets spilled down from terraces decked with olive groves, orchards, and meadows. Goats roamed, seemingly at will, more agile than the sheep and cattle grazing the luxuriant greensward. There were formal gardens, opulent as any in Durbrecht, and others of more natural shape, displaying a vivid array of wild flowers. Paths wandered the terraces, and long flights of white stone steps. The entire center of the island had been shaped by sorcery to cup this jewel as if in a careful fist.

And on the topmost tier, so high the observers on the galleass must tilt back their heads, necks craned, to gaze upward to where it stood bright against the sky, was the white tower, like a sword raised in defiance of the Sky Lords. A single straight stairway ran to its foot, a door of blue wood there, no other openings. It seemed a very simple structure to emanate so great a sensation of sorcerous power, and Rwyan studied it in awe. Within lay the greatest secrets of her kind.

She staggered as the galleass drifted to a halt, her attention diverted from the tower to the rush of activity initiated by their docking. Two of Lyakan's Changed sprang to the wharf, securing the ship as two more ran out the gangplank. All came from their rowing benches to assist the newcome sorcerers to disembark. There were none amongst the crowd gathered on the pier: all there were Truemen.

Chiara was aflutter with undisguised excitement as they traversed the plank to meet the welcome of the residents. Rwyan, for all she was enchanted with the beauty of her new surroundings, was less stimulated. Before long, she knew, Lyakan would take his galleass back across the Fend and the sea-gates would close behind him. It felt to her that they would close, too, on Daviot; that he must be shut off from her by all the weight of ocean and distance and duty. She turned her attention a moment back, to the ship and the Fend beyond, and then she sighed, and took a breath, and shaped her lips in a smile as she walked toward her future.

In the weeks that followed Rwyan's departure, I grew surly. I thought more of my loss than of learning and gave short answers to those who inquired after my abrupt change of mood. My mind was occupied with memories of Rwyan. I indulged in the pointless exercise of self-pity. It was foolishness: what was, was. I knew that; it made my grief no easier. I sank into sullen despair, that exacerbated by my healing leg. I progressed from crutch to staff and then was able to limp without support, chafing at confinement within the College. None but Urt and Cleton knew the reason for my black mood, but it was impossible it should go unnoticed—questions were asked my friends. I am confident neither Cleton nor Urt (who were both interrogated) gave much away, but the College authorities were subtle and very adept in drawing out answers. Such is, after all, a part of the Mnemonikos's talent, and it may be employed to more ends than the investigation of a story. Whatever was said or not, the conclusions drawn were correct: that I had become engaged in an affair with a member of the Sorcerous College recently departed for the Sentinels. I was brought before a tribunal, that judgment of some kind might be delivered.

Decius presided, and it was to his sunlit chambers I was summoned. He sat as usual behind his desk, but to right and left, on high-backed chairs, sat four of the College dignitaries. Keran was one, beside him, Ardyon; on the master's right were Bael and Lewynn, who taught geography. I could read none of their faces; I was not invited to sit.

Without preamble, Decius asked me, "Is it true you dallied with a student of sorcery?"

I saw no profit in equivocation and answered him, "Yes."

"For how long?" he demanded.

I said, "A year."

His brows rose at that, his round face become owlish in its surprise. "Yet none suspected," he murmured. "You must have had help."

I was not sure if he asked a question or made a statement and so offered him no response: I was prepared to accept whatever punishment this College court deemed fit, but I would not betray my friends.

"He's great ingenuity," Bael said. I was uncertain whether that was praise or condemnation.

Decius nodded, so that the sun coming through the window at his back flickered bright on his pate. I was somewhat blinded by the light, so I could not see his eyes clearly. He said, "Hmm," and was silent awhile.

Ardyon leaned toward the master and murmured something I could not make out, save, I think, for the names Cleton and Urt. Decius nodded again in response and made a small gesture, as if quieting a restive hound. I waited. I felt my healing leg begin to throb dully.

Then Decius asked me, "How did you think it should end, this affair?"

I said, "It has not. I love her." Ardyon's explosive nasal inhalation told me I spoke too fiercely, and it came to me I might well face expulsion. In a milder tone I added, "I had not thought beyond that — that I love her."

"Yet you know such" — Decius appeared for some reason to find the subject delicate — "*friendships* are not encouraged."

"Nor," I ventured, "forbidden."

Close on the heels of my realization that I might soon be thrown out of the College came another. Were I expelled, I could return home to Whitefish village, and that was not overly far from the Sentinels: I could obtain a boat (it was a measure of my mood that I did not consider *how* I should acquire it) and sail to the islands; find Rwyan there. Of course, that would mean throwing away these last few years, turning my back on all I had learned, and there remained some small rational part of my mind that warned me I should not find entry to the Sentinels easy, and that Rwyan might not be allowed, or might not wish, to leave. Balanced against my desire for her, it was a negligible weight.

"Not forbidden," Decius said, "but neither encouraged. That for both sides' sake. Did it not occur to you that she has a duty, as do you, and that your . . . love . . . should conflict with that loyalty?"

I wondered why he found that simple word, *love*, so hard to say. It did not occur to me then, in my youth and my loss, that his love was entirely for the College and all it stood for; that he found it difficult, indeed near impossible, to comprehend that a man might find a greater passion.

I said, "I suppose so. Yes; but I hoped . . ."

Decius gestured that I continue. I squinted into the light, shrugged, and said honestly, "I did not think too far ahead, master. I hoped we might both remain in Durbrecht . . . or find ourselves assigned residents to the same keep . . . or . . ." I shook my head and shrugged again.

He said, "Your Rwyan is gone to the Sentinels, where none but sorcerers are permitted residence. Even did you somehow find your way there, you would not be allowed to remain. Ergo, your affair could not have succeeded."

It seemed, almost, he read my mind; I was taken aback that he knew so much. I should not have been, of course: there was little enough went unnoticed by the College, and this matter had been investigated. I ducked my head and muttered a reluctant negative.

Then he startled me again by asking, "Would you throw away these years? Do you wish to leave us?"

We had a saying in Whitefish village concerning the fish caught betwixt net and hook. I understood it fully in that instant. I knew that if I said yes, I might walk away, free to go seeking Rwyan. And if I did? I had no way of knowing to which of the Sentinels she had gone. Even did I somehow succeed in landing on the right island, I must still find my love. I did not doubt but that Decius spoke the truth when he warned me I should not be allowed to remain. And would Rwyan forsake her duty, quit her calling to come away with me?

I hesitated, my head spinning. I fidgeted, indecisive, easing my weight from throbbing leg to good and back again. The sun was warm on my face, hiding the expressions of the men who watched me, awaiting my answer. I thought then of that message Rwyan had left me. My talent, my trained memory, brought it back precise: *Tell Daviot that I love him. Tell him that I shall always love him, but I cannot refuse my duty. I must go where I am bid, as must he in time. Tell him I pray he recovers. Tell him I shall never forget.*

Rwyan had accepted her duty. Could I do less and remain the man she loved?

To Decius I said, "No. I'd not leave."

As I spoke, I was unsure whether I chose the net or the hook. I knew I felt a dreadful pain.

I heard the master say, "Then we must consider your future. Do you return to your lessons, and we shall inform you."

I nodded wearily. I had not thought to find my fate still undecided. I turned and limped from the room.

I had been engaged with Telek in the herbarium, and I returned there. The herbalist-chirurgeon greeted me with a sympathetic smile and waved me back to my classification of the dried plants. Cleton contrived to place himself at my side and inquired in a whisper how I had fared.

I told him my fate was as yet unfixed, and he scowled, and tapped the plaster still encasing his arm, and said, "In the God's name, what more do they want? Rwyan's gone and you choose to remain. What's to decide?"

"Whether I'm fit to stay, I suppose," I whispered back. "Or not."

My friend cursed roundly and very soundly and said, "Do we visit the Horseman tonight? A few tankards of Lyam's ale might wash that cloud from your face."

I had not known my expression was so black. Nor did I feel much appetite for ale, or even company. Neither did I much wish to be alone: solitude would afford too much space for doubt. But I was still banned the city. I said, "I cannot. I am commanded to remain here." At that moment, the College seemed to me a prison.

Cleton grinned and said, "Even with your leg, the walls should not be hard to climb."

I was tempted. I was also very confused, torn between the desire to be alone and that for his stout company. I almost agreed, but then I thought of the cost—surely expulsion, was such disobedience discovered.

I shook my head, saying, "No, I think not."

"By the God," he returned, "you've been long enough confined. A visit to the Horseman would surely ease your miseries. Better, a visit to Allya's. Thais asks after you, you know."

I had not thought of Thais, nor wished to now, and what appeared to me his casual dismissal of Rwyan roused me to anger. I glowered and said primly, "I've no wish to visit Thais. Nor would I risk my future here. Do you not think I've lost enough already?"

Poor Cleton's smile melted in the heat of my response, and he raised a placatory hand. "Forgive me," he asked. "I was not thinking."

I grunted a reply. I knew he sought only to cheer me and so felt guilty at my anger—which served to fuel it more. We spent the remainder of the afternoon in prickly silence, both working with a fervor that surely must have impressed our tutor.

"I told them nothing," I said, "save what they knew. Of you and Lyr I said nothing at all."

Urt set the chimney of a lamp in place and pinched out the taper before turning to face me. His coarse gray hair was reddened by the flame; his whiteless eyes were placid. His smile was not: it was very confident.

"I did not think you would," he said.

Cleton was rummaging through our wardrobe, seeking a suitable shirt for his planned excursion. Over his shoulder he said, "But they likely guess. By the God! Ardyon asked me enough questions."

"The warden spoke at length with me." Urt nodded gravely. "But you know that. And that I said no more than I must, I hope."

"Of course." I set a hand on his shoulder, which was sinewy and muscular, and smiled. "I could find no better friend," I said.

Urt seemed embarrassed, his eyes flickering to Cleton. I saw my Trueman comrade frown at such open expression of friendship with one of the Changed, and removed my hand. Thinking to mend our differences, I amended my statement: "I could hope for no better friends than the both of you."

Cleton was visibly taken somewhat aback to find himself ranked alongside a Changed servant in my estimation, but he took it gracefully and hid his frown behind his chosen shirt.

Urt's expression grew solemn then, and he fixed me with his dark stare. "Still, Master Cleton is right," he said. "Save I think they know, rather than guess."

Cleton struggled with his shirt. We take our bodies for granted, never thinking how the loss of a limb's use hampers us until we must perforce do without. Urt went to help him, and as Cleton's head emerged from the collar he frowned anew, but for a different cause now. "Then surely," he said, "they'd have had me before that tribunal."

"Perhaps not." Urt shook his head, and in his eyes I thought I found some emotion I could not define. "You are son of the aeldor of Madbry, Master Cleton, and that carries some weight. More, you're a good student."

Cleton laughed carelessly. The sound struck me like a cold wave: it failed entirely to register what I heard in Urt's voice, saw in his eyes.

Still chuckling, he stood as Urt tied the laces of his shirt. "Daviot's a better student than I," he declared. "And my birth means nothing here."

"Think you not?" asked Urt.

His husky voice was carefully modulated, but still I thought he spoke with unaccustomed openness in Cleton's presence. I thought he seemed almost reckless, as if he felt some dice were cast, determining a future I failed to comprehend. I waited, suddenly nervous.

"Son of an aeldor, son of a fisherman." Cleton extended his arms that Urt might fasten his cuffs; flourished the linen. "Son of a koryphon, even. All are the same in this College, all equal."

Something flashed an instant in Urt's eyes, gone almost before I saw it. "Some are more equal," he said in a soft voice, "some less."

"Nonsense," Cleton said.

I said, "Do you explain, my friend?"

Cleton opened his mouth to elaborate, then recognized I spoke to Urt and fell silent, his frown returned. Whether because I looked to the Changed for answer or because I again openly named him friend, I neither knew nor cared.

Urt paused an instant. I thought him unwilling to speak for Cleton's presence and smiled encouragement, motioning him to continue. He hesitated still, and I said, "Shall we conspirators hold secrets from one another? Go on, friend."

He smiled briefly. A flash of sharp white teeth. "Some command a greater influence than others," he said, "no matter the society. Do you not learn that from your studies of politics?"

I saw Cleton's frown dissolve into an expression of curiosity. He settled on his bed and allowed Urt to tug on his boots. They shone bright with fresh polish—the Changed's work. I waited, foreboding mounting.

Urt said, "How is this College financed?"

Cleton answered him, "The Lord Protector and the koryphon fund us, of course. And merchants, nobles, donate."

"And the Lord Protector and the koryphon are funded by taxes, no?" Urt said. "And the koryphon has his power from the Lord Protector, and both rest on the support of the aeldors, who tax those within their holdings, no?"

"How else should it be?" asked Cleton. He selected a tunic and let Urt drape the garment over his shoulders. "That's the natural order of things."

Very softly, so that I alone heard him, Urt said, "Perhaps." Then louder: "But what if the aeldors held those taxes for themselves? What if the Lord Protector and the koryphon received no tithe?"

"That," said Cleton, coldly now, "would be sedition. And rightly punished as such."

"It would surely be punished," Urt agreed, which was not a full agreement. "But—a supposition only, of course—what should happen did the aeldors withdraw their support?"

"Chaos!" Cleton snapped. "By the God, the Sky Lords would overwhelm us did all not work together. Dharbek would collapse."

"I speak only of this College," said Urt, carefully. "That the goodwill of an aeldor is worth more than a fisherman's."

Or, the Changed's. He did not have to say it. I recognized his gist; I felt surprise that he commanded such a grasp of the webwork of politics and privilege that underpinned decisions. I said, "You think I might be punished whilst Cleton goes free."

"I think the good opinion of Master Cleton's father likely carries a greater weight than does yours," he said. And coughed a small laugh that might have been apologetic, "Whilst mine carries none at all."

"You're Changed," Cleton said.

He was smiling as he took up his purse, weighing the coin therein, happily oblivious of Urt's discomfort or my reservations. "Well," he said, "if I cannot persuade you to join me, I shall be on my way. Do I give Thais your regards?"

I said, "No," and he shrugged, and waved, and strode from the chamber.

The door closed behind him and Urt said, "Do you require anything?"

And I answered, "Yes. I'd talk with you, if you will."

His expression was entirely bland as he said, "I am at your command. I am your servant."

"You are my friend," I said. "Or at least, I hope you are."

"Yes, I am." His expression shifted—I grew moment by moment more adept in its translation—and I saw apology in his eyes. "Forgive me, Daviot. Sometimes . . ."

His lean shoulders rose and fell. I ventured to finish for him: "Sometimes the attitude of Truemen is offensive. I apologize for Cleton."

That elicited a brief smile. "How should you apologize for another?" he murmured.

I shrugged in turn and said, "On behalf of my kind."

"Your kind is rare," he said. "Cleton's the more common."

I nodded, not knowing what to say: it was the truth. I compromised with, "He means no ill."

"No." Urt looked a moment out the window, then returned his gaze to me. "Few do."

There was something hidden behind his response; something sad in his voice and in his eyes. I rose from the bed and crossed to the ale keg. I filled two mugs, passing him one and motioning for him to sit.

"You're a strange fellow, Daviot," he murmured. "Why do you show me such kindness?"

It had not occurred to me that I did: I treated him as felt natural to me. I frowned and said, "How else should I deal with you?"

He said, "As do other Truemen."

"You're my friend," I said.

He laughed at that, and raised his mug in toast, and said, "Yes. Perhaps someday I shall have the chance to prove it you."

"You have already," I told him, and what had begun as an answering smile froze on my lips. "You proved it in carrying my messages to Rwyan." I sought to conceal my sudden misery behind my tankard.

Urt said, "I'm sorry for what happened." And paused a moment before adding, "But I meant in a greater way than as courier."

"No service could be greater," I said.

"Perhaps."

He smiled, but I thought the expression was now designed to allay further inquiry. I asked, "How, perhaps?"

He shook his head and sipped his ale. "Does the opportunity come, you shall know," he said.

"Do you explain now?" I asked.

His lips closed, pursing. His eyes grew dark: unfathomable, and he shook his head. "No, I cannot. And I presume on our friendship to ask that you inquire no further."

I was intrigued. I forgot my misery as I sensed some mystery here. There was such hint in what he said of things unknown, unsuspected, of areas of knowledge beyond my ken, I was mightily tempted to press him. There was also, on his face and in his voice, a warning— that he would not speak, and that did I demand explanation, our friendship should be threatened. It was valuable to me, that friendship, and so I respected his wishes. I nodded and made some gesture of acceptance. "Do you so wish," I said.

He smiled with unfeigned pleasure and said, "Thank you, Daviot."

And I, in my youth, heard such warmth in those three simple words, I was embarrassed. I think I blushed. I know I said, "I'd not pry, my friend," and sought to turn our conversation onto safer ground. "What do you think will happen to me? To us? Shall I be allowed to stay?"

Urt paused again, then said, "I suspect you will. Likely there'll be some small punishment—you'll be confined longer to the College grounds; something of that sort. But it's common knowledge you're considered too good a Mnemonikos that you'll be let go."

"You're very confident," I said.

He grinned and answered, "We Changed hear much. There's some advantage in our situation, for Truemen seem to think we've not ears, or memories, but we've both; and servants talk."

"And you?" I asked.

He did not immediately answer but rose and took my mug for refilling with his own, which in itself was a compliment—a measure of his confidence in my sympathy. I awaited his reply. It seemed all the foreboding I had felt, the shiftings of his face, his recklessness, co-alesced in his answer, and as he gave it, I felt a fresh weight added to my burden of unhappiness.

"It is rumored I shall be sent away." He raised a hand to silence my instinctive protest. "To argue it would be pointless; I ask that you accept. Do you argue, you can only make your own situation worse."

I felt new pain. Not so fierce as at Rwyan's departure, but still hurtful. I asked, "Where?"

Urt shrugged. "Likely the Border Cities," he said.

I raised my hand, half minded to dash my mug to the floor. There was such certainty in his voice, I could not doubt but that he had this information from the servants of the tutors, the warden, the master; from that network of anonymous Changed that moved unnoticed through human society. Was I the only Trueman to see their faces, to perceive them as beings in their own right, to credit them with emo-tions, with sentience? Resentment grew, allied with frustration and new-seeded anger.

Urt said mildly, "Do you shatter that mug I must clean the floor again."

I snarled and lowered my hand. I said, "That's not fair."

"Fair?" He smiled, and the curving of his lips was cynical. "I am Changed, Daviot."

"I'll tell them I coerced you," I declared. "I'll say I gave you no choice but to carry my messages."

"And they would say I should have gone to Ardyon," he returned me. "That my duty to the College precedes any personal loyalty."

I could not argue: it was the truth.

"And it should only do you harm," he went on. "Better that you stay silent. Apologize, and accept whatever punishment is meted out; finish your studies."

He gave me advice, and it was sound. Vague through my anger came the thought that most men would find it strange a Changed should assume to advise a Trueman. I asked him, "Why?"

"Why should you remain?" he asked in turn. "Or why do I counsel that you do?"

"Both," I said.

"The one because it should be a great waste of your talent. You've the makings of a fine Rememberer, and you've worked hard for that. To quit the College now would be to throw away the years you've spent in Durbrecht. What would you do else? I doubt you could return to that village of yours and become a fisherman. Would you join some warband, be a soldier?" He paused, as if to let his words sink in. Outside, the day darkened, allowing the lanterns' light greater play on his hair and face. He was very solemn: I thought of prophets. "The other? In part for the same reasons, in part because I am your friend, and I do not enjoy waste."

"Whilst you are banished to the Border Cities!" I cried.

"It's not quite banishment," he said. "That we must part saddens me. But that should have come to pass in any event, no?"

Again he spoke only the truth, which made it no easier to swallow. It was less the fact of parting than its manner that troubled me. It was somehow comforting to think of Urt continuing at the College, perhaps impressing some student come after me with his humanity; perhaps to open another's eyes. I said, "It is not fair to punish you for my sins."

He said, "I shared them. I knew—perhaps better than you—the risks we took. I knew judgment would be delivered, were we discovered."

"Yet still you aided me," I said.

"You are my friend," he said. "What else should I do?"

I looked him square in the eye then and said, "Have I ever the opportunity to repay you, Urt, you've but to name it."

He nodded, once, and said, "I know that, Daviot."

"Perhaps they'll allow you stay," I said. "At least until I go out a Storyman."

I knew, or sensed, that I clutched at straws. Urt confirmed it with a shake of his head.

"Perhaps we'll meet again," I said, still clutching.

"Perhaps," he allowed. "I hope we may."

It had grown dark now, and the clatter of hammers, the drone of saws, had ceased. Occasionally there came a shout from the yards outside; mostly the night was silent.

"Save you've need of anything, I'd best go."

Urt rose. I shook my head. I wanted to say more, but there were no words, only a sadness in me that was colored with the fire of anger. Was this what it was to be a Mnemonikos? To see one's loves, one's friends, all left behind? I had known it should be a lonely path to take, but that awareness had been intellectual, unreal. Now it was emotional, personal. It hurt. I watched him take his tankard to the closet and rinse the mug. He set it down beside the keg and came to stand before me.

"The tribunal will deliver its verdict soon," he said. "I'd ask you heed my advice when they call you."

"Yes." I knew not what else to say. I rose and took his hand as I would any Trueman's. "The God go with you, Urt."

His grasp was powerful as he said, "I do not think the God cares much about we Changed, Daviot. But still, my thanks."

He loosed his grip and went out the door.

Cleton returned at some point, but I was unaware of his presence until the impatient tapping on our door woke me. I raised my head from the pillow, noticing from the quality of the light that it was only a little while after sunrise. Then I realized the tapping lacked the softer sound of flesh and knuckle but was rather the sharp rattle of wood on wood. Such as a caduceus would make. I sprang naked from my bed, motioning Cleton back as he stirred, and went to the door.

Ardyon stood there, his cadaverous face impassive. I felt my stomach lurch. I had believed myself resigned: I had been wrong.

I said, "Day's greetings, warden."

He nodded, sniffed, and said without preamble, "Dress. You're summoned to the master."

I said, "Yes," and stood back, thinking he would enter; perhaps to watch over me for fear I should escape from the window. Instead, he shook his head and waved his caduceus to indicate I hurry, closing the door on me as I retreated.

Cleton was sitting up, his blue eyes worried. "The verdict?" he asked.

I said, "Ardyon awaits me," and affected a smile I hoped was brave, "with his trusty caduceus."

I went into the alcove to splash my face. I satisfied a suddenly urgent need to urinate. I wondered if the sound I heard was the tap of the warden's staff against his thigh, or the thudding of my heart. I dragged on clothes. I could not understand why I was so nervous. I had believed Urt when he told me I should not be expelled. I had not thought I cared so much.

Cleton said, "The God grant it goes well."

I nodded, shoving shirt-tails into my breeks. I ran fingers through my hair, took a deep breath, and crossed back to the door.

Ardyon seemed not at all impatient. I studied his face, seeking some clue to my impending fate, but he gave me nothing, only ducked his head as if in approval of my haste, and set off down the corridor. I limped after him. I dared not speak. Even had I, I do not believe he would have answered. He was a man who took his duties very seriously; he did not consider explanations to be amongst them.

We went down the stairs into the yard. I caught the smell of breakfast wafting from the refectory. My stomach rumbled, either from hunger or trepidation. The sky was aquamarine, the sun not yet visible above our walls. A breeze stirred, warm. I licked my lips and followed the warden into the building that held the master's quarters.

We halted at the familiar door and Ardyon applied his caduceus. A voice came muffled through the wood, and he swung the portal open, motioning me inside. I stepped past him and started as I heard the door close behind me, leaving me alone with Decius.

I had expected to find those others who had sat in judgment present, but Decius was alone behind his desk. For an errant moment I wondered if he spent the nights there, if he ever left. Perhaps he was crippled and lived all his life behind that desk. I said, "Day's greetings, master." I was surprised my voice did not quaver.

Decius answered formally and beckoned me closer. His chambers lay to the west side of the College and thus were sunlit only in the afternoons. I had always been summoned before him later in the day: now I could see his round face clearly, unmasked by opposing light. It was concerned, as if he were a father confronted with a naughty child, bound to deliver some reprimand, but not much taken with the notion. He cleared his throat and frowned. I waited.

"We have debated your case at length, Daviot," he said, "and it is decided you shall not be expelled."

He studied me. I thought he waited for some response, and so I said, "Thank you, master."

He smiled very briefly and said, "There are some consider you a risk, a bad influence. They'd see you ejected."

I thought, *Ardyon*, and wondered who else.

Decius said, "Others believe you one of the most promising students we've had. But even so . . ."

He ran a hand across the smooth skin of his pate, which I had never seen him do before. I could not be sure what the gesture meant.

He cleared his throat again and said, "For my own part, I believe you might one day be a tutor. Master, even."

I was amazed. I gasped and stuttered, "Thank you."

He waved dismissal of my gratitude. "But you've that in you as to arouse doubts. This latest matter"—he shook his head—"you knew it was frowned on, but still you continued. You suborned others to your cause. . . . That you should not have done."

"No," I said, thinking perhaps I might win Urt a reprieve did I humble myself; thinking of his advice. "I should not have. I apologize for that, master. For all I did."

Decius nodded and caught me out in my false humility: "Do you then repudiate your mage?"

I swallowed, recognizing the trap. Dismiss Rwyan? I could not do that. Would not! I said, "I cannot, master. I love her still."

I saw his face cloud at that, and my sense of self-preservation prompted me to add: "Even though I shall likely never see her again."

It seemed to mollify him. At least he nodded and murmured, "Likely not. A Storyman fares better alone. Do you serve out that time, and then, should you become a tutor . . ." He smiled. I thought it the smile of a man who suggests some course he does not truly believe in, or properly understand. "Then you might take a wife. Or find a mistress. This Thais, for example. Is she not satisfactory?"

Once more he succeeded in taking me aback. Thais? How had he discovered her existence? Cleton had not told me he made any mention of the cyprian. I wondered if there was anything the master did not know. I wondered if he was a sorcerer, besides head of our College. I gulped and said, "Yes. I suppose so. She's . . ." I faltered. "She was . . . satisfactory."

"Then I'd suggest you take what pleasure you need there," Decius said. "And from henceforth leave alone those others."

I had no intention whatsoever of following that advice: I nodded.

He nodded in return and said, "So, to your future. You shall remain amongst us, but—on probation. Do you err again, it must be the last time. You understand?"

I said, "Yes, master."

"And do you accept?" he asked.

Again I said, "Yes, master."

"Then understand the strictures that apply," he said. "You will not depart the grounds without specific permission. Nor shall you attempt to contact this Rwyan in any way."

I said, "Yes, master," thinking I began to sound like some timid Changed.

"When you are allowed to leave the College grounds," he went on, "it shall be only in company with two others. One may be Cleton."

His expression seemed to me to invite thanks for that favor, so I repeated my iteration: "Thank you, master."

He paused again, musing, as if he mulled his next words. I continued to wait. I wondered why I was allowed Cleton's company, he having been integral to my affair. Perhaps Decius believed his influence would draw me back to the safer pursuits of the street of green lanterns; perhaps the master thought to keep his bad eggs in the single basket. I was not about to question the decision.

Then he said, "By this year's end, you'll have all the learning we can give you for now. Next spring, you go out a Storyman."

"Master?" He had the ability to surprise me still. I wondered if it was amusement I deciphered in his eyes.

"A Storyman, Daviot. Did you not expect that?"

Now it was my turn to pause. Of course I had expected it: it was the next step. Why else was I here? But to be told this news in such circumstances left me befuddled. I had thought it more likely I should be kept close to the College, until such time as I was deemed sound. I saw that Decius expected a verbal response, and said honestly, "I was not sure, master. I thought perhaps . . ."

I shrugged, lost for words. Decius said, "We've lost too many in these last attacks. There's a need for good Storymen; more, I think, in the days to come."

I was not sure what he meant by that. I had heard no rumors to suggest the Sky Lords came again. Was he privy to secret knowledge? Certainly, he seemed so far omniscient.

When I said nothing more, he continued: "So you shall be sent out at winter's end. Cleton, too. You may tell him that."

I chanted another of my "Yes, master's," aware that he had so far made no mention of Urt. My future was secure, and Cleton's; but what of my Changed comrade? For an instant I debated the wisdom of inquiry, knowing even as I did that it was the safer course to play the penitent, to humbly accept, and say no more than yes and no and thank you. Urt himself had counseled me to that course, and likely inquiry after his fate would serve only to harm us both: I remained dutifully silent.

Decius sat awhile, as if pondering whether to say more. I stood, doing my best not to fidget as my healing leg began to itch horribly.

Finally, the master raised a hand, waving me toward the door, saying, "Enough. You've lessons still. Go."

I said, "Yes, master; thank you," and turned away.

I was tempted to run but settled for a more dignified, if somewhat brisk, walk to my chamber. I was surprised (startlement seemed the order of this day) to find Cleton there.

"I waited," he said, unnecessarily. "What happened?"

"We stay," I told him, and then explained all Decius had told me.

"The God be praised!" He clapped my shoulder. "Next spring, eh? I'm not sorry I missed my breakfast. Not for such good news."

"Did you not have Urt bring food?" I asked.

His answer was casual: "I've not seen Urt this morning." It struck me like a blow.

"Where is he?" I demanded.

Cleton took a step back as I faced him. He shrugged and said, "I've no idea."

I did. I mouthed a string of curses that might have blistered even Garat's ears and shouldered past my friend in search of my other. Cleton hurried to catch me, his expression puzzled.

"What's amiss?" he asked, to which I answered simply, "Urt."

To give him his due, he recognized my concern and took a share, falling into step at my side as I flung myself down corridors and stairs into the yard. I was grateful that he asked no further questions: I was in no mood to give kindly answers.

Together we pushed our way through students going to their lessons. Our own would soon commence, but I cared not at all. I thought Ardyon the most likely to answer my fear, and the refectory the most likely place to find the warden—I took Cleton there.

Ardyon was moving toward the door as I entered. He was in conversation with Clydd and a tutor of politics, Faron. I set myself in their path, ignoring raised brows and the warden's ominous sniff.

I said, "Urt! Where is he?"

Ardyon's deep-sunk eyes met my gaze with massive indifference. He said, "Remember you are yet on probation. You will address your superiors in suitable manner." His voice was flat; and heavy with threat.

I felt Cleton's good hand on my arm. It held me back from striking the warden, which I think Ardyon knew, for he brought his caduceus to rest on his shoulder. The staff was solid enough to do me harm: I did not care.

However, I controlled my anger and forced my voice to semblance of civility. "I have not seen Urt this morning, warden," I said. "I'd be grateful to know his whereabouts."

The skin was stretched so taut across the bones of Ardyon's face, it was bland as a mask. He sniffed now. I thought the sound suggested relish. He chose to address my statement: "You were with the master, no? How then should you have seen your servant?"

I clenched my teeth and fought the impulse to drive my fist against his face as I realized he toyed with me. And that it could mean only the confirmation of my fears. I swallowed, took a deep breath, and said, "By your leave, warden, I'd know he's well."

"I believe he is," said Ardyon.

I hated him in that moment, and he saw it in my eyes. I saw his fingers fasten tighter about the caduceus. At his side, Faron made an impatient gesture, and Clydd frowned. I think neither approved of the warden's game, but nor did they speak to end it.

I said, "He's in the College?" Only after thinking to add a dutiful, "warden."

Ardyon shook his head; slowly, his sunken gaze never leaving my face. "No longer. He's sent to Karysvar."

A Border City: Urt had been entirely correct in all his assumptions. Or known even as we spoke that the decision was made. I thought he had likely held that knowledge from me to ease our parting. I felt my jaw drop. My fists ached from their clenching. I said in a very hollow voice, "Already. Why?"

It was not a question to which I anticipated a response. I knew the reason: I asked it of the One God, or the Three, or fate; whatever was the power that plucked the strings of my life.

Ardyon, however, elected to answer me: "Because he proved untrustworthy; because he betrayed his duty to the College. You may hold yourself accountable for his fate."

That was a vicious sally. The tutors, even, thought it so. Faron made a disapproving sound, frowning at the warden; Clydd said warningly, "There's naught to be done about it, Daviot."

I barely heard them. I stared at Ardyon. Cleton had let go my arm, but now I felt his hand lock on my shirt, at the back, ready to haul me away from attacking the cadaverous disciplinarian.

Ardyon said, "Have you no lessons this day?"

Cleton said, "Yes, warden," and, "Daviot, we'd best be gone."

He put his arm around my shoulders. I let him turn me away: there was nothing I could do, save throw away the future. Urt was gone.

As I retreated, Ardyon said, "Another servant will be appointed you."

Over my shoulder I said bitterly, "He'll not be Urt."

I heard Ardyon say, "So much fuss over a Changed."

I shouted, "He was my friend!"

I had never heard Ardyon laugh. It was as well Cleton held me firm.

The Sky Lords appeared again not long after my fruitless confrontation with Ardyon—a score of airboats that succeeded in depositing two centuries of Kho'rabi in the city. They were destroyed, airboats and warriors alike, but only at terrible cost. They were not the last, and before the summer was ended Durbrecht took on a ravaged look. The tallest towers were broken; the walls stood gapped as the jaws of old men. Cavities showed in the streets where buildings had burned; where pleasant gardens had stood there were now patches of weeds, growing amongst the fire-blackened stumps of dead trees. We knew disease that summer, and folk fled the city. Those who remained spoke of ruin, of defeat. A palpable aura of fear hung over Durbrecht.

I was crazed that summer, when I was as much a soldier as a student. I transmuted grief into physical action. I took no pleasure in it; it was, rather, a means of suppressing emotion, and I fought with a cold intensity. I earned a new reputation as a fighter. I was not proud of myself, but I was admired by my fellows. Indeed, I was appointed commur of a student band and hailed as a leader.

As autumn drew on the attacks eased, finally ceasing when the weather grew cold, the skies become heavy with rafts of gray cloud that drove rain and hail against the land. It seemed odd to me that the Sky Lords had found ways by which to overcome the Worldwinds but not, it appeared, the seasons. Perhaps they did not travel well in rain. Nor, as winter settled over Durbrecht, in snow.

It was a hard winter. Ice crusted the shore of the Treppanek, and despite the depleted population, food was in short supply. Too many farmers had suffered, too many fields been burned, too many men called to the warbands. Even so, there was some sense of relief as day after anticipatory day passed without a Coming.

I thought much of Rwyan and Urt that winter, and with the fighting ended there was no longer any convenient receptacle into which I might channel my fears: my mood grew once more black. I endeavored to hide it from all save Cleton, who—still chafing under the encumbrance of his too-slowly mending arm—became impatient with me. I had spoken so little of Rwyan during that summer, he had come to think her forgotten, and when I appointed him confidant of my fears, he scolded me for harboring so futile a passion.

We had, as Ardyon had promised, been given a new servant. He was of equine descent, named Harl, and whilst he was attentive to all our needs, he lacked Urt's wit or sensibility. He avoided those conversations I attempted to induce, responding in blunt monosyllables and mumbled protestations of ignorance, so that I gave up after a while and (I confess this with no small measure of guilt) came to think of him as dull and bovine. I suspect he had been admonished by the warden to avoid my proffered friendship, or feared he should suffer Urt's fate.

It was a miserable winter, and for all it seemed likely the turning of the year must see a renewal of the Sky Lords' attacks, I was glad of spring's advent. I had sooner be out awandering than cooped another season in the city.

The feast day of Daeran was traditionally the eve of a Storyman's departure. The day was spent in preparation (which took little enough time) and farewells, and in the evening those going out dined with the master at the head table.

There were but five of us that year, where usually there would have been twenty or more: the Sky Lords had taken a toll of the College no less than of the city. We were each of us kitted out with sturdy boots, a change of clothing, a good cloak of oiled wool, a pouch of herbal remedies, and a purse containing a few durrim. In better times we might have been given horses or mules, but those beasts not eaten were earmarked for military use, so we had only our feet on which to begin our journeying.

As dusk fell and Durbrecht readied for a night of celebration (it seemed to me the citizenry had forgotten the summer's terror; or looked to find what pleasure might be had ere it began again), we bathed and dressed in our finest clothes, then made our way to the refectory.

The whole College was assembled, standing silent as Decius beckoned us forward. He gave us each that staff that marks the Story-man and is, besides, a useful weapon, and ushered us to seats at the center of the high table. We were served wine in honor of our departure, and as we ate the master assigned us our destinations. I was to take ship west along the Treppanek to Arbryn and from thence make my way southward down the coast as far as Mhorvyn. Such a journey would take the better part of a year, save I should succeed in gaining myself a horse, and from Mhorvyn Keep I was to send word of my arrival and await further instructions. I wondered if I was sent to the west coast of Kellambek because Rwyan was domiciled to the east and Urt to the north. I kept my wondering to myself.

I did not enjoy that feast, for all the food was excellent and the wine the finest our cellars had. I ate and drank and responded to questions and advice with glib precision, thinking all the time that soon the width of Dharbek should stand betwixt Rwyan and I. Had I not become somewhat skilled in dissimulation, I should have allowed my mask to slip and spoken out; but I did not: I continued in the part I had played the past year. I smiled and voiced soft grateful words, marveling that none (save perhaps Cleton) saw through me. No less that I felt so little excitement at this great adventure. It was, after all, the culmination of my training, of the time and energy I had given to the College of the Mnemonikos. It was the natural result of my ten-ure, and I went out into dramatic times. I should, I knew, have been exhilarated, but I could only pretend. I accepted because I saw no alternative. Inside, I felt resentment that fate, embodied in the earnest, smiling faces all around me, could so order my destiny, and Rwyan's, and Urt's.

Still, I hid my feelings skillfully as any mummer, thanked Decius and the rest for all they had taught me (for which I *was* grateful), and behaved generally as did my fellow viators.

Toward midnight Decius announced his intention of finding his bed, which was cue the feast should end. He saluted us a final time, wished us well, and quit the dining hall. We Storymen bade one another farewell and went to our chambers. I felt neither tired nor alert but in a somber, contemplative mood. Cleton was mightily excited; I felt a curious indifference. I could not share his enthusiasm for our impending departure, but nor had I any wish to remain in Durbrecht. I could not define my mood well: I felt resigned as a rudderless boat, willing to let the irresistible pressure of the tides drive me where they would. If I could not be with Rwyan, it mattered nothing where I was, or where I went. I slumped on my bed, accepting the tankard Cleton drew me.

He said, "In the God's name, Daviot, does our parting truly sadden you so?"

I knew he jested and that he sought to lift my spirits. I thought, too, that he looked to throw a bridge across the rift that had grown between us, so I erected a smile and said, "It shall be strange without you, my friend."

He nodded, his own smile faltering a moment, and said, "Yes, it shall." Then he cheered and added, "But we knew it should come, eh? And what an adventure lies ahead!"

We neither of us knew what truth he spoke, and as he raised his mug in toast, I felt a melancholy that had nothing to do with Rwyan or Urt descend upon me. I raised my own mug and drank, but as I did I thought on how I *should* miss Cleton's company and felt sorry that we had drifted apart. I looked into his pale blue eyes and said earnestly, "You've been a good friend, Cleton, and you've my thanks."

"For what?" He laughed, refusing to join me in depression. "By the God, I'd have been bored without you."

That night I dreamed that I wandered afoot through an oak wood where a thin new moon silvered the gray mist that hung amidst the gnarled trees. I could hear sounds—the wash of surf, the clatter of metal, of tramping boots and shouting men—but only faint, as if from a great distance or as if the mist dampened sound. I could see dim shapes, but none came near, and when I attempted to approach, they receded. Overhead, I could hear the beat of massive wings, but when I looked to the sky, it was as gray as the mist, only the moon visible. I knew I was lost, and that I must find the edge of the wood before I became as one with its spectral inhabitants, but there were no paths and the holt seemed endless. I heard Rwyan calling me, and then from another direction, Urt, so that I faltered, turning this way and that, unsure to whom I should go, nor certain I should find either. I was wading through deep leaf mold in answer to Rwyan's call, stumbling over concealed roots, branches tugging at me as if to hold me, when I awoke.

The day was dull, torn between winter's failing grip and spring's fresh promise. Rafts of pewter cloud hung low, assaulted from the east by a promisingly bright sun. Birds sang, their melodies far easier on the ear than the sounds Cleton made at his ablutions. I waited for him to finish and then attended to my own toilet.

He was to travel overland to Dorsbry on the Treppanek's north bank and would not leave until midmorning, whilst I must soon be gone. We clasped hands and said our last farewells, and I shouldered my pack, took up my staff, and quit the chamber that had been my home for the past five years without a backward glance.

The College yards were empty so early, save for scurrying Changed, and I spent a moment staring around, thinking that I should feel some greater emotion. I felt nothing but a vague pleasure at the notion of being again on a deck. I saw Decius watching me from his window and smiled as I remembered that I had once wondered if he had legs. He saluted me and I raised my staff in answer, then strode toward the gates.

Ardyon was there. Ensuring the Changed gatemen did their duty, I presumed. I was not at all inclined to bid the warden any fond farewell, but it was impossible to escape his notice or to ignore him. I looked him in the eye and nodded.

He sniffed and said, "Day's greetings, Storyman."

I answered, "Day's greetings, warden," with no warmth in my voice.

He sniffed again and clasped his caduceus in both hands against his narrow chest. "The God go with you," he said.

I said, "My thanks," still cold.

His cadaverous features remained impassive as ever, but there was about his stance some hesitancy, and I surmised he wished to say something more, so I waited.

Finally he said, "Concerning the servant—Urt. I had no choice in that matter, save to do what I did."

I looked at his sunken eyes and said, "Perhaps not; but that does not make it right. Think you he enjoys such treatment? To be shunted hither and yon, like some beast?"

His expression did not alter, but in his sniff I thought I discerned amazement. He said, as if the words were all the explanation needed, "He's Changed."

"Think you the Changed have no feelings?" I asked coolly.

Behind his back I saw the gatemen staring, their eyes wide and startled. I am not sure whether in amazement at what I said, or that I dared say it to Ardyon. I did not care: it was too late for him to punish me now.

I think he frowned then. At least his brows shifted a fraction upward, and he shook his head slowly. "You're the oddest student I've ever known," he said.

I shouldered past him and ducked my head to the gatemen, crying, "Day's greetings and farewell, my friends."

There was a pause, and then I heard them each call, "Day's greetings and farewell, Storyman."

I smiled at that, striding away from the College, thinking that I scored a small victory.

The *Dragon* was a single-masted galley captained by a westcoaster named Nyal, whose good nature prompted me to revise my opinion of westcoasters. He stood a head taller than I and seemed composed mostly of thick black hair, out of which eyes and teeth sparkled cheerfully. He boasted a crew of twelve bull-bred oarsmen and carried on board his sister, Lwya, her husband, Drach, and their daughter, Morwenna. The family, he explained, were fleeing Durbrecht for fear of the Sky Lords, planning to return to Arbryn, where Drach hoped to reestablish his chandlery. Drach advised me that their home had been partially destroyed in the last Coming and that he had sold his business at a loss, but that he preferred to settle his family in some location safer than Durbrecht, which he believed was singled out for destruction by the Sky Lords as it contained the Sorcerous College.

All this I learned before we reached midstream: Drach was a voluble fellow and was convinced a Storyman must have the ear of the koryphon, if not that of Gahan himself.

I expressed myself innocent of such connections and asked him if he thought Arbryn should be safe, whereupon he nodded enthusiastically, expounding his theory that the Sky Lords looked to destroy Dharbek's centers of magic, leaving alone the lesser settlements.

"But Arbryn's a keep," I said, "and a commur-mage, surely."

"Of course," he answered me. "The aeldor Thyrsk's the holder, and Donal the commur-mage. But the Sky Lords'll not come so far west—Arbryn's too small. No, the Dark Ones'll concentrate on the Sentinels, and Durbrecht, on Kherbryn. They'll not bother with such small fry."

There was ephemeral truth in his supposition, and I had no great desire to blunt his optimism, but his careless—or so it seemed to me— dismissal of the Sentinels (and thus of Rwyan) irked me. I said, "But do the Sentinels fall, there'll be no defense against the Sky Lords. They'll come unchecked, and do they conquer Durbrecht and Kherbryn, there'll be none to stand against them. How shall Arbryn fare then?"

I felt immediately guilty, for both Lwya and Morwenna hung upon my words as if I was some font of wisdom, and at this dour pronouncement they paled and gasped, the daughter reaching for her mother's hand. She was a pretty thing, a few years younger than I, and had my heart not belonged to Rwyan, I believe I might have sought a closer acquaintance. As it was, I regretted my stark declaration. So I smiled heartily and said, "Better to place your trust in the sorcerers and the Lord Protector. Pray the Sentinels deny the Sky Lords passage, and that the warbands slay those Kho'rabi who set foot on our soil."

Lwya, whose dark good looks foretold her daughter's future, murmured a heartfelt "Amen," to that, and Morwenna nodded eagerly, her great black eyes intent upon my face.

Drach tugged on his beard, his brow wrinkled as he considered my words. "I do not *wish* it," he said. "The God knows, I'd see them blasted from the sky, but still I think—"

He broke off as his wife touched his arm. I suspect they held me in such awe as to fear I might denounce them as traitors. Perhaps I flatter myself. I did, however, remember that my duty as Storyman was to instill courage in the folk I encountered, so I said, "There's no denying Durbrecht took a beating this past year, but Trevid has his engineers building even greater war machines, and the Sorcerous College bends all its efforts to the finding of greater magicks. The Sentinels still stand and shall be strengthened the more. The Sky Lords shall not defeat us! Remember the story of Anduran."

I spun out that tale of past glories, when the aeldor led his warband against a Kho'rabi force three times their number and held the invaders at bay until the Lord Protector, Padyr, came to his aid, with the sorcerer, Wynn, and the enemy were slaughtered to a man. It was one of the great old tales, and they had doubtless heard it a hundred times before, but (though I say it myself) I was a skillful story-spinner, and I held them rapt as Nyal pointed the *Dragon* westward.

As twilight dimmed the Treppanek, Nyal brought us in to a place named Darbryn, a village that served as an overnight stop to passing traffic, with a ferryboat and an inn. I suggested that I sleep on deck, thinking to hoard my coin, but Drach insisted I accept a room at his expense. I am not sure whether he looked to make amends for fleeing Durbrecht, or if he felt intimacy with a Storyman loaned him prestige. It mattered little to me: I accepted with alacrity.

As the women bathed and we drank ale with Nyal, he said, "I trust you don't think me a coward, Daviot. Nor that I lack faith in the sorcerers or Lord Protector. I fought with the militia this last year, but I've Lwya and Morwenna to think of, and I'd not see them fall to the Sky Lords. Had you a wife, or a daughter, you'd understand."

That cut me somewhat, but how could he know? I smiled and reassured him I doubted neither his courage nor his loyalty and wished them safe refuge in Arbryn.

Nyal grunted and said, "A man's first loyalty's to his kith and kin, no?"

I agreed and asked him if he was not wed, at which he shook his head and said bluntly, "I was. The cursed Sky Lords slew her."

I voiced condolences and asked, "In Arbryn?"

He shook his head again, setting the mass of his darkly curling hair to waving, and answered me, "On the Treppanek, east of Durbrecht. She sailed with me. We were Rorsbry-bound two summers past when an airboat passed over." He drained his mug in one long gulp and shouted for more. "They were crippled—low overhead—and they dropped their God-cursed fire on the ship. Kytha died, and half my crew. The ship sank. Had it not been for Drach, here . . ."

All this he told me in a low monotone that I recognized was a chain binding his grief. His dark eyes were expressionless, but as his voice tailed off, I saw tears run down his cheeks, leaving moist trails over his tan. He coughed and rubbed at his face. "Drach loaned me the coin to purchase the *Dragon* and new oarsmen," he finished.

I said, "I'm sorry," and he grinned without humor and returned me, "Why? It was not your doing."

I shrugged, not knowing what else to say. And then I had a kind of revelation. I realized at that moment what I had not seen before— that I had become lost in my own grief, which was but a single small fish in a shoal of woes. It was arrogance and selfishness to think I swum alone: all around me there were folk had suffered as much or more, and to single out myself, to allow self-pity free rein, was a weakness, an act of egoism. I doubted Rwyan would approve. I vowed to set aside my own concerns and attend more carefully those of others.

That night, in the room I shared with Drach, I slept soundly, and when I woke I felt enlivened, as I had not since Rwyan's going. I would not forget Rwyan, but neither would I dwell any longer on her loss.

Thus my journey passed far more enjoyably than I had anticipated. I practiced my storytelling on my fellow passengers and even the crew—Nyal was a kinder master than Kerym and treated his Changed oarsmen, if not as equals, then at least better than mere beasts—and studied the riparian landscape with eyes that seemed newly opened. When I thought of Rwyan (which was still often enough), it was with a sweetly fond nostalgia that was only sometimes pierced by the barbs of my dismissed grief. I had, I suppose, accepted what Cleton had told me: that our parting was inevitable and that to grieve over that which I could not change was a pointless scourge.

And then we came to Arbryn.

Thyrsk was aeldor here, and I had it from Nyal that he had but one son, Kalydon, and that his wife was dead of a fever these past three years. I knew no more, save that Arbryn prospered—which I could see from the pastel-painted houses and well-tended gardens— thanks to its advantageous position, being well-situated to handle trade from farther down the coast and the Treppanek, both. I thought it a pleasant, sleepy place that appeared untouched by the Sky Lords. The streets were clean, and I was greeted with cheerful cries as I walked toward the high stone tower that stood like the axle hub of a wheel at Arbryn's center, behind its own wall, and showed no sign of attack.

Four days I lingered there, wandering the town by day's light, welcomed in the taverns and the squares where I told my stories, passing the evenings in Thyrsk's hall. The hold's sorcerer sent word to Durbrecht along that magical chain that connects the keeps of Dharbek, informing the College of my safe arrival, but what response, if any, came back, I know not. Storymen are governed by few orders, save to tell their tales and keep their eyes and ears open, and I was at liberty to choose my own path and my own timetable. It was a heady freedom.

12

Aside from the practice of our calling, there are three prime considerations about a Storyman's life that seem seldom to occur to our listeners, who appear to believe we arrive by magic and depart by the same process.

The first is the act of traveling itself. I was commanded to go from Arbryn to Mhorvyn before the year's end; the *how* of it was left to me. I had one pair of stout boots, and save in heavy rain when my healed leg was wont to ache, I was fit as any soldier. The length of Kellambek, however, is a considerable distance, and the more time I spent traveling, the less I should have to speak and listen. I had some few coins, but insufficient to purchase a horse or a mule. I could hope to find passage with some merchant's caravan or at some point to obtain a mount, but in the meanwhile I had only my feet.

The second consideration is food. An empty belly makes for slow walking and a short temper. Indeed, it was not unknown for Storymen to starve in the wilder parts of Dharbek's interior. I did not anticipate that fate, for my tales would earn me sustenance, and if they did not—well, this was a fertile landscape, and I could likely scavenge enough to see me through.

Third is warmth: the road grows cold and wet at times. Indeed, this is why we wanderers were sent out at the year's turning, when we might expect clement weather at the start of our journeying. I knew there should be rain along my way, but summer would come soon enough, and by winter I hoped to be ensconced in Mhorvyn Keep.

Consequently, I set out from Arbryn in fine spirits. I had ventured to hope Thyrsk might gift me with a mount, but his generosity did not stretch quite so far, and I departed afoot. I thought that did I acquit myself well enough as I progressed, I might earn such a reputation as would persuade some aeldor to present me with a horse come the spring foaling. (Optimism is a necessary part of a Storyman's nature; without it we should tread a very hard road.) It was a thing I could hope for, and meanwhile I had no complaints. I set out along the paved road that followed the coast south to Dunnysbar.

I reached the village after nightfall, my arrival announced by a pack of dogs that came yapping at my heels. I applied my staff and my boots, being in no great good humor, and sent my attackers snarling into the shadows as I made my way toward the light of a hostelry. I was welcomed there and promised all the ale I could drink in return for a story or two, though I had to pay for my dinner and chose the free accommodation of the stables over the cost of a room.

The next two nights I slept beside the road, warmed by a fire of fallen branches, fed the first on a rabbit I snared, hungry the second. The third night I found shelter in a farm, where I was fed and offered a place by the hearth, which I shared with four great shaggy dogs. Such is a Storyman's lot.

In Darsvyn Keep I found a welcome equal to that I got in Arbryn, and I lingered there five days. Ventran was a taciturn man, but his wife, Gwenndynne, more than made up for her husband's solemnity, and their children—of whom there were five, and all young—took after her: I spent a large part of each evening in that keep with a child on either knee, another hung about my neck, and the rest at my feet. Ventran was of the College's opinion—that the Sky Lords planned invasion. The keep's sorcerer, a fair-haired young man from east Draggonek whose name was Tyris, agreed, and the four of us sat long into the night, discussing the Lord Protector's preparations and what the year should bring.

That was an alarming development of the Sky Lords' magic.

I first had the news from Kaern, aeldor of Dursbar, some eight weeks after leaving Arbryn. Spring was already turning into summer in these milder western climes, and I had been three days in Dursbar without news of Durbrecht or the east since my departure. I had dared hope the attacks of the previous year should not be repeated, that the gloomy prognostications of the College and of Kherbryn had been unfounded, that the Sky Lords had given up. I was wrong: only the tactics had changed.

It was early one fine evening, the sun still bright on the slate rooftops of Dursbar, when I was invited to attend Kaern in his private chambers and found the aeldor with Trethyn, who was the commur-mage here. Kaern was a young man, come only recently to his station following the death of his father in a hunting accident. Trethyn was twice his age. Both were typical westcoasters: dark of hair and swarthy of complexion, their faces tending to a stern demeanor. On this bright evening they were both grim, and as Kaern motioned me to a chair and pushed a cup toward me, I felt the chill fingers of presentiment dance down my spine.

"There's news come from Durbrecht," Kaern said as I filled my cup with the golden wine for which his hold was famous.

In itself this was not surprising: the Sorcerous College acted as a gathering house for information, receiving and digesting reports from the keep sorcerers and disseminating that information throughout Dharbek. It was as if an unseen web spread over the land, every touch upon its fabric notified to Durbrecht, from whence news was sent along the magical strands to all the far-flung holds. From the sober faces of my two companions, however, and from the heavy tone of Kaern's voice, I realized this news was grave. I swallowed wine and waited.

"The Sky Lords are returned," the aeldor said.

I nodded, thinking that in this young man the taciturnity that appeared a natural characteristic of the westcoasters was somewhat magnified.

He appeared disinclined to elaborate, and so I asked, "They attack again? In numbers?"

Kaern shook his head and looked to Trethyn, gesturing that the sorcerer should answer.

The commur-mage said, "No. This is different."

They shared a glance, as if, having summoned me, they now debated the wisdom of imparting their news. Or perhaps Kaern deferred to his commur-mage. I thought to encourage them. I asked, "How, different?"

Trethyn stroked his gray-streaked beard and said, "They do not attack. At least, they have come only twice against Durbrecht; twice, too, against Kherbryn."

I frowned, curbing impatience even as I cursed their reticence. Had they been other than aeldor and commur-mage, I should have sought to draw them out with my Storyman's guile. With such as these, however, it was not meet: I held my tongue and waited.

Kaern said, "Neither city was much harmed."

Trethyn said, "The Sentinels destroyed half of each fleet and crippled more.".

Kaern said, "Those that remained were all destroyed."

I smiled at that, nodding enthusiastically. I assumed they thought to reassure me. I wished they would get to the heart of the matter.

"But," said Trethyn, "the Sky Lords play a different game these days."

He reached for the decanter, filling his cup. Kaern sat silent, staring darkly at the sunlit rectangle of the window.

I was chafed. I prompted him: "A different game?"

He ducked his head once and said, "Yes. They've a new tactic, it seems."

He fell silent again. I looked from him to Kaern, willing them to loose their tight westcoaster tongues. It seemed a long time before he continued. I was tempted to shake the words from him.

At last he said, "They employ smaller vessels. Skyboats a fraction the size of their usual craft."

I could contain my impatience no longer. I said, "Surely then they're a lesser threat. Save they bring the Kho'rabi knights in numbers, how can they hope to conquer us?"

It was Kaern who answered. I think my tone or my expression roused him from his silence, but still he spoke obliquely. He said, "Was it not the belief of both your College and Trethyn's that the attacks of these past years were in the nature of scouting missions?"

There was a new—and somewhat unexpected—authority in his voice: I nodded and answered him, "Yes. We suspected they sought to test our defenses. We thought they must probe, readying for the Great Coming."

The aeldor snorted bitter laughter. He looked no longer out the window but directly into my eyes as he said, "I've some training in the art of warfare, and I'd not send centuries of men out scouting. That's a task for a few, light-mounted to travel fast, unnoticed."

I began to see it. I said, "Small airboats . . ."

Kaern nodded agreement. "Small and swift; enough they are able, often as not, to slip unharmed past the Sentinels."

"And return word of what they find?" I gasped. "We'd suspected they'd found such magic as to send word back."

Now it was my turn to fall silent as Trethyn said, "Worse. They'd found those magicks, yes. But none too reliable over such distances; also, we'd found the way to block their messages, to disrupt them."

"Then how," I asked carefully, aware that my voice came hollow with dread, "is this worse?"

The sorcerer ran nails that I noticed for the first time were chewed down and grimed with dirt through his beard before he answered. Then: "They've found the means to entirely control the elementals. Thus to overcome the Worldwinds."

I gaped, horrified. Into my mind came a precise memory of those half-seen creatures I had observed sporting about the Sky Lords' vessels. I had thought then that they propelled the airboats, that their fundamental power was bound to the Ahn's cause. I had never suspected, never anticipated, they might overcome the Worldwinds. None had. Forgetting all protocol, ignoring all courtesy, I motioned for the sorcerer to continue.

If he noticed my imperious gesture, he paid it no heed. He said, "These smaller boats are able to come and return at will."

This was alarming news. "And the Sentinels?" I cried. "The Sorcerous College? Can they not halt these boats? Not destroy them?"

"Some few," he replied. "Not enough. The road our magic took is different—we Dhar have never attempted to control the elemental spirits."

An old memory, tucked away in one of those compartments dead Martus had spoken of, sprang into my mind. I said, "We once mastered the dragons."

"Once, yes," said Trethyn. "But the dragons were creatures of flesh and blood, and thus the Dragonmasters were able to attune their minds to the creatures'. The spirits of the air are different—we've no control of them."

"Why speak of dragons?" Kaern asked. "The dragons are dead, and the Dragonmasters with them. This danger belongs to this day, and to our tomorrows."

Trethyn grunted his agreement. I shrugged: they were right. What use to think of dragons now, here? I said, "Does Durbrecht anticipate invasion then?"

The sorcerer turned his face to the aeldor. Kaern said formally, as if by rote, "The Lord Protector Gahan bids us stand ready. We cannot know how strong this new magic waxes, but do they learn to harness the spirits in numbers . . ." He paused, his eyes closing a moment, as if what he told me sat heavy on his tongue and he had rather not say it. "It is thought the Sky Lords shall attack this year or next."

Trethyn said, "The Sorcerous College believes it will be next year at the earliest."

I said, "But if they are able to ignore the Worldwinds . . . If they can evade the magic of the Sentinels—"

He silenced me with a raised hand. "As yet—so we believe—this newfound power over the elementals is not strong enough they can harness the spirits in sufficient numbers to their larger vessels. At least, not in such numbers as to make invasion feasible."

"Yet," said Kaern. His voice was as bleak as his face.

I said, "Then we've a year to ready for war. Shall you sorcerers not find a means to defeat even the elementals?"

Trethyn shook his head. Amidst the gray and black of his beard, I saw stained teeth bared in a sour grin. He said, "Within a year? No. It's our belief the Sky Lords have spent decades—perhaps centuries— finding the gramaryes of binding. Have you any idea what such magic entails?"

I shook my head. I felt dulled; helpless. I thought abruptly of Rwyan. I heard Trethyn saying, ". . . inconceivable power. We'd need revise all our thinking, all we've learned."

I nodded. It seemed the skin was drawn taut over the bones of my face. My mouth was dry: I filled my empty cup and drank deep.

In the wine I found a straw of hope and snatched it. I said, "It would not be the first Coming. We've defeated the Sky Lords before. Shall this be so different?"

Trethyn took the straw from me and broke it. "Mightily different," he said. "Before, they traveled on the whim of the Worldwinds. Oh, they harnessed the spirits of the air to aid them, but not even with that assistance could they entirely defy the winds. Did your College not teach you that?"

There was such asperity in his voice as to offend, had I not recognized it was fear that honed the edge. I nodded and said, "Yes, I was taught that."

And I was: the Comings followed the cycles of the Worldwinds, and that gusting was capricious. Not all the Sky Lords' dread craft reached our shores—many soared too high, to drift on across the western ocean into oblivion, more were brought down by the Sentinels. Sufficient grounded as to be a blight, to render the Sky Lords a terror, and the Kho'rabi warriors were creatures out of nightmare— but never enough of them to accomplish their dream of conquest. And we Dhar had, each time, that cycle of recuperation, of preparation: when the Worldwinds turned again, we were always ready. Now, did the Ahn wizards obtain such power over the elementals as to come and go at will, they could deliver the Kho'rabi at any time, and their airboats return to their far-off land to bring more against us. More and more and more, until—I endeavored to deny the thought, but could not—until they conquered us. I shuddered and said softly, "I see it."

"It is not a pleasant vision," said Trethyn, no louder.

"This is not," Kaern said, "a thing to voice abroad. The God willing, we'll not see these new airboats so far west. Until the time comes, the common folk are not to know."

"Shall you not prepare?" I asked: the aeldor was not alone in owning some knowledge of strategy. "How shall you hide it, must you raise levies?"

He grunted acceptance of my judgment and said, "We aeldors enlarge our warbands and commission ships. Yes—we prepare. But until we are sure, I'd not see panic spread."

To this Trethyn added, "There are already refugees come west to escape the attacks of yesteryear. Should such news become common parlance, likely the cities and the east would be deserted."

"And your resources be strained," I said. Then: "You expect the fighting to be in the east."

"And the cities," said Kaern. "Do the Sky Lords fight a sensible war, they'll seek to overcome three centers first—the Sentinels, Durbrecht, and Kherbryn. Take those, and Dharbek fights in disarray."

Rwyan! The cold fingers I had felt on entering this room became claws, scoring my soul. I could only duck my head, horrified. I was helpless. I could do nothing, save hope; or pray to a God I was no longer sure existed.

"This goes no farther," said the aeldor, formal again. "It is deemed necessary to inform you Storymen, but none others."

"No," I said. "My word on it."

The sun was close to the sea now, and the window was a rectangle of brilliance. I could hear the squalling of gulls and the noises of folk in the yard below. The smells of cooking drifted, mingled with the scent of the ocean. It was a pleasant evening, tranquil. I felt as I had when a child, watching storm clouds build over the Fend, knowing that soon the wind should howl and lightning dance. Then, I could anticipate the shelter of our cottage, the storm shut out. Now, I thought there should be no shelter from the storm.

"So, a brave face," said Kaern, rising. "Tell cheerful tales, Storyman. And hold your lips sealed on this matter."

"Yes," I said. And for the first time added, "My lord aeldor."

I did as I was commanded, trudging from hold to village to town with the most glorious of my tales. I spoke of Fyrach and the Great Dragon, of the battle of Tenbry Keep, of Petur's duel with the Kho'rabi. In hamlets where fishing boats clustered the shoreline I told of Jeryd and the Whale, and Dramydd's Voyage. In farms and lonely foresters' huts I spoke of Beryl and the Magic Tree, of Shadram and the Great Bull of Corvyn, of Marais the Cattle King, and the hermit Denus. When—as was inevitable—I was asked for news of Durbrecht, I told of the city's splendors and of its valiant stand against the Sky Lords. I spoke of my own battles, and those of others I had heard, all slanted so that we appeared invincible, the Sky Lords an enemy soon defeated by might of magic and the wisdom of the Lord Protector.

I was hailed a master of my calling; I felt I was a deceiver.

And though I did my best to quell my burgeoning fear, I thought too often of Rwyan, and how she should fare did the Sky Lords come against the Sentinels as Kaern and Trethyn predicted. Too often I found myself watching the sky as I walked.

Early in that summer, I wandered a little way inland, following a road that wound gently up through low hills whose slopes were all thick with cork oak, the crests with pine. The sun was not quite at zenith, and I had halted atop one hill, electing to wait out the midday heat beneath the cooling canopy of trees. I had fared well at my last stop and been gifted with a fresh loaf, a thick wedge of good yellow cheese, and a skin of pale wine; now I intended to eat, drink a little wine, and indulge in the west coast custom of dozing awhile.

As I ate, I surveyed the gentle panorama spread before me. Brynisvar, I calculated, lay beyond the third ridgeline. At the foot of the slope facing me stood a farmhouse. Perhaps I would halt there and tell a tale before moving on. Likely the farmer and his folk would be too busy. I sipped wine and gazed idly at the sky. It was a blue not seen in the east or over Durbrecht, a lapis lazuli blue of incredible clarity. To the northeast I saw a shape that neither soared nor hovered but came straight on. At first it was but a speck, and I assumed it some bird intent on whatever business propels avians to hurry. As it drew closer, I saw that it was no bird. I stoppered my wineskin and sprang to my feet.

Soon I could see clearly the cylinder of blood red, the occult sigils of the Sky Lords' magic painted on the flanks. They pulsed and throbbed. Beneath hung a black basket. Around the craft, the air shimmered, roiling like steam from a kettle. Within that disturbance I saw elementals darting, whirling too swift for precise definition. The skyboat came closer still, and I saw that it was small, that the basket could hold no more than ten men. It was at the same time familiar and strange. It bore the configuration of an airboat, but that cloud of miasmic dread, dark, that was the customary signature of the Sky Lords was absent. I felt no chill, save that of shock, nor that mind-numbing horror that usually accompanied such craft. I pressed close against the trunk of the sheltering pine. And felt my breath catch in my throat as the vessel halted.

Trethyn had told me; Kaern had told me. Still I could scarcely credit the evidence of my own eyes: the tiny airboat halted and hovered. The wind was from the west but held no dominion over this craft. It hung steady as any falcon over the farmhouse in the valley.

The aftertaste of wine turned sour in my mouth: I spat. I reached cautiously for my canteen, afraid I should be seen. I drank and hung the canteen with my pack, on my back, ready to flee. I had my staff and my knife—I should stand no chance against Kho'rabi were I spotted.

The airboat turned slowly around, sinking toward the ground. It landed, light as any feather, the red cylinder still airborne, only the black basket touching the sward before the farmhouse. It had been seen by the folk there. Of course it had been seen! I had been too preoccupied, too amazed, to think of them until now, when they came from their home to face this unprecedented apparition.

There were four men, armed with nothing more than farm implements. Two clutched pitchforks, one a scythe, the last a mattock. Three dogs clamored about their feet. From the rear of the building I saw three women emerge, their skirts gathered up as they scurried for the oak thicket behind the house.

From the basket came nine black-armored Kho'rabi. A tenth Sky Lord remained behind. He, I supposed, must be the wizard, retaining control of the spirits that even now danced and darted about the shape of the airboat.

I suffered a terrible dilemma then. These farmers stood no chance against such warriors. Less even than I, who had fought Kho'rabi. Should I go to their aid? Should I align myself with them in hopeless defense? Or should I watch, hidden? Safe. A coward?

I calculated the distance between my safe position and the farm and knew that I could not reach it in time. Knew, also, that my presence should make no difference to the outcome. That was inevitable: I watched, and wondered the while if I was craven.

The dogs attacked first. They were large—such hounds as can protect flocks from wolves or bring down a man—and they were brave. The Kho'rabi dispatched them with a casual efficiency. I watched as swords swung and the dogs died. Watched as the Kho'rabi advanced on the men, who were no less courageous. They flailed their poor weapons and fell to Ahn steel without a blow struck. I saw the greensward painted red.

Then the wizard gestured, and I suppose he shouted, for the Kho'rabi ran past the bodies of their victims, around the farmhouse, to the timber beyond. I do not know whether he guessed the women hid there or knew it by his magic; nor did I see the women slain. I remained hidden, waiting, as the black figures disappeared amongst the oaks and in a while came back, their blades sheathed. I hoped the women had escaped; I did not think they had.

I watched as the Kho'rabi entered the building, emerged with sacks and slabs of meat that they stowed on board their vessel. Some brought containers to the farm's well, that they filled and put on board. Then they regained the basket, and the airboat rose vertically, turned its nose a little north of east, and moved away.

I wiped sweat from my brow and unlocked my fingers from my staff. They ached from the strength of my grip. I stared after the receding shape and saw that it moved toward Brynisvar. It came to me there was no keep there, no sorcerer or warband to confront the Sky Lords. I did not know whether they intended to attack, but I felt compelled to act. I had stood a hidden witness to massacre, and I could not go on so neutral: I quit the cover of my pine and began to run.

For a moment I considered searching for the women, but dismissed the thought. Were they slain, I could do nothing for them; did they survive, they would go back to the farm. I had small appetite to face them, whichever was their fate. Perhaps I might acquit myself better in Brynisvar. Perhaps I might bring warning, or at least lend my own martial skills to the defense. It was no aeldor's hold, but there were enough able-bodied men there that the Kho'rabi—did they intend attack—should find it a harder task than the wanton slaughter of innocent farmers: I ran.

I had never run so hard. The God knew, Keran had worked us mercilessly in Durbrecht, but now my feet flew. Sweat ran hot and then chilled; I felt my lungs burn, my muscles protest. I became an automaton as I sped across the valley, climbed the farther slope. I saw the airboat high above, ahead. The Sky Lords seemed in no great hurry. Sometimes, even, their vessel hovered, or soared off to left or right. I thought perhaps they mapped the land. Perhaps they assessed its defenses, its population. Perhaps they would disappear altogether, and I come heart-strained and useless into Brynisvar, my haste all wasted. I did not care: it was as though I must atone for my helplessness, scourge myself with the effort of this headlong pace. I flung myself over the crest of one hill and ran toward the next.

Then, where the hills flattened to form a small plateau, I saw Brynisvar. I calculated the distance as I raced toward its walls.

I could see the airboat off to the north, not very high, moving away down the intervening valley. I thought I might have run uselessly, but still I did not stop, and as I went down the slope I saw the bloodred cylinder begin to describe a wide curve, eastward. I no longer wondered whether they planned an attack. I wanted only to reach the plateau, to warn the inhabitants. I did not think any there had seen the craft.

I crossed a wooden bridge, onto the road beyond. The trail began to climb, and for a while Brynisvar was lost to sight; the airboat, too. I hurled myself up the slope. I felt I could run until my heart burst.

Then walls of clay-chinked wood stood before me, barely higher than my head, gates standing open, through them a wide thoroughfare flanked by rustic houses that devolved on a broad central square. I began to shout as I entered the place.

"The Sky Lords! Ware the Sky Lords!"

My voice came out a whispery croak, but still folk turned to watch my progress. No doubt they wondered what brought a stranger in such haste; perhaps they thought me mad. I collected a retinue of barking dogs and laughing children that ran with me to the square. I halted there and with that cessation of movement regained feeling. It seemed a furnace roared within my chest. My vision blurred as blood pounded inside my skull. I struggled to draw air into lungs I thought collapsed. My old forgotten wound throbbed. I knew I had never run so hard or so swift. Through tears I saw a timber cella, a polished bell in its little tower atop the structure. My legs were unsteady as I stumbled to the temple, worse as I mounted the rough ladder to the bell. My hands shook as I rang the alarm and from my vantage point turned my eyes to the sky, seeking the airboat. It was south of Brynisvar now. I pointed.

Below me, a lean young man in the robe of a mantis shouted, demanding to know what I did. I waved him be silent, but he paid me no heed. A crowd was gathering, summoned by the bell. I let go the striker and retreated down the ladder.

The mantis seized my arm and said, "Who are you? Are you insane? Why do you ring the bell?"

I opened my mouth to speak, but found my mouth so dry I managed only a croak. I pointed to the south. Mantis and crowd looked to where I pointed, and on the priest's face I saw blank incomprehension, the suspicion he held the arm of a madman. He let me go and took a pace back. I groaned as I saw that the rooftops of Brynisvar hid the airboat. From the crowd several brawny men came to flank the mantis, protective. I heard one say, "He's crazed," another: "That's a Storyman's staff, no?"

I nodded and retrieved my staff, barely evading the teeth of a snapping dog. I gestured they be patient and raised my canteen to my lips. I almost laughed as I realized I had dropped my wineskin. The water was tepid, and a good deal dribbled down my chin, doubtless adding to the impression of insanity. Still, it loosed my tongue.

I said, "The Sky Lords are here," and pointed once more to the south.

There was a murmur of apprehension at that, and for a moment I faced only backs as all turned to study the sky. The airboat was still hidden, and when the crowd swung around again, I perceived I was judged crazy. I said, "I am Daviot, late of Durbrecht. I am a Storyman, and a little while ago I saw Kho'rabi land and slaughter a farmer's people."

The mantis was quick-witted, for which I blessed him. He said to one of the men standing beside him, "Find Krystin. Bring her here."

I poured water over my face and head. I said, "Krystin?"

The mantis said, "Commur-mage of Tryrsbry Keep."

I came close then to conviction that the God does exist and sometimes favors us. I said, "There's a warband here?"

The mantis said, "A squadron only."

He was not yet, I saw, convinced of my sanity. I nodded and rested on my staff. The square was abuzz, more folk arriving momentarily.

Then a man I recognized as a jennym pushed a way through the crowd. He was short and very muscular, dressed in new leather, a long sword sheathed across his back. He carried a kettle helm, and he was frowning. On his heels came a slender woman in the black and silver gear of her calling; her hair was blond, bound in a loose tail. She faced me as the jennym, having cleared her path, stood aside.

"I am Krystin, commur-mage of Tryrsbry Keep," she said, and stabbed a thumb at the short man. "This is Barus."

The mantis said, "He warns of the Sky Lords."

Krystin glanced at him, and he fell silent. Her eyes were the same blue as the sky, and her features were those of a classical statue. She gestured for me to speak.

I told her who I was and what I'd seen, and she motioned for Barus to mount the cella's tower. He went up the ladder with an agility that belied his shape and from the top peered around. The square fell silent, waiting. I watched his swarthy face turn around the circuit of the compass, and as it faced the west, I saw it blacken. He came down the ladder faster than he had climbed, nodded once to Krystin, and pushed back through the onlookers without a word.

Krystin fixed me with her blue gaze. "Can you ride?" she asked.

I nodded, and she said, "Then come."

The mantis said, "What is it? Krystin, do you explain?"

She answered him: "There's not the time, Anacletus."

She was already moving away, me with her. The mantis reached for her arm, then hesitated and drew back his hand. He said, "There's danger? His tale's true?"

"Do Storymen lie?" she returned enigmatically. Then added, "I think there's no danger to Brynisvar. Nor reason to spread panic, eh?"

The mantis recognized the warning and ducked his head. Krystin said softer, "This is a thing of no great account, Anacletus. But still— perhaps best you mount a watch till you've word from me."

We were past the edge of the crowd now, striding toward a stable where soldiers stood mounted, Barus at their head. I asked the commur-mage, "What of the farm? Perhaps the women survived."

She glanced at me and shook her head. "Think you it's likely?" she asked.

I said, "No," and she nodded.

"Here." Barus thrust the reins of a tall gray mare at me. "She's something of a temper, but she can run."

I took the reins and swung astride.

The mare was equipped with a cavalry saddle, set with a lance bucket and fixing loop: I stowed my staff there. She snorted and began to fret, curvetting so that she bumped her haunches against the animals to either side. I hauled the reins tight, forcing her plunging head down, and stroked her neck, murmuring softly the while. She gentled, and Barus granted me a grudgingly approving nod.

Krystin raised a hand, pointing to the gate through which I had entered Brynisvar, and lifted her black gelding to a trot. As we went down the avenue, I brought my mare alongside and asked, "Where do we go? What if they attack this place?"

She answered me, "Ten, you said? Nine Kho'rabi and a wizard?" And when I confirmed it: "There's near two hundred men in Brynisvar, and most of them archers. I think not even the Sky Lords would take those odds."

"Then where do we ride?" I asked.

We were at the gates now, and just past them she reined in a moment, not answering me as she studied the sky. I saw the airboat again. It quartered the blue like a hawk, hovering to the west, then moving slowly southward. Krystin's eyes were closed and her lips moved, though she made no sound. I recognized the practice of magic and held my tongue until she was done.

"After them," she said, and turned her horse's head to the south, driving heels against the black flanks.

We rode along Brynisvar's wall to the edge of the plateau at a canter. A trail led down there, running into the woods. In moments the sky was hidden beneath a canopy of branches, but Krystin was like a questing hound, not slowing our pace even as she closed her eyes and raised her face up. I knew she had established some kind of linkage to the Sky Lords through her sortilege. Rwyan had spoken somewhat of the ability—it was as though the magic that propelled the airboat gave off a scent, occult, that was discernible on that mysterious plane to those gifted with the occult talent. Certainly, Krystin had no hesitation in pursuing the vessel.

I had no desire to disturb her concentration and so stayed silent, but neither did I feel much enthusiasm for a chase that must surely run random through these western woods. I thought we should do better to find high ground and track the Sky Lords' progress to some destination. I let my mare fall back to flank Barus and put this notion to him.

He gave me a somewhat contemptuous look and shook his head. "This is not our first chase," he said. "Do we stay close enough, we can take them when they land."

I craned my head back, seeking to find the sky through the webwork of boughs. The afternoon was not much advanced, and as best I could tell from the filtered light, we likely had a long ride ahead of us. Still, it was easier work than running.

"It was fortunate you were in Brynisvar," I said.

Barus nodded. "Recruiting for Tryrsbry's warband. Seeking potential sorcerers." He chuckled. "Or Storymen. We found you instead."

I could not tell if he intended insult, nor cared much. It seemed he had taken a dislike to me, and his opprobrious manner prompted a mutual disregard, but I elected to hide my feelings: the making of enemies serves a Storyman ill. So I only grunted and continued in silence, letting my gray mare move a little way apart. Barus paid me no further attention, and I concentrated on Krystin, who yet ran ahead like a hunting dog leading her pack.

As we rode deeper into the hinterland, the terrain grew rougher, the hills steeper and higher, the valleys smaller. The timber thickened, so that we rode more often than not beneath a roofing of branches, the sky obscured. But Krystin never faltered, and as the afternoon gave way to evening and we climbed a hogback spread thick with tall pines, she found our quarry.

The commur-mage raised a hand as we approached the crest. I slowed my gray even as Barus motioned for me to halt. Farther up the slope, Krystin dismounted, leading her black down to where we waited. I sprang from the saddle, clamping a hand over the mare's nostrils as I saw her about to whicker. The jennym beckoned two soldiers over, whispering orders, and the men began to collect horses, leading them away to flatter ground. I gave them the gray's reins.

Barus said, "Stay with the horses, Storyman. This is warrior's work."

I shook my head and saw his face blacken. He was about to speak when Krystin grasped his arm. "This is neither the time nor the place to argue," she said.

"Nor to carry excess baggage," Barus replied.

The commur-mage ignored him, turning to me. "Can you fight?" she asked.

"I'm Durbrecht-trained," I told her, thinking that answer enough. I heard Barus snort softly and added, "I've fought Kho'rabi ere now."

Krystin nodded and said, "All well, we'll not fight them. Only kill them."

Barus said, "I'll not play nursemaid."

I said, "I'll not need such care."

His dark eyes narrowed under the rim of his helm, and I thought him about to protest, but Krystin silenced him with a look and said, "So be it. *On my order, jennym.* Daviot comes with us."

Barus ground his teeth. I wondered why he objected so to my presence, then dismissed the thought as Krystin waved the troop close.

There were, with me, twenty-one—odds none too favorable against ten Kho'rabi, and one of them a wizard. I waited to see what stratagem the commur-mage had planned.

She said, "The Sky Lords are landed over this ridge. Barus, do you come with me to spy the lie of the land. You others wait here, and in the God's name keep those horses quiet."

I glanced back: the horses were set on a picket line amongst the trees. I prayed my gray should not vent her temper. Then I heard the faint sounds of climbing and turned to see Krystin and Barus moving stealthily toward the crest. Before any could halt me, I followed them.

Barus favored me with an angry glare, Krystin with a look I could not interpret. I paid heed to neither. I was a Storyman: it was my duty to observe. The commur-mage motioned me to caution and I nodded, moving on hands and knees to the ridgeline, easing forward on my belly.

The pines thinned there, and the downslope was bare of cover. At the foot there was grass and a pool of clear blue water where rocks dammed a little stream. It was an idyllic setting. A breeze blew down the valley, setting the timber on the far slope to sighing. The sun was yet high enough the water glittered, gurgling merrily along its way. I noticed that no birds sang even as I stared at the red cylinder of the airboat that floated stationary to the north. I saw four of the Kho'rabi gathering wood, five bringing their spoils from the black carrier basket. The tenth—the wizard, I assumed—stood beneath the boat, his head tilted back, his arms spread wide. The disruption of the air surrounding the vessel was more noticeable as the shadows lengthened, an aura that shimmered and shifted like sunlit mist. Within it I saw the elementals more clearly. They were ethereal creatures, little more substantial than the aura itself, half the size of a man, all changing shades of blue and silver, with hints of darkness where eyes and mouths would be. I wondered what part they might take in the coming battle; and if Krystin's magic should be strong enough to overcome them and the Kho'rabi wizard both.

Then I felt a tug on my arm and turned to find Barus calling me back: warily, I retreated.

We joined the others. I saw the Tryrsbry men had bows strung now. Krystin beckoned them close and whispered a report.

"We wait until sunset," she said. "Let them settle to their dinner and think themselves safe. They build a fire, which shall light them for us. Loose your shafts on my order."

"Horses?" Barus asked, and the commur-mage shook her blond head: "No, that slope's too strewn with rubble, and we'd need bring the animals up beforehand. Arrows and a charge on foot is the way."

The jennym nodded his agreement. I said, "What of the wizard?"

Krystin said, "He's mine."

I said, "And the elementals? What of them?"

She frowned and returned me, "*What* of them?"

I heard Barus snigger softly, as if I once more exhibited ignorance. I once more ignored him, frowning in my turn as I asked Krystin, "Shall they not fight for the Sky Lords?"

She smiled, but in a friendly manner, and said, "No. The Kho'rabi wizards bind the spirits to their cause, but they'll offer us no hurt. Do they approach you, ignore them—they're harmless."

I said, "I'd thought . . ."

And fell silent as Barus murmured, "This Storyman knows little, eh?"

Krystin said, "Barus," in a tone of reprimand and brought her face close to mine. We were both somewhat sweaty after our half day of hard riding, but hers was sweet and pleasantly musky. The breath that touched my face was sweeter still as she said, "The elementals own no allegiance save what's imposed on them by the Sky Lords' magic. They are bound to their task by sorcery, not desire, and once the Kho'rabi wizard dies, they'll run free. Think of them as a team of horses hitched to the airboat."

I nodded, digesting this information. It occurred to me that a team of stampeding horses could be dangerous, but Krystin seemed confident, and so I said nothing. She smiled; I returned it, thinking that she was very beautiful. Not as my Rwyan, but in the manner of ancient statues, as if she were Danae come down from her mountains to once more hunt the earth.

Barus, who had followed our exchange and appeared to like it not at all, said in a carefully modulated voice, "He's no weapon save that dagger."

I grinned at him, motioned him to wait, and crept down to the horses.

The gray mare eyed me irritably as I approached, and I murmured gently, seeking to reassure her; willing her the while to remain silent. She tossed her head and stamped a hoof, but the carpet of pine needles dulled the sound, and she—the God bless her—only huffed air. I stroked her neck, thinking that there were considerable advantages to a mount trained for cavalry work, and took my staff from the saddle. It was a length of hickory thick around as my wrist, and slightly taller than I. Each end was capped with metal, and the entire length was banded with metal rings into which were etched the symbols of my calling. Trained as I was in the use of a quarterstaff, it was a weapon to be reckoned with. I brought it back to where my companions waited and flourished it at Barus.

He eyed it dubiously and shrugged. Krystin, however, nodded and said, "It will do, needs must. But go wary."

I smiled at her and said, "Lady, this shall not be my first skirmish with Kho'rabi." Then I feared she should think I boasted (which I did) and added, "And all well, your bowmen shall slay them before it comes to close quarters."

"All well," she murmured, and looked to the sky. "So, now we wait."

"You did well to bring word."

I looked up to find Krystin close. She rested on her elbows, her hair spilling back from her sculpted features. Her tunic did little to conceal the shape beneath. I shrugged and said, "It was fortunate you were in Brynisvar."

She turned her head, brushing back an errant wave of pale gold, her eyes firm on mine. "Perhaps it was destiny," she said.

I found her gaze and her tone both disconcerting. "Perhaps," I said.

She smiled, looking past me to where Barus lay, and lowered her voice so that I must draw closer to hear: "Pay no heed to Barus. He's a jealous man, even without the right."

I felt further confused. I shrugged again and said, "Certainly, he seems not to like me much."

"There are few he does like," she said, "and none who are not of the West Coast."

"You're not," I said. "Of the West Coast."

"No." She shook her head so that it seemed for a moment she was encompassed in curtains of light. "I was born in Tannisvar. The College sent me here to serve Yrdan."

"Aeldor of Tryrsbry?" I asked.

She said, "Yes."

I asked her, "How long have you been Tryrsbry's commur-mage?"

She said, "A year. Arlyss, who was commur-mage before me, was slain by the Sky Lords."

"Not long, then," I said, thinking that we were of an age, and that she had established her authority well in so short a time. "Yet Barus accepts you readily enough—for one not West Coast born."

She chuckled softly and said, "My sex and my calling give me certain advantages, Daviot."

I said, "Yes," and saw white teeth flash as her lips parted.

Across the valley the sun touched rimrock. Below, darkness gathered. I heard the wind sigh through the pines. It was almost time. I looked to Krystin and found her studying my face, her lips still curved in a smile entirely enigmatic.

She said, "When this is done, shall you come back to Tryrsbry?"

I nodded, and she said, "Good." Then she stretched, prompting me to think of cats, and said, "So. Do we go about our business?"

I took up my staff. I saw a soldier pass Krystin a bow, a quiver filled with arrows fletched in black and silver and red. To my left, Barus had a shaft already nocked, a tight savage smile on his mouth. We began to climb. Behind us the sun fell rapidly, as if, having touched the topmost peaks, it was drawn down to wherever it went at night. In balance, the shadow that had filled the valley bottom began to climb the slope. Stars showed, and a quarter-filled moon. Bats fluttered overhead. Apart from the sound of the wind, these hills were very quiet.

We reached the crest, and there was noise. A fire crackled, spitting sparks at the darkened sky, outlining the Kho'rabi, who talked as they lounged about the blaze. It was strange to hear them speak; stranger still the vague familiarity of their tongue, as if I could almost understand. I counted the full complement: they had set no watch. Nor did they wear their black armor, which stood in neat piles away from the fire. The airboat was a red shadow along the valley, the sigils on its flanks glowing faintly. I could no longer discern the elementals. I saw the Tryrsbry warriors spread along the hogback. I was to Krystin's right, Barus to her left. The jennym wet a thumb, held it to the wind. Krystin took two shafts from her quiver, cupping each head in right and left hands. She whispered something I could not hear and blew softly into each fist. Then she stabbed one arrow lightly into the ground and nocked the other. She looked to Barus and nodded, then both rose to a kneeling position, bowstrings coming back to touch their cheeks as they sighted down the shafts. I saw a Sky Lord spring to his feet, head cocked as he peered toward our position. I thought: *The wizard; he senses magic.*

"Now!"

Krystin loosed her arrow as she shouted, the second readied before the echo came back off the far valley wall. The Kho'rabi who had climbed to his feet took three steps back as the shaft struck his chest. It was driven deep, but still he raised his hands, pointing at our position. He did his best to speak—to voice a cantrip, I guessed—but Krystin's arrow had pierced a lung and blood filled his mouth, slurring his words. I saw a glow, like witchfire, dance about his outthrust hands, and then the slim column of the second arrow sprout beside the first. His spell died stillborn. The blood that came from his mouth was black in the firelight. The witchfire radiance shone bright an instant and then was gone. He fell down, his arms spread wide, and for a while his legs kicked, propelling him back as if he sought to flee. Then he was still.

The dusk was full of shouting now and that particular whistling an arrow makes as it travels its deadly path. The Tryrsbry bowmen were expert: their shafts flew straight and true. The Kho'rabi fell around their fire, most barely to their feet, two as they drew blades. I heard Barus roar and joined unthinking in the rush down the slope. I saw Krystin drive her short-sword deep between the wizard's ribs, slash his throat. I saw a Sky Lord before me. He was on his knees and wore two arrows in his chest, and blood came in long streamers from his parted lips. His breath was a choking exhalation. I thought he looked no monster, stripped of his dread armor, but only a hurting man, not much different in appearance from we Dhar. I thought of what I had seen that noonday, at the farm: I stove in his ribs and windpipe. I looked about, seeking another, and saw a warrior from whose belly and left shoulder shafts protruded swing his blade awkwardly at Barus. The jennym parried the cut and returned a sideways swing—the stroke Keran dubbed the Headsman. The Sky Lord's skull was parted from his neck. I sprang away as liquid gouted. All around the Tryrsbry men dispatched those Kho'rabi not slain by the arrows; slit the throats of those already dead.

Suddenly, from where the airboat hung, there came a loud rustling, a wailing akin to a building wind. It grew in volume, rapidly, until it was a howling fit to pierce the ears. I saw the sigils on the vessel's sides pulsate, brightening so that they stood out clear in the darkness. Several of the Tryrsbry men pressed hands protective to their heads. I stared, my own ears ringing, threatening to burst. It seemed there was something of triumph in the howling, as if myriad thin voices rose in gleeful chorus. It reached a crescendo, and I felt myself buffeted as by a wind. For an instant I saw leering faces flutter around me. I felt spectral hands tug at my hair, touch my face. It was like the caress of falling snow. I looked into the blank dark eyes of the elementals. I saw them whirl about the fire, stirring the blaze to a conflagration. I saw them hover above the dead Kho'rabi wizard, long fingers plucking at his wounds, dabbling in his spilled blood. Then they gathered about Krystin, a whirlwind of flickering, barely visible shapes that stroked her cheeks and hair. Some few clutched at her hands; I swear one kissed her on the lips. Then they were gone, rushing into the night sky, lost to sight.

I stood rooted to the spot. I thought on what a tale I should have to tell. I looked toward the airboat, thinking it a great prize. Perhaps with that for a trophy, our sorcerers would learn the secrets of the Sky Lords; perhaps learn the manner of the craft's construction, plumb the secrets of its propulsion. We might find the means to build our own and meet the Sky Lords in aerial combat.

The airboat exploded.

It sounds dramatic in the telling—*the airboat exploded!*—but in reality it was not. It was not like the airboats I had seen destroyed over Durbrecht or the Fend. There was no fireball, no blast of sound and fury. Instead, it seemed to sigh, not much louder than the wind amongst the pines, or a tired horse. It tugged on the cords connecting it to the basket, drifting a little way south as the wind took it, no longer held by the power of the trapped elementals. Then the sigils blazed, tongues of flame—real, not occult—licked at the sides, and there was a soft report. The airboat collapsed inward, like an emptied wineskin. For a moment the night was bright with its burning, malodorous with sulphur stench. I watched aghast as it fell onto the basket and all was consumed.

Krystin interpreted my expression. "It is ever thus," she said. "The Kho'rabi wizards set magicks on the craft, that we not capture one."

I said, "I had hoped we might. We could learn much."

She answered me, "As did I, the first time. But it seems the boats are bound by sorcery to their captains—the wizard's death both frees the elementals and ensures the destruction of the boat."

"Then . . ." I said, and broke off as she turned to Barus.

"Do you see these burned." She gestured at the bodies, which the jennym set to heaving onto the two fires. To me she said, "Should we not try to take a wizard alive? Was that to be your question, Daviot?"

I nodded.

Krystin chuckled, not unkindly, and shook her head. "No Kho'rabi is ever taken alive," she said. "Neither warrior nor wizard. We've tried it and lost good men in the attempt; without success. That we can slay them must be enough—at least these shall not carry word of our defenses to their masters."

I said, "No," and put a hand over my nostrils as the corpses began to burn.

W e rode some way from the scene of our ambush before we
halted. I suspected Krystin was as anxious as I to put distance between us and the funeral pyres. Surely she rode in
silence, seeming lost in her own thoughts. Perhaps she used
her talent to communicate our victory. I was not sure, nor did she
vouchsafe me an explanation or I see fit to question her. I hoped to do
that later, for my head was abuzz with all I'd seen this day. For now,
however, I curbed my tongue. And then, when we reined in, we were
busy awhile with the picketing of the horses, the construction of a fire,
and the preparation of food. I did my share, tending the gray mare,
evading the teeth she snapped at me even as I hoped I might be gifted
the beast. Temper or no, she was a sound runner and would be a boon
in my wandering. I rubbed her down and watered her, left her cropping grass as I went to the fire.

The Tryrsbry men were sharing boasts of their prowess, passing
a wineskin back and forth as they spoke of past battles. Barus was

with them, giving me a dour look as I came close. Krystin sat a little way off, and I went toward her, then hesitated, thinking perhaps she preferred solitude. She looked up and touched the grass at her side. I smiled and settled there. The moon was high by now, filling the clearing she had chosen with a wan light. It transformed her hair to silver, her features even more statuesque.

"You fought well," she said.

"A wounded man?" I shook my head. "There's little valor in such killing."

She shrugged, nodded, said, "He was a Kho'rabi. To slay a Kho'rabi is to fight well. One less enemy."

I made no reply.

She said, "They'd destroy us, Daviot. They'd have this land and see we Dhar slain to the last child."

I said, "Yes. I know that, but even so . . ."

She was percipient; she said, "What other choice do they leave us? With the Sky Lords, it's kill or be killed, nothing else."

I sighed and said, "I know; and I've done my share. But even so . . . sometimes I grow weary of it. Sometimes I wish it were otherwise."

"But it's not," she said.

I thought her about to say more, but then Barus stood before us, a callused finger pointed at my chest. "Do you ply your trade, Storyman," he said, "and entertain us with a tale."

His breath was perfumed with the wine that thickened his tongue, and it was less request than demand. From the corner of my eye I saw Krystin stiffen, her features contoured with irritation. I had no great liking for his manner, but neither any wish to provoke an argument with refusal: I nodded curtly and climbed to my feet.

The others of the troop were of more genial manner than the surly jennym and welcomed me with enthusiasm as I settled by their fire. Krystin joined us, and I paused a moment, selecting the tale. I decided they should hear of Ramach and the battle of Cambar Wood: it fit my odd mood well that I should tell of a victorious aeldor leaving the hurst a monument to the fallen. My audience was dutifully silent as I spoke, and I ended with my own experience there.

When I was done, Barus snorted and said, "Foolishness! The God-cursed Sky Lords deserve no monuments. The flames are enough for them."

I said, "The aeldor Ramach deemed them brave; worthy foes."

"Then Ramach was a fool." He reached for the wineskin, tilting it to his mouth. "The Sky Lords are a blight on our land, and I'd not honor them."

Krystin said, "Barus," her tone a warning. He turned away, refusing to meet her eyes, and she looked to me with a smile. "Do you give us another, Daviot?"

I said, "As you wish," and told them of Fyrach and the Great Dragon.

I am not sure why I chose that particular story. Perhaps I felt it occupied ground sufficiently neutral that Barus should be mollified. Perhaps I looked to investigate their feelings in regard to the dragons. Whichever, the one worked, and the other told me no more than I knew already. All listened attentively, and all save Barus voiced approval when I was done. One even said, "What allies the dragons would make now, eh?"

That elicited laughter, in which I joined, though I then said, "Could we but find them again and persuade them to our cause."

Krystin said, "Yes. Were they not dead."

I said, "Can we be sure they are? Might some not live still?"

The commur-mage shrugged, offering no response.

I said, "Of course, to find them would mean crossing the country of the wild Changed."

She gave me a look then that was oddly familiar. I recognized it in a memory: Rekyn had worn that same expression once. So, too, had Rwyan, when I had spoken of my fantasies, though then I had been more concerned with other matters, and not so much interested in plumbing her knowledge as the secrets of her body.

"Storyman's fancies," Barus grunted. "Dragons? The dragons are gone, and no Trueman dirties his feet in the soil of Ur-Dharbek."

"The wild Changed live there," I said, "and surely dirt is dirt, wherever it lies."

The jennym spat and found a second wineskin. When he had swallowed—deep—he said, "Changed dirt is not for Truemen. Who'd consort with such beasts? The Changed are animals, no more. The God knows, they were created for dragon fodder, and they're good for nothing else."

It was too much: into my mind's eye came an image of Urt, who was certainly no animal, whose company I much preferred to this uncouth fellow. I said, "In Durbrecht I named a Changed my friend."

It was a challenge and recognized as such. Silence fell, and for a moment it seemed even Barus was lost for words. He tossed the wineskin aside and stared at me. His expression suggested he looked on an abomination. When he spoke, his voice was cold for all its wine-rough slurring.

"Are you then a Trueman? Or did your mother lie with beasts?"

In the timber an owl sounded. The crackling of the fire was suddenly very loud. It seemed the wind held back its breath. I heard a horse nicker softly. My staff lay at my feet; Barus's long blade was sheathed and rested across his thighs.

Krystin said, "Barus! You go too far."

He smiled, not looking at her but straight at me. I thought he seemed more bestial than any Changed. I met his stare and said, "No, my father was a Trueman. Aditus, he is called." I was pleased my voice remained so calm. I paused deliberately and asked him, "Did you know your father's name?"

It was a crude sally, but subtlety was wasted on such as he. Someone chuckled nervously. Barus's face flushed dark, his lips thinned in a snarl of unalloyed rage. I saw his right hand close about his sword's hilt. I saw the blade slide out a little way. I tensed.

"Enough! I tell you both—*enough!"*

Krystin had not moved or touched her own sword. She had no need—there was such authority in her voice we both froze. I felt immediately embarrassed that I had allowed my irritation a hold, that I had sunk to the jennym's level. Barus rammed his sword home in the scabbard. His eyes were narrowed, as if he fixed my face in his memory, and there was the promise of murder there.

"Barus, I'll not warn you a second time. You insult a guest of Tryrsbry Keep, and do you continue you'll answer to Yrdan. After me." It seemed her eyes shone as she glared at him. I thought of the two, it should likely be her punishment was the worse. Then she turned that blue gaze on me. "And you, Daviot—is this fitting for a Storyman? To trade insults like some common tavern brawler?"

I shook my head and said, "No. My apologies, lady."

"I'm no lady," she returned me, echoing Rekyn, "and what apology you offer is best directed at Barus, not me."

I caught my refusal before it was voiced and said, "My apologies, jennym."

Barus said nothing. Krystin said, "Barus . . ."

He scowled, less like a warrior in that moment than a willful child caught in some mischief.

"Barus . . ."

He said, "My apologies, Storyman," and promptly rose to his feet, kicking the wineskin aside as he strode into the shadows.

Krystin rose and went after him. I wondered what transpired between them. I could not believe they were lovers, nor could I hear what was said. I felt a hand nudge me and turned to find the wineskin proffered. I murmured thanks and swallowed long. The soldier who had passed it me said, "Barus makes a bad enemy, Storyman. Best watch your back do you linger in the keep."

I nodded and asked him, "Why does he take such objection to me?"

The soldier glanced away, ascertaining Barus was gone out of earshot before he said, "He'd bed our commur-mage, would she but have him." He chuckled and winked lewdly. "But she'll not, and that puts him in foul temper. The worse that he sees the way Krystin favors you."

Late the next day we arrived in Tryrsbry. It was a sizable place, a good many leagues inland, the town spreading across the mouth of a fertile valley, the keep perched above, a little way up the north wall. A river descended the slope there, its course shifted to moat the hold, and we clattered across a wooden bridge into the yard. It was not so grand a keep as Thyrsk's tower in Arbryn but more akin to Cambar, plain for all I could see this was a wealthy bailiwick.

We left our mounts to be stabled, Krystin taking me with her to meet Yrdan. Barus prowled like some foul-tempered black dog alongside. Since that night we had not spoken, and whilst he had offered no further insult, he did not conceal his dislike. I was minded of the friendly soldier's advice—to watch my back.

The aeldor's welcome went some way to compensate for his jennym's animosity. We found him in private chambers, engaged in a game of catch-dice with his wife and two daughters, who—fortunately for them—favored their mother. Yrdan was an ugly man. He wore the typical dark locks and swarthy skin of a westcoaster, but his nose was huge and hooked, and his jaw excessively broad, displaying twin rows of overlarge and entirely separate teeth as he smiled. He was short and his legs were bowed, so that he must tilt back his head to find my eyes. In stark contrast to his looks, his temperament was sunny, and he greeted us with a cheerful roar, embracing Krystin as if she were kin, shaking my hand, and shouting for a daughter to pour us ale before he took report of our encounter with the Sky Lords.

Krystin's account was succinct, and when she was done, Yrdan said to me, "I bid you welcome, Daviot Storyman. You've bed and board in Tryrsbry as long as you choose. Now, do you tell the tale?"

I agreed readily and told him all I had witnessed. After, he nodded and said, "That was well done," then laughed as he slapped his malformed thighs. "I'd not have managed such a race. And nor shall you again. Do you take that horse as my thanks-gift?"

I said, "You are kind, my lord."

He returned me, "Yrdan, Daviot." Then he winked: "And, am I honest with you, there's few with much liking for that mare, and she with none for anyone."

"She has something of temper," I agreed solemnly.

Yrdan bellowed laughter and beckoned his wife and daughters forward. "I am remiss," he said. "I forget my courtly manners in this rough place. So . . ."

His wife was named Raene, and she stood a head taller than her husband. She possessed that sultry handsomeness common to the women of the West Coast, and her beauty was emphasized by his homeliness. I noticed, however, that when her eyes fell on him (which was frequently), they were filled with an absolute adoration. The daughters—Danae and Kyra—were as lovely as their mother, of marriageable age (I soon learned they were courted by the sons of several neighbors), and of dispositions akin to their father's. It was a cheerful audience, marred only by Barus's darkly looming presence.

Soon enough, though, the jennym left to attend his soldierly duties, and Yrdan suggested Krystin show me to my quarters. The commur-mage led me to a chamber on an upper level, a simple room but furnished comfortably and with a splendid view along the valley. She left me there, promising to send servants with hot water, and her company to the dining hall. I saw that her chambers were across the corridor.

Not long after, four Changed brought in a tub. I thanked them, seeking in their faces and their replies some indication as to the keep's attitude to their kind. Yrdan and his family had treated me well, but I was a Trueman, and I thought perhaps their benevolence did not extend to those beast-bred, that perhaps Barus expressed the common feeling.

The servants, however, seemed quite at ease, answering me with smiles, and I decided that the jennym was likely extreme in his views. Indeed, this was confirmed when I repaired to the dining hall. The Changed I saw there appeared happy, exchanging pleasantries with the men of the warband and their womenfolk; all save Barus and a handful of others, whom they treated with a wary deference. Yrdan accorded them much the same casual courtesy as he dealt the few Trueman servitors, and—Barus and his cohorts apart—I thought the Changed well served in this friendly keep.

It was a fine meal, and I enjoyed it and the company in equal measure. I was honored with a seat at the high table, between Danae and Kyra, whose questions occupied me throughout. They were a

flirtatious pair, and I was grateful for the lessons taught me in Durbrecht, that I was able to meet their sallies without discomfort or
offense: I had no wish to upset so genial a host as Yrdan. Even so, I
was somewhat relieved when the aeldor rescued me from their attentions with the request I entertain the hall with a story or two.

I chose the tale of Mallach the Swordsmith, and that of Aedyl
Whitehair, and both were received so well, a third was called for. I
spoke of Corun and the Witch of Elandur, and the hour was late
before I was done.

Yrdan called a halt then, thanking me for my tales and repeating
his offer of hospitality for so long as I cared to remain in Tryrsbry. I
told him I would linger there awhile, for now that I had a sound horse
to carry me south, I might journey more leisurely. He chuckled at
that, and winked, and tapped his massive nose, declaring me caught
by his cunning gift. Even on such short acquaintance, I liked this
aeldor greatly.

The candles that lit the corridors were guttered low as Krystin
and I returned to the floor we shared. The commur-mage had shed
her black and silver leathers for a gown of dark blue, and her hair was
bound up in a net of silver set with little beads of jet. Her neck was
long and slender, and she now appeared entirely feminine, without
hint of the martial air her travel gear afforded. We came to my door
and halted.

I said, "Goodnight, Krystin."

She gave no answer, only looked at me. In the dim light her eyes
were dark, unfathomable. She put a hand to her head, removing the
net, and shook her hair loose. I stood silent, watching the play of light
over her blond tresses. She took my hand and drew me toward her
chambers; and I did not resist.

There was an outer room lit by a single lantern, across which she
led me to a sleeping chamber. That was dark, save for the faint moonlight entering through the open window. It fell on a wide bed. She
closed the door behind us and faced me.

I said, "Krystin . . ."

I am unsure how I might have finished that sentence because
Krystin placed her hands around my neck and kissed me, and she
needed no sorcery save her presence after that. It had been so long
since last I lay with any woman.

She told me, after, that I spoke Rwyan's name. I apologized, and
she said it did not matter, though I think it did, and in those later
nights I was more careful and said only "Krystin."

"Shall this not make problems for you?" I asked.

She lay within the compass of my arms, her cheek against my chest, her hair a soft golden fan that shifted gently as she spoke.

"I've no lover in this keep." Her breath was warm against my skin. "Before, in Durbrecht—but here, no."

"Barus would have you," I said.

She snorted laughter and rose on her elbows to rest her weight on me, all down the length of my body. I felt myself begin to stir again as she spoke.

"We cannot always have what we want, eh?" Her smile was mischievous and seductive. "And poor Barus shall never have me. You, though . . ." Her hand moved, sliding between us. She laughed again, softer. "You, though, Daviot . . ."

Later, as the first pale hint of dawn lit the sky, she said, "Likely Barus shall not dare offend you further. Surely not within the precincts of the keep. But still, perhaps best you stay close by me."

I nodded gravely and said, "I shall, Krystin. I shall endeavor to remain as close as possible."

"How close?" she asked. "Do you show me?"

I did, and then we fell asleep, our limbs entwined.

It was full light when we woke, and later ere we rose to dress and break our fast. I was very hungry.

We went smiling to the dining hall and begged some bread and tea from the Changed servants, who were by now preparing for the midday meal. Those of the household we encountered smiled as they saw us, and when the warband found us deep in conversation they chuckled and muttered amongst themselves. I could guess the direction of their comments. Barus saw us and scowled blacker than ever, but he said nothing to me or Krystin, only found himself a chair and shouted for ale. Nor did Yrdan or Raene do more than smile benignly on us, though Danae and Kyra both giggled together and gave us long, appraising looks, as if they shared some secret with us.

That afternoon Krystin showed me the town. It was, as I had surmised, a prosperous place. There were taverns and squares where, in the days that followed, I pursued my calling, crowds gathering to hear my tales. It seemed my reputation grew, and that was a boon, for it enabled me to speak with more of the common folk, to assess their mood, as the College had ordered. I found them mostly careless of the Sky Lords' threat, for there had been no raids in this vicinity and they trusted in Yrdan and his commur-mage to protect them. They had heard of the craft that approached Brynisvar; that it had been destroyed with all its crew served to reinforce their confidence. I thought them complacent. I thought this West Coast had been fortunately sheltered.

I voiced my thoughts to Yrdan and for a while saw his mien grow serious. There was, he agreed, a feeling on this side of Dharbek that the Sky Lords were no great danger. "But fear not, Daviot," he said. "Does it come to fighting, the West Coast shall take its part. Meanwhile"—he smiled and tapped that massive nose, leaning closer as if to impart a secret—"Kherbryn promises us engineers, that we may build those war-engines that defend the cities of the east. Gahan sends them to us even now, I hear."

I was relieved to hear such news and thought once again that perhaps I took too much on myself, assumed a weight of responsibility beyond my station. Surely it was vanity to think that I alone was aware of the terrible danger the Sky Lords represented. These aeldors were not fools, nor blind; neither were the sorcerers. To think I was the only one who saw the danger was to insult them: I vowed to curb my ego.

So the days passed, happily. If aught marred them, it was my curiosity, for I retained my desire to question Krystin on the matter of the wild Changed.

She was not, of course, always with me. Three times she rode out after sightings of the airboats, and she had duties to which she must attend, and some of those private. But when we were apart, she contrived to leave me in company of friends or find some task for Barus that ensured we should not meet. As much as she was able, she stayed with me, and there grew between us a friendship perhaps more lasting than our transitory passion. It was on that that I relied for satisfaction of my curiosity.

We had ridden out one morning, along the valley into the wilder country beyond. We took with us food and a skin of wine, and when the hot summer sun approached its zenith, we halted where a brook traversed a little tree-girt meadow. I remember the sky was a cloudless blue, and the lazy buzz of insects. Our horses grazed some little distance off, apart—my mare had, it seemed, no more fondness for her own kind than for mine. Krystin and I stretched languidly on the sward, sharing the wineskin. I felt wonderfully comfortable.

I said, "Krystin, do you tell me of the wild Changed?"

For an instant I saw her beautiful face assume the cold stillness of a statue. I was uncertain what I saw in her eyes, for she sat up, denying me clear sight, but I thought it anger, or doubt, or even disappointment.

She said, "What of them, Daviot?"

Her voice was entirely normal. It sounded uninterested, even bored, as if she felt there were far better topics to discuss on such a day, in such a place. I suspected the tone assumed.

I said, "I don't know. Only that whenever I've asked a sorcerer about them, I see a particular expression, as if I trespass on forbidden ground. And none give plain answers."

"Perhaps there are none to give," she said; then laughed. "Perhaps we sorcerers guard our secrets."

I sensed prevarication and said, "Is it forbidden you speak of them, tell me, and I'll hold my silence."

Her laugh was entirely genuine then. "And shall you curb that Storyman's curiosity, my love? Is such a thing possible?"

I shrugged, knowing the answer; not wanting to voice it.

She said, "Did your Rwyan not tell you?"

(Such was our relationship that we had told one another of our lost lovers and sometimes spoke their names without fear of giving hurt.)

"Not much," I said. "No more than anyone does."

"And how much is that?" she asked.

I said, "That they dwell in Ur-Dharbek, put there by the first sorcerers as"—Barus's term seemed most apt—"dragon fodder. That those Changed liberated by their owners may cross the Slammerkin if they wish, but none may come back. I've the feeling the Border Cities are no longer defense against the dragons but are there to hold out the wild Changed. And if the dragons *are* dead, then surely Ur-Dharbek must now be a veritable kingdom of the Changed."

Krystin laughed again. Perhaps too lightly? I was not sure. She said, "Perhaps it is. What matter? Do the freed ones choose to cross the Slammerkin, why would they come back?"

"I don't know," I said.

"And what you don't know troubles you, eh?" She turned onto her belly, chin cupped in her hands as she regarded me, hair that captured sunlight falling across her face. "By the God, Daviot, you're a Storyman."

I nodded and smiled. "To learn is my duty," I declared.

"And shall you next seek the secrets of my calling?" she asked.

I said, "I've not that talent." I smiled as I said it, but I was nonetheless aware she gave me no answers.

She hesitated a moment, plucking a frond of grass that she placed between her teeth, nibbling. Then she said, "We say little of the wild Changed because we know little of them. Ur-Dharbek is closed to us —no Trueman goes there, and we sorcerers are no exception."

"But," I said, and paused, feeling myself on uncertain ground, "why not?"

Krystin answered me with, "Why should we? Is Dharbek too small for you? Would you conquer this kingdom of the Changed?"

I said, "No. But still I wonder. Urt would not speak of the place, either."

"Perhaps Urt knew no more than I," she said. "Which is little enough more than you."

"Are you not curious?" I asked.

She said bluntly, "No. I've enough here in Tryrsbry to occupy me. I've the Sky Lords, for one thing."

I said, "Yes, of course. But even so . . ."

She tossed her grass blade away and rolled onto her back, reaching for my hand. "Even so, my Storyman. I've not your thirst for knowledge. I am but a humble commur-mage, with a keep to protect; I'm happy with my lot. Though I could be made happier. . . ."

She drew my hand closer. She had removed her tunic and wore only breeks and a shirt of fine silk. Thin silk that clung like a second skin, and no undergarments. I felt the warmth of her flesh and the quickening beat of her heart. I put my curiosity aside. I did not, then, consider that perhaps she evaded my questions. I did not, then, care.

That came later, and even then I was not sure. Perhaps it was only coincidence. Perhaps Krystin had no hand in it; or no more hand than her duty demanded.

What happened was that three days later, I was ordered to quit Tryrsbry.

I had known I must, but the days had melted one into the next, and I had lingered longer than I should, even with a horse to carry me on. I had set the decision aside, aware that the sorcerers in the keeps I had already visited would send word back to Durbrecht; aware that Krystin would have reported my arrival and should report my departure when it came. Perhaps it was only that. But I could not help but wonder that the order came so soon after that abortive conversation. The timing was such as fitted the sending of an occult message and the returning of an answer.

Krystin told me as we prepared for the evening meal. She had been about her sorcerous business that afternoon, and I had passed the day in the town. This was our first time alone since morning.

She took my hands and looked into my eyes. "Word came from Durbrecht," she said abruptly. "You are commanded to go on."

She looked sad. I believe she was, for all we had both known from the start this must come. I felt a coldness in my belly—as before, with Rwyan, I thought that *knowing* a thing and *accepting* it were very different. I swallowed and ducked my head. She put her arms about my neck and kissed me lengthily.

When we drew apart she said, "Tomorrow. Daviot, I am sorry."

I nodded and stroked her cheek. I said, "Yes." I did not know what else to say. I felt that an interval had ended, an idyll stolen from out of time.

She smiled. I thought of tragic statues. For a while we stood in silence, holding one another. Then Krystin said, "I shall not forget you, Storyman."

I said, "Nor I you, my commur-mage."

"You'd not, eh?" She chuckled. I did not feel much like laughing, but I forced myself. She said, "So, do we go down with brave faces?"

I said, "Yes."

Yrdan was already informed and promised me such provisions as should see me comfortably through to the next keep, which was Cymbry. I thanked him for his largesse, and when the meal was done, I believe I excelled myself in my storytelling, for all I felt no great enthusiasm. All the time I could see Barus smirking. I was determined he should not see my melancholy.

Krystin and I slept little that night. We said our farewells with few words and came the morning went out to the stables, attended by Yrdan and his family. The aeldor clasped my hand, and Raene embraced me; both daughters planted moist kisses on my cheek. I held Krystin a last time, then mounted the gray mare, who snorted and set to prancing. I raised a hand in farewell and heeled my irritable horse to a canter. I did not look back.

Tryrsbry lay a league or more behind me when I heard the hoof-beats. I was making for the coast road, thinking the sight of the sea should cheer my megrims. The trail was broad, winding up the flank of a shallow valley where cork oaks grew, and I could see the rider coming fast after me. I reined in, thinking some messenger was sent from Yrdan's keep; I was curious as to why. The morning was bright and I squinted, seeking to recognize the horseman. It was not Krystin —that blond head I should have known instantly—and I waited at the road's center. I saw an unfamiliar bay stallion, a man in the leathers of the warband in the saddle. As he came closer, I recognized Barus. Almost, I took my staff from its bucket; then thought better of it. The jennym would surely offer me no harm, and I'd no wish to be the first to make a hostile move.

He snatched his mount to a brutal halt, wheeling the animal in a circle that lifted dust in a swirling cloud. I saw that he wore no armor and that his long sword was hung across his back. He studied me in silence, his face begrimed. His horse blew hard. There was a lather of yellowish sweat on its chest and neck.

I said, "Day's greetings, jennym."

He said, "Thought you to depart without an accounting between us, Storyman?"

I frowned, for all I could guess the reason, and said, "An accounting? An accounting for what?"

He said, "For insults given. For . . . Krystin."

I realized I had been wrong in thinking he would not offer me harm. I watched his face, awaiting those telltale signs that warn of attack. I thought that he could free his blade and swing before I might bring my staff from its fixings. I set my knees firm against the mare's ribs, and she, trained for battle, blew her own whistling challenge, her ears flattening. Barus's mount answered with a snort. Its eyes rolled. I thought he had ridden the poor beast very hard, and so it might well respond slower. Still, I'd no great desire to fight him.

I said, "Barus, for insults given, I've apologized. As for Krystin — Krystin's her own woman; the choice was hers to make."

His nostrils flared, much like those of his horse. I saw his eyes narrow. He was bareheaded, his black thatch bound with a sweaty cloth. I thought that if I could land one sound blow against his skull, the impending combat should be ended. And then that a single cut from his sword should end it just as well. A quarterstaff is a most effective weapon (which is, of course, the reason the College gave us wanderers the poles), but it is a weapon best employed on foot. I thought that if he pressed the affair, I must endeavor to persuade him down from his horse, or seek to knock him down before he cut me.

He said, "Your cursed Storyman's tongue beguiled her. Had you not come to Tryrsbry . . ."

I said, "I'm gone from Tryrsbry now. Do you pursue your suit." I shrugged.

He shook his head, not taking his eyes from my face. "Too late," he said. "What's done is done."

I said, "In the God's name, Barus, this is pointless! What shall you achieve by fighting me?"

He corrected me: "By *slaying* you, Storyman."

I ignored his interruption. I continued: "Yrdan will have your head. Think you my death shall bring Krystin to your bed? I tell you no."

"How shall they know?" he asked, and smiled. I thought of snarling dogs, of rapacious wolves. He jabbed a dirty thumb in the direction of the timber. "Do I leave your body up there, amongst the trees . . . the Sky Lords, perhaps; or bandits. Whichever, time shall pass ere you're found."

"And my horse?" I asked him. "What of her? Shall she not return to her familiar stable, and so bring warning?"

That gave him pause, as I had hoped. He was, after all, one of Yrdan's warband, and a horse was a thing prized and honored: he would hesitate to kill my mare.

I had underestimated his cunning and his hatred. He spat and said, "Your horse I'll tether. It shall take her some time to break free."

The mare whickered then, as if she understood the import of our conversation. She tossed her head, and I felt her tremble under me. I thought her anxious to give battle. Then I thought that Barus had first encountered me afoot: likely he allowed me but poor equestrian skills. I thanked Cleton for his lessons then; and Keran for all his. He it was had first told me an angry man may be weakened by his rage, that fury is a flame best burned cold.

I said, deliberately, "You'd stoop to murder then, like some common footpad. Does Yrdan know his jennym owns so little honor?"

He barked laughter. "The Headsman, bastard! As I slew that Kho'rabi, so shall I cut you to size."

I said, "The Sky Lord was wounded, coward. He wore two arrows. Think you I shall be so easy?"

He gave me back, "Yes!" and brought his right hand up to the hilt of his long sword.

I gave my mare a length of rein. I drove my heels hard against her flanks, and she—sweet creature!—screamed and hurled herself forward, against the bay stallion.

Her chest struck the stallion as he reared in defense. He was blown by the gallop: he was slow. He screamed in turn, flung off balance. Barus was thrown atilt in the saddle, and his blade flailed empty air. I had my staff out from the bucket, and though I could not deliver a firm blow, I rammed the tip against the jennym's chest. Barus made a sound midway between a shriek of rage and a cry of pain. I thrust again. He was thrown to the ground.

I sprang down, leaving my mare to her own fight, and ran around the snorting horses. Barus was clambering to his feet. His dark face was ugly, no longer like a dog's but akin now to that of a wild boar brought to bay—all blind fury and the need to inflict harm. He was also fast as a boar, and near as strong. He saw my staff swing at his skull and succeeded in both gaining his feet and moving clear of the blow. My hopes of ending the battle swiftly evaporated. I held the staff in both hands, across my chest, advancing.

Barus roared and swung a double-handed cut; I raised my staff and beat it off. Seasoned hickory is almost as strong as iron, and this pole was bound and tipped with metal: I felt the impact, and so did the jennym. We each paced a step back, feinting, assessing one another.

I said, "A question, Barus—one you failed to answer. *Did* your mother know your father's name?"

He gave me no reply save a blow. I said, "It's common knowledge in the keep, Barus, that you'll never have Krystin. They laugh at you."

That sally (crude as the first, I admit; but I was fighting for my life) served its purpose: he screamed and delivered a flurry of blows. I countered, defensive at first, but then with knocks to ribs and forearms. He was a skilled swordsman, and powerful, and I knew that he needed land only one serious cut to take the victory; but I was no laggard with the quarterstaff. Also, he fought enraged, which state— as Keran often enough advised us—consumes energy fast, whilst I fought coldly. It was as when I had gone out against the Sky Lords in Durbrecht: I perceived Barus as an obstacle, a thing insensate, a receptacle for my own cold anger.

We drew apart. He was panting. I saw spittle slick on his chin. I said, "Krystin told me she'd as soon bed you as—"

The sentence went unfinished. With a howl of naked hatred, Barus launched a terrible attack. The long sword seemed weightless in his hands. It pounded against my guard, the staff vibrating, sparks flying as edged steel struck the metal banding. I retreated, aware that at my back two horses snorted. I thought they no longer fought, but I had no wish to find myself driven between them or against the hooves of either. I thought my mare as likely to kick me as my opponent. I deflected a blow and riposted, catching the jennym's elbow. I saw his face pale at that and gave him two more steps, then cracked his elbow again.

He cursed, and his next cut was weaker. I risked a swift sidelong glance and saw the horses on the grass beside the road. They, it seemed, had settled their differences and now grazed between wary looks at us two. I backed a little way across the trail. Barus, his teeth bared, came at me. I parried and succeeded in tapping his elbow a third time. Could I but get past his guard to deliver a strong enough blow, I could shatter the bone. I thought that I had best not kill him, lest it be my head Yrdan took. Even so, I was tempted: I felt, now, that I had the victory in sight.

I retreated almost to the meadow, feigning weariness. I let the quarterstaff fall a little under the onslaught, as if the pole grew heavy in my hands. I aped the jennym's panting. Barus glowered, his eyes now quite mad. He grunted a hoarse battle cry and lifted his blade high. I watched it rise and cringed. I saw triumph anticipated in his eyes. I sprang forward, my staff crisscrossing before me, fast. It landed twice, hard against his ribs, and then I swung the pole up, taking his descending cut and forcing his blade away to the side. For an instant we looked directly into one another's eyes. His were wide and shocked. I reversed my stroke, dropping the staff to hook his knees. I knocked his legs from under him, and before his back touched the dirt of the trail I swung the staff against his skull.

I might have killed him with that blow, but I held back. I'd no wish to make an enemy of Yrdan, to find myself posted outlaw. Even so, I saw his eyes and mouth spring wide, then close. The sword fell at his side, and I stamped a boot down, trapping the blade. Barus groaned and stirred: he was remarkably strong. I tapped him, almost gently, on the point of his chin, and he lay still.

For a while I stood poised to strike again, thinking he perhaps feigned unconsciousness. When he made no further move, I kicked the sword away and stooped beside him. A colorful bruise was spreading down his right temple and cheek. I checked the pulses in his neck and wrists and listened a moment to his stertorous breath, assuring myself he lived. Then I rose and went to his horse.

The bay stallion showed me the whites of its eyes, pawing ground as I approached. I set my staff down and murmured to the beast, calming it enough that it allowed me to take its halter and lead it to where its master lay. I took Barus's sword and used it as a tethering peg. Then I rummaged swiftly over the saddle, finding cords there sufficient to my purpose. I returned to Barus and hauled him up. He was heavy, and he moaned softly as I got him on his feet and lifted his arms across the saddle. The stallion stamped and nickered as I pushed the insensible jennym across its back. I lashed him in place and secured his sword. Then I looped the horse's reins around the saddlehorn and slapped the beast's rump. The stallion snorted a protest and cantered back the way it had come, back toward Tryrsbry. Barus flopped like a sack.

I watched until I was confident the animal would take him home and then went to my gray mare.

She looked up from her grazing and snapped yellow teeth at my hand as I took the reins. I forgave her: she had proven her usefulness this day. She showed no sign of wounds, and so I collected my staff and once more climbed astride, turning her up the slope.

As I rode away, I set to wondering how Barus would feel when he woke. I hoped he should regain consciousness before he reached the keep: his embarrassment would have been a thing to savor. I wondered what explanation he would offer. I realized that my melancholy had entirely disappeared. I began to laugh aloud.

14

When I reached Cymbry, I was met by the commur-magus of that keep. He was a thin, bald man, Cuentin by name, and he greeted me with a smile. He was dressed extravagantly for his calling and his sex, and I discerned a subtle rouging of his cheeks, a touch of kohl about his eyes. Rings glittered on his fingers.

"You'll be Daviot the Storyman, I'd guess," he said. "I've a message for you."

I climbed down from the saddle, snatching the gray mare's bridle as Cuentin made to stroke her neck and she made to bite his hand.

"She's of somewhat sour temper," I warned him. "A message, you say?"

He nodded, moving a few cautious steps clear of the horse. His eyes were so dark as to be almost devoid of white, but they sparkled with amusement as they studied my face. He said, "From Tryrsbry," as if he savored his news and would draw its imparting out as long as possible. "From the commur-mage Krystin."

I waited with ill-assumed patience. What message would Krystin send? I had not thought to see her or hear from her again. Like all those others from my past, all those who had shaped and formed my life, I had believed her left behind, living only in my memory. I had chosen to look ahead — I was not sure I wanted a message from Krystin.

Cuentin said, "It appears that the very day you quit Tryrsbry the jennym of Yrdan's warband was set upon by brigands. Seven or eight, he claims — he was fortunate to survive."

I held my face straight. I said, "Seven or eight, eh? He was indeed fortunate."

Cuentin said, "Yes," and I could see he struggled not to laugh. "A very strange attack, it was."

I began to like this commur-magus. I chose to play his game and assumed an expression of curiosity. "How so, strange?" I asked him.

He said, "Well, as the jennym — Barus is his name, but you'd know that, I suppose — has it, he was out riding alone, when these seven or eight brigands sprang from ambush. He gave a fine account of himself, slaying at least three and wounding more, but then he was clubbed down and lost his senses. He remembers nothing after that."

"Nothing?" I inquired.

"Nothing." Cuentin paused, laughter hidden behind the clearing of his throat. Then he said, "It appears these brigands then secured him on his horse and set the beast free. It returned — by Krystin's account — to Tryrsbry Keep with the valiant Barus slung across the saddle . . . How did she put it? Yes — like a sack of potatoes. Now, is that not strange? I wonder why these ferocious bandits let him live? And why they failed to take his horse? Think you there's a story there, Daviot?"

Solemnly, I answered him, "It would seem so, Cuentin."

"But you're southward bound," he said, "so perhaps you'll never learn it."

"No," I said. "Likely not."

He nodded. "Krystin also said to bid you the God's speed."

I said, "For which, my thanks — to her and you."

He smiled wide, his eyes moving from my face to the staff set beside my saddle. "That's a sturdy pole," he remarked casually. "I imagine it must serve you well."

"It does," I said. "At need."

He said, "Yes," and began to laugh aloud.

I could not help but join him, and he took my arm in a companionable way as we traversed the yard. As we came closer to the stables, he stifled his laughter and said more seriously, "I've encountered Barus a time or two, and he's a surly fellow. Still, it does not do to spread rumors about a jennym, so perhaps we'd best keep this tale betwixt we two, eh?"

"Barus," I said, "is not a fellow I care to think of much."

"No," Cuentin agreed. "You'll find our Tevach more genial." He smiled mischievously. "Perhaps because he's no desire for me."

"Nor I," I said, not wishing there to be any misunderstanding between us.

Cuentin took no offense at this, but raised his hands in mock objection. "Fear not," he said. "I understand from Krystin that your tastes lie elsewhere. Albeit they tend toward we sorcerers, eh?"

I smiled and nodded, waving back the Changed stableman who came to tend my mare. I warned him of her temperament, and he left me to unsaddle her, contenting himself with the preparation of a stall.

I was glad of the interruption, for Cuentin's news disturbed me somewhat. Just as I had once before grown aware of societies overlapping one another—of Changed living amongst Truemen, simultaneously seen and invisible—so now I perceived that the sorcerers were a further layer in these complex, secretive strata. I had known my arrival and departure should be reported from keep to keep, but only that. It now seemed the sorcerers exchanged more detailed messages, gossip even. Perhaps it was only Krystin's fondness for me that had prompted her to tell Barus's tale to Cuentin, but it came unnervingly fast on the order to quit Tryrsbry, which had come soon after my questioning her about the wild Changed. I wondered if my progress was monitored. Perhaps I traveled under the cloud of my affair with Rwyan, my friendship with Urt. Perhaps the interest in the Changed I had shown in Durbrecht, my disobedience of the unwritten rules, yet branded me a rebel. It was an odd sensation to consider that I might be "watched" in this fashion; it was irksome to think that I could do nothing about it—was my burgeoning suspicion correct, I could hardly question Cuentin or any of his kind. To do so would only reinforce whatever doubts existed about my probity. *If* such doubts existed and my sudden unease was not solely a product of egotism.

I set to currying the mare, barely aware of her irritable snapping, instinctively avoiding the sudden lurches with which she sought to trap me against the bars of the stall. I finished tending my ungrateful horse and turned to the patient Cuentin.

"So," he said, "do I bring you to Gunnar."

I shouldered my saddlebags, took up my staff, and went with him into the tower of the keep.

By the time we found the aeldor, I had learned that he was wed to Dagma, had three sons—Donal, Connar, and Gustan—and a single daughter, Maere; that Dagma was pregnant, all three sons betrothed, and that Maere possessed a temper of erratic nature. Cuentin was a font of information.

I found the aeldor and his wife a solemn, even dour couple, and their sons not much different. By contrast, Maere, who was little more than a child, was a lively girl. All were dark, and all save Maere seemed to me of that West Coast character I had, overall, come to expect. Still, they made me welcome enough, and I remained in Cymbry some days.

While I was there, I was a dutiful Storyman. I asked no untoward questions, pried not at all, but only told my tales and thanked them for their praise. What questions I did ask were entirely within the aegis of my calling. I decided that if I were indeed monitored, it was not by the aeldors but by their sorcerers.

And if that were the case, Cuentin was a most subtle observer. I spent much time in his company and found him amusing and informative. From him I learned that the Sky Lords' little airboats were seen with increasing frequency all over Dharbek, seeming not to concentrate on any particular area but randomly across the land, whilst the larger vessels had been seen not at all this year. With the aid of Gunnar's jennym (who did indeed prove a most likable fellow), Cuentin had slain three groups of Kho'rabi. He spoke openly of the elementals harnessed to the Sky Lords' purpose, and it came to me that not everyone saw the ethereal creatures so clearly as did I. It was Cuentin's opinion that the blood gift that made him a sorcerer and me a Mnemonikos also granted us the ability to perceive the aerial spirits more readily. I wondered if that same blood rendered us more aware of the subtle currents flowing through our world, of the existence of societies within societies. That thought I kept to myself.

I rode once with him and Tevach after word came of a sighting, and I saw the Kho'rabi slain with the same efficiency as Krystin's band had demonstrated. I once more witnessed the liberation of the elementals, and it was as strange and disquieting an experience as before. I asked Cuentin his opinion of such magic and got back no more answers than before.

"It lies beyond my ken," he told me. "Their sorcery takes a weirdling path. And the God knows, do they bring it to full strength"—his lips curved in sour approximation of a smile—"then we shall see the Great Coming, and Dharbek fight for her life."

To hear this voiced by one usually so sanguine was somehow more alarming than those predictions issued by folk of more saturnine disposition. I said, "And what of you sorcerers?"

I realized we had begun to speak in terms of conclusion, not supposition. It was an ugly realization.

Cuentin shrugged wearily. "Shall we be enough?" he asked. "The God knows, the sorcerous talent is hardly commonplace. The College is already depleted to strengthen the Sentinels; all Dharbek's scoured for initiates—with not much success. Do the Sky Lords come in force . . ."

He shrugged again, letting the sentence tail away like the filthy smoke rising from the pyre. I chose then to take a chance: the moment, and the direction of our conversation, were opportune. I asked him, "What of the Border Cities? Might sorcerers not come from those?"

He answered me without, I felt, forethought. "And leave the Slammerkin undefended? Unwise, my friend." Then he broke off, his dark eyes suddenly enigmatic. I could not tell if I had caught him off guard. "There are fewer of us to man the Border Cities now, scarce enough to ward all Dharbek. And as we know naught of the land beyond . . . What if the Sky Lords grounded across the Slammerkin? What if they established themselves in Ur-Dharbek? We might then face landward invasion from the north, besides the aerial attack. No, better hold the Border Cities manned against that danger than risk the Kho'rabi coming over the Slammerkin."

It was a sound argument, the logic irrefutable. Perhaps—even likely—it was sincere, but for an instant I had thought to see something in his eyes, on his face, that hinted at secrets, at knowledge held back. I was tempted to say something of the wild Changed; I thought better of it.

If Cuentin guessed I had sought to probe, he gave no sign, and Tevach approached us then to announce his grisly work completed. We mounted our horses and rode away, my curiosity still unsatisfied.

It continued thus as I progressed southward. I was given ready welcome wherever I halted, and with my sturdy (if still ill-tempered) mare to carry me, I was able to meander between the populous coastal plain and the wilder hinterland much at will. The common folk were not much informed of events in the wider world, nor much interested. They went about their lives as usual, the little airboats considered a nuisance rather than a threat. They had become a thing accommodated into the daily round, much as were the cycles of the Sky Lords' Comings—a matter for the Lord Protector and his lieutenants, the aeldors and the sorcerers. And as for those authorities—well, their attitude was not, I thought, very different. Engineers sent from Kherbryn appeared in the keeps, supervising the construction of the war-engines, and the aeldors appeared to feel such weapons should combine with the powers of their sorcerers to defeat any attack. I encountered no other sorcerers so open as Cuentin, nor so voluble, and if they—like him—thought the war-engines insufficient to their purpose, they kept that belief from me. As Sastaine came and went, I found no more answers, only more questions.

And one in particular that set my conscience an agonizing dilemma.

I had passed several days in Thornbar, some way inland from the coast. It was a town built around a hill, the entire foot ringed with a high palisade, the houses climbing higgledy-piggledy up the slope to break against the stone wall of the keep. That sat atop the apex of the hill like some vast monument. From my chamber I could look out over the town to the distant valley sides. It was, I thought, an eagle's view.

I left with my saddlebags stocked well by the aeldor Morfus and the gray mare plumper for the abundance of good oats she had been eating of late. We were both somewhat overfed, and I thought to pare us down a little with more arduous rural wandering. I struck out to the east. There were villages and hamlets in the back country that were seldom visited, isolated places virtually forgotten, even by we Storymen.

The valley holding Thornbar was wide and steep-walled, and I had lingered over my departure. Consequently dusk caught us climbing the east slope. This was densely wooded, the trail a narrow path of hard-packed dirt flanked by ancient oaks. The night was moonless, and I'd no wish to find myself knocked from the saddle by an unseen branch, that being an occasional device of my faithless steed. I decided that the first decent resting place should be our halt for the night.

Toward the crest I found a suitable spot. The trees thinned here, allowing grass to grow, and I heard water sounds nearby. I dismounted and led the mare off the trail. There was an open space where a spring bubbled up from a rocky fountain, babbling away into the darkness across a tiny mountain meadow. I let the mare drink and set a hobble on her forelegs. I rubbed her down (I yet hoped such attentions might sweeten her temper) and doled her out some oats. She gobbled them, protesting when I would give her no more, and then grumpily set to cropping grass. I spread my blanket and moved into the trees in search of dry wood for my fire. I had an armful of branches when I saw the light.

It came from the south, where the valley wall was broken by a shallow cleft. It was not much distance off, and I saw that it should be hidden from Thornbar by the folding terrain. I wondered what it presaged. Perhaps some other travelers; if so, a sizable group, for it was a big fire. I felt no great need or desire for company, but curiosity prompted me to set down my burden and make my way through the trees to discover who lit the blaze. It occurred to me that brigands were not unknown in these parts, and therefore I approached cautiously. I thought that if it were bandits, I would regain my horse and return to Thornbar with word. If it proved no more than some merchant's caravan, I would, from sense of duty, make myself known and regale them with a tale or two.

It was neither, but still it was as well I came thieflike.

I could see the fire clearly through the oaks, growing ever larger as I drew nearer. Sparks climbed the sky in fiery echo of the stars. I saw the ground break up before me, forming a rocky bowl, at the bottom of which the blaze was built. Light reflected off the stone, and I counted four figures, which was not many for so large a conflagration. I could see no horses. I halted on the edge of the timber, hugging the shadows. I cursed myself for leaving my staff. I dropped onto my belly and crawled to the rim of the bowl. Boulders and trees hid me as I peered down. I stifled a gasp of surprise as I realized the figures below were not Truemen, neither honest merchants nor ill-purposed outlaws, but Changed. I frowned, wondering what they did, building such a blaze here, and from where they had come. I could think only that they were indentured to Thornbar, to the keep or the town, and had slipped away. For what purpose, I had not the least idea. Perhaps some secret ceremony known only to their kind? I knew from Urt that the Changed met away from the eyes of men, that there were rituals they performed in private—marriages and the like—but not of any that would bring four Changed into the hills by night to build a fire.

Then something turned my gaze skyward. Perhaps it was some sixth sense; perhaps some shifting of the air, a pressure so subtle as to be felt only by instinct. I know only that I looked up and saw an airboat descending. Almost, I rose and fled. Certainly I felt sweat burst hot on my brow, and then immediately cool so that I shivered. I tensed, a hand clamping about a gnarled root. I swallowed, willing my body to blend with the ground, with the shadows. The Kho'rabi wizards were able to sense the presence of magic, that I knew. Could they also sense me? I think that had the airboat not been so close, I should have taken to my heels. But it was, and I knew that if I fled now, the Sky Lords must surely see me and pursue me; and slay me. For a moment I was a child again, returned to the beach of Whitefish village: I longed to void my bowels. Those, too, I willed to silence and stillness.

The skyboat came from the east, silent as a hunting owl. The fire's glow lit its underside. I thought of burning blood. I could see very clearly the elementals that sported about the craft. They seemed better defined in the fire's light. I counted faces in the black basket hung beneath: ten, as before, lit ruddy. I watched the boat come down to hover awhile. It was on a level then with my position, and I thought —I knew!—the Kho'rabi looked directly at me. I held my breath. I sought to make myself one with the rock, a shadow amongst shadows. I closed my eyes an instant, and when they opened, I saw the vessel sink, close by the fire. The basket touched ground, and the occupants sprang clear. The Kho'rabi wizard raised his hands, chanting in that odd, almost-understandable language. Then he joined the others, who faced the four Changed.

They spoke together.

It was a while before that sank in. I huddled, watching them, listening. The fire—a guiding beacon, I realized—lit them clear, and the stone bowl magnified their speech. I heard the Kho'rabi speak and the Changed respond, but long moments passed before that fact registered on my bewildered senses. I could not decipher what they said, and it seemed they had some difficulty, as if one side or the other spoke a learned tongue. But converse they did, which was another oddity in this night of amazements.

They seemed not quite friendly, somewhat wary of one another, but nonetheless it was obvious an alliance existed here. I watched as the Changed prepared food and all sat down to eat; and after, the Changed brought out sacks that were stowed on board the airboat. I had no sense of time's passing, nor was I any longer aware of my fear. It remained with me, but it was dulled, pressed down into unimportance under the tremendous weight of my curiosity. What I witnessed was unprecedented. I prayed to the God I doubted that I might live to tell the tale.

I heard a wolf howl far away across the hills, the call answered by another that was closer. I heard an owl. Indeed, for some time the bird perched close by, studying me as if uncertain whether I was a living man or carrion. After a while it launched itself, swooping across the bowl. The Kho'rabi were on their feet at that, for all the bird's passage was almost soundless. Those black-armored warriors, however, came upright on the instant, and I saw that three held nocked bows of dark, lacquered wood. I felt my heart thunder then, watching their eyes scan the slopes. I thought that if they chose to investigate, I would run. Perhaps in the darkness amongst the trees they would miss me. A pessimistic voice whispered in my ear, telling me I was a fool, that the time to flee was long gone, and were I spotted only death awaited. I forced myself to breathe evenly and did not move. The Kho'rabi wizard said something, answered by one of the Changed, and the bowmen eased their strings and settled back by the fire. The shadows filled, thickening, as the night grew older. I felt my muscles stiffen. The ground felt cold.

Then the Sky Lords returned to their vessel. The Changed saluted. The wizard spoke, and the elementals floating about the airboat stirred. It was like watching a mist lit by firelight. There was a sighing, mournful music, and the airboat rose, straight up into the night. I scarce dared turn my head to watch, and when I did, my neck protested the movement. I saw the airboat hover, turn toward the south, and then it was gone, lost against the sky, a shadow prowling the night. I returned my gaze to the Changed. They stood awhile, watching, then kicked the fire dead and clambered limber over the rocks. For a fearful moment I thought they came my way, but they cleared the bowl east of my position and ran away through the trees.

I waited until I was certain I was alone. Then I rose, groaning as my rigid muscles unlocked. I stretched, working feeling back into my body, and walked slowly to the clearing where the gray mare waited. She lifted her head as I approached and whickered softly. I blessed her for her patience and her silence, but when I moved to stroke her muzzle, she rolled her eyes and bared her yellow teeth. I contented myself with murmured thanks of which she took no notice.

I unstoppered my wineskin and swallowed a long draught. My stomach rumbled, and I found cheese and bread and settled on my blanket. I set my staff close to hand. It was foolish of me, but I no longer cared to light a fire. My mind was racing, and I peered constantly about, wondering if the night hid watching eyes. I decided the mare should give me warning if ambush threatened and did my best to order my thoughts.

My first impulse was to saddle the gray and ride headlong for Thornbar Keep, to bring word to Morfus of Changed treachery. Then I thought that perhaps the Changed I had seen had not come from Thornbar. I thought that it should not matter much, the outcome would be much the same. Did I go to the aeldor with my tale, what course could he take but to announce betrayal, to inform the Lord Protector and his fellow aeldors that Changed and Sky Lords came together? And for what purpose other than betrayal of Dharbek? That would be his duty, and I did not think Morfus was a man to shirk his duty, nor entertain such doubts as I. Even did he seek to hold it secret, such news—such a fear—would surely not stay hidden long, but would become public knowledge.

And what then? A pogrom? A purging of the Changed? Or their

banishment across the Slammerkin to Ur-Dharbek, those—perhaps innocent—who survived? My troubled mind conjured an image of Truemen and Changed locked in bloody strife. I was not sure who would win.

And where, I wondered as the night grew chill and my soul yet colder, should that leave we Truemen? We depended too much on the services of the Changed that our world might continue smooth without them. We relied on their labor: our society would collapse without them. It was an alarming thought.

But so was the notion that all across the land the Changed played the part of spies for the Sky Lords; that the Kho'rabi had eyes and ears throughout Dharbek. That did they mount their Great Coming, the Changed might rise to stab we Truemen in the back.

Fear counterbalanced fear; confusion stood paramount. The bread I chewed threatened to clog my throat: I spat it out and rinsed my mouth with wine. I did not know what to do. My duty as a Trueman was clear—to warn Morfus, to urge he send word to Kherbryn and to Durbrecht. I thought that did I do my duty, I condemned Urt and all his kind to massacre.

Then I wondered if he knew. And with that wondering came a fresh consideration—What if those Changed I had seen were some outlaw group? What if they acted alone? Were that the case, I should be responsible for the suffering of thousands of innocent Changed. I felt a horror of such bloodshed. I felt torn.

I looked to the sky and saw it brightening with dawn's approach. It was empty of enlightenment. I wished I had not seen that cursed fire; that I had quit Thornbar earlier, or later, or gone another way. I cursed myself and fate, but what was, was, and all my wishing could not change it. I threw back my head and bellowed a curse.

The rising sun found me squatted on my blanket, oblivious to the dew or the chorus of the birds. Curious rabbits studied me and were ignored. I was no wiser, nor any more decided.

I wished Rwyan or Urt were here, that I might ask them what I should do. I wished there were someone with whom I might share this dreadful burden. Its weight ground me down.

I was still sitting as the sun climbed to its noonday zenith. My mare had given up her demands for oats and set sullenly to cropping the grass. I was, I think, more than a little mad then.

I had no answers, only the prospect of terrible slaughter did I do my duty, the prospect of dreadful bloodshed did I not. I could not convince myself of the rectitude of either course. I felt that down the one path lay betrayal of my people, down the other betrayal of the Changed.

I reached a compromise. Perhaps it was born of cowardice. I know not, only that it seemed to me the sole path I might take and still hold true to my own conscience: I decided I would hold my tongue.

I decided (or perhaps I merely sought to justify my indecision) that the Sky Lords did not yet command such power over the elementals that they could launch their Great Coming. Therefore Dharbek was at least a little while safe. Meanwhile, I would endeavor to discover if the Changed—all of them—did indeed conspire against we Truemen, or if only some faction allied with the Kho'rabi. Should I find such a plot existed, then I would make known all I had seen, all I might by then have learned. I should face awful punishment, but until such time as I could *know*, I would hold silent.

I prayed I did the right thing.

I rode south with my secret. It was a burden I had rather not carried, but it dwelt with me, an incubus I could not shed save at risk of birthing its mate. In the keeps I told my tales and conversed with commurs-magus and -mage, aeldors and jennyms, soldiers and common folk, as Daviot the Storyman, thinking all the time that I was now Daviot the Betrayer by their lights. Often I was tempted to blurt it out. Often I smiled and spoke and pretended all was well as I felt guilt beat a cold tocsin in my heart. Often I wondered if the sorcerers saw through me, or into me, and only played some arcane game with me, allowing me to mire myself ever deeper in treachery. Nights I lay often awake, the gladiators of doubt and guilt battling in my head. But I said nothing; it was as if a lock lay upon my tongue, keyed by irresolution.

It was a place too small to own a name: no more than seven rough cottages set within a cleared space in the woods, animal pens nearby, and vegetable patches. I saw that there were seven houses as I approached, and I wondered if that was an omen of some kind. Are three and seven not luck's numbers? I was met by a pack of barking dogs, sizable hounds of assorted colors and a uniformity of large teeth. One—the leader of the pack, I supposed—dared snap at my mare's fetlocks. Her ears were already flattened, her nostrils flared. She liked dogs no better than any other living thing, and she sent this particular hound howling into retreat, the rest deciding caution was the better part of valor. I was nearly unseated by her display, and by the time I had her calmed, we had an audience.

They were mostly women, the only males a handful of children who stared wide-eyed at my ferocious steed. One stepped forward, two small faces peering from behind the protection of her skirts.

"You own a fiercesome horse, stranger," she said. She seemed not at all afraid, only sensibly wary. "Do you tether her secure, I'll bid you welcome. We've ale, and food enough to spare."

I said, "Thank you," and climbed down.

I led the mare to a pen where hogs snuffled and lashed her reins to the fence.

The woman said, "Tyr, do you fetch a bucket of fresh water and see her turned out. But be careful of the beast."

A boy darted from behind her skirts. He was a sturdy lad, his head a thatch of fine brown hair. I said, "Perhaps best I tend the mare. She's a temper, as you've seen."

"No matter," the woman said. "Tyr's a way with animals, and he'll not let her harm him."

She seemed so confident I saw no reason to argue. I looked at her and smiled. I said, "I am Daviot, a Storyman."

"Well, the day's greetings, Daviot Storyman," she returned. "I am Pele."

She was tall as I, and slender, her features delicate. Strands of silky, honey-colored hair escaped from beneath a headscarf. I saw that her eyes were green and somewhat slanted and realized with a shock that she was Changed, a cat-bred female. I hid my surprise behind a courtly bow, at which she chuckled and said, "We've little ceremony here, my friend."

She showed none of the deference the Changed customarily granted Truemen. I let my eyes move past her to the others. I saw that of the seven women, three were Changed. Yet it was Pele who spoke for all, and she who named the Trueman females. It was as if, in the absence of their menfolk, all there regarded her as leader.

Pele brought me to her cottage and poured me a mug of very good ale. It was the midpart of the afternoon and I had eaten, but from courtesy and a desire to avoid affront I accepted the platter of cold pork and a wedge of bread she offered me. As I ate, she busied herself with domestic tasks, talking the while. Her daughter, who was named Alyn, assisted her when the child was not studying me with huge eyes that made me think of kittens. The cottage was small but built sound. It would hold off the cold of winter; now the single window and the door stood open.

"So what brings you here?" asked Pele. "We see few strangers in these wild parts, and never a Storyman before."

"I was at Thornbar Keep," I said. "I thought to wander the hinterland awhile."

She nodded, as if this were not at all strange. She said, "Sometimes the Truemen go in to Thornbar."

"To sell your produce?" I asked.

She said, "Yes, and to buy such tools and stuff as we cannot make or grow."

"It's a lonely place," I said.

She laughed at that, reaching up to brush an errant strand of golden hair from her eyes. She was kneading bread, and she left a white smear of flour on her forehead. She said, "There's company enough. But still—a Storyman shall liven the evening, do you elect to stay."

"Do you offer such hospitality," I said, "I'll gladly accept."

" 'Tis yours for the asking." She gestured at our surroundings. "You've the choice of a room shared with Tyr and Alyn, or the hearthside."

"The hearth is good enough for me," I said.

"Then be welcome. Save . . ." She paused a moment. I thought her, albeit on only short acquaintance, unusually hesitant. "Not all approve of us. Perhaps you'd best reserve your decision until Maerk returns."

I asked, "Your husband?"

She answered, "My man. We're not wed in the Church's eyes."

I laughed then and said, "That matters nothing to me. I've not the niceties of some mantis."

"It's not that," she returned me, and looked me straight in the eye. "Maerk's a Trueman."

I could not conceal my surprise, and she saw it. Her fine features darkened a fraction; not, I thought, with embarrassment, but with defiance. I swallowed a mouthful of ale. Alyn studied me solemnly.

I said, "Is that why not all approve of you?"

Pele nodded. "And why we seldom visit Thornbar. There's some would see us punished. It's why we live here; in part, at least."

I shall not tell you I was not taken aback. That would be a lie. It was not unknown for Truemen and Changed to consort casually. Indeed, there had been establishments in Durbrecht that boasted the exoticism of Changed cyprians, and I had heard tales of women who enjoyed the services of Changed lovers. But it was not a thing done openly. It was a thing denounced by the Church, furtive, and marriage was unknown. The slurs Barus had cast my way were indicative of the common feeling: a couple such as Pele and Maerk must inevitably find themselves outcast. I could not help but glance at Alyn.

Pele saw the direction of my gaze and shook her head. "I was wed before," she said softly, "and widowed. My babies are both Changed; Maerk bought us after."

My brows must have risen at that. Certainly the thought entered my mind that Maerk had purchased himself a cyprian of a kind. I think it did not show, but Pele was quick as any feline, and as good at gauging mood. She reached beneath her blouse and drew out a disk, held around her slim neck by a leather thong. Silently, she held it toward me: it was such a disk as freed Changed were given, stamped with the marks of authority. I had seen such disks in the hands of beggars.

Pele said, "He was a carpenter then. He saved and borrowed until he was able to buy me. Then he set me free. His family cast him out for that."

Her voice challenged me to object. I said, "He must be a good man."

She said, "He is. And more—he loves me; and I him. Can you understand that, Daviot Storyman? Do you know what love is?"

I said, "I know what it is. In Durbrecht . . ."

I shrugged, and could not help the sigh I vented. I had believed my memories of Rwyan under tighter rein, but this story brought them back. I thought that we might have found some refuge such as this hamlet, some lonely place far from our duties. Then I thought of the secret I carried and knew that once duty is accepted, it cannot be escaped. I said, "She was a sorcerer. They sent her to the Sentinels, and me here."

Pele nodded as if she understood. I suppose she did. She said, "Perhaps you'll find her again."

I said, "I think not."

She drew me another mug and stood before me then. "We are not the only ones," she said. "Of the families in this place there are two Changed and three Trueman. Two are of mixed blood—Maerk and I, Durs and Ylle. Durs is of canine stock."

Perhaps she anticipated outrage, or criticism, but I felt none. I was, as I have said, surprised, but I had witnessed stranger things of late, and to express disapproval of such arrangements would have been a betrayal of my belief that there was, in truth, no longer very much difference between my kind and hers. Still, she seemed to expect a response. I am not sure why I said what I did; the words sprang unpremeditated from my mouth: "I had a friend in Durbrecht of canine stock. His name was Urt."

She said, "A friend?"

Her tone was casual, neutral. Perhaps purposefully so. She looked at me with her head cocked slightly to one side. That I was Trueman and she Changed meant nothing, and everything. I do not believe she judged me, but I felt a tremendous need to explain: I told her of my friendship with Urt.

When I was done, she nodded and returned to her bread. After a while she said, "He was a good friend."

I said, "Yes. Perhaps the best I've known—he risked much for me."

"And was rewarded with exile."

She glanced up as she said that, watching me with enigmatic eyes. I did feel judged then, as if I stood in place of all my Trueman kind. I answered her, "That was not my choice. I argued it."

Again she nodded. Then she smiled and said, "I think Urt found a good friend in you, Daviot."

I returned her smile, but mine was cynical. "It seems my friendship brings poor reward," I said.

"The same might well enough be said of Maerk and I." Pele shrugged. It was a lazy, feline movement. "This world deems us different and would not see Trueman and Changed together. Save as master and servant."

"Or dragon bait," I said.

"That was long and long ago." She chuckled. "So long ago, none but you Storymen remember those old ways."

"And yet," I said, "Ur-Dharbek still stands a barrier between this country and the land of the dragons."

"Old habits die hard," she said. "And Ur-Dharbek is not much different now to the Forgotten Country, I think."

I said, "Save the wild Changed dwell there in freedom."

I looked to cast a hook in the waters of her knowledge. This was no sorcerer, but a woman of the Changed who appeared to me entirely open and honest. I thought perhaps to land a catch of information.

Instead, I got a laugh, a shrug, and, "So it is said. But I've no idea."

"Should you and Maerk," I asked, "and all these others, not be received better there?"

She said again, "I've no idea," and then: "Why should it be different? If Ur-Dharbek is indeed a kingdom of we Changed, then should attitudes not likely be the same? Save in reverse? I'd not see Maerk reviled by my kind."

I digested this. It had not properly occurred to me that the Changed would indulge the same prejudices as Truemen. I had thought, albeit vaguely, that if Ur-Dharbek harbored a Changed society, if it was now a country in its own right, then it should be a free society, a country without such partiality. In this, Pele was wiser than I. Why should Ur-Dharbek be different? Indeed, the wild Changed must have greater reason to detest the Truemen who had made them to be prey for the dragons and now used them as servants. As slaves, in fact, for the Changed of Dharbek had few enough rights. That should surely be a weight of suffering's memory. I found no ready answer.

"No," Pele said as I sat silent, "I think we do better here. We are left alone, and we've a good enough life. Besides, Ur-Dharbek is a very long way off."

I said, "That's true," with such unconscious solemnity that we both laughed.

Then Tyr came in. He carried my saddlebags and my staff, which he set at my feet. He faced me with that dignity only children can command. "I've seen your horse settled," he told me. "She's *very* ill-tempered. When I took off her saddle, she tried to bite me."

"I apologize for my disagreeable horse," I said, "and thank you for tending her. Perhaps I'd best look to her needs from now on, though."

He thought about this a moment, then nodded solemnly and said, "If you wish. Besides, if you're to ride her, you'd best learn to handle her."

I said, "Yes, I had," trying very hard not to offend him by laughing at his earnestness.

Pele rescued us both with the suggestion that he go select a chicken for our dinner, and he ran out with Alyn hard on his heels.

"You've fine children," I said.

"Yes. It's a pity I can have no more." She looked a moment pensive, then shrugged and said, "But the seed of Changed and Trueman mixes no better than that of cat and dog."

I could think of nothing to say to that and so held my tongue, watching as she set her bread in the oven and began to prepare vegetables. It was a scene of such domesticity as I had not encountered in some time. I had been mostly in the keeps and towns of late, and there such things were done out of sight by Changed servants, whose offices I accepted unthinking. Sitting here, I contemplated again what life with Rwyan might have been like, had we not been born with our respective talents. I began to feel nostalgia for a life I had never known, nor likely ever should. Melancholy threatened—I pushed it back: there were far greater events afoot.

I watched Pele's deft movements, thinking how graceful she was. I thought she could not know of Changed dealing with the Sky Lords, for if she did, surely she would not make me so welcome. Unless . . . an ugly notion imposed itself . . . she sought only to lure me into a false sense of security. And then? Would Maerk appear, and others, and look to slay me? I shook my head: what I had seen and what I had failed to do surely seduced me into mistrust where only honest welcome was offered. These people could not know my secret. Nor were they likely to consort with the Sky Lords—Changed and Truemen living together in harmony, wed in all eyes save those of the Church? No, surely they would not. Rather, this was an idyll of a kind, an indication of how things could be, were inbred prejudice denied.

I grew the more convinced of this when Maerk appeared. He was a blunt-featured man, swarthy and hairy as any other westcoaster but with a ready smile that lit his face as he came in.

He cried, "Day's greetings, Storyman," as he crossed the room to plant a resounding kiss on Pele's flour-smudged cheek, holding her close a moment before drawing himself a mug of ale and pulling up a chair. I saw that his forearms were corded with such muscle as a carpenter or a forester develops, and his shoulders were wide. When he took my hand, his grip was powerful.

"I found Tyr and Alyn amidst the wreckage of a chicken," he explained, "and they told me we'd a visitor. Pele's made you welcome, I trust?"

"Most welcome." I flourished my mug. "My thanks to you both."

Maerk made a dismissive gesture. "The God knows, we see few enough strangers here that we'd turn a man away," he said. "And a Storyman, to boot? No, never. But you'll earn your bread, I warn you."

I said, "Gladly." I felt my random suspicions dissipate.

"No doubt you've tidings aplenty," said Maerk, but when I began to speak, he hushed me, telling me to save word of the greater world for later, when all might gather to hear it. "We manage well enough without," he said, "that I can wait awhile; and you not delay your storytelling with twice-told news."

I agreed. He said to Pele, "We took a deer. We'll dress the meat tomorrow."

She nodded, smiling at him, and in both their eyes I saw a devotion warm as any hearthfire. She went outside then, to check her children's labors, and Maerk grew serious awhile.

"You understand our situation here?" he asked me. "Pele's explained things?"

"She has," I said.

"And you've no"—he paused, shrugging his broad shoulders so that I feared his tunic might burst—"objections?"

"None," I assured him.

He said, "Good. Then we speak of it no further."

Nor did we. Instead, he brought me to their well, where we washed, and then sat down to drink more ale as Pele set the chicken to roasting. She was an excellent cook: I ate well that day.

When we had finished, it was twilight, and with replenished mugs we quit the cottage for the square outside. Maerk shouted that the evening's entertainment began, and from the other buildings folk brought out chairs and blankets, setting them in a circle, at the center of which I stood. I spoke first of events in the world beyond, which produced some grunts of surprise and some of alarm. I thought these lonely folk had very little commerce with the rest of Dharbek, that they knew so little of the Sky Lords' activities. I mentioned the little airboats and several shouted that they had seen the craft, but none in a way that suggested more than curiosity. I watched their faces and the way their bodies moved, and I decided there was not one here had any truck with the Kho'rabi. These people wanted only to be left alone. I could not help wondering how they should act did it come to war. Did the Great Coming we Mnemonikos and the sorcerers feared descend on Dharbek, what would these folk do? I hoped, did that Coming materialize, they would be left in peace. I thought it a vain hope, for should that invasion commence, I did not think there would be any corner of Kellambek or Draggonek left untouched.

Such fears I hid. I told them stories as the moon climbed above us and the surrounding forest filled with night sounds. I used all my skill, for I wanted badly to repay their hospitality, and I had sooner entertained them than any aeldor in his tower.

And as I recounted my tales of greatness and glory, I thought that were I to fulfill the duty laid on me by Durbrecht, I must at the year's end send word to the College of this village and its folk. It was a thing I had not encountered before—Changed and Truemen living in such equality—and I did not think the College knew of such a thing. I was by no means sure I would. They appeared to me so happy, so contented with the life they had made for themselves, I felt loath to make public their existence. I thought that they should likely find that censure that had driven them into isolation returned, did I speak of them. Some disapproving aeldor would visit them, or a zealous mantis. I thought them better left alone. I already had one great secret: I thought this should be another, smaller confidence.

I spoke to the best of my ability and should cheerfully have continued (aided by the mugs Maerk passed me) all night, had the children not begun to yawn. As it was, I reached the conclusion of Daryk's tale, and Pele announced it time to halt. Alyn was asleep in her arms, and Tyr, for all he fought to hold his eyes open and protested the curtailment, lay curled kittenish and sleepy at her feet. I promised more on the morrow and bade my newfound friends goodnight, going with my hosts to their cottage.

I slept the night by their hearth, and the next morning aided Maerk in dressing the deer (of which he promised me a portion when I left). I passed a pleasant day in his company and spent a second night storytelling. I was invited to remain as long as I wished, and I was greatly tempted to linger. But I steeled myself and refused: there were matters I must investigate that, for the sake of my conscience, I could not ignore. I thanked them and, my saddlebags bulky with good venison, prepared to leave.

I chose to continue inland. Maerk had pointed me to a trail he assured me would eventually lead to a village named Dryn, some five days' distant on horseback. He and Pele and all their kindly neighbors walked with me to the trail's beginning. They wished me good journey, but it was Pele's parting words impressed me most.

She set a hand upon my knee and tilted back her head to look me in the eyes. "I hope you find your Rwyan again," she said. "Your friend Urt, too. Perhaps then you'll find what you seek."

I started at that, prompting the mare to toss her head and stamp. Even as I gentled the restive horse, I wondered what Pele meant, what she saw in me, or guessed; what she knew. Pele stepped back, but her green feline eyes remained intent on my face, and I felt she looked deep inside me, into the places I held closed and hidden. I frowned and asked her, "What do I seek, then?"

"Peace?" She shrugged, the single word more question than statement. "I know not, Daviot; only that there *is* something."

I swallowed, confused. Did this cat-bred woman possess the talent for magic, that she could discern my innermost doubts? I met her clear gaze and said, "How do you know that, Pele?"

She smiled, and waved a careless hand, and said, "Sometimes it is in your eyes, sometimes in your voice. I'd not pry, but I see it there. And I hope you find whatever it is."

There was such kindness in her voice, I felt my eyes moisten. I nodded and smiled, and then I rode away.

I felt I had learned something there that would aid me when the time came that I must decide what to tell and what to hold back. Those folk were, though they knew it not, pivotal to the world's future. I think had they known it, Pele would have nodded sagely and Maerk would have laughed; and both told me they sought only to live their lives in peace, not shift the course of Dharbek. Still, I felt gifted as I left them. I thought they had showed me an unsuspected road, confirmed my own feelings about Changed and Truemen, and for that I was truly grateful.

I still, however, did not know which course I should eventually take. But now I felt somehow better equipped to make that decision when the time came.

I continued inland as the year aged and autumn came aknocking on summer's door, on to Dryn, on to the wild places where the land rose up to join the foothills of the massif. Often as not I slept rough; the villages were few and scattered here, towns a rarity, keeps scarcer still. I was greeted with enthusiasm—these places had not seen a Storyman in years. And everywhere I went, I watched and listened and asked questions, but I learned no more than I already knew. There were fewer Changed in these isolated places than were found on the more populous coastal plain, and those I encountered seemed content enough. I could not believe they took any part in conspiracy—if conspiracy, indeed, existed. Had I not been Durbrecht-trained, I think I should have begun to doubt my memory, to think that meeting I had witnessed a figment of my imagination, a dream. But I knew it was not so. I could recall it clear, every detail, and it remained a worm gnawing at the heart of my conscience. Still, I saw no further sign of collusion betwixt Changed and Sky Lords, saw no more clandestine rendezvous. Indeed, I saw not much more sign of the Sky Lords themselves. A boat sometimes, not often and never close, so that I began to wonder if the Kho'rabi gave up their voyaging or confined it to the coast. I thought I should learn no more in the wild hinterland, but only where folk gathered in the larger towns. The gray mare and I were both leaner now, at the peak of our strength, and I decided it was time to return westward.

•   •   •

It was a pretty ride, through a landscape painted with autumn's colors, the air crisp by day, chill by night, but as I came on the coast I realized I had dawdled longer inland than I had intended. Fog met me as I approached Trevyn, rolling in off the western sea to blanket the land, cold and damp. I drew my cloak tight and came on the hold like some ghost rider, my mare, whose coat matched the brume, all but invisible. It was the midpart of the day, close on noon, but if the sun shone, it was lost above the fog, and I located the gates only by the braziers that burned there.

Inside the walls it was not much better—a twilight lit by the diffuse glow of windows and the lanterns carried by passersby. I knew Trevyn to be a sizable place, but I could barely make out the houses to either side in the gloom, and despite the directions I got, I lost myself five times before I found the keep.

It sat beside the sea. I could hear waves lapping against the western wall. I thought there would be no boats out today. I announced myself to the gate-guards and was brought by a Changed ostler to the stables. My mare was in foul mood, and I saw to her myself before proceeding to the tower, warning the ostler against her temper. I felt cheerful, anticipating a bath (I had slept by the trail the past three days) and perhaps a mug of mulled ale, a good hot meal. Instead, I found myself brought immediately before the aeldor Chrystof and his commur-magus, Nevyn. Neither appeared overjoyed to see me.

Chrystof was a gaunt man of advanced years; a widower, I understood, and childless, with a left arm withered by an old wound got from the Sky Lords. Nevyn was younger, perhaps a decade older than I, plump, his hair dark as the aeldor's was silver. They sat in high-backed chairs either side of a roaring fire, a jug set close enough to the flames that the spiced wine I could smell should be kept warm. A rug covered Chrystof's legs. He appeared feeble, gone into his dotage.

I said, "Day's greetings, my lord aeldor; commur-magus."

Chrystof nodded and returned the salutation in a hoarse voice. I noticed that his eyes were yellowed with age and the proximity of death. Nevyn only studied me with a cold speculative gaze. I was not invited to sit, although a third chair stood close by, nor was I offered wine. I ran a hand over my fog-wet hair, feeling suddenly chilled despite the warmth of the fire.

Without preamble, Nevyn demanded, "Where have you been, Storyman? We thought to see you long since."

I hesitated, surprised it was the sorcerer who spoke, and by the imperious question. A Storyman had no set itinerary but was free to wander at will. Word was, of course, passed from keep to keep, of our arrivals and departures, but we were not bound to follow any fixed route or timetable. Nor was it usual to question our comings and goings: I sensed something amiss here. I thought again that perhaps my progress was watched more closely than my fellows'. I said, "Did you expect me ere now, I apologize. I rode inland a way."

"A long way inland," said Nevyn, and sniffed disapprovingly. For an instant I saw Ardyon's cadaverous features imposed over his. "Half the summer inland."

I shrugged, not liking his tone or the way he studied me. I said, "The aeldor Yrdan of Tryrsbry was kind enough to gift me with a horse. I thought to use that advantage to wander the isolated settlements. Most had not seen a Storyman in too long."

I had thought that mention of an aeldor's kindness should remind them of courtesy: it did not. Chrystof grunted and motioned with his cup, which Nevyn promptly filled. He still made no move to offer me wine. He sipped his own and said, "You left Thornbar Keep weeks ago. Where have you been since then?"

"Riding," I said. I began to grow impatient with his manner, but I hid my irritation, wondering at the reason for this unusual interrogation. "There were none of your kind where I went."

My answer was deliberately ambiguous. Nevyn grunted, drawing a hand over the purple stain the wine had left on his upper lip. For a while he stared at me. Then: "Word has come from Durbrecht—you are to make no more such forays."

"What?" I frowned, entirely unable to conceal my surprise. Such a command was unprecedented. "Am I to forsake my calling then?"

The sorcerer ignored my outburst. "You are to pursue your calling as you are bid," he said. "Your duty is to proceed south down the coast, to Mhorvyn."

I stared at him. I was struck by his pomposity; struck more by the nature of this command. He took my silence and my expression for doubt and turned to Chrystof for confirmation. The aeldor had been looking into the flames throughout this exchange, but now he swung his gaunt head in my direction. He nodded and said, "It is so, Storyman."

I could not doubt it; I could wonder why: I asked.

Nevyn answered me obliquely. "You're to be in Mhorvyn by Bannas Eve," he said. "And go there by the coast road. Without deviation."

I asked again, "Why?"

The plump commur-magus shrugged. "Perhaps your College would have report of our preparations." He sipped more wine. "Perhaps Durbrecht feels your talent is better employed where folk live, not wandering lonely through the hills."

"Folk live there," I said. I forbore to add, "Folk kinder than you." "Do they not have need of Storymen?"

Nevyn stooped to fetch the jug from the hearth; filled his cup. I grew wearied of this insulting behavior.

He asked me, "Do you question the orders of your College?"

This took me aback. "Yes" would have been the honest answer, but I was not, I admitted to myself, any longer entirely honest. Were I, I should have long since spoken of what I had seen. Consequently, I said, "No, I do not question the command; I wonder at its reason."

I thought perhaps he would answer me with word that I was no longer trusted. That Durbrecht would have me in clear sight; at least, where sorcerers might monitor my progress and my doings. I could not, of course, voice this thought: to do so would mean revealing secrets I was not yet ready to impart. I awaited his response.

That came with a smug and careless smile. "Perhaps Durbrecht sees a wider picture," he said, and added an insult as calculated as any Barus had given me. "Remember we gird against the Sky Lords, Storyman. Do they come, shall it be against some foresters' hamlet or against the keeps? Which do you think?"

I thought that I had sooner dealt with him as I had dealt with Barus. I held my staff, and I thought that it should have been most satisfying to deliver him a sound crack. I gripped the pole tighter. Nevyn saw and drew himself a little upright in his chair. I thought perhaps he readied his magic to throw against me: I forced myself to calm and said, "Doubtless both our Colleges see the wider picture—I had thought to allow the plain folk of this land a glimpse. After all, these great holds—the towns—are warded by such as you, and news is easier to find. But in the lonely places—should they not know, too?"

I was rather pleased with my diplomacy. It went unnoticed by Nevyn. He waved a dismissive hand and said, "Do the Sky Lords attack, it shall be against the keeps, not the hamlets. Surely, then, better to ply your calling where folk gather, not waste it on the empty woods."

It was an effective counter. Nevyn was pompous, insulting, but he was no fool. I saw we reached impasse in our verbal duel and allowed his point with a silent nod. He smiled and told me, "In any event, you are commanded—the coast road to Mhorvyn, without diversions."

"I'd not," I said carefully, "argue the wisdom of my College. So be it, then."

"I'm glad," he returned me, "that we reach agreement."

I nodded again. I wondered fleetingly if he saw through me; if his talent allowed him to perceive what I hid. I decided not—I thought that were it so, he should have ordered me seized and imprisoned. I thought that this was such a man as would order a pogrom did he learn what I had seen. I stood in stolid silence.

Chrystof stirred himself then, as if he noticed for the first time that I stood dripping on his carpet. "You're wet," he said.

"The fog," I replied.

He turned slowly to the window, the lines creasing his face etched deeper as he frowned. "Ah, yes. It's foggy. Nevyn, do you see him given a room?"

The sorcerer nodded and reached to a plaited cord hanging by the hearth. He tugged it. I suppose that somewhere a bell rang. I thought that Nevyn was the power in this keep. Chrystof said, "A room, and a hot tub. Tonight you'll entertain us, eh, Storyman?"

"As is my calling," I agreed.

There came a soft tapping on the door then, and when Nevyn bade the caller enter, a Changed servant came in. He was of canine stock, blunt featured, with a pug nose and loose jowls. He bowed, his eyes downcast as he murmured, "Masters?"

Nevyn issued curt instructions, and the Changed nodded deferentially, not raising his eyes as he stood back to let me pass. I gathered up my saddlebags and my staff and quit the chamber. In the corridor outside, the Changed asked if he might carry my bags. I thanked him and told him no, at which he seemed disconcerted.

"I'm well used to fending for myself," I told him, "and not much to having folk fetch and carry for me."

At that he gave me a swift sidelong glance, and I saw his eyes for the first time. They were mournful as a hound's, and in them I thought I discerned both surprise and curiosity. He said, "As you will, master."

"I'm Daviot, a Storyman," I said. "How are you called?"

"Thom, master," he returned me.

His voice was soft and had in it the same quality of submission as his eyes. I wondered how his kind fared in this keep. I said, "Well met, Thom. Shall you listen to me tonight?"

He looked at me again, and this time I was sure I saw surprise. "Listen to you, master?" He seemed not to understand.

"Yes," I said. "When I tell my tales in the hall."

"I'm a body-servant, master."

He touched the tunic he wore, which was of some coarse green cloth, edged with red. I had sometimes seen servants decked in such manner, but not often; it seemed to me an affectation. I assumed Chrystof—or perhaps Nevyn—elected to dress the servants thus. I asked him: "Do all the Changed of Trevyn wear such uniforms?"

He said, "Yes, master."

"To mark your duties?" I asked, and he gave me back another "Yes, master."

I smiled, seeking to put him at his ease; and failed. He was, I thought, taciturn as Bors, though whether that was a natural trait or an imposition of this keep, I could not tell. I was, however, aware that my questions made him uneasy, and so I curbed them, contenting myself with following him to the chamber assigned me.

That was small and devoid of decoration. A single window showed the fog gray outside, filling the room with wan and miserable light. There was a narrow bed and a chest, a washstand and a lantern suspended from the ceiling, nothing more. It was chill and slightly damp: I wondered if this was the usual hospitality of Trevyn Keep, or some insulting punishment dreamed up by Nevyn. I thought I should not remain here long.

"Do you wait awhile, master, and I'll fetch a brazier," Thom said. "Or shall I bring you to the baths?"

I was quite rank and so opted for the latter. I was surprised when I climbed into the tub to see Thom strip off his tunic. "What are you doing?" I asked him.

He said, "Master?" as if quite taken aback by my question.

I said, "Why are you undressing?"

"To bathe you, master."

This I had never encountered. Even in the most sybaritic of keeps, men bathed themselves. I waved him back, succeeding in splashing hot water over the floor. "That," I declared, "is not my custom."

"Master?" He seemed utterly confused.

I said, "Thom, I've not been bathed since I was a child. I'm grown now and quite capable of tending myself."

He pursed his lips, his hands fidgeting awkwardly with his tunic. His chest was broad and very hairy. It seemed to me both amusing and obscene that so muscular a fellow should bathe another, but he was clearly accustomed to such service and seemed not to know how he should react to my refusal. I had no wish to upset him nor to lead him into trouble, but neither was I prepared to let him bathe me.

I tried to ease his quandary. I said, "Thom, do you find a brazier to warm my room, and see a change of clothes set out, that shall be ample service. This"—I gestured with the soap I held—"I'd sooner manage by myself."

He said, "Yes, master; as you command. I'll return immediately I'm done."

I said, "I'm a Rememberer, Thom—I can find my own way back."

Even so, for a moment or two he stood with tunic in hand, staring at me. It was the first time he had looked me directly in the eyes. I smiled and nodded, and watched as he dressed, then quit the chamber. I sat a moment, frowning as I pondered the oddities of this strange keep. Then I succumbed to the luxury of hot water and sank into the tub until only my face remained above the surface.

My room was warmer when I returned. Thom had set a brazier below the window and lit the lantern. Clean clothes were laid neatly on the bed, and the Changed sat on the chest, industriously polishing the metal trappings of my staff. It had not shone so since first I got it, and when I tugged off my boots—Thom insisting on helping me—he set to imparting the same luster to the worn leather. He had brought in a small table, on it a pewter jug that gave off an enticing odor of spiced wine and a single cup. He filled it, and I drank as he polished.

"Do you find another cup and join me?" I asked.

"Master?"

He looked up from his work, meeting my gaze for the second time. I gestured with the cup. "Take wine with me."

"Master!" This time it was not a question but a startled refusal. His mournful eyes were shocked.

My own widened. I asked him, "Is it forbidden, then? May I not invite you to join me?"

He said, "I'm Changed, master."

I said, "I know that, Thom," and he nodded as if a point were made, and returned to his polishing. Then halted again as I said, "But still I ask you."

He licked his lips, eyes flickering a moment from side to side, as if he thought we might be observed or overheard. He reminded me more than ever of a dog—such as has the misfortune to find an unkind master and spend its life in anticipation of beatings. Very softly, he said, "Truemen and Changed do not drink together in Trevyn Keep, master."

He was clearly so nervous now that I did not repeat my invitation. Instead, I told him, "It is not so in Durbrecht, Thom," which was not entirely true, but his ministrations reminded me of Urt, and I sought to establish some rapport between us.

He made a small gesture and said, "We are not in Durbrecht, master, but in Trevyn Keep."

"Alone in this room," I said. "Who should know?"

I saw his lips shape the name *Nevyn*, but he made no sound, only bent more industriously to his task. I thought the sorcerer a malign influence, that he instilled such fear in the Changed, but I sought to hide the anger I felt. I waited awhile, then asked him, "Is there so little commerce betwixt Truemen and Changed here?"

"We are servants, master," he replied. "It is not our place to drink with Truemen."

So meek was his tone, so redolent of submission, I found my ire stoked. I thought of the rude welcome I had received, and the orders so casually issued, the insult Nevyn had delivered me. I set my cup aside and bent closer to the kneeling Changed.

"Your place?" I demanded, mild as I was able. "This keep should fall were it not supported by your kind. Who'd polish their boots, eh? Who'd cook their food, or tend their horses? I say you're good enough to drink with me, and does Nevyn gainsay me, he's a fool. I've known Changed I'd far sooner share a cup with than many a Trueman. Have you no feelings, man?"

Almost, I said *pride*. In my sudden anger I was not aware I named Thom a man. I was, however, aware that my vehemence frightened him, for he lurched back, sprawling on the floor, from where he stared at me, much as a Trueman might stare at a rabid beast. I made a placatory gesture and beckoned him closer. He ignored it, easing away from me, as if afraid I should impart some contagion.

I sighed and said more gently, "Thom, in Durbrecht I named a Changed my friend; and he, me. I was proud he did. I think there is little difference between us, save what's imposed by such as Nevyn, and I see no reason why you should not take a cup of wine with me, save you *choose* not."

His eyes were very wide and his lips were drawn back from his teeth in atavistic memory of his ancestry. As suddenly as my anger had arisen, so did the realization that if he reported this outburst to Nevyn, I must be surely marked a dissident, again branded a rebel. Was I watched now, his report would damn me. I feared I had gone too far, revealed my feelings too openly. I shook my head and fell silent.

I saw Thom's lips close slowly over his yellow teeth, then move. I thought it some expression of fear or outrage, but then a sound emerged, faint: a name.

He whispered, "Urt."

I was amazed. I said, "You know Urt?"

Thom shook his head. I thought to press him; thought better of it. I waited as he gathered himself, no longer crouching defensively but squatting as he had done before. Absently, he reached out to find the boot he had dropped. No less absently, he began to polish again. I suspected he took refuge in familiar action. I waited: there was a mystery here I thought should be lost did I pursue it too eagerly.

Finally, his eyes intent on the boot, he murmured, "Urt's Friend. We speak of you, master."

"Urt called me Daviot," I said. And for Thom's sake added, "When we were alone."

The Changed nodded, and I saw his lips shape my name. Gently, I asked him, "How have you heard of me, Thom?"

He hesitated, glancing up, then down again. I thought he debated the wisdom of confiding in me. I curbed my impatience. It seemed a long time before he said, "We . . . speak, Master . . . *Daviot.*"

"How?" I asked.

I wondered if I stumbled on a thing unknown to other Truemen. That the Changed of Durbrecht communicated with one another, that I had long known. But that this servant of a keep on Kellambek's west coast should know of Urt, know of me—that was a startling revelation. I did not believe the College of the Mnemonikos was aware of this. If so, it was a well-kept secret. Were the sorcerers? Were they aware, then perhaps my feeling of being watched was explained. I had inquired openly of the wild Changed, of Ur-Dharbek, and my sympathies were known in Durbrecht. Perhaps that was the reason I was commanded to proceed directly from keep to keep, that the sorcerers might observe me, eavesdroppers to my possible sedition.

Thom shrugged and polished, and when he spoke again, it was with lowered eyes and a voice so soft I must bend close to hear him. "Oarsmen come down the coast, Master . . . Daviot. . . . There are servants in the taverns, porters. . . . Merchants employ us. They speak . . . we hear . . . sometimes."

He shrugged again and fell silent. I saw that he was very frightened. I prompted him gently: "I'll not betray you, Thom. What you tell me shall be our secret—you've my word on that."

He looked at me again. It was the look a whipped dog gives when offered some kindness: gratitude and fear mingled. He said, "Word came of Urt and you." Then he smiled, a wary, tentative expression. "Urt's Friend, you are named."

I returned his smile. I felt proud of that appellation. "We *were* friends," I said. And then, "What word of Urt?"

"None . . . Daviot." I thought he savored the saying of my name; nervously, like indulgence in forbidden fruit. "Not since he was sent to the Slammerkin."

A hope faded at that, though its flame was not entirely dimmed. I recognized it was wildest optimism to think I'd find news of Urt so far south, but what I had found opened wide vistas of possibility. It seemed that that hidden society I had perceived in Durbrecht must extend throughout Dharbek. Stretched thin by distance, yes, but nonetheless there—a network of the Changed, unseen, passing word of their kind wherever Changed met Changed, their presence, their unquestioning servitude, so familiar to most Truemen it was taken for granted. I was disappointed that Thom could tell me no more of Urt; I was wildly excited by what I learned.

"Daviot?" I heard him ask. "You'll say nothing of this?"

"You've my word," I promised. "Should it earn you punishment?"

"Likely." He ducked his head. "The commur-magus has little liking for us."

"And Nevyn's the power here?" I asked.

"Yes," he told me. "Lord Chrystof's no blood-heir; the commur-mage is named his successor."

I grunted. It explained Nevyn's presumption. I thought he should make an unkind master. "He shall have nothing from me," I said.

Thom said, "Thank you."

He set my boots aside—they gleamed bright as my staff—and rose to his feet. For an instant I debated the wisdom of questioning him about the Changed I had seen aiding the Sky Lords. I decided against such risk: did he know aught of that, it was unlikely he would reveal it to me, for all I was named a friend. Did he not, then I should put my freedom in jeopardy, perhaps my life. I saw then what subterfuge and deceit bring—inevitable mistrust. It crossed my mind (a fleeting, guilty thought) that Thom might be some spy of Nevyn's, sent to lure me into confession. I held my secret to myself. Still, he had revealed things I had not known: I took a small chance, hoping to enlarge my gains.

"Might word be gotten to Urt?" I asked.

"Perhaps," Thom allowed. "It would be difficult."

"Were it possible," I said, "I'd have him know I wander Kellambek. I'd have him know he's still my friend; that I hope we shall meet again, someday."

Thom nodded thoughtfully. "Can I pass word," he said, "I shall. . . . There might be a boat."

"He was sent to Karysvar," I said, "on the Slammerkin."

Thom said, "Yes."

I was not sure whether he confirmed my words or his own prior knowledge. I went on: "He might have gone into Ur-Dharbek, to the wild Changed."

Thom said, "Perhaps," and his face became masked. "Then he'll not get word."

I had gone too far. The features of the Changed are rooted deep enough in their animal ancestors that they are difficult to read; at the same time, they are sufficiently removed from their forebears that their bodies no longer display the clear reactions of beasts. Even so, I had conversed with them enough I saw Thom was perturbed. His reaction was not dissimilar to that of the sorcerers I had questioned on the same subject. I recognized that he would say no more than they, and that did I press him I should lose his confidence altogether. So I shrugged and said, "No, I suppose not. Still, I hope he shall get my message."

"Yes."

Thom seemed torn now between the formal "master" and the use of my given name. I was pleased he chose the latter but knew I had made him uncomfortable when he inquired what further service I might require or if he should bring me to the dining hall.

I was hungry: he guided me to the hall.

Neither the aeldor nor the commur-magus was present, which troubled me not at all, and I was given a cheerful welcome by the warband. The warriors were led by a jennym whose name was Darus, and from him I learned that Nevyn had been some dozen years in the keep and was not popular. I commented on the servants' tunics— those tending us in the hall wore gray bordered with silver—and Darus advised me that was Nevyn's doing. He spoke somewhat of the Sky Lords, but save for sightings of a few of the little airboats (Trevyn Keep had encountered no landings), I garnered no more information than I already had. War-engines were constructed, but it was Darus's belief the west coast was safe. I thought him dangerously wrong but said nothing, suspecting that did I voice my opinion that in a year or two the Sky Lords would likely mount their Great Coming, I should earn Nevyn's further displeasure and my sojourn in Trevyn Keep be even less pleasant. Instead, the fog yet lingering, I passed the afternoon telling stories to a hall of bored soldiers. I noticed, as I spoke, that the Changed disappeared.

That evening I saw Chrystof escorted into the hall by two burly Changed in the uniforms of body-servants. He seemed not quite aware of his surroundings, as if he were more accustomed to his private chambers, and he sat at the high table with only Nevyn for company. I was not invited to join them, but Nevyn called in a commanding tone that I should demonstrate my talent once the tables were cleared and the servants gone. The warband seemed not to find this unusual but drew their own ale without comment. I was pleased to see that a handful of Changed, Thom amongst them, gave furtive ear from shadowy doorways. I thought this an unhappy keep, and (a small and, I admit, spiteful revenge) that I should mention it on my return to Durbrecht.

That night I found my brazier renewed and a covered jug of wine placed on the table. Thom had set a warming pan in my bed, and my riding gear had been laundered. I thanked him for such services, but when I sought to draw him again into conversation he grew reticent. I feared I had startled him too much with speaking of the wild Changed and made no more effort to press him.

That night I dreamed once more of the wood beyond Cambar Keep. It was the first time the dream had come in weeks, and as I groped my way amongst the mist-shrouded oaks, I thought I saw the faint shapes of tiny airboats through the gray canopy overhead. I heard again that strange beating sound, as of massive wings, but whatever made it did not disturb the brume, and I could only wander, struggling to discern from which direction came the voices, Rwyan's and Urt's, that called to me even as I hid from the spectral shapes of the warriors fighting there.

I woke to dim, gray light, thinking for a moment that I dreamed still. Then Thom knocked, and I realized the fog remained outside, a shroud spread miserable over the hold. It seemed fitting.

I greeted the Changed and refused his ministrations, electing to dress myself as he found small tasks to occupy his hands. I broke my fast and went to visit my mare. She appeared content enough to rest in her stall, and I asked that Thom be my guide into the town. He must get permission for that, which Nevyn granted with some reluctance. I was reassured by the sorcerer's disinclination—it suggested Thom was not his spy—and had Thom bring me to a tavern, the plazas being emptied of traffic by the weather.

I bought the Changed a tankard, but he would not sit with me, going instead to an area where others of his kind gathered. At least they heard me. I passed the day there, gleaning what news I could (which was little enough) and had no more need to buy my own ale, for as word passed around that the Sword entertained a Storyman, the inn filled up and the landlord refused my coin.

I was three days in Trevyn Keep before the fog lifted and I was able to use Nevyn's own admonitions to continue on my way. I spoke as much as I was able with Thom, but he was more guarded for all I avoided any mention of Ur-Dharbek or the wild Changed. He spoke freely enough of his own life and the lives of his fellow servants, but not at all of those matters that most intrigued me. Still, I felt I had collected a further piece to the puzzle I saw was my homeland. I hoped to gather more along the way to Mhorvyn. I hoped one day I should find more answers than questions.

I've few fond memories of that place, and I was not at all sorry to leave it; only for the Changed who must toil under Nevyn's command. I was happy to see the fog clear and had my mare saddled immediately I had taken my morning meal. I bade farewell to Thom and to Darus and his warband. The aeldor Chrystof, I was informed, had taken to his bed, and the only good-bye I got from Nevyn was a curt reminder that I should not deviate from the coast road.

That, I followed southward, the sea never far away, so that I halted in fishing villages as often as in the keeps. I obeyed the orders sent from Durbrecht, never remaining longer than a few days in any one place. Nowhere did I encounter another like Trevyn Keep; everywhere I saw with clearer eyes that the Changed, even when treated kindly, went unseen, faceless servitors to we Truemen.

I rode through the autumn into winter, which was milder on this west coast than those I had known in Whitefish village or Durbrecht, and a day before the dawning of Bannas Eve I came to Mhorvyn. It was the climax of my year's wandering; it was also, I found, a crossroads.

Mhorvyn was the largest hold I had seen since departing Durbrecht, and unlike any other. It sat upon a rocky island that hung like a teardrop from the southernmost tip of Dharbek, connected to the land by a causeway that at high tide was hidden beneath the waves of the southern ocean. Landward, the bailiwick was given over to farms and orchards, and a village of fisherfolk spread along the shore facing the hold. The day I came there was squally, a biting wind driving rafts of gray cloud in off the sea, a wintry sun snatching brief glances through the scud. I halted on the shore, studying the road that ran, it seemed, across the waves. The tide was on the ebb, and water spilled from the stone, leaving behind pools and pungent strings of seaweed. My mare argued my decision to proceed, and it was a while before I could urge her out onto the causeway. It was a strange sensation to ride that path, the sea stretching out sullen and wind-tossed to either side, salt spray lashing us. It seemed almost that my mare trod the waves, like some seahorse out of legend. She liked it not at all, and I must admit I was not sorry to reach the sturdy barbican that granted ingress to the island. Walls of blue-black stone extended from the little tower around the whole of Mhorvyn; within, the buildings of the town seemed to tumble down at random over the flanks of a low hill surmounted by the great tower of the keep. I was brought there by a cheerful soldier, who led me at a brisk pace through a maze of narrow streets decorated in readiness for Bannas Eve. From him I learned that word had been sent ahead to expect me, and that all Mhorvyn looked forward to enjoying my tales as part of the festival celebrations.

I got no less a cheerful welcome in the keep itself. Yanydd was the aeldor here, a sturdy man in his middle years, handsome and thick-bearded, and he filled me a tankard himself as he introduced me to his family and the folk of the keep. His wife was a woman of startling beauty whose name was Dorae; she seemed too young to have borne three sons. They were named Rhys, Maric, and Ador, the eldest about my own age, his brothers younger by a year apiece. The commur-mage was older, her hair gray and her face, for all it was not unhandsome, lined and weatherbeaten. Her name was Laena.

It was close on dusk, and the hall was redolent of roasting meat and ale. Cypress boughs and sprigs of mistletoe hung about the walls, and on every door was pinned a dried oak leaf and a token of the God. The keep had a festive air that combined with the pleasant manner of Yanydd and his kin to put me at my ease. I saw that the Changed of this place wore no symbols of their station as in Trevyn and appeared comfortable with their lot. I thought this should be a better hold than many in which to pass the midwinter festival.

Courteously, Yanydd invited me to bathe and find my chamber before submitting myself to the inevitable barrage of questions and the dispensation of my duty as a Storyman. I accepted gladly, and a Changed servant was directed to escort me to my quarters.

They were, I found, luxurious. The bed was wide, the stone floor covered with a gaily patterned carpet, and coals glowed in a small hearth, on which a jug of mulled ale steamed. There was a garderobe, and a tall window afforded a view over the rooftops of the town to the sea beyond. I tossed my staff and saddlebags on the bed and flung open the window, inhaling the salt-scented air as I studied the busy streets below.

The Changed—he was feline-bred and named, I had learned, Lan —waited patiently. I contemplated interrogation but decided it was the wiser course to approach gently, cautiously, lest I scare him as I had done Thom. So I closed the window and gave him a smile.

"Shall you celebrate this Bannas Eve, Lan?" I asked.

Unlike Thom, he met my gaze and answered my smile with his own. "Yes, master," he said. "Lord Yanydd has all his people celebrate."

I said, "My name is Daviot, Lan."

He answered me, "Yes, I know that," and hesitated a moment before adding, "Daviot."

That both pleased and surprised me, but I had no wish to frighten him off and so said, "I'd not earn you trouble, Lan. Is it your custom to call me 'master,' then so be it; but I'd be happy with 'Daviot.'"

He nodded, his expression sage, and after a moment said, "Perhaps in private, Daviot. But in the halls, better I title you 'Master Daviot.'"

I deemed him quicker of wit than Thom and far less cowed, which reinforced my impression that this was a friendly keep. I said, "As you wish."

He smiled again at that and said, "Yes," gravely, as if he took the suggestion under consideration and reached his own conclusions.

It came to me that he did; and with that realization another thought: that he accepted what must surely be odd behavior in a Trueman with unusual alacrity. I asked him, "Have you heard of me, Lan?"

"All Mhorvyn knows a Storyman was due this Bannas Eve," he said, which was prevarication.

"That's not what I meant." I said it gently, smiling lest he think it a reprimand. "And I suspect you know that."

"How should I?" he asked.

His rounded face was bland, his tone subtle, so that the question sounded entirely innocent; or cautious. I saw that he was no simpleton but quick of wit and careful. Also, I sensed in him an air of confidence. I chose to show somewhat of what I knew. I said, "I thought perhaps word had come. In Trevyn Keep I learned you name me Urt's Friend."

He said, "Yes," and his smile grew wider. It was as though a mask dropped from his face. "Word came; and so you are known to us."

I nodded, holding my smile in place even as I marveled at what I heard—word came ahead of me, as if the Changed communicated near as efficiently as the sorcerers. I felt a pang of guilt (small and soon enough consumed beneath my wonder) that I succeeded so well in combining deceit with honesty, revealing my own knowledge that I might pick more from his responses. Casually, I asked him how.

"There was a boat," he said. "The crew had word of you."

Of course: the craft that plied the coasts of Dharbek were manned by Changed, the caravans of the merchants were manned by Changed, and all moved from hold to hold, from town to town. They were the messengers. In the halls and holds Changed servants heard their masters speak and passed on word of what they heard to others —in the taverns, the markets, the docks: the places those who traveled visited. It was an effective network. I wondered if Lan knew of his kind dealing with the Sky Lords; and I knew that if I broached that topic, he would admit no more.

I asked him, "Do any other Truemen know of this?"

"I do not think so." He shook his head. "To most we've no faces, nor eyes or ears. You are unusual, Daviot. You *see* us."

I shrugged. It seemed to me no great thing to recognize the Changed as beings with feelings, identities, to perceive them as individuals, and yet I knew I was odd in this. I was more surprised that Lan should so readily confide in me. Also, I admit to feeling flattered.

I said, "Nor shall they know of it from me."

And was again surprised when he gave me back a calm, "Why not?"

I had no ready answer, save that I sought to protect the innocent.

"Because," I said, and halted. It was near impossible to express in words my confused emotions. "Because . . . Urt was my friend, and he was punished for my transgression."

"Your mage," Lan said, and nodded as if that were justification enough.

Now I gaped. He knew of Rwyan? Was all my life open to the Changed? This cat-bred servant appeared to know more about me than my own kind. I closed my mouth and asked him needlessly, "You know of that?"

"From the Changed of Durbrecht," he replied. "When Urt was sent north, word spread of why—and of you."

I swallowed, staring at him, not knowing what to say.

He looked me in the eyes then, directly, and in his I saw an absolute candor. "These matters are best kept secret," he said. "For your sake as much as mine. Lord Yanydd—Laena—are kind enough, but I think if they knew . . . they would feel it their duty to alert Kherbryn, Durbrecht. I think that if the Lord Protector or the sorcerers knew, there would be . . . measures . . . taken."

All I could think of to say was "Yes."

"And did they," Lan went on, "then you would be punished with us. I suspect Truemen would deem you a turncoat."

I nodded, dumbstruck. Marvel piled on marvel here. This was no ordinary servitor, neither any ordinary Changed. There was suddenly an authority to him, a sophistication I had seen only once before—in Urt. I thought that if anyone could satisfy my curiosity about Ur-Dharbek and the wild Changed, it must be Lan. I wondered if I dared ask him.

I said, "Who are you, Lan? *What* are you?"

"A servant." He shrugged lazily. "A Changed man descended from cats. A nobody."

I said, "I do not think so."

"Here"—he waved a hand, indicating the chamber and the keep together—"I am only that. What else should I be?"

I said, "I don't know."

He said, "Also, I am a friend. Perhaps someday that shall count for something."

I said, "This day. You place great trust in me."

"And you in me," he said. "Is it misplaced?"

I shook my head and said slowly, "No. Though I've myriad questions I'd ask you."

"Perhaps I shall answer them," he returned. "But now, do I see to your bath ere folk wonder at your absence?"

I saw the mask descend upon his face again, his expression become one of patient servility. I thought this was the only face most Truemen saw. I wondered if behind it, hidden deep in his eyes, I saw amusement. Abruptly, I wondered if Lan played with me; if perhaps he gave me back my own game, leading me into revelation, even as I thought to draw him out. I gave him a quizzical look, but he offered me nothing more, and I nodded. When the door closed on him, I stood for long moments, staring at the wood.

I had no further opportunity to speak with Lan that day, for when he returned with a tub he was accompanied by two sturdy Changed of taurine stock and played the part of courteous, efficient servant, seeing to the filling of the tub and leaving me alone with a minimum of dutiful words. I bathed and, dressed in my finest clothes (which were not very fine at all), made my way to the hall.

Yanydd called me to the high table, seating me between himself and Laena, and as the meal was served I was occupied, as the aeldor had promised, with a barrage of questions.

We spoke of the Sky Lords and the likelihood of the Great Coming, of the war-engines and the mood of the common folk, and of what I had seen during my year of travel. Of that topic I gave a censored version, wondering the while if Laena somehow sensed my dissembling. Her eyes never left my face as I spoke, but her voice was soft when she voiced an opinion or a question, and I thought she did not see through me.

In return I got back what news they had. The little airboats (Yanydd and Laena believed them scouts for impending invasion) had been seen less frequently of late, as if the onset of winter curbed their intrusions; or, the aeldor declared in somber tone, they had gleaned all the information they required. He had filled his storehouses against the possibility of siege and made preparation as best he could to find shelter for the fishermen and farmers of his holding.

"The Sky Lords have the advantage there," he murmured, "the God curse them. We cannot be all the time on alert, unsure what we face or when it shall come. The folk of this west coast are not so used to the attacks as the rest of Dharbek, and I'd not see panic spread with constant reminders to go wary. So my people forget—the God knows, they've lives to live and work to do without one eye all the time on the sky."

"The Sentinels shall send warning," Laena promised.

Yanydd said, "Yes. But do the Sky Lords refine these new-found powers, how much warning?"

At that, the commur-mage could only sigh and shrug and tell him, "As much they may."

"Which may not be enough" was his glum response. "Do they now own full command of the elementals, perhaps they've the strength to overcome the Sentinels and be on us apace. And do they bring that strength against Kherbryn and Durbrecht, what then? Chaos, with every keep in the land fighting alone!"

"To overcome the Sentinels, even with their new powers, that shall be hard," Laena returned. "No less to take Kherbryn or Durbrecht."

"I pray it be so," said Yanydd, and barked a laugh I thought was not much humorous. "I pray all our fears prove unfounded and they do not come at all."

"We've faced them before and given them to the Pale Friend," said Rhys fiercely. "We'll do the same, do they dare invasion."

His father nodded, smiling at the young man's bravado. "I think that are our fears proven true, it shall be a Coming such as we've not known before," he said, and turned to me. "Daviot, you've faced Kho'rabi—how think you?"

"I know them for terrible warriors," I said, and found myself again the center of attention as Rhys and his brothers pressed me for a detailed account.

They gazed rapt as I spoke, drinking in my every word. Rhys, as

I have told you, was about my age, Maric and Ador not much younger, but as I spoke, I felt older. I thought I had seen and done things of which these young men were entirely innocent, and that those experiences had taught me that the glory of battle is in the dreaming of it, not the doing. I wondered if I was the only man in Dharbek who thought at all of peace.

I was grateful to Dorae for her intervention. Had she not spoken up, I should likely have found myself commandeered by her sons. She it was reminded us that Bannas Eve approached, and with it the seasonal celebrations—a time for joy, not tales of bloody battle. She suggested I be allowed to regale the hall with more fitting stories.

Thus I was provided a table for a platform, in the center of the hall, with all the warband and all the keep's folk, both Truemen and Changed, gathered around as I told the tale of Gwynnyd and the Ghost.

I think I told it well. Certainly, when I was done there was a moment's hush, and I saw several glance around nervously, toward the shadows, before they applauded me. I bowed and drank ale to wet my tongue, then launched into the story of the aeldor Kyrd and the Wise Woman of Tyrvan.

By the time that tale was spun the hour was late, and Yanydd reminded the hall we must rise early on the morrow, for the Bannas Eve services. There was a shout of disagreement from Rhys and his brothers, but Dorae bade them be silent, and they concurred, albeit with obvious reluctance, and I was allowed to climb down from my dais.

As we prepared to leave the hall, Laena took my arm. "We must speak," she said. "Tomorrow or the next day."

I said, "Yes, as you wish," hoping she did not notice the alarm her words roused in me.

Likely she sought no more than a fuller accounting of my travels, that she might send back to Durbrecht word of all I had seen, of my thoughts concerning the mood of the land. But I could not help but wonder if something more lay beneath that simple statement.

I had, however, no chance to investigate, for servants came with torches to bring us to our rooms. Lan was my escort, and I followed him in troubled silence. I must hope Laena suspected nothing; and pray I did the right thing in holding secret all I knew of the Changed and that mysterious transaction I had witnessed.

I was startled from my musings by Lan's voice.

"Is aught amiss, Daviot?"

I saw that we had come to my door. It stood open, Lan waiting with his torch. I forced a smile and beckoned him in.

"What troubles you?" he asked.

His voice was entirely solicitous, and for an instant I was tempted to tell him all. I thought that had he been Urt, I should; that Urt would have counsel for me, perhaps answers. But I was not yet ready to trust Lan quite so far. I saw that the wine jug still stood upon the hearth, and that there were two cups. I filled them both and passed him one.

"Laena would speak with me," I said, and knew my tone was nervous.

Lan waved a casual hand. "Laena does not judge you," he said. "I think she seeks only that report all Storymen must make. There's no magic in that, save in her sending word to Durbrecht."

"Do the sorcerers watch me?" I asked. I realized I accepted without question that he should have such knowledge. "I've wondered about that."

He paused an instant before replying. "They pay you special attention, Daviot. That should not surprise you—that you befriended Urt so openly; your affair with Rwyan; the due you give we Changed; things you said in Durbrecht—such behavior is unusual enough you are noticed by the rulers of this land."

My face must have expressed alarm at that, for Lan chuckled and added, "I think you've not too much to fear. Save you give them greater cause for concern, I think you shall be safe."

He appeared entirely at ease; I was not. I heard the shutters rattle over my window, buffeted by a wind that seemed, for all the chamber was warm, to pierce my bones. Almost, I blurted out that I concealed secrets greater than those entrusted me by this strange Changed. But I did not—I did not yet quite trust Lan that far. Instead, I asked him, "Have you any word of Urt or Rwyan?"

"Of Rwyan, none," he said. "There are no Changed on the Sentinels, and so I can tell you only that she was brought safely to the islands. Of Urt? Urt went to Karysvar, where he is, as best I know, a servant to a merchant named Connys. News from so far north is hard to get."

"You seem," I said, "to get news aplenty."

Lan nodded, again as if this were entirely normal. "This hold is famed for its orchards and its tobacco," he explained. "Craft from both coasts come to Mhorvyn, and traders by land. All bring news, but seldom from farther north than the Treppanek."

It was more than I had hoped for. Rwyan was resident on the second Sentinel, about which I could do nothing, but if Urt was still in Karysvar . . . Perhaps someday I might go there and find this merchant. I smiled at the thought.

"You'd find them again?" Lan asked.

"Could I." I ducked my head and sighed. "But I doubt I shall. At least, not Rwyan. I think she must be forever lost to me. But perhaps someday I might meet Urt again. I should like that."

"If he's still there."

Lan's voice was soft, the sentence less statement than unguarded thought. I looked up, catching his eye—and saw the mask descend even as I said, "Where should he go?"

The feline Changed shrugged, not replying.

I said, "Across the Slammerkin, Lan? To join the wild Changed?"

Again, he shrugged. "Some do."

There was hesitation in his voice. I thought he regretted that slip. I suspected he knew more than he revealed. I thought he had revealed so much, what he hid must surely be of great import. I thought we both, for all we exposed ourselves, held back secrets still. I knew mine: I wondered what Lan's were. I said, "I know nothing of the wild Changed; nothing of Ur-Dharbek. It seems none do, save perhaps the sorcerers. And they're closemouthed on that subject."

"Nor I," he said. "Save Truemen gave Ur-Dharbek to the Changed that the dragons leave them be. Our lot, it seems."

I said, "I'd go there. I'd know what's there."

The mask remained a veil over his true feelings, but I thought I discerned amazement as he looked at me. "Think you a Trueman should find a welcome there?" he asked. "Be there any to welcome him."

"Have the dragons eaten them, then?" I returned.

He laughed aloud at that. "Dragons, Daviot? Surely the dragons are all dead; the stuff of your stories now, and no more."

"Be that so," I said, "then perhaps the wild Changed prosper."

"Perhaps." He seemed to me to hold his expression bland. "I'd not know."

I had taken too many steps along this path to turn back: I pressed on. "Are the dragons gone, what reason for the Border Cities?" I asked, deliberately making my tone one of idle curiosity.

"What reason for any city?" Lan echoed an answer I had got before. "They trade along the Slammerkin just as they do along the Treppanek. They exist for that and no more reason, likely."

I saw he would give me no more. It was the same bland claim of ignorance I got each time I broached this subject. Perhaps he really knew nothing; I suspected he hid knowledge. I was about to speak again when he flung back his arms, yawning noisily, as if weariness suddenly took him.

"Forgive me." He became once more the humble servant. "I think perhaps I should find my bed, and you yours. The services of Bannas Eve start early, and I'd get some sleep ere I commence my duties."

I nodded, aware our conversation was ended. Save I commanded him—which would surely undo his confidence in me; and was not, anyway, in my nature—I should have no more from Lan this night.

"Yes." I smiled as he rose, collecting my cup and the jug from the hearth. "But I hope we shall speak again."

"I think we shall," he said. "Goodnight, Daviot."

I said, "Goodnight, Lan. And my thanks."

"For what?" He paused at the door. His face was composed in an unreadable expression.

"For all you've told me," I said. "For . . . trust."

"Trust is like a sword, Daviot; it cuts both ways."

Before I had opportunity to comment, he was gone, the door closed quietly behind him.

We Truemen went afoot into the town the next day, leaving the Changed behind to prepare for the feasting as Yanydd led us in procession around the walls of Mhorvyn. The sleet had blown away inland, but the wind still blew harsh, sending waves in crashing progression against the rocky shoreline. A few brave gulls fought the gusting, but they were the only interruption of an otherwise featureless and sullen sky. I hugged my cloak close, the wind ofttimes so strong, I must lean against it. Laena clutched my arm as if she feared it might blow her away, her lined face creased deeper as she studied the heavens.

In the lee of a building, where the blast could no longer steal the words unheard, she said, "Bannas Eve is not often so unkind. Last year the sun shone."

There was a note of trepidation in her voice that prompted me to wonder. "Where I was born," I said, "the weather is much like this on Bannas Eve."

We passed beyond shelter then, and she fell silent, gripping my arm again, her face hidden in the hood of her cloak. I looked at the sky. It seemed not at all out of the ordinary to me: in Whitefish village we'd name such weather squally and expect it, until Matran at the least. I wondered why it disturbed the commur-mage so. I did not know her well, and she gave an impression of taciturnity, but I sensed she was concerned. It might have been the cold or the wind, but her shoulders were braced rigid under her cloak, and the eyes she turned upon the sky were narrowed as if she sought something there.

"I doubt even the Sky Lords can master such a wind," I said.

It was a flippant comment. I did not believe she looked for sign of aerial attack, but her unease communicated and I looked to diffuse it with a joke. Her answer took me aback.

"Think you not?" she said.

I said, "Surely not! In winter? Besides, a wind like this must surely deny them grounding."

We came to another open space then, and she did not reply until we stood again protected. We had completed our circuit and now walked the winding streets, returning slowly in the direction of the keep. From either side folk waved cedar twigs or clusters of dried oak leaves, their shouts loud, so that I must put my face close to Laena's to hear her answer. Even then she kept her voice low.

"Not a grounding," she said. "Not a Coming, even. But I tell you, Daviot Storyman, that this weather is unseasonal."

I shrugged. I was yet heir to my father's weather lore, and I knew that what was customary was never graved in stone. I said, "Do you tell me this is the Sky Lords' doing?"

She gave me a wan smile then, one that spoke of doubt, of self and opinion. "They bind the elemental spirits to their command, no?"

She awaited a response, and so I ducked my head and gave her, "Yes. But as yet only to their little airboats, surely. The sorcerers I've encountered this past year seem largely of the belief they can do no more for a while. A twelvemonth, perhaps; perhaps longer, before they can bind those creatures to their great ships."

"And likely all those sorcerers are right," said Laena. "I do not speak of airboats, but of this weather."

Her voice was low and held not much expression, as if she spoke of a thing she had sooner not contemplated and was loath to say openly. That somehow lent her words a greater impact. I grunted, surprised (I seemed to spend much of my time in Mhorvyn surprised by one thing or another), and said, "You believe they control the weather now?"

She had pushed back the hood of her cloak, and so I saw the pursing of her lips, the doubt that shone clear in her eyes. "Not believe," she said. "Wonder, perhaps. I tell you—for years Mhorvyn has seen the sun shine on Bannas Eve. But now . . ." She shook her head and tilted it to indicate the sky.

I said, "Weather is no fixed thing, Laena. What's been for years can change."

She said, "Yes. But still I wonder. . . . Do they gain true control over the elementals, might they not bend the weather itself to their will?"

That was a thought I had not entertained; nor much cared to now. It was a terrifying prospect. It was somehow even worse than the belief that the Sky Lords commanded the elementals like carthorses. I heard my own voice grow dull with horror as I asked her, "Can that be? Is such a thing possible?"

"I know not," she said. "I know nothing of such magic, but I know they control the aerial spirits in ways I cannot comprehend. If they can do that—if they can harness the elementals to their vessels— might they not also harness the elements themselves?"

I thought of the churning sea surrounding this island hold, of such storms as could isolate the rock. I thought of the craft that plied the coasts, the Treppanek and the Slammerkin, all harbor-locked or sunk by raging waves and howling winds. I thought of warships toss- ing useless at anchor, of fishing craft idle on the beaches. I thought of harvests lost and orchards wasted. I looked to the sky and hoped that Laena's fears be all misplaced.

"Perhaps," she continued, and took my arm even though we walked sheltered. Her fingers pressed hard. "Only perhaps, Daviot. Perhaps such fears are groundless; perhaps I become a scaremonger in my dotage. I've put the thought to my College, and it's debated there. None other knows it, save Yanydd. I trust you shall hold silent, too. Were such a thought voiced abroad . . ."

"I'll hold it close," I said. Another secret to my hoard: they built apace. "None shall have this from me. But why do you tell me?"

At that she smiled more genuinely. "Are you not a Storyman?" she asked. "Are you Mnemonikos not the recipients of all our lore, of all our history? And be I right, then this is indeed historic. One at least of your talent should know."

I ducked my head, in confirmation and gratitude, both. I felt suddenly more confident. Did Laena so entrust me with her secret thoughts, then surely she could not suspect me of harboring my own.

We approached the keep now, and across the open space before its walls the wind howled with renewed ferocity. I saw the aeldor's banners whipped, snapping and crackling by the gusting, and thought of omens. What little smoke rose from the banked fires was lost against the dreary sky, nor were either stars or moon visible.

It was a relief to stand behind closed doors, even though the hall was chill and dim, without lanterns or blazing hearthfire. Changed servants came to take our cloaks; others stood expectant about the room, tapers and tinder boxes ready in their hands. Yanydd went to a clepsydra and tapped the glass, urging the last drops to fall. I think we all were pleased when he announced it sunset. The hall was filled then with the rasp of flint on steel, and myriad small flames moved like fireflies as the Changed set to lighting the lanterns, to building up the fire. The warband cheered as warmth and light drove off the chill, and then again as kegs of ale were broached.

Laena brought me to where the aeldor and his wife stood, conversing with the jennym of the warband. Callum was a man in his middle years, his hair and beard already gray, his face scarred and stern, save when he smiled, which was often. Now, it was entirely serious, and as I approached he nodded to Yanydd and marched briskly away.

"He goes to check the causeway," Yanydd explained.

Dorae said, "This weather . . ." and shook her head.

Yanydd and Laena exchanged a swift glance, and I saw the aeldor's eyes flicker in my direction, the subtle nod the commur-mage returned. He said, "Unusual, certainly. But likely it will blow itself out by dawn."

"I pray it does," his wife returned. "A storm on Bannas Eve bodes ill for the new year."

She had no notion of Laena's suspicion, I saw. Yanydd caught my eye and smiled gravely, as if we were conspirators together. I smiled back and said, "On the east coast, the winter is all storms," and our conversation turned to idle matters as servants came with trays of tidbits.

Soon after, the doors opened to admit Callum, windswept and damp, and mouthing curses concerning wind and wave and causeway.

A mug of ale cheered him, however, and before long he was inquiring after the impending feast. I thought that should be a while coming, but when Yanydd sent to the kitchens, he got back word that all was ready. It seemed the Changed had toiled through the day: those religious observances applying to we Truemen did not affect them, save to make their tasks the harder for want of light. Even so, Yanydd was kinder than most to his menials, for once the meal was served, they were dismissed to their own feasting, and we Truemen left to fend for ourselves.

The mantis gave a blessing, and we set to. I ate abundantly and drank my fill. My breeks were tight when I pushed back my chair and rose in answer to the shouted demands for a tale.

For Rhys and his brothers, I told of Damyd's Battle. A kithara was brought out for that, and a tambour, which made a fine accompaniment. Then, as all around men and women called for their own favorites, I told them of Cambar's oak wood, wondering how they might respond. I was gratified to hear them murmur solemn agreement that the wood was a fit monument to brave men. Still, I followed that with more traditional stories—of great battles and courageous warriors, of wise aeldors and Lords Protector. I felt welcomed here in Mhorvyn, but I knew that ere long I must speak with Laena, and she send report to Durbrecht; and that after I should be commanded on, to wander more or return. My first year as a Storyman was ended this night. I had no idea what the next should bring.

Bannas Eve became Lantaine: a new year was born. In
Yanydd's hall we hailed Lantaine's dawning as outside the
keep's stout walls the wind beat fiercer. The aeldor's proph-
ecy proved wrong: the storm did not blow itself out by dawn,
but rather grew more intense. Shutters vibrated under the onslaught;
tongues of winded flame flung sparks into the hall; word came the
island was cut off, the causeway drowned, no boats likely to put out in
such a tempest. When I ventured out, I saw the sky black with sullen
cloud and lightning dancing over the roiling sea. I had witnessed
storms as bad, or worse, as a child, but this—perhaps because of
Laena's glum augury—seemed to me different. I thought it should not
soon end.

Nor did it. It blew for seven days, and I began to think the
commur-mage correct in her belief, though I could scarce comprehend
how the Sky Lords might bend the weather itself to their will. It lent a
somber undercurrent to the seasonal festivities that, by common con-

sent, we elected to ignore. We worked the harder at revelry, for all it was no easy thing to smile and dismiss the ravaging of wind and wave as Lantaine duties were dispensed. Yanydd must, of course, go out amongst the people of his holding, and I had my Storyman's duty, which brought me out to the taverns and alehouses with my tales. On orders of the aeldor, Callum gave me an escort of four stout soldiers, who made themselves a barrier betwixt the wind and me as we struggled against the ferocious gusting. That alone was often strong enough to blow a man off his feet, but also there were roof tiles hurled like missiles down the streets, and shutters torn loose and flung like straws. I saw several folk injured; the keep's herbalist-chirurgeon was much in demand. In the harbor three boats were sunk, and for all that Lantaine the causeway lay under angry water.

I spoke of it to Lan. He knew already of Laena's belief (which knowledge no longer surprised me: I had soon enough come to accept that there was little the Changed did not know) but claimed ignorance of the storm's source.

"Be it the Sky Lords' doing," he said one evening as I prepared for the night's feasting, "then their magic must be wondrous powerful."

"And wondrous disruptive," I said. "Is all Dharbek assaulted like this, there can be no commerce."

"No" was all he gave me back.

"But neither can they attack," I said, and added a cautious, "surely. Such a gale must deny them grounding, no?"

"I'd think it so," he said. "Save they've such magicks as can deny the storm."

He seemed quite sanguine, as if neither storm nor source bothered him overmuch, and I could not decide if that was simple indifference or something else. I had no way to press him, however, save by open accusation, and that I avoided. Our relationship was built on mutual confidences but was not yet quite friendship. I felt he dealt with me honestly for the most part, and when I sensed reticence, I could not decide whether it stemmed from genuine ignorance or a refusal to tell me all he knew. I had sought to learn more of Ur-Dharbek and the wild Changed but with no better success than before: he continued to claim a lack of knowledge with a fixity I could only think of as dogged. Rather than jeopardize our rapport, I elected to leave that matter be. I had, anyway, other preoccupations.

Chief amongst them was my report to Laena, and that meeting I approached with some trepidation.

The gray-haired mage showed me only friendship throughout my sojourn in Mhorvyn, but still I hoarded such secrets as prompted me to anticipate that meeting with no great enthusiasm. As it was, Lan was again proven right, and the fears I created for myself were the worst I must face. It was the second day of Lantaine that she suggested we withdraw to her chambers, that I might tell her of my year. I agreed without demur (I had little option, and I felt I had sooner confront the affair than allow the maggot of fear to gnaw further) and so found myself ensconced in a comfortable room, settled in a deep-cushioned chair before a blazing fire. Laena took a seat opposite and offered me mulled wine. I thought perhaps it might contain some electuary to loosen my tongue and so, pleading a sufficiency already drunk and more to come, refused. Laena showed neither surprise nor disappointment and filled herself a cup. As she drank, I began to suspect myself of paranoia. Neither did she seek to employ her talent in any quarrying of my mind, but only asked that I tell her of my wanderings.

I spoke freely enough, holding back what I knew of the Changed and that mysterious encounter I had witnessed; in all other specifics I was honest. Laena heard me out, interrupting from time to time to ask that I repeat some observation or clarify some point. Occasionally she raised a hand to silence me and sat awhile with closed eyes, her lips moving without sound.

I asked her what she did, and she told me, "I've not your talent, Daviot, else I'd be Mnemonikos and not mage. I must employ my magic to commit all this to memory."

"Your magic will hold it all?" I asked.

"Long enough," she answered. "Not as you do, but until what you tell me is passed to Durbrecht. That I'll do once we're finished, and then it will fade and I'll recall no more than my own natural memory retains." She chuckled then and added: "That shall not be very much, nor for very long," which set me more at ease.

So I gave my report, and Laena dismissed me.

"It will take a while for this to reach Durbrecht," she advised me, "and then some days ere word comes back. I'll tell you as soon I may what orders your College has."

"I hope," I said, gesturing at the closed shutters, "that I'll be allowed to stay here until then."

Laena nodded, smiling a trifle wanly as she cocked an ear to the wind's howling. "I think there'll be no choice in that," she said. "Until this weather breaks at least."

I nodded and left her to her magic. She gave no sign that she suspected me of dissimulation, and whilst I could not entirely dismiss unease, I was somewhat relieved. I felt I was granted a reprieve, at least until Durbrecht returned word.

That took longer than was usual. I had anticipated a response within six or seven days, but none came in that time and I began once more to fret. Was my case such as occasioned lengthy deliberation? Or did this freakish weather somehow disrupt the channels of occult communication? I did not know, nor had I any wish to question Laena, for fear she wonder at my impatience. I had no one in whom I could entirely and honestly confide. Lan was the nearest to that ideal, but even to him I could not tell all, and when I ventured to express some small measure of my concern, he only bade me wait, seeming no more disturbed by this than by the weather.

And then the storm died, the wind's place taken by snow. The louring black that had spanned the heavens took on a livid hue, and a white curtain fell over Mhorvyn. This, I was told by Lan and Yanydd and Laena—indeed, by all I asked—was unprecedented. Snow was rare enough here; snow in such quantity was unknown. I had seen enough in Durbrecht, but very little in Whitefish village. There, what fell was soon translated into rain or sleet, the salty seaside air melting the flakes even as they descended. It should have been thus here, but the precipitation came so thick and strong, it blanketed the island between dawn and dusk and after built steadily up. It was a marvel to many—who had never seen snow—and to the children sheer delight. They rampaged through the streets, tossing snowballs, rolling in the stuff, constructing forts and follies even as gangs of Changed were set to clearing the roads and walks and roofs. It was, in truth, a pretty scene, the keep and all the rooftops decked pristine, but at the same time unnerving.

I went about the town as usual, wrapped in my cloak, my boots padded against the chill, listening as much as I spoke. None connected either storm or snowfall with the Sky Lords, but all wondered at such weather. Some talked of omens, some zealots of the God's wrath; fishermen complained of lost catches, merchants of undelivered goods, farmers of blighted crops. Most looked to me for answers, as if I were a soothsayer. I told them I did not know, and I hid my burgeoning suspicion that this was indeed the Sky Lords' doing.

Then word came. It was not good.

Yanydd summoned me to his private quarters, where I found Laena already settled by the fire. The aeldor stood by the window, staring morosely over the white snowscape of his holding. He turned as I entered, and I saw from his face and the commur-mage's that this should be no idle conversation. He waved me to a chair, inviting me to fill a cup. I did so and sat waiting, nervous again.

"Durbrecht's returned word," Yanydd said. "Laena, do you tell him?"

The sorceress nodded and set down her cup, folding her hands as if the chill pervaded her bones even in this warm room.

"First," she said, "you are to leave us as soon you may."

I glanced toward the window. Through the glass I saw only whiteness. I wondered how I should travel in such conditions.

"Not yet." Laena interpreted my look correctly. "Your College and mine agree you must wait until this snow ceases and the roads are passable."

"How bad is it?" I asked.

"Exceedingly." Her tone was grave; I shared her chill. "Dharbek lies snowbound. The storm wrecked shipping the lengths of the Slammerkin and the Treppanek, both; also down the coasts. Roads are blocked, and whole keeps, towns, are cut off. There has never been such a winter."

I said, "I know," and she gestured apology, murmuring, "Forgive me, Daviot. Of course you'd know."

I asked her, "Magic? Is it the Sky Lords' doing?"

Her face was answer enough, the words redundant. "Durbrecht fears it so," she said, "and Kherbryn agrees. We cannot understand how, but there seems no other explanation."

I raised my cup; drained it. Yanydd cursed, and silently I joined him. Almost, I told them all I knew. I thought that if the Sky Lords now commanded the elements themselves, if the Kho'rabi wizards sent tempests and blizzards against us, they must surely soon mount the Great Coming. I thought that every scrap of information should likely be of use; and then that all my reasons for holding back pertained still. It was the Changed dug Mhorvyn clear; it was the Changed risked the causeway to fetch wood for our fires. Did ships venture out, it would be Changed crewed them; it would be Changed toiled to open the roads. To tell of those few I had seen in alliance with the Kho'rabi was surely to betray the many, to bring down suffering on the innocent. Urt should suffer, and Lan; poor cowed Thom, and Pele and her children. Betrayal was balanced by betrayal—of the Changed, or perhaps of my own Trueman kind. I was caught between, trapped by my own instinctive decision to hold my tongue. I felt wretched: I hid my expression, reaching for the wine jug.

"We cannot believe they'll attack yet." I set the jug aside, composing myself as Laena spoke again. "Not in such weather."

She shrugged, looking to Yanydd. The aeldor said, "This must hamper them no less than us. It makes no sense to invade a land of blocked roads. How should they fight, how travel?"

"They've their skyboats," I said. "Shall they need roads?"

"They must!" Yanydd's fist set his cup to bouncing. "Shall they send skyboats against every keep? Can they have so vast a fleet? Even do they concentrate their attacks on the great holds—seize Kherbryn and Durbrecht, even—still there should be sufficient lesser holdings to fight them. No, it's my belief they must look to establish bridgeheads, do they plan real conquest. And what use a snowbound bridgehead?"

He fell silent, righting his spilled cup. I suspected his fierce words were a defiance based on hope, rather than genuine belief.

Laena said, "Yanydd believes they seek to grind us down. To disrupt the land and then send an armada against us."

"And you?" I asked, meaning both her and the Sorcerous College.

"That likely Yanydd's correct," she replied. "That they shall send such weather against us as will blight our crops and wreck our ships —leave all Dharbek in chaos. Then that they shall end their sending and mount the Great Coming."

I thought a moment on all I had learned in Durbrecht of military strategy, of past campaigns. None had been fought in winter, not the great battles. The transportation of armies was too difficult in winter. We Dhar fought our battles under the sun. Did the Ahn? Was winter truly an encumbrance to the Sky Lords? Yanydd's prognostication made sense. The storm that had raged, the snow that followed, did not. None of this made sense, save that terrible powers were brought against us. I said, "Then we've time yet, be you right."

"Yes." Laena nodded. "But how much, we cannot know. Do they command the very elements, then this snow may cease as swift as it began."

"Durbrecht's no better notion?" I asked.

"We suspect . . ." She paused, seeming a moment lost. Then: "We suspect that their magic cannot entirely dominate the seasons. That they must bend nature to their will, shaping it, rather than controlling it utterly. Therefore, it seems unlikely they shall attack before spring."

I glanced again at the window, wondering how long that season should be in coming.

"We looked to fight them," Yanydd said, "sooner or later. It comes sooner."

I thought that Laena whispered, "Too soon," but her head was bowed, and I could not be sure. I said, "So I am to leave as soon I may. Where do I go?"

The commur-mage looked up, meeting my eyes. "East, around the coast," she said. "Then north, to Durbrecht."

I had not dared hope I might see my home again so soon; I had not at all thought to see it in such circumstances. I said, "And my commission? Do I say aught of all this?"

"Yes." Laena ducked her head. "The Lord Protector deems it timely the people know what they face, that they be full ready. Durbrecht commands you tell brave stories, that you embolden the people. And learn all you may of their mood. Do you find any place unready, you are to report from the next sound keep. You are to hold nothing back."

You are to hold nothing back. Almost, I laughed at the irony of it; almost, I wept. I only nodded and said gravely, "Yes, so I shall."

As dusk fell that night—which was then merely a darkening of the white, a transposition of faint day's light by silvery night's—I told Lan I must soon depart, and why.

He nodded as he stoked my fire. "I think that shall be a hard journey," he said. "But you'll see your home again, at least."

"It shall be no great homecoming," I returned. "Not with such grim news."

He added a log to the blaze and turned to face me. "At least you've the chance, Daviot."

I was immediately chastened: Lan, as a Changed, would never have that privilege. Gently, I asked him, "Where are you from, Lan?"

"My parents served Kembry Keep," he said. "I was born there. I came here when I was ten years."

"Would you go back?" I asked.

He studied me a moment, his expression enigmatic. Then he shrugged and said, "One keep is much as another to we Changed. Lord Yanydd is kinder than the aeldor of Kembry, but otherwise there's little difference."

"But your parents," I said. "Would you not see them again, were it possible?"

"It's not," he said. "I cannot travel as do you, free. Why dwell on the impossible?"

His tone was fatalistic, and I could not discern any regret in his expression or stance. I frowned: I spent much time dwelling on the seemingly impossible. I pondered the possibility of peace with the Sky Lords, I thought on the condition of the Changed, I wondered about the dragons of legend. It seemed to me that dreams were necessary. I said as much to Lan.

He smiled then and said, "Perhaps that is a difference between us, Daviot. We Changed have not the same feelings for family and past as you Truemen. Our lot is different—perhaps dreams should only bring us pain."

"You've no feelings for your family?" I asked him.

"I think not as you do," he answered. "Magic made us from the beasts, and beasts have few feelings for their sires, eh?"

"But you are not beasts," I cried. "Don't name yourself an animal!"

"I don't," he said gently. "But neither do I claim the same affection for kin and hearth as Truemen."

I nodded, accepting. I thought perhaps I grew so ardent in my feelings for the Changed that I began to think them mirrors to my image. But they were not—as Lan pointed out, they were descended from animals, and though they were now (of this I should not be dissuaded) become far more than their progenitors, still they lived their lives to a different rhythm than I and my kind. It did not render them inferior, only different.

"But dreams," I said. "Surely you have dreams?"

"Yes," he allowed me, "but they are *our* dreams, and not like yours, I think."

"Tell me," I asked. "What are they?"

He shook his head, his expression veiled. "We hold our dreams private, Daviot."

His voice was quiet, but in it I heard steel. I thought a moment to press him, and then that such as he had little enough privacy I should presume to intrude on those small areas that were his alone; not if I thought to name myself his friend. I said, "As you wish," and he smiled again, nodding his gratitude.

"Perhaps one day you shall know them," he said.

I said, "That should be an honor, Lan."

He looked at me awhile, as if I puzzled him, and then he said softly, "You are a strange man, Daviot."

The snowfall continued fourteen days, and then the sky cleared. It was good to see the blue again and the sun, for all the temperature dropped so low Mhorvyn now lay beneath a covering of white frozen hard as stone. There was no wind; the air was a knife. Water froze in the wells and cisterns, and the smoke of bonfires hung thick as folk sought to melt a way to the precious liquid. Streets that had previously resounded to the scrape of shovels now rang with the clang of pickaxes. To touch metal with ungloved fingers was to lose flesh. Yanydd opened his warehouses to distribute food stored against the possibility of siege. Ice sheeted in the harbor and the coves. The fishermen, though now able to put out, reported a dearth of fish. From the mainland, the farmers reported the ground iron hard, defying plow or harrow.

It was the same, so Laena advised me, throughout Dharbek, worse in the north. Both the Slammerkin and Treppanek were frozen over, and folk already spoke of famine. I had no great eagerness to travel in such conditions, but I had my orders and so I prepared to leave.

My last meal in Mhorvyn Keep was a solemn affair, for whilst the aeldor and the commur-mage still held their belief of Sky Lords' magic private, it was quite impossible to quell suspicion. I had heard talk in the town, and the warband openly mooted the likelihood of occult manipulation. Also, these honest folk had grown fond of me, and I of them; I had not felt so grieved by departure since leaving Krystin in Tryrsbry.

Still, I put on as cheerful a face as I could muster and thanked them for their hospitality, urging they remain in the warmth of the hall when I at last rose to gather up my packs. I had sooner it be that way, I told them, and in deference to my wishes they came only so far as the great door.

Yanydd saw me well provisioned, my saddlebags bulked out with food and extra clothing (what little was not already on my back), and I went to the stables swathed like some mummer. My gray mare was shaggy under her winter coat and plumped by grain and leisure. She objected to the saddle, and it took some time and some adroit maneuvering to get her readied. She sensed departure and welcomed it not at all. As I led her out, I found Lan watching me. We had already said our farewells, and I was surprised to find him there. Obviously, he had slipped away from the keep, for he wore only tunic and breeks and shivered despite the braziers that warmed the stable.

"This weather suits me ill," he said, "but there's a thing I'd give you."

I clutched the mare's bridle as she stamped and gnashed her teeth, wondering what this thing could be. The Changed had few enough possessions they could afford to donate parting gifts. Thinking to be kind, I said, "Your company's been gift enough, my friend, and all you've told me—your trust. There's no need for more."

He smiled and brought something from under his tunic, holding it toward me. It was a length of plaited hair, red and white and black, woven in alternating strands. I tethered my irritable horse and took it from him. I was not sure what it was, save a trinket given in token of burgeoning friendship, of trust between us.

I said, "My thanks," and Lan raised a hand, silencing me.

"I'll likely be missed ere long," he said, "and you must go. But I wanted you to have this. There are Changed who will know its meaning and give you help, should you need it."

There was an urgency in his voice that told me this bangle was far more than some simple token. I nodded, and he gestured that I hold out my wrist so that he might tie the thing in place.

Again I said, "My thanks," and was about to ask elucidation, but he smiled and clasped my hand and said, "It may prove useful, Daviot. Ward it well, and do Truemen ask what it is, say no more than a trinket."

Then, before I could say more, he moved away, swift into the shadows at the stable's farther end. I heard a door thud closed. I looked at the bracelet, touched it, wondering at his enigmatic words as I pulled on the gloves that were another gift of this keep. The gray mare kicked a stall, reminding me that folk looked to see me emerge: I loosed her tether and led her out into the icy air.

Yanydd and his kinfolk saluted from the door, and I raised a hand in answer, then I mounted and turned my horse to the gates, on through them into the streets of the town. There were few folk abroad, save the Changed working to clear the terrible weight of snow, and to them I nodded as I passed.

I continued downhill to the barbican, where the guardsmen huddling around their brazier bade me ride careful over the causeway. I saw no sign of hazard from the sea, which lay as calm as any ocean in winter, but as I ventured out onto the neck I (or more precisely, my mare) found it slick with treacherous ice. She shrilled a protest as her hooves slithered on the sleek black surface, fighting the reins so that after a while spent in useless argument I dismounted and walked her across. We both of us were thankful to reach the farther side, for all it seemed even colder, and I paused, calming her.

The village here was all but lost under the snow, the cottages white mounds marked by their chimneys and the dark shapes of cleared doorways. All down the beach the boats lay drawn up from the water, their nets and rigging ice-rimed, glittering under the cold sun. It was a sight both beautiful and terrible. I wound my scarf closer about my face and turned my back on Yanydd's holding, climbing the gently sloping land in a northeasterly direction.

I could not afford to delay. With luck I should reach shelter by nightfall; without the blessing of fortune I must sleep out, and I was by no means certain either my mare or I could survive a night in such awful cold. I put heels to her flanks and urged her to a canter. She responded eagerly. I think she hoped to outrun the chill.

We climbed away from the village, up through the blighted orchards and the plantations. That far the way was cleared; then we faced the unhidden effects of the blizzard.

The road disappeared. Before us lay a seemingly unending snowfield, barely interrupted by rocks that would normally have stood tall as a mounted man, and snow-drowned trees. I slowed the mare, not wishing to founder in some drift, and wondered how we should survive: it seemed impossible that we could cross such a depth of snow.

That night I found the steading Yanydd had promised and took shelter there, repaying hospitality with a story and the answering of many questions. The farm folk were not much heartened by what I told them, but I urged them to a faith I could not quite share, and in the morning they saw me well fed, vowing themselves ready for whatever might come.

They had no better idea than I what that should be.

I went on, eastward now, around the southern edge of Kellambek. It was a longer route than the trade road across the massif, but I'd no desire to chance the mountains in such weather. I'd lay no odds on surviving that and thought none could argue my choice. Did Durbrecht wish me hasten, I'd make poor speed dead.

Even so, it was no easy path I chose. Indeed, for most of the way there was no path visible, and I must go by instinct, guided by instructions received and what few signs of the marked road remained. There were but three keeps between Morvyn and Whitefish village and few enough settlements. The land rose up to meet the tumbling flanks of the massif, where the great central mountains fell down into the southern sea, and those slopes were the domain of shepherds, empty of much other habitation. There was no natural shelter, and as the day aged I grew worried.

The sun westered fast and a wind got up, edged as a razor, skirling snow in ghostly clouds. As dusk fell, worry became fear. My mare needed rest and warm stabling; I no less a fire and walls about me. Here there was nothing: the landscape was smooth as a clean-scraped plate. I pressed on for want of alternative. Then, past a huddling ridge of snow, in the slope's lee, I saw what I took to be a shepherd's hut. I saw a chimney but no smoke nor light. I wondered why no dogs gave warning of my approach. I felt uneasy: the sun was lost behind the ridge and twilight shrouded the lee, shadow vying with the sparkle of starlight and moonglow. I reined in and hallooed the place. When only silence answered, I shouldered the door open and went inside.

I found a single room, sizable and neat. It was sparsely furnished, the hearth cold. It was eerie.

My gray mare nickered impatiently, urging me to haste in search of stable and fodder. There was an outbuilding, but it was mired so deep in snow, I saw no way to clear an entrance and elected to grant my horse the hospitality of the cottage. I took her reins and brought her inside. She promptly kicked a chair. I bade her show some better manners, which she answered with a snort and snapping teeth, and so I stripped her down and rubbed her off, then doled her a measure of oats. That soothed her, and as she ate I set logs in the hearth and got a fire started. I was somewhat guilty at rendering this tidy home a stable, but I saw no other choice. I thought I should restore it on the morrow.

I ate. I even found a jar of distilled wine and helped myself to a cup or two. Then, with murmured thanks to my unwitting hosts, I stretched myself on the larger of the three beds and went to sleep.

That night I had a strange dream. I recall it as clearly as those others I have told. Indeed, it was linked to those others, as if some spirit of that oak grove beyond Cambar had touched me and set the dream in my head; save it now seemed to unfold like a story I could not quite understand. This is what I dreamed:

I stood again in the hurst, again enveloped in swirling gray mist, but now a brume cold as the night outside. Icicles hung from the oaks, and the ground was thick with snow. I looked about, once more finding the spectral figures of warriors locked in battle. Not of my own volition, I shouted and they ceased their fighting, all lowering their blades and axes as they turned toward me. I felt very afraid, for all they offered me no harm but only stood, a silent circle, watching me or waiting on me to shout again. I felt they expected something from me, but did not know what.

Then all were gone, and in their place stood a great throng of Changed, and they, too, were silent. Unthinking, I took my left hand from my staff and held it up, that all might see the bracelet I wore. The Changed murmured at that, but their voices were like the wash of waves and I could not discern precise words, nor gauge the import of what they said. I raised my hand higher, and it was as if my ears were unstoppered. What they said was "Urt's Friend," and the mist and the snow were gone, the wood lit by warm sunlight.

I raised my head. For a moment I was blinded by the sun, then my vision cleared and I saw the sky cloudless, and then abruptly filled with shadow. I heard a sound like distant thunder or the rumble of water over rocks. I felt something immense approached, something awesome and terrible in its grandeur. I raised both amulet and staff, not knowing why they should protect me or if they would. The branches of the oaks trembled; leaves fell. I was suddenly aware I stood alone. I wanted to run and could not. I wanted to cower and could not. I could only stare as the darkness coalesced.

I cried out then; I did not know whether in fear or triumph.

Perhaps both, for what I saw was confirmation of a dream, a merging of hope and wonder, and very terrible.

I saw a dragon.

It was vast. Great wings, leathery and clawed like a bat's, beat rhythmically, holding the massive bulk of the body stationary above me. I felt the beating of its wings as must a ship's sail bellied by a storm. I felt its breath hot on my face, dry and arid as sun-baked stone. I saw such jaws as might easily encompass a horse and its rider, set with fangs akin to sword blades. A serpentine neck extended from huge shoulders, the body hided in smooth glossy blue, sleek as armor. The limbs were heavy with muscle, the forequarters shorter than the hind, all ended in articulated paws that were tipped with sharp, curved talons, all large enough to grasp a man. A tail limber as an octopus's tentacle lashed behind. I should have been smashed down by the wind of its hovering, but I was not. I stood staring, my gaze met by great yellow eyes that observed me with an alien intelligence. I felt myself judged.

What conclusions this oneiric beast reached, I did not know. I was trapped by its yellow orbs as surely as any rabbit was ever held by an eagle's implacable stare. I was lost. I felt no longer myself but a husk, as if the dragon leached out my spirit, as if it looked not at me but into me, into those secret places I kept hidden.

Then the beast craned back its great craggy head and screamed. It was the howl of a hunter, the shriek of a storm wind, the grinding of rocks in the bowels of the world. All of those: it dinned inside my head and drove me at last to my knees. And when I rose, the dragon was gone.

I opened my eyes and yelled in unalloyed terror as I felt hot breath on my face, saw eyes that I knew were real peering down at me.

My mare snorted and backed from the bed, tumbling furniture on her way. I sat up, groaning, rubbing at my eyes. I felt weary, as if I had not slept at all. I thought the dream should vanish, but it did not: it remained precise in my memory. I staggered from the bed, my legs unsteady as I found the water bucket and drank deep before giving the pail over to my horse. I was trembling, and sweat beaded my brow. I took the jug of distilled wine and gulped a cup, then sat, slumped against the table.

It was an effort to rise. I conjured the image of the dragon. I wondered if it was a true image or merely the product of my imagination. I went to the fire and stoked the embers, adding a few logs against the cold pervading the room.

My mare had soiled the floor, and I cleared her dung before

heating what was left of last night's stew. I fed her and tidied the cottage, then broke my own fast and doused the fire. I saddled her and led her out, still bemused by the odd dream. I swung the door closed and mounted. A trickle of smoke rose from the chimney, soon lost against the dawntime gray. It was very cold, but the sun flirted on the rim of the eastern horizon, and I thought the worst of the night's chill should be soon gone. I felt no wish to linger.

I never learned what became of the inhabitants of that cottage, though I was told their names the next night, when I sheltered in another lonely shepherd's hut. The general opinion was that their bodies would be found come the thaw. If the thaw came: none were too sure of that.

Were they killed by this occult winter, they were not the only ones. The toll of lives and livestock was heavy throughout all Dharbek. Folk died in the lonely places, of hunger, of the cold; in the cities and settlements, too, as food grew short; fishermen drowned as ice-caked boats capsized. Deer froze in the wilderness, and wolves came down from the highlands to prey on penned sheep and cattle. I saw it all as I wound my way eastward, thankful that I survived.

I was rounding the southern coast, and Whitefish village lay not too far distant. I came to Amsbry on a day the wind hurled frozen snow like needles against my face, and I was grateful for the warmth of Perryn's hall, the strong stone walls and stout wood shutters. It stood like an eagle's aerie atop a cliff, and beyond the land ran down broken to the east coast. They were on short rations—all Dharbek was on short rations now, I heard—but it seemed rich fare to me after long days sharing what poor shepherds and farmers could spare. I reported all I had seen along my way to Kydal, who was commurmage there and not much older than I, and I had back what news she could give me. It was not much, nor different from all I'd got along my way: unlikely winter prevailed, famine threatened, the Great Coming was anticipated. I remained three days and then set off for Tarvyn, which lay some nine days away.

Those nine days stretched into thirty.

I quit Amsbry with the sun a silver disk in a steel-hard sky. There was no cloud, and the snowfields shone bright, undisturbed by wind. By the midpart of the day a breeze came out of the east. I paid it no attention at first, more concerned with boiling my tea. Then my mare whickered, and when I glanced toward her, I saw she stood with head raised, her nostrils flared. She seemed expectant, and I thought perhaps she caught the scent of wolves and rose warily. A flank of hillside loomed above us, a shallow valley below, pines straggling thin over the slope. I saw no sign of predators and went to where the mare stood. She greeted me with an almost amiable snort, her head tossing, her hooves pawing. I saw that her ears were up and her eyes not rolling, which I took for confidence. I did not understand her behavior: she seemed frisky, coltish, which was not at all her way. I stroked her neck, and to my surprise she allowed it, even going so far as to nudge me in return. I frowned; then gasped as I smelled what she had sooner known: the breeze was such a draught as heralds spring.

That night we found shelter in a village. Rhysbry, it was called, and it boasted a tiny inn where I was made welcome, bed and board offered in return for my stories. I told but one: the folk of that place, who had passed the last months snowbound, were entirely occupied with the weather's shifting. All their talk was of the breeze; of its scent and strength, its promise. Spring came, they said, and soon the snow should be gone. My weather lore was no less than theirs, and I must agree it *was* a spring wind; but even knowing all I did of the sorcerers' beliefs, still I could scarcely credit so sudden an ending of the Sky Lords' winter.

The next day, however, the gusting came again, and the sky was a warmer blue, the sun golden, and the air warm enough I shed my scarf. By noon, I rode without my cloak. By dusk, my mare's hooves left deep prints in which water puddled, and when I halted at a shepherd's cottage, I must walk her awhile to cool her. That night I threw off my blanket.

As I readied for departure the shepherd, whose name was Tarys, gave me warning.

"You ride for Tarvyn, no?" he said, and when I confirmed this: "Then best ride careful, Daviot. 'Tween here and the keep, the way's all valleys and ravines, and does spring come on us swift as this God-cursed winter, there'll be flooding with the melt."

He stabbed a thumb skyward in emphasis. I looked up and saw a spring sky; the air was balmy, and I suspected he might well be correct. I thanked him, and he ducked his white head, declaring that he'd not see a Storyman drowned. I mounted my mare and turned her east, thinking that he gave me sound advice: I came to accept the winter fled.

Clear of the high country, the slopes were forested, and all that day water dripped relentlessly from the branches overhead, and the snow beneath my mare's hooves grew soft, rivulets forming to trickle downslope. For all I sweated under it, I donned my cloak. I studied the valley bottoms and ravines carefully and saw the streams there swollen, no longer iced, but running swifter and gray with snowmelt. In the afternoon, as I crossed a valley, I heard a rumbling from the far slope and saw a great mass of snow break loose, trees and boulders tossing in its passage, leaving behind a scar of muddy brown earth. I began to worry again.

I found no shelter that night, for I was forced to detour from my route by three more avalanches. I made camp atop a ridge spread with looming cedars that no longer dripped, which in itself was disturbing, for they should not have dried so soon. Neither should the ground there have been visible yet. It was as though the seasons accelerated, winter fleeing before onrushing spring in a matter of days. I wondered what manner of summer might follow.

Whatever it should be, I did not think I should need wait long to find out. Day by steady day, the temperature rose. I could no longer follow my chosen path, for I must all the time ride around landslips or find some way over streams become rivers, rivers swollen to torrents. Valleys lay waterlogged, bridges were washed away, and fords become impassable. Pastureland was rendered quagmire, swaths cut through timber. I saw animals—sheep and cattle and horses, deer and wild pigs, twice bears—washed drowned and bloated past me. Sometimes I saw human bodies, tumbled by so swift, I could not tell whether they were Truemen or Changed. When I found the road, it was awash with mud and ofttimes blocked by the detritus of landslides. Farms and villages stood wet and miserable, and everywhere folk told sad tales of ruined planting, of fields lost to the excessive melt, of deaths by drowning or landslide. They forecast a poor harvest, if any harvest at all might be reaped. And all the while the heat increased, until all the snow was gone and it seemed Kellambek was become a land of swamps and lakes. It seethed under the sun, vapors rising thick as mist from ground that dried as rapidly as it had flooded. Save our world was somehow drawn closer into the sun's orbit, there could no longer be any doubt that frightening magic was brought against us.

By the time I reached Tarvyn, the floods were gone and the earth baked as if midsummer were come. Rivers that had run in spate were now thin streams, streams were dry gutters. Trees that had been denied the chance to bud stood withered, what grass had not been washed away lay sere. There were fires in the hills and dread throughout the land.

Tarvyn Keep stood beside the sea, where the southern ocean met the Fend. The sun sparkled off slow waves and the still air was heavy with the odor of rotting seaweed. Boats stood along the beach with tar oozing melted from their caulking, their crews lounging idle, paying me only the slightest attention, as if the heat leached out their curiosity. I rode in shirt-sleeves, a cloth wound around my forehead to hold off the sweat that would otherwise blind me. My gray mare had long since lost her springtime friskiness and walked sullen, her head low, panting in the excessive heat. She seemed not even to have the vitality of her usual ill temper. Nor was I in much better fettle. This heat — and belief in its origin — drained hope as surely as it leached energy. I thought it must be very hard to fight in such weather.

We plodded slowly to the keep's entrance, and I announced myself to gatemen whose look reminded me of boiled lobsters. They waved me by as if that effort cost them dear. As I crossed the yard, I saw folk all languid in the heat, stripped to decency's minimum of clothing. There was no breeze, for all the sea was but a stone's throw distant, and the aeldor's banners hung limp from the tower. I dismounted, shirt and breeks clinging wet to my body, and walked my horse into the stable. It was thankfully a little cooler there, but not much, and the Changed ostlers who came to offer help plodded like their equine forebears. I gave them the warning that had become my custom and saw to the mare myself. She made no protest as I removed her tack and rubbed her down, not even her habitual attempt to bite me. I thought I had rather suffer her temper than see her thus.

I gave her oats and water and went to find Madrys, whose holding this was.

He was in the hall, a thin young man whose red hair was plastered slick to his skull. He rose to greet me, and when I made my excuses for this late arrival, he waved a weary hand and told me he knew of the road's difficulties. He introduced me to his wife, Rynne, whose pale yellow gown was patched dark at breast and armpits. She held a baby that mewled, his tiny face bright red; for him and all the children, I felt most sorry. There was an air of lassitude in this hall; only the commur-magus Tyrral, seeming unaffected by the heat. I was invited to take ale chilled in the well and sat sipping as Changed servants fanned us. Their efforts seemed only to stir the overheated air that had succeeded in pervading even the cool stone of the keep.

I gave brief report of my journey from Amsbry and had back the news that Tarvyn had not long since seen two of the Sky Lords' little craft, as if they came to check their occult handiwork. Madrys appeared resigned or drained of optimism, though he assured me his warband stood ready to fight. Tyrral was more sanguine. Indeed, he treated his aeldor brusquely, as if the younger man's apathetic mood irritated him. As soon as was polite, I asked if I might bathe and change — and was shocked to be told fresh water was in short supply. I had thought the snowmelt must fill the aquifers.

I remained only a few days in Tarvyn. I gave them my best stories, tales of glorious victories and great battles, but received only a lackluster response. For all Tyrral put on a brave face, there was a feeling of despair about the keep, as if aeldor and warband had already given up. It saddened me, but also it threatened to affect my own spirits.

Also, I was now close enough to Whitefish village I thought of reunions, of seeing again my kinfolk and childhood friends, and that spurred me to impatience. So, pleading an urgency imposed by my delayed arrival, I made my excuses soon as was decent and left that sad keep behind me.

Within seven days I saw the boundary stones that marked the limit of Madrys's holding and the commencement of Cambar land. Within seven more I came home.

18

It is a strange experience to go home after years away in a wider world. I had left Whitefish village an innocent, eager to experience the marvels of Durbrecht and all that lay beyond. Even then, I had had that double-edged gift of memory, and it fixed my home in my mind as it had been and was that day I departed. The village and its folk had been all my world, and I could yet conjure clear those impressions of my youth, so that—for all I knew I had changed—still I perceived my home immutable, preserved thus in my mind as the lapidaries set insects or flowers in glass. But places and people, both, shrink as we grow. Things change, and yesterday is a country of the memory that is no longer quite what you recall; even for a Mnemonikos.

I came north up the inland road, turning to the coast along the track that crested the pine-clad cliffs of my infancy to run down to Whitefish village. The meadowland there was parched, the grass sere, the soil cracked as an ancient face. The trees stood desiccated, needles fallen too soon crackling under my gray mare's hooves. I halted atop the bluff, suddenly nervous. Below me stood a huddle of rude cottages such as should barely fill one of Durbrecht's plazas. Along the beach stood fishing boats, beyond them the Fend, brilliant under the remorseless sun. There was no breeze—I had not felt a breeze in days— and the village baked. It seemed to me a poor, rough place, and I felt ashamed to think it so: I heeled my mare and took her down the slope.

I felt an odd admixture of anticipated pleasure and wariness as I reined in outside my parents' cottage (I could no longer properly think of it as home) and dismounted. A woman with gray streaking her hair rose from a chair set in the shade of a sailcloth canopy, wiping hands slimed with fish scales on her grubby apron. Her hands were rough and red and her face darker than I recalled. I felt my heart lurch. I said, "Mam," and she smiled and cried out, "Daviot," and ran to embrace me. I hugged her. Her head reached no farther than my chest. She seemed frail. When she leaned back to study my face, there were tears in her eyes, and she gazed at me as if she could not believe I was truly there.

I said, "You're well?" and she nodded, and held me tighter, and began to cry against my shirt. Almost, I wept for the joy of seeing her again. I felt embarrassed, but after a while she stilled her weeping and let me go, wiping at her eyes.

All in a rush she said, "Oh, Daviot, you've come home. You've grown so. Shall you stay?"

"Only for a little while," I said. I felt abruptly awkward, not wishing to dampen her joy with news I'd soon be gone. "I'm ordered north, to Cambar first, but then on."

She stared at me, smiling as only a mother ever does. "You're taller," she said. "And so grand, with your fine horse. Is that a Storyman's staff? Are you truly a Rememberer now?"

"Yes," I told her, and she beamed.

"Your father will be so proud." She touched my cheek. "I'm proud. Our Daviot—a Storyman!"

I shrugged, embarrassed, and asked, "Where is Da?"

"At the beach," she said. "Daviot, he'll be so pleased to see you."

I said, "And Delia and Tonium—where are they?"

My mother blinked then, and sniffed, and I saw pain in her eyes. "Tonium was drowned," she said, at which I felt a stab of grief for all we'd not much liked one another. "Delia wed a lad from Cambar— Kaene—and lives there now."

I said, "I didn't know about Tonium. I'm sorry."

She shook her head, dismissing grief. Fisherfolk learn that early. "How should you?" she asked. "You away in Durbrecht. We heard the city was attacked, and I feared for you. Oh, Daviot, it's so good to see you. Are you truly well? You look thin. Do you eat enough?"

Those questions mothers ask came in a flood that I could scarcely dam with my answers. I felt twelve years old, but finally she took my hands and declared that we must find my father, lest I spend all my time repeating myself. I asked that I first might stable my mare, and so she walked with me to Robus's barn, where I rubbed down the gray horse and saw her watered. I warned Robus of her temper, and he studied her and me with wary eyes, as if I came back some lord, unsure how he should address me. I thought him plumper than ever, and aged. I promised him a story later; I promised all the village a story, but after I had greeted my father and my other kin. As my mother and I walked to the beach, he was trotting amongst the cottages, shouting the news that Daviot was come home a Storyman.

My father sat with Battus and Thorus, working on their boat. Save that gray streaked their hair and their faces wore more lines, the years might not have passed. Then they rose, and I saw that for all that time and hardship had left their marks, still these three were hale. My father took my hand. He must tilt back his head to meet my eyes. Then he smiled and said, "Daviot," and took me in his arms, which told me he was still strong, for I felt my chest crushed, my breath expelled by his fierce embrace. I felt a great surge of love for this aged man, so that my throat clogged and for a while I could not speak, only hold him and whisper, "Da," as if I were a child again.

Thorus and Battus each shook my hand, and Thorus pointed to the knife I wore. He said, "You've the blade still."

"I'd not lose a good knife," I told him, and he nodded, taciturn as ever.

Work ceased: we went to Thorym's aleshop. He, a tad gaunter but otherwise not much changed, greeted me as a long-lost friend. He filled us mugs in welcome as all the village folk gathered.

It was strange to see their faces again, sprung sudden on me without the softening acceptance of slow-passing time. Tellurin and Corum both came, grown men now, with shy-eyed wives at their sides, children staring nervously from the shelter of their mothers' skirts.

A mantis arrived, not my old tutor (he had died two years agone, of a summer fever) but a thin young man, intense of face, whose name was Dysian.

We drank; I was plied with questions. I asked how they had fared through the winter, and how they did now in this tropic summer.

The answer was no more, neither better nor worse, than I had expected. I had heard much the same along my way and should hear it all up the coast. The winter had been harsh—the Fend too storm-tossed for safe fishing, the catches too poor; some had drowned; some had died of the cold. The sudden thaw, the sudden summer made things no better—without a wind, the fishing remained hard; it seemed the ocean grew too warm, there were few fish. There had been no winter planting, nor in the brief spring; now there was no point— seedlings died in this heat. Water was in short supply, the brooks arid, the springs become drying puddles.

The afternoon aged. A mild spring evening should have followed, but it seemed the sun's passage was hindered, the hard gold-silver disk lingering like a glaring eye in the unbroken blue above. I opened my purse to hand Thorym hoarded durrim, that the ale keep coming. None seemed disposed to leave, and after a while, by some unspoken agreement, a meager feast took shape. I felt both proud and guilty that I be deemed worthy of the honor and determined that they should have the very best of me when I told my tales.

So we ate and drank as the sun moved slowly westward, sultry twilight finally cloaking the village in shadow. The heat did not abate, as if the gibbous moon that climbed above the Fend took the sun's place to scorch the land. I thought then of how this used to be so peaceful a time. The sea's slow wash had been a lullaby then, the breeze a balm; men would gather to sup ale, and mothers would set children abed. Innocent days: gone now. I looked about, aware of tension, aware that folk drank less to slake thirst than in search of comfort. There was a somewhat fevered air to their celebrating, as if my presence afforded an excuse to indulge, perhaps to forget for a little while what cares should face them with the morrow's dawning. I found a sadness growing in me, for them and all Dharbek. When I rose to speak, I think I made good my promise to myself: no aeldor in his keep ever had better storytelling of me.

By the time I was done, full night had advanced. Mothers gathered reluctant children and folk began to drift away. In time only those who had been closest, and Dysian, remained. The women left us, all save my mother, who sat beside me, sometimes touching my sleeve as if to reassure herself I was truly there.

Corum said, "So you've fought the Sky Lords, eh?"

I nodded, not much wishing to speak of that, for my mother's sake and my own. Dysian muttered, "May the God curse them. May he destroy them all. He'll not allow the cursed Dark Ones to overrun his chosen country."

I considered his faith blind. It seemed to me the God, if he existed, paid Dharbek little heed. Still, I'd no wish to make the Church my enemy, and so I said mildly, "I'd not venture to interpret the God's will, but it's the opinion of Durbrecht and the Lord Protector that likely the Sky Lords plan their Great Coming this year, or next. . . . No one is sure. The God willing, the sorcerers will find ways to strengthen the Sentinels and halt them—"

I broke off as Dysian snorted and my mother gasped. My father said, "What should we do?"

It was strange to hear my father ask advice of me: things change. I said, "Do they come, I doubt they'll attack the villages."

I spoke with far more confidence than I felt, but I'd no desire to see fresh tears in my mother's eyes or rob my father of hope. I held back my doubts and kept my secrets close.

My mother yawned then, and I realized it was only my presence kept her. The moon was overhead by now, and were I not come home, she'd have been long abed. No less the others, who seemed now to linger only in hope of comfort I could not give them, save with soft words that skirted around what I believed was the truth. I emptied my mug and declared myself weary.

"How long shall you stay?" my father asked.

I hesitated. I was both tempted to linger and eager to be gone. It was far easier to assume a brave face amongst strangers, to tell folk I'd not met before and should soon enough leave that all should be well, but amongst these old friends, my parents, it was hard. Almost, I told him I must depart with the dawn, but I thought that should be unkind, that it were almost better I had not halted here at all. So I smiled and said, "Tomorrow, Da. But then I'd best go on. They'll have sent word from Tarvyn, and Cambar must expect me."

"Best not keep the aeldor waiting," he said, in a voice aimed at reminding the others that his son consorted with the mighty.

That night I slept in my old bed and dreamed I was a child again, carefree.

I woke to the smell of baking. My mother knelt by the hearth, smiling as I emerged, indicating the biscuits she made. They had always been a favorite delicacy, and I voiced my thanks even as I wondered if she could afford such largesse. I thought it should hurt her more did I protest and so said nothing, but went out to the well. As I drew up the bucket, I saw the rope was lengthened: I used only a little water.

We ate—the biscuits and thin porridge—and spoke of the years betwixt my departure and now. I said little of Rwyan, and save for expressing sympathy, they were tactful enough not to press me. I promised I should visit Delia. Then we all three walked to the beach, where Thorus and Battus waited. It was not long past dawn, but already the sand was hot, the air turgid. There were no clouds nor any breeze, and the sun seemed to blister the sky. The Fend rolled lazy, as if this awful heat robbed even the sea of vitality. We launched the boat, and I usurped Thorus at the oars—it was pointless to raise the sail. I brought us out to the fishing grounds and sat panting. My body had forgotten what hard work this was.

From the tiller my father fixed me with a look I remembered well. It was the way he had studied me when I was caught in some unadmitted prank. It was a look that said he knew what I held back, but had sooner I confess of my own volition. I felt immediately guilty.

He stared at me awhile longer and then said, "So, do you tell us? There are no women or children to frighten out here, and we'd know the worst if it's to come."

I had thought I hid my true feelings. From any others I likely had, but these had known me from my birthing, and my father saw deep into me, past my defenses. I wished then I had not come home. I sighed and began to speak.

I told them all I had seen, and all I believed (save for that one sighting of Kho'rabi and Changed together), and when I was done, there was silence, broken only by the mewing of optimistic gulls.

I was thankful that we spoke no more on such matters. By unspoken consent we turned our conversation to the mundane—or what in such times passed for mundane—talk of catches and the problems this heat afforded honest fishermen. We went a long way out, farther than ever I had been as a boy, far enough the southernmost of the Sentinels was just visible, low against the horizon. I wondered if Rwyan might be on that island. Perhaps she turned her blind eyes to the sea and found a boat there and thought of the fisherman's son she had loved. I pushed those thoughts away and took a hand as we set the net. There was still too much pain in those memories.

Our catch was poor, and after some hours we turned for land. It was the midpart of the afternoon then, and I sat helping my father with his floats as my mother prepared our evening meal.

We ate alone, but when the meal was done went back to Thorym's aleshop, where folk already gathered in expectance of my stories. The night was no cooler than before, and it seemed to me that even the bats darting amongst the cottages flew slower. It was the bats, seeming tiny reminders of my oneiric dragon, that prompted me to recount one of the oldest of all the tales.

It was the story of the Last Dragon, and seldom told. Indeed, it was argued in Durbrecht that it had no place in our canon, for its veracity was disputed. One school of thought maintained that it was our duty to tell only such stories as were anchored firm in historic evidence, and as this had no such authority, it was best forgotten. Another, however, held that all the folk tales had a place, being part of our past gone into legend. I thought there was no harm in such old tales, and much to be lost did we forget them. Besides, I liked the story for itself.

When I was done telling it, there was a murmur of appreciation and some few chuckles.

"In the God's name," my father declared, "what allies the dragons should make, eh? Think on it—did the Dragonmasters live still, they might bring the beasts out against the Sky Lords. That should give them something to think about, no?"

There was laughter at his words, but I felt an odd chill run down my spine. He echoed things I'd said in Durbrecht; things I'd wondered on since. I felt—I could not define it—a kind of presentiment, as if, unwitting, he spoke with an augur's tongue. I shaped a smile and laughed with the rest.

Thorym said, "That they would, were they not all dead and gone."

Dysian said, his tone censorious, "The dragons preyed on men; the God gave us magic to use against them. Better put your faith in him than creatures of legend."

I saw my father cast a dark look the mantis's way, and my mother touch his sleeve as if in warning. I thought this intense young priest was not much liked in the village, but none spoke up against him.

I said easily, "Should it not be a fine thing, though, Dysian, if the God saw fit to give us back Dragonmasters and dragons for allies?"

He said, "What use such dreams? Both are long gone, and we must trust in the God, not fables."

I shrugged, and motioned for Thorym to fill his mug (at which, I noticed, he did not protest), and said, still casual, "But *did* the God see fit . . . our sorcerers might ride the sky to bring their God-given magic against the Kho'rabi wizards and their boats."

"Pah!" was all his answer, and he sank his long face in his mug. I grinned across his head at my father.

However, we spoke no more of dragons. I told another tale—that of Naeris and the White Horse—which was acceptable to Dysian and held the others rapt until its ending, and by then the hour was again late and folk began to disperse. I'd no wish to face more questions and so murmured to my mother that I'd find my bed, as I must depart on the morrow. I suspect she'd have sat all night awake to spend more time with me, but I saw her eyes grew heavy. Nor would I see my father spend more of his hard-earned durrim. My own hoard dwindled, and I had determined to leave some small coin in gratitude and as succor against the harsher times foreseen, so I said my goodnights and rose, offering my mother my arm.

That night I dreamed I walked in Cambar Wood again, and again the dragon hovered, and again I felt the creature judged me. I woke sweaty and confused and lay a long time awake listening to the small night-sounds of the cottage, the faint call of the sea. I pondered long on that and all the other dreams, wondering if they were some random invention of my imagination, conjurations of the bits and pieces of knowledge I accrued, or sendings from some power I could not define.

I fell asleep again sometime before dawn and did not wake until my parents' movements roused me. I rose quickly, knowing that a parting no easier than before awaited me, and anxious to have it done. I bathed and dressed, thinking to put on my mended shirt, and then packed my saddlebags. Behind the curtain veiling my bed I quietly counted what coin I had left. I held back a few durrim for myself and concealed the rest beneath a pillow. My parents would find it after I was gone, when it should be too late they insist I take it back. Bags and staff in hand, I went out to break my fast.

We ate—grilled fish this morning—and I kissed my mother, embraced my father. They both put on brave faces as they escorted me to the barn and watched me saddle the gray mare. My mother cried a warning as the horse snapped her displeasure, and I assured her this was a daily ritual to which I was long accustomed and she need not worry. (Useless advice to any mother!) I gave Robus a durrim for the stabling and mounted. I had thought to escape without fuss, but as I walked out I found Thorus and Battus, Tellurin and Corum, waiting to see me off: there was an exchange of good wishes, a clasping of hands. I feared my mother would weep. I leaned down to kiss her once more, raised a hand to my father, and turned away. My mare aided me then, for she rolled her eyes as the village folk pressed close around and set to bucking. I fought her still, but none came near after that and I was able to ride out with no prolonged farewells. They trailed after me to the cliff path, as if I were some lord with his retinue, and I waved once, and heeled the mare, and urged her swift up the slope.

19

The white banners of mourning hung listless over Cambar's tower, and all the keep folk wore the ribbons on their sleeves. I was saddened when the gatemen told me Bardan was dead, slain the past year in battle with the Sky Lords, for I held fond memories of that bluff and kindly warrior. Sarun was aeldor now, and once I'd seen my mare stabled, I went to pay my respects.

I found the heir seated in the hall, alone save for a handful of warriors and a few servants. He was not much changed physically, but as he studied me with those hawkish eyes, I discerned a greater authority in him, an air of somewhat weary responsibility. At first he did not know me: I bowed, formally announcing myself, and he gave such a start as set the great gray hounds lounging at his feet to barking. He shouted them silent and looked me up and down, a slow smile stretching his narrow lips.

"In the God's name," he said at last, "Rekyn gave word of your coming, but I'd not recognize you. You've grown, Daviot. You went from here a stripling lad; you come back a man, grown. A full-fledged Storyman, at that."

I smiled and shrugged. He called that ale be served me, waving me to a seat across from him. Before I accepted, I said, "Sympathy for your loss, Lord Sarun; honor to your father. He lives in my memory, may the Pale Friend grant him peace."

Sarun nodded, his smile an instant bleak. "He died well," he said. "For all his years, his sword was blooded when he fell."

"The Dowager Lady Andolyne?" I asked. "She's hale?"

"Hale, aye," he answered. "Hale, but grieving yet. There's much happened here since you last saw this keep. You've had word?"

"No." I shook my head. "I was five years in Durbrecht, studying. This last, I've traveled the west coast. I've had no word at all."

He grunted, toying with his cup, and offered no immediate elaboration. I saw now he had changed more than I at first suspected. It was not physical but a hardening of his eye, a harshening of his voice, as if the years had set a steeliness in him, honing him. He seemed tense, ready to spring. He made me think of a sheathed sword.

"The Lady Gwennet is well?" I asked when he did not speak.

"Aye, she's with child," he told me. "Our second. My mother's with her now, and Garat."

"May the God favor mother and child, both," I said formally.

"Life goes on." He drank. "Some die, some are born. I think there shall be more die ere long."

"You believe the Sky Lords will attack this year?" I asked.

"It seems likely." He shrugged and favored me with a sour grin. "But do they or not, still we'll know death here—from famine or fevers, does this cursed heat not abate."

He confirmed what I already feared or knew. I inquired after his brother.

"Thadwyn's wed," was his reply, "and gone to Ryrsbry Keep now I've an heir."

"And Rekyn?" I asked. "Andyrt?"

"Rekyn's yet commur-mage," he said. "She's out hunting one of the Sky Lords' God-cursed boats."

"They're seen again?" I watched him toy with the ribbon wound about his sleeve. "I've not encountered any since the year turned."

"Aye." He barked an angry laugh. "They're seen again and have been since this unnatural summer began. They come and go like God-cursed hornets, and for every one we destroy, there seem two more. Rekyn's her work cut out."

He made no mention of Andyrt, and I supposed the jennym rode with the commur-mage. I said as much, and Sarun shook his head.

"Andyrt was slain," he said. "Two years agone, now. The great skyboats came thick that year."

I stared, momentarily lost for words. Foolish as it was, I had never thought Andyrt might die. In the eye of my memory I saw the jennym clear, as he had looked that day he came to Whitefish village and let a simple fisherman's son carry his helm. Andyrt it was had first helped me astride a horse, had promised a place in Cambar's warband, did I not become Mnemonikos. Andyrt had shown me the oak grove. I counted him a friend; I felt an emptiness open inside me. It was as if another piece of my past were stolen, gone like Rwyan, like Urt or Cleton. Save they, as best I could know, lived still while Andyrt was irrevocably gone.

I heard Sarun say, "I'm sorry, Daviot. You were close, no?"

I nodded, reaching for my cup. I drank deep and forced grief back. To Sarun I said, "He was a good man."

"He was," said the aeldor. "May the Pale Friend grant him peace."

I'd no wish to dwell on loss, and so I asked, "One child already, you said?"

"A boy. His name is Bardaen, after my father." Sarun's stern face softened. "He's scarce four years yet, but he bears himself well. You shall meet him later."

"I should like that," I said. "It's good to be here again, Lord Sarun."

"Plain Sarun will do," he told me. "I've poor patience with ceremony."

Like your father, I thought: I smiled.

"So," he declared, "would you bathe and rest? You come from Tarvyn, I understand, and that's lengthy road."

"I stopped along the way," I told him, "at Whitefish village last. But, yes—I'd scrub the dust away."

I was, in fact, not very dirty, thanks to my mother's ministrations, but the thought of a tub, of hot water, was pleasant.

"So be it." Sarun beckoned a servant and gave the Changed instructions that I be shown to a chamber and a bath provided. "Tonight you can tell all you've witnessed along your way. Rekyn should be returned by then, and we'd both hear what mood pertains in the villages."

"You shall," I promised, and followed the servant from the hall.

•   •   •

It felt near as strange to be in Cambar as it had to return to Whitefish village. In many ways a Storyman's life is timeless. Save we be given permanent duty in some keep, we travel. Save we be summoned to the College as Mnemonikos-tutor or some other senior office, we travel. We put down no roots, name only Durbrecht our true home (and that not often seen), and so have none of those unnoticed calendars that mark the passing of time for other folk. We see no children grow, build no homes, our possessions are only such as we can carry. We exist in a curious limbo, and to come back in so short a span to two places so important to me was somewhat unsettling.

The more so when I was brought to the chamber I'd occupied on my first sojourn here.

I set my staff against the wall and crossed to the window. The shutters were closed in a vain attempt to fend off the heat, and I threw them open, leaning on the wide sill. The land lay hazy before me, shimmering under the sun, but in the distance I could just make out the oak wood. It was a gray-green shadow, vague as the grove of my dreams. I thought I did not much wish to go there again. I turned away, smiling at the patiently waiting servant. My sleeves were rolled and Lan's bracelet in clear view, but the Changed seemed not to recognize the ornament. I crossed my arms, deliberately turning the knotted hair, but still the blunt face showed no expression save patience. I thought perhaps he saw only a bangle, meaningless, and that thought introduced another: did the bracelet mean nothing to him, then not all the Changed could be privy to the mysterious society Lan had shown me.

I smiled at him and said, "I am Daviot. Your name?"

"Tal," he said. "Shall I arrange your bath, Master Daviot?"

I nodded.

He left the room and I stood awhile, absently turning the bracelet, pondering Lan's words. *There are Changed who will know its meaning and give you help, should you need it. It may prove useful, Daviot. Ward it well, and do Truemen ask what it is, say no more than a trinket.* There had seemed to me then, and did still now, a promise given with the gift. It had seemed to me a passport of some kind into that society Lan had revealed, and I had assumed it should be recognized by all the Changed. Now it appeared otherwise. I began to wonder if the culture of the Changed was no less intricately layered than that of Truemen. Perhaps Lan represented some faction, some group from which Tal was isolated. I thought Urt must be a member—Lan had known of him, and our friendship had clearly counted in my favor. I studied the bracelet, frowning, more intrigued than ever.

Then Tal came back, two hulking bull-bred Changed bearing a

tub and water, and I set aside my musings in favor of the idler luxury of the bath.

As I lay there I heard a clattering from the yard below, as of armored riders, and distantly I thought I heard Rekyn's name called. I leaped from the tub, careless of the puddles I left behind as I crossed to the window and peered down. I saw a double squadron of horsemen dismounting, Cambar's plaid bright through the dust that cloaked them. Rekyn was there, dust on her face and raven hair, paling her black leathern gear. I saw bodies lifted down, and several wounded. I turned away, seeking a towel, and when I returned to the window, Rekyn was gone. I was eager to see her at closer quarters: I dried myself hurriedly and dressed no less hastily, then quit the chamber for the hall.

It was empty, save for servants, and when I inquired after the whereabouts of the commur-mage and Sarun, I was told they spoke in the aeldor's private quarters. I deemed it unseemly I should disturb them there and so waited in the hall. Before long, warriors began to drift in, those who had gone with Rekyn travel-stained and weary, those who had remained about the keep no less agog for word. A Kho'rabi vessel had been sighted, and Rekyn had led two squadrons in pursuit. In the ensuing fight five men had died and nine more been wounded. It was a victory, but comrades were slain; in the aftermath, the heat of battle cooled now, they seemed poised between elation and mourning. I saw women led weeping from the hall, and others joyous in their relief that their menfolk survived. I drew a mug of ale and found myself an obscure corner, where I should not intrude.

Then I was summoned to Sarun's chambers, and the news I got was dramatic as the summer lightning that struck out of the sun-scorched sky.

The aeldor sat pale-faced behind his father's desk, a dagger turning restlessly in his hands, as if he would find some target for the blade. Rekyn sprawled in a chair, still dusty. She seemed shocked, her green eyes dark with doubt. On both their faces I saw expressions of disbelief. I felt uneasy: this chamber held an atmosphere that set my skin to prickling.

Rekyn said, "Day's greetings, Daviot," and laughed bitterly. It sounded as though dust clogged her throat. "If that be right on such a day."

I had anticipated a warmer welcome and felt a moment hurt. "Day's greetings, Rekyn," I returned cautiously. "It's good to see you again. Sarun told me of Andyrt, and I—"

She shook her head, stilling my tongue. "Old grief," she said.

Her voice was curt, but I saw the flash of pain in her eyes. It dawned on me that she and Andyrt had been lovers.

Sarun gestured at a chair, and I sat, nervous. Their bodies no less than their faces told me some matter of tremendous import awaited announcement.

There was silence awhile, as if they both digested unpalatable news. I watched them, alert. I had seen such expressions before, on the faces of bereaved folk who cannot entirely grasp that a beloved is dead and would yet reject the irrevocable. I shifted uncomfortably in my chair. Then Sarun let go a gusty sigh and indicated Rekyn should speak.

The commur-mage turned toward me. She was older but little different, save for faint lines upon her brow, the arcs that curved from her nostrils to the corners of her mouth. She swallowed a long measure of ale and closed her eyes a moment.

Then, without preamble, she said, "The Lord Protector Gahan is dead."

"What?" I started forward in my chair: I understood her preoccupation now. Gahan was not old. He had fewer years than my father. "How? Have the Sky Lords attacked Kherbryn?"

"No." Rekyn shook her head. "He took a sickness, a little while agone. None thought it serious. Only just now, when I sent word of the Kho'rabi, did I hear of his death."

She broke off, as if she could scarce believe what she told me. I had never thought to see her so disconcerted. I looked to Sarun and on his face saw alarm. I said, "There's no doubt?" I knew there could not be; I wanted there to be.

"None." Rekyn's voice was bereft of its usual confidence. "Four days ago, he died. The palace herbalists—the chirurgeons—none could name the illness or the cure. They were helpless. They could only watch as he died."

"How could . . . ?" My voice tailed off. Suddenly the heat in the room seemed more than I could bear. I loosed my shirt and, all protocol forgotten, reached for a mug, drew myself ale. Sarun offered no objection; he seemed not to notice.

"How could the Lord Protector take ill?" Rekyn shrugged, her brief smile sour. "Like any man, Daviot. Like any mortal man. There are some suggest he was poisoned."

My mouth dropped open at that. It was unthinkable! The Lord Protector was guardian of Dharbek, temporal head of the Church, commander of all our soldiers: the keystone of our world.

"Who'd poison him?" I asked, aghast.

"Were that known, they'd be dead now," Rekyn answered. "It's a suspicion only."

"No Dhar." Sarun spoke, his voice grim. "I'd stake my life no Dhar would commit such a crime. Surely it was the Sky Lords."

"Perhaps." Rekyn saw me frown as I wondered how even the Sky Lords with all their occult powers might gain access to the Lord Protector, and she addressed herself to me. "They've a new tactic now —the God be praised we've not seen it here yet. They tow rafts behind their skyboats, loaded with the rotting carcasses of dead animals. They cut the rafts loose to fall on the cities, scattering the fouled meat. In this heat . . ."

She shrugged expressively. I felt my mouth go dry. In this heat there was already disease abroad. Not bad here along the coast, but in crowded cities, where likely refugees fled to swell the busy streets, it must be a dreadful weapon. It seemed to me an abomination. I said, "Was that the cause?"

"None know," she replied. "Only that Gahan took sick and died. I doubt the Lord Protector could have been fouled thus. I know for certain only that he *is* dead."

"Taerl is Lord Protector now. Or shall be, after the ceremonies." Sarun barked a bitter laugh. "Sad ceremonies those shall be, eh? Gahan's funeral followed by Taerl's dedication."

"Taerl's no more than a lad." I spoke softly: I thought that must be a dreadful responsibility, to assume the mantle of Lord Protector so young.

"He's sixteen years." Rekyn echoed my own thoughts. "In the God's name, what a burden to set on him. Even with Jareth appointed Regent."

"Jareth?" Sarun sent the dagger clattering across the desk as he rose to fill his mug. "Jareth's likely to prove the heavier burden."

I knew what prompted his distaste. Jareth was koryphon of Mardbrecht, the greatest of the Border Cities. That alone vested him with much power. That he was wed to Gahan's younger sister gave him more—a claim, after Taerl (who was not yet wed), to the office of Lord Protector. Did Taerl die childless, Jareth could claim the High Throne of Kherbryn by marriage right. He was not a popular man, Jareth. It was said he made the land along the Slammerkin his kingdom, and that his tithes were enforced with a strictness bordering on the extortionate. It was said he built himself a palace to rival Gahan's, and that he lusted after the office of Lord Protector. He had his sycophants, but I wondered how many would take his cause in battle, for he was also said to be a leader who commanded from behind.

Even as I nodded, Sarun muttered, "There are enough must object to his regency. Did he claim Kherbryn for his own . . ."

I asked, "Would he dare?"

Sarun only fixed me with a dour look; it was Rekyn who answered, "Jareth and Yraele have a daughter, no?"

I said, "Avralle, yes."

"Who is," Rekyn went on, "now fourteen years of age."

I saw it in the instant. It had not occurred to me before, because I had not thought Gahan should die so soon. I gasped and blurted out, "And in two more shall be of marriageable age."

"Indeed," Rekyn said. "And is Jareth regent for those two years, he might well persuade Taerl to choose his daughter for a wife."

"Which should bind Jareth closer still," I murmured.

"Closer?" Sarun interrupted with a snarl. "By the God, it should in all effect give him Kherbryn. He'd be Lord Protector in all but name. Perhaps that, too, does his ambition run higher than his courage."

"And there are enough object to Jareth that some," Rekyn turned sharp eyes on the young aeldor, "might oppose him."

"Civil war?" I looked from one to the other. "When the Sky Lords threaten the Great Coming?"

"Not all see so far ahead as you," said Rekyn. "There are some might well forget the greater threat."

"I think," said Sarun, "that which is the greater threat—Jareth or the Sky Lords—is a matter of some debate."

I asked, "Why did Gahan name him regent?"

"That shall likely remain a mystery." Rekyn's voice was tired, and as she went to fill her cup, she groaned, stretching her back as if too long asaddle. "Gahan was on his deathbed when he named Jareth. Perhaps he could think of no other. Perhaps—"

Sarun's laughter cut her off. It sounded to me like the barking of an angry hound. "Jareth came south fast enough once he'd word. By the God, he must have killed horses to reach Kherbryn so swift!"

"Perhaps Yraele persuaded Gahan," Rekyn went on. "She's ambitious for her husband. However it came about, the fact remains."

"Perhaps Jareth had Gahan poisoned."

Sarun ignored Rekyn's gasp. He could not ignore her words, for they came furnace-hot and sharp as edged steel. "Hold such thoughts to yourself, Sarun. For Cambar's sake! For the sake of Gwennet and Bardaen; for your unborn! Were that voiced abroad, how long do you think you'd live?"

Sarun shrugged, though he now wore a somewhat shamefaced

expression. He took up his dagger again, running a thumb along the edge. "I'll not voice them," he muttered. "But I'll wager I'm not the only one to hold them. For the God's sake, Rekyn—can you tell me you've not wondered? Gahan dead so sudden, and Jareth come arunning? Perhaps magic was used on Gahan, to slay him or persuade him."

"No sorcerer would stoop so low!" Now the commur-mage's voice was a whiplash. "I know not what killed the Lord Protector, but there's no sorcerer come out of Durbrecht would soil themselves so."

Sarun looked chastened. Indeed, I found Rekyn frightening then. I said, "But Taerl shall be Lord Protector, Jareth only Regent. And that no longer than it takes Taerl to attain his twenty-one years."

"For three of which Jareth shall stand at his shoulder," Sarun said, but softer now. "Whispering in his ear; and perhaps in two, his whispering shall persuade Taerl to wed Avralle. What do you know of Taerl, Daviot?"

I was a moment taken aback. I frowned, harvesting memories. Then I said, "Not very much, save he's Gahan's son by Elvyre, who is six years dead. He spent two years in Mardbrecht; two in Durbrecht. It's said he's a quiet fellow, with a great love of horses."

"He's young and feckless," said Sarun. "He'd sooner ride than govern. Oh"—this with a glance at Rekyn that said he did not forget her warnings—"I'd not speak against him. Were Gahan yet alive, I'd not doubt the boy should be whipped into shape, and I'd pledge fealty when the time came. But now? Do the Sky Lords come, Jareth will command; and Jareth's not the man for that task. In the God's name, I like this situation not at all."

"I suspect your sentiments are shared throughout Dharbek." Rekyn spoke dryly. "Indeed, I'd wager this very conversation echoes up and down the land. But still it remains that Jareth *is* named regent. The why of it may be questioned, but there is no doubt at all that Gahan named him. And with what we face, accord is needed, not argument."

Sarun nodded, but his face was sour. "Think you Jareth shall command us well?" he asked. "Do we face the Great Coming as you sorcerers believe, shall Jareth lead us or sit safe in Kherbryn?"

"Do the Sky Lords come as I believe," Rekyn said, "then I think Jareth shall be no safer in Kherbryn than any other place. I think there shall be nowhere safe in Dharbek."

I sat listening with half an ear, offering no further comment. They spoke somewhat in circles now, of factions and rivalries, of blood lines and marriage treaties, of who should support Jareth and who oppose. Did it come to open war, I thought Sarun should lead

Cambar's men in rebellion, so fervent was his dislike. I was not sure Rekyn would support him. I thought that—just as the commur-mage had said—there must be keeps throughout all Dharbek ringing to the same words. I thought this death could not have come at a worse time. Gahan was popular; better, he was wise. He was a leader, which it appeared Taerl could not yet be. And was Sarun's animosity shared, then Jareth's appointment seemed more likely to foment dissent than promote union. I felt an awful fear that the Sky Lords should mount their Great Coming against a land torn by civil strife.

I heard Rekyn ask a question and let go my musings.

"You understand, Daviot, that what's been said here must remain between us? You'll not speak of it elsewhere?"

Almost, I smiled: I grew well versed in the keeping of secrets. I said, "I understand: I'd not betray you. But when I return to Durbrecht? The College will have an accounting of me then, and I'll be asked what mood pertains where I've been. Am I to hold silence then?"

Neither spoke immediately, and when an answer came, it came from Rekyn. It seemed Sarun deferred to her in such matters. "I think," she said slowly, as if each word unwound her thoughts, "that you had best speak openly then. Your College and mine both have say and sway in Dharbek's affairs, and perhaps it were better the mood of the holds be known. But not until you return, eh?"

I was glad to find my bed that night, though sleep was harder found. I lay on sweat-damp sheets, the air thick, the light of the now-full moon seeming warm as if the sun yet held sway. How long I lay awake I was not sure, but I did eventually sleep, for the dream came back.

It came distorted, without its usual strange coherence, so that when I woke, I retained only fragments, as if my memory failed me. I was once more in the wood, but there was no mist, and I looked across a sun-washed sea to distant islands. Then the sky grew black, and dread possessed me. I heard the weird singing of elementals, and through the darkness came the red cylinders of the Sky Lords' boats. I cowered, and the sky was black no longer but the color of blood. Beams rose from the islands, clawing at the skyboats. Where they struck, the skyboats blazed and fell, but there were so many that each gap was on the instant filled. They covered the heavens from horizon to horizon. I heard Rwyan scream my name, and I stood on a beach of bleached white stone, my love beside me.

She said, "Daviot, hurry! We've little time. Save we act, all's lost."

I turned to ask her what she meant, but a great wave rose up, that I saw was made by the beating of a dragon's wings. A shadow passed over me, and my head rang with the creature's scream.

It landed on a cliff where black pines grew, Whitefish village below. Then cliff became city wall and the village became Durbrecht. The city burned, the walls lay ruined, and where the College of the Mnemonikos should have stood was an open place, at its center a splendid catafalque surrounded by mourners. I glimpsed Urt amidst the rubble, Rwyan at his side, and took a step toward them, then was frozen by the dragon's scream.

I stared up, unable to disobey the imperative in that cry. The dragon perched on its hindquarters, a jet-armored Kho'rabi clutched in one sword-taloned paw. The Kho'rabi swung a useless blade against skin impervious to his blows. The dragon raised the struggling man. I watched aghast as the great head dropped, jaws opening, and the dragon bit the Kho'rabi. The body fell separated, and the dragon opened its jaws wide, again emitting that piercing scream. I was suddenly surrounded by Kho'rabi, but they ignored me, raising long bows to send black arrows volleying at the dragon. The missiles made no impression on the sleek blue hide, and the dragon seemed not to notice them, save it spread its wings and beat them three times, which sent the Sky Lords tumbling like windblown leaves. I could not understand why I was not blown away, but I stood untouched and alone as the beast folded its vast wings and fixed me with its yellow stare.

It seemed less terrible, albeit indifferent to the corpses strewn about its taloned feet. I thought its look benign. It seemed to call me, and I beckoned Rwyan and Urt on as I began to climb the broken wall. I knew that could I reach it, the beast must give me answers, though I did not know the questions I should ask. I scrambled upward, but as I approached the dragon, the sky was filled again with the Kho'rabi vessels, and it spread its wings, readying to fly. I shouted, begging it to wait, but it launched itself, and the beating of its wings tumbled me down. I heard Rwyan say, "Daviot, we must—"

—And I woke.

The sheet was tangled at my feet, and sweat drenched me. My head ached and my limbs were heavy as I rose, stumbling to the pitcher. The water was tepid, but I drank and doused my head, and then stood, my chest heaving, against the sill, staring out. It was not yet full dawn, but the sky already possessed a leaden intensity, and the air was hot as noon on a midsummer day. The keep's thick stone was warm as an oven's. The yard below was silent, but I could still hear the sound of the dragon's wings. The chamber seemed suddenly too small. I turned from the window and washed, then pulled on shirt and breeks, my boots, and went out.

Changed servants moved sleepily about the hall. I thought they seemed less troubled by the heat than Truemen, though their movements were leisurely. I asked a cat-bred woman if I might have tea, making sure she caught sight of my bracelet. She showed no more sign of recognition than Tal, but she brought me tea and fruit and bread, for which I thanked her.

I broke my fast and sat awhile as the warband appeared. Of Rekyn or Sarun, there was no sign, but Andolyne came in holding Bardaen's hand. The dowager gave me the day's greetings and took a place with a weary sigh, favoring me with a wan smile.

"Oh, but this heat, Daviot," she murmured. "I can hardly bear it, but poor Gwennet . . ."

"She's close?" I asked, and Andolyne nodded, answering me, "Garat stays by her. He says any day now." She shook her head. "Sad times, no? That a babe be born with Gahan dead and the Great Coming likely."

"Sad times indeed," I agreed. "But all well . . ."

Bardaen set to tugging at my sleeve then, demanding a story, and I took him on my knee, giving him the tale of Dryff and the Boar of Draggonek. By the time that was told, the hall had filled and Rekyn found me. I looked at her with brows raised in question, and she nodded, ruffling Bardaen's hair. By unspoken consent, we said nothing of Gahan or what had passed in Sarun's chamber, but talked instead of calmer days. She'd have a full accounting of all my time in Durbrecht and after, and I found myself recalling memories tucked away in the drawers of that mnemonic chest that dead Martus had described. I went into no great detail about my friendship with Urt or my too-brief time with Rwyan, and I said nothing at all of Lan's bracelet or that sighting of Kho'rabi and Changed together. It saddened me that I should be less than honest with so old a friend, but I thought Rekyn's first duty was to Dharbek and to Cambar, and that did I reveal my secrets, she would likely see no choice but to report them to her College. I felt trapped in my own dissemblance.

If Rekyn sensed my concealments, she gave no sign but suggested we walk into the town. She would, she promised, bring me to the cottage that Delia shared with Kaenc. I agreed, though first I'd see my horse was well—this heat was no kinder to animals than to men, and we had a long journey ahead of us, was I to make my way north up the coast and then along the Treppanek to Durbrecht.

We went to the stables, where a Changed ostler with a bandage about his forearm advised me my mare was indeed as foul-tempered as I had warned. I looked her over (it seemed by now she tolerated me somewhat or had decided to call a truce) and found her fit enough. Rekyn eyed her and said softly, " 'Twas Andyrt first put you on a horse, no?"

I said, "It was; and by the God, I ached after."

She chuckled at that, as I'd hoped she should, and shook her head, murmuring, "Old grief. Best left behind."

I nodded, saying no more. Mnemonikos are not alone in harboring memories. Ours are just clearer, held with a precision, a clarity, that is ofttimes heartbreaking.

We walked leisurely from the keep into a town drained and dulled by the oppressive heat. Awnings that would not in a normal year have been unfurled until months later shaded the buildings, and the few folk we saw moved lethargic. Most held to the shade. We went down to where the fisherfolk beached their craft, and Rekyn pointed out a cottage.

"Do you go greet your sister," she suggested, "and I'll await you in the Flying Fish."

I nodded, studying the cottage. It was twin to my parents', with a little yard before, a vegetable patch behind. The vegetable patch was arid, what few shoots showed, withered and limp. The smell of rotting seaweed hung familiar in the air. I thought it should be good to see Delia again: she had always been my favorite. Eager, I went to the door, which stood open beneath a canopy fashioned from an old sail, and called her name.

My sister came out, an inquiring frown on her pretty face. She wore a scarf about her hair, and her hands were floured. I knew her immediately, for all she was a woman now, full grown and become beautiful.

She stared at me a moment, recognition dawning slowly. I said, "Do you not know your brother, Delia?" and her face lit up, and I was almost felled as she flung herself into my arms.

"Daviot! Is it truly you, Daviot? I scarce knew you. You're a Storyman? Shall you stay?"

She led me inside as she spoke, the words a tumble, question piling on question—all those things a sister demands of a brother not seen in many years. I answered her as she saw me seated at a rough table, a cup set in my hands and thin yellow beer poured me. She was well, yes; and happy: Kaene was a good husband. He was out fishing now—the God grant him success—in a boat half-owned, hopefully soon theirs, save this weather leached the Fend of fish. They had no children as yet—a blessing, given such troublous times—but later . . . And I? Had I been to Whitefish village? I'd heard of Tonium's death? Mam and Da, they were well? She and Kaene sailed south as time and work allowed. . . . Where had I been, where did I go? Did I stay in the keep? I'd heard, then, of Bardan's death?

We tossed news back and forth, and I could hardly drink my beer for holding of her hands. It was good to see her again.

In time, I told her I must go, that Rekyn awaited me and I'd duties now. She offered me bed and board, which I declined, explaining it was expected I should stay in the keep. I thought the feeding of an extra mouth should cost her and Kaene dear. I promised to come back, had I the opportunity, and assured her that I looked forward to meeting Kaene. I might well speak in one of the taverns, I told her, and she bade me let her know which that she might hear me. Her pride in my accomplishments embarrassed me. We embraced, and I walked away.

I found Rekyn in the Flying Fish, a tankard of ale before her. She called for another as I took a chair. When it was brought, I asked, "Does Cambar suffer much?"

"No worse than any other hold." Rekyn leaned back, stretching out her long legs. She wore her leathers still and her sword, as if she thought she might be momentarily called to battle. "Sarun's set stores aside, but does this heat continue, he'll likely need open his warehouses to feed the hold-folk."

Her voice was grim, and I studied her face before I spoke again. "Does your College not seek answers?" I asked her.

"Seek, aye," she returned me with a cynical chuckle. "But find? As yet, no. The Kho'rabi wizards command such magicks as we've never guessed at—they surpass us in the occult talent. And Jareth commands our armies now." She raised her mug in mockery of a toast. "By the God, Daviot! Gahan could not have died at a worse time. Dharbek suffers now; by Sastaine, we'll know famine. There's disease in the cities, and that must worsen as this heat continues. Did you know there's been rioting in Durbrecht?"

I shook my head, horrified.

"In Durbrecht and in Kherbryn, too," she went on. "This last sevenday, word came that a merchant's caravan was ambushed crossing the massif. In Lynnisvar a grain boat was attacked by starving folk, and the aeldor must bring his warband to drive them off. Does it continue so, we'll see chaos before the Sky Lords come."

"Surely Jareth must take some action," I said, though I was unsure what might be done.

Rekyn shrugged and drained her tankard. I called for more ale. When we were alone again, Rekyn said, "The Changed grow troublesome, too. We've not seen it here as yet, but there are Changed have fled their masters to go wild into the mountains, or to cross the Slammerkin. Not too many as yet, but should enough take flight . . . the God knows, we'd see chaos then."

The results of that action I had already pondered. I thought— fleetingly—that did Truemen treat the Changed better, they should be more likely to stand by us. I did not think that was a view to put to Rekyn now, and so I said, "They go to Ur-Dharbek? Can that be a kinder land?"

"Who'd know?" she gave me back, and laughed again, with a bitterness I'd not before seen in her. "Jareth, perhaps? He's, after all, from the greatest of the Border Cities."

Old memories flung themselves to the forefront of my mind; old questions came, too tempting to ignore. "Is there truly so little known of Ur-Dharbek?" I asked.

I watched Rekyn's face as I voiced the question and as she answered. I was not certain what I saw there: alarm, perhaps, or concern, though for what I could not guess.

She said obliquely, "You've an interest in that place, eh?"

I spread dismissive hands. "I've an interest in all this land: I'm a Storyman."

"But your College told you nothing?"

I suspected she dissembled. Not for the first time, I wondered why. I answered, "Nothing more than all know."

"But you'd know more than all?" Her eyes locked on my face. "Why, Daviot? Is there so little in this land that you must delve the mysteries of Ur-Dharbek?"

"Are there mysteries?" I returned.

She chuckled then, her head shaking slightly as if in disbelief of my persistence. I thought the laugh better humored. "This interest in the Changed has brought you trouble ere now, no?" Her eyes did not leave my face. I was once more minded of the dragon's gaze, but now I frowned surprise that she should know this. She saw it and said, "Oh, Daviot, take off that startled look, and I'll tell you what you'd likely learn in time, save I suspect you already guess somewhat of it."

There seemed real amusement in her eyes now. We both supped before she spoke again.

"Are you not told to bring back word of what you see along your Storyman's road? Of the keeps' moods, their readiness for war?" Her fine, dark brows rose, and I nodded mute agreement. "And no less are we sorcerers commanded to report on you. Had you not thought as much?"

I said, "I'd wondered—aye, I'd suspected it was so."

"Then a word of warning," she said gently, "from a friend. Have a care what questions you ask. Perhaps show less of this feeling for the Changed. Your friendship with your servant served you ill, no?"

I was abruptly aware of the bracelet on my wrist. Almost, I took my hand from the table to hide the bangle, then knew it for foolishness. Did Rekyn know it for what it was, then it was too late to hide it. Did she not, then best make nothing of it. I said defensively, "He was my friend. Is that wrong?"

"In some folk's eyes, it is," she said. "I'd not say it so, but there are others. . . . Jareth, for example, is known to scorn the Changed."

I said, "Without them, we'd know chaos. You said that much yourself."

"So I did." She nodded. "And so it is; or would be, did worse come to worst."

Her voice trailed off, and for a moment she stared into her ale. Her face was clouded, and she toyed absently with a strand of dark hair. I had not thought to see Rekyn so irresolute. I waited, sensing she reached a decision of some kind. I was agog but curbed my impatience, for I felt she was about to speak of things, if not forbidden, then seldom said. I was minded of conversations with Lan: I thought perhaps another piece of the puzzle should come my way. Rekyn raised her head to look me in the eye again, and I saw her choice was made.

"Likely I should not tell you this," she said quietly, "but I've a feeling about you. I cannot explain it, save"—she smiled and sighed a laugh—"save were I a seer, I'd tell you destiny sits on your shoulder. So—you've wandered abroad enough to see how much we depend on the Changed?"

I said, "Without them, Dharbek should be helpless, I think."

"We've come to depend on them perhaps too much." Her handsome face was grave now, and her eyes flickered about the room, as if to ensure she was not overheard. "And likely there are those amongst them know it. I think those who flee across the Slammerkin must."

She paused. I saw this was no easy thing for her to say and asked, "But shall you sorcerers not employ your magicks to create more? Enough to replace those who flee?"

I was surprised when she shook her head; amazed at her words. She said, "No, Daviot. We cannot."

My jaw gaped, and I could not suppress the gasp that escaped. Rekyn frowned, green eyes flashing a warning. I closed my mouth and set my hands about my tankard as if to anchor myself, leaning toward her across the table.

"We cannot," she went on in a voice only I might hear. "There's none can say exactly why, though some claim it's to do with our migration south. We found that talent when we dwelt in Ur-Dharbek, they say; when the dragons hunted us and we must create prey for them. Since we crossed the Slammerkin, we've had no need for the talent. Instead, our magic was bent to conquering Draggonek and Kellambek, and then to defeating the Sky Lords."

She fell silent as the serving woman came asking if our mugs needed replenishment. We drained them and sat unspeaking as the red-haired woman fetched us fresh. Then Rekyn continued: "All the efforts of my College were given to the creation of the Sentinels, to mastering those gramaryes that enable us to meet the Kho'rabi wizards in battle. We saw the Changed already made bred young—there seemed little need to create more through magic when nature gave us sufficient. Now, it appears we've forgotten the way of it."

"How can you forget?" I asked.

Her lips curved in a smile empty of humor. "We're not Mnemonikos, Daviot," she said. "Perhaps did we not guard our secrets so close, but had entrusted those gramaryes to your kind. . . . But no matter; we did not, and there it is."

"But," I asked, bewildered, "how can you forget a talent? Surely once developed—"

"Perhaps *forget* is the wrong word," she said. "Perhaps it's that we took our talent down a different road; perhaps it was some thing intrinsic to Ur-Dharbek, or our need then. Whatever, we've lost it now."

"Do you say that the sorcerous talent is a thing of the land?" I must remember to hold my voice low, as if we engaged only in casual conversation, and that was no easy discipline. "That *where* you are shapes *what* you are?"

"Some do," she told me. "For my own part, I know not. But I could not take some beast and make of it a Changed."

I shook my head even as a thought burst inside. I stared at Rekyn and said low-voiced, "Do you say we Dhar somehow gained the talent whilst we sojourned in Ur-Dharbek? *Because* we lingered there?"

It was rhetoric: I sought to pin down my sudden thought, but still she confirmed me, "Some say it so, aye."

"Then if they be correct," I murmured, "shall the wild Changed not develop sorcerous abilities?"

It was as though a shutter lifted to expose a bright-lit room, or a torch were ignited to spill brilliance where before there had been only shadow, and I was dazzled. I felt pieces of the puzzle join; there was no complete picture yet, but I saw its outline grow clearer.

Rekyn faced me square across the table, and I was again minded of the dragon's gaze. "Likely," she said. "It's suspected, at least."

I said, "By the God!" For all the heat, I felt a chill course down my spine.

"Now do you understand why your interest in the wild Changed has found such disapproval?" she asked me, and when I nodded, dumbstruck: "I should not have told you this. Such knowledge is forbidden, and I break a vow in the doing. Do you voice it, then likely you and I both shall find ourselves on the scaffold."

I nodded. I was too intrigued then to feel any fear. That would come later, but in that moment I felt only awe; and a tremendous curiosity. I asked her, "How many know this?"

"We sorcerers," she said, "the master of your College, the Lord Protector, the koryphons; none others. It's a secret close-guarded."

I licked my lips, staring at her. Close-guarded? Aye, for what should be the outcome did the folk of Dharbek—Truemen and Changed both—learn of this? Even were it no more than suspicion, it must turn our world on its head. I thought the Changed should surely abandon the land to flee north, to gain that power that was now the sole property of their masters. I thought Truemen should fight to halt them. I thought there should surely be such chaos delivered us all as must hand Dharbek like some festival gift to the Sky Lords. I stared at Rekyn and felt fear stir behind my wonderment.

"Did you speak aught of this," she said carefully, "then likely Sarun—or any aeldor—would have your tongue torn out before execution. And mine with it."

I said, "Aye," aware my voice came hushed and hoarse. "Save not *likely*, but surely. But Rekyn, why do you tell me?"

She shrugged then, a smile haunting her mouth as puzzlement misted her eyes. "I cannot say," she told me. "Not beyond that I've a feeling about you. I can explain it no better, save perhaps the telling shall serve to bind your questioning tongue."

"Bind it?" I snorted bitter laughter. "Rekyn, you float a lure before my curiosity and tell me do I chase it, I must die."

"Were you not already chasing it, in your own way?" she gave me back. "You go from keep to keep asking your questions—What does this sorcerer know of the wild Changed? What that of Ur-Dharbek? You show open friendship of the Changed; you deal with them as equals, never hiding your beliefs. Oh, Daviot, leave off that face! I've told you we've a duty to observe, just as you do. In the

God's name, my friend, you hold the history of the Dhar in your head; you've knowledge few others possess. With all of that and clear evidence you perceive the Changed as little different to Truemen, think you you've not raised hackles? There are some have urged you be called back to Durbrecht—found some position within your College, where your curiosity might be tight-reined, you all the time watched. Save you've won yourself a reputation as the finest Storyman in decades, you'd be there now; and warded close as any prisoner."

I was, I must admit, flattered that I had earned such a reputation. I was also shocked that the College of the Mnemonikos should curb investigation: I had thought we Rememberers were above such things, that it was our bounden duty to seek knowledge, no matter where it lead. I was, too, alarmed: I'd no wish to lose my freedom or my life.

"Shall I be?" I asked somewhat nervously.

"No." Rekyn shook her head, smiling warmly. I was grateful for that reassurance. "So long as you watch your tongue, you're safe. And now you know the reason for the doubts you've raised, perhaps you'll step a little wary."

"I shall," I vowed. I made that promise to myself as much as her. It was not, I thought, the same as promising I'd do nothing.

"Then we shall speak no more of this," she declared. "I've a fondness for you—I'd not see you end on the scaffold."

I smiled my gratitude and asked, "One last question?" And when she sighed and gestured, I continued: "What purpose the Border Cities?"

"Much like the Sentinels," she replied. "Save they ward the Slammerkin shore."

"Against invasion?" I frowned. "Can the wild Changed have become so powerful?"

Rekyn confirmed it. "Against that fear," she said. "Against the possibility the wild Changed find magic and look to use it against us."

I emptied my mug in silence. A thousand thoughts buzzed in my head, each one birthing myriad others. I thought I should like to be alone awhile to digest all this, but Rekyn set her tankard down and suggested we return to the keep. I nodded dumbly and followed her out.

Part III

Destiny's Weaving

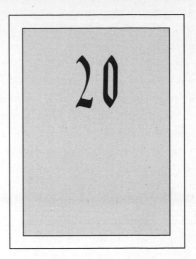

20

Rwyan had learned much since first she came to the Sentinels, but never the magic of unlearning. Sometimes she wished she might possess such knowledge, to obliterate that memory of Daviot that lay always in the hinder part of her mind like a wound that would not heal. It was a foolish notion, impossible to achieve, and she berated herself for entertaining such useless fancies. She had a duty here; the God knew, if the worst fears of the sorcerers were realized, she had a desperate duty ahead. But still she could not forget him.

She had tried. She had taken a lover briefly and when his attentions grew boring to her, another, but he had lasted no longer, and after that she had spurned all advances. Now none looked to bed her but accepted her as celibate, which was, they murmured when they thought she should not hear, a pity. That amused her, for she agreed; but could find no way to change her feelings. Sometimes she allowed herself to wonder if Daviot felt the same way, or if he now followed his Storyman's road with a woman or found comfort in the keeps. But did he, she told herself, still he'd not forget her—his talent would not allow that.

She sighed, dabbing at her face with a sleeve. There should have been a breeze so high atop the cliffs, but there was none. The pines stood silent under a sky that seemed a canopy of hammered blue, so bright as to shine silvery. Had she turned her head, she knew the vast column of the tower looming above the island would have blinded even her occult sight. The sun was a merciless eye, searing all it surveyed. The Fend spread like puddled mercury, calm as a millpond. No sails broke that expanse; even the gulls that rode the warm air seemed lethargic, their mewing dulled, as if they lacked the vitality to protest such heat. Rwyan wondered how long the Sky Lords would maintain this magic, and if the sorcerers of Dharbek should ever find a countering sortilege. She wondered how Daviot fared in such weather.

Too often, she dreamed of him, and those dreams were strange. She had mentioned them to Chiara—who dismissed them as no more than foolish fancy—and to the adepts, who were more sympathetic, if little more helpful. None could offer either interpretation or remedy, and the draughts the island's herbalist had prescribed had served only to lock her longer in that oneiric world she walked with Daviot.

With Daviot and others she did not recognize.

She sighed again, closing her eyes against the blinding sky, and allowed her mind to wander.

At first she had dreamed of their shared past, of times together and the things they had done, embarrassed when she woke by the flush that suffused her cheeks, the pleasant languor that pervaded her limbs. But then, gradually, the tenor of the dreams had changed, past memories fading into a strangely shifting pattern.

Sometimes she would see Daviot striding purposefully down a lonely road, she hurrying behind. An airboat would drift unnoticed above him, and she would call out, but he seemed not to hear or to ignore her, and then she would run after him, laboring up a slope he climbed with ease, to disappear over the crest. She would reach the ridgetop and find the road ahead empty, the surrounding fields sere, the woodland bleak. She would stare about, calling his name, but there was never an answering shout, and night would fall as she stood alone.

Sometimes she would find herself in a crowd, in a town square or the hall of a keep or the common room of an inn, always at the rear as Daviot intoned some tale she could not properly hear. She would endeavor to push through the throng, to announce herself, but always, before she could reach him, his tale would end and she find herself suddenly alone again, passersby ignoring her as if she were invisible.

Those dreams she could explain to herself. They seemed obvious as the earlier, happier, conflations of memory. But now . . . for some time now she had found the dreams menacing and mysterious and could not at all understand them.

She would glimpse Daviot in a clearing in a misty wood, all gnarled and ancient oaks, the grass littered with the empty armor of Dhar warriors and Kho'rabi, as if once, long ago, a battle had been fought amongst the trees. She would hear him call her name, and sometimes others she did not know. She would see him turning warily around, as if he saw what was invisible to her, and she would go toward him, aware that danger threatened. She would see a Changed she guessed was Urt moving slowly through the mist from the far trees and know they must meet, come together to save Daviot from . . . she did not know what, save that overhead there came a sound like thunder, as if gigantic wings beat against the sky. She would look up then, but see nothing, only darkness and fog torn by the reiving of Kho'rabi wizardry, and hear Daviot call her name, forlorn. She could never come close to him, no matter how hard she tried, and even as she heard him shout, the mist would thicken, swirling, until she stood alone and there was no sound at all.

From those dreams she would wake trembling, held a moment in panic's fist, instinctively gathering her power to send against . . . nothing; only the dawn light pervading her chamber. And then she would attempt to set the dreams aside, to tell herself they were no more than the fevered imaginings of a foolish lovesick woman who had better forget what she could not have and bend her mind to what was real.

But as with the man himself, she could not quite dismiss the images. They lingered, a mental redolence she could never fully shake off. Nor did learning or labor, or nostrums or advice, serve to rid her of either the dreams or the memories, for all she threw herself into her duties with an energy designed to exorcise the ghosts.

That, at least, was one benefit: she did not languish, and if she pined, then her pining prompted her to work the harder. Hard enough she progressed, the older adepts Advised her, swifter than most Talented. Within the first year she had been raised, no longer a humble student, little more than a source of occult power for those more skilled than she, but tutored in the usage of that power, in its summoning and direction. By the end of her second year, she was declared adept; now she joined the others in the white tower, working with the crystals to focus that terrible energy on the intruding skyboats.

That had been unexpected knowledge, that the crystals both augmented and focused the natural abilities of the sorcerers. That was a thing no more than hinted at in Durbrecht, known for sure only to the senior Adepts and those consigned (Rwyan was almost tempted to think, *condemned*) to the Sentinels. Even the Lord Protector was vouchsafed only deliberately vague knowledge of some sorcerous device, and the Mnemonikos knew nothing at all. Rwyan and all those like her were sworn to secrecy.

They were called crystals, but they were far more than that: as different to the baubles cut and polished by the lapidaries as were those ornaments to pebbles. They had first come, she had learned, from Tartarus, the Forgotten Country. The earliest Dhar sorcerers had found (none could any longer say how) that the stones strengthened their natural power; through the stones they had learned to commune with the dragons and become Dragonmasters. The stones came south with the people, hoarded by the sorcerers, as they went into Ur-Dharbek, and then on, across the Slammerkin and the Treppanek. And all the time, the sorcerers had drawn strength from the stones, as if they lived symbiotic, the glittering chunks of quartzlike material invested with a crystalline vitality that none could properly understand or explain, only use.

With them, to those standing always in close proximity, there was a growth of power. It was, Rwyan thought, as if the crystals were hearthfires on a winter night, their blaze warming those closest to them, useless to any standing beyond the aegis of the heat. Thus were only the most talented of the College sent to the islands, only the most gifted of those allowed entry to the guarded chambers that held the strange stones; Chiara was somewhat piqued that she could not yet attend. Rwyan wondered if the crystals and her dreams were somehow linked.

It was an idle musing. She could no more understand the workings of the stones than those long versed in their use: they granted power, not knowledge. Neither was their employment without hazard —to remain in close proximity for too long resulted in madness or in a draining of the occult talent, as if the flow of power became reversed, leaving the victim a mindless shell. No sorcerer remained indefinitely on the Sentinels, and the crystals were shielded behind walls of lead and stone, exposed only at need. Were she not dismissed earlier, she knew she must depart the island in ten or fifteen years—a lifetime!— to live in Durbrecht or find place in some keep as commur-mage. Meanwhile, however, she sensed her powers expanding, growing, as if accelerated by the unseen pulsing of the crystals. She knew there was a dreadful insensate energy in the stone behind her and that it might be shaped and directed, by those with the talent, to blast the Sky Lords' vessels from the heavens.

She thought it sad (though she was careful to hold the notion to herself alone) that such occult power be used bellicose. She wondered what might be achieved, did the Sky Lords not force her kind to bend the crystals to warfare. She supposed she was not, for all she owned recognized ability, a good mage: Chiara would never have entertained such thoughts.

But then Chiara had never sat with Daviot, building an imaginary world of *maybe* and *perhaps* and fanciful supposition, where dragons still flew and peace was forced on Kho'rabi and Dhar alike.

And I think of Daviot again! I must not; I cannot, for it hurts too much.

She rose, shaking out a gown damp with sweat, and "looked" a last time across the smooth surface of the Fend. It was as though the sea steamed; the coastline of Kellambek was a shadowy blur on the horizon, a faint, dark line drawn through the shimmering heat.

Had Daviot ever sailed such a sea? Might he, even now, stand somewhere on that vague shore, staring toward the Sentinels, remembering?

She brushed an errant strand of hair now more golden than red from her face and turned away, resolute. There were duties to attend, lessons; come dusk, she must take a turn on watch in the tower. The vigilance of the Sentinels was never-ending: to allow thoughts of Daviot to intrude when she must be alert against the danger of the Sky Lords was to be derelict of her duty. She found the path and began the long descent.

She had reached the foot of the path when the summons came: *The Sky Lords come! To your posts, now!*

She registered confirmation and her presence, and began to run toward the tower, all thoughts of bath and fresher clothes forgotten.

She was but one of the many racing to Dharbek's defense, the island become abruptly a place of organized confusion. No more than a handful of Adepts would join their talents directly to the crystals' power, but for that score there would be another, living conduits between the wielders and the human fodder lending their ability to those who sent the magicks against the intruders. She had liked the experience not at all, when she had been amongst the suppliers of occult strength. It was needful and she had submitted without demur, but she could never quite overcome the feeling it was a thing vampiric, as if the used—no matter the purpose or the need—gave up some part of their souls. She enjoyed it little more when she took the part of conduit, for there seemed to her something of the pander about that, and always, after, she must find a tub and scrub herself. She was glad (albeit a gladness tinged with guilt) that now she would stand amongst the senders, distanced from the others.

All these talented, she thought, *with such power in them, and all of it bent to destruction. We can wash the sky with fire, but not one of us can truly find an answer to the Sky Lords' magic. Must it be so, always?*

The thought was traitorous, and she pushed it away, composing her mind in readiness for what was to come. She was at the tower's door. Alrys and Demaeter stood there, ushering her inside, pointing unnecessarily to the arched opening on her left, where sorcerers already mounted the winding stairway to the column's topmost level. The stairway rose, spiraling up the tower's interior, lit now by globes of heatless white floating overhead, the walls unbroken by door or window until there came a second arched entry. Here the twenty channelers gathered, settling into high-backed chairs placed in a circle in a bare chamber. Rwyan clambered on until she reached the topmost level, where the tower stood open to the sky. There were no chairs here, nor decoration of any kind, only the chest-high walls that granted a wide view over the Fend, and the pedestal supporting the crystal, that no more than waist-high, carved of black basalt, the stone in a hollow at the center, the shields removed.

It was so small a thing to hold such power. She might have held it in both her hands, and it looked no more than a knob of agate, lumpy, and banded with layers of pale color, all shifting and shining under the sun. So small, so insignificant to those without the talent; to the sorcerers, so powerful, its strength a palpable force. Rwyan felt the familiar tingling run through her body, as if all her nerves throbbed. It was a seductive sensation: there were some had fallen so deeply under that crystalline spell, they gave up their minds, even their lives to it. She shuddered, fighting off the temptation to touch the stone, to feel its power and let it drink of hers. That would come soon enough; instead, she directed her attention to the sky.

There was no disruption of the blue. Neither gulls nor kittiwakes, indeed no birds at all, ventured close to the roofless chamber, and she could not "see" the promised skyboats. She turned her face toward Gwyllym, whose mental broadcast had sounded this alarm. He had the watch, with Jhone and Maethyrene, and she could even now feel the faint vibration deep inside her skull that told her he communed with those below. His eyes were closed in concentration, and so she "looked" to the others. Jhone stood with her head raised, cocked slightly to one side, as if she listened to the silence. Maethyrene was turning, frowning as she counted the Adepts emerging from the arched doorway. Rwyan caught her eye and raised her brows in silent question.

The hunchbacked woman nodded, jabbing a thumb skyward. "No doubt of it, they come." Her voice was deep and musical. It seemed almost she sang the words. "Either a full-blown skyboat or a flock of those God-cursed little ones."

Jhone said, "They come swift. The little boats, I think."

Gwyllym said, "All below stand ready. Do we prepare?"

They grouped about the pedestal. Rwyan waited nervously for Maethyrene's command.

"Let us be ready."

She said it mildly, but none were slow to obey. Rwyan stared at the crystal, opening her mind to its magic, feeling it enter her, shocking as sudden immersion in freezing water, startling as an unexpected blow. For an instant nausea gripped her and she gagged, her sight gone. Then calm, the linkage with the minds below, not conscious, but as if she drank of naked power, was become insuperable. It was a heady sensation and always at first disconcerting. She was herself individual and at the same time a part of a greater whole, a unit in the gestalt formed with her fellows, joined in purpose and power. As her vision cleared, she "saw" the crystal pulsing, faint streamers of multihued light flickering like umbilical cords between the stone and those around it. She had not known she staggered until she became aware of Gwyllym's thick arm about her shoulders. She smiled her thanks and turned as he did, eastward, to where the enemy came.

They were the little boats, a score or more, bloodred cylinders hung within the disruption of the air caused by the elementals that drew them onward. Beneath were suspended the black baskets, like dories, containing the Sky Lords. She felt the weirdling magic of the aerial spirits, wild, angered by such enslavement, and beyond that the cold confidence of the Kho'rabi wizards, the implacable meshing of their sorcery, defensive and eager to strike.

Now!

Maethyrene's command was swifter than speech; obeyed no slower. As one, all twenty sorcerers summoned the power and sent it against the Kho'rabi vessels. Light pierced the sky, brighter than the sun, redly glittering lances of brilliance striking at the sanguine vessels, the sable baskets.

Five exploded. Rwyan felt the dying, the painful stab as human life ceased, assuaged by the rejoicing of the elementals as the spirits were freed, the sense of triumph that came from her companions. Terydd gloated: he enjoyed this too much. From Jhone and Gwyllym she felt a sorrow akin to her own, but steeled with the certainty that this battle must be fought. She gathered herself, pushing regret aside. The crystal pulsed—the Dhar sent out their minds in waves of pure destructive energy.

Light flashed, magic dueling with magic. That of the Sentinel was visible, that of the Kho'rabi wizards unseen, but still it was akin to the blades of master swordsmen, an occult struggle, parry and riposte, attack and counter. More skyboats burst in balls of searing fire. Rwyan heard the howling of the elementals; felt the grim determination of the Sky Lords, their anger.

Again and again the terrible beams struck out. The skyboats were reduced to twelve now; now seven. Five shot by safe, all the power of the guiding wizards bent on staving off the magic of the Dhar, on driving the elementals like madly lashed horses to the shore beyond the Fend. Of the remaining two, one erupted directly overhead. Rwyan felt the heat of its destruction; felt stuff touch her and struggled against horror as she knew blood and pieces of flesh rained on her. As though from far away, she heard Waende scream and saw the brown-haired woman scrubbing at a face all bloodied, ignoring the sparks that smoldered on her gown. Beyond the tower's retaining wall she saw the second skyboat falling, flame and smoke streamered behind. The Kho'rabi wizard was slain and the spirits he controlled fled —she could feel the absence: the vessel was no more than a burning boat, rudderless, impotent now.

It drifted toward the mainland, southward a little, the canopy of the supporting balloon blazing, the basket beneath afire. The dark shapes of men leaped from amongst the flames, falling down and down to the waiting sea. Rwyan felt Jhone's prompting and gathered herself, preparatory to striking again. Abruptly there was no need: flame ate the canopy, and the gas inside exploded. For a moment a ball of fire hung in the sky, a small second sun. The basket, trailing oily smoke, fell away. It seemed to fall forever, and then the sky was clear.

Gone. The God be praised, they're gone.

Maethyrene's sending was more relief than triumph.

There are no more. Yet.

Jhone slapped absently at a curl of scorching hair.

Aye, it's done.

Gwyllym sent word to those below.

Rwyan felt the linkages break, threads of occult energy tugging at her mind as if reluctant to quit their hold, and stepped an instinctive pace back as she broke her own communion with the crystal. The stone ceased its fervent pulsing, and she felt again that sense of loss, as if something precious were snatched from her. She dismissed it, fighting the desire to remain awhile longer one with the stone, blind a moment before she summoned her weaker magic to restore her "sight." Across the width of the tower's top she "saw" Waende weeping, Terydd holding her, using a sleeve to wipe blood from his lover's face. She looked down and "saw" her own gown stained. She felt weary, drained, and more than a little queasy; she was uncertain whether because she had slain men or because of the crystal.

"Enough." Gwyllym sounded not much better, but he squared his great shoulders and forced a tired smile. "Jhone, Maethyrene, do we remain until fresh watchers come? You others may go; rest. You did well. Those designated for tonight's watch will be replaced."

Rwyan needed no more prompting.

In her chamber, she shed her gown and filled a tub. The green linen was speckled with droplets of red and the pinhole marks of burning. In better times it might have been abandoned, but since the supply ships came so infrequently now, she decided it must be washed and repaired. But later; now she wanted only to languish in the bath, then scrub herself clean.

Scrub my flesh clean, she thought. *Inside, I shall still feel soiled.*

She could not understand why: she had done her duty, left no choice by the Sky Lords. She was unsure exactly what she felt . . . guilty? Certainly, such encounters as this day's left her with the feeling she was rendered somehow unclean. Yet the enmity of the Ahn was implacable—the God knew, she had felt that, like a foul dark wave coming from the skyboats—and there were few others of her kind felt any compunction at slaying the ancient enemy. Not all exulted in the fight, as did Terydd and some of his ilk; some, like Maethyrene, radiated a solemn resignation, but none felt any real regret. So why did she? Almost, she could wish she were less gifted, her talent weaker, so that she had not been chosen for the Sentinels but ordered to some keep. There seemed to her something close to obscenity in the battles the Sentinels fought, as if evil were brought out to oppose evil. Likely it should be a simpler life in a keep.

Would it, though? she wondered as she sank herself in the tub. *The keep sorcerers fight when the Sky Lords ground their boats, so what difference? Either way men die.*

She began to wash hair matted with blood, coated with ash, watching the water change color. *Perhaps,* she mused, *it's to do with the crystal. Or to do with me, solely. Perhaps I'm not the stuff from which true patriots are fashioned. Perhaps I've not the stomach for war and should be no better as a commur-mage. Perhaps I listened too close to Daviot, when he spoke of our driving the Ahn from their homeland. When he spoke of—no! I'll not think of him.*

Angry with herself, she rose to find the pump and sluice her body. It was always, she realized, after she had linked with the crystal that she thought the most of Daviot, dreamed the more. It was as though the stone opened some portal to grant memory better ingress. She dried herself (thinking it was near pointless in such heat) and tugged on a clean gown. She was hungry, and there would be company in the refectory to alleviate her megrims.

When she found it, the long room was already crowded: such magic as had been used today edged the appetite. Rwyan "saw" Gwyllym—like her, fresh bathed—deep in conversation with Cyraene and Gynael, Chiara listening even as her eyes wandered. The blond woman saw Rwyan and waved, indicating a place beside her. Rwyan smiled, somewhat tentatively, and nodded, making her way across the room. She hoped that with more senior sorcerers present, Chiara would not babble as usual about the day's events, not evince such bloodthirsty fervor. She wondered if she grew testy: in Durbrecht she had not thought of Chiara's chatter as babbling. Likely, she decided as she joined them, it was because Chiara found such pleasure in those things Rwyan herself found distasteful. She supposed they both had changed since coming here. She held her smile in place, aware that otherwise she might have scowled, as Chiara greeted her eagerly, already speaking of the fight.

"Better than a score, so Gwyllym says; and all but five destroyed. I wish to the God I'd been with you."

Rwyan waved that one of that day's servitors bring her ale and food. "Do you?" she asked. "It was not very pleasant. I've been washing off Kho'rabi blood."

"Dark blood that can no longer threaten Dharbek," said Chiara fiercely. "Like battle honors."

Rwyan fought irritation. "Poor Waende was drenched," she said, looking around. "Is she here? Is she well?"

Gynael said, "She's abed. Not hungry, she says, and somewhat disturbed. Marthyn gave her a sleeping draught."

"Best she not take a watch for a while," said Gwyllym. "But you, Rwyan, are you well?"

"Save for a burned gown." She smiled. She'd not say here she felt unclean. "Save for that, aye."

"Good." He nodded kindly. "Me, I've an appetite after that squabble."

"How," asked Chiara, "can you name it a squabble?"

"Easily." Gwyllym chuckled, catching Rwyan's eye and winking. "Now, shall we speak of gentler matters?"

Chiara was about to protest, but Cyraene patted her hand and bade her quiet. Rwyan could not decide whether she wanted to laugh or shake her friend as Chiara pouted, but at least she obeyed her lover, and the conversation moved away from the fight.

Not far: it was difficult to avoid discussion of the Sky Lords, of their newfound magic, and the likely imminence of the Great Coming.

None there doubted its approach; the sole question was when, and on that opinions differed. Rwyan favored no one opinion over another. Sometimes, secretly, she entertained the wish that somehow there be a peace forged; but that was surely no more than idle indulgence: the Dhar would not give back the land taken from the Ahn, any more than the Sky Lords would relinquish their claim. Not willingly; not without it be forced on them both. And how should that be accomplished?

Unless, came the errant thought, *Daviot's dreams be true, and we find the dragons and make them our allies.*

"Rwyan?" Gwyllym's voice intruded on her musing. "Where do you go, Rwyan?"

Before she could shape a reply, Chiara said, "Dreaming again! Of whom, Rwyan?"

"I thought," she said, favoring her friend with a glare, "that it were better to end this war before too many die."

"Were there a way, aye." Gwyllym nodded soberly, his craggy face grave. "But there is no way; not that I can see."

"Destroy the Sky Lords!" Chiara's pretty face became a harpy's mask, her voice strident. "Send every one of their God-cursed skyboats down in flames! Build boats of our own, to take the battle to them and lay waste their land!"

Her hands clenched in angry fists; her blue eyes flashed. Rwyan heard Gwyllym sigh, thinking he grew as bored with Chiara's fanaticism as she. Even Cyraene looked askance at the younger woman.

Gynael said, "You know we cannot build such boats. We can only endeavor to destroy theirs."

Her tone was soft, as if she delivered a reprimand to a willful child. Chiara turned defiant eyes on the silver-haired woman, lips parting to reply. Before she had chance to speak, Cyraene took her hand, still fisted, and patted gently. "Little one," she murmured, "you must learn to curb that ardor. You waste your anger, dreaming of what cannot be. We've our magic; they, theirs—so it is, and we must accept it."

For a moment, Chiara seemed about to argue, but then she nodded, her flushed cheeks paling. Rwyan was surprised Cyraene could affect her so; and grateful, for she was in no mood to suffer another eruption. Mildly, she said, "Were it only possible to speak with the Kho'rabi. Perhaps . . ."

Chiara interrupted with a snort laden with contempt. "You listened too much to Daviot, Rwyan. His mad dreams taint you. I give you Cyraene's advice—leave off dreaming of what cannot be."

Rwyan shrugged agreement, not wishing to fuel argument. Tempers grew short in such heat, and likely Chiara was right: Daviot had seeded an idea in her, and likely it was wild as the notion of Dhar airboats, or living dragons.

"Gently, gently." Gwyllym's tone was moderate, but beneath lay the steel of authority. "Could we build skyboats, aye—but we cannot. Could we speak with the Sky Lords, aye—but we cannot. We can only do our duty, and that shall be hard do we quarrel amongst ourselves."

Rwyan said, "Forgive me," thinking she had done little to warrant apology. Still, she'd not lose Chiara's friendship, for all the woman grew tiresome. *Had I such vehemence,* she thought, *I'd likely be happier. Surely I'd not entertain such doubts as plague me.*

Almost, she smiled at that—another impossibility—but she held her face solemn, attentive again as Gynael said slowly, "Upward of a score, Gwyllym? Why so many, think you?"

The big man shrugged, rough-hewn features expressing incomprehension.

Gynael lowered her wrinkled face as if in thought. "As many came against every one of the Sentinels, and as many were felled. Would they make such a sacrifice? It seems costly to me."

"The Sky Lords count lives cheap," said Cyraene.

"True," Gynael said, her hoarse voice contemplative. "But even so, it seems to me a terrible waste. It prompts me to wonder if all their scouting is not done. If they've garnered all the knowledge of Dharbek they need." She smiled sadly. "I think that what we saw today was a testing; perhaps the last. We've seen none of the great vessels in a year or more; nor lately the little skyboats. Now, of a sudden, they come like flies to a midden. Why should that be, think you?"

Her rheumy eyes found Rwyan's face, and as none other spoke, Rwyan said, "They'd know what magicks we command. Discover if we've learned aught to defeat them this past year."

"I think it so," said Gynael. "I think they sacrifice their little boats to gain that knowledge."

Beside her, Rwyan felt Chiara stiffen and "saw" her hand find Cyraene's. The dark-haired woman's face was paled, her lower lip worried by her sharp white teeth. Across the table Gwyllym sat with clouded visage, his eyes intent on Gynael. His deep voice was a rumble as he said, "The Great Coming."

"I'd guess it so." Gynael nodded, then smiled as if amused by their expressions. "Why such startled faces? Is this not what we expected?"

Aye, Rwyan thought, *it is. But to expect a thing and to face it are not the same. We are not ready; we've not the magic.*

"I'd thought," said Cyraene, her voice hushed, "to have more time. To find the key to defeating their magic . . ."

Her words tailed off. Gwyllym vented a bass chuckle devoid of humor. "As the seasons they send against us," he murmured, "so the clock runs faster."

"Too fast," whispered Cyraene.

That night, Rwyan dreamed she flew. She sat astride a great winged creature that was simultaneously incorporeal and substantial. She felt the beat of massive wings, the rise and fall of vast ribs, the rush of air that washed her face and streamered her hair, but she could not see the beast. No matter how hard she tried, she could not quite capture its image, so that even as she knew she hurtled through a sky darkening to star-pocked night, borne aloft by what she knew must be a dragon, she felt she was alone, upheld by nothing more than a dream. She grew afraid then, thinking that she must tumble down to the sea below. And Daviot was there, before her, her arms about his waist, her cheek rested snug against his back. She raised her face to nuzzle his hair, and he turned, smiling confidently.

He said, "You see? The dragons live still."

And she asked, "Where do we go?"

He pointed ahead, and Rwyan saw they had flown through the night, the darkness gone, replaced by the rising sun lifting from a horizon spread with three mountainous islands.

She asked, "Is that not the domain of the Sky Lords?"

And he answered only, "Aye."

Then, from one island, there rose a skyboat, rushing toward them. Rwyan saw the sigils glowing malign along the flanks of the bloodred cylinder and heard the eerie singing of the elementals. In the black basket beneath the cylinder, she saw the glint of sun on metal as bows were drawn. She felt the Kho'rabi wizards summon their magicks to send against her, against Daviot, and readied her own, unsure her strength should be enough to defeat so many.

She said, "Daviot, I'm afraid."

And he answered her, "What other choice is there?"

Rwyan woke then, the question still loud inside her head. She could not understand it; nor, all that day, could she forget it. She told no one, for she could not believe any on the island should own the answer; and it was, after all, only a dream.

In the tense days that followed, the dream returned nightly, always the same, unchanged and inexplicable. Rwyan set it aside as best she could and endeavored to concentrate on her duties. That was no easy task, for like all on the island, she waited on the summons to battle. When she walked abroad, she was not alone in looking often at the sky, and all the time that part of her attuned to the minds around her listened for the call that should send her to the tower and the crystal, to war.

One night a storm arose and she neither dreamed nor slept very much for the crash of thunder and the vivid illumination of the lightning that danced across the sky. She dared hope the tempest was herald of the occult summer's ending, but she was disappointed: the heat did not abate, and the next morning the air was again cloying, the sun a baleful eye overhead.

Then, when the storm was gone as if it, too, had been only a dream, her life was irrevocably changed.

21

The sun, although barely a handspan above the horizon, transformed the sky to a sheet of flawless blue silvered by the
rising heat. The boundary line separating the heavens from
the unbroken surface of the ocean was indiscernible, air and
water merging in burnished union. No motion of waves disturbed the
one, nor cloud the other: only the shimmering blue existed, fierce as a
furnace, painful to observe and soul-destroyingly empty. The corus-
cating glory of the dawn was a brief memory, the interim between
darkness and day burned off in an eye's blink, like gossamer feather
fallen in fire. What little cool the night had brought was gone as
swiftly, replaced by the intensity of the ascending sun.

The man turned slitted eyes from his observation to study the
rock on which he lay, optimism flaring and dying as swiftly as the
dawn. It had not changed since he had last seen it, despite his hope
that he was somehow, in some manner he could not comprehend,
caught in a dream that would end with the night. That forlorn solace

evaporated as he cast his eyes—what color were they? he wondered—
over the oblong slab of unblemished white.

It was exactly as he recalled, and he knew that if he summoned
the energy to rise and step out its confines, it would measure fifty
paces by nineteen, slanting a little upward after the thirtieth pace,
sloping about its perimeter into the ocean. That vast womb seemed to
wait, patient, knowing that in time it would have him, just as it had
welcomed the bleached bones he had cast upon its waters, as much to
introduce some disturbance, some leavening of the awful monotony,
as to rid the stone of the empty-eyed reminders that death stood close
by his shoulder. They had provided a small measure of grim amusement as he tossed them out over the featureless water, watching the
splashes, wondering what features had fleshed the skulls, what musculature once decorated the bones of arms and legs, the cages of the ribs.
He doubted they had been fat, not in this place; but what expressions had they worn when death reached out to touch them, telling
them the time had come? He grimaced at the melancholy thought,
wondering what his own would be, wondering what he looked like
now.

His body—those parts of it he was able to see—was tanned and
hard, the belly flat, the muscles firm, laced with corded sinew. His
fingers told him his mouth was wide and full-lipped, his nose broad;
the hair that fell long about his face was straight and black; but the
composition of his features, for all his attempts to catch his reflection
in the sea, remained a mystery. As much a mystery as his name, or
how he came to be here.

He eased stiffly to a sitting position, limbs grown adjusted to the
hard contours of the stone cramping, his mouth dry, the tongue sticky,
salted with the scent of the sea. To stand was an effort that spun his
head, exploding brilliance behind his eyes, but he forced himself to it,
flexing shoulders, turning a neck stiffened in fretful sleep to and fro
until his body had resumed some degree of mobility. He performed a
series of exercises he could not remember learning, their execution
ingrained, habit.

Then with nothing better to do, he sat again, sighing.

He did not know how he had come here, nor how long he had
been on this desolate slab, as unsure of those things as he was of . . .
everything.

It was easier to enumerate those things he did not know than his
knowledge of himself or his whereabouts. He did not know his name
or the place of his birth; he did not know how this ocean that surrounded him was named; he had no idea how he came here, which in
turn led to the thought that he did not know if he had enemies, or

friends, a family, a wife, or children. He did not know what he looked like, or how many years he had lived, or how he had lived them.

He knew so little: and that was the most frightening thing of all.

It seemed he was born full-grown upon this rock, birthed by the ocean itself perhaps, that awesome mother waiting to take him back, watching implacable as the sun fried his brain and pitched him into madness.

What might he do then? Plunge into the depths and drown? Or die withered by thirst and heat, his skin tightening over his bones until it cracked and fell away, leaving, finally, only a skeleton, perhaps for some other such as he to find. He was aware that he did not fear death in the same way that he knew such exercises as loosened his cramped limbs, but not how or why, and that blankness, that absence of memory, of self-knowledge, was the most galling aspect of this strange limbo.

He grunted, rising again, seeking in movement refuge from such melancholy contemplation. He was not dead yet, and whilst blood still pulsed in his veins, he would not give up, not turn to find death but flee from that embrace. He shaded his eyes, staring over the remorseless blue toward the scattering of similar rocks that jutted above the water. They were empty of life, though he suspected they held their caches of bones, offering no escape. He had thought of swimming to the closest—until he had seen the dark fins that occasionally clove the surface of the sea, judging from their size that the bodies beneath were sufficiently large to possess maws capable of swallowing him. In time, perhaps that would seem the more preferable option; but not yet. No: he was not ready yet.

He walked to the farther extension of the rock and crouched on the rim, peering down. Yesterday—or was it before yesterday? Time blurred in the amnesiac miasma of his memory—he had caught two crabs here, where the stone slab descended in a sharper curve to form a shallow bowl before slanting at a steeper angle into the depths. There had been more, moving about the pool, but he had been able to snatch up only two before the rest scuttled to the safety of the ocean. Neither was large, though he had received a painful abrasion from the pincers of one before smashing its shell against the stone, and the extraction of the raw meat did more to tell him his teeth were sound than assuage his hunger. But they had offered some sustenance: now there were none, and the scraps of broken carapace he had set out in faint hope of catching fresh water should rain fall or dew form were empty, dry as his own arid mouth. He swept them aside, seeing them fly over the smooth surface of the ocean, watching the small splashes they made, and pushed wearily to his feet.

Back, fifty paces to where the rock swept gently into the water, the stone was already warm beneath his bare soles. Soon it would be too hot to tread, and he would huddle, drawing in upon himself, seeking to reduce the area of skin exposed to the sun, cupping his hands over his head as he felt the rays burn into his mind, removing them only when he felt the heat become too great to bear and it seemed his flesh must take flame and burn. Then he would fight the temptation to dive into the seductive water, knowing that he must either give himself up or emerge salt-caked, easier prey to his fiery enemy, those parts of him already burned screaming silently at the saline caress.

The darkness was little better, though it brought a slight lessening of the heat, for then it seemed the ocean woke, great bodies moving within its suspension, half-seen things rising and diving, black bulks etched by the same moonlight that silvered the water, filigree patterns formed by the ripples. He looked then on stars he could not name, though he knew instinctively—or felt he did—in which direction north lay, and east, south, west, though he could not say what lands boundaried the water. Indeed, he could not say that the sea ended, could not be sure it did not extend forever, circling back on itself, this unknown world in which he found himself ocean-girt and he the only living human creature on it. Save that he felt in his bones his homeland lay to the east; and that others had preceded him: there was skeletal evidence of that.

He clung to the belief that he had come here through human agency: thus might he hope to escape by the same means. Perhaps some vessel would pass and take him off. Or grant him the boon of a boat; water and some means of shelter, at least.

Or perhaps not, said the unseen figure waiting at his shoulder. *If men cast you away here, why should men succor you? Why should they not pass you by?*

"Because they are men," he answered, "and not all men can be so cruel."

Can they not? Death asked mildly. *Do you know that?*

He paused before he shook his head and said, "No," hearing soft laughter at the admission.

"You are not there," he said, "I am talking to myself. Perhaps I am going mad."

Perhaps, came the response.

"No," he said, and shivered despite the heat, and drew his hands down over his face, tasting the sweat that already beaded his palms. "Go away."

He forced his watering eyes to focus, studying his hands, hearing

Death's soft chuckling—or the steady murmuring of the sea, he was not sure which—as he fought despair.

They looked strong, his hands, callused about the bases of fingers and thumbs, across the palms, as if accustomed to wielding some implement. Hair grew dark from the backs, divided by the pale traceries of old scars, that patterning continued along his forearms: the blazons of remembrance. He sensed his past there, knowledge of himself: what he was, and what he had been, elusive as a rainbow's ending. He struggled to pursue the hints, to chase them down, like a man seeking to define a fading dream. It was as if he tried to clutch fog in his hands: hopeless. He blinked as heavy droplets of perspiration ran down his forehead and clung thick to his lashes, clouding his vision like tears: he wiped at his face, his concentration breaking. He ground his teeth and shook his head lest he weep, unaware that innate pride shaped the movement, glancing up to see the sun risen higher, wondering how much longer he could last.

Not long; not without shade and fresh water, food. Already his lips cracked, and it seemed he could feel the swelling of his tongue, the engorged flesh cloying to the roof of his dehydrating mouth, tender against his teeth. Soon his skin would blister, likely the relentless shimmer of sky and ocean would blind him, and then . . .

I shall have you, said Death.

"But not yet," he answered.

Why not? demanded the unseen speaker, gently. *You must come to me in the end, and what reason is there to prolong this suffering?*

"I do not know who I am," he said. "I want to remember."

Is that a reason? Death laughed, dismissive as the softly echoing sea. *Does it matter who you are? You are a man alone on a rock in an unknown sea. What more need you know?*

"Who I am," he said. "What I am."

You are nothing, said Death. *You are a sack of flesh stretched over bone that soon will scorch and wither and come to me.*

"Then wait," he said. "Wait until I am ready."

You draw out your agony, said Death. *No more than that. You condemn yourself to needless suffering. There is no one to witness this, no honor in it.*

Honor: he felt the sharded strings of his memory tugged. "There is me," he said.

And you are no one, Death countered. *Come to me.*

"No!" He shouted now, the sound startling him, so that he looked up and saw the sun had passed its zenith and was moving toward the western horizon. "You see?" he told his adversary; told himself. "I have survived another day."

Death did not answer, and the man slumped afresh, his breath a ragged panting that seared his lungs until the sun once more touched the water, a great ball of burning gold that lanced flame over the soft undulations of waves, the sky darkening to the east, as if the descending orb drew behind it a curtain. It disappeared, and for a little while the sky was a glory of crimson, of salmon, of coral. Then blue velvet pricked with stars and the slender crescent of the moon. The air cooled, and he sighed, luxuriating in that benison, heaving unsteadily to his feet, that he might feel the faint breeze that briefly wafted the air over all his tortured body. He felt his sweat dry and become cold; something splashed, unseen in the darkness. He groaned, lowering himself, and curled upon the rock, closing eyes that still saw the sun, reminding him that so long as he clung to life, he must face it again.

Finally, he slept.

The next day, he woke as the first rays spread like molten metal over the sea.

His lids were heavy, the orbs beneath hot, itching as though their moisture were leached out and drawn into the sun. He thought of rising, but the effort seemed too much and he lay watching the water grow brighter, until it became too bright, driving pinpricks of pain into his skull. His skin, too, felt it, crawling with the heat, and that galvanized him to action: he husked a curse and tottered to his feet. Perhaps there would be crabs again in the pool. Slowly, delicate as a dancer or a drunken man, he moved toward the farther end of the rock. The fifty paces had become eighty now, and the incline steeper. His muscles felt drained of moisture, knotting, movement painful. He halted at the rim, closing his eyes against the nausea that gripped him, fighting the dizziness that roiled his senses as he lowered himself cautiously to his knees.

The pool remained empty, as if the taking of the two crustaceans had rendered it forbidden territory to their fellows, the clear water shimmering, pricked with myriad points of brilliance that stabbed his vision, inflaming the dull ache inside his skull so that it pounded against the confining bone.

This is quite pointless, said Death. *You will find neither food nor water. There is only suffering here.*

"And you," the man answered, curling up on the rock, his knees drawn up to his chest, his arms encircling his spinning head.

And me, Death agreed affably. *Your true companion.*

"You name yourself my friend?" he demanded.

Of course, Death said. *Do I not offer you release from this pain?*

"Then tell me who I am," he challenged. "Tell me that, and then perhaps I will come to you."

Do you not know? asked Death.

"No!" he croaked. "I cannot *remember*. Tell me!"

I could, Death said. *I know it as I know all men's names. Come to me, and I shall tell you.*

The man thought on that awhile, still huddled, his eyes closed. It seemed to him, not knowing himself, that he was not afraid of dying but loved life more. "Not yet," he said.

Death's laughter was soft: the lap of undulant water on stone. *Why delay it? Why suffer? You have no hope—come to me.*

"I live," he said.

But you do not know who you are, Death said.

"But still I live."

Crouched, curled, his arms wrapped about his head, he could not see, but he thought Death shrugged, negligently. "Tell me who I am," he repeated, "and then perhaps I shall agree."

There was a shadow on the featureless sea, a blur of darkness that flickered in and out of his sight on the swell. Perhaps it was some trick of Death's, to convince him of the futility of clinging so obstinately to the frayed thread of his life. But as he squinted, willing the vision to be real, it coalesced into solidity: a boat, blue painted, propelled toward him by four sweeps, the shapes of men at prow and stern. He fell to his knees, careless of the abrading rock, bracing himself on trembling hands, and mouthed a silent prayer of thanks. He did not know if there was a god or gods; or if there were, whether or not he believed in any deity, but still he gave up thanks, and said to Death, "You see? You shall not have me yet. I have beaten you."

Death gave back no answer: the boat came closer. He thought it a fishing boat, though why he could not say, nor how he should know one vessel from another. He knew only that it offered salvation: he raised his arms, waving.

None on the craft returned his wave, and rather than coming straight on, to where its passengers might find landing, it turned aside. The man's mouth, already open, gaped wider at that, and he croaked a hoarse denial, forcing himself to rise, tottering ungainly as he turned to stare in horror, hands outthrust, as if he would draw the boat to him. Almost, he plunged into the sea, to swim to the vessel, but for all his fear it should abandon him, he knew the effort of traversing that distance would be too great, that he must drown before he could reach his goal.

He peered through narrowed lids as it swept down the brief length of the rock, its outline shimmering in the heat haze, vague through the curtain of sweat that coursed his face. Four burly men manned the oars, he thought, and another the tiller. A man and a woman stood at the prow, their faces mere blurs, though he felt they studied him.

As if they fear me, he thought. And then, *Why? What am I, that anyone should fear me? Who am I?*

The moments it took for the craft to go by were an eternity in which hope died; then flared anew as the boat turned, circling the rock. He stood, turning with it, his head spinning with the motion, so that boat and sea and sky merged in a whirling of brilliance. He did not know he fell, did not feel his wasted body strike the stone. He no longer cared: in that instant Death might have claimed him and he gone unprotesting; that should have been preferable to this rise and fall of hope, this torment. He closed his eyes, teeth grinding, hands knotting into fists. Had his body been capable of producing such moisture, he would have wept, for despair consumed him then. And then through despair came anger: did these folk toy with him, he would not grant them the satisfaction of his suffering. He would face them and curse them as a man, on his feet. He did not know why that was so important, but he forced his eyes open and his body upright. He could barely stand, and the sun was fire on his skin, and for a while he could see nothing save the molten light of the water and the sky.

Then shapes formed, six, standing in a semicircle before him, between him and the boat, that held to the rock by a seventh figure who clutched the painter and eyed him warily. No less the others: six men in loose shirts and breeks of linen, short-swords in their hands, their expressions guarded. The woman wore a shift of the same plain linen, hair the color of polished copper shining in the sun drawn back from the oval of her face in a loose tail. She was lovely, he realized, and at the same time that she was blind: her eyes were large and green and fixed intently on him, but she studied him with something that was more than sight.

He thought, *Magic, she wields magic,* and did not know how he knew it.

He looked from their faces to the blades, and into his mind unbidden came the thought that he could not defeat them all, not so weak, not unarmed. He straightened, realizing he had dropped to a crouch, his hands extended, the fingers held rigid, ready to strike.

Almost, he laughed at himself, barely able to stand like a man, but preparing to fight. *What am I?* he wondered, and said as best he could past swollen tongue, from dry throat, "I am . . ." and fell silent, shaking his head. But not so much he should lose sight of them. "Who are you? Do you come to save me or to slay me?"

They frowned at that and exchanged sidelong glances, one to the other, and a tall broad-shouldered man in whose big hand the short-sword seemed no more than a knife said something he could not comprehend.

He decided they were not intending to kill him: was that their intent, they should surely have struck by now. He said, "Water," and when the tall man's face furrowed afresh, he gestured at his mouth, aping the act of drinking. The tall man spoke again, but still the words remained incomprehensible.

He waited, thinking that he could not stand much longer, that whatever innate discipline had set him on his feet must soon give sway to weakness and he fall down. He did not know why that thought was so distasteful; he wondered why he could not understand these people, or they him. He said, "Water, for the love of . . ."

He could not think whose love should merit that gift, but he heard the woman speak and saw the tall man nod, then turn to another, smaller, and murmur something that sent the slighter figure stepping backward to the boat.

A canteen was passed him, cautiously, as if the donor feared he might strike out.

He mumbled, "My thanks," and brought the flask to his lips.

As he raised it, the tall man spoke warningly and touched swordpoint to flesh. The others moved a little way apart, muttering low. Again, he could not say how he knew they voiced cantrips, but it seemed the air crackled with the power they summoned. *Do they slay me now*, he thought, *at least I shall die with my thirst slaked*. He essayed a smile, ignoring the touch of steel against his throat as he began to drink.

At first there was no taste, only an easing of a pain become so familiar, he had not known he felt it. He let the blessed moisture trickle over his tongue, into his throat, and moaned at the pleasure. He began to swallow, the water tepid, but to him like some mountain spring, cool and achingly desirable.

When the tall man took the canteen from him, he snarled, trying to retain it, to gulp down more. He was too weak to resist, but from the corners of his eyes he saw the others tense. He thought, *Like warriors. Like warriors who fight with magic.* He raised his hands, licking off the droplets spilled there, and saw the woman draw closer.

She touched the canteen, and then pointed at his mouth and at his belly, clutching her own midriff in parody of sickness. He guessed she told him that to drink too much should harm him, and he nodded. She smiled and touched her breast, uttering a single word. At first he did not understand, and she repeated it, indicating herself again. He wondered what she meant, but then she touched the tall man and said a word, and he surmised she spoke their names.

Their names were unfamiliar, as if his tongue were not shaped to utter them, but he did his best, encouraged by the woman, and finally managed: "Rwyan," and "Gwyllym."

The woman nodded confirmation, smiling, which he found reassuring, and stabbed a finger at his chest. He said, "I do not remember," and shrugged. She pointed again, pantomiming her failure to understand: he shrugged again and shook his head helplessly.

She turned away then and spoke with the one whose name sounded like Gwyllym, which seemed as odd a name as hers, though why that should be, he could not say, and the tall man nodded and called to the others. They drew closer, surrounding him, and one went to the boat, returning with shackles. Proximate, he felt their magic on his skin, like the sting of salt, and the prick of their swords, and offered no protest as they fettered him, his wrists and ankles cuffed, connected by a chain. He wondered why they were so afraid of him.

They walked him to the boat then, and though he did his best to tread out the length of the rock, his knees buckled and he would have fallen had the tall man not given him the support of a brawny arm. He felt ashamed when he could not climb unaided on board but must be lifted, babe-like, and set down in the prow, huddling there, the man and the woman watchful to either side as the others settled to tiller and sweeps.

He watched the rock recede as the oarsmen backed the boat, thinking that Death might appear to admit defeat, to acknowledge his victory, but there was nothing, only a length of bleached white stone that seemed to float on the blue expanse of sea, and he turned away. He did not know if he was rescued or brought to some other fate, but they had given him water and so, he assumed, intended him to live at least a while longer. Did they mean to slay him, he hoped he might die fittingly.

He struggled to focus his eyes on their course, to see where they went, but he was consumed with a tremendous lassitude, as if rescue drained him of the last reserves of his energy; as if, his fate now placed in the hands of others, he might for a little while let go his hold. The motion of the boat was gentle, a pleasant rocking that lulled him, for all he could not understand why he was chained or why he provoked such fear in his rescuers. *I live,* he thought. *For now that must be enough, though I'd dearly know my name.* Lethargy crept over him, and he closed his eyes, letting the weariness take him.

· · ·

When next he woke, shadows told him dusk had fallen. He saw that he was in a room plastered white, beams of dark wood spanning the ceiling, a glassed lantern suspended from the centermost, a single window, shuttered against the heat, set in one wall. Two men, brawny and with swords belted to their waists, settled on chairs. There was little furniture besides the bed: a small table, the two chairs, pegs on which clothing might be hung. There seemed no more to learn for now, and he lay back; his fetters were not uncomfortable, and the bed was very soft. He felt stronger, enough that he might test his bonds. They remained in place, affixed to head and foot of the bed, but soft cloth now warded his wrists and ankles against chafing, and his body was slick with some unguent that soothed and cooled his sunburned skin. He slowly turned his head and saw a man, a stranger, and the woman called Rwyan, seated across the room. He opened his mouth, feeling more ointment on his lips, and said, "Please, water."

They turned to him at that and spoke, and the man quit the room with a nervous backward glance. The woman rose, filling a pannikin that she brought to the bed. He was not so much recovered as he had thought, and she slid an arm about his shoulders to raise him that he might drink. He would have gulped, but she allowed him only a sip, and then another, doling the water slowly into his parched mouth, speaking all the while in a soft, calm voice. When the pannikin was emptied, he smiled his gratitude, and she lowered him gently back.

As she returned the cup, the door opened to reveal an angular, round-shouldered man carrying a bulky satchel, moonlight glinting on a hairless pate. The prisoner watched as the bald man spoke with the woman, then snapped his fingers, the action producing a flame that he touched to the lantern. As light filled the room, the prisoner saw that the woman now wore a loose gown of green and that her hair was unbound. He thought again how lovely she was, but then his view was blocked by the bald man, who touched his chest and said, "Marthyn," which seemed to be his name.

He said no more but set down his satchel and began to rummage through the contents. When he produced a phial and measured out some drops of a pale yellow liquid, the prisoner hesitated only an instant before swallowing the decoction: for reasons he could not define, he felt safer in Rwyan's presence, and when she saw him hesitate, she smiled and nodded encouragement.

The liquid was tasteless; it filled him with a pleasant languor, so that he drifted midway between sleep and waking as the man called Marthyn examined his body and applied a fresh coating of the unguent. He was only dimly aware of the men who entered, on

316 / ANGUS WELLS

Marthyn's call, to remove his fetters and turn him gently over. He was asleep when the manacles were replaced.

Light filtering through the shutters woke him next, though whether one night, or several, had passed, he could not guess. Rwyan was gone, and the man who had sat with her, in their places two men who might have been twins. They turned toward him as he stirred, and in their eyes he saw suspicion. *Not fear*, he thought, *but wariness. As if they were confident, but yet cautious.* He said, "Rwyan?" and one of them shook his head, pointing at the door, then touched his chest and said, "Darys." The other stabbed a thumb and said, "Valryn." The prisoner repeated their names and said, "I'm hungry."

Darys shrugged and brought him water, which he drank, the liquid prompting his stomach to rumble, so that Darys chuckled and spoke with Valryn, who went to the door and called through it.

After a while, Marthyn came to apply a fresh coating of the unguent and feed him droplets of a blue liquid, then spooned broth between his lips. It was a small bowl, but it filled him as if it were a feast, and afterward he slept again.

He woke to day's light, once more not knowing how much time had passed, thinking it likely not much, for Darys and Valryn still played the parts of nurses, or guards. He needed badly to void his bowels, which was difficult to express, though he at last succeeded; Valryn drew his sword as Darys unlocked his fetters and helped him rise. The chains were fixed again about his wrists and ankles, and he was brought to an alcove. He was chagrined that he must still rely on another to walk, more that both men watched as he satisfied his need. He found some small comfort in the thought it were better men observed him than that Rwyan or some other woman had been present.

After, he was returned to the bed and chained again in place.

So the days passed, at first in confusion but then to an emerging pattern. He drifted less, remained longer awake. Under Marthyn's ministrations his body healed, sun-ravaged skin becoming whole, his strength returning. He ate; at first only broth or gruel, but then more solid food—fruits and vegetables and meat. He saw that his guardian nurses were changed daily, and that while they were usually men, sometimes women took a turn. He liked none of them so well as Rwyan, for she seemed the only one not much afraid of him, nor so wary. Most seemed to perceive him as they might a wild animal, half-tamed and potentially dangerous. He knew somehow that he was strong and that he could fight, but he felt no animosity toward these people—save they kept him chained—and he did not understand why they held him so. He wished he understood their speech, or they his, for then he could tell them he intended no harm and would not seek to hurt his saviors. Rather, that he was indebted to them, that he owed them his life and would lay it down before offering them injury.

As he recovered, so his curiosity increased. He was a full-grown man, but of his life he remained innocent as a babe, as if the sea itself had birthed him on that miserable rock. He was of different stock to the folk who tended him—their language told him that much—but from whence he came and in what land he found himself, he had not the least idea. He determined to learn and commenced to ply those who sat with him with questions. It was a dissatisfying process, a matter of gestures and repetitions that enabled him to identify objects, to learn simple words. His mind, it appeared, was quick enough, for he soon could ask for water, or food, the latrine; he could offer thanks and greet newcomers, but true communication remained impossible. He gleaned more from the attitudes of his tutors: some refused to indulge him, some were reluctant, some few enthusiastic; but in all of them he felt still that wariness, and in some a loathing he could not at all understand. It emphasized his loneliness.

In time he was strong enough to stand and walk unaided, and then confinement began to chafe. He pantomimed excursion and felt resentful when he was at first refused. Rwyan was the most sympathetic, and to her he put, as eloquently as he might, his desire to walk abroad. She understood, and nodded, and later spoke with Marthyn, who frowned tremendously and muttered, mostly to himself, in a tone the prisoner knew was dubious. Marthyn left and returned with Gwyllym and several others, who stood in animated conversation as the man lay chained, watching their faces, cursing his incomprehension. He beamed and said in their language, "My thanks," when finally his fetters were unlocked and they informed him he should be allowed to leave the room.

He was given a shirt and breeks, which reminded him for the first time of his nudity, though he did not feel embarrassed by that. The manacles were a worse indignity, but at least the chains were lengthened enough he might walk without too much difficulty. When he ventured out, two men were always with him, swords sheathed on their belts and heavy staffs in their hands. He did not mind: to walk again under the open sky was a joy, for all he must bear the curious stares of all he encountered, as if he were some strangeling beast taught to walk upright.

Within a span of seven days he was fully limber, recuperated from his ordeal, vigorous enough he should, had he not been hampered by the chains, have outdistanced his escort. He was allowed the freedom of the open spaces but not the buildings, and those he avoided anyway, for there were always folk about them, and their reaction to his presence disturbed him. He preferred to wander the terraces and the heights, especially when he discovered Rwyan might be often found there.

When he found her, he would sit, a respectful distance off, and seek to plumb her mind. She offered no objection but took the role of pedagogue as if it were a welcome relief from troubled thoughts he could not comprehend, only wonder at. As best he could, he expressed his gratitude, telling her he owed her people his life. He felt she understood; he did not understand why she smiled so sadly. He thought there was much strangeness in the world.

One night, alone in his room—he was still chained, and both the door and the single window were locked, but none now remained with him—he remembered his name. He did not know how it came back, it was simply, suddenly, there in his mind, and when he said it aloud, it was familiar: "Tezdal." He felt more whole for that, as if such knowledge of identity anchored him firmer in his confused world; he felt less a cipher.

In the morning, when the door was opened and his guards entered with food, he touched his chest and said proudly, "I am Tezdal."

They looked sharply at him, and one fingered his sword, but then they spoke, and soon Gwyllym appeared, and the hunchbacked woman called Maethyrene, who pointed at him and spoke his name as if it were a question.

He nodded, smiling, and said, "Yes, I am Tezdal."

Gwyllym spoke, but save for a few words and phrases the pattern and meaning remained a puzzle to Tezdal. He thought the big man both pleased and excited, Maethyrene equally disturbed, and then himself grew alarmed as they urged him to dress, suddenly impatient. He had thought they should be pleased by this small prize hooked from the fog of his amnesia, but it seemed instead to galvanize them, as if the utterance of his name rendered him somehow more dangerous. He was allowed no breakfast but was hurried from the room to a long colonnaded building, its white stucco brilliant in the morning sunlight. There was nowhere cool even so early in the day, but inside the building the heat was not so fierce, the hall to which he was brought shadowed and very quiet. His alarm increased as he was pushed roughly to a chair and his chains fastened, securing him in place. For an instant anger flared at such treatment, and he strained against his bonds. Then he saw a sword drawn partway from the scabbard and the unmasked hatred in the bearer's eyes, and he subsided, panting and more than a little afraid: it came to him, for the first time, that there were some here would willingly slay him.

He sat, waiting as the hall's quiet calm was lost to uproar, folk he had known only as tranquil bursting in with voices raised and startled eyes studying him with unfathomable expressions. For a while confusion reigned, the chamber filling, becoming crowded, and he could only look about, wondering what occasioned such excitement.

He saw Rwyan amongst the throng, but she was deep in urgent conversation with Gwyllym and gave him no more than a tentative smile, as if she, too, were become unsure of his intentions or his probity. Marthyn came, to place a hand upon his brow and stare into his eyes. *As if,* Tezdal thought, *he checks me for fever, or madness. Why is my name so important?* Then, as Marthyn moved away and all began to take chairs, facing him like some court of inquisition, he thought, *Perhaps it is not my name but my remembering of it.* He wished he understood their language better.

But he did not, and he could only sit silent as they debated . . . *My fate,* he thought as one after the other rose to speak, enough gesturing in his direction that he could entertain no doubt but that they spoke of him. He could not be sure, but from the looks some wore, the tenor of their speech, he suspected they called for his death, as if his remembering of his name condemned him, branding him guilty of crimes of which he had no knowledge. Others seemed less sanguine, but he could not much better interpret their voices or their faces, only hope they spoke up on his behalf.

Surely, he thought as the morning aged and the colloquy went on, *they would not take me off the rock and nurse me back to health only to execute me because I claim a name. I am not their enemy; I am not a danger to them. Having saved me, why then slay me?*

The shifting of the light filtering through the shutters told him noon had passed before a decision was reached. What it was, he could not tell, only that he was loosed from the chair and marched from the hall. He tried to find Rwyan in the crowd, hoping to glean some information from her face, some indication of his fate, but she was lost to sight, armed men pressing him close on all sides, as if they feared he might somehow escape, and he was brought to the great white tower.

He had never ventured close to that keep before: the aura of power he had felt the first time he saw it had persuaded him to avoid the place. He did not understand why, only that he felt easier keeping his distance, as if the tower plucked forgotten memories, were in some way he did not comprehend threatening. Now he was escorted to the doors, through to a flight of stairs that wound windowless upward, and uneasiness grew.

He fought the sensation, refusing to give way to fear. Perhaps they intended to fling him from the parapet; if so, he would die as a man should. He steeled himself as a door was opened and he stood beneath the sky. The aura was stronger here, and his eyes were drawn irrevocably to the crystal resting on a pedestal of black stone at the center of the floor. It seemed possessed of occult life, pulsing as the unroofed area filled. Somehow he knew these people communicated with the stone, though how or for what purpose, he had no idea, save that it must be to do with him.

Then his arms were gripped, and he was urged closer to the crystal. He felt a great reluctance, but would not let it show, and so walked straight-backed forward, as if he were not at all afraid. Seven gathered in a circle about the pedestal. Amongst them he recognized Rwyan and Gwyllym, Maethyrene; the others were strange to him. His belly lurched as they began their ritual: he told himself that was only hunger and knew he lied. He watched, compelled, as the stone shone brighter, lines of glittering light flashing out to touch the seven, bathing them in scintillating nimbus. Then he cried out and fought his captors as the light embraced him, and he felt touched by nameless power, as if unfleshed fingers probed his mind. Darkness fell.

22

Rwyan sat sipping tea and thinking as she studied the sleeping man.

Tezdal. An odd name, a Kho'rabi name: there was power in names.

By the God, but his remembering of his own had demonstrated that. It had thrown the island into uproar, as if that small retrieval had rendered him abruptly no longer a curiosity but a threat. And yet surely he was the same man who had come gently enough to seek out her company, come seeking knowledge to fill the vacuum of his amnesia. He had worked hard to express his gratitude; had, as best she could understand him, told her he offered no harm, was indebted to his saviors. She had believed him then—should she not now? Should the remembering of his name so change the situation some now called for his execution? They had known what he was from the start, when the fishing boat had sighted him, alone and naked on that forsaken rock. He could scarcely have been aught else but one of the Sky

Lords fallen from a burning airboat. They had agreed he should be rescued and brought back to the island, that they might learn what they could from the first Kho'rabi ever taken alive. They had never thought to find a man without recollection of his past, all his awareness limited to his brief existence on the stone.

And that had been the irony of it, that his memory was gone, and he had no more idea who or what he was than some storm-beached fish. Had he possessed his memory then, he would have been questioned, the occult power of the crystal bent to plumbing whatever secrets he held. Amnesiac, his mind was locked secure, was innocent as a babe's, denying them entry. They had not known quite what to do and so had delayed decision.

Some, even then, had spoken for his death, and that had seemed to Rwyan, for all she knew he was the enemy, akin to seeking the death of a child. It seemed to her that his loss of memory obliterated his past, as if he were truly newborn. So she had spoken against so extreme a measure, suggesting that his innocence was no enmity but a chance to learn, perhaps eventually to communicate with the Sky Lords. Gwyllym had supported her, Maethyrene, Jhone, and Marthyn, enough others the vote had come down in Tezdal's favor: he should be granted his life, so long as he represented no threat.

Now he had won back his name, and the cry went up again, born of ancient hate, of inbred fear, that with that first step taken, he should become again a Sky Lord and therefore should die.

"And what use that?" Gwyllym had demanded. "We'd as well have left him on that rock and saved ourselves the effort of a hard day's rowing. We wanted him alive, that we might question him; we got him alive. Were we wrong, then?"

"Aye," some had said in answer. "Wrong to save him, wrong to nurse him, wrong to let him live now."

"Are our worst fears realized, and the Great Coming imminent," Gynael had said, "then that should be a waste. Alive, what might we not learn from him?"

"What use is a man without his memory?" had come the countering argument, from Demaeter.

"What danger from a man without his memory?" Rwyan had asked. "To slay him now would be murder, no more."

"To slay a Kho'rabi is not murder!" Demaeter had shouted, outraged. "It cannot be."

"He's an extra mouth to feed when food grows short," Cyraene had said. "He cannot speak our language—what can we learn from him?"

"What we hoped to learn before," Gwyllym had declared, and asked that Marthyn speak.

"His name," the herbalist had said, "is the key. Without that, there could be no unlocking of his mind. Now that he's remembered it, however . . . it's my belief we may use the crystal's power to gift him our tongue."

As cries of protest had risen, Gwyllym had shouted, "That was ever our intention! In the God's name, did you dissenters think to learn his? Do we give him our language, then perhaps we can unpick the strands of his memory and all our efforts not be wasted."

Some had argued then that it was a dangerous course, that Tezdal might be a Kho'rabi wizard and that to bring him to the crystal serve only to augment his power. Also, that he might in some manner harm the stone; or that, empowered by magic, he find some means to harm the Sentinels themselves.

And Gynael had climbed stiffly to her feet and managed somehow, for all her eyes were rheumy, to imbue her gaze with scorn. "Are we so weak, then?" she had demanded. "Shall we not set a warding on him? Even be he a wizard and not a mere warrior, think you he's so powerful he shall overcome all of us? I say we've an opportunity here none have before known. I say we betray ourselves do we not seize it."

It had been those hoarse-spoken words, Rwyan thought, that had swayed the conclave. There had been some further debate, but opposition had faltered, and finally it had been agreed Tezdal be brought to the crystal and they endeavor to put the Dhar language in his head. Rwyan had felt sorry for the uncomprehending man as he was hauled away to the white tower.

That had been seven days ago, and for all that time Tezdal had slept, not waking even when Marthyn dripped broth laced with restorative herbs between his lips. He had drunk and slept on. He soiled the bed and did not wake when he was lifted off, the sheets replaced. His chest rose and fell, breath came soft from his mouth, but his eyes did not open. Rwyan wondered if the gramarye had sent his mind into limbo, if perhaps the crystal had absorbed him in some way, leaving behind an empty husk.

She had much time to wonder, for it was agreed that of all on the island, she was the one most sympathetic to the sleeping man. She was the one most likely to win his trust. Hers was the company he had sought out, and therefore hers was the face most likely to reassure him when—*if*—he woke. Marthyn had confided in her his doubts: Tezdal might not wake, but sleep his life away. He might wake mad; he might regain consciousness aware he was a Sky Lord taken by the Dhar. He might awake still empty of his memory. Whichever, it was better Rwyan's be the face he saw first; and better he remain securely chained.

It was a duty not entirely to her taste, for it held the flavor of trust betrayed. But she could not refuse, for she was yet a mage, with duty to her land acknowledged, and though it was no easy task to spend her days and nights cooped in the little room "watching" him sleep, she accepted. There was, too, that she pitied him. She could not now perceive him as an enemy: he was only a man, alone in an unfamiliar world; perhaps, even as he slept, aware that around him were folk would slay him, had they their way. She could not help but feel sorry for him. And somehow, he reminded her of Daviot. There was something—she could not precisely define it—about his look, the angle of his jaw, the shape of his skull, his glossy dark hair, that summoned those memories she had easier lived without. Almost, she had mused, as if blood were shared; as if the fisherman's son from Kellambek and the Kho'rabi knight had some ancient ancestral linkage.

She sighed and rose, stretching muscles cramped from too long without movement, turning her occult sight on the window. Dusk was fallen. She heard the milch cows lowing, goats bleating; from the olive groves a nightingale sang. She lit the lantern, not wanting Tezdal to wake—if he should wake, ever—to darkness. He had suffered, she thought, frights enough.

She went to the door, smiling at herself as she eased it open, as if she had sooner not disturb him than wake him with the sound. She stepped outside, arching her back and tilting her head, wishing for a breeze that was not there. She turned her face skyward, finding the gibbous moon hung low in the east. At least there had been no more skyboats come since that raid that had delivered Tezdal.

Which likely means, she thought, *that Gynael was right, and that was a final probing of our defenses. In which case, how long before the Great Coming? Have the Sky Lords learned all they need now? Do their manufactories build the armada? Their wizards harness the elementals?*

The waiting, she decided, was the hardest part.

And do they come soon, what shall happen to Tezdal?

She heard a sound then, unfamiliar and therefore distinct, through the murmur of voices, the calling of the goats and the nightbirds. It was the sound of metal chinking, as if chains were tested. She spun around, mouth opening to smile and cry out at the same time as she "saw" her charge.

He shifted on the bed, stirring as might a man waking from a very deep sleep, turning slowly, first on one side, then the other, arms and legs extending so that his chains were strained in their fastenings. Rwyan went to him, drawing up a stool, leaning over him.

His eyes opened.

For a moment they were sleep-fogged, unfocused, then intelligence sparked, and recognition.

"I'm thirsty."

She smiled and said, "Yes, Tezdal," and fetched a cup, holding it to his lips.

He drank and said, "My thanks," then raised an arm as far as the chain allowed and said, "You bind me still. Why? Am I so dangerous?"

She said, "Some fear you are, or might be. Do you remember my name?"

He said, "Rwyan," and smiled. "You were always the kindest."

Then amazement widened his eyes, and his jaw dropped open. "I understand you." He said it slowly, as if testing the words, as if they fit unfamiliar on his tongue. "I speak your language."

She said, "Yes. How much do you remember?"

He frowned then, and thought awhile, and finally said, "I woke with my name. Tezdal. That seemed to frighten some of you, and I was taken to a hall, where people spoke. I thought they discussed what to do with me. Then I was brought to that tower and to a jewel that shone. A magic stone, that gave off light and . . . touched me. After that . . ."

He shrugged, rattling the chains. Rwyan said, "It was decided to gift you with our tongue. We channeled the crystal's power to teach you, that we might converse." He nodded, staring at her face, wonder on his. Rwyan continued, "That was seven days ago. You've slept since. I feared . . ." She laughed and shook her head. "Needlessly, it seems. What else do you remember?"

His face darkened then. "A rock," he said. "A bare forsaken rock in a sea I did not know. I spoke with Death there. A boat came—you were on it, and you took me off. You and a tall man called Gwyllym. You brought me here and nursed me back to health. Then I remembered who I am."

"Who are you?" she asked.

He said, "I am Tezdal," and frowned again. "But more than that . . ." The chains rattled as he shook them. "I know you chain me, but I do not know why. I do not know where I came from, or why you fear me."

"I don't fear you," she said.

"Then loose me."

She shook her head. "I cannot. That must be decided by others."

"Am I dangerous?" he asked, his face puzzled now. "Am I a madman? A criminal?"

"No, neither of those." Now she frowned. "You're a Sky Lord; a Kho'rabi."

Lines creased his forehead. "I don't understand. What are those names?"

"You don't know?"

"I've heard them said, I think. But . . ." His head turned in slow negation. "They mean nothing to me."

Rwyan's lips pursed. There seemed no guile in him: she believed him. She said, "I must summon others. Do you wait, Tezdal, and perhaps they'll agree you may be loosed."

"I should like that," he said, so solemnly she must smile.

She nodded and closed her eyes, sending out a call. *He wakes. He speaks our language now, but I think he remembers no more.*

We come. Wait.

She opened her eyes. It was easier to focus her talent for sight with them open, and long ingrained habit. She smiled reassuringly and said, "Not long. They come now."

"You're a sorcerer." His voice was hushed, as if the fact had not sunk in before. "Are all here sorcerers?"

"We are," she said. "We defend Dharbek."

"Dharbek?" His face expressed incomprehension.

"You've much to learn," she told him. "Be patient. We must all of us be patient."

His smile grew cynical then, and he shook his chains. "I've little choice, eh?"

Rwyan said, "No. Not yet, at least."

It was again full council and, save Tezdal was not this time present, as heated as before.

Gwyllym spoke: "In the God's name, we argue around and around like a dog chasing its own tail—getting nowhere. He hides nothing. He's nothing to hide! How much proof do you need?"

Demaeter said, "More. Enough we can be sure that sending him to Durbrecht shall not be sending a viper to the land's heart."

"I think he's hardly a viper," Gynael said, her hoarse voice become a rasping croak from the lengthy debate. "He seems to me more like a man lost, adrift from both his homeland and his own past."

"Save he be a Kho'rabi wizard," said Cyraene. "And conceals his power."

"There's no magic in him." Marthyn's voice was edged with irritation. "On that I'd stake my life."

"Perhaps you do," said Alrys.

"May the God grant me patience." Marthyn shook his head, adding in what was not quite a whisper, "I need it, dealing with fools."

"I'd not deem it foolish to be wary." Alrys chose to ignore the slur. "Do we err, then better it be on the side of caution."

"Do we take your cautious path," Marthyn returned, "then he'll live out his life on this island."

"Save he be executed," Cyraene said.

"No." Demaeter shook his head. "On that at least we're agreed— to execute him now should be akin to murder."

"Unless he *is* a wizard," Cyraene muttered.

"In which case," said Gynael wearily, "he's a wizard so accomplished as to defeat all our investigations. In which case, he's likely more dangerous here than on the mainland. In which case, it must surely be safer to send him to Durbrecht."

Maethyrene lent her support: "We can learn nothing more here."

"No; on that, at least, we seem in accord." Gwyllym rose to address the assembly. His sheer bulk commanded attention: Rwyan hoped it should command agreement. "Does he remain here, it shall be as a man without a past. What shall he be, then? A servant? We've never had servants; we've no Changed to fetch and carry for us. Shall we make a menial of him?"

Cyraene muttered, "It should be fitting," and Alrys chuckled, nodding agreement.

Rwyan said, "Was it not that first made the Ahn our enemy? Shall we repeat that mistake?"

Faces turned in shock toward her, outrage writ there. That she questioned was, their eyes said, grossest assumption. She was grateful for Gwyllym's calm smile.

"There's truth in that," he said, voice raised over angry muttering, "but I'd not now debate our past. Save I say we should not forgo our ancient customs. I'd not see him made a servant any more than I'd have Changed on the Sentinels. Can we agree on that?"

There was a murmur of acceptance, a ducking of heads; reluctantly from Cyraene, Alrys.

Gwyllym waited until he had silence again. Then: "So, here he's useless to us—as has been said, another mouth to feed. We cannot restore his memory, and without that he's nothing. In Durbrecht, however . . ." He paused, gray eyes moving slowly from face to face. "In Durbrecht is the College of the Mnemonikos, whose talent is remembering; who understand memory better than we and possess such techniques as might restore his. I say we send him there."

"And our own College," Gynael said, forestalling Demaeter's

protest, "which can surely deal with one forgetful Kho'rabi; wizard, or no."

"And on the way?" the plump sorcerer demanded. "What of that?"

There was a pause. Into it, Rwyan dared speak again. "I've spent more time with him than any of you, and I tell you he's no threat. He deems us saviors, himself indebted."

"Perhaps," said Cyraene, her voice smooth, venom in the words, "you've grown too close. Did you not once disgrace yourself with a Rememberer?"

Rwyan felt a chill at that reminder; instantly replaced with anger's heat. "I loved a man, aye," she said. It was an effort to hold her voice calm: she had sooner slapped the woman. "And when I was bade come here, I left him. I know my duty."

"And have you found another man?" Cyraene asked with malevolent mildness. "One no more suitable?"

"I've not," Rwyan answered curtly; and could not resist adding, "neither do I cull the newcome for lovers."

The older woman's face paled with affront, but as her mouth opened to vent reply, Gwyllym said, "Enough! Shall we squabble like spiteful children, or speak as adults?"

Rwyan said, "I'm sorry." Cyraene shrugged, arranging her gown.

Demaeter said, "I ask again—what of the journey to Durbrecht? How can we know him secure along the way?"

"Deliver him from keep to keep," suggested Jhone. "Let the commur-mages take him, with a squadron from each warband."

"Slow," said Alrys.

"And," said Gynael, "unlikely to be much welcomed by the aeldors. Are our fears realized and the Great Coming begun, the keeps shall need their sorcerers and their soldiers."

Gwyllym ducked his head. "That's true," he said. "A boat should be simpler and swifter. But first—are we agreed that he goes to Durbrecht?"

Again a pause, a murmuring as individual discussions were voiced; finally a nodding, a rumble of consent.

"So be it." Gwyllym turned slowly, eliciting agreement from each of them. "He goes to Durbrecht. Now let us debate the how of it."

Maethyrene said, "A supply ship?"

"When shall the next come?" Alrys demanded. "Most are commandeered to supply the holdings."

"We might request one of Durbrecht," Jhone suggested.

"And be refused," said Demaeter. "Or wait the God knows how long."

"Send to Carsbry then," Jhone offered. "Let Pyrrin divert a boat or send one of his own galleys."

"Has he one to send," said Gwyllym thoughtfully. "And there's another thing—I'd see Tezdal delivered whole, alive. Think you a galley out of Carsbry, with warriors on board, should treat a captive Sky Lord kindly? Remember, both Pyrrin's sons were slain."

"They'd more likely slay him," said Cyraene. Rwyan thought she concealed her pleasure at the notion.

"We could protect him," Maethyrene said. "Send our own escort."

Cyraene's protest was genuine: "We've a duty here! We dare not weaken our defenses."

"Then it would seem we reach impasse." Demaeter folded chubby hands across his belly. "For I'll not agree to sending him anywhere save he's warded by magic."

Gwyllym frowned, nodding acceptance. Rwyan said, "Perhaps there is another way."

Again, their faces turned toward her, some still hostile, others curious. Gwyllym motioned that she explain, and she said, "I think that the warbands *would* likely slay him, perhaps even some keep sorcerers. I'd suggest he go clandestine—that we advise only Durbrecht of his coming and none others. We might send one of our own boats to Carsbry and find some ship going north from there."

"Not without he's warded," said Demaeter obstinately. "And as Cyraene points out, we cannot spare guards for such a journey."

"We might," Cyraene said, her eyes sparkling as they fixed on Rwyan, "send *one*. Perhaps one powerful enough to hold the Kho'rabi in check, but not so great as to weaken the island's magic."

Demaeter nodded, Alrys voiced agreement; others joined them.

Rwyan saw a trap set and sprung: she was not sure she minded. She said, "I'd go, be it your wish."

Jhone said warningly, "It would be no easy journey, child."

"Yet we're agreed it must be done," said Cyraene.

Rwyan found Gwyllym studying her speculatively. She said, "I swear Tezdal is no threat. I trust him."

"With your life?" asked Gynael.

"With my life," answered Rwyan.

Cyraene smiled feigned friendship and said, "I say we accept Rwyan's proposal."

Gwyllym asked, "Are you sure?" And when Rwyan ducked her head, "Let us vote on it."

It was soon cast. Some there were glad enough to see themselves rid of the Kho'rabi, some of Rwyan; her friends voted honestly, in favor of what seemed to them the best proposal. It was decided she should go with Tezdal to Carsbry, claiming herself a mage returning from a sojourn on the island. She would ask of the aeldor Pyrrin that he arrange passage north for them, to Durbrecht if that were possible, if not, then to some other keep closer to the Treppanek, where she might find another ship. She would be given coin enough to facilitate the journey; they wished her the God's speed.

There was only a single point of dissent: Demaeter would send Tezdal out in chains. Rwyan had not known she commanded such eloquence as she argued that.

How, she demanded, might such bonds be explained? They should look most odd, no? Was Tezdal a prisoner, then surely he would be delivered to the aeldor. And what manner of prisoner would come from the Sentinels, save a Sky Lord? Which announcement they were surely agreed was not to be bruited abroad for fear Tezdal be slain out of hand.

No, she told the fat sorcerer with a firmness she had not known she possessed, was this subterfuge to work, then all must appear normal. There could be no chains.

And should he regain his full memory and turn on her?

He would not, of that she was certain; too, she was not without defenses. She had the talent, no? She could ward herself well enough against a single man, surely?

"I believe you can," said Maethyrene. "But even so—do we agree he goes unfettered—you must still explain his presence. He cannot be your servant, for we've no servants here. What is he then? Why does he accompany you?"

There was a murmur of agreement, of doubt. Cyraene frowned as if disappointed. Rwyan thought a moment on the argument and smiled. "I am blind," she said, "so let him be my eyes. A man hired off a supply ship to act as guide and servant. The God willing, that explanation should satisfy most folk."

Demaeter voiced protest but the rest nodded approvingly, and once more it had been Gynael who set the seal on it.

"I am old and I grow weary," she had said. "I'd eat, and find my bed. Rwyan's the way of it, and wise for one so young. We'd send the Kho'rabi to Durbrecht, and it seems to me that save we do it as Rwyan suggests, he'll likely be torn apart on suspicion alone. Be that the case, then we've wasted all our time, and I've not so much to waste. I say be done! These are perilous times, and they call for desperate measures. Is Rwyan confident, then let him go loosed as she suggests. I trust her."

Gwyllym had lent his support, but the silver-haired woman had swayed the doubters, so that his vote was little more than a formality: it was finally agreed, the details settled. It was left to Rwyan to advise Tezdal.

She had not realized how nervous she had been until she quit the hall and walked out into the baking heat of the afternoon: it seemed cooler than that shadowed interior. She paused, opening hands she had not known she clenched, and saw the indentations her nails had left in her palms. *Why do I care so much?* she asked herself, and could offer no rational answer, save that she did and would not see Tezdal either slain or made a mindless servitor. *Is it wrong? The God knows, he is a Sky Lord, and they are our enemy.* Then: *No! He was a Sky Lord; now he's just a lost and lonely man and likely trusts no one but me. Is that reason enough?*

She made her way toward his room—his cell—lost in thought, careless of those she passed, even when several called to her wanting to know the council's decision. To them she gave vague answer, barely aware of what she said, absorbed in her musings.

Everything she had told the Adepts was true. She *did* trust Tezdal; she did not believe he would harm her. There was something about him, something in his demeanor, that told her he spoke honestly when he spoke of owing his life.

But do I betray him? she wondered as the path wound through a grove where goats and sheep ambled lazily about her. *I take him from imprisonment here, but surely to another kind of jail, in Durbrecht. What shall they do with him there, the Mnemonikos and the sorcerers of the College? Shall he be chained again, fed and watered like some animal, his mind a toy to be dissected?*

She "saw" the tiny cottage, the door locked, and paused, not yet quite ready to break her news; needing to be sure in her own mind that what she gave him was gift, not curse.

At least he'll not be condemned to live out his life here. She gasped, recognizing the shape of her thought: its inherent significance. *Condemned? Is that how I see this island, as a prison? I'd not spend my life here, only such time as the crystal allows, and yet . . . God! Have I hidden my feelings even from myself? Am I a traitor to my College, to my talent and my duty?*

She felt her head spin and reached out to clutch a low-hung branch. The gnarled wood was rough beneath her hand, warm; she pressed her forehead against it a moment, her mouth dry.

Are my motives selfish? Do I seek my own freedom, Tezdal the key? Surely not—I had accepted my lot before he came. I was . . . resigned. At least, not unhappy. Or not very.

332 / ANGUS WELLS

An ant ran busy over her hand, forerunner of a column, the insects' passage relentless, her hand merely an obstacle to overcome.
She "watched" them, thinking:

*Like the Sky Lords. Amongst whose number I must not forget Tezdal was
counted; if not now, then once. And like these ants, the Sky Lords are relentless,
they intend to overcome my country. Then I do my duty in bringing him to
Durbrecht, and at least along the way he shall enjoy a measure of freedom.
Surely that must be for the best; surely.*

She straightened, blowing softly to dislodge the ants still clinging
to her skin, and went toward the cottage.

The lock was newly fixed—there was no need of locks here—and
the key hung from a nail beside. She took it down and swung the door
open. Tezdal sat on the single chair, a length of chain securing him to
the bed.

As if he were some half-wild animal, not yet to be quite trusted. She
smiled at him and said, "Day's greetings, Tezdal."

He rose. *He always rises,* she thought, noticing it for the first time.
He is a genteel man.

He said, "Day's greetings, Rwyan. Is my fate decided?"

Certainly his wits were sharp enough. She said, a little nervous
now, "How do you know we spoke of you?"

He shrugged and said, "I've been left alone all day. Usually, you
come; at least, someone. When none came since I was fed, I
thought . . ."

She motioned that he sit. He ducked his head in approximation
of a bow and went to the bed, waiting until she took the chair.

"We did," she said without further preamble. "You are to go to
Durbrecht."

"Durbrecht?" He frowned. "You've spoken of Durbrecht. A
great city, no? Where you were taught to use your magic."

"My College is there." She nodded. "But also the College of the
Mnemonikos—the Rememberers."

He smiled politely and asked her, "Why?" as if they spoke not of
his future, of his fate, but of some jaunt.

"It's our belief," she answered, "that they might restore your
memory."

"I should welcome that." His smile became a rueful grin. "At
least, I think I should. I do not feel . . . whole . . . not knowing
quite who I am; or what. Is it far?"

"Yes." *A lifetime far.* "We must first cross to the mainland, then
take a ship north."

Tezdal grinned at that and rattled his chains. "Shall I wear these
still?" he asked.

Rwyan shook her head. "No. They'll be struck off."

He said, "Good," and his smile was broad.

He listened attentively as she outlined the journey and the part he must play; what had been decided in conclave.

When she was done, he said, "I am not a servant, Rwyan." His expression was troubled; he seemed affronted at the notion of such subterfuge. "I do not know how I know this, but I do."

Rwyan said gently, "As do I, but for your own sake you must pretend."

"Why?" he asked, a moment obstinate.

"Because you are—because you *were* Kho'rabi," she said. "A Sky Lord; enemy to Dharbek. There are those who'd kill you for that, on the mainland."

"You've spoken somewhat of this," he murmured. "Of these Sky Lords, the Kho'rabi. But if I was, I am not now. Can I be something I do not remember? Someone of whom I have no knowledge? I am not your enemy, Rwyan. Not yours, or your people's."

"I know that," she said, "but on the mainland . . . Dharbek has suffered much; does now. This heat . . ." She gestured at the shuttered window. "That is the Sky Lords' doing."

"Their magic must be strong," he said.

"It is," she said.

"And they are your enemy?"

She nodded.

"Then they are mine. My life is yours, Rwyan; it has been since you took me off that rock."

"Folk on the mainland will not know that," she said. "Do they even suspect you were Kho'rabi, they would slay you. That's why you must pretend. Only play the part of servant until you are come safe to Durbrecht."

She "watched" him as he thought it through. *By the God, he looks like Daviot when he sits thus, pondering.*

An errant thought then: *Daviot. Might it be I shall find him again, along the way? Or in Durbrecht?*

"You look sad, Rwyan."

Tezdal's voice startled her back to full attention. She smiled and said, "I thought of someone from long ago. You remind me of him."

He nodded gravely and asked her, "Did you love him, that his memory makes you look so sad?"

And that, she thought, *is exactly like Daviot: to strike directly to the heart of a thing.* She ducked her head and said, "Yes, I did."

"Then," he said, "why are you apart?"

"We'd different talents." She shrugged, not much wanting to pick at those old wounds. "Mine was for sorcery; his for memory. I was sent here; he's a Rememberer."

"Shall he be in this Durbrecht?" he asked.

"I think not," she said. "I think he likely wanders Dharbek now, as a Storyman."

"What's that?" he asked. "A Storyman?"

Rwyan told him, and when she was done, he said, "Then perhaps you'll meet him along the way."

"Perhaps." She smiled, denying herself the brief flare of hope his words kindled. Then caught the import of what he said: "You accept? That you must act the servant?"

"Do you wish it?"

She was not quite sure whether he asked her or made a statement. She said, "It's needful."

"Be it your wish then." He stood, executing a cursory bow. "Then so be it."

"Thank you," she said.

The Feast of Daeran was past before I sighted Carsbry, my belly grumbling its anticipation of Pyrrin's hospitality. Betwixt this keep and Cambar, the land was ravaged, famine a growing threat, disease stirring. This should have been a season of growth, of plenty; it was, instead, a time of hardship. I went often hungry: I thought I should rest awhile in Carsbry and fatten myself a little before continuing up the coast.

The hold was a pretty sight in the midmorning sun, despite the arid fields, and I paused by a stand of black pine, studying the place. It sprawled around a gentle bay, the houses spreading in twinned arcs from the centerpiece of the keep, that standing watchful over the harbor and the inland road alike. Moles extended out into the placid waters of the Fend, ensuring safe anchorage for sea-borne traffic, and I saw galleasses moored there, and galleys, warlike amongst the smaller fishing craft. It still seemed odd there was no wind. I nudged my mare and set her to the road.

No less odd than the absence of a breeze was the listless attitude of the folk I encountered. I should by now have become accustomed to that apathy, but still it struck me as strange that the arrival of a Storyman should elicit so little excitement. I thought the implacable heat drained more than physical energy; it seemed to rob the people of that animating vitality that had always carried us defiant through hardship.

I halted at the keep's gate, announcing myself to the soldiers lounging there. They wore no armor but only breeks and plain shirts draped with Carsbry's plaid. For all they still wore swords, I thought them ill prepared against attack should the Sky Lords come. My name taken with no great display of interest, the pyke commanding waved me carelessly by and I heeled my mare across the sun-hot cobbles of the yard. Pyrrin's banners hung limp from the tower, which appeared so far the condition of his holding. When I looked to the walls, I was encouraged to see a trio of the war-engines standing ready, with missiles piled beside—presumably not all here was lassitude.

I found the stables and rubbed down the mare, saw her watered and fed, the Changed ostlers warned of her temper, and made my way to the hall.

Pyrrin sat dicing with his warband. He was a man at the midpoint of his life, no longer youthful, but not yet given up to age. I judged him some ten years or more my senior and likely overfond of his food and ale. Fat began to overlay his muscle, and his pale brown hair was thinning. I thought his features spoke of indulgence, though his manner was amiable enough. He greeted me kindly, calling that ale be served me, and introduced me around.

His wife—the lady Allenore—greeted me from where she sat sewing with her women. She was as like her husband they might have been sister and brother, save her hair was thick, albeit weighted with sweat. The commur-magus was an elderly fellow, Varius by name. He was portly and disfigured by a dreadful burn that marred the left side of his otherwise cheerful face. He told me later that Kho'rabi magic had left its mark, and from others I learned that despite his years and girth, he was a formidable fighter. The jennym was a lean, hard-looking fellow named Robyrt. He alone amongst the commanders wore leathers and seemed ready to fight.

We drank and traded news. I had little enough: what change I had observed along my road was for the worse. They seemed not much concerned by Taerl's succession or Jareth's regency, or were loath to air their views in my presence. They told me there had been, some weeks ago, an expedition of the Sky Lords come against the Sentinels. Not, they hastened to advise me, the great airboats, but a horde of the little craft. All save a handful had been destroyed, and those few Kho'rabi who had reached the shore were all slain. Of greater and more recent interest was the arrival of a sorcerer in Carsbry, bound for Durbrecht with a servant in tow. She awaited, they said, the departure of a trading galley which should leave on the morrow.

I was immediately intrigued. "A servant?" I asked. "I thought there were no Changed on the Sentinels."

"Nor are there," said Varius, "and nor's he."

"A strange fellow," Robyrt offered. "Did he not accompany a sorcerer, I'd think him likely a Kho'rabi. He's a look about him."

"They came here only yesterday," said Pyrrin, "and have hardly emerged from their chambers. Had Varius not received word from the Sentinels, I'd wonder but if she doesn't look to hide him."

She? I felt my heart start beneath my ribs. It was like a blow, and for a while I was without breath, heart and head aswirl. It could not be . . . surely not . . . it could not be: that should be too much to dare hope. Worse, if it were and *she* was Durbrecht-bound. To find her only to lose her again? That should be more than I could bear.

I heard Pyrrin say, "Daviot? What ails you, man? By the God, but you're gone white. Are you ill?"

I shook my head, not yet able to speak. My throat was clogged with hope; and fear, also, that I might regain and again lose so much. All their eyes were on me. The aeldor pushed a mug to my hand, asking the while if I'd have him summon the keep's herbalist. On his face I saw the fear I brought disease into his hall. I was not sure what I saw on Varius's, but I recalled Rekyn's warning that I was observed by her kind. So: did this plump, scarred magus suspect the reason for my discomfort?

In that instant I did not care. I forced down ale and asked, "She?"

It must have seemed to them a strange question. My whole demeanor must have seemed strange. I did not care.

It was Pyrrin who answered, "Aye, *she*. Rwyan, her name."
Rwyan!

I knew not what I did then. Reason was gone, sense: my body reacted of its own. I sprang to my feet, sending my chair clattering over, my head turning, eyes ranging the hall in search of her.
Rwyan!

Robyrt came upright with me, his sword drawn and raised to cut me down. I ignored him: all my eyes knew was that she was not there. I took a step away from the table, turned. They must have believed me crazed. Across the hall, Allenore had dropped her embroidery, hands pressed frozen to her mouth. Her women clustered about her, as if her presence should protect them from this madman. Robyrt stood defensive before Pyrrin, who was himself on his feet, a dagger in his hand. The warband came with naked blades. I saw, as if from outside my body, that some held spears readied to cast. I could not see Rwyan. There was a silence broken by Varius's calm voice.

"Aye, Rwyan. A blind mage with hair like burnished copper. Bound on tomorrow's tide for Durbrecht. Now do you sit down and gather up your senses? Or must we bind you?"

I groaned, or wailed—I know not to this day which; but I righted my fallen chair and sat.

Varius filled my mug and bade me drink. I obeyed. I was suddenly gripped with a terrible fear that the sorcerer, or the aeldor, or the jennym, would order me bound, have me locked away until Rwyan was departed. I sat and drank as swords were sheathed and spears lowered. I was the focus of attention. I noticed that Robyrt had taken Pyrrin's seat, putting the length of the table between the aeldor and me, and that his blade rested ready across his thighs. I gestured apology and mumbled, "Forgive me, my lord Pyrrin; lady Allenore. I . . ." I shook my head. "She's here? In the keep now?"

Pyrrin nodded. From his expression it was obvious he had not the least idea what went on. All he saw was a Storyman seemingly made mad by mention of a woman's name. Robyrt was all undisguised suspicion, as if I were a slavering red-eyed hound. From behind me I heard a voice murmur, "Berserker." I took deep breaths, forcing myself if not to calm, then at least to its semblance, enough to reassure them I was not an immediate danger. Oh, by the God! She might walk in at any moment. I did not know what I might do then. I burned with impatience; with a maelstrom of emotions, hope and fear all mixed. It was all I could do to hold my seat.

All eyes were on me: an explanation was called for. Hoarse-voiced, I said, "We were lovers once, in Durbrecht. I've not seen her since; I'd not thought to see her again."

Pyrrin favored me with a look somewhere between amazement and pity. "By the God!" he said softly. "And she's come here now; and you. What odds on that, eh?"

Varius said, "Perhaps better had you come here tomorrow, or the day after. But . . ." He shrugged, that side of his face still mobile twisting in approximation of a sympathetic smile.

I said, "But I did not. She's in her quarters now?" My voice sounded strangled.

The sorcerer nodded. "She and her man, aye."

A hideous doubt assailed me. Her man; her servant? There were no servants on the Sentinels, I knew that much. So who was this fellow? Had Rwyan a lover? Jealousy flared. Irrational, unjustified, but no less fierce for that. I had found comfort in Krystin's arms, had I not? How then could I burn so hot at thought of Rwyan with another? What right had I? None, fairly—which made no difference at all. What's fair to do with love?

I swallowed down the lump that seemed to clog my throat, drank ale, and asked in as calm a tone as I could manage, "I thought the sorcerers of the Sentinels had no truck with servants?"

"Nor do they, usually." I could tell from Varius's expression that he saw the direction of my thinking. "But neither are many blind. This fellow's servant and guide both; hired to ease her passage. No more than that."

I think I sighed then. I know I felt relieved; and as quickly suspicious again. Perhaps Varius looked only to soothe me, to avoid public disturbance. Certainly, my behavior so far provided him with concern enough. I said, "I see." And then, "But—"

I bit back the words. Rwyan was blind, aye. Of course she was; of course I knew that. Knew it as surely as I knew she had no need of men to play the watchdog. With the gift of her talent she could "see" as well as any sighted woman. Jealousy flared anew: a servant, a guide? I saw that Varius waited on me, no less Pyrrin. Robyrt sat alert, his blade still drawn. My mind raced. Did Rwyan stoop to sophistry that she might bring a lover with her?

My hosts still waited on me. I said, "But I had never thought to find her again."

It sounded weak to me, but they appeared satisfied; at least none made comment. I raised my mug and set it down empty. Were this a story or a balladeer's song, Rwyan should enter the hall now, fall into my arms and go with me into some sunlit future. But it was not: there still lay a wall between us, our callings. There was still this mysterious *servant*. I summoned that empty dignity men rely on in such situations: had Rwyan come here with a lover, she should not see me disadvantaged. I should be strong; I should dismiss him. And her, needs be.

I said, "Does she take her meals in the hall?" And when Pyrrin told me aye, "Then likely I'll see her betimes. Meanwhile"—I gestured at my dusty shirt—"if I might bathe?"

The aeldor nodded enthusiastically. I suspect he was pleased enough to be rid of me awhile. I thought, aware of the undisguised curiosity emanating from Allenore and her ladies, that the hall should soon enough be abuzz with gossip. What a tale I made—the Storyman and the sorcerer, love thwarted not once but twice: a tale to moisten eyes. I rose, dignified, taking up my saddlebags and staff as Pyrrin called a Changed servant and charged the fellow with escorting me to a chamber, seeing a bath drawn.

I bowed and followed the Changed—cat-bred, I dimly noticed—from the hall. As we departed, I thought I heard conversation erupt. I had no doubt it concerned me. I revised my notions of lingering here: I should quit Carsbry as soon I might.

But meanwhile I should meet Rwyan again. I was no longer sure I welcomed that.

Ryl was the Changed's name. That much I noted, but little else. All thoughts of exploring his unseen world fled me as I was brought to my chamber. I thought entirely of Rwyan.

Here in Carsbry.

With an unneeded servant.

Taking ship tomorrow.

In Durbrecht, Telek had taught how sometimes ill-conceived humors may so affect the heart that that organ falters in its task. Its pumping becomes irregular, blood thins along its course, or spurts; breath comes short. At worst, the heart ceases its work altogether. As I lay in my tub, I thought I suffered so. I feared my heart should burst. I felt it pound against my ribs, as if demanding exit. I could not remain still for long but must scrub at the grime, soap my hair, and leap from the tub. Only to pace the floor in a fury of indecision. Should I return to the hall? Should I wait? Ryl had taken my boots to polish, my spare shirt and breeks to clean. All at my request; with the request he hurry, return them to me as soon as he was done—I'd not meet Rwyan clad vagabond. I believe the unfortunate fellow was somewhat frightened of my manner. I went to the window, aware I sucked breath as does a drowning man. I pressed against the sill, forcing my labored breathing even.

Below was the yard, bright in the sun, ordinary. A farrier's hammer clattered; horses nickered; a few folk moved slowly about their ordinary tasks. From the kitchens came the odor of cooking food to remind me the midday meal should not be long. I wondered if Rwyan should eat in the hall, as Pyrrin had said, or remain in her chamber. I wondered, if she did, if I should go to her. I wondered what I should say, did this mysterious servant prove my worst fears true. I wondered if she knew yet I was here in Carsbry.

I started as Ryl's knocking announced the return of my clothes. I gave him effusive thanks and waved him away, tugging on cleaned shirt and breeks, my gleaming boots. I tidied hair overlong in need of cutting. I picked up my staff and set it down. I turned Lan's bracelet around my wrist. I wanted to go; and I wanted to stay. I wanted to see

Rwyan; and I was afraid. I could not decide if it were better we meet in the crowded hall or alone. I thought of finding her chamber—Ryl or some other servant would surely know where she was quartered—and then of what I might find there. Indecision became an agony. Hope and fear lay balanced. Finally, I could wait no longer—whatever lay in store, I'd face it and know it, for worse or better. I took a deep breath and flung through the door, into the corridor beyond.

I had thought perhaps she might be quartered on this same level and we meet by chance, privately, but the corridor was empty. I walked to the stairs. Sweat that had little to do with the heat beaded my brow; my fresh shirt felt limp on my back. I straightened my spine and went down the winding stairway to the hall.

Pyrrin sat with Allenore and Varius at the high table. There were two empty chairs and a sudden silence as I appeared. All up and down the room eyes turned toward me. The aeldor beckoned, and I went to join him. The crossing of that hall seemed to take a long time. I sat as, slowly, conversation started up again. Faces still looked my way, when they were not turned, anticipatory, toward the door through which Rwyan must come. In gratitude, I must say that Pyrrin and his wife and Varius did their best to set me at my ease; also, that they faced an impossible task. I accepted the wine offered me and drank faster than was my wont. I smiled and made small talk, all the while waiting. It was an effort of will to keep my eyes from the door. I swear that waiting was worse than any battle I have fought. I had sooner face Kho'rabi knights than endure that again.

I was turned in Allenore's direction, responding to some question, when I heard the silence fall. I saw Allenore's pale brows rise, a hand clench in nervous fist. I felt a chill, as if iced water were spilled down my back, and at the same time hot. I broke off in midsentence, careless of my manners as I turned.

Rwyan stood beneath the arch of the door. She wore a loose gown of cream linen, gathered at the waist by a narrow belt of braided leather. Her hair, lighter than I remembered it, was piled up, so that her neck appeared a fragile column, tanned the color of wild honey. Her face was that same perfect oval that lived, vivid, in my memory, the planes and lines of jaw and cheeks and nose ideal. Her lips were full and red. I remembered their taste with agonizing clarity. Her eyes were that lovely ocean green. I saw them spring wide as her talent gave her sight of me and then, before any others there could see it, return to normal. Save she affected a blankness I knew was false.

I held my breath, unaware I did, as I directed my attention to the man at her side.

He was tall, about my own height, and I suppose he looked

somewhat like me. At least, his skin was dark and his hair black, his eyes a blue that might be gray. His face was impassive, but I saw that his gaze flickered swiftly over the entire hall, as if, from habit, he checked the diners, the shadowed corners. I thought that a fighter's look. He wore plain shirt and breeks of unbleached linen, the blouse sleeveless, exposing muscular arms. Rwyan's right hand rested on his forearm, and I hated him for that touch, for that familiarity. I saw her murmur something to him, and he reply, casting a hooded glance in my direction. Or perhaps it was in the direction of the high table only, and my assumption born of jealousy. As they came forward, I saw that he walked loose-limbed: a warrior's stride. This was not, I thought, any servant.

My mouth was dry as they approached. I knew Rwyan could "see" me; knew with absolute certainty she was aware of my presence. I could not understand this pretense. I wet my mouth with wine. My heart was a battle drum under my ribs. I rose from my seat, about to speak, to say her name, but Pyrrin preempted me.

"Rwyan," he said, not much at his ease, "we've another guest. The Storyman, Daviot. You . . . know . . . him, I believe."

I saw her hand tighten on her *servant's* arm. Her head cocked. To anyone who did not know she could "see," it would have seemed she merely turned her face as the blind do. That the movement set her eyes directly on mine should have seemed pure accident. I stared at her, utterly confused.

She said, "Daviot?" and in her voice there was something I could not define. Was it pleasure or surprise? Alarm? I could not tell, only gape, my heart aching, and say, "Rwyan."

Solicitous, Pyrrin eased back a chair. I stared as the dark-haired *servant* guided her to it, saw her seated, and took station behind. My confusion increased apace—she treated the man as if he were a servant, and I could scarce believe my gentle Rwyan would deal so with a lover. Not save she'd changed dramatically during her sojourn on the Sentinels.

She said, "Daviot, it's been a long time. You're hale?"

Her voice was soft as I recalled, melodic; the cool disinterest I heard was strident. More—she could "see" I was in good health. What game was this? Almost I asked it aloud, but then I thought that if she maintained this pretense of disability, there must be a reason. Also (I am now ashamed to admit) that if she played some game with me, I would play her back, move for move. I would stand on my pompous dignity. I'd not play the heart-broke lover but be the sophisticated man.

I said, "I'm well, my thanks. And you?"

She said, "Save I must rely on a guide in unfamiliar places, aye —
I'm well."

For all I was mightily confused, both by her behavior and my
own troubled feelings, I recognized that for a warning. She'd no need
of guides and so must have some reason for leaning on this silent
fellow's arm. I'd know it there and then, and had our companions not
bent themselves to setting us both at our ease, I'd have taken her aside
to have the reason. But I could not; I must sit and converse as if there
were no longer aught between us save old memories. I hated it.

A myriad questions bubbled in my head; accusations rose unspoken, and words of love. Whatever doubts I'd known or what intentions, I could not deny I loved her still. I gazed at her and knew that
with utmost certainty. Was this fellow her paramour, still I loved her.
I'd slay him if I must, to win her back. I loved her still; still doubt
lingered. I was like a man dying of thirst and come upon a spring,
wondering if the water be pure or poisoned. I studied her face and
longed to touch her, to kiss her, to hold her. Images of our time in
Durbrecht spun through my mind, salt on the wounds of my doubt. I
cursed those protocols, the warning her deception gave me, that
bound me to polite conversation. I ate without noticing what I put in
my mouth. I watched hers and remembered the taste of her lips,
whilst she, all that anguished time, maintained a horrid calm.

She returned to Durbrecht, she advised me, summoned back by
her College, a man hired to be her guide and servant. And I? Where
had I been? Where did I go now?

After, when better sense returned, I realized she directed our
conversation with a subtlety worthy of my own calling, prompting me
to talk whilst she sat, head tilted in attitude of attention, "watching"
me. To this day I cannot say whether Varius was all the time aware
she could "see," or deceived by her pretense. Certainly the rest were,
and I did not then consider the scarred sorcerer, only my love.

Or rather, my love and the man standing dutifully behind her
chair. He had said nothing, and Rwyan had not offered his name. His
presence bewildered me. There was that about him suggested he was
a warrior — his stance, the way his gaze shifted to encompass the hall
whilst seeming not to shift at all, the marks on his forearms that only a
blade could have left — and yet he deferred to Rwyan obediently as
any Changed. He was a conundrum. No less this camouflage of blindness Rwyan wore, or her attitude toward me.

When the meal ended, I did not know if I was relieved or further
tormented. Rwyan made some excuse to return to her chambers, and I
must watch her take her *servant's* arm again and walk from the hall
without a backward glance. I'd go after her, but I could not: Varius

was there, a sorcerer, well able to send word to Durbrecht of my behavior, to speak with Pyrrin and have me confined till Rwyan was gone. Perhaps later—when the keep slept. Then, perhaps, I might find her and have answers of her. Meanwhile, I'd not give myself away, not to Varius or to her. Did she scorn me, I'd not concede her the satisfaction of my unhappiness. Instead, I heeded the aeldor's request for a tale: my duty; I cursed that duty then.

I did not give of my best, but still I was applauded, and by the time I was done, the long afternoon had progressed. I was allowed to escape and for a while contemplated finding Rwyan's chamber. I decided not and went instead to the stables. Had I thought to find solace of my horse, I was disappointed. She greeted me with a nicker and a snapping of her teeth, as if the comfort of a stable restored her ill temper. I snarled at her and made my way back to the yard.

Robyrt was there, drilling a squad of sweat-drenched soldiers. I watched and then asked if I might join their exercise.

The jennym gave me an expressionless look and nodded. He found me kit and a wooden practice sword, presenting himself as my opponent.

As I laced the padded leathers, he said, "You've my sympathy, Storyman. You love her still, eh?"

"Is it so obvious?" I asked.

Solemnly, he said, "To any man with eyes in his head."

But to her? I mouthed a foul curse and took up my sword.

Robyrt said, "Practice only, Daviot."

I had not thought my face was so naked. I nodded and went on guard.

As what passed for twilight in these unnatural times spread faint shadows over the yard, Robyrt called a halt. I was awash with sweat and had not few bruises, though not so many as the jennym, who complimented me on my swordwork. He reminded me of Andyrt. He got me salve of the keep's herbalist, and I returned to my chamber, presenting poor Ryl with dusty boots and a shirt in dire need of laundering. He took them meekly and had a bath brought in. I soaked my aches away, at least those imparted by Robyrt's stave, and rubbed my bruises with the unguent. The thought of facing Rwyan at another civilized table was painful. I felt my hope recede.

Quite what I hoped for that crazed day I do not know. I was still a Storyman, bound by my duty to wander up the coast to the Treppanek and thence to Durbrecht. She was to take ship on the morrow. To Durbrecht, aye; but what chance of finding her again there? She would be in her College, I in mine until I was sent out again. Or the Sky Lords might come. And even did they not, still our old infraction should be remembered, and we watched, kept apart. And I could not know if she loved me still or spurned me now. It was hopeless, and I no longer had the wild innocence of youth to bolster my optimism. At best—did she not turn me away—I might hope to snatch one night with her. The which should likely render a second parting the more painful.

I ground my teeth in helpless frustration, possessed of something akin to panic. I could not decide whether to go early or late to the hall. I knew that I must spend the evening telling tales. I wondered if Rwyan would remain to listen. I thought it should be anguish to be so bound by duty and protocol, not knowing where I stood, she there, untouchable, proximity the worst distance.

Ryl brought back my boots and the promise of a fresh-washed shirt come morning. I thanked him and reached a decision.

"Ryl," I asked, "where is the sorcerer Rwyan quartered?"

"Across the way," he told me. "Three doors along the corridor."

"And her servant?"

If he suspected my motives, he gave no sign. Only said, "In the smaller room beside. The fourth door."

Separate rooms meant nothing, but it was a straw to clutch. I smiled and nodded and said, "My thanks. I've no further need of you."

I waited only so long as it took him to fetch two bull-bred Changed to remove my tub, and then enough they'd have quit the corridor. I smoothed my damp hair and went out.

Three doors along.

I paced the flags with a heart I thought must announce my approach with its hectic beat. I thanked the God I was not sure existed that the corridor remained empty. I halted, dry-mouthed, at Rwyan's door. I raised a fisted hand, and hesitated.

What if she lay there with her *servant*?

What if she turned me away?

What if she laughed at me?

I drew a breath as if about to plunge into the depths of the Fend and struck the door.

Her voice came back, asking who it was.

I said, "Daviot."

And the door was hurled open and she stood before me, "looking" directly into my eyes with such an expression of pain and fear, I could only put my arms around her and hold her close.

Into her hair I said, "Rwyan. Rwyan, I love you."

Against my chest she said, "I love you, Daviot. I was afraid . . ."

She raised her face, and I saw she smiled and that her eyes held tears. I kissed her. I felt her lips respond, her arms tighten about me. All doubt vanished. I heeled the door closed.

When we drew a little way apart—not separate, not past the compass of our arms, but enough we might catch breath—I saw the room was empty. I said, "I feared . . ." just as she said, "I was afraid . . ."

We laughed and kissed again, and all the years between that moment and our parting were gone. I had my Rwyan back, and in that instant I decided I would not lose her again. Not duty nor all the width of Dharbek should be allowed to come between us. I'd not let my College or hers gainsay us. I'd quit my calling to have her, and deny Durbrecht, even Kherbryn itself, to keep her.

I said, "I love you, Rwyan. I've always loved you."

She touched my face, her fingers gentle, exploring the contours of my cheeks, my jaw and mouth and forehead. It was as if, with touch, she would confirm what her occult vision told her: that I was here and real. She said, "I feared I'd forget you. I tried sometimes; but I could not. I dreamed of you. Oh, Daviot, to find you here and not come to you, to act as I did—that was so hard."

I still did not understand, but that seemed now not to matter at all, only that I held her and she loved me. I said, "You took my heart; you own it still. I was afraid . . . when I saw you with . . ."

She said, "Tezdal," and her lovely face grew troubled.

Through my joy I felt a brief pang of recent fear. I said, "Who is he? Why do you pretend you cannot see? You've no need of a guide. I thought, perhaps, he was"—the word sat bitter on my tongue; I forced it out—"your lover."

"No." She shook her head, that glorious hair brushing my cheek. I drank its scent. "He's not my lover. But . . ."

The sentence tailed away, a shadow fallen on her face. I stroked her cheek, traced the outline of her lips. Beyond her, I could see the bed: immediate temptation. But in her voice I heard I knew not what: I bade my desire begone. It refused, but quieted enough I might hear her out.

She said, "Daviot, this is a tale for only your ears. I must have your promise."

"You've my heart," I said, "and all the promises I can give you."

She smiled at that, but not without some measure of gravity, of discomfort. I felt again a stab of doubt; not that she loved me but that somehow this Tezdal—a strange name, surely—might come between us. I said, "Do you bid me silent, my lady, then my silence is yours. My word on it."

She nodded and said, "There's much to tell."

Then, from the corridor outside came voices, the tread of passing feet. Rwyan said, "Oh, by the God, they go to the hall."

I said, "Let them."

She shook her head, frowning now. "We cannot, Daviot. I dare not . . . none must suspect . . ."

I said, "Rwyan, I'll not let you go again."

I bent my head to kiss her, but she set a hand against my lips. She was troubled and I hesitated. I held her still, and she me, and I sensed she was in no way eager to break that hold. I wondered why she frowned.

She said, "Daviot, do you trust me?"

I ducked my head in earnest confirmation.

"Then do you trust me a little longer. Only go to the hall; let no one see you leave this chamber. Act as before—as if we are now strangers—"

I interrupted her: "Rwyan, they say you sail tomorrow, and I'll not lose you again."

I saw pain on her face then. She said, "Only in the hall, my love. Be the Storyman there, and I some woman from your past, dismissed now."

I said, "Never dismissed!"

Again she silenced me with a touch. "After, when the keep sleeps, come to me and I'll explain. *My* word on that."

Reluctantly, I nodded and said, "Do you so bid me. But shall you stay to hear me?"

She smiled then, and no sun ever shone brighter. She said, "I'll stay. But impatiently; I pray they'll not delay you there."

It was all I could do not to kiss her, fold her in my arms, and carry her to the bed, but there was an urgency in her voice, a plea in her blind eyes: I quelled the impulse as the sounds outside grew louder. I said, "I fear my throat grows sore in this heat. I fear I'll not be able to speak too long."

She laughed then, softly, and raised her face to mine, brushing me with her lips. Then pushed me away, saying, "Good. Now go, I beg you."

I loosed my hold on her. I stroked her cheek and turned to the door, listening. I heard voices receding and opened the door a crack. The footsteps faded, and I swung the portal wide. As I went out I said, "I'll not lose you again, Rwyan."

She nodded, but in her eyes I saw doubt. I ignored it: I had none any longer. I closed the door. The man—Tezdal, she had named him —stood watching me. Our eyes met, and he nodded, as if in greeting or approval, but neither of us spoke. I walked away.

That noonday meal had been hard, but this was worse. To have held my Rwyan again, to know again she loved me, and now to pretend . . . it was no easy task. I wondered if Varius or Robyrt saw it in my eyes, in the glances I could not help sending her way as we sat at table and conversed as civilized folk do: politely, formally, impersonally. And all the time agog for the evening to end, to go to her. If they did suspect, they said nothing, nor gave any hint. She was superb, playing the blind woman, cool in the presence of a forgotten lover.

I ate with better appetite and drank little, and when the tables were cleared, I rose at Pyrrin's request to take a place at the hall's center. I was pleased to see the aeldor's Changed servitors were allowed to remain; better pleased that Rwyan did. I gave of my best that night, and if my earlier performance had been lackluster, I compensated for it now. I gave them Aerlyn's Wedding and Daeran's Revenge, then roughened my voice (which elicited a small, secret smile from Rwyan) as I commenced the tale of Marwenne's Ride. When that was told, I downed a mug of ale, as if to soothe a speech-sored throat. There were shouts that I go on, but I pled my fear I should lose my voice altogether and so not be able to speak on the morrow. I was eloquent, and the hour grew late. Pyrrin accepted my excuse, announcing his own intention of finding his bed: the hall began to clear.

I watched Rwyan depart on Tezdal's arm, consumed no longer with jealousy but with impatience now, and more than a little curiosity. As soon as seemed decent, I said my own goodnights and found my room.

Ryl had laid out my laundered clothes and lit the lantern. A jug of wine and a single glass stood on the table. I left them lie, easing my door a crack ajar. A few servants yet moved along the corridor, and I resisted the temptation to ignore them—Rwyan had entrusted me with secrecy, and I would not betray her. I crossed to the window, my fingers tapping an impatient tattoo on the sill. The night hung hot and heavy, and I thought the sky seemed not so dark as it should be, as if the Sky Lord's magic held back the sun from its rightful setting. I wondered what secrets Rwyan would reveal; mostly I thought of lying with her again.

Then, driven by an impulse I did not stop to define, I folded my gear and filled my saddlebags, setting them with my staff. I knew not what the future held for me, only that I could not bear to let Rwyan go again. I returned to the door and, finding the corridor silent, went to her room.

Her door opened on my knock, and she came into my arms. For a while we said only words of love, and when we spoke of other things we were naked on a rumpled bed. I licked sweet salty sweat from the gentle mound of her belly as she sighed and tangled fingers in my hair. A single lantern burned across the room, its wick trimmed low so that light fell golden on her skin. Her blind eyes were huge; I thought she had never looked so lovely.

She said, "Daviot, we must talk."

I raised my lips, not willingly, from her flesh and nodded.

She eased higher, resting back against the pillows. Her hair fell like golden flame over her smooth shoulders. I heard such gravity in her voice, I made no move to kiss her or hold her but only took her hands in mine. For now that seemed enough.

She studied my face a moment, as if gauging my reaction. Then she said, "Tezdal is a Sky Lord."

"*What?*"

I'd have been off the bed and running to alert the keep had Rwyan not flung her arms around my neck to hold me back. Even so, I dragged her halfway upright, my feet upon the floor, my hands moving to disentangle her arms.

"Daviot, no!" she cried. Then softer, "Listen! I beg you, listen. He's no danger—he's no memory."

"What?" I said again.

That seemed to me so dreadful a loss, I sat back. I was bemused. Why did Rwyan protect a Sky Lord? She took my hands again, kneeling before me. Lust stirred, even through my amazement. She shook her head, spilling her glorious hair back, and "looked" me in the eye.

"He's no memory," she repeated. "Save that his name is Tezdal, he remembers nothing of his past."

I said, "But he's a Sky Lord? You know this?"

"We do," she said, and told me of his finding on the rock and his sojourn on the island, the design the sorcerers had drawn.

When she was done, I was silent awhile. It seemed to me so enormous a thing, I must take precious time to digest it. I said, "Did Pyrrin know this, he'd slay the Kho'rabi."

"Hence my deception," she said. "Save I can deliver him safe to Durbrecht, he'd as well have died when we destroyed his airboat."

I nodded. I thought perhaps that had been the better course; then that had events not run to this pattern, I'd not have met Rwyan again.

I supposed that in a way I should be grateful to my enemy. I said, "He's no memory at all? You're confident he does not deceive you?"

"We dug and dug," she said. "We used our magic on him. Save we were convinced, think you we'd take such risk?"

"I suppose not." I shook my head slowly. Then: "Robyrt wonders at his looks. He said"—I paused, conjuring the jennym's words— " 'Did he not accompany a sorcerer, I'd think him likely a Kho'rabi. He's a look about him.' By the God, Rwyan, does Robyrt wonder, what of Varius?"

She licked her lips. They gleamed moist in the lantern's light, and I wanted badly to taste them. She said, "I think perhaps Varius suspects but chooses to remain silent. Likely he feels that if the Sentinels elect to employ such subterfuge, there must be a reason and he best advised to hold his own counsel."

"Pyrrin would not," I said, remembering details heard along my road. "He lost sons to the Sky Lords."

"That's why I must deceive them," she said, "all of them. The God willing, we'll not be questioned on the boat."

I said automatically, "The ship. You plan to take one of those craft in the harbor?"

She ducked her head, hair falling in a burnished curtain over shoulders and breasts. She shook it back, and when I saw her face again, it was solemn; mournful, even.

She said, "The *Sprite*. We sail tomorrow, on the morning tide."

I said, "Rwyan, you face terrible danger. Should the master learn, I doubt he'd scruple to cast the Sky Lord overboard. Or to bring you to the nearest aeldor, charged with treason."

She said, "Still, it's the safest course. We agreed on that."

I said, "Still, he's a Sky Lord; our enemy. Can you be safe with him?"

She said, "Aye. He considers me a savior—that he owes me his life. He's sworn to defend me."

I did not much like that. I frowned and said, "I'd see you better guarded."

She smiled and squeezed my hands. "I'm a sorcerer, Daviot," she said. "I'm not without defenses."

My frown grew deeper. She let go my hands, placing hers upon my cheeks, her eyes surveying my face as if she'd embed my image in her memory. She said, "Can your College and mine only unlock his memory, think you what advantages we might gain. I *must* bring him to Durbrecht."

Her face became grave again, and in her voice I heard regret. I said, "You're fond of him."

No doubt my voice expressed my resentment. Certainly, Rwyan leaned toward me, kissing me softly, before she said, "Fond of him, aye. But I love you, Daviot. There can be no other for me. For Tezdal I feel . . . pity, I suppose. I think that when I've done my duty, he shall be a prisoner again. Likely they'll seek to drain his mind, and when that's done . . ."

She shrugged; I nodded. I think I loved her more in that moment than I ever had before. Suddenly it seemed to me a wonderful thing that she could feel such compassion for an enemy; and awful that she was bound by her duty to do a thing that must cause her pain. But this was my Rwyan, and there was steel beneath her soft flesh. I put my arms around her, drawing her close against my chest.

"Duty's a harsh master," I said, "but the Sky Lord could have no sweeter warder."

I felt her lips move against my skin, her voice muffled. "Aye, harsh," she murmured. "That it brings me back to you, only to lose you again."

"You'll not," I said into her hair.

She tilted back her head to find my eyes. In hers I saw tears. I brushed them away as she said, "How can I not? I must sail tomorrow; you must go your own way."

I said, "Not without you."

She said, "Oh, Daviot, don't torment me. This second parting shall hurt enough."

There was such anguish in her voice, such pain writ on her face, that I could only pull her to me, my lips on her neck, her cheeks, as I said defiantly, "I'll not let duty come between us again."

"How can it not?" she moaned. "Please, Daviot, say no more of this—it hurts too much. Only hold me; love me."

I did, but even as we lay together through that sleepless night, I knew my decision was made. I cared nothing for the consequences. Let fate treat me as it would, I'd not lose her again.

Came the first light of dawn, and I rose. It was no easy thing to quit Rwyan's bed; easier, albeit not without some feeling of guilt, to deceive her. That was needful, I told myself: a small lie now, that there be none in our future. I gathered up my scattered clothes and tugged them on. Rwyan lay languid amidst the disarrayed sheets, and I bent to kiss her.

"A little while longer," she pleaded, her arms about my neck. "Only a little while."

The scent of her body was musky in my nostrils, and it was very hard to say her nay, but I did.

"The keep begins to stir," I said. "I'd not leave you ever, but if none must suspect, better I go now."

Reluctantly, she nodded. "Shall you break your fast in the hall?" she asked.

I sighed and shook my head and told her honestly, "To see you there and continue this pretense should be too hard. I'll busy myself elsewhere and not see you go. But Rwyan . . . know that I love you. That I always have and always shall."

She said, "I do," and there were tears in her eyes.

We kissed, and I must disentangle myself. As I went to the door, she said, "This is a hard duty, Daviot. I wish to the God it were otherwise."

Almost then I told her, but I bit back the words, knowing she'd forbid me, even to alerting Varius or Pyrrin of my intention. Her sense of duty was ever stronger than mine. Instead, I said, "Perhaps we'll meet again ere long," and before she could do more than smile sadly, I was out the door.

The corridor was thankfully empty, and I crossed swiftly to my own chamber. My staff and saddlebags lay where I'd left them, and when I looked from my window, I saw the yard was yet empty, pearly with thin gray mist in the dawnlight. I took my gear and tossed it out, noting where it fell. Then I filled a glass with wine, for courage, and drank it down. For fear my room be checked and suspicion aroused, I rumpled my bed as if I'd slept there. Then I went out again.

Few stirred as yet, and those all Changed servants who paid me scant attention as I made my way from the keep. I trusted they'd say nothing, and were they questioned later, they could say only that they had seen me go by. Did any ask, I hoped they'd assume I went abroad early, to wander the town. I did not believe any would guess what I intended.

I found my gear and slunk like some latecome thief across the yard: there was one farewell I'd not forgo.

Horses nickered drowsily as I entered the stable. My gray mare met me with an irritable stare, as if she feared I'd saddle her and take her from this comfort. I stroked her muzzle, which she accepted but a moment before endeavoring to bite my hand. I wished her well. I thought she'd find a good home here, likely a softer life than the Storyman's road. I was somewhat surprised to realize how much I should miss her; but my choice lay between her company and Rwyan's, and that was no choice at all. I left her with her nose buried in the manger.

I traversed the yard again, this time toward the gates. I went boldly—the walls were high for climbing, and that furtive exit was more likely to attract attention than if I behaved as if all were well. Still I felt that eyes locked on me as I approached, and it was not easy to saunter casually, all the time waiting for a voice—Robyrt's or Varius's or Pyrrin's—to hail me and demand to know where I went, with staff and bags, at such an early hour.

I was grateful for the negligent attitude of Pyrrin's gatemen: they were half asleep still and barely glanced my way as I ambled by, nodding to them. One gave me the day's greetings, and I answered in kind. Likely they found nothing odd in a Storyman going out so early, but even so, I waited on the summons that should bring me back as I found the avenue leading down to the harbor.

Low warehouses stood silent here, their frontages facing toward the sea. I paused where two afforded me a shadowy hiding place, scanning the nearest mole. There was no breeze, and the air no longer carried the odors of seaweed and tar and fish—the still-familiar scents of my childhood—but rather a metallic hint of the heat to come. It was already warm, even though the eastern horizon as yet showed only a glimmer of sunlight. It was a reddish gold: it reminded me of Rwyan's hair. I studied the ships riding at anchor. The *Sprite,* she'd said; I looked for it.

I could not find the vessel: I left the cover of the warehouses and set to pacing the harbor, south to north.

It was very quiet. There were no Truemen about save me; Changed crewmen slept on open decks, quite unaware of my inspection. Rwyan had said her ship sailed on the morning tide. The tides even were changed in this unnatural summer, defeating my childhood memories of their swell and ebb, but from the look of the water I guessed the turning should not come before midmorning. There were no fishing boats along the beach—I assumed them out, taken on the night's ebb. I thought the harbor should not wake until the sun was full risen. I continued my stealthy inspection.

I could not read; there was no need. But neither could any save a handful of Dhar. The nobles, a few sorcerers—such folk as sometimes wished to record messages privately. What could not be said in honest speech was illustrated, like a tavern sign or a ship's name, and that was how I recognized the *Sprite.*

She was a galleass, her three sails furled, her sweeps stowed inboard. She was painted a brilliant scarlet, and on her plump bow was an ethereal figure, a silvery-haired woman clad in wispy blue robes that became waves about her waist, one arm raised to point ahead. I had no doubt this was Rwyan's ship. I halted.

She rode high in the water—if she was to take on cargo, that should be loaded later (how much later? how soon?)—and I could not see her deck. I looked to her oarports and saw twelve openings. So: twenty-four oarsmen whose benches must lie directly beneath the topdeck, more crew to handle her sails; likely all sleeping on board. There was no gangplank run out, but from bow and stern extended heavy cables, lashed firm to the wharfside bollards. Below them were portholes that must open into cabins fore and aft. The latter, I decided, was most likely the master's, and he might well sleep there now;

the forrard quarters would be for such passengers as should soon come aboard. If the master remained with his vessel, I could not chance waking him: I walked silently to the bow.

I stood at another watershed in my life, and I shall not deny I was afraid. I could turn back now; go back to Pyrrin's keep with neither questions nor accusations leveled. I was ordered by my College to travel up this coast by land, and I had no idea what punishment should be mine did I betray that duty. I could neither ask for nor purchase passage—that would be denied me. If Rwyan knew what I intended, I thought she would deny me. If I did my duty—remained in Carsbry—I must let Rwyan go; I should likely never see her again. That thought I could not bear. Of the outcome, I thought not at all.

It was too late for second thoughts: I buckled my saddlebags across my back, fixed my staff beneath them, and took hold of the mooring line. I swung clear of the mole, teeth gritting as my hands almost slipped from the cable. My weight carried me down, the *Sprite* shifting in the water. For a moment I feared I should be crushed between galleass and wharfside, that the movement alert the sleeping crew to what I did. Momentarily I anticipated faces, shouts; defeat. Then the ship righted, water slapping about my heels. Her boards groaned softly. I swung my legs up, hooking dripping boots over the rope, and began to inch my way along.

It was no easy journey, encumbered by staff and bags, the line greasy and wet, the *Sprite* all the time swaying as if undecided between allowing me my goal and squashing me like some unwelcome bug. Had I not been propelled by the greater fear of forever losing Rwyan, I believe I might well have let go, dropped into the water of the harbor and swum hangdog ashore. But that fear gave me strength: I clung limpetlike or, more correctly I suppose, like a determined rat, intent on reaching the riches on board.

From my inverted point of view, I saw the forrard port come closer. I almost fell as I nudged its glassed shutter wide. I hung, swaying precariously, listening for shout of alarm. None came, nor face to the opening; the galleass remained silent, save for that multitude of sounds a ship makes at anchor. The thudding of my heart seemed to me louder. I took a breath and got one hand on the lower edge of the port. This would be the hardest part, the point at which I was most likely to fail. I clenched my teeth and let go the rope.

I got my free hand on the porthole's sill as my body crashed against the bow. My face hit the planks, and I felt pain erupt in my nose and jaw. My head spun; I was winded. I thought my fingers must snap, so fierce did I grip my hold. Blood ran from my nostrils. I thought I must be found. I held my breath, ears straining then as much as the muscles in my aching arms. There was silence still: I found some purchase with my toes and desperately hauled myself up. I got one elbow on the sill—the second—and then I was inside, stifling a cry as my injured face struck wood again.

I rolled onto my back: bloodstains would doubtless occasion questions. I inspected my teeth and found none broken; nor was my nose, for all it hurt ferociously. I lay panting, my head tilted back until the trickling from my nostrils ceased. I inspected my surroundings. The cabin was small, the outer wall curved, following the shape of the prow; the inner was straight, dividing this berth from its matching fellow. There was a narrow bunk with storage space below, a bench seat that was also a cupboard, a table hinged to fasten against the wall, nothing more; nor anywhere to hide. I picked up my staff and went to the door.

I pressed an ear to the wood and heard nothing. I could not dare hope the crew would sleep much longer, only pray none came below before I found some better refuge. I eased the door ajar and set an eye to the crack. I looked out on the rowing gallery. The oarsmen's benches were set to either side, roofed by the topdeck, which was open down the center. The masts were bedded here, and between them were hatches affording access to the holds and bilges. Aft was a single door that must, I surmised, open into the stern cabin. To either side, ladders rose to the upper deck. I glanced that way and saw the sky was brighter. I heard movement above, as of bodies rising, the sound of stentorian yawns and the beginnings of conversation. I had no more time to waste: I scurried to the nearest hatch.

A short ladder carried me into darkness. The air was redolent of past cargoes, thick and unpleasantly warm. I could see nothing, only grope my way forrard until I reached the stemson. I crouched there, hidden as best I could manage behind one upward-curving rib, slipping off my bags and thinking of the tinderbox within. To strike a spark was too great a risk, and I resisted that temptation. I hoped there should be no cargo taken on from Carsbry.

Time ran slow in that stygian gloom, its passage marked only by the muffled sounds from overhead. I thought the crew must break their fast, but I could smell only the musty odors of my hiding place. I lost track of time; I dozed, and woke as footsteps echoed directly above me. Wood creaked, and I supposed the oarsmen found their benches. I heard shouts, faint through the intervening planks, then felt the ship roll as she cast off. A whistle shrilled, there were muffled thuds, the craft vibrated, trembling slightly. I felt her heave—the bow coming around—and then the familiar undulation of vessel through water. I thought of finding my way above and decided to wait, at least until we were too far from Carsbry for the master to willingly turn back.

More time went slowly by. I curbed my growing impatience. I sweated profusely, the air heady. I grew hungry; thirsty, too. When I deemed us well out onto the Fend, I climbed the ladder and shoved back the hatch.

I had not often seen overmuch expression on the bovine faces of the bull-bred Changed, but those of the oarsmen showed stark surprise as I appeared. One bellowed; several lost their stroke. From the stern came a shout, part inquiry, part anger. I climbed out, blinded by the light as I came into the sun, so that I could only stand, hand raised to shade my dazzled eyes. I heard the same voice shout, this time in bewilderment.

Then a voice I knew, closer, said, "Daviot?" as if she could not believe the evidence of her senses. Then, firmer, "Daviot! What in the God's name are you thinking of?"

I said, "You."

I felt at some disadvantage. The sun now stood directly overhead, and I had lurked in darkness long enough it took some while for my eyes to adjust. Rwyan's voice had sounded as much angry as surprised.

I heard the other voice shout from the stern, "You know this fellow, mage?"

And Rwyan answer, "Aye. He's a Storyman; Daviot by name."

"What does he on my ship?" I assumed this was the master. "By the God, are Storymen become stowaways now? Or is he some pirate?"

"He's a Storyman," Rwyan called, "but what he does here, I can only guess."

My sight returned slowly, and I saw the oarsmen had resumed their task, bending over their sweeps, ignoring me as if divorced from this drama. I saw other Changed faces peering down, and then Rwyan's, Tezdal at her side. The Sky Lord seemed somewhat amused; Rwyan not at all. I grinned and said, "I'll not lose you again."

Her expression then was one of naked disbelief: she seemed not quite able to accept I was there. I went up the forrard ladder to where she stood. Four burly Changed moved toward me, marlinespikes in their hands. Rwyan gestured them back, calling to the captain, "He's no danger, Master Tyron," and to me, softer, "only a fool."

"A fool in love," I said. "I could not bear to let you go."

Her expression changed. It was as though sun and shadow chased one another across her face. I saw disbelief become pleasure, that turn to anger, then exasperation as she shook her head and beckoned me to follow her. We went to the bow. Master Tyron came after us.

He was a squat, barrel-chested man, tanned dark as ancient leather, his head bald save for a fringe of white hair. He wore a short, wide-bladed sword such as sailors favor, and his right hand curled around the hilt as he studied me. His eyes were a piercing blue; they fixed me as if I were some loathsome creature come slithering out of the depths to soil his ship.

"I'd have an explanation," he declared. His voice was gruff, hoarse from shouting orders or from outrage. "I'm commissioned to deliver you, lady, and your man here. Not some stowaway Storyman who slinks on board. When?"

This last was barked at me. I said, "This morning, captain. At dawn."

He grunted, muttering something about a careless watch and punishments to come, and said to me, "How?"

I told him, and he grunted again. Then: "Why?"

I hesitated. I'd no wish to needlessly deliver trouble on Rwyan. I said, "I'd go to Durbrecht, captain. With this lady. She knew nothing of this."

Tyron said, "I'm minded to put you overboard. Carsbry's not too far a swim."

I could not help but glance shoreward at that: there was a suggestion of firm purpose in his tone. I saw the coast shimmering faint in the distance; I doubted I could swim so far.

Rwyan said, "No!" and when I turned toward her, I saw genuine alarm on her lovely face.

Tyron snorted. "You say you know him? Is he crazed?"

She said, "No."

Tyron's gaze swung from me to her. I watched his fingers clench on his sword. "You had nothing to do with his trespass?" he demanded.

Rwyan and I said, "No," together. I added, "On my word as a Storyman, captain."

Tyron considered this awhile. Finally he said, "Then I place him in your charge, mage. You decide what's to be done with him; but I'll have payment from his College or yours for his passage."

Without further ado, granting me a last smoldering stare, he spun and stumped his way aft, shouting irritably at the crew as he went.

Rwyan faced me, and I was abruptly embarrassed. I said, "I could not bear to let you go."

She said, "You keep repeating that, Daviot," and sighed. "Shall you tell them that in Durbrecht? Think you it shall be explanation enough?"

I looked at her. She wore a blouse of unbleached linen and a skirt of the same material, dyed blue and divided for ease of traveling. There was no wind to ruffle her hair, and it floated loose about her troubled face. I reached to touch her cheek, but she drew back. That hurt.

I said, "Are you not glad to see me?"

She said, "No!" Then, "Yes." Then, "In the God's name, Daviot, *are* you crazed?"

I shook my head; I shrugged and fiddled with my staff. I could think of no proper answer. I had not thought much at all beyond this moment, and it was not progressing as I had anticipated. I was abruptly reminded of childhood transgressions and my mother's stern face.

Rwyan said, "This is madness. What do you hope to achieve?"

"I thought . . ." My voice faltered. I shrugged again and said, "I'd not thought too much. Save of losing you again."

"Think you I don't feel that hurt?" She seemed torn between anger and fondness. "But we've both a duty, and it forces us apart."

I said obstinately, "I'd not have it so. I'd be with you, always."

She closed her eyes a moment, as if wearied by my insistence, then met my gaze. "That cannot be, my love." Her voice was no longer angry, but gentle as if she chided some recalcitrant child. "We both know that. I'd have it otherwise no less than you; but I cannot. Nor does your presence help."

I had hoped for warmer welcome. "At least I'm with you," I said. "Save you elect to have Tyron put in and deliver me ashore."

She said, "Aye," in a contemplative tone that chilled my blood. "What else should I do?"

"Let me come with you," I said.

"To Durbrecht?" She shook her head and sighed. "And what then?"

I said, "That's in the future, Rwyan. We can be together ere we reach Durbrecht."

"I think you *are* gone mad," she said. "You speak of a future measured in days, weeks at best. And then? How should your College and mine greet our arrival together? Think you either should look kindly on this escapade?"

I opened my mouth to speak, but she gestured me silent and I obeyed. There was a fierceness in her blind eyes that warned me I had better hold my tongue.

She said, "Do we put in at the next harbor, you might . . . no! By now they'll know you gone from Carsbry and guess the reason why. Varius will send word on—to every keep along the coast, and do you land it shall likely be into confinement; certainly disgrace. And do you come with me to Durbrecht—the same."

She paused, thinking, and I said, "Then the choice lies between some little time together and none at all. Let me stay."

She said, "Perhaps does Tyron put you ashore at the next keep, it shall not be so bad," and my heart sunk.

I said, "I'd take the chance, to be with you. Even for a little while."

As if I had not spoken, she continued: "Aye. That way your disobedience shall be the lesser; equally the punishment."

Horrified, I asked, "Shall you truly do this to me?"

She "looked" me in the eye and nodded. "For your own sake, Daviot." Her voice was earnest, as if she'd have me understand that what she proposed brought her pain, too; but still she'd do it. "What else is there? Do I let you remain on board, then surely when we come to Durbrecht, your College must reject you. Likely you'd be cast out."

I said, "Then so be it."

I spoke unthinking, careless of aught save my thwarted need for her. I felt embarrassed, aye; but also the glimmerings of anger, that she remain so practical whilst I was wild with love.

She gasped, her eyes wide as she "stared" at me. "Do you know what you say?" she asked.

I nodded. "This duty you place so high tore us apart before," I said. "I'd no say then, for you were gone and naught I could do about it; save dream of you. I'd not thought to find you again; but I did, and if the God exists, he surely meant that to be. If not, then he's a trickster. I know only that I found you, and I'd not again lose you. I care nothing for the consequences! Does my College reject me for that, then let it."

For long moments she studied me in silence, wonder on her lovely face. Then she said, "You'd reject your calling? You'd be no longer Mnemonikos? For love of me?"

"For love of you," I said.

Tears welled in her eyes, but when I moved again to touch her, still she held me back with a gesture. "This is no easy burden you lay on me, Daviot," she murmured.

I said, "I cannot help that, Rwyan. I love you, and for you I'd forsake my College. Anything!"

Softly, she whispered, "So much. Oh, Daviot . . ."

I thought her persuaded; that I should be allowed to travel with her at least as far as Durbrecht. But then she shook her head and said, "No. I cannot agree to that. I cannot let you destroy yourself."

"You don't," I said earnestly, "save you turn me away. This duty that holds us apart—that's what destroys me."

She took my hands then, her face so sad, I must fight the urge to hold her close. I thought she would not then welcome that. She said, "Daviot, Daviot, what are we if we renege our duty? Our talents are gifts—"

I interrupted, fierce: "Or curses, that they deny us what we want."

"Are we children, then?" she asked me. "To stamp and fret when we may not have exactly what we wish?"

"Not children," I replied. "Children don't fall in love."

She closed her eyes again, head bowed a moment. "You do not make this easy," she murmured.

"I cannot," I said. "You name my talent a gift? My talent blazons your face on my memory. I close my eyes, and I see you. I remember every moment we had together, all we said; like a blade turned in my heart. I'd thought to live with that, but when I saw you again, I knew I could not. I knew I could not let you go."

"What choice have we?" Her hands squeezed tight; there was pain in her voice and on her face. "Oh, Daviot, perhaps it were better had we never met."

"No!" I said loud.

"What else can we do?" she asked me. "I must bring Tezdal to Durbrecht—my duty—"

"Then do your duty," I said. "But when it's done, why should we not be together?"

"Storyman and sorcerer?" She shook her head vigorously, hair tossing in red-gold waves. "Durbrecht would not allow it."

"Durbrecht be damned then!" I cried. "Must I choose betwixt my College and you, Rwyan, it's you I choose."

She "looked" at me with something akin to awe in her eyes, and when she spoke, her voice was soft, almost fearful. "Do you know what should be done, were you to say that in Durbrecht?"

I shook my head.

Rwyan hesitated a moment. Then said, "What I tell you now is forbidden knowledge. None save we sorcerers and the masters of your College know it. I break trust in telling you."

She paused. I said, "Tell me, if you will." I felt afraid.

She said slowly, "When I was sent away, then you might have quit your calling without reproof. But now—oh, Daviot, you chose that staff, chose the Storyman's road, and now you've been abroad too long. Do you choose now to turn your back—in the Sorcerous College there is a crystal; it empowers magic. You'd be taken there, and the crystal used to destroy your memory. All you've learned, all you've seen and done, would be taken from you."

The sweat that cloaked me was suddenly cold. I shivered; my mouth felt dry, but still I wanted to spit. I felt a chill lump curdle in my belly. I said, each word thick, "My choice is made, Rwyan. I'd have you."

She made a small strange noise. Tears flowed ignored down her cheeks. I longed to kiss them away, but she held my hands still, very tight now. She said, "Can you truly love me so much?"

I said, "Yes."

She said, "We fear the Great Coming. There's a need of Storymen."

I said, "I'm not the only one. There are others."

She said, "And sorcerers? Think you there are sufficient of my kind?"

Before I could reply, she tossed her head, indicating the cloudless sky, the placid sea, the absence of wind, the heat, and said, "The Sky Lords command great magic, Daviot, and we've not the answer to it. How much of this can Dharbek take? How long before the Great Coming? Daviot, I am *needed*. My talent is needed, to defend our land."

I said, hearing my own voice come hollow with dread, "What do you say, Rwyan?"

She wept openly now, tears glittering in silver tracks down her face. Her voice was clogged with grief. "That I cannot give up my calling, my love. Not even for you."

In that awful moment when I saw all my mad hopes dashed, my pain became anger, entirely selfish. I snatched my hands from her grasp, took a single backward step, staring at her with disbelieving eyes.

"Do I mean so little to you?" I asked, low-voiced.

"You mean everything to me," she said.

"How so?" I raised my hands, clenched in frustration.

I had forgotten Tezdal until I felt my wrists gripped from behind, a foot land hard against an ankle, tangling my legs so that I fell. I had not forgotten my training. I went limp, bringing him down with me, and twisted as I fell. One hand broke loose. I drove an elbow against his ribs and turned, about to drive my knuckles into his face, at that point between the eyes where the bone can be broken and smashed back into the brain. I was consumed with grief, and it made me mad.

I heard Rwyan scream, "No!" and was gripped by a terrible force.

I had never felt magic before. It was as if ice filled my veins, freezing my arm before my blow could land. It was as if every meal I'd eaten turned sour in my belly. It was as if all my muscles cramped together in knots of sudden pain. I groaned, my eyes awash with tears. I am not sure if her magic put them there or only my grief. I was dimly aware of the Sky Lord contorted in the same painful posture.

Then it ended. It was simply gone, as swift as she'd delivered it. I pushed to hands and knees, head hanging as my body remembered. Then I climbed to my feet.

Rwyan said, "Tezdal! Daviot intended me no harm. Do you leave him be."

Tezdal rose and ducked his head in acceptance. "As you wish, Rwyan." And to me, "Forgive me, Daviot. I thought you meant to strike her."

I shook my head. He offered me that curious, curt bow and moved away to the farther bulwark. I turned to Rwyan.

Softly, she said, "You take leave of your senses."

I shrugged.

She said, "I love you, Daviot."

I said, "But not enough."

She made that little whimpering sound again, and through my anger and my grief, my selfish pride, I felt remorse. I loved her, no matter she'd surrender me.

"What should you do?" she asked. "Were you no longer Mnemonikos?"

"Go home," I said surly. "Be a fisherman again; or join a warband."

"That should be sad loss." She moved toward me and took my hands again. I did not withdraw: I felt an awful lassitude, as if waning hope drained out my energy. I stood dumb as she spoke, her voice gentle and earnest. "I cannot forswear my duty; not when Dharbek stands in such need. Nor should you, but rather go on."

"I wish," I said, forlorn, "that we fought no war with the Sky Lords. That we had no duty, but you and I be free to go our own way."

"And I," she said. "But it's not so; and so we have no choice."

I swallowed. Her face swum misty before me, and I realized that I wept. I knew these tears were not the product of magic, save that love's a kind of magic. I nodded, accepting defeat.

Rwyan let go my hands and cupped my face. Her lips touched mine, careless of the crew, careless of Tyron, who doubtless watched us from the stern. Her kiss tasted salty. She pulled away and said, "I'll advise our captain he's to put in at the next hold."

I nodded and watched her walk away. I rubbed at my eyes; I felt exhausted. I slumped against the bulwark, sliding to the deck. Across the forecastle, Tezdal studied me.

"You love her very much."

I grunted agreement, and he said, "You should not be parted."

I chuckled sourly. "I've little choice, it seems."

He said, "Duty is important, but I do not understand why you cannot be together."

"Nor I," I answered him, "save it's so here."

He appeared entirely sympathetic. It did not seem at all strange to me that I should engage in such a conversation with a Sky Lord. He said, "You fight well."

"I was taught in Durbrecht," I said.

"Where I go."

His dark face showed no sign of trepidation, only curiosity. I wondered if he knew what likely lay in store. I felt sorry for him then. I said, "Aye."

He said, "It is hard, having no memory. It seems to me a man is diminished by that. He cannot properly know who he is."

I realized he sought to comfort me: I smiled and said, "No. But in Durbrecht I think they shall restore yours."

He nodded solemnly. "I hope so. Even do I remember we are supposed to be enemies."

"Supposed?" I said. "Dhar and Ahn have fought down the ages. You Sky Lords *are* our enemy; just as we are yours."

"I am not your enemy, Daviot," he returned me. "Rwyan—your people—saved my life. I cannot be the enemy of someone who saved my life. How could that be? It would not be . . . right."

I thought on that awhile, then said, "No."

He smiled and turned toward the stern, watching Rwyan as she spoke with the shipmaster. I leaned my head against the bulwark, staring at the blank sky. The sun was gone a little past its zenith, and the heat was ferocious. My shirt was limp with sweat, soiled from my sojourn in the hold. I tugged it off, using it to towel my face and chest. As I reached for my saddlebags, a crewman came diffidently toward me. He was massive, one of the bull-bred, and seemed built better for a charge than so hesitant an approach.

"Would you have me wash that, master?"

A huge hand gestured at my shirt.

I said, "My thanks, but there's no great need."

He came a pace closer. His head was slightly lowered, as if he lacked the nerve to look me in the eye. "It's no trouble, master," he said. His voice was a deep, bass rumble. "It's soiled, and I've others need tending."

I thought perhaps he looked to curry favor. I smiled my gratitude. "Very well, then. Here."

I held out the shirt—in my left hand, on whose wrist I wore Lan's bracelet. The Changed took it, and as he did our eyes met. He held my gaze an instant, then turned away. I wondered if I had truly seen interest flicker in those bland bovine orbs.

He halted, stepping aside and bowing as Rwyan came back, and I forgot him, looking at her face. She had wiped away her tears, but her eyes were red. She held herself very straight, which I thought was from effort of will alone. Wearily, I climbed to my feet, pulling on a clean shirt.

She said, "Tyron advises me we can dock in Ynisvar on the morrow."

I nodded, unspeaking. I had nothing left to say; nothing I had not already repeated, to no avail.

She said, "Soon after dawn, he says."

I ducked my head again.

Rwyan sighed noisily. "This is not as I'd have it," she murmured. "Do you believe that?"

I said, "Yes," and turned, resting my arms on the gunwale, staring out across the Fend. It was too hard at that moment to see her.

She came to join me, close, and that, too, was hard. She said, "Do you also believe I love you?"

Again I said, "Yes," and in my hurt could not resist adding, "but not so much as your duty."

It was a shabby rejoinder that I instantly regretted. I should have told her so then, but I was sunk deep in my self-pity and could not. I heard her stifle a gasp, as if my words stung, and then she said, "Daviot, you are unkind. Could it be otherwise, think you I'd not go gladly with you? As your wife or your woman, always by your side?"

"But," I said, not turning my head, "it's not otherwise. Is it?"

She said softly, "No."

I said, "Then there's no more to say. Save farewell."

I heard her shift then and knew she studied me. I refused to meet her eyes. I held mine firm on the unyielding sea, knowing that did I see her face, I'd weep and beg her to rethink, plead with her. A moment more, and she turned away. I heard her footsteps go soft across the deck, and I was left alone. My heart felt empty as the cloudless sky.

She spent the remainder of that day in her cabin, and I did not move until the sky darkened and the smell of grilling fish tempted my nostrils. I had forgotten hunger, but now my belly rumbled prodigiously, reminding me that no matter how we suffer, life goes on. I had no appetite, however, and made no effort to join the group around the cookstove. What matter if I starved now?

I heard steps approach, and the savory odor of charcoal grilled fish was stronger. I turned to find Tezdal standing with a plate and a mug of ale. He smiled warily and set down his burden.

"Even so," he said, "you must eat."

I snorted and looked past him down the deck. Rwyan sat with Tyron, half the Changed crewmen a little way separate. The rest still manned the sweeps, driving the *Sprite* remorselessly onward, toward our landfall in Ynisvar.

The Sky Lord followed the direction of my gaze. "She loves you, Daviot. This gives her pain."

"But she's her duty," I said.

"She's strong," he told me, "she's honor. You should admire her for that."

Sourly, I said, "I do. But also I love her."

He nodded. "Perhaps when I regain my memory, I shall find I love someone."

I said, "I hope not."

He frowned then and asked me, "Because I'll know, but not have her?"

I said, "Yes. It's hard to love someone you cannot have."

He studied me thoughtfully. Then he said, "But surely better than never to love at all."

I must think about that. My memories of Rwyan brought me pain, but would I be without them? I answered him, "Perhaps you're right."

He smiled gravely. Then: "Did you go to her cabin tonight, I do not think she'd turn you away."

Perhaps not. But surely that would be to rub salt into open wounds. I'd wounds enough: I shook my head. "Perhaps she'd not, but I think I could not bear that. I'd sooner be gone now than suffer more."

"It's your choice," he said, and offered me that odd half bow. I watched him return along the deck, finding a place at Rwyan's side. I had not thought to envy a Sky Lord. I glanced at the plate he'd left; then I sank down and began to eat.

The sky grew slowly black, and Tyron ordered his running lights set. A Changed came by me with a taper and gathered up my plate. Then another came with a replenished mug. I took the tankard and thanked him. He said, "My pleasure, master," and I automatically said, "I am called Daviot."

His smile was ponderous as the beast from which he originated, but he said, "My pleasure, Daviot."

I sipped the second mug, vaguely surprised that I felt no wish to drown my sorrows. I saw Rwyan come down the deck, her face turned toward me. I hid behind my upraised mug, and when I set it down, she was gone. Then Tezdal went into the cabin beside hers, and I thought on what he'd said. It was still too painful to contemplate joining her. I thought it would be akin to opening a wound. I stretched on the forecastle, my back against the starboard bulwark, and stared at the stars.

A bulky shape blocked my view, an outstretched hand offering my laundered shirt. I said, "My thanks. How are you named?"

"Ayl," came the rumbling answer, "Daviot."

I nodded. I was too weary, too lost in my apathy, to question him further. He stood a moment longer, his face in shadow so that I could not discern what expression lay there, then he said, "Sleep well, Daviot," and left me to my thoughts.

I dreamed that night as the *Sprite* clove through the Fend, northward; odd, fitful dreams, all fragmented like my hopes.

I was in the oak wood again, blinded by the sunlight that poured down through the leafy branches, so that I caught only momentary glimpses of the figures flitting between the mossy boles. But when I moved toward them, they were gone, and from my back I heard Urt shout my name. I turned in that direction and saw my Changed friend standing with Ayl and Lan, all pointing past me, alarm on their faces.

I turned again and saw Rwyan, tears running bright in the sunlight down her face. I said, "Rwyan, I love you," and opened my arms, but Tezdal stepped between us and said, "She's honor, Storyman; she's strong."

I said, "Yes. Would I had her strength." And then a hand of Kho'rabi charged the clearing, and I took up my staff to defend Rwyan.

Tezdal stood beside me, armored in the Dhar fashion, a longsword in his hands. We attacked together, but for each Sky Lord we slew, another came out of the surrounding trees, like black ants boiling from a disturbed nest.

We were forced back, to where Rwyan stood, and she said, "I must use my magic."

I said, "It's not enough," and she returned me, "Still, I must try. It's all we have."

I shouted, "No, there's more," not knowing what I meant until I heard the thunder of great wings and saw the clearing darkened by the body that fell from the sky.

It was the dragon, and it descended on the Kho'rabi with a dreadful fury. I pressed back, an arm protective about Rwyan, and then I was aloft, soaring over jagged peaks and rocky valleys, my face battered by wind. The sky was dark with thunderheads, and lightning danced across the land. I looked around and saw Rwyan mounted astride a dragon, diminutive on that massive back, dwarfed by the vast wings that beat a rhythm loud as the thunder itself. Urt, I saw, rode another; and beyond him, Tezdal. It seemed not at all strange that we rode dragons.

I heard Rwyan call to me, "Where do we go?"

I shouted, "I don't know."

She cried, "But Daviot, you're the Dragonmaster."

I opened my mouth to ask her what she meant, but the sky filled with a shrieking sound . . .

Which came from Tyron's whistle, shrilling announcement of dawn, rousing those Changed allowed to sleep from their rest.

I sat up, rubbing at sleep-fogged eyes. The sky was gray, the sun a pale hint along the eastern horizon, the air, out here upon the Fend, cooler than on land at this hour. I clambered to my feet, working kinks from my muscles, oneiric images still vivid in my mind. A solitary gull winged across our path, taking my gaze with it—it made for land, for the shore that held Ynisvar and likely my final parting from Rwyan.

I heard Tyron's whistle sound again, and then his voice raised in outrage. He shouted at the tillerman, ordering a change of course: the *Sprite* held steady on her line. I blinked, staring down the deck, unease stirring. Then I gaped as I saw Tyron draw his wide sword and swing the blade at the steersman's head. The Changed ducked the blow with an agility I had not known the bull-bred possessed, and the captain's sword carved splinters from the tiller. I took up my staff, my eyes still intent on the poop, and saw Tyron seized, his arms pinned beneath the massive biceps of a crewman. His sword fell to the deck. He struggled, shouting furiously as he was carried to the port side. His shouting faded as he was flung overboard; I could not hear the splash.

I shouted, "Rwyan! Mutiny!" and sprang to meet the Changed who advanced toward me, Ayl at their head.

He bellowed, "Easy, Daviot! No harm shall come you, do you put down your staff."

I swung the pole at his head. He raised a hand and caught it easily as if I were a child flailing a willow switch: I had not fully realized what strength lay in these bull-bred bodies. He pulled on the staff, and I was flung sideways, crashing against the bulwark there, winded. I saw my staff go spinning away across the water. I saw Tezdal appear, then Rwyan, my view interrupted by the Changed who fell upon me. I crouched, propelling myself up and forward, punching at faces and chests that seemed impervious to my blows. Hands strong as manacles gripped me, and I was held immobile. I could do nothing as my knife—Thorus's parting gift that I'd had so long—was taken and sent after my staff into the Fend.

I saw Rwyan shout, hands raised to weave patterns in the air that I knew should produce magic. Two Changed roared and dropped as if poleaxed. Another sprang down to the lower deck. Ayl shouted, "No harm! As you fear her wrath, no harm!"

The oarsmen left their benches now, converging on Rwyan and Tezdal. I saw the Sky Lord leap forward, defending her. He had done better to rely on her magic: a fist struck his head, and he went down. Rwyan felled the attacker, and the rest hesitated, spreading out before her. They no longer seemed bovine but more akin to those wild bulls that roam the slopes of the Geffyn. Then I saw Ayl reach into his belt and fetch out a length of chain that glittered in the sun. He clutched the thing in one fisted hand and ran forrard along the deck. I saw that he moved behind Rwyan and opened my mouth to shout a warning. A hand that covered half my face clamped down, stifling the cry, so that I could only watch, helpless, as Ayl leaped down.

Rwyan turned too late. The Changed was already at her back, his fingers oddly delicate as he snapped the necklace in place. Rwyan screamed, and there was such horror in her shout, it wrenched my soul. I struggled uselessly. At last the suffocating hand let go.

I shouted, "Do you harm her, I'll kill you!"

Ayl called back, "No harm, Daviot. We'd have you all alive."

I cried, "Rwyan! Rwyan!"

She moaned, unsteady on her feet, swaying as if stunned. She said, "Daviot? Daviot, I'm blind."

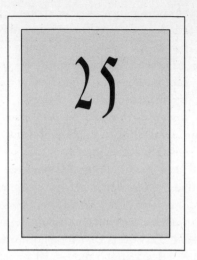

The *Sprite* was Ayl's command now. Brisk orders sent the rowers back to their sweeps, the galleass continuing northward. More had the unconscious Tezdal carried to where I stood, no longer struggling but entirely preoccupied with Rwyan. Ayl himself brought her to the upper deck and gently set her down before me. He nodded to my captors, and they let me go. I'd no fight left in me, only fear for Rwyan: I put my arms around her, holding her close, protective. She clutched me tight; she shook, and I was uncertain whether from terror or anger.

Ayl said, "There's no harm done her, only her magic checked."

I stared at him a moment, then at the necklace. It was a linkage of plain silver loops, small and very bright, fastened with a tiny lock. At its midpoint, glowing against Rwyan's throat, was a crystal that pulsed myriad rainbow hues in the morning sun.

I said, "What is it?"

"Magic," Ayl answered me. "Magic to fight magic. You'll not remove it, and only hurt her trying."

I glared at him. "What do you intend?"

He said, "No harm; only a journey."

I cursed. Garat should have been proud of those curses.

Ayl heard me out, impassive, then said, "Daviot, it was your ill luck brought you to this. And good fortune gave you that talisman." He indicated the hair woven about my wrist.

I said, "Lan's gift?"

"Aye." He ducked his massive head. "That charm marks you as a friend. Were that not on your wrist, you'd be swimming ashore now."

I said, "But instead I'm your prisoner."

He said, "Yes; or guest, do you prefer. It need not be a hard confinement, and where we go, you'll garner such stories as shall make you the envy of your kind."

"Where do we go?" I asked, and he chuckled, tapping finger to nose. I said, "Rwyan's blind."

"Only whilst she wears that trinket," he replied. "It may be removed in time."

I'd have questioned him further, but he waved me silent, ordering that we be taken to Tyron's cabin, and I could only obey. I moved slowly, holding Rwyan tight all the time. She clung to me as might a drowning man cling to a spar or a raft. Her steps were faltering, and all the time she wept silently.

The Changed were oddly courteous as they herded us to our prison. Tezdal was laid on the captain's bed, and I guided Rwyan to its foot, settling her there as the cabin door closed and I heard a key turned in the lock. I went immediately to the ports. They showed me the Fend, its surface scarred by our wake. Then bodies blocked my view, and there came the ring of hammers on nails as bars were pounded into place. I turned away, going back to Rwyan.

She sat with her head thrown back, hands busy at the necklace. Her face was wet with tears, and pale. I sat beside her, and she started, head moving from side to side as if she hoped the movement should grant her sight.

I said, "It's me."

I had never before thought of her as truly blind. Now she seemed so helpless, I almost wept for her. I put my arms around her; she rested her head on my shoulder.

Hoarsely, she said, "This cursed necklace must hold a crystal."

I repeated what Ayl had said, and she sighed agreement. When next she spoke, it was so soft, I must bend my head to hear: "Then I must wear it until they take it off."

She found the thought abhorrent. She did not voice it aloud, but I knew it from her tone, from the tension in her body. I said, "Let me try."

She told me it should be no use, but still I made the attempt. I poked and pried until she cried out, telling me I choked her: the links were forged too strong, and the lock defied all my attempts at picking. I examined the cabin for tools—anything that might snap the cursed thing, or force the lock—but there was nothing. I supposed our captors had removed all possible weapons. Without tools, it could not be broken; even with a blade or lever it should have been dangerous. I gave up and took her in my arms again, holding her and stroking her hair as I murmured helpless reassurances. It was the most I could do: it was not enough. I told myself that at least we were together. I was grateful for that: I had never seen Rwyan so frightened, and—am I honest—I was myself not a little afraid.

In time her trembling ceased, a measure of calm returned, or resignation, and she wiped at her eyes. I told her I must leave her awhile to examine Tezdal, and she nodded wearily. I stroked her cheek and went to the Sky Lord.

A bruise flowered over one side of his face, but as best I could tell, he was not otherwise damaged. I made him comfortable, all the while explaining what I did to Rwyan, who sat straight-backed, staring blindly ahead, her hands locked as if in prayer. I suspected she struggled to keep them from the necklace; surely, her knuckles shone white.

I turned my attention to the cabin. I had some inkling now of where we likely went, and I thought we should be confined here for some time. It was, at least, a reasonably comfortable prison. It occupied the width of the stern, and Tyron's bunk was wide enough for two. For all they were now stoutly barred, the ports let in light and air. There was a curtained alcove that held a watergate; a bench along one wall, and a table cut with holes to secure cups and a flask of wine. I filled one and brought it to Rwyan: her hands shook as she drank, droplets falling unnoticed on her linen shirt.

I raised another to Tezdal's lips, and he opened his eyes. The cup was knocked aside as he came upright, hands raised ready to attack. I seized his wrists; Rwyan cried out.

I said, "Tezdal, all's well," and he sank back, recognition dawning. He groaned, warily touching his swollen face.

I retrieved the fallen cup and filled it again. Then I must once more explain. He stared at Rwyan as I spoke, then said, "Lady, do they harm you, I shall slay them; or die attempting it."

I was not sure I welcomed his chivalry, but Rwyan gave a wan smile in the direction of his voice. "They are many, Tezdal, and I think that for now we can only accept we are prisoners."

He nodded, frowning, and immediately set to exploring the cabin. I found my place by Rwyan's side and put an arm around her. She took my free hand in both of hers.

I said, "It seems you'll not be rid of me after all."

I sought to cheer her, but she ignored the sally, head turning as she followed Tezdal's prowling. He had no better luck than I in loosening the bars; nor, indeed, do I know what we hoped to do, had we removed them. Dive into the Fend and bring poor blind Rwyan somehow to the shore? We'd likely have drowned. I suppose we did those things men feel are expected of them in such circumstances; done less in real hope of escape than in the need to occupy ourselves, to maintain our waning denial of defeat.

Finally he must admit himself beaten and settle on the bench, his dark face flushed with anger.

He asked Rwyan, "Shall that thing harm you?"

Sunlight filtered through the bars, and the rays sparked brilliance from the little stone on her throat. Save for its malign power, it was a pretty bauble. I stared at it, hating it and the Changed who had put it there. She said, "It robs me of my talent. I cannot see or work magic." Her voice faltered, and her hands clenched tighter on mine. "But save I wear it overlong, it shall do no lasting harm."

Fear curdled anew in my belly. I asked, "How long?"

She said, "Is it like those we use, then some years."

That was a small measure of relief. I said, "I think we'll reach our destination ere then."

"Our destination?" Her head cocked, her face turned awkwardly toward me. She seemed utterly vulnerable. I stared at her sightless eyes and fought back tears; I regretted those harsh words spoken earlier. "What's our destination?"

I said, "Ur-Dharbek, save I miss my guess."

"Ur-Dharbek?" She moved her head as if seeking some glimpse of me. "How can you know that?"

I said, "I don't *know* it, not for sure; but . . ."

My words came in a flood, as if a dam were breached—all those secrets, the suspicions I'd held to myself, I now revealed. A part of me was afraid such honesty should earn Rwyan's displeasure, that she might judge me and find me lacking; another part knew only relief that I should have no more secrets from her.

I told her all I'd learned during the months of my wandering, everything I'd seen. I held back nothing, and as I spoke, it was as though the sundry disparate pieces of the puzzle I'd sensed fell clearer into place. I told of seeing Changed and Sky Lords in congress; that the Changed communicated; of the bracelet Lan had given me, and what he'd said. I spoke of what Rekyn had told me, of the Border Cities and the Dhar's lost ability to create more Changed.

"I think," I said, "that Rekyn spoke the truth better than she knew—that the wild Changed do more than just survive in Ur-Dharbek. I suspect they've a society there, and that they've found crystals; the use of magic. I think we're taken there, though why I cannot say."

Rwyan said, "By the God," in a hushed voice, her own fears forgotten in light of the picture I painted. Then: "Daviot, why did you not speak of this before?"

"I'd not much to say," I returned her. "That I suspected?"

"You saw Changed and Sky Lords come together!"

Her voice accused me. I said, "Aye, the once, in a lonely place. Had I spoken out then, what should the outcome have been? A pogrom? Good honest folk like Pele and Maerke made suffer? Innocent Changed punished for crimes not theirs?"

I think that had we not found ourselves in such circumstances, Rwyan would likely have reported all this to Ynisvar's mage, certainly to her College. Such was her sense of duty. But then, had matters proceeded normally, I'd have been put ashore at Ynisvar and she known none of it. As it was, I found it a palliation to unburden myself, even though she stiffened and pulled away from me, her forehead creased in a frown.

I'd believed her lost twice now: I'd not lose her again. I said, "Rwyan, do you believe me a traitor?"

She made no reply, as if she pondered the question. I went on, "Had I spoken of all this, think you the keeps should not have sent the warbands out against the Changed? Guilty and innocent alike? Think you there'd not have been terrible bloodshed?"

I waited until she nodded silent agreement. "And think you we Dhar treat the Changed fairly?" I asked her. "In Durbrecht, I named Urt my friend, and he gave no offense save to aid you and I to meet. He did no more than Cleton, yet he was banished to Karysvar—sold off, as if he'd no say in his own fate; no more say than any Changed. We *made* them, Rwyan—as if we Dhar were gods, to build life and govern it. We made them prey for the dragons, to save ourselves; and then to be our servants, too many treated as if they were still beasts.

"But they're not! They've feelings like any Trueman. I've had kindness of them, and I've seen fear in them. I've played with their children. In the name of this God you call on, they have children and marry and love, just like Truemen. Yet we see them as beasts still, to be bought and sold, their lives decided for them, as if they'd not minds of their own, could not think. I know they do. I know them for folk neither worse nor better than we Truemen.

"So—knowing that—should I have consigned them to pogrom, to annihilation? I saw only a handful deal with the Sky Lords—perhaps some renegade group, gone into the hills. I know not; only that I'd not see such as Pele and her little ones, or Urt, brought down for a thing not their doing. I tell you, Rwyan, our hands are not clean in this."

There was a long silence. Tezdal sat across the cabin, his bruised face grave as he studied us. I felt the galleass shift course slightly, moving farther out to sea. Ayl looked to avoid shipping, I supposed. At that moment I did not care. I thought nothing at all of the future, only of Rwyan's response.

The moments stretched out. I feared she condemned me, that that sense of duty she held so firm must stand a barrier between us, my confession the death knell of our love.

But this was my Rwyan, who was ever a woman unique. She took my hand, and my heart leaped. She said, "Daviot. Oh, Daviot, how long you've lived with this."

I said, "There was no one I dared tell. Save you."

She said, "You give me much to think on. I'd not seen the picture so large till now."

"You don't condemn me?" I asked. "You don't name me traitor?"

"Most would." She smiled. Faint, I thought. "I think likely all would. But then, I think any other Storyman would have straightway reported what he'd seen; and none save you perceive it so."

"I could not do otherwise." I shrugged, seeking those words that might explain a decision I had not properly comprehended then and did not entirely now. "I feared to see the innocent suffer."

"You'd ever a fine conscience," she murmured, and her smile grew warm. "I cannot condemn you for that. Traitor? No, for you did only what you believed was right. And shall I condemn the man I love?"

I sighed and touched her cheek, knowing I had not lost her. Rather, I had found her again, more truly than before, for there was no longer anything hidden between us, only honesty and trust. I felt a great wash of relief.

She leaned against me and said, "Now, do you tell me why we're kidnapped? Why we are taken to Ur-Dharbek?"

I said, "I think the Changed perhaps inhabit Ur-Dharbek just as we Truemen occupy Draggonek and Kellambek; perhaps they've cities. It would seem they've the means of communicating with their kin in Dharbek, and they must possess some knowledge of magic."

I hesitated then, for what I now suspected must surely frighten Rwyan, and she had already suffered enough. But she urged I go on.

I said, "Perhaps they'd learn to use it better; or learn how you employ your talent. Perhaps they took me for what I know of Dharbek. And Tezdal . . ." I glanced at the Sky Lord. His presence opened vistas of speculation for which I cared little. "Perhaps they league with the Kho'rabi. . . ."

I was surprised to hear Tezdal laugh. I turned toward him, motioning that he explain.

"Save they can give back my memory," he said, "what use shall I be? Can your sorcerers not return it, shall these others? And I owe my life to Rwyan. I'll not betray that debt."

His eyes challenged me to refute him. I could not: I ducked my head in agreement. I think it was in that instant I came truly to accept him. He was no longer a Sky Lord but only a comrade, caught in shared adversity. I believed him and trusted him, and that was a strange realization. But then, it was a strange day.

We sat awhile in silence, digesting all we'd said. Then Tezdal asked, "Shall the Sentinels not bring their magic against this boat?"

"Why?" Rwyan stirred in my embrace. "Save they've cause for suspicion, this shall appear only another ship traveling up the coast."

"But when we do not arrive in this Durbrecht of yours?" he asked.

"Then the Sorcerous College will wonder," she replied. "But it shall be too late then, no?"

"Perhaps not." I was by no means certain I welcomed the direction of my thoughts, for they led to a parting of our ways. "Your College expects us?"

Rwyan nodded. "Word was sent secretly."

I said, "The coast of Draggonek's a longer reach than the Treppanek. So do we fail to arrive, shall the sorcerers not alert the keeps? We might be halted ere we reach Ur-Dharbek."

"Perhaps." Her voice was thoughtful; I heard uncertainty. "But the precise time of our arrival was never known, so they might assume the ship sunk, do the Sky Lords attack. Or Ayl has some plan."

She touched the silver links as she spoke, nervously, and I kissed her hair. Quiet against my chest she whispered, "Daviot, whatever becomes us, know that I love you."

I smiled at that, elation for a moment the hottest of my emotions. There seemed not much more to say, and we fell again into silence.

•   •   •

The days passed, the one blending furnace-hot into the next. We were fed well enough, and at night allowed brief freedom to walk the deck. We spent our time in talk and such fitful sleep as prisoners find, needed less for its restoration than as refuge from boredom. I told my tales, first those I thought should not offend Tezdal, then all of them. He showed no affront when I spoke of the battles between his people and mine, but rather a keen interest, as if he hoped to find in the stories some clue to his past, some reminder of who he was. I sought to help him down that road. I employed all those techniques taught me in Durbrecht, employed every artifice at my disposal; but none worked. His past remained a mystery.

He showed me those exercises his body remembered, telling me how he'd used them on the rock, and we performed the routines together.

Rwyan told of his finding, and of her life before and after. We confessed to the lovers we'd taken and consigned them to our separate pasts. We talked of magic, openly; of that possessed by the Dhar sorcerers and of that strange command of the elementals and the weather that the Sky Lords owned. I learned much of Dharbek's sorcerers, and she of what it is to be a Storyman.

At night, in whispers, Rwyan and I spoke of our dreams and were surprised at the similarities we discovered. It was as though our minds had somehow remained all the time linked, despite the leagues and years that had lain between us.

I spoke to Tezdal of our history, of the age-old enmity between our peoples. And we agreed that we were not enemies, nor ever should be. We clasped hands in friendship and vowed we should never fight one another.

He knew nothing of the Changed, and I told him of their place in Dharbek's history and of my own feelings concerning their status. We all of us talked at length of that, debating pro and con, and both Tezdal and Rwyan came to see the Changed and their status through my eyes.

"But still," Tezdal said one sweltering afternoon as we lounged within the cabin, "they put that necklace on Rwyan. I cannot forgive them for that."

"Nor I," I said fierce, her hand in mine.

She startled me then. She said, "Can you not, after all you've said of them? You speak of your sympathy for them persuasively enough; I come to agree. You tell me there's now scant difference betwixt Truemen and Changed, and that we are wrong to treat them as we do.

Perhaps they see no other choice, save this—that they must take a sorcerer, to win some measure of freedom. To win—by your lights, Daviot—such respect as we should accord them by right. I'd not have come willing on this journey, and had I my talent unfettered, I'd use it against them. Ayl knows that, so what choice has he but to bind me? I think he must believe that what he does, he does for all his kind: his duty. Is that the case, then I can forgive them."

I sat surprised, mulling her words. I think it is ofttimes easier to see the wider picture, to deal in abstract notions, than in those matters personal to us. I thought then that if she could forgive, so must I. I felt humbled by her kindness.

I said, "Do you forgive it, Rwyan, then I must."

She gave me back, "I'd not have either of you seek revenge on my behalf. I'd have us all survive this adventure."

I stared at her, marveling. It seemed to me this woman I loved all the time revealed fresh depths. I said, softly, "As you wish."

She smiled and turned her sightless eyes toward Tezdal. He scowled but then sighed and said, "I like it not. I'd have an accounting of them for these insults. But . . . would you have it so, Rwyan, then I obey."

That was a solemn moment. I felt I learned much from Rwyan, that I came to understandings I'd not have found alone.

But still we were prisoners, and whilst we'd given up much hope of escape, we could not help but wonder what our fate should be.

The *Sprite* must have been well provisioned, for our rations were adequate and we continued northward without delay. I began to wonder if the Changed intended to row all the way to Ur-Dharbek without halting. But then one night I woke, at first uncertain what brought me from sleep. I felt a change I could not define and lay awhile with open eyes and straining ears, Rwyan's breath soft against my chest. Something was different, and it troubled me. I eased my arm from under Rwyan's slight weight and sat up. She stirred, reaching for me.

I said, "Something's happening. Do you wait here."

She murmured agreement, and I climbed from the bunk. Tezdal woke at the sound and came with me to the portholes.

The bars occluded full sight of the sky, but by dint of much crouching and craning of my head I was able to make a guess we had changed course. It seemed to me we no longer went north but had turned in a westerly direction.

I went back to Rwyan, Tezdal with me. I said, "I think we make for land."

She said, "But we cannot be close to Ur-Dharbek yet."

I said, "No, we must be still along Dharbek's coast."

"Then why?" she asked. "Surely they'll not put us ashore in Dharbek."

I thought a moment, then said, "Perhaps they take on fresh provisions."

We could not tell, only wait.

In time our momentum eased, and the galleass hove to. The ports told me nothing, save that the night was starry and we had turned west. We heard activity—the pad of feet and muffled voices, faint cries as if from ship to shore. Tezdal and I pressed our ears to the door but learned nothing from that solid barrier. I thought I heard the noise a gentle sea makes, washing against rocks. Then we felt the ship sway slightly and heard such sounds as suggested hatches were lifted. I decided I was correct in my assumption.

There was a splashing then, as of dipped oars, and the *Sprite* shifted again. I felt the bow come around and hurried to the ports.

Rwyan called, "What goes on, Daviot?"

Her voice was nervous, and I said, "I think Ayl made landfall, to take on stores. Now we turn for the open sea again."

I *was* right: sternward I saw the dark mass of a rocky coastline, pines etched stark by a westering moon, a soft swell breaking luminous on a tiny cove. For an instant I glimpsed a fire—a signal beacon —that was dimmed even as I watched. I pressed my face to the narrow opening, seeing the coast recede. The *Sprite* headed east of north, seeking the wider reaches of the Fend again. Soon there was nothing to see except the moonlit stretch of the ocean: I returned to Rwyan's side.

We did not sleep again that night but sat talking of its events as the prow came around once more, once more on a northerly tack.

We agreed that Ayl had brought the vessel in to restock, and that was suggestive of even greater organization amongst the Changed than I had suspected. It suggested we were expected; and was that so, then perhaps our kidnap—at least Rwyan's, and perhaps Tezdal's— had been planned from the beginning.

"How could they know?" Rwyan asked. "My arrival in Carsbry was not announced."

"Perhaps Ayl simply acted on the opportunity," I offered. "He saw the chance to take a sorcerer and seized it."

"But how arrange this resupplying?" she said.

"Would word not have been sent?" I asked. "If not of you, then that the *Sprite* quit Carsbry?"

"That, yes," she told me.

"And in the keeps, folk talk," I said. "They speak of the comings and goings of Truemen, of vessels, in hearing of the Changed, never thinking the Changed have ears. The Changed are faceless to most Truemen; they speak in the presence of the Changed as they would before horses or dogs. It's as I told you—Truemen do not *see* the Changed."

Rwyan held my hand as we spoke, and I felt her grip tighten at that. She gasped softly, her eyes, for all they saw nothing now, wide as full realization sank in.

"Then nothing's secret," she said, her voice a whisper. "As if the walls of every keep had ears."

"Yes," I said, "and all through Dharbek, the Changed listen and pass word between themselves."

Tezdal said, "Even so, how could they know this ship would go to that particular cove?"

I said, "I think likely they didn't. I think it was likely just one cove of many where Changed wait."

"By the God!" Rwyan's voice was shocked. "Be that the case, then there's a great conspiracy afoot."

I said, "Aye, and I think we go to the heart of it."

I believed I was right; I was also afraid that I was right. It seemed that all the pieces of the puzzle I had observed grew daily clearer, fitting one into the next. I believed it was the Changed's intention to bring a sorcerer to Ur-Dharbek, perhaps to save a Sky Lord—an ally. I suspected I was brought along only because—as Ayl had suggested—I wore Lan's bracelet, which marked me as a friend. I thought I should be safe; I suspected Tezdal should be safe. I did not know how they might treat Rwyan, and that frightened me. Should they seek to employ her magic against the Truemen of Dharbek, I'd no doubt she would refuse. . . . I could only guess what might be the outcome of such refusal. Was Ur-Dharbek filled with Changed, Tezdal and I should be poor champions.

I debated putting these thoughts into words. I suppose it was a kind of cowardice that I did not: instead, I told myself I should only frighten Rwyan, and she be better comforted by my silence. But then, the enormity of the conspiracy only just burgeoning, I was myself alarmed enough, and more than a little confused. So I held my tongue, and put an arm around her, and told her we could do nothing save wait.

One morning when it seemed we had sailed forever and should likely go on and on until we came to the ends of the world, there was a most marvelous thing occurred.

We sat in the cabin, accustomed by now to its stuffy confines, to

air that moved only when our actions stirred it, to sweat-damp clothing, and to that lethargy excessive heat and inaction produce. Rwyan
shifted on the bench, turning her head from side to side. I saw she
frowned and thought her troubled, but when I asked what disturbed
her, she only raised a hand and said, "Do you not feel it?"

Without waiting for an answer, she rose and groped her way to
the nearest port. I followed her, Tezdal close on my heels. I saw
Rwyan smile. And then I recognized what gave her such pleasure.

There was a breeze.

I felt it on my face, a caress I had resigned to memory alone. It
was like a lover's touch; like Rwyan's fingers gentle on my skin. I
moved my head; I opened my mouth to taste it on my tongue. I scarce
dared believe it was there. I wondered if we fell into madness.

Then Tezdal said, "A wind," in a voice filled with wonder.

I swallowed, almost afraid to believe. I felt the sweat that beaded
my brow chill, and bellowed laughter, taking Rwyan by the shoulders
and dancing her around, drawing her close as I shouted, "Aye! By the
God, you're right! There's a breeze!"

We clung together, laughing, pressing our faces to the ports that
we might savor this simple, wondrous, impossible thing.

It grew stronger. We heard orders called, and then a sound I
knew well and had not thought to hear again—the marvelous sound of
dropped canvas, of bellying sails. We staggered as the *Sprite* heeled
over, the floor tilting under us so that we, so long accustomed to even
boards, to the absence of any real movement, were pitched across the
cabin, fetching up in a tangle on the bunk.

I saw Tezdal frown, worried, and cried, "Ayl tacks, only that.
He'd catch the wind."

I hugged Rwyan, and for a while we only laughed and bathed in
that glorious breeze.

But then her face grew serious, and she pulled away. I said,
"What's wrong?"

And she gave me back, "Do you not see what this means? What
it must mean?"

I said, "That the Sky Lords' magic is gone."

"That, yes," she said. "But how long have we been at sea? Where
are we now?"

I thought a moment. Realization dawned: I said, "Ur-Dharbek."

Rwyan said, "Aye. The magic's not gone; we've only passed beyond its aegis. We reach our destination—we've come to the
Changed's country."

26

It was the midpart of the morning that I heard the familiar sounds that herald land—the snap of furling sails, the slap of waves on stone, the mewing of gulls. Then the boards shifted under my feet, and I heard voices, greetings shouted, those creaks and groans a harboring vessel makes. The motion of the galle-ass ceased, replaced by a gentle rocking, as of craft at anchor. I set my face to the starboard port and saw gray stone. I waited with bated breath, a hand on Rwyan's shoulder, Tezdal wary on her farther side.

The cabin door opened, and Ayl beckoned us out.

It was strange to stand again under a summer sky unsullied by magic. Gulls wheeled screaming overhead, and a salt-scented breeze blew off the sea. The sun stood bright in the eastern quadrant, and to the north I saw billows of white cumulus moving on the wind. It had been too long since I'd seen cloud.

I described it all to Rwyan as I helped her up the ladder to the topdeck. How the *Sprite* stood within the shelter of a curving bay, headlands like protective horns extending north and south, fishing boats drawn up on a beach of gray-silver sand all strewn with seaweed, nets hung out to dry just as they'd be in any fishing village of Dharbek. I told her of the plank we must cross to the mole of rough stone, flagged along its upper level, and of the village I saw and the Changed who watched us.

It was a village so similar to Whitefish, I hesitated, staring, so that Ayl must urge me on. He did it courteously enough, but I think he was amused by my amazement, and I talked all the while we passed through the onlookers toward the buildings.

They were cottages of stuccoed stone, white and bright blue and pink, with vegetable gardens and chicken coops, outhouses and storage sheds, frames for the nets. They flanked a road that went away inland from the harbor, broadening to a village square where the cottages stood thickest. I saw a mill, its sails creaking around, and what I took to be an alehouse, racks of fish curing in the sun. All that was missing was a cella. The folk who fell into step behind us might have been ordinary villagers, too, for here there were only we three Truemen to mark any difference between our kind and theirs. They stood tall and short, not many plump, male and female and children, dressed like any honest, hardworking folk, all curious. Only the children came near, brave as children are, darting close to stare up at our faces, a few touching us. I thought they had likely never seen Truemen.

We came to the square, and Ayl directed us to the building I had thought an alehouse—which, indeed, it was—and sat us at a table, for all the world as if we were guests, not prisoners. A gray-haired Changed came, not in the least hesitant, with mugs of ale and a plate of crisp dried fish. He smiled when I caught his eye, but not in any triumphant way. It seemed to me he did not gloat at the sight of Truemen taken captive but smiled only as would any innkeeper at his patrons. The ale was cool and brewed well.

I waited for Ayl to speak, thinking this little village unlikely to be our final destination, and after several hearty swigs of his beer, he said, "No doubt you guess we're come to Ur-Dharbek. Do you think of escape, know that the Slammerkin lies leagues distant, and the magic of the Border Cities shall deny you return no less than we."

I said, "Then you cannot go back?"

He laughed, as if I made a splendid joke, and shook his shaggy head. "I'd not," he said. "I've fulfilled my commission, and now I'll live amongst my own kind; free."

"And us?" I asked him. "Where do we go?"

"To Trebizar," he answered me. "To the Raethe—the Council."

I frowned inquiry.

He said, "Trebizar is our capital, where the Raethe sits."

I did not properly comprehend this talk of a council: I told him so.

He said, "We've no Lord Protector in Ur-Dharbek, neither koryphons, nor aeldors, nor churchmen. We live free here, and the Raethe is our government."

I coughed ale, I was so surprised. I asked him, "Do you not fight, then? Are there not rivals for power?"

"Our fight," he gave me back, with such solemnity I thought at first he jested, "is for freedom alone. The freedom of all Changed to live as they will, not as servitors but freemen, equal to any."

I nodded slowly, realizing he was entirely earnest. He said, "I'd thought you saw this, Daviot. Urt claims it so, and Lan."

I turned the bracelet around my wrist. Surprised anew, I said, "Urt? You've word of Urt?"

"Urt's in Trebizar," he said, as if this were not at all surprising. Then chuckled as I gaped. "He crossed the Slammerkin and now dwells in Trebizar. He's a seat in the Raethe."

That Urt should find prominence did not surprise me. That he was hale, and I should before too long meet him, delighted me. But there were other considerations I could not overlook: I gestured at Rwyan and said, "Shall you take off that cursed necklace now?"

Ayl's smile faded, his expression become grave. He turned his gaze on Rwyan and asked her, "Were it removed, what should you do?"

She said, "My best to return to home. I've a duty there with the Great Coming imminent."

I deemed that needlessly honest, but Ayl appeared pleased with her candor. He ducked his head and said, "Lady, I admire your integrity. But we've all a duty, no? And mine is to deliver you safe to Trebizar."

I asked him bluntly, "Why?"

He said, "The Raethe shall explain."

"And take off the necklace?" I asked.

"Likely," he replied. "I think it may be safely removed there."

"Why there?" I demanded. "But not here?"

At that he smiled, and tapped his nose, and would give me no more explanation. I thought of all I'd heard, all I'd wondered and surmised, of crystals and magic.

"And what of Tezdal?" Rwyan asked.

He said, "You shall all be safe. No harm shall come you, do you but accede to the Council."

"Accede?" Rwyan frowned and found my hand. "What does that mean?"

"The Raethe shall explain," Ayl told her. "You'll learn their wishes soon enough."

And with that we must be satisfied, though I liked not the sound of it. Nor Rwyan, whose fingers clenched tight on mine as the bull-bred Changed pushed back his chair and bade us remain.

We could not have easily done otherwise, for his fellow crewmen were there and watched us as he quit the alehouse. They offered no overt hostility, but still I had the feeling we'd be soon enough constrained did we disobey. I felt confident we stood in no immediate danger: I believed Ayl in that, but still there remained the reason for our kidnap. Also, I was greatly intrigued by all Ayl had said. Clearly, Ur-Dharbek was not the barbaric wasteland we Dhar imagined but a country civilized and organized. I could not deny I was curious to observe this place at first hand.

Which opportunity came soon enough.

Ayl reappeared, summoning us out, and when we stepped again into the square, I saw a wagon drawn up. It was a sizable vehicle with four deep-chested bay horses hitched to the pole, the bed surmounted by a wattle cage. This, I assumed, was to be our transport to Trebizar.

I was correct: Ayl motioned us on board.

I said, "You speak of freedom, Ayl, but treat us as prisoners."

He gave me back, "Did Truemen not treat we Changed as they do, you'd not be dealt with so. But . . ."

He shrugged huge shoulders. I could not fairly dispute his argument, nor contest his strength. Rwyan touched my arm, and I handed her on board. I climbed after her, and Tezdal sprang up behind. Ayl swung the gate closed, fastened with a length of chain and a sturdy-looking lock. Rough benches had been fixed along the sides, and cushions and blankets scattered the floor. It was not uncomfortable. I tested the bars and found them solid. At least we had a view.

Ayl took the forward seat, another bull-bred at his side, and the wagon lumbered out of the square.

Out of the village the road climbed a shallow cliff where black pines grew and birds sang, emphasizing the normality of the weather. Beyond the rim spread fields, sheep and cattle grazing there, hogs grunting over pastures walled with stone. It was a landscape not much different to that of my home. Somewhat harsher, I thought, the hursts I saw comprised mostly of firs and spruce, with not much oak or beech, but the grass green enough, which was a pleasant sight of itself after Dharbek's arid summer.

I thought to ask Ayl about that, and he told me, "The Sky Lords' quarrel is with Dharbek, not this land. We give them no offense, and they do not send their magic against us."

"Do you ally with them?" I asked.

"The Raethe shall explain," he answered, as if by rote.

I said, "On the west coast I saw Changed meet Sky Lords."

He only shrugged and called the horses to a faster pace. I thought he left more unsaid than spoken, and that I should get no more answers from him. I settled on the bench beside Rwyan, took her hand, and described to her the countryside we traversed.

The road we took was hard-packed dirt for most of its length, but as the sun went down and twilight fell over the land, the wagon's wheels began to drum on stone. I saw that we now moved along a paved track, and soon stone walls flanked our path. Ahead were lights; and then out of the dusk came a village.

There was no wall, nor any keep, only a sprawl of houses and barns clustering about the road as if the inhabitants felt no need of defense. It seemed to me a very open place. Ayl brought the wagon to a halt in a wide plaza, where the smell of smoke and cooking food hung homely in the air, and unlocked our cage.

A Changed whose ancestors had been, I suspected, canine, stood framed in a lighted doorway, studying us with obvious but not impolite interest. He gave Ayl cheerful greeting, and the bull-bred answered him in kind. As I stepped up onto the porch and saw his face full lit, I saw that he was old, his features seamed and kindly.

He ducked his head as if I were some traveler come welcome to his establishment and said, "Greetings. I am Thyr."

I nodded and told him my name, and he smiled and said, "Ah, yes. Urt's friend the Storyman."

My eyes widened at that, that I was known even here, and Thyr chuckled and said, "Your fame travels far, Daviot. Welcome to Bezimar."

Ayl gave him Rwyan's and Tezdal's names, and he stepped aside, inviting us to enter. My curiosity mounted apace.

It seemed we entered an hostlery. The room was large, an empty hearth against the far wall, a counter on which stood mugs and bottles to one side, chairs and tables across the floor. There were folk drinking, who looked up as we came in, their conversation ceasing. Thyr led us to a door, ushering us into a chamber dominated by a single long dining table. Tall windows stood on one wall. I noticed they were glassed, affording a view of the yard behind, where I saw the wagon brought. Thyr tapped a keg and filled mugs. I stared around, finding no difference between this place and any inn of Dharbek.

Ayl noticed my inspection and smiled. "What did you expect?" he asked. "That we should live in caves? Or lair in the fields?"

I said, "I did not know what to expect."

He chuckled then and said, "We're not so different, Daviot."

I went to a window, tapped the glass. I said, "You've manufactories?"

He nodded. "Glazieries and metal shops and breweries. We are not uncivilized."

I said, "No. Save you take prisoners."

"And Truemen do not?" he returned. "Was I not Tyron's prisoner? Had I wished, could I have quit his service? I could not—no more than might a bull owned by a farmer! Are we Changed not imprisoned in Dharbek?"

Such argument I'd used myself: I could not dispute him, and so I smiled and ducked my head in acknowledgment. Surprise piled on surprise in this place, not least that Ayl spoke so eloquently. I had always found the bull-bred Changed as prosaic as their bovine forebears, but this fellow was articulate and more than a little skilled in debate. I deemed it wiser to make no remark on that, lest I offend him. So far, he proved a most courteous jailer, and I'd not change that. I returned to the table and found a place by Rwyan.

She had listened in silence to our exchange, but now she ventured to question Ayl. She fingered the crystal at her throat and asked, "You've the talent for magic now?"

I saw Ayl hesitate at that and sensed there were some matters he'd sooner not discuss; or was forbidden to discuss. He said, "Not I, lady."

This was obvious prevarication. Rwyan smiled. "Not all Truemen have it, only a few. Is it so here?"

I thought the Changed embarrassed then, as if he regretted his role. He said, "Doubtless all shall be explained in Trebizar."

Rwyan said, "But you've crystals. Some of you must have learned their use, else I'd not wear this."

Ayl said, "No," and then, "I'll see does Thyr have our dinner ready."

He rose and went to the door. His companion (a dark, silent fellow whose name was Glyn) remained with us, and so we did not speak of what he'd said—or rather, left unsaid—until later, when we were alone.

Before that opportunity came, we dined well. Thyr set a fine table, and we ate our fill, the food washed down with dark beer. Then Ayl declared that we should find our beds, as we must depart early. Thyr carried a lantern before us up gently creaking stairs, and we were shown rooms. Tezdal was directed into one, and the door locked on him, Thyr turned to Rwyan and me. Once again he succeeded in surprising me.

"Shall you share a chamber?" he asked. "Or take separate quarters?"

Before I could overcome my amazement, Rwyan said, "We'll share."

Thyr smiled and said, "Then here," indicating a door across the way from Tezdal's room.

Save we were not allowed a lantern and the windows were locked shut, it was a chamber no different to many I'd known in Dharbek. I described it to Rwyan as the door was closed, and I heard a key turn in the lock.

"They treat us well," she said.

I said, "Yes," crossing to the window.

She said, "We treated Tezdal well enough, but still we planned to use him."

I looked out over the sleeping town. A dog barked twice and was after silent. The moon stood high, close on its full, shining on shingled roofs and smokeless stone chimneys. It was all so ordinary, so normal, I could scarce believe we were in Ur-Dharbek, behind a locked door. I put my arms around Rwyan. I said, "Tezdal is—*was*—a Sky Lord—our enemy."

Her smile was equivocal. "Think you the Changed do not see Truemen as enemies?" she asked me.

I said, "Perhaps. But we are treated so kindly, it's hard to think they mean us harm."

"Perhaps not harm," she said, "but use. That, I think."

I said, "I'll not let them harm you."

Rwyan held me at arm's length then, her face turned up as if she could see me clear. She said, "I'm not a fool, Daviot. No matter how kind they treat us, still we're in their power, and neither you nor I can do aught about it."

I was chastened. "I'm sorry. Are you afraid?"

She laughed then, soft, and said, "Of course I am. I'd be a fool otherwise. But I'll not let my fear overcome my sense."

Oh, my lovely, brave Rwyan! I could only hold her then and ask that God I doubted that she be kept safe, unharmed, her talent returned. And holding her, desire stirred, pent long weeks in shipboard chastity. I raised her face and kissed her.

•   •   •

The morning found us entwined in limbs and rumpled sheets. I was grateful that Ayl knocked upon the door without entering, as might some less discreet jailer, and bade us prepare to leave.

Tezdal, Rwyan, and I broke our fast and were once more locked in the wattle cage. Thyr nodded grave farewell as the wagon lumbered away. I held Rwyan's hand. I could not help but feel happy, for all our future remained a mystery.

It was early yet, the sun barely a handbreadth over the horizon, and the air held a slight chill. The moon still lingered in the west, but the sky was soon blued and scudded with white cloud. Birds sang loud, and for a while two dogs paced the wagon. Few folk were abroad, and they paused only briefly in their tasks to watch us go by. I thought that a prison cage traversing the roads of Dharbek should have attracted far greater attention.

We left the little town behind, and soon the paved road became again a track, running through farmland. Through the wattles I could see ahead the looming shadow of highlands. The road appeared to lead that way, and from the position of the sun I calculated that we traveled in a northwesterly direction. I supposed Trebizar must lie in the heart of Ur-Dharbek, likely in those hills.

That afternoon we rode through orchards, the trees heavy with apples and pears, and Glyn sprang down to pick handfuls of the fruit which he shared with us. I saw few buildings, but those were neat and well ordered, with wells and windmills and guardian hounds that came out baying warning of our approach. That night we slept in a farm, the three of us together in one small room beneath the thatched roof. There was one window, tiny and shuttered because it held no glass.

Tezdal examined the roof and said, "We might dig through that easily."

I said, "Remember, Rwyan's blind."

She said, "It should be useless anyway. Even could we reach the Slammerkin, we'd face the magic of the Border Cities."

I thought of what Rekyn had told me then, and of Ayl's words, and repeated them back: " 'The magic of the Border Cities shall deny you return no less than we.' Is that truly so?"

Rwyan nodded. The room was dim, and I could barely make out the movement of her head, but her voice came clear enough. "Those cities guard the Slammerkin shore. Their magic is shaped to ward the north, to hold back any Changed who might seek to return; or dragons, do they still exist."

I said, "But we're neither Changed nor dragons."

She said, "No matter. The magic of those cities is not so particular. *Anything* coming south over the Slammerkin should be destroyed."

Tezdal said, "Even you? You're a sorcerer."

Her laugh was soft in the gloom, and self-mocking. "Not now," she said. "Not whilst I wear this necklace. I'd be consumed with you."

Tezdal cursed and punched the roof, releasing a downfall of dust and straw.

Rwyan said, "We can do nothing, save go on."

"And hope," I said, finding her in the dark.

She leaned against me, her head on my shoulder. "Aye," she murmured. "And hope."

We went on, past farms and hamlets, sometimes towns. None were walled; I saw no keeps nor any sign of warbands. We slept under a roof when such comfort was available, under the stars when it was not. The nights held a chill now, and Ayl obtained us all blankets, and as we progressed farther inland, he allowed us more often out of our cage. Those nights we slept beside the road, we sat around a fire, and that was oddly merry, as if we were all companions on some journey of discovery.

I ventured to ask Ayl if he was not afraid we might flee, for there were no constraints set on us, and even those nights we slept in beds, the doors were no longer locked.

He chuckled and asked me in turn, "Where should you flee, Daviot?"

I shrugged and gestured vaguely to the south. I was not serious, and he knew it: this was become a kind of game between us, a slow gleaning of information. He said, "That's a long way, and even did you succeed in stealing a boat, your sorcerers deal unkindly with vessels coming south out of this land."

"You brought the *Sprite* north," I said.

"Aye, north," he returned me, "and far out to sea. The attention of the Border Cities is not much directed that way."

"They only pen you here?" I asked.

He nodded gravely. "It's deemed senseless to hold a Changed who'd flee to this land," he said. "We who choose to cross the Slammerkin are thought dangerous—Dharbek well rid of us."

I said, "You seem not very dangerous to me, Ayl."

He laughed at that. "But I'm a terrible freebooter. I stole the *Sprite*, no? And took three Truemen prisoner."

Those events I had pushed to the back of my mind marched forward, and I perceived an ambiguity in his good humor. I thought to test the mettle of our relationship then: I said, "Aye, that you did. And put the captain overboard."

Firelight played on his massy face as he nodded soberly. "I did," he said. "But Tyron was also thrown a float; and that was a greater kindness than he'd show me. Did fortune favor him, he made the shore."

I said, "That should be a long swim, even with a float."

He asked, "Think you he deserved better?"

I made a noncommittal gesture. Rwyan said, "Did he drown, shall his death not weight your conscience?"

Ayl turned toward her, and on his face I saw an expression I could not interpret. Still looking at her, he said to me, "Do you describe what I show you, Daviot."

I frowned and ducked my head. He unlaced his shirt and rose, tugging off the garment and turning his back. I gasped: his skin was dark and across the swarthy surface, from the width of his huge shoulders to the narrowing of his waist, there was a pattern of pale scars, ridged welts that could have only one source.

In a voice frightening for its calm, he said, "I was tillerman then. A storm was rising, and I argued Tyron's command that we sail. He ordered me whipped. Two of my fellows were lost in that storm. So— no, lady, my conscience shall not be troubled."

I heard Rwyan suck in a sharp breath, her face creased in expression of pity.

Softly, Tezdal said, "Did any mark me thus, I'd kill him."

Ayl drew on his shirt and sat again. "I think I dealt him kind," he said.

I nodded.

And then a thought struck me: that Ayl knew much of this land he could not, was all he told me true, have visited. Did the Border Cities make so effective a barrier, there could be no commerce between Ur-Dharbek and Dharbek, for all traffic must go in but the single direction and none come back. How then could he know of Trebizar, of this Council—of this road, even?

I asked him that straight out and saw a mask fall over his face. He said, "Perhaps the Raethe shall explain," and went to where the horses grazed.

I recognized dismissal and pressed no more. Perhaps in mysterious Trebizar I should find the answer.

The next day we entered a forest where the air hung misty blue, scented sweet with sap, and birds chorused our passing. The trail was wide and rutted with wagon tracks as if much used. Ayl told me it was the main highway to Trebizar, and around noon we came on a caravan halted for the midday meal. A merchant led the party, but there seemed scant difference between him and the nine drovers tending the wide-horned oxen. I thought that were we in Dharbek, they should all have been Changed and he a Trueman.

They bade Ayl and Glyn welcome and offered to share their food. I was surprised that we were released from the cage and given platters of a vegetable stew, with hunks of hard bread and even a mug apiece of ale. They watched us surreptitiously, as if we were marvelous creatures they could not quite bring themselves to approach. I was not entirely comfortable under such scrutiny, but still I did not feel much like a prisoner. From their conversation I gathered they were outward bound from Trebizar, carrying manufactured goods to the settlements along the way, intending to return with salted fish and other such goods as should be found on the coast. In Dharbek a caravan like this would have gone armed, but these Changed carried only such knives as they'd need daily, and goads to prod the oxen. Not even the merchant wore a sword.

I ventured to inquire after such lack of weaponry; and found my question met with shocked stares.

"What need?" asked the merchant, whose name was Ylin. "Who'd harm us?"

I said, "Outlaws; robbers," and he gazed at me as if I were crazed.

Ayl said, "Dharbek's a different land, Ylin."

"Indeed it must be." Ylin shook his head as if the notion of footpads or bandits were hard of digestion. "That an honest merchant cannot travel the roads safe without weapons? Now that's a thing, eh?"

His drovers nodded agreement, and I realized their eyes were on us now as if we were barbarians. That was a very odd feeling. I suppose I began to feel something of what the Changed underwent in my homeland.

When we parted, Ylin called after us, "Beware those robbers, Ayl," as if it were a great joke.

We traversed the forest all that day and as twilight came down made camp beside a spring that welled up from a rocky mound. Unasked, unthinking, Tezdal and I set to gathering wood for our fire while Ayl and Glyn tended the horses. We built a blaze and water was set to boiling. An owl hooted soft amongst the timber, and far off a wolf howled, answered from a distance.

I passed Rwyan a mug of tea that she cupped between her hands for warmth. I thought that summer ended; that I caught autumn's advent on the breeze. I draped my blanket about her shoulders, and she murmured thanks that warmed me better than the tea.

Ayl said, "Those clothes are thin. I'll get us stouter gear when next we find a town."

I said, "Ylin was surprised when I spoke of outlaws. Are there truly none here?"

The Changed shook his head absently. It seemed to me he took that absence for granted.

"We do not live like Truemen," he said. "Just as we've no aeldors or the like, so we've no outlaws."

"No criminals at all?" I asked.

He made a movement of his shoulders, not quite a shrug, and said, "Sometimes folk argue . . . sometimes there's a fight . . . but such matters are settled amongst neighbors. There are no malefactors as you describe."

Bluntly, I asked him, "How so? You've no aeldors, you say, nor any authority save this Raethe, it seems. What's to stop some malcontent from becoming a thief, a bandit?"

He thought awhile before answering. Then he said, "We are Changed, Daviot. We do not think or act like Truemen."

"Yet," I said, "there seems no longer very much difference between your kind and mine."

"In some ways there's not." He hesitated, frowning as if he pondered an unfamiliar thought; one alien and consequently difficult of definition or expression. "I suppose our birthing renders us somewhat different. You Truemen made us to be prey for the dragons, and then to be your slaves. That gives us common cause, I think; so we've not such rivalries as you know. We'd sooner help one another than steal. Think on it—there have been Changed in Ur-Dharbek since Truemen quit the land, and they must survive the dragons. Did they not work together, they'd have died. And now? Now those newcome are fugitives, fleeing slavery—another common cause. Did we prey on one another, then I think none should survive."

This seemed to me idyllic. Indeed, it seemed to me almost incredible. Yet I'd seen Ylin's unfeigned surprise and the startled expressions of his drovers: I could scarce doubt the truth of it.

And I'd another matter to pursue. I said, "You speak of dragons. Are there dragons still?"

Ayl's great hands spread to shape a gesture of ignorance. "I'd not know," he said. "I'm newcome here. In Trebizar they'll likely know."

It seemed to me this Trebizar must prove a cornucopia of answers: I looked forward to reaching the place. Then I thought of what it might well mean for Rwyan and somewhat revised my thought.

The forest saw us through another day of travel and then ended on heathland. Its edge was boundaried by the town Ayl had promised, and that was the largest place I had seen here. Again I was struck by the absence of walls; and by the size of the buildings, which rose three and four stories, all higgledy-piggledy, as if levels were added at random whim. The streets were mostly dirt, only those immediately adjacent to the center paved, but clean, and busy with such traffic as is common to any crossroads town.

In the morning we broke our fast with fruit and cheese and bread, and then Ayl left us in Glyn's care as he went out to obtain us warmer clothing.

He returned with gear that fit us well enough—shirts of heavy cotton and jerkins of stout leather, breeks of the same material, boots for Rwyan, cloaks for her and Tezdal. I wondered what climate lay ahead: for all the Sky Lords' magic was not brought against this land, still it was hard now to imagine anything other than endless summer.

But as we trundled out across the heath, I felt a wind blow cool from the north, and when I looked that way, I saw great banks of darkened cloud patrol the horizon. I thought there was even rain falling over the distant line of hills.

We rode toward those uplands, through stands of gorse and bright yellow broom. Birches and pines grew in scattered stands, and the day was loud with birdsong. I saw raptors ride the sky and thought again of dragons. Indeed, when we slept that night within a hurst of lonely pine trees, I dreamed again but not as before. It seemed my reveries took on a different tenor.

I stood not in the oak wood but on some craggy highland. A wind blew strong out of a storm-dark sky, and far away I saw lightning whip the land. I looked about, but I was alone . . . and then not alone, though I could not make out what stood so close. I saw only vast yellow eyes, solemn and stately, observing me in silence. They seemed to me ancient, those eyes, and I thought they must hold all time's secrets locked within their orbit.

I said, "What do you want of me?" but got no answer. I felt that they judged me.

Then . . . to say I *heard* is wrong, for there was no voice save inside my mind, as if these observers spoke directly to the channels of my nerves, to the innate substance of my being. Nor were there words, but rather only feeling, an emotion. . . . So then into my mind came a summons, a calling. It was as if they bade me join them, come to them.

Then silence and darkness.

I woke filled with a terrible yearning, as if I should be somewhere I was not, and could not go swift enough to satisfy the oneiric demand still lingering, a resonance in the conduits of my blood. I shivered and felt Rwyan wake within the compass of my arms. She made a small, almost tearful sound and clutched me. I stroked her hair, murmuring, thinking she'd suffered a nightmare.

Against my chest she said, "I dreamed," and repeated back exactly what I'd dreamed, identical in every specific.

I frowned and told her I'd had the same, and then, suspicious, I looked around our camp.

The fire was burned down to embers, but the night was bright with moon and starlight. Ayl and Glyn slept on. I saw Tezdal sitting up, and on his swarthy face such an expression as gave me answer to my question even before I voiced it. Still, I whispered my inquiry, and he nodded, wide-eyed, peering about as if he anticipated the momentary appearance of those great eyes.

"What does it mean?" he asked.

Rwyan said, "It was like a call. As if something would draw us to it."

"Or to them," I said.

"What them?" asked Tezdal.

I said, "The dragons." I could think of nothing else.

"Can they live still?" Rwyan asked.

I said, "I don't know."

"And do they," she said, "how could they know of us?"

I said again, "I don't know. But is it not very strange that we all three had the same dream?"

She said, "Yes."

I thought her frightened and held her tighter, stroking her hair. I found as much comfort there as she: this new aspect of the dream disturbed me in ways I could not properly define.

When dawn came, I ventured to ask Ayl and Glyn if they had been troubled with dreams, but they only shook their heads and told me no, and I left it. I was not sure why, only that I felt this was a thing private to we three and best not revealed to the Changed.

Most nights afterward the dream came back, though not on those we found shelter in farm or village. It was as though it were a thing of the wild places, and surely in it there was a wildness, a sense of absolute freedom. I felt less and less troubled, though I perceived in that silent observation an element of danger, as if I stood under judgment.

I felt in equal measure that did I fail, I should suffer, and that I should not fail. But I could not say how I might fail or know why I was judged; nor what might be the outcome, whichever way the scales tipped.

All this I discussed with Rwyan and Tezdal, whenever we found occasion, and they shared my feelings.

Then, when the rising land we crossed became the foothills of the mountains, the dreams came less and less frequently. I felt an odd sense of loss, for the yearning I'd known from the first remained still and shaped a vacuum in my soul, as if some great prize almost within my grasp were snatched away.

I have said before that Ur-Dharbek was a land of surprises: its capital did not disappoint.

We crested the mountains through a pass loomed all around with great peaks, the sky no longer the pristine blue of the lowlands but a steely color, as much gray as blue. Dull cloud streamed overhead, and there was a constant wind, often fierce so that it sang amongst the stones. For a full day, from dawn to dusk, we traversed the pass, and then pure wonder was revealed.

We had made our camp within the shadows of the gorge, finding its egress a little after sunrise. The road descended here, down into a verdant bowl cupped within the encircling peaks like a jewel held in stony hands. Great stands of deodar spread dark green before us, the colors softening on the lower slopes to the shades and hues of autumnal woodland, high green pastures. Far off toward the notional center of the bowl (that cirque defied eye's sure measurement), I thought I detected a hint of blue, as if a lake lay faint in the distance.

The road ran true through the woods, and as we descended I noticed first that the wind dropped away, and then that the temperature rose. Not to summer's heat but to the clean freshness of autumn, so that we shed our cloaks, and later our jerkins, to ride shirt-sleeved. Above us, the sky was no longer gray but again blue, as if the ringing hills denied inclemency entry. All this I described to Rwyan.

She said, "Yet we climbed for what? Five days? It should not be so warm, save . . ."

She paused, head turning as if she'd test the air. Tezdal said, "This place reminds me of your island."

And Rwyan nodded and said, "Aye. There's likely magic abroad here."

I looked about with different eyes. I thought that if magic did indeed shape this place, then did the Changed command it, they were powerful sorcerers. And yet I'd seen no evidence of magic elsewhere, no mages in the settlements, no hint of talent amongst the folk we'd encountered. Perhaps it was some natural gift, and none of Changed making; perhaps these hills were rich with crystals. Perhaps what sorcerers the Changed had all dwelled here. Questions buzzed like troublesome flies, and I could find no answers; only ever-increasing curiosity.

Down we went, the road falling gently for two days, the woodland thinning as we came to level ground. We passed meadows where placid cows and black-faced sheep grazed; fields of corn; orchards; solitary farms and tiny hamlets where we were given shelter and hearty country food. We crossed rivers bridged with wood and stone, and the trees scattered into the hursts of gentle, lowland climes — hickory and walnut, oak and birch and ash. It was a bucolic landscape; and entirely unnatural. I was certain that we drew near to Trebizar, and companion to my wonderment there grew a sense of unease. We approached Ayl's goal, and there should be taken decisions that must surely affect all our lives. I began to brood on what fate awaited us.

Then I saw the city, distant at first but growing ever more distinct as Ayl lifted the horses to a swifter pace.

It was lacustrine, built along the shores of the lake that lay like a blue jewel at the center of this amazing cirque. It was not large, either in spread or height. Set beside Durbrecht, it should have been dwarfed; indeed, it seemed no greater than many of the holds I'd known in Kellambek. No structure stood taller than two stories, and only a few were built of stone at their lower levels, the upper all timbered, with balconies and colonnaded walks. I had not expected walls, and there were none; neither any towers nor other fortifications. Piers thrust out into the lake, and I saw boats moored there, more out on the water, white sails bellied in the breeze.

Ayl turned, speaking over his shoulder: "We come to Trebizar."

I set an arm about Rwyan, speaking low of what lay before us.

And then I gasped, my fingers digging hard against her flesh, as I saw what lay beyond the city.

I could scarce credit the evidence my eyes gave me. I closed them, thinking it should be gone when next I looked. It was not: they hung low on the shore past Trebizar, still as basking sharks. I stared, the configuration of those bloodred cylinders familiar, the sigils painted down their sides pulsing faintly in the sun, more on the black baskets beneath. I saw the mooring lines, and the disturbance of the air where elementals shifted in their occult traces like restive horses. My mouth was abruptly dry. I licked my lips; swallowed against the lump that seemed to clog my throat.

"What is it?" Rwyan asked.

Hoarse, I said, "Skyboats."

"What?" Amazement and fear to match my own echoed in her voice. "How can that be?"

I said, "I know not. Only that they are there—skyboats."

From the corner of my eye, I saw Tezdal staring at the craft. He seemed only curious: there was no sign of recognition on his face.

Then the buildings blocked our view, the skyboats lost. It was as though I hallucinated. I knew I had not. I stared around, thinking to see Kho'rabi come storming at us. I saw only a wide avenue flanked by low buildings, pavements of smooth flagstones either side of the road. Folk moved there—Changed going about their business as if this were an ordinary town, the day normal; as if there were no Sky Lords' craft moored beside that perfect lake. I saw all this with a strange tremendous clarity, as if pure shock heightened senses already trained to record all I saw. The buildings were decorated, doors and balconies and shutters all cut with simple patterns, sunbursts and crescent moons, scatterings of stars. Pillars were carved, twined round with vines in bas-relief, clusters of acorns, and ears of wheat. The folk we passed were dressed not much differently to us, the males in breeks and shirts and jerkins, the females in plain gowns or masculine attire softened with scarves and ribbons, little displays of white lace. None wore weapons other than plain belt knives; a few carried staffs, as if they were herdsmen come in to trade. There were children, babes and older, playing in the streets or watching us go by. We passed

horsemen and some carts. I realized I felt none of that awful unnerving dread that came with the presence of the Sky Lords.

What dread I felt was created by sight of the airboats alone. By
what their presence here likely meant.

I started as the wagon halted.

We stood in a large square, the avenue continuing north, others
entering from east and west. I could see the lake shining blue between
the buildings to the east. I could not see the skyboats.

Our guardians sprang down. Glyn looked to the horses; Ayl
came to the rear of the wagon. Our cage was not locked, and when he
beckoned us out, I let Tezdal go first, handing Rwyan down to him
before I followed.

"Come."

Ayl indicated that we enter the closest building. It was of stone
about its base, wood above. Wide double doors hung open beneath a
veranda, glassed windows to either side. I could see no space that was
not covered with decorative carving, and from the veranda's roof
hung numerous baskets filled with plants that trailed creepers, all covered with little flowers of blue and red and white. I smelled ale and
food cooking, and as we went through the doors I saw this was an
inn. I stared: I had expected a prison. Sight of the Kho'rabi vessels
had dislodged all notions of companionship, of discovery and adventure. Curiosity was replaced with unease. I took Rwyan's elbow to
guide her across the floor.

It was not yet noon, and there were not many patrons at the
tables. Those present favored us with curious glances but said nothing
to us or to our warders. (Warders? I was no longer sure what was our
relationship with Ayl and Glyn.)

We found a table to the side, a little way apart, and Ayl went to
where the landlord stood scrubbing tankards. I watched as they
spoke, but I could not hear what was said. I examined the room,
which was like any taproom, save perhaps cleaner than many in
Dharbek. Rwyan held my hand in a tight grip.

Ayl joined us and said, "The Raethe sits now, likely until dusk or
past. So do we eat?"

"And then?" I asked him.

"Then I think perhaps best you remain here until your presence
is required," he said.

I said, "Those were skyboats I saw, no?"

He said calmly, "They were."

I said, "What truck do you have with the Sky Lords?"

He said, "Doubtless the Raethe shall explain. If it sees fit."

I ground my teeth in helpless anger. Clearly I'd have no answers of Ayl. Either he lacked the knowledge, or he chose to hold it from me. I grunted and said, "So be it."

He ducked his head again and then leaned closer, his voice dropping to a bass rumble that none save we might hear. "Do you heed my advice, Daviot," he said, "you'll curb your impatience. Only wait, and you'll have your answers. And that necklace Rwyan wears be sooner removed."

I frowned, unsure whether he issued honest advice or a non-too-subtle threat. Certainly, I believed he prevaricated where the Sky Lords were concerned. I'd have spoken up, but Rwyan squeezed my hand in warning, and I bit back my retort and nodded my acceptance.

Ayl lounged back, as if he'd not a problem in all the world. He appeared entirely at ease, unsurprised and comfortable as any regular visitor to this inn, any inhabitant of Trebizar—like a man come home. I supposed he was; and then that, had he not lied to us from the start, he could not be. Had he told the truth, then he could be no more familiar with this place than we Truemen. Nor any better acquainted with the road or the towns—I perceived fresh mystery here.

I studied his face as brimming mugs were set before us and thought of another oddity. No payment was asked, neither here nor in any place we had halted. The landlord only set down the tankards, nodded casual greeting, glanced at Rwyan, Tezdal, and me as if he were not at all surprised to find three Truemen seated in his taproom, and walked away.

I said, "It seems we were expected."

Ayl lowered his tankard only long enough to nod.

"Nor's payment asked," I said.

Ayl said, "No."

I said, "Is that the way here? Is there no currency?"

"We've coinage," he said. "But those on the Raethe's business travel free."

"How are you recognized?" I asked. "You wear no badge of office that I can see."

He chuckled then, gesturing with his mug. "Think you it's a common sight," he said, "three Truemen on our roads?"

That, I must admit, was likely rare; I asked him, "How did you know the road, Ayl?"

He shook his shaggy head, and I saw the mask again drop over his features. "Daviot," he said kindly enough, but nonetheless firmly, "doubtless you're agog with curiosity, but it's not my place to answer your questions. Do you follow that advice I gave and bide your time. Ask of the Raethe, not me."

His eyes met mine, and I saw that he would speak no more of such matters. I shrugged and drank ale, our conversation becoming a desultory affair, designed more to fill the awkward silence than satisfy the questions that teemed in my head.

We sat thus as our tankards were refilled and food served us. I was uncomfortable, and that somewhat leached my appetite. Rwyan, too, was nervous, but Tezdal seemed not at all discomfited. I supposed that for him all had been strange since his awakening on the rock, and consequently this no odder than any other situation. I wondered how he should react did we encounter Kho'rabi. Should that engage his memory; might some Sky Lord present here recognize him? For all I'd done my best, I'd had no success in restoring him his lost past. I wondered should I feel so kindly toward him did he return to what he'd been. Or for that matter, he to me.

I pondered all this as our table was cleared and Ayl interrupted my silent musing.

"For now," he said, "you must remain here. But I understand the rooms are comfortable, and there's a bathhouse."

"I'd see this fabulous city," I said.

At which the Changed smiled apologetically and told me no, repeating that until the Council granted us audience, we must confine ourselves to the inn.

Rwyan said, "A hot tub should be a luxury."

She squeezed my hand as she spoke, which I took to be a warning or a request, and so I acceded. I thought my agreement afforded Ayl some measure of relief, as if he'd avoid open argument. That surprised me, for I now saw us more truly as captives, and I wondered why he should concern himself with my wants or displeasures.

He sent Glyn to arrange it and called the landlord to show us to our chambers. Once again, Rwyan and I were given shared quarters, Tezdal in the adjoining room. Unusually after so much latitude, our doors were locked. My unease waxed, and I inspected the chamber as Rwyan took her bath.

It was as Ayl had promised. A wide bed spread with fresh linen stood against one wall between two windows. I checked them both and found them secured beyond my undoing. They gave a view of rooftops, a section of street, the lake blue beyond the farther houses. I could not see the skyboats. There was a wardrobe and a washstand; a screened partition hid a commode. There were two comfortable wooden chairs set either side of a small table, on which stood a decanter of pale wine and two glasses, a flask of water. The floor was spread with colorful rugs and a lantern hung from the ceiling. It felt suddenly like a cell: I paced impatiently.

Rwyan came back perfumed with sandalwood, and I led her around the room, that she familiarize herself with its furniture. Then Glyn escorted me to the bathhouse. I was aware the Changed stood sentry outside as I scrubbed myself. This sudden concern with our security disturbed me, and I bathed swiftly, going back damp to the room.

The door was locked behind me, and I crossed to where Rwyan sat on the wide bed.

"I cannot understand this concern," I said. "Why lock doors now? Why deny us the freedom we've had so far? In the God's name, we're in the heart of Ur-Dharbek—we could scarce hope to escape from here."

She touched me and, finding me still somewhat moist, began to towel my hair.

"I think there must be things here they'd not yet have us know," she said. "How many skyboats did you see?"

I took my head from under her busy toweling. "Perhaps a score. Hardly enough for invasion. At least, not yet."

"You believe it so?" She dropped the towel. I picked it up; flung it aside.

"What else?" I said. "I've seen Changed and Sky Lords together; their airboats here. Do they not agree it, then I think they must talk of it. Alliance, at the least . . . discussion of terms, of strategy. . . . The Sky Lords defy the Sentinels now, so the Border Cities should likely prove no greater obstacle."

"Aye," she said soft. "Doubtless they should strike down no few skyboats, do they mount the Great Coming. But not enough, do they come in numbers. The God knows, they've always found ways past us, and now . . . now do they attack across the Fend *and* across the Slammerkin; do the Changed of Dharbek rise to support them . . ."

She'd no need of elaboration. The land already bled under the wounding of that unnatural summer. Jareth was regent, deemed weak, his elevation a source of discontent amongst the aeldors. Was the Great Coming launched, did the Changed rise—I shivered at the thought. Better than any save this woman who sat with me, I knew how subtle were the secret ways of the folk we Truemen had made, how surely they communicated, that their eyes and ears were everywhere, hidden by their very station. It was as if the sorcerers had created some hydra, a monster invisible until it struck.

"Dharbek's lost," I said.

Rwyan ducked her head. "And the Changed have magic now," she whispered, fingering the necklace glinting at her throat. "They can do this. They've made this valley, and as you describe it, only great magic could create such a place. I think the hills must hold an abundance of crystals. Changed have dwelt here long enough, they absorb the magic. They develop the talent!"

"But surely long exposure destroys," I said. "You told me that. It brings madness."

"Is war not madness?" she returned. "But yes, I told you that. And so it is—for Truemen. Perhaps the Changed are different; perhaps the crystals do not destroy them."

"Then why take you?" I wondered, though I'd already a horrid suspicion. "Can they do all this, what need of you?"

"I'm not sure," she said, and shuddered, so that I put my arms about her and held her close as her voice dropped low. "Save . . ."

"Save what?" I prompted, thinking I'd not welcome the answer.

Nor did I: Rwyan said, "Save they'd plumb my mind. Learn Dharbek's secrets—our usage of those crystals that ward the Fend, the Slammerkin—learn the limits of our magic."

She trembled in my arms. I felt her tears against my chest. I raised my head, staring blindly at the ceiling. Beams stood dark against white plaster. They reminded me of gallows trees: I lowered my face to Rwyan's hair.

She pulled back a little way. I looked into her blind eyes, the green shining tearful now. She said, "Daviot, I cannot betray Dharbek."

I studied her face. I saw a strength I dreaded, a determination I feared. I read the direction of her thought. I'd run from that compass save it should have been a betrayal of this woman I loved, of the strength that made her what she was. I owed her better than that, and so I said, "What can you do, does worse come to worst?"

And she smiled—so brave, my Rwyan!—and told me, "Perhaps it shall not come to that. But does it—what choice have I, save to defy them?"

Almost, I said that she should speak out, answer whatever questions were asked, give whatever information was demanded; only survive, because without her my life should have no meaning. But that was selfishness and insulting to her courage. And I think she'd have scorned me had I said it aloud. So instead, I said, "The God will it not come to that."

A small laugh then; and: "The God, Daviot? I'd thought you doubted his existence."

"I do," I said. "But be I wrong, then I ask he spare you. You deserve better."

"I doubt," she said, "that 'deserve' comes into this. It seems to me more happenstance—that I helped bring down Tezdal's skyboat; that I was there when we found him. That he came to trust me, and I was chosen to escort him to Durbrecht. Even that the *Sprite* was the ship chosen. All happenstance, no?"

I wondered if she sought to strengthen her resolve with words or set aside contemplation of that resolution. If so, I'd help her: I said, "Happenstance? Or is there a pattern, and I've a part in it? Had we not met, should you have been sent so soon to the Sentinels? Had I not come to Carsbry when I did, I'd not have found you. Had Lan not given me this token—which he'd not have done save I knew Urt, who helped you and I to meet—then Ayl should surely have cast me overboard, and we'd not be together here. Aye, surely there's a pattern too subtle for mere happenstance. It seems more like our fates are linked."

I looked to comfort her (and am I honest, myself), but as I spoke, I saw a kind of truth in what I said. There *was* a pattern of some kind; at least an interweaving of our lives that surely ran more certain than random accident might dictate. It was as if we were fated to come together, and whether that was the God's will or nebulous destiny, it seemed to me to become more real even as I spoke. I warmed to the subject.

"And the dreams," I said. "That on the Sentinels you dreamed of me; not randomly, but as if you shared my dreams. And here—those judging eyes. Surely that cannot be happenstance."

Her head tilted as if she saw me, and on her lovely face a frown set twinned creases between her eyes. Her lips pursed, luscious, so that I must struggle not to kiss them. Not yet; not whilst she seemed to find solace in my words.

"Perhaps it's so," she murmured. Then frowned deeper: "But Tezdal shared that latter dream."

"And had Tezdal not been on that skyboat," I said, "you'd not have found him on the rock, not come to Carsbry. I'd not have found you there, nor stowed away."

"Then he's a part of this pattern," she said.

I'd seen it more in terms of we two, but I nodded and said, "I suppose he must be."

"And Urt?" she asked. "That you knew him in Durbrecht, and had you not, he'd not have been sent to Karysvar, nor come here. Surely there's another part?"

I nodded, though Rwyan could not see that, and murmured, "Yes, surely."

I was frowning now. I had begun this wordplay intending nothing more than to comfort Rwyan. Now I began to wonder if we did not unravel threads of subconscious knowledge, somehow untangling strands of awareness to form a clearer picture . . . of what? That I could not say; not yet. But I felt we explored something here that I must pursue. That might—whatever ruled our destinies willing—afford us escape from our predicament.

"What is it?" Rwyan's hands touched my face. "What silences you?"

"Urt *is* here," I said. "Ayl told us that, no?"

"And a voice in their government," she said.

"Then sooner or later we'll speak." I took her hands and kissed the palms. "And I can ask him if he's shared our dreams."

"Daviot!" She gripped both my hands, firm. "Do you say all this is truly so? Can it be?"

This straw seemed to me stronger. I said, "I'll not tell you for certain, aye. But is it not strange, this interweaving of all our lives?"

She said, "Yes," and once more pursed her lips in thought.

I could no longer resist: I kissed them. Her arms wound about my neck, and we lay upon the bed. Against my mouth Rwyan said, "What if we're summoned by this Raethe?"

I answered her, "They sit late, Ayl said. And do they not, then they must wait."

She laughed, and helped me find the lacings of her shirt.

We were in that room three days before the summons came. Ayl brought us out, with Glyn and five thickset bull-bred Changed in attendance. We were marched across the square and down a street that ended on the lake's shore. It was early in the day, and I saw the skyboats clear as we were directed out along a pier. They were huge, floating like vast airborne slugs, their crimson flanks a bloody contrast to the pure blue of the water. I thought the baskets must hold a plenitude of Kho'rabi. Amongst them, like minnows swimming with whales, were the little scout vessels. It seemed to me the half-seen elementals sporting about the craft grew more agitated under my observance. I thought I heard their keening, but that might have been only the wind off the lake. Then Ayl tapped my shoulder, indicating I should board a skiff.

He took the tiller, and Glyn lowered the sail. There was room for only two more of our escort: we left the others on the pier. Rwyan took my hand. Her palm was damp, and when I looked at her face, I saw her jaw set firm, her lips a resolute line. Tezdal reached out and took her other hand. I could not resent that intimacy.

She smiled thinly and said, "Perhaps this necklace shall be removed now."

I said, "Yes, all well."

She said, "Where do we go?"

"Across the lake," I answered.

The wind, which seemed not to affect the town much, was brisk out here, and we sped over the blue water. Wavelets lapped against the hull, and did I not look back to where the skyboats hung or wonder what lay ahead, I might have enjoyed the journey. Instead, I looked to the far shore, where a solitary building grew steadily larger.

It stood close to the shore, shining in the sun, for it was made all of white stone such as I'd not seen before in this unknown country. It was no more than a single level, and circular, with a portico running around its walls. I had the impression of a temple, surely of a place of power, though its architecture was plain. A pathway of the same pale stone stretched from the portico to a pier, where Ayl brought the skiff in.

We were handed ashore. Ayl beckoned us to follow, the rest falling into step behind. I saw that vivid flowers grew in profusion about the building, and insects filled the still air with their buzzing; but there were no birds. We climbed seven steps up to the portico and faced a door of wood shaved and bleached to match the stone. A brass gong hung there, and a mallet. Ayl took the hammer and struck a single ringing note that echoed sonorous down the colonnades. The door swung open on silent hinges. A woman—cat-bred, I thought—appeared. She seemed no different to any Changed female save that she wore a circlet of gold about her brow. Ayl ducked his head, and she nodded in reply, motioning us forward. As the door closed behind us, I realized Ayl and the others still stood outside.

"Do you follow me."

It was not a question nor quite a command, but the woman turned and walked away as if she entertained no doubt but that we should obey. I thought she was not very old, perhaps younger than Rwyan, but possessed of such imperious confidence that she seemed ageless.

We crossed a broad vestibule that was, as best I judged, all seamless white marble to an inner door. The woman pushed it open and stood aside. We went through into a circular chamber lit bright by the windows that marched along the walls. My eyes narrowed against the

glare, for it seemed that sunlight was reflected off every surface there.
I was reminded of Decius's chamber, unable to properly define the
figures that occupied the tiered benches I faced. I suppose that was
the intention: to set us at an immediate disadvantage.

Rwyan felt my hesitation and asked, "What is it?"

I told her, and as I did, my vision adjusted enough that I could
better make out the room.

We stood on a kind of balcony, a semicircular balustrade opening
on a short flight of steps that descended to an oval faced by the
benches. The floor was yellow, not quite gold, and blinding; all else
was white, save the clothing of our interviewers. That was a mixture
of mundane homespun, simple leather, and brighter robes and gowns
in a variety of colors. I thought perhaps fifty Changed sat studying us.

"Do you step down."

The voice came from the midst of the watchers. As we obeyed, I
looked for Urt, but the sun was in my eyes, and I could not find him.

The same voice said, "I am Geran, spokesman for the Raethe of
Trebizar. You are hale? Your quarters are comfortable?"

I said, "Yes. Why are we here?"

Someone laughed at that and said, "You told us he was direct,
Urt."

He *was* present then: I felt more hopeful. I said, "Shall you remove Rwyan's necklace now?"

"Shall that be done?"

I recognized Geran's voice. There was a murmur of assent, and a
Changed with an equine look about his long face stepped down from
the benches. He was in his middle years, his hair a dull brown. He
wore a robe that trailed the floor, dark green chased with silver patterning. Like the female who had delivered us here, he wore a golden
circlet about his brow. I noticed that his hands were spatulate as he
raised them to Rwyan's neck.

He sprang the lock and slipped the silver links from her throat.
She sighed as if a weight were lifted from her and turned her head
from side to side. I saw her talent fill her eyes and smiled.

She said, "I can see again." Her voice was joyful.

The horse-faced man pocketed the necklace and trod a pace
backward. "We'd not inflict needless hurt," he said.

From the benches someone said, "That's the province of
Truemen."

"Not all."

I recognized that voice! I squinted into the light, seeking Urt.
I found him on the seventh tier. He seemed unchanged. Perhaps

smaller, or I had grown since Durbrecht, but not at all aged. He gave me a small smile, but on his face I read concern. He ducked his head a fraction, acknowledging me, and made a gesture difficult of interpretation. I thought perhaps he warned me to tread wary.

The spokesman said, "We'd not keep you blind, mage. But know this—your talent is limited here, bound by our magic. It is a small thing, but do you attempt to use it against any Changed or any guest, then what follows shall make your blindness seem a pleasure."

Rwyan nodded. She stared directly at the seated figures. (Once more gifted with occult vision, she could see them better than I.) She said, "Why am I here?"

A new voice said, "Because we'd have you here."

"Why?" she demanded.

"You presume!" The speaker was clearly angered. "Ours to ask, yours but to answer."

"And do I choose not?"

I saw a figure rise, limned in sunlight, indistinct. I thought it was a female. One arm flung out, and I heard Urt cry, "No!"

I sprang before Rwyan. Tezdal was at my side, both our bodies interposed between Rwyan and the standing figure. I thought we should be struck down. I was certain this Changed—perhaps all those present—commanded magic.

Urt said, "Do we condemn Truemen and ourselves use their ways? Shall we rise bellicose against every little argument?"

"What other language do Truemen understand?"

"Some, kindness. Some seek to redress wrong. Not all are evil."

"Not this one? This mage? One of those who made us and make us their servants?"

Rwyan said, "There are no servants on the Sentinels."

"But enough in Dharbek," came the response. "I tell you again— finally!—that you'll answer, not ask."

"You command like a Trueman born, Allanyn."

Urt's words were dry. I'd heard that tone before, used on Cleton, sometimes on Ardyon. Almost, I smiled. The one called Allanyn, however, found it not at all amusing. Her angry shriek was entirely female, and feline. I saw her arm drop as she rounded on my old friend. And friend still, I dared hope.

She said, "You insult me, Urt. Newcome to the Raethe, do you assume to slight me?"

The spokesman said, "Newcome or old, Allanyn, all have equal place here."

"I'll not be called a Trueman!" Allanyn snarled.

Mildly, Urt said, "I'd never name you that."

Was it an apology, it sounded mightily like an insult. Allanyn appeared confused, unsure whether to take affront or allow appeasement. She remained on her feet, staring past her fellows at Urt as if she contemplated turning the full force of her rage on him.

Geran said, "Allanyn, do you sit? Better that we reach agreement before we resort to threat."

I liked the sound of that not at all.

Rwyan pushed between Tezdal and me then. She seemed undeterred by Allanyn's rage or any threat of reprisal. I clutched her arm and said urgently, "No! Rwyan, hold your tongue."

Allanyn said, "Your lover gives sound advice, mage."

I thought to deflect her anger. I said, "I'd know why we're here no less than Rwyan."

Allanyn said, "These Truemen are presumptuous."

I shrugged and said, "We were kidnapped, brought prisoner here. Is it so odd we'd know the why of it?"

One of them chuckled and said, "That seems reasonable enough."

Allanyn spat, for all the world like her forebears thwarted in some savage design.

Urt said, "Reason is usually the sounder course. From my own experience in Dharbek, I tell you that kindness brings a surer result than the lash."

There was murmur of voices then. Some I thought in agreement, others opposed. I thought there were factions here, and that Urt sought to defend us. I hoped he should prevail.

The debate died away. Geran stood, his back to we three as he studied his fellows. One by one, they either nodded or shook their heads. I could not see clearly enough I might make out which faction won. The spokesman told me.

"You, Daviot, are here by accident, though I suspect we shall find a use for your Storyman's talent. The mage because we'd glean knowledge of her magic—"

Rwyan interrupted him, defiant. "I'll give you nothing!" she cried. "I'll not betray Dharbek!"

As if she'd not spoken, the Changed continued, "The Sky Lord Tezdal, we'd return to his own."

Rwyan said, "There *is* alliance!"

Geran ducked his head. "We treat with the Sky Lords, aye. Should we rather allow our brethren to continue under the Trueman's yoke? Must we go to war to free them, then war it shall be."

"And how many die?" Rwyan asked. "Changed and Truemen both. And Sky Lords."

"Reason?" Allanyn's voice rang contemptuous. "There's no reasoning with this one."

I said, "Tezdal's no memory."

"That we can right," the spokesman said, and turned to Tezdal. "Would you have back your memory, Lord Tezdal?"

Tezdal frowned. He glanced at Rwyan and at me; I saw hope flash in his eyes, and suspicion. He said, "I'd know who I am, aye. But you should know this—Rwyan saved my life, and I have sworn to defend her. I'll not see her harmed; neither Daviot, who is my friend. Who looks to harm them shall answer to me. Be I Sky Lord or no, that vow I'll honor."

I knew in the instant of his speaking that even were his memory restored and he become again a Kho'rabi, he would honor that promise.

The spokesman nodded gravely, as if he, too, acknowledged Tezdal's integrity. But then he said, "Do we first give you back your past and you be whole again; then do you decide where lie your loyalties."

Softly, I heard Tezdal murmur, "That I already know."

Rwyan said, "Are you truly able? Those techniques of the Mnemonikos known to Daviot have failed. Shall you succeed where he could not?"

"And doubtless you and your fellow sorcerers attempted it." Geran's voice held an echo of laughter. "However, where Truemen failed, I believe we may succeed."

"You must," said Rwyan, "command powerful magicks."

I saw that she sought to learn something of their powers. No less the spokesman, for he smiled and said, "Lady, we do."

"And do you refuse us, you'll soon enough witness them firsthand," said Allanyn.

Rwyan turned her eyes to where the cat-bred woman sat. "I tell you again," she said, "that I'll not betray Dharbek. What I know of our magic, I'll not give you."

Allanyn snorted spiteful laughter. "This wastes our time. The mage cannot be reasoned with. I say we end this dalliance, and use the crystals on her without delay. Let her defy *them*!"

I cried out, "No!" And soft in Rwyan's ear as fresh debate erupted, "Would you goad them needlessly? This one would have your life."

Before she could answer, Urt spoke. "Reason may yet prevail." His voice rose over babble. I had not known he was capable of so commanding a tone. "Do you but hear me out?"

"Do you plead for your Trueman friends, no."

That was Allanyn, her rejection echoed by others of her sympathy. More called that Urt be heard, and finally the spokesman quelled their argument, motioning that Urt speak.

He said, "I think us agreed on one thing—that the Lord Tezdal be restored his memory. Is that not so, Rwyan?"

Rwyan said, "That was ever my intent."

"Daviot?"

I nodded and said, "Aye."

"And such restoration was attempted by the sorcerers of Dharbek, who failed?"

I could only nod. Rwyan said, "Obviously," her tone a deliberate provocation.

Urt ignored it. He said, "Then can we succeed where you could not, the strength of our magic must be proven, no?"

I sensed a trap; I wondered where he took us, down what road. Did he look to protect us from Allanyn's wrath or to betray us? I thought I could no longer entirely rely on his friendship: like Rwyan, he must surely define his loyalties here. I hesitated to answer.

Rwyan did not. She said carelessly, "Can you give Tezdal back his memory, then in that I must acknowledge your magic the stronger."

Urt nodded gravely. Allanyn spat and said, "In that and more, mage. I say again—this wastes our time. I say we prevaricate no longer but put her to the test."

As a murmur of agreement arose, Geran stood, arms raised until he had again silence. "Let Urt have his say."

Allanyn's cohorts fell quiet, reluctantly. Urt said, "Allanyn speaks true—that magic we command surpasses yours now. Does the Raethe choose it, then your mind can be drained of all its knowledge. Willing or unwilling, you've not the strength to resist."

His tone was urgent, but I could not decide whether he warned Rwyan in friendship or in threat. I wondered how well I could know him now, after so long. Well enough to recognize a warning? Did he ask our cooperation that Rwyan might survive intact? Or did he only threaten, and I hope in vain that we'd found an ally?

I heard Rwyan say, "You shall slay me ere I betray Dharbek."

I cursed the sunlight that denied me clear sight of Urt's face. I could see him only as an outline, standing amidst his fellows, and must judge his intent from his voice alone. And that, I realized, was surely modulated as much for his companions as for Rwyan or me. Did he seek to aid us, he could not risk revealing his purpose.

He said, "Lady, there should be no need. Are you given to the crystals, you'll tell us all, without let or hindrance. You'll have no choice; and after, your mind should be a void."

The chamber was warm, but I felt cold. I dared not speak.

Rwyan said, "My case is stated. Do you put yours?"

Some little hope there. Urt said, "We are not those meek Changed you know in Dharbek. We've power here, and I'd show it you. Do you witness our strength, and then decide."

Rwyan said, "My decision was taken long ago, when I took those vows my College requires."

I must admire her courage. At the same time I was possessed of a great desire to shake her violently, to clap a hand over her mouth and agree on her behalf. She appeared bent on destroying herself. The thought of my lovely Rwyan reduced to a mindless husk (I had absolutely no doubt Urt spoke true in that) set a cold and sour knot in my gut.

I heard Allanyn mutter, "Time wastes."

Urt said, "Do you watch us restore the Lord Tezdal his memory and know our power. After, you may agree to what we ask and remain whole; or—"

"I'll take her for a servant," Allanyn said, the sally met with laughter from her supporters.

I could hold silent no longer. I turned to Rwyan and said, "Rwyan, for the God's sake—for my sake!—agree to this at least."

She faced me with an unfathomable expression. "Would you ask me to betray myself?" she demanded.

I was caught, my choice betwixt net and hook. I'd have her live, whole. But did I seek to persuade her to forswear her duty, I knew I should lose her. I groaned and shook my head. "Not that," I said. "But the time's not yet come for that. I say only that you agree to what Urt suggests—observe their power, and after decide."

She held my troubled gaze awhile, then calmly she turned to the assembly: "So be it. Do you show me what you can do."

Surely it took them aback, for none spoke awhile, not even fierce Allanyn. And then Geran said, "Very well. Let us prepare."

They came down from their tiered benches then, all of them, gathering about us, and Geran said, "This shall take some little while. Do you go with these," and we were surrounded by Changed wearing the golden circlets on their brows.

Tezdal made to leave with us, but the spokesman touched his arm and said, "Lord Tezdal, do you wait here. Your companions shall not be harmed."

Tezdal shook his head, protesting. He pulled loose of Geran's hand and moved toward us. The spokesman gestured, and Changed stepped close as if by accident but nonetheless blocking Tezdal's way. I thought the Sky Lord would fight them, but Rwyan called out, "Tezdal, do you obey. There's no harm shall come us yet," and he frowned, hesitating. Rwyan called again, and he nodded. He seemed bewildered but made no further move to join us.

The movement of the throng hid him, and Geran nodded approvingly. "That was sensibly done, lady. You show wisdom." He touched the band around his temples and said, "This signifies the talent. All those who wear these circlets command the gift of magic."

He spoke mildly, but I recognized the warning. I was thankful Rwyan acknowledged it: she said, "I'll not attempt to use my own power."

Geran smiled as if he admired her audacity. "Then do you go, and when all is ready, you'll be sent for."

A tall, thin-faced Changed touched my elbow, indicating that I follow him. There were seven of the gifted attended us, and as they herded us away, I caught a glimpse of Urt through the crowd. He met my stare with a bland expression that told me nothing. I saw that he did not wear a circlet.

Folk made way for us as we were led from the audience chamber, their expressions a mixture of curiosity and hostility. On some faces I thought I saw pity. On one I saw unhidden hatred, and for all I'd not seen her clearly until now, I knew this was Allanyn. And that she was an implacable enemy.

She was tall and slender, and had it not been for the malign fire burning in her ocher eyes, I'd have thought her beautiful. Her hair was russet, falling loose about a narrow face dominated by those huge, fierce eyes. Her lips were narrow and mobile, curving in a smile as she studied me. She was undoubtedly feline: she had that sinuous grace, that predatory languor. The yellow gown she wore hid it no better than her smile hid her animosity. I'd not have been surprised had she extended claws. She wore a golden band about her brow.

Lightly, as if she were not at all afraid, Rwyan said, "That one bears us little love, I think."

"Best ward your tongue, lady." The thin-faced Changed spoke soft, and not without a hint of sympathy. "Allanyn's one of our strongest, and she bears no love at all for Truemen."

Rwyan nodded as if this were a tidbit of knowledge not unsuspected and gave the fellow a cheery smile. "My thanks for the warning," she murmured. "But does Allanyn govern here or all the Raethe?"

"All have a voice," said the Changed, his tone low enough that only we might hear, "but Allanyn's is very loud."

"Indeed," said Rwyan, and laughed.

I was uncertain whether she was genuine in her apparent lack of concern, or only put on a brave face. For my own part, I'll admit I was mightily nervous. I felt little doubt but that Tezdal's memory should be restored him, nor any more that such demonstration of power should fail to persuade Rwyan. I knew with an awful certainty that she would refuse to give up her secrets willingly but rather fight the Changed to the end. I found her hand and forced a smile I knew was hollow.

28

We were marched along a windowless corridor that should have been dark but was not. Instead it glowed with a pale radiance that seemed to emanate from the surrounding stone itself. I had not seen its like, but Rwyan smiled as if such a marvel were familiar. Her expression suggested some private confirmation, but when I frowned a question, she only shook her head, indicating I remain silent.

I obeyed: it seemed she was in command now. I marveled that she could be so calm when all I felt was mounting trepidation.

We came to a door that appeared cut from a single slab of stone, and a Changed pushed it open, gesturing that we enter. The door closed behind us, and I looked about.

We stood in a square chamber that was neither quite a cell nor such a room as should be offered guests. Walls and floor and ceiling were all of the same white stone, unadorned. Light came from a single window, falling bright over two chairs of black wood that were the only furnishings. No latch or handle marred the pristine surface of the door, and when I tried to shift it, it remained resolutely sealed.

Rwyan said, "That shall do no good, Daviot. We can only wait."

I grunted, crossing to the window. The rectangular opening was glassed, without hinges or shutters. I wondered how air might enter, and if we were left here to suffocate. Anger stirred, tainted with panic, and I struck the glass. That only hurt my fist.

Rwyan set a hand on my shoulder and said, "You'll not break it, my love. We're prisoners here until they choose to release us."

I asked, "Your magic?"

And she shook her head. "I'm helpless here. Do you not sense it?"

It was my turn to shake my head. She gestured at the walls. "Magic surrounds us; I feel it on my skin, like a storm building. This place is mortared with crystals that leach my power."

"But you can see," I said.

"That little they allow," she told me, "and no more. They've far greater command than I suspected."

"Then why," I asked, "are they not destroyed, made mad?"

She shrugged and said, "We've spoken of this before, no? These wild Changed are—different. . . . And mad? Do you believe Allanyn is sane?"

I thought of the rank hate I'd seen in those ocher eyes and shook my head again. Rwyan's hand descended to fall around my waist. She rested her head on my shoulder. She said, "Do you heed your own advice and be patient. I'd know the fuller measure of their power and of their intentions, before . . . I decide what I must do. I cannot give them what they ask, not willing."

Something in her tone chilled me, deep in the marrow of my bones. I thought she must fear that terrible decision, that for her was no decision at all. I turned to face her, my hands on her shoulders, holding her at arm's length that I might see her clear. I said, "Do you refuse, they'll take it, and—" I sighed and drew her close, my face buried in her hair.

She said, calm against my chest, "And leave me mindless. I'd not have that."

I said, "Nor I!"

She moved within my arms, leaning back a little that she might "look" directly at my face. "And surrounded by this power, my own is as nothing. I'll not be able to match them—neither defy them nor fight them."

I said, "Then you can only submit."

"No!" Her hands moved upward to cup my cheeks, to hold

steady my head that I look into her eyes. I saw her resolve and felt fear. She said, "But you . . ."

I said, "Me? What power have I?"

She said, "That given you by your College."

I choked out a sour laugh. "The power of a Storyman? Shall I recite them a tale to change their minds, then?"

"Not that." Her eyes held mine transfixed. "But one of those other skills taught you in Durbrecht."

I did not want to hear what I feared she'd ask: I could not refuse. "Rwyan, don't ask this of me."

She said, "I must; and you must agree."

I groaned. I thought I should choke on the constriction that filled my throat. Or empty my belly over this cursed white magic floor.

As if from far away yet very clear, I heard Rwyan say, "They'll not watch you so close. You wear that talisman that marks you as their friend. And you've the skill."

I shook my head and mumbled, "No."

She said, "You'd rather see my mind drained? Left empty, like some discarded bowl of bone?"

I closed my eyes and shook my head and said through gritted teeth, "No."

She said, "Then does worse come to worst, you must kill me."

I opened my eyes and stood a moment blind, stunned and silent. There was a ghastly logic in what she asked, and damnation did I either refuse or agree. I said, "I cannot."

She said fierce, "You must! Do they use their crystals on me, I shall betray Dharbek, betray what I am. I'll not go willing to that; neither would I be mindless. Sooner dead!"

I blinked, my cheeks wet. It seemed the room spun. I felt Rwyan's hands upon my cheeks, and it seemed they burned me. I loved her. I could only admire her courage. And hate her determination. I said again, "I cannot. Rwyan, don't ask this of me."

She said, "I must. I've no one else."

That, I could not argue. I had anyway no arguments left; neither hope. I saw only despair ahead. Silently I cursed Ayl for his kidnap. The sorcerers who'd sent Rwyan out with Tezdal, myself; even Rwyan, that she should ask this dreadful duty of me.

Rwyan said, "One blow, Daviot my love. Only that."

I groaned, shaking my head.

She said, "Do you love me, you cannot refuse."

I said, "No." I did not know whether I confirmed her words or denied them.

She said, "It were better I die than live mindless. Better I die than betray Dharbek."

I said, "It were better you live whole."

She nodded gravely. How could she be so calm? She said, "Aye, and if I can, I shall. But if that's not to be, I ask this boon of you."

I said, "I'd give my life willing for yours, Rwyan. But this? I doubt I *could* strike that blow."

Urgent, she said, "You must, be it needed. You will, do you love me."

It was hard to meet the implacable gaze of those great green eyes. They bored into me, alight with determination. Under my hands her bones seemed suddenly fragile. I saw the slender column of her neck and knew that I might snap it with a blow; might drive a fist against her face to send fragmented shards of bone into her skull. Keran had taught me well. I felt my breath come short, in gasps that seared my throat. It was as though a hand clamped hard about my heart. Blood pounded in my head, drumming loud in my ears. I thought my tears must flow sanguine. I burned and was chill, together. Had I not loved her so well, I'd have hated her for the imposition of this awful burden. Had I not loved her so strong, I'd have refused her.

I said hoarse and hollow, the words torn slowly out, "Do you truly ask it, then so be it."

She said, "I do truly ask it."

I said, "But not yet. Not now."

She said, "No. Not whilst hope exists. But does the time come."

I said, "Then I'll do it."

She drew my head down, and kissed me gently, and whispered, "My brave, strong Daviot. My love."

Brave? I was a coward then. I asked the God I'd cursed and doubted that this burden be taken from me. That he work one of those miracles the Church promises, to take us both from this place, safe and together. Almost, I asked that I might die first. But not quite, for that should have been betrayal, and Rwyan taught me momentarily to be strong. Had she the strength to ask this of me, should I be so weak as to fail her? Almost. Oh, almost. But not quite. It was as if I drew strength from her; as if that pure purpose that invested her being bled into me. I held her close and kissed her fierce. Both our mouths were wet with tears.

When we at last drew apart, I said, "I cannot vouch for Urt's loyalty, but did you not think the Raethe stood divided as to our fate?" I felt not much conviction. I thought that if factions did exist within the Council, then it was as likely Urt argued simply to thwart

Allanyn as to aid us. That what we'd witnessed was some internecine struggle for power. I found it hard then to believe he was still my good true friend; but still I said, "Be that so, then perhaps he's some plan to save us."

Rwyan said, "To save us? Think you he'd betray his own kind?"

"Perhaps not that," I answered. "But perhaps there's some way he might save us without betraying the Changed."

I wanted to believe. At the same time, I feared such hope—did I grasp it as my heart dictated, I thought I should lose that resolve Rwyan gave me. I feared I should succumb to hope and delay my blow until it was too late and thus betray my love. I dared not hope; I could not say that to Rwyan. So instead I said, "I pray it be so."

When the sun was some time passed overhead and shadows lengthened outside, we were summoned.

Four gifted Changed escorted us through curving corridors lit by magic to a blank door. They halted there, and though none knocked or called out, the door swung open. We went through, descending a flight of wide stairs to the bowels of the hall, where an arch opened onto a large, circular chamber.

This was lit by that same occult radiance, and I stared about, wide-eyed with wonder.

Not least at sight of Tezdal.

I had seen him only in the plain garb of Dharbek or that simple gear Ayl had given us. Neither had I seen a Sky Lord undressed of all his armor. Now this man I named my friend stood before me in the clothing of his Ahn homeland.

His hair was oiled and dressed, drawn back tight from his swarthy face to fall in a long tail behind. He wore a shirt of what I took to be black silk, a crimson sash about his waist, a long dagger sheathed there in a silver scabbard. Sable breeks belled over calf-high boots of soft crimson hide, and over all this he wore a sleeveless crimson robe that descended to his ankles, all sewn with glyphs of rainbow threads that flickered and shone in the light. Lord Tezdal, the Changed had named him, and he looked the lord now, save that his face wore an expression of confusion and some embarrassment as he greeted us.

No less grand were the Sky Lords standing close.

Better than a score of them there were, and all garbed in similar magnificence. I saw that all their shirts and breeks and boots were of the same black and crimson hues, but each robe was a different color, with different symbols. They studied us with cold curiosity. Two fingered daggers, as if they'd as soon draw the blades and slay us as leave us witnesses to the ceremony. When Tezdal greeted us as friends, they favored him with disapproving glances.

I looked for Urt and found Allanyn instead. Her eyes sparkled with malice, and I thought that did the Sky Lords attack, she'd not attempt to stay them; rather aid them. She stood with others of the gifted Changed. Beside the Sky Lords, their homely garb was drab, their brightest colors those circlets they wore in evidence of their talent.

I looked about the chamber and felt an unnamable power. I felt my skin prickled, like tiny nails scraping. My mouth was dry. Overhead the vault curved, only the floor flat, all white. Toward its center stood a ring of slim white columns, natural as stalagmites, save for their uniformity. Each rose an arm's length from its neighbor, and atop each column rested a crystal, larger mates to the stone Rwyan had worn. They pulsed as if invested with arcane life, shimmering a spectrum of pale colors. I thought of those jellyfish that drift shining in the ocean and poison whatever comes within the aegis of their filaments. At the center of that circle stood a construction like a bier, draped with a golden cloth. I had never before set foot in any place of magic, but I should have known this for such a location, even had Rwyan not clutched my hand so that I felt her tremble, or seen the crystals.

Our escort moved to join their fellows, and from the group stepped Geran.

"We'd restore Lord Tezdal his memory," he said. "Do you witness this and know our power. As you value your lives and his, do not interfere."

I nodded. Rwyan said, "Are these all your crystals?"

"No." Geran made a small negative movement of his head. "This valley is rich with them."

Rwyan nodded as if a belief were confirmed and murmured, "I thought as much."

"So do you stand here," Geran said. "Silent."

He turned away, devoid of any doubt but that we should obey. I caught Tezdal's eye. I thought him none too happy. I smiled encouragement. No matter the situation, I counted him a friend; and thought it a dreadful thing to have no memory.

The Sky Lords grouped close around him, murmuring in their own language. They brought him to the bier, and he climbed onto the platform, stretching out with arms folded across his chest. They stood a moment there, intoning what I thought must be a prayer, then went to join the Changed sorcerers.

All found a place about the columns, all reaching out so that their fingers rested lightly on the crystals. The stones shone brighter with that contact. I felt Rwyan's grip tighten and glanced sidelong at her face. Her expression frightened me, for it was one of longing and loathing combined. She shuddered, her lips drawn taut, as if she fought some private impulse. Her eyes shone, intent on the pulsing jewels. I loosed her hand and put my arm around her shoulders, pulling her close. She was heated, as if a fever gripped her. I remembered all she'd told me of the crystals and thought they called her. I moved behind her, both my arms around her waist: I thought I might need hold her back. She moaned softly and clutched my wrists, pressing against me. In other circumstances I'd have found that contact erotic; here I felt only awe, and more than a little fear.

No word was spoken, but I sensed communion. Pale light, almost lost under the radiance of the walls, began to shroud each figure. It came from the crystals, flickering tentative at first over hands, climbing arms, flowing swifter, liquid over bodies until all were encompassed in that faint nimbus. Some strained rigid, others stood limp. Some heads flung back as if in ecstasy, others drooped, slack-jawed. I saw Allanyn's eyes close, her wide mouth stretched in a smile. A thin trickle of saliva ran down her pointed chin. The light coming from the walls dimmed as the nimbus gained strength. I thought the crystals drew power from the sorcerers in equal measure to their call on the stones. A radiance that was all colors and none bathed the figures and flowed inward, over Tezdal. I saw him shudder, his body tensing. His eyes sprang wide, then closed. He made a sound that was part sigh and part cry, loud in the chamber's silence. He relaxed, and the glow grew stronger still, until it hid him from my sight, shimmering like pale flame.

How long we stood watching this ceremony, I've no idea. Time had no meaning in this vault. It was as though the crystals imposed their own chronology, dismissing those measurements that we breathing, blooded creatures set to mark their own pace. I know only that the glow dimmed, then was gone, swift as snuffed candle's flame, and it was as if I woke.

I felt Rwyan let go her hold on my wrists and lean against me with a sigh, as if she were exhausted. I exhaled a gusty breath, staring at the bier.

Tezdal lay still, only the slow rise and fall of his chest to announce he lived. Around him hung faint light. I was reminded of that shimmering that surrounded the Sky Lords' vessels. I saw that from each crystal there extended a pale tendril of radiance. I looked to the sorcerers.

They came slowly from their task, the Kho'rabi wizards swifter than the Changed. Allanyn was the slowest. She seemed reluctant to leave go the stones she touched. When she did, it was with a shudder, her eyes glazed, focusing only gradually. She licked her lips and wiped a sleeve across the spittle decking her chin. When she saw me watching, her lips pursed a moment. I thought she'd speak, but all she did was smile and turn away. Still there was something triumphant in her look.

Geran came toward us. His long equine face was grave, his eyes somewhat dulled. I thought him wearied.

He said, "So it's done. Or nearly."

Rwyan straightened in my arms. "I see only Tezdal, sleeping," she said.

The spokesman smiled. "Lady, you know great magic was practiced this day."

She gave him back, "Magic, surely. Great magic? Of that I see no evidence."

The horse-faced Changed shrugged. "What we've done here shall be clear enough in time. Lord Tezdal shall sleep awhile, but when he wakes, he'll have back his memory."

"And know himself a Sky Lord." Allanyn approached us from the side, all her spiteful composure regained. "Know you for his enemies."

Rwyan faced her with a calm visage. "Shall he have all his memories?" she asked. "All those since we found him?"

Her voice was mild, inquiring. It confused Allanyn, who frowned and made an impatient gesture.

Geran answered, "All, lady. Both those he lost and those he gained in your company."

Rwyan nodded solemnly. "Then he'll remember his sworn vow," she said. "He'll remember Daviot and I are his friends."

Allanyn liked that not at all.

We were taken from the vault to another chamber. Not that sparse cell we'd occupied before, but a more spacious room, clearly intended for overnight occupation. It was furnished as would be the chamber of a good tavern: comfortably, with all necessary requisites; but of that same blank white stone, and without decoration. There was a window—again of sealed glass—and through it I saw night had fallen. There was a table set with food and wine. We found our appetites were returned.

Rwyan filled a goblet and drank thirstily before she spoke. I was somewhat dazed by what I'd witnessed, and now that we were alone again, I felt trepidation return.

I said, "Tezdal shall have back his memory?"

Rwyan nodded, her face thoughtful. It seemed she took that restoration for a sure conclusion. She said, "They've far greater power than I suspected."

"They convince you?" I asked.

And then I must drink wine to assuage the dread her answer should give. My hand trembled as I raised the cup.

She said, "They do."

I set the goblet down. The wine soured in my belly. I steeled myself, meeting her calm gaze. I must ask a question now for which I'd no taste.

I suppose my expression was clear enough, for Rwyan gave me a wan smile and shook her head and said, "Not yet, my love. We've time yet."

I sighed and filled my cup again. A few drops fell to the table. They shone in the sourceless light.

Rwyan said, "I'd see Tezdal wake and know the fuller measure of their abilities. And I think they'll not force me ere then."

I nodded. "How long shall that be?"

She shrugged. "I've no idea. Such magic is unknown in Dharbek."

Had I been sure of the God's existence, I'd have sung his praises then, for that small gift of time. No less, I'd have prayed that man I deemed my friend sleep on: I'd have betrayed him for Rwyan's sake.

I said, "Think you he'll truly honor his vow, are all his memories restored?"

"I believe he'll try," she answered. "But does he wake a Sky Lord reborn, he must surely find his loyalties divided."

"And you," I asked, "will not reconsider?"

The look she gave me was answer enough, words redundant. I felt ashamed: her resolve was so much stronger than my own.

She smiled at me then. "Have faith, Daviot. Until that moment comes, we've hope. I'll not believe we've come so far only to die here."

I forced a smile in answer. I saw no reason why Trebizar should not be that place the Pale Friend came for us. Our fate seemed to me only delayed, no more. I thought that did the magic of the Changed work its miracle on Tezdal or not, still that demand should be made of Rwyan; and she refuse. And then I must be bound by my promise, else I betray her and betray our love; and that I would not do. So I foresaw only that we had a little time; that too soon must come the moment I should strike her, and then—doubtless—be myself slain. That mattered nothing: without Rwyan, nothing mattered.

I heard her say, "Put off that glum face, my love. We've time yet, and hope."

I stretched out my lips in facsimile of a smile and did my best to assume a cheerful manner that would match hers. "Yes," I said, "and they feed us well."

"And give us a most pleasant chamber, no?"

Her eyes moved sideways, in the direction of the bed.

I felt an urgency then: we had, I thought, so little time left us. I rose and went around the table. Rwyan rose to meet me, and we embraced, our kisses ardent. Of a sudden we were on the bed and not much slower naked. I was entirely unaware of the occult light dimming, for the moon's glow took its place, silvery on her skin.

When the sun was risen a hand's span above the walls, our door was opened and Urt stood there.

He said, "Day's greetings, Daviot; Rwyan."

She answered him in kind, calmly, as if his appearance afforded her no surprise. I hesitated, no longer sure whether I looked on a friend or an enemy. He wore a shirt of homespun linen that was not quite white, and plain brown brecks, soft boots: nothing much different to what I'd known him to wear about the College. There was nothing to mark his elevation; in Durbrecht he'd have passed as a servant Changed, unremarkable. I studied his face—clear now—and saw lines etched there that had not been present in Dharbek. In his eyes I saw—I was not sure—a graving, perhaps, of age. He seemed somehow older in more than mere years, weighted by knowledge and experience. I wondered what that had been, and what it was.

I said, "Day's greetings, Urt," cautiously.

He smiled—regretfully, I thought. "Doubtless you grow bored of confinement. Would you walk awhile in the garden?"

I asked, "Tezdal wakes?"

"Not yet." He shook his head. "Perhaps the gifted must work their magic again. But meanwhile . . ." He gestured at the corridor beyond the open door.

Rwyan said, "It should be pleasant. Eh, Daviot?"

I shrugged and nodded; and we followed him out.

He was alone, which surprised me, and as we paced the corridor, I asked, "Are you not afraid, Urt? To be alone with us?"

He gave a little chuckle and met my stare. "Would you harm me then, Daviot?"

I said, "I'd slay any man who harms Rwyan." And thought of Allanyn, and so added, "Or any woman."

He said softly, "I offer you no harm."

He spoke companionably enough, but I sensed a hesitancy. I sought to read his face, the language of his body, but without success. I wondered if he hid his feelings. My own were utterly confused. Was he still my friend? Or was he now committed to the strategies of the Changed? Did I walk with an ally or an enemy? I could not know, only follow.

We came to a door of plain wood, latched, and Urt thrust it open, waving us through.

Now we stood beneath the portico, the garden spread before us. The air was pleasantly fresh, neither possessed of summer's heat nor cooled by autumn's advancement, but poised on that enlivening axis between the two. I thought it should have been turned more decisive between the seasons, and then that this valley was, indeed, a place governed by magic. The sky was blue, decorated here and there with drifting billows of pristine cumulus. The absence of birds was strange. Urt beckoned us as he set out along a path that wound amongst hornbeams and hazels. In moments, the Council building was lost to sight. It was as if we strolled some wildwood.

In a while Urt halted by a pond surrounded by drooping willows and green alders, fed by a little stream. Without preamble he said, "I am commanded to speak with you; to convince you."

Rwyan said, "You waste your breath, Urt."

He said, "Lady, I know that; but still I'd speak with you. Shall you hear me out?"

His tone was urgent, and in his eyes I saw such a look as brought back memories of Durbrecht. I motioned that he continue; Rwyan ducked her head in agreement.

He said, "It cannot be long before Lord Tezdal wakes and you are forced to a decision."

Rwyan said, "That's already made."

"Only hear me," he asked. "Do you refuse the demands of the Raethe, you know the outcome."

Rwyan said, "That was made plain enough."

Urt hesitated a moment, staring at the pond. I saw the pebbled bottom, trout drifting there, stationary in the current as their pale eyes scanned the surface, awaiting insects. I envied them their simple lives. Urt faced us again, and in his eyes I saw only sincerity and concern. I wondered if he dissembled.

He said, "I told them as much, but I discharge my duty—I was ordered to speak with you of this, and that I've done. I can return with clear conscience."

I said, "Then have we aught else to say?"

I put it curt and got back a look of rueful reproach. "Daviot, you've reason enough to doubt me, but I am your friend yet. I'd find some way around this that shall leave you both unharmed."

I asked him bluntly, "Why?"

And he gave me back, "For Durbrecht. Because I've no liking for Allanyn's ways; no lust for war."

I began to speak—to scorn him, to accuse him of treachery—but Rwyan touched my arm and bade me hold silent. I obeyed.

He smiled his thanks. "Had Allanyn her way, you, Rwyan, should be already emptied by the crystals; and you, Daviot, slain."

Rwyan said, "But you delayed that course."

I asked again, "Why?"

"Aye." Urt nodded briefly to Rwyan. To me he said, "For sake of our friendship; because I loathe her methods."

I frowned and would have spoken, but Urt raised a hand to silence me. "We've not much time and much to say." He smiled a crooked grin. "Nor am I altogether trusted—Allanyn may well send watchers ere long. So do you hear me out and after judge whether we be still friends, or no?"

Rwyan touched my hand, urging I agree: I nodded.

"There are two factions within the Raethe," Urt continued, "of which Allanyn's is the greater. Born here she was, and she's filled with the power the crystals give. No Changed sorcerer was ever stronger than Allanyn, and too many fear her. I suspect she's crazed, but still she's the ear of the many who would take her path."

"Which is?" asked Rwyan.

Urt said simply, "War. Allanyn and her followers would ally with the Sky Lords to destroy you Dhar Truemen, or make of you what you made of us—servants."

"And the Sky Lords?" I asked. "Are they not Truemen? Shall they be only your allies and nothing more?"

He answered me, "The Sky Lords would take back Kellambek for their own, no more. They've dreamed of that for centuries—a holy quest to regain their homeland—and the agreement made is that they shall have Kellambek, we Changed the rest."

"And you?" I asked him.

"I'd see my fellow Changed shed their bonds," he said. "I'd see them equal to you Truemen. Was that not once your thought, Daviot?"

I looked into his dark eyes and could only nod. "But not through bloodshed," I said. "Not by war."

He said, "Perhaps there's no other way. I think there are not many Truemen think as you do."

I said slowly, "No. But even so . . . war? Do the Sky Lords mount the Great Coming, the Changed rise—Dharbek should run red, and Changed and Truemen bleed and die alike."

Soberly, he said, "Yes. And so I'd find some other way—if there is another way. I and a few like me, who've little love for Allanyn's path. Does Allanyn prevail, I think the world shall not be better; only turned on its head. Where Changed now are, there'd be Truemen. And no doubt they'd plot to overturn it all again. I think that way should be only bloodshed, unending."

I said, "War should be a great undertaking, Urt. Could the Changed hope to win?"

"Allanyn believes we should," he said, "and she's command of our army. Does she have her way, the Sky Lords will attack across both the Fend and the Slammerkin. Do they overcome the Border Cities, then we Changed shall march south whilst our kin in Dharbek rise. The slaughter would be terrible, I think."

I asked, "How should your kin know when to rise?"

He smiled. "You know we communicate?" And when I nodded: "There's more to it than you suspect, Daviot; and you're likely the only Trueman to have understood so much. I've not the time to explain it all now, but . . ."

He paused, hesitant again, looking a moment at the pool where the trout rose hungry. Then: "Do you trust me?"

It was a blunt question, demanding a blunt answer. I said, "I don't know, Urt."

Hurt showed in his eyes, but then he shrugged. "Why should you? Perhaps, though, I might convince you. I think I cannot now, with words, but perhaps with another way."

I frowned, waiting. I scarce dared allow the little spark of hope his words kindled.

He said, "Tonight I'll come to you with all the proof I can give; I can do no more."

This puzzled me. "And am I convinced?" I asked. "What then?"

He laughed: a short, sad bark. "I know not. I can see no way to thwart Allanyn, to avoid war. Perhaps when you've all the knowledge I can give you . . . perhaps you'll see some way."

Rwyan said, "You speak for peace, Urt?"

He thought awhile, then ducked his head and said, "I'd free my kind, but not at cost of their lives. Neither do I believe all Truemen are evil. This world of ours must change, but I cannot believe Allanyn's is the way. Even though I see no other."

Rwyan surprised me then, for she asked what seemed to me a

very strange question in these circumstances. She said, "Urt, do you dream?"

He looked no less startled than I. His eyes narrowed, framing a question of his own even as he nodded.

Rwyan said, "Of what?"

He paused before he answered, as if the recollection were not altogether pleasant. I thought he braced himself before he said, "Of dragons, sometimes; of riding the skies with those creatures. You and Daviot with me. I feel, sometimes, they call me. I see their eyes, as if they sat in judgment."

Rwyan laughed and clapped her hands. "The pattern! By the God, it's the same dream."

Urt stared at her as if he thought her mad. Some lesser version of that doubt crossed my mind, too—I'd looked only to comfort her with those musings, not taken them so serious myself. But now . . . now I began to wonder. Slowly, I said, "We share that dream. I've known it, and Rwyan; Tezdal, too."

"But there are no dragons left," he said. It sounded somehow like a catechism. "I remember in Durbrecht, Daviot, that you spoke of them."

"And was laughed at," I said. "But even so, those dreams return, time and time again. And even when we were parted, Rwyan shared them; then Tezdal. Now you."

His expression was blank, empty of understanding. "Do you explain?"

I said, "I cannot."

Rwyan said, "I believe there's a pattern, Urt. Some weaving of destiny joins us, perhaps sends us these dreams."

"To what end?" he asked. Warily, I thought.

And now Rwyan must frown and shrug and tell him, "That I cannot say. But I feel it a good omen."

Urt nodded without much conviction. Then his head turned, cocked in attitude of attention. Urgently, he said, "Are you questioned, say only that I sought to persuade you; naught of anything else."

His hearing was far more acute than mine: he caught the approaching footsteps long before Allanyn stalked into the clearing. She wore a gown of emerald green that emphasized the feline grace of her movements. Her hair was gathered up, the golden band bright on her brow. Her eyes shone spiteful.

"So," she demanded, "are they persuaded?"

"I put our case," said Urt. "They consider it."

Allanyn studied him a moment. Then, lazy as a cat toying with a trapped mouse, turned to us. For long moments she only eyed us, her lips parting to expose sharp white teeth.

"They *consider* it?" Her tone was mocking, oily with malice. I was uncertain whether her spite was meant for us or Urt. "They've not so much time they should dwell overlong on a matter foregone. Before this winter's out our Sky Lord allies shall have all their ships and all their warriors in place. By summer's advent—by Ennas Day—we'll be ready—our battle shall commence then, Urt. In Dharbek, our people will rise; and from across the seas and over the Slammerkin will come the skyboats. Ere then, I'll have this mage's knowledge, willing or not."

Her voice rose triumphant as the sentence ended; I felt Rwyan's hand find mine. Brave, she said, "Not willing, Allanyn."

The feline Changed smiled at that, horridly. Her eyes returned to Urt. "Perhaps the mage should be better persuaded by other methods. Perhaps we should put her lover to torture and let his pain deliver our arguments."

Her tone was casual: I felt a chill. I was prepared to die, but I'd not thought to be tortured. I saw Urt frown his distaste and shake his head. In a voice so calm it was an insult, he said, "Would you soil us with such methods, Allanyn?"

Her ocher eyes blazed. She stiffened. She said, "I'd have those answers we require; and soon."

"The Raethe has agreed," he gave her back, "that they've until the Lord Tezdal wakes. Do you now assume to command us all?"

I thought she might fling her magic at him for that. I could not doubt but that these two *were* enemies. I watched as Allanyn spun round, striding back the way she'd come. Over her shoulder she hurled a parting sally heavy with threat: "Not yet, Urt. But when that day comes, beware."

29

By Ennas Day! By summer's beginning: it seemed to me time ran faster now. Those days on board the *Sprite*, the slow trek to Trebizar—they seemed an idyll, a leisurely journey for which we now paid the price. I thought it could not be long before Tezdal woke and I must strike that blow I dreaded. And after —Allanyn's threat vivid in my memory—I thought I should likely face not clean death but slow torture. I saw no escape. How could there be? Even was Urt still truly a friend, still there seemed to me nothing he could do. He had admitted he saw no answers; neither had he suggested any means by which we might evade Allanyn's wrath. Indeed, likely the wrath of all the Changed did we attempt escape. Which seemed to me impossible. . . .

My thoughts ran around and around in circles. . . .

The Sky Lords prepared the Great Coming. . . . The Changed prepared for war. . . . The fylie of the Kho'rabi should soon descend on Dharbek from both east and north. . . . The wild Changed go bellicose across the Slammerkin. . . . The Changed of Dharbek rise like some invisible army. . . . The land would run red.

I'd not be there to witness that carnage; nor Rwyan. I wondered if time's clock might have run different had I spoken of what I'd seen that night when I saw Changed and Sky Lords together. I'd still no doubt but that pogrom should have ensued, but might that not have been the lesser abomination? Could my warning have changed history's course? Had I delivered my country all unsuspecting to destruction?

I slumped morose in a chair as twilight fell over the gardens, my head all aspin with awful doubt. Rwyan spoke to me of hope, but I could find little place for such optimism. She spoke of the pattern, but I could see only the snapping of its threads here in Trebizar. I thought death should be welcome; sooner the Pale Friend's embrace than witness of what must surely come.

I ate a few mouthfuls of the meal they brought us, my appetite quite gone, and would not be cheered by Rwyan's optimism. I could not be: I saw no space for hope. I drank wine that had no taste. I wanted only to hold her and for a little while push back the bloody darkness that loomed about me.

She held me. She kissed me and stroked my hair. But she would do no more: she told me we must wait, that Urt would make good his promise of revelation. I thought that revelation should be poor comfort.

Then, when the sky was all velvet blue and filled with stars, Urt came. For an instant I dared hope he had some plan—that he'd somehow spirit us away. I was unsure I'd even want that—not knowing we left behind the destruction of my homeland.

I need not have tormented myself so: he had no plan, only a crystal.

He came in furtive, motioning we be silent as he eased the door ajar and went to the table. From a pouch on his belt he extracted a glowing stone. It was larger than that obscene jewel Rwyan had worn; not so large as those in the crypt where Tezdal—so he advised us— slept still. He set it down and unthinking wiped his hands against his tunic, as if the crystal left behind some physical taint.

"Lady." He addressed himself to Rwyan. "I think you'll know the use of this. Do you show Daviot, and before morning I must have it back." He shrugged, his eyes mournful. "I can do no more. Perhaps you'll find an answer in the stone."

I said, "Shall it free us? Shall it grant Rwyan power?"

He said, "I think not that, but perhaps understanding. I've not the talent for it, but the gifted use these stones—they send them south to Dharbek, to the Changed there; to spread the word."

He hesitated an instant, as if some dire secret were revealed. I was reminded of that clandestine meeting I had witnessed, when Changed and Sky Lords came furtive together. I said, "In Kellambek I saw your people and Kho'rabi meet by night. Was this the reason?"

Urt nodded. "Likely. Those little boats the Sky Lords command defy Dhar magic to bring the stones south."

I grunted as that mystery was resolved and gestured that he continue.

He said, "Perhaps do you commune with this, we three can find some way . . ." He shook his head helplessly. Then smiled without sign of humor. "You asked for proof of my friendship, Daviot? Well, is it known I give you this, I'm dead. This secret is close-guarded, and should the gifted learn what I do, my life is forfeit. Allanyn shaped this crystal herself, and she'd not hesitate to take my life."

He spoke with absolute conviction, and as I watched his face, I felt my doubts dissolve. It seemed a weight lifted off me.

He was once again the old friend of my youth, the one who had first shown me that secret world of the Changed. The true friend who'd carried my messages to Rwyan and hers back to me. Without him, I'd not have known my love: I thought then that it was he had first set my feet on the road that brought me here. I suppose I might have hated him for that, but all I felt was love, our comradeship rekindled. I went to him, taking his hand as I'd done so long ago in Durbrecht.

His smile grew warm at that, and he answered my grip firm. There was no need of words, for which I was thankful—I had none at that moment. I felt only shame that I'd doubted him and heartfelt regret that this world we Truemen made should force enmity on us. Urt was not my enemy, nor I his: those roles were chosen for us by the past. I felt sad that our tomorrows looked to be soon ended.

He said, "I dare not delay. Allanyn already seeks to brand me traitor. 'Trueman's Friend,' she names me."

Still gripping his hand, I said, "Is that a crime, Urt?"

"To some; to Allanyn surely." His grin brought me memories of his usual good humor. "Was it not ever the way—that Changed and Trueman live apart? Our situations reverse, eh, Daviot?"

"I think," I said, "that had I a choice, I'd sooner face Ardyon than Allanyn."

His grin faded at that, his expression become again grave. He said, "Aye. Ardyon seems as nothing beside her."

As we spoke, Rwyan studied the crystal. She did not touch it; she seemed to me wary of the stone, as someone loath to handle a sword might regard the blade they know they must soon wield. Her face was troubled as she turned toward us. "Does this give us answers, Urt, shall you be with us in their deliverance?"

He met her sightless gaze unflinching and said, "I'll not betray my people, Rwyan; but can you find a way to avoid this war and free my kind—then, aye. What aid is mine to give, you shall have."

"Good."

Rwyan returned to her observation of the crystal. I looked from her to Urt. There was much we had to say to one another; there was not the time to say it. He smiled grimly and said, "I cannot linger, lest I bring suspicion on you. Do you employ that thing, and I'll come back ere dawn."

I said, "Shall it be safe till then?"

"All well," he answered. "Save the Lord Tezdal wakes. Does that happen, we're lost."

I nodded, and he clasped my hand again. "Daviot, for good or ill, I *am* your friend," and then he was gone.

I turned to Rwyan. "What is it?" I asked her.

She said, "Am I right, then such magic as should delight you, Daviot. Am I right, this stone holds memories."

I gaped, going to her side. The crystal lay on the table. It was the size of my clenched fist, a pale blue that pulsed faintly, like water struck by sunlight. Sparks of pink fluttered through it. It was a pretty thing. It seemed quite harmless, save for the strange sense of slumbering power emanating from it. Or did it slumber? I experienced a strange sensation as I came near. I thought the crystal . . . eager . . . as if it anticipated contact. I felt suddenly nervous. I felt . . . I can only describe it as a call, in the channels of my blood, in the roots of my brain. Perhaps it was only that I knew the stone for an occult thing; perhaps otherwise I should have thought it only some chunk of quartz, grist to the lapidaries and no more.

I asked, "Can you use it? I thought your talent denied you here."

Rwyan licked her lips and said, "Be this so powerful as I suspect, I think it shall commune with us both. I believe it asks to be unlocked, and it shall overcome those gramaryes that limit me."

I saw that she felt scant enthusiasm for that contact. "Do you fear a trick?"

Her smile was fleeting. She said, "Such thought had crossed my mind."

I said, "Then leave it be."

She said, "Do you not trust Urt, then?"

I shook my head. "I trust him. But he's no sorcerer. Might Allanyn have let him bring this?"

She closed her eyes a moment, then forced a smile. "Let us find out," she said. "Do you sit and take my hand and not let go."

I took a chair beside her. Her hand was warm in mine, our fingers interlaced. I felt wary as she reached toward the stone. I saw it pulse brighter as her free hand drew near. The stone flickered more red than blue. It seemed to me hungry. Rwyan set her fingertips on the crystal, and it became all brightness, like spilling blood. Her hand was lost in the glow. I heard her murmur, the words too low I might discern them. I felt the magic engulf me, flowing out from the stone in a torrent of occult power, Rwyan the conduit.

I cannot properly describe that sensation: as it is with dreams, so ordinary words, mundane concepts, are insufficient to the task. As in dreams, I saw clearly, I was aware, and yet all was governed by an indefinable logic, defying rational analysis. Knowledge was instantaneous, a flood that washed over me and into me. There was no order, save what my mind must impose that I be able to digest it all. Understanding was imparted wordlessly, instinctive as the child's first inhalation.

I must use inadequate words to describe what entered me.

I saw the Changed left behind in Ur-Dharbek by we Truemen, that they be living safeguard against the dragons. I felt their fear, their anger: I *was* Changed. I was aware of their survival, of time's slow passing like impossibly long summer, nurturing resentment of their unfair fate as they hid from the predators. Too many died.

Images, then, of crystals, of discovery, of burgeoning awareness, the sense of wonder as the talent was discovered, the Changed found the gift of magic. Never so many of them they might overcome the Border Cities I saw built, guardians of the Slammerkin, an occult wall to Dharbek's north, but enough they could defend themselves, conceal themselves from the dragons and then drive off the sky hunters.

Time then, slowly passing, the world turning, the dragons no longer a threat save to children, become creatures of legend. A bountiful time ensuing, peaceful, the gifted coming to better understanding of the magic they used unthinking, the slowly burgeoning realization it stemmed from the crystals.

A hunt: to gather the occult stones and bring them where they should be hidden from Truemen, piled to build the magic of the Changed—to this valley of Trebizar. The first of the gifted formed the Raethe, and Trebizar became the heart of Ur-Dharbek, power spreading. . . . I saw the wastes mastered by Changed magic, made a pleasant land, a secret, contented land, save for . . . the memories these crystals held, always reminding those gifted with the talent of what had been, of Truemen's treachery. And those memories nowhere stronger than in Trebizar, amongst the gifted of the Raethe.

I choked on bile as waves of bitter resentment, of raw hatred beat over me. I knew then that Allanyn had held this stone and was mad, consumed by crystalline dreams of revenge. I knew that all those Changed possessed of the strongest talent were crazed. I felt an awful guilt for what my kind had made of these folk.

I saw, too, that their magic took a different path to that of the Dhar sorcerers. These Changed lived closer to the earth than we, and their magic—once the dragons were gone—was not needed in defense of their land, but employed to render the wastes habitable. I saw that most were peaceable, and in that found some small hope.

And then despair as events unfolded in my mind, and I saw the first Kho'rabi skyboat, driven north by Sentinels and Border Cities, come drifting down to land, to make alliance with the wild Changed.

To those most gifted—those bent fiercest on revenge—it was a boon unimaginable.

As the paths of Changed and Truemen's magic had diverged, so had that commanded by the Sky Lords. Their will was bent on conquering the Worldwinds, on binding the elementals to their cause, that they mount the Great Coming and take back their ancestral land. In the wild Changed they found allies both physical and magical: they joined in union.

Changed had always come north over the Slammerkin—the rebels and the discontented, the dreamers. But only north: now the Sky Lords showed how that barrier might be crossed southward.

Their great invasion craft were whales in the ocean of the sky; their little skyboats were barracuda, swift. They evaded the magic of the Dhar. They carried wild Changed south to speak with the oppressed and kindle the dream that grew amongst their northern kin. To we Truemen these agitators were faceless as their servile southern brethren—they came and went unnoticed. Thus was the flame of discontent fanned, the torch of rebellion lit; thus would the Changed of Dharbek know when the time was come.

I saw the whole design now, or the larger part of it. I saw how Ayl had his knowledge of this land. I saw those little pieces of the puzzle I'd recognized as I wandered fall into place. It was a terrifying alliance. I knew it must shatter Dharbek. I saw how blind we Dhar had been, and were still.

It began already, for the crystal told me it was Allanyn's agent had poisoned Gahan, and that Jareth's ascendancy delivered the land to disunion. I saw that soon the Kho'rabi would mass in Ur-Dharbek, and that from Ahn-feshang would come such an invasion fleet as must surely overwhelm the Sentinels, whilst from the north would come that other, Sky Lords and Changed together.

From the crystal came a sense of immediacy, of anticipation. A sense of terrible hunger.

I was barely aware when the flood of images, of impressions, ceased. I knew that my head ached and my mouth was dry, that my eyes felt scorched as if I'd wept. I felt a touch upon my shoulder and found a cup of wine pressed to my lips. I drank and looked into Rwyan's eyes. Her face was pale and grave.

I said, "Can there be any doubt?"

She shook her head. "But perhaps some hope," she said.

I frowned and drank again. I was not used to this communication with the occult. I said, "What did you see that gives you hope?"

She filled a cup and drank herself before replying. I saw that the crystal was no longer bright, but only faintly pulsing now. Beyond the window night reigned. The knowledge of centuries had flooded through my aching head, but the angle of the moon told me it was scarce midnight.

Rwyan said, "The talent brings its own curse here. Allanyn and her ilk are quite mad."

I said, "Old news, Rwyan; poor news."

I did not mean to speak so sharp. I felt fear and despair in equal measure: now more than ever I could see no hope.

Rwyan ignored my poor humor. She set down her cup and said, "But not all are crazed. Neither all the Changed, nor all the Raethe. Urt's sane enough, for one."

I said, "And is but one; and helpless against Allanyn."

She said, "Save he finds allies."

"Allies?" I shook my head. "Allanyn's strong in the Raethe— Urt's own warning, no? And what I saw suggested only bloody war."

She said, "Those folk we encountered along the road here—were they bellicose?"

I shook my head again and wished I'd not.

Rwyan said, "I saw much of a peaceful land. The fiercest hatred resides in the gifted, I think."

I said, "The gifted hold the power, it seemed to me."

She nodded slowly and gave me back, "True, but I suspect Allanyn and her faction lead these folk into war; and hide much from them. Did you not recognize the undercurrents?"

I began to shake my head and thought better of it. Instead I only said no.

She said, "Forgive me: I assume talent in you," and vented a short bitter laugh.

I thought at first she laughed at me, but then she sighed and pushed back her hair and made a small conciliatory gesture. I saw a great sadness in her eyes, and had the crystal not still stood between us, I'd have reached out to take her hand. I felt too weary to rise and go around the table. Instead, I mustered a smile and asked that she explain.

She closed her eyes a moment, as if gathering her thoughts. "I think I understand why these crystals are close-guarded. Were they used often, they'd show all their secrets, even to those without the talent. As it is—in the God's name, Allanyn and her followers deserve to die!"

I had never heard such anger in her voice, nor seen it on her face. She had an enviable capacity for forgiveness, but now I saw and heard only implacable rage. She seemed to me like one of those messengers the priests claim the God sometimes sends, avenging. I frowned and asked, "What is it?"

She gestured at the crystal. "These stones record memories," she said. "Memories, and more. By the God, aye! They record so much more; but that hidden, to be found only by those with the talent."

She shook her head and filled her cup. I watched her drink, thinking I'd not seen her so disturbed. I waited agog.

She swallowed wine and said, "Are they used frequently, they absorb the emotions of the user. Desires, lusts, dreams—all are recorded. But deep, like the lees in a wine cup, lost to most under the weight of that other knowledge they hold.

"Listen—those messengers the Sky Lords have carried south, they give the Changed of Dharbek a dream, give them a share of the hate. They promise riches, a domain of the Changed, but say nothing of the bloodshed that dream must entail. Or what shall follow."

Her eyes were fierce on mine, as if she'd impress comprehension with her gaze alone. I shrugged, not yet understanding.

She said, "The message those crystals bear is shaped by the gifted, by Allanyn and her kind. And she hides too much."

I said, "Urt told us the stones are a close-guarded secret."

She nodded. "And save a sorcerer plumbs their depths, they tell only so much as Allanyn would reveal."

I asked, "What does she hide?"

Rwyan said, "Allanyn seeks not to free her kind but to rule them. Already this Raethe is less than that honest government Ayl spoke of, but rather controlled by Allanyn and those gifted who choose her path. Or are seduced by these crystals."

"How can that be?" I said. "Surely the crystals are only tools of you sorcerers?"

"No." She shook her head, the movement both weary and angry. "I believe the crystals have a life of their own. Perhaps they think; perhaps they've absorbed so much fear, so much resentment, down all those long ages the Changed suffered that they give it back." She laughed again; I did not like the sound. "I curse Allanyn, but perhaps I should curse the crystals. Perhaps, unwitting, she's only their creature."

She paused, drawing deep breaths. It was as though the enormity of what she'd learned required an effort to tell. I filled her cup and mine, and waited. I felt a great dread.

"Allanyn seeks war," she said. "She'd see all Truemen ground down; slain or enslaved. But then, that victory won, she'd make herself ruler of all the Changed. She'd see only the gifted in the Raethe — save it should be no longer the Raethe but her court. She'd be mistress of all Dharbek, and to gain that end she'd sacrifice her people."

In my mouth wine became bitter. I swallowed, and it seemed to burn my throat. I saw no hope at all in this, only rank despair. I could envisage no means to thwart Allanyn or escape her clutches. I thought that did she learn we'd communed with the crystal, we were surely dead. And Urt, for he must be discovered. I wondered suddenly if he knew these secrets or only suspected. I said, "We must warn Urt. Is he convinced of Allanyn's treachery, perhaps he may rally others."

"Aye," Rwyan gave me back, "and still there's Tezdal. And the pattern."

The pattern! Almost I wished I'd not spun out that fancy, for it now seemed to me no more than that—a Storyman's fable, one of those tales we spin for the entertainment of children. Like Jarrold's Magic Pig or Ealyn's Wondrous Boat. I thought perhaps Rwyan clung to belief as prop to waning hope, the need to believe greater than the reality. The pattern! I could weave a pattern at will, from my imagination. Now I looked at reality, and all I could see were threads unraveling, the strands of our lives dwindling like yarn set in flame.

I rose on legs that shuddered and protested the movement, and went to the washstand, splashing cool water over my burning face.

Rwyan sat still, seeming lost in thought. When I returned to the table she said, "Could I but show those not yet gone over to Allanyn's cause what she intends."

I said, "You'll not have that chance. They'd not trust a Dhar mage."

She said, "No," sadly, and sighed. "Oh, Daviot, our world's gone far astray, no?"

I ducked my head, wincing at the pain. "Better had we never made the Changed. Better had we never enslaved the Ahn."

Rwyan said, "But we did, and now we pay the price. Save we can find some answer. But by the God, I'll not concede Allanyn the victory, nor see this war begun, can I do aught to halt it."

"Nor I," I declared, though I could scarce see what we two prisoners might do. "When Urt comes, we'll tell him."

She said, "And Tezdal. I'd have him know, too."

"Yes." I nodded agreement, ignoring pain. "But I think he'll not dissuade his fellow Sky Lords from their course. Even is he persuaded himself."

We fell silent then, wrapped in depressing musing. I looked to the window and saw the moon was gone past its zenith. Stars speckled the sky, and dawn was hours distant. I wondered when Urt would come. Then if he would: I thought that did Allanyn suspect him—of treachery, she'd name it—it should be an exquisite torture to allow this glimpse of her intent. To show us and then "discover" the crystal; thus to condemn us and Urt together. I yawned. I felt mightily weary, and my head still ached. Across the table Rwyan's face looked drawn, shadows beneath her eyes like dark half moons. She stared moodily at the crystal. I looked at the thing, wondering if I truly felt a sense of triumph emanating from its pale blue depths, or if that was merely a fancy of my troubled mind.

My eyes felt weighted with despair, and I closed them. That eased the pain in my skull a little, and I set my elbows on the table, resting my face on my hands. A gray fog seemed to cloud my vision, and for an instant I thought I dreamed again of that oak grove beyond Cambar, but I saw only the gray void. I did not know I slept.

Nor, till I woke, that I dreamed. I'd not dreamed since first we came within the aegis of Trebizar's magic.

What I dreamed was this:

I sat slumped at the table. Rwyan remained seated across its width, the crystal still between us like some barrier to hope, but the glow coming from the walls dimmed, the radiance slowly fading to black. It was the black of deepest starless night, or the depths of the sea. I drifted there: it was strangely comforting, and I thought perhaps

I'd remain forever, give up my body and all its cares, and only wander this lightless, soundless place, rid of destructive hope, of responsibility —become a creature of limbo.

But then I heard Rwyan say, "You cannot, Daviot. Remember the pattern."

My body raised its head and said, "Why not? I can do nothing. You can do nothing. Nor Urt or Tezdal. We are all of us helpless. The world turns as it will. Come with me."

She shook her head. "No. I'll not give up hope. I'd thought you'd not. I'd thought better of you."

I shrugged, embarrassed. I felt then as must a fish caught on a line: I'd find those black deeps again, but I was called back, drawn up toward the light by love of Rwyan.

I looked into her eyes, and they were no longer hers but the vast orbs of my oneiric dragon. And the walls were gone, and the garden, and I was ringed by those eyes, all of them fixed on me. They seemed to accuse me of cowardice; they seemed to judge me. I felt ashamed then of my weakness and straightened in my chair, meeting that implacable gaze.

I said, "What do you ask of me? What must I do?"

There was no verbal answer, but rather an emotion—I'd known this before, but it was stronger now, become an imperative—that summoned me. It was a call that rang in my blood, in the very fibers of my being. It was akin to that sensation I'd felt from the crystal, and different, warmer somehow. So strong it was that I rose, standing and turning slowly around, finding only those eyes calling me.

I felt I stood at a threshold, and that did I not step across, I must lose . . . I was not sure what I should lose. Rwyan? Hope? Pride? Integrity? All those, I felt, and more: myself. And at the same time I felt that did I take that step, it must deliver something vast and dreadful. I felt I should be cursed whichever course I chose. I was afraid then, as I'd never been before. I knew I was summoned, and that it was no longer a vague dreamy feeling, but a call so strong I ached to answer it. I felt that did I fail, I must stand condemned and lost forever. That I should find neither that peace the darkness offered nor any other, but only anguish.

I said, "Where shall I go? How shall I come to you?"

And the voice that was not a voice told me I should know, that I already took the first steps. And at that I felt a great gladness, and also a great fear, for it seemed I embarked on a terrible journey.

But I told the eyes, "Yes. As you will," and at that they seemed no longer to judge me so much but to praise me and wish me well along my journey.

And then I saw Rwyan stood beside me, and she took my hand and smiled. And Urt was there, and Tezdal, and we four stood together, encircled by the great yellow eyes. It was as if we stood close to the sun, or several suns, which warmed us with their approval, and bade us hurry and be welcome.

I saw the table again and the crystal, which now pulsed fierce, as if angered. Then from out of the light cast by the eyes reached a hand, a man's, and took the stone, drawing back amongst the yellow orbs that were all the boundary of this dream world. I stared, trying to see past the light, to know whose hand this was, but I could not. Instead, I heard the rustle of vast wings unfolding and felt the wind of their beating. It was a stormy force, but though I knew it should, it did not beat me down but only washed around me as the crystal was carried up, aloft and away into darkness.

Colors then, such as form against shuttered lids, the myriad sparklings of blood in flesh. I opened my eyes and raised my head. I sat slumped across the table, Rwyan in like position, sleeping yet. I looked around and saw we sat still within our quarters, the night outside not yet lit by dawn's early light. The room was shadowed, but even as I blinked and rubbed my eyes, the walls and ceiling began again to glow, and soon the chamber was lit bright as day.

Rwyan woke then and stared at me with a puzzled, questioning expression. I'd no need to ask, but still I did: "You dreamed?"

She nodded, not speaking until she'd filled a cup with water and drunk. Then she said, "Yes. I dreamed." She shook her head, frowning. "It was strange . . . of eyes that . . . summoned . . . me. A promise."

My own mouth was very dry: I got myself water. I wondered if this was part of the pattern. I thought that had Urt and Tezdal experienced the same dream, then it must surely find its roots in some reality beyond my comprehension. I said, "I felt I was asked to make a choice."

She said, "And did you?"

I ducked my head and answered her, "Yes. They called me and I agreed to go; though I know not where."

"Nor I," she said, and glanced at the crystal, dormant between us. "Perhaps that's unlocked some power. Perhaps in using it, we opened a door. Or sent a message."

I sighed and blew out a mournful chuckle. "Then dragons shall come down from the sky to carry us off from this place." I gestured at the walls, the sealed door and window. "But first they'll need overcome the magic of the Changed."

Rwyan said, "Perhaps they will."

"And we best hope they'll not devour us," I said. "Was that not their habit?"

She said, "I felt no threat in my dream, save that I betray myself."

"Which you'd not do," I said. "Oh, Rwyan, could it be so, I'd welcome dragons. But I cannot dare hope they shall be our saviors."

She smiled wearily and was about to speak, but then the door flung open and Urt came rushing in.

His gray hair was awry, and on his face was an expression that mingled fear and wonder in equal measure. He stared at us, his eyes wide. I thought perhaps his "treachery" was discovered and that Allanyn should appear on his heels. I had not known I rose until I heard my chair clatter on the marbled floor.

He turned his startled face to Rwyan and said, "Those dreams you spoke of? Just now—there were eyes. . . . They asked me to go with them. . . . You were there, and Tezdal."

He snatched up the wine flask and a cup, filled the goblet, and drained it. Rwyan cast a triumphant glance my way and went to where he stood. I saw that he shook.

Rwyan set a hand on his shoulder. "We, too, Urt. Daviot and I had the same dream."

He sighed. "What does it mean?" His eyes demanded answers of us.

Rwyan said, "I cannot say for certain. But that there's hope, I think."

He asked, "Of what? They were dragons, no?"

He shuddered. It came to me then that he had cause to fear the dragons. As the Kho'rabi were the nightmares of my childhood, so must the dragons have been the monsters of his. Did the Changed possess the memories of their ancestors as the beasts from which they were shaped owned memories, then dragons must surely be creatures of naked terror. Their threat must be implanted in his blood, passed down generation to generation. I went to stand beside him, setting a hand firm on his other shoulder. I could smell his discomfort, and through his shirt I felt the trembling that racked his frame.

I said, "They offered us no harm, Urt. Did you feel threat in them?"

He shook his head and licked his lips. I saw his nostrils flare, as if he'd test the air for scent of danger. He said slowly, "No. But they were dragons still."

Rwyan said, "But not dangerous. Not to us. I think these dragons are our friends."

Urt said, "Dragons friend to Changed? Can that be?"

I said, "Perhaps. Surely what we dreamed was friendly."

Urt swallowed and ducked his head. "That's true," he said. "But I understand this not at all."

Softly, I said, "Nor I."

Rwyan said, "I believe we are told something. That we must stand together, surely. But more—though what, I cannot say; not yet."

Urt said, "The Lord Tezdal was there."

Rwyan said, "Yes. We four are called in some way."

"We four?" Urt's shuddering gradually subsided. "How so?"

Rwyan said, "I've as many questions as you, and no more answers. But perhaps—" She paused, her brow creased as she pondered. "Think on it—you, Urt, are Changed. Tezdal is a Sky Lord. Daviot's a Trueman and a Rememberer. I am a mage. Do we not stand as symbols for the folk who must suffer does this war begin?"

I said, "What of the gifted Changed? What of the Kho'rabi wizards?"

"As I say, I've more questions than answers." Rwyan shrugged. "But perhaps the gifted Changed and the Kho'rabi wizards are too far gone in hatred to hear this call."

Call to what? I thought, but I said nothing.

Rwyan said, "Or perhaps we hear it only because we four are ready. Perhaps because we'd sooner see peace than war. Perhaps because we join together in common purpose, and what we are—Truemen or Changed, Sky Lord or Dhar—does not matter to us. I know not. But I do not believe these dragons intend you harm, Urt. Not you, or any of us."

Urt was calmer now, though I could see he was still not much at ease with the notion of dragons, even were they only the creatures of dream. I squeezed his shoulder and said, "Is Rwyan right, then we've naught to fear. Is she wrong—why then, we only suffer odd dreams. And there's a more immediate danger."

I gestured at the crystal. Outside, the sky assumed that utter blankness that precedes the first light of dawn. I thought we'd not much time, and was Urt still unnerved, it were better we told him quickly what we'd learned, what Rwyan had learned, that he have time to compose himself before he must replace the stone. I thought he'd likely need composure for that, lest Allanyn discover our complicity.

Rwyan nodded. We found seats, and she began to speak.

She'd not a Storyman's skill with words and I'd have told it more succinct, but she spoke with such fervor, I saw Urt was convinced. I watched as his face—seldom so readable—expressed first amazement tinged with disbelief, then burgeoning conviction, and finally outrage to match what I'd seen on Rwyan's. When she was done, he snarled. I saw the animal in him then.

He said, "She stands condemned! Traitor, she! And all her kind. Little wonder the gifted guard these stones so close."

He seemed so angry I took his arm. "Urt, do you speak of this carelessly, I think we shall all be slain."

He nodded. That animal rage was suddenly replaced with grief. He said, "I'd doubted her ways, but I'd not suspected this. None of us suspected this. She'd lay us all on the altar of her ambition."

"None of you?" I asked hopefully. "How many of you are there? Enough to oppose her, expose her?"

"No." He shook his head. "We are but a few, a handful. The Raethe is mostly gifted now. I found a place because I know of Durbrecht and Karysvar; there are a few more like me, without the talent. But Allanyn and her followers are the stronger."

"Might you convince the gifted?" I asked.

He laughed at that, though it was more a bark. "It should be hard to convince even my friends," he said. "What should I tell them? That the gifted are insane? That the crystals seduce them? That Allanyn leads us to war only that she might rule us? They'd ask me how I come by this information, no? And how should I prove it? Shall I tell them I have it from a mage of the Dhar and a Storyman? Allanyn should have my head, did the rest not slay me first."

I voiced acknowledgment with a curse. "Impasse then. Is all we've learned useless?"

"I might slay her," Urt said. "Perhaps I might succeed."

"That should be hard," said Rwyan. "And you undoubtedly die. Surely after, likely before."

He said, "I'd save my people," doggedly.

Rwyan said, "And I'd save mine, but I think that attempting Allanyn's assassination should lead only to your death. I think you'd serve your people better alive."

He said, "To what end? To watch us go to war, that Allanyn rule us?"

"Remember the dreams," she said. And when both Urt and I looked at her askance: "Perhaps there's some answer there. Is it not strange that we should learn of Allanyn's designs and straightway dream again?"

Urt grunted; I shrugged. We neither of us had any ready answer.

Rwyan said, "We've time yet, too—until Tezdal wakes, at least. I'd know if he shared this; and perhaps we'll dream again and get some better answer."

I could think of no other option, and so I only nodded, keeping silent.

Urt said, "Perhaps," with little real conviction in his voice.

"Then best you get this stone returned," Rwyan said, "ere it's missed. And when you can, come back."

Urt nodded and gingerly took up the crystal. He dropped it in the pouch as might a man set down some horrid insect. He looked weary, bereft of hope. "As soon I may," he promised, and raised a hand in farewell.

The door closed behind him, and I turned to Rwyan. "This looks not at all well."

She said, "No. But I'll not yet relinquish hope."

I smiled at her bravery and touched her cheek. She rubbed against me, feline, and yawned hugely.

I said, "Do we get what sleep we can?"

She said, "Aye," and we stretched, fully clad, on the bed.

It seemed my eyes had barely closed before we were roused. I groaned, my vision foggy, and sat up. I saw Allanyn and two others of the gifted standing close. Allanyn's face wore a triumphant sneer. Her eyes were bright with unpleasant anticipation.

She said, "Come. The Lord Tezdal wakes."

The vault felt pregnant with anticipation. I saw it on the faces of the Sky Lords, in the narrowing of their dark eyes and the set of their shoulders; no less in the gifted Changed. In Allanyn it was most apparent; but where the interest of the rest seemed entirely for Tezdal, hers was as much directed at us. I thought she gloated, savoring what was to come. I put an arm about Rwyan, and she leaned close and whispered, "You'll not forget your promise, Daviot."

She intended no insult to my Storyman's memory: it was not a question. I answered her, "What of the pattern?"

She said, "Only does the time come."

I said, "Yes," and sighed.

Then all my attention was on the supine form of the Kho'rabi I named a friend.

He lay still on the cloth-draped bier. The crystals surrounding him sat adumbral on their pedestals, as if their light were gone into the restoration of his memory and now they slumbered. Somehow, I had no doubt but that it was restored him. It seemed, for all they no longer pulsed or flickered, that the stones radiated a sense of satisfaction. I watched, breath bated, as the Sky Lords took positions about the dais. Three stood at the head, two at the foot, the others to either side. All raised their arms, extended palms downward over the silent form, and spoke together.

I could not understand their language, but I saw that Tezdal responded. I saw his chest rise steeper than before. I heard the gusty exhalation of his breath. He made a sound, sigh and groan together, as if aroused from deepest slumber. His eyes opened, blank a moment, then lit by intelligence. He rose on his elbows, peering about, eyes narrowed, his brow creased. Then he said something in his own tongue.

The Sky Lords clustered close. A Changed came forward, bringing a goblet that one of the Ahn brought to Tezdal's lips. He drank deep and wiped his mouth, then swung his legs from the bier and stood upright. For an instant he swayed, eyes closed as he shook his head, but then he straightened, shaking off the hands that would assist him. He looked slowly around, finding my eyes and Rwyan's. He ducked his head slightly, acknowledging our presence, but his expression was unreadable. I felt Rwyan tense within the compass of my arm.

Then Allanyn blocked my view. She insinuated herself between the Sky Lords—which I saw affronted them—to face Tezdal. In the language of the Dhar she said, "Lord Tezdal, are you again whole? Have you all your memory again?"

Tezdal answered her in the same language: "I do."

His voice was cold, as if he found her impertinent, which Allanyn minded not at all. She gave him her back as she spun to face us.

"So it is done! You see our power now; and now you've a choice to make."

Her smile was feral: I thought she hoped for Rwyan's refusal. I tensed, my heart sinking as I shaped my hand to strike the blow I dreaded.

Rwyan said, "Perhaps. But ere I make that choice, I'd speak with Tezdal."

Allanyn's lovely face became a mask of rage. "What?" she cried. "You'd dictate terms? I tell you—choose now, or it shall be done for you."

I moved a small distance from Rwyan's side, enough I'd have sufficient room to strike. A sour weight sat deep in my belly. For an instant my vision clouded red. For an instant I thought to spring at Allanyn, to let my blow shatter her hateful face. But I'd made that promise. To renege on that would be to betray Rwyan—and likely leave her to suffer the angry devices of the Changed alone. I should be dead; nor had I any great confidence I *could* slay Allanyn. I ground my teeth and curbed the impulse. I stood ready to slay my love, and as I did I cursed every turn of the fate that had brought us to this moment.

Rwyan said, "Not yet," and I was uncertain whether she directed her words at me or at the raging Allanyn.

Then she said, "Is your magic truly so powerful as you claim, then Tezdal has back *all* his memories. Both those that make him a Sky Lord and those that make him my friend."

I watched as Allanyn's lips drew back from her sharp white teeth in an entirely feline snarl. Her hands rose, beginning to weave a pattern in the air. Had she not been so consumed with rage, she'd have got the spell out clear and blasted Rwyan on the spot.

But she spluttered, and before she could complete the cantrip, Tezdal had her by the wrists, forcing her arms down, turning her to face him. I could not see her expression, but I saw her shoulders strain beneath her gown and heard her howl of fury. Sky Lords and Changed spoke together then, urgently, their voices raised in a babble of protest and anger. I saw the crystals begin to pulse and felt that tingling on my skin that warned of burgeoning occult power. From the corner of my eye I saw Rwyan's slight smile, as if she scored a victory. I thought at best she bought us a little time.

Then Tezdal's voice came clear and cold through the hubbub.

"The lady Rwyan speaks true! She's debt-claim on me, and I am sworn to defend her."

He let go Allanyn's wrists, and the Changed woman sprang back. The Sky Lords drew closer to Tezdal, as if they'd defend him against her magic. Their faces were a mixture of confusion and outrage. I thought that did Allanyn or any other gifted look to employ magic, I should witness a horrendous duel. I supposed it might end the alliance; I wondered if Rwyan planned this.

Then Geran pushed to the fore, hands raised in placatory gesture. "My friends," he said, "do we fall to fighting amongst ourselves? Shall we squabble over this Dhar sorceress? Calm yourselves, I say, lest all our dreams be wasted."

Another Changed took Allanyn's arm: she shook him off even as he murmured urgently. But more drew near, setting themselves between her and the Sky Lords, succeeding in forcing her reluctantly back.

Geran said, "So, do we becalm ourselves? All of us!"

This last was directed at Allanyn, who allowed herself to be placated. I saw her force a smile and heard her say, "Forgive me, my lords. I grow impatient with the rank presumption of this mage. I'd see our venture commence as soon it may, and her pointless defiance angers me."

The Sky Lords murmured in their own tongue. I sensed they found her display unseemly. I thought these were likely folk much given to protocol. Dismissing my earlier curse, I prayed they were much given to honor.

One, gray in his oiled beard, said, "Your apology is accepted, lady. But this matter of Lord Tezdal's vow is a troubling thing."

Allanyn said, "Surely such a vow is worthless. Lord Tezdal was not himself when that oath was sworn."

She had better held silent. I saw that in the stiffening of the Sky Lords' backs, the frowns that twisted their features. The speaker said, "A vow is a vow." His voice was cold. "Save he's his honor, a man is nothing. The gods shall not forgive an oath-breaker."

Allanyn would have spoken again. I hoped she would, for her words seemed to drive a wedge between these allies, but Geran forestalled her. He said, "Aye, there's much truth in that. And a conundrum, also."

He was a diplomat, that one, and cunning: all fell silent, waiting on him.

He said, "I'd not besmirch Lord Tezdal's honor—nor would any here! But when one vow stands in opposition to another? What then?" He paused: he had their attention. "Lord Tezdal is Kho'rabi—Dedicated—and so sworn to the Great Conquest. That vow was made knowingly, when he possessed all his senses and was entirely himself. This other, surely, was made when he was—forgive me, my lord—less than entire. His memory was gone, taken from him by Truemen's sorcery. No fault of his, that; but were he not victim of that magic, would he have sworn that vow? I think not, and so I'd ask he set aside that latter—lesser!—vow, in honor of the greater."

This was sophistry worthy of Durbrecht! Almost I could admire Geran's slippery tongue. He spoke so earnestly, sincerity dripping, his expression one of concern, suggesting he might share the dilemma he outlined. I glanced at Rwyan, dreading she'd bid me strike, and saw her smiling still, seeming possessed of a confidence I could not share. I looked to Tezdal and saw him perturbed, his eyes narrowed as if he considered Geran's words. The other Sky Lords waited on him. I felt my future and Rwyan's waited on him.

Finally he nodded and said, "There's much to consider in that. But still—as Zenodar says, a vow is a vow."

"Even were you not yourself?" asked Geran. "My lord, surely there was a theft here—Dhar magic stole your memory."

"In battle," Tezdal said, and smiled directly at Rwyan. "There was no theft intended—only death."

"Aye, they'd have taken your life!" said Geran. "They'd have slain you, save their magic was not so great."

"And well might have slain me, after," Tezdal replied, "when they found me on that rock, or when they took me to the island. But they did not, and from Rwyan I had only kindness."

"Surely in service of their own ends," Geran said, "and for no other reason. Surely they let you live only that they might plunder your mind of its knowledge."

"True." Tezdal ducked his head, solemnly; then raised his face to Geran, "Just as you'd plunder this lady's."

"Surely there's a difference." Geran smiled, stroking his long jaw. "We offer this mage a choice. What we ask of her, she may give us freely. Only does she refuse would we resort to those other measures."

Tezdal smiled back. His gaze flickered in Allanyn's direction. I thought I saw disbelief on his face, as if he doubted the feline Changed should offer such option. He said, "What choice is that? Has Rwyan not sworn a vow to defend her land? You ask her to renege, to forfeit her honor. I know her, and I tell you that for her that's no choice at all."

From behind Geran came Allanyn's outraged shriek: "She's a Trueman mage! What honor there?"

The look Tezdal sent her way was utterly cold; warm as his eyes swung back to Rwyan. "Much," he said. "I know this lady, and I tell you she's the honor of a Kho'rabi."

There was startlement at that; gasps from several of the Sky Lords, a puzzled frown from Zenodar. Geran—seeking to retrieve his argument, I thought—said, "But an enemy, still. Of your people and mine."

Tezdal said, "Perhaps. But do I fight, I'd have my battles with such honorable people."

I heard Allanyn mutter, "Honor!" as if the word were an abomination. Tezdal ignored her; Geran, too. He said, "Yet we must have her knowledge, lest the Border Cities and the Sentinels destroy the fleets."

Tezdal nodded. "Yes. But still I made a vow. That remains."

"When you were helpless," Geran said. I thought he sounded not quite so confident now. "When you'd no memory of those other vows. When you were not, properly, Kho'rabi."

"Which means?" asked Tezdal.

"That you are once more whole," said Geran. "That you are again yourself—the Lord Tezdal Kashijan of Ahn-feshang—and owe allegiance only to the Cause; to the Attul-ki, to the Conquest. Our magic it was gave you back your life, gave you back your memories! Shall you forget that?"

Tezdal said, "No," in a voice so coldly imperious, the horse-faced Changed flinched. "Nor shall I forget my honor."

"Then where do we stand?" asked Geran. His oily confidence was gone now: I could not—for all I felt not at all happy—help but smile.

"The Lady Rwyan would have full proof," said Tezdal, and turned again to Rwyan. "Is that not so?"

Rwyan said simply, "It is. I'd hear from you alone that this sortilege has done its work."

"Then you shall," he said.

Rwyan only smiled and nodded. I relaxed a fraction: I felt she'd earned us a little more time. I felt we lived our lives in increments now, snatching moments from the ravening jaws of hungry fate.

Tezdal nodded in response and looked again to Geran. "So shall it be," he declared. "The lady Rwyan shall have her proof from me, and then . . ." He frowned, some measure of confidence departing. "But first, I'd dine and speak with my fellows. So do you return the lady Rwyan and Daviot the Storyman to their quarters? Unharmed, eh? And treat them with the respect they deserve."

Neither Geran nor the other gifted liked that much. I saw Allanyn's face pale, two spots of angry color on her cheeks, but neither she nor any of them argued, so commanding was Tezdal. I saw Rwyan's smile grow broader, and when I caught Tezdal's eye, he grinned. I wondered what game he played. Was it all some thing of honor that I could not properly comprehend? I knew nothing of the Sky Lords—save as ferocious enemies—but I had the feeling he sought to help us.

I could not see how, save that he gave us a brief respite from the inevitable. I told myself that must be enough for now.

There was a tapping at our door. It took me a while to wonder why our captors should now deign to announce their entry: I called that they come in.

The door opened, and Tezdal stood there.

He was alone. He wore the shirt and breeks and boots of the vault, but not the crimson robe, and on his face was an expression I could not interpret.

He said, "Daviot," as if in greeting or inquiry, and looked past me to Rwyan and spoke her name. And then, "May I enter?"

I shrugged and beckoned him in. I wondered why he bothered with such formality: was he our friend, he must surely know himself welcome; if not, why should he concern himself with niceties?

He smiled slightly and gave me a brief formal bow. Rwyan said, "Tezdal. Enter, and welcome."

His smile grew warmer. I frowned and stood back. He closed the door and turned to face us. Rwyan ushered him to a chair and gestured at the decanter, for all the world as if we entertained some unexpected guest whose presence was an unanticipated pleasure.

Tezdal shook his head. "I've learned much about myself. And about other things."

I saw his eyes cloud as he spoke, and lines appear across his brow. He ran a hand over his hair as if its arrangement sat unfamiliar on his skull. I took a seat across the table, beside Rwyan. I studied this man I thought my friend, who might well now be my implacable enemy. I read confusion in his stance, doubt in his eyes. I waited, certain he should unfold some new chapter of my life and Rwyan's, not knowing what it might be, good or ill.

Rwyan said, "Do you tell us?"

Her voice was calm. I felt sweat bead my brow, for all the room was pleasantly cool.

Tezdal said, "I've my memory back. All of it."

His voice was controlled. I watched a tic throb on his temple. Rwyan said, "Then tell us all of it."

He nodded and began to speak. I listened, marveling at the magic the Changed commanded, thinking how such talent might benefit we Mnemonikos.

He was born on the seventh day of the seventh month in the Year of the Eagle, which is holy to Vachyn, God of the Skies: a birthing day of great portent. His father was Tairaz Kashijan; his mother, Nazrene, formerly of the Isadur, and so in his veins flowed the High Blood of the Ahn. On the sixteenth day he was carried, wrapped in his swaddling clothes, to the temple of the Three, where his parents, as was custom, offered him in service to the gods. They were proud when the Attul-ki pricked his flesh with the sacred knife and he did not scream.

The blood, the priests said, ran true in this one, this child was truly Kho'rabi, and so he was named Tezdal, which in the language of the Ahn means both "brave" and "honor."

At the age of seven years he underwent the rituals of consecration. He smiled and did not struggle when the priests lowered him into the earth that was Byr's, nor did he protest when the dirt struck his face. He smiled and did not close his eyes when they sank him beneath the waves that are Dach's. When they lashed him to the tiny airboat and sent the craft into the sky that is Vachyn's, he laughed aloud. Then they said, "This one shall be a credit to the Kashijan. He will be a mighty warrior, and his life and his death a monument to the Ahn." That night, as all the folk of the Kashijan and the Isadur, those of both the High and Low Blood, and all their retainers, feasted, Tezdal drank his first wine and, in a voice steady for one so young, raised his cup in toast to the Great Conquest. It pleased him to be born at such a time, when the Attul-ki promised a turning of the winds, a strengthening of their holy magic, that should see him of an age to ride the sky across the Kheryn-veyhn to regain the Homeland.

The next day, his head still somewhat fuddled by the wine, he was taken by his father to the Jentan-dho in Asanaj and given into the care of the Tachennen who would be his teachers and his guardians until he was of an age to wear the warrior's braid, and call himself a man, and go back into the world a true Kho'rabi. Even then, as he turned from his father and went with the Tachennen into the House of Warriors, he did not cry or look back.

For eight years Tezdal remained in the Jentan-dho. There he learned the Seven Paths of the Warrior, and the Three Ways of the Gods. He was visited by his parents on the seventh day of each seventh month, and on that day sacred to the people when the prophet Attul first set foot on the soil of Ahn-feshang. On these occasions he greeted his father and his mother with suitable deference, neither weeping nor seeking undue favor. He was, the Tachennen said, their finest pupil, a true Warrior of the Blood. Once, his mother found it necessary to stifle a cry of alarm when she saw his right arm bound and strapped useless to his side. It had been broken, Tezdal told her, in training on the Second Path; it hurt him not at all. His father said nothing to the boy but inquired of the Tachennen, who advised him the damage was done in combat with the practice swords, when Tezdal faced three opponents.

Tairaz Kashijan had nodded and asked, "And the others?"

"Had the blades been true kachen," the Tachennen had answered, "then they should all be slain."

Tairaz had nodded again at this and asked, "Did he conduct himself well?"

"He did not cry out," the Tachennen had said. "He had bested one when the blow landed. He fought on and won single-handed."

"That is good," Tairaz had declared. "But he should not have allowed the wounding."

By his thirteenth year, Tezdal had mastered the Seven Paths and none could defeat him, save by sheer weight of numbers, in the melees. He waited eagerly for manhood and the promised Conquest.

Such was the dream of all within the Jentan-dho. It was to that end that the warriors named themselves the Dedicated, and since the Attul-ki had given the people the Great Dream, it was the hope of all the Ahn.

Once they had dwelt in the Homeland, far to the west across the Kheryn-veyhn. Their gods were the Three and in the way of gods had seen fit to test their worshippers. The cursed Dhar had come out of the north, a locust plague across the land. Their priests and sorcerers stood united in enmity of the Ahn, who then had owned but little magic and been too few in numbers to oppose the invaders. Worshippers of the one god were the Dhar, and they had torn down the temples of the Three and burned the sacred groves, driven the people into hiding or slavery. This was the first testing, and the Ahn had held true and would not forsake the Three, and in answer to that faith the gods had sent the prophet Attul a vision.

In the accoutrements of warriors they had appeared—Byr with promise of a new land; from Vachyn, lordship of the sky; from Dach, safe passage over the sea. "Go," they had told Attul, "go east across the Kheryn-veyhn with all the people. A new land awaits you there, where you shall grow strong again, and in time come back to conquer what is rightfully yours."

The promise had burned hot in Attul, and the word had spread amongst the people, and in the secret places of the land the Dhar named Kellambek, the Ahn had built their boats, readying for the journey. Attul had led them and guided them in the exodus, and the gods made good their promises. Dach had granted them the crossing, safe, and Vachyn sent the wind to speed them on their way to the land Byr made for them, which they named Ahn-feshang—the New Place of the People. Attul had set his feet on the new land and given thanks to the triumvirate, and the Three had taken him up, to dwell as one with them.

The Ahn, the promise of the gods yet bright, had found a welcome in Ahn-feshang, and soon they spread throughout the islands, of which there were three—Ahn-zel, Ahn-khem, and Ahn-wa. Byr had been kind in his building: the land was lush, with wooded mountains and grassy valleys, where game was plentiful. Dach gave them rivers of clean water and pleasant beaches and filled the sea with fish. But what gift Vachyn gave was not yet clear.

The Ahn prospered, but the testing was not yet done. Fertile as was the new land, still the islands suffered the ravages of the elements. There were typhoons, and tidal waves, and volcanoes that vented their might against the heavens. This was the second testing, and there were many then who doubted the gods and so fell forsaken. But to those whose faith endured, the Three gave such magic as the world had never known. To those whose faith was strongest they gave power over the elements—the ability to defy the storms, to calm the waves, to soothe the earth-fires. To these sorcerers the Ahn looked for salvation, naming them the Attul-ki, which means "Children of Attul," and they took the place of the hetmen and the attars, leading the Ahn safe through this second trial.

To them the Three gave word of the final testing, which was trial and prize both, for it was that the people should return to the Homeland to drive out the Dhar and take back what was theirs.

Then did Vachyn bestow his gift. He showed the Attul-ki the way of constructing the great airboats, how the skins might be filled with the breath of the volcanoes, to ride the Worldwinds and carry the Kho'rabi knights across the Kheryn-veyhn to smite the Dhar.

This was the longest of the three trials, for the magic of the Attul-ki was yet as that of infants, albeit powerful, and not even they could master the winds but must travel only on Vachyn's whim. They persevered, and in reward Vachyn taught them that magic that granted them mastery over the spirits of the air. Slowly, they learned to bind the elemental spirits to their craft, like horses to a chariot, and then were they able to defy the Worldwinds and go against the Dhar usurpers at will.

To this great dream the Kho'rabi were dedicated, for the Three yet chose to test their followers, and those who sailed the sky to the Homeland did not return but gave their lives in service to the triumvirate, that the Dhar never forget but dwell in fear of the Comings.

And for such faith the Three gave due reward: the Attul-ki grew ever more accomplished in their magicks and found ways to bind the elementals in greater numbers to their purpose. In time they saw the final trial approach and warned the people to ready themselves. It should be soon, they said. Not this year or the next, but soon enough as gods count time.

For a while they sent the great airboats against the Dhar, with sorcerer-priests of such power aboard that they were able to send back word, of what magicks the enemy commanded, and the manner of their defenses. Then came a breathing space, for the Dhar found new sorceries to thwart the people and prevent the sending back of word. Then did the Attul-ki bend all their will and all their wits to the dream. They decreed there should be no more attacks for a while, but only small vessels—such as might carry no more than ten men—go out. But these were the key to the Conquest, for the Children of Attul bound to them such numbers of elementals that the boats might return to Ahn-feshang, defying the sorcery of the Dhar and the gusting of the Worldwinds both. And from these scouts came reliable word of fortresses and cities and holds, of the deployment of soldiery, and the resources of the enemy.

And more—they found allies, who vowed to aid them in the conquest of the Dhar.

Then all the people saw that the final trial was near and readied for the Great Conquest. Across all Ahn-feshang they labored to construct the armada, none sparing wealth or possessions or strength but all bound to the single promised purpose: the Conquest.

On the seventh day of the seventh month of Tezdal's fifteenth year, Tairaz Kashijan, accompanied by the lady Nazrene and a retinue of one hundred Kho'rabi knights, attended the ceremonies in the Jentan-dho in Asanaj. They watched as their son performed the obeisances to the Three and to the Tachennen. Then Tairaz stepped forward and silently bound his son's hair in the warrior's braid. Tezdal rose from his knees and bowed. Tairaz presented him with the kachen of manhood and clapped his hands. The five most senior of the Kashijan warriors came forward, full armored as befitted so solemn a ritual, to strip the young man and dress him in his own armor. Tezdal thanked them eloquently and waited as his mother led forward a horse. It was such a beast as fit a Kho'rabi knight, a testament to the wealth of the Kashijan family, a jet stallion of pure blood. Tezdal shouted, "For the Three and for the Conquest," and severed the head with a single cut.

There was shouting after that, and an end to formality. The families Kashijan and Isadur had supplied the Jentan-dho with food and wine enough that all found their beds that night with bellies filled and heads aswim. In the morning Tezdal departed much as he had come: his head pounding, without a backward glance. He rode a stallion that matched exactly the beast he had slain.

On his return to the Kashijan estates he found the members of both families awaiting him. There followed seven days of feasting, culminating in his betrothal to his cousin, the lady Retze Isadur. She was a pretty girl, and he was pleased with his parents' choice.

On the eighth day Retze departed with her family to the Isadur estates, and Tezdal did not see her, save on feast days and holy days, for three years. Then, in his eighteenth year, which was Retze's sixteenth, they were wed. From the Isadur family they received an estate in the mountains of Ahn-khem, with a sizable manor house, nine farmsteads, and a retinue of fifty servants. The Kashijan gifted them with three hundred Kho'rabi, fully equipped and well-mounted. Tezdal was happy in all ways but one: the Great Conquest was promised soon and he lusted for that battle.

His voice tailed off like a dying wind, and upon his face I saw an expression of naked grief. I heard Rwyan gasp and knew she "saw" that same pain. I said, "Tezdal, what is it?"

He said, "My boat was felled," and offered Rwyan a tortured smile. "By the magicks you threw against us. I was believed slain; died with the rest. That word was sent to Retze, and she mourned a year, then . . ."

He swallowed, choking on the words. I saw tears lucent in his eyes, running slowly down his cheeks. Rwyan stretched a hand across the table, taking his. I rose and filled a goblet with wine, passed it to him. He smiled wan thanks and drained the cup.

Then he sighed and finished, "Retze took the Way of Honor."

I'd no real need of explanation, but still I asked.

I think I was so startled by all I'd learned, so numbed by this incredible insight into the ways of the Ahn, I felt a need of words to set it all firm in my mind. Surely I intended him no more pain.

But it was there in his eyes and his voice as he told me, "She slew herself. Such is our way, in defeat or loss of a loved one."

Rwyan said, "Tezdal, I'm sorry. Had I known . . ."

He laughed at that, a bitter sound, and asked, "Should you have done different? Not flung your magicks at us?"

Rwyan shook her head. "No. But still I grieve for your loss."

He sighed and closed his eyes a moment. When they opened, they were bright with tears. He seemed not at all ashamed to show his grief, which I think was a measure of his strength. He said, "I believe you, Rwyan. I honor you as a worthy foe; I honor you as a friend." A twisted smile stretched out his lips. "By the Three, but were this world of ours different!"

I said, "I'd have it otherwise, Tezdal. I share your grief."

He ducked his head. I watched as he wiped his eyes, not knowing what else to say; not knowing how this should affect Rwyan's fate and mine.

It was a while before he raised his head, and when he did, his expression was bleak. I liked it not at all: torment was graved there. He said, "I am sworn by the Three to fight you. To destroy you. But I cannot name you enemies." He shook his head. "They set a heavy burden on us, our gods."

I said, "What shall you do?"

He smiled at that and barked a laugh that held no humor, but only anguish. He said, "My avowed duty is to give you over to the Changed. To see your secrets, Rwyan, sucked out, that we may take back the Homeland. To slay you, Daviot, if I must; and then go south, to war."

Rwyan said, "And shall you?"

He wiped a hand down over his fresh-shaved jaw and looked her in the eye. "I feel myself divided," he said. "I am Kho'rabi; I am also your friend. I am sworn to defeat you and defend you, both. I see no choice left me save the Way of Honor."

He touched the hilt of the long dagger sheathed at his waist and offered us a death's-head smile.

I opened my mouth to protest, to tell him there must be another way, but Rwyan spoke while useless words still spun unshaped in my head.

"The Way of Honor?" Her voice was gentle as a blade sheathed in velvet. "Suicide? I thought you sworn to defend me. Do you take this Way of Honor, how think you I shall fare? Or Daviot? Would you give us into Allanyn's hands?"

That was cruel, I thought. I saw Tezdal wince, his eyes starting wide, then narrowing. I thought him snared in the trap of his Kho'rabi honor; and that that was Rwyan's intention. I understood that code of honor better now. I understood the Sky Lords better than any Dhar. I had such knowledge as would delight my College. And it was useless. Or so I thought: I failed to accord Rwyan her just due.

Tezdal said, "What choice have I? Shall I betray my people, and stand damned in the eyes of the Three? Shall I betray you, and damn myself? I am lost, Rwyan! I am no longer entirely Kho'rabi; neither am I Dhar. I see no other way."

I was startled by Rwyan's response.

She asked him, quietly, "Have you dreamed, Tezdal?"

He was no less surprised than I. He stared at her as if she were gone mad. She sat, calm, her beautiful blind eyes intent upon his troubled face, brows arched in question.

He said, "You know I have. Along the road to Trebizar . . ."

Rwyan nodded: confirmation of old, shared knowledge. "Then, aye," she said. "But since? Whilst you lay in that vault?"

Tezdal frowned. His shoulders rose a little, and fell. He gestured with his right hand, helplessly. Then he said, "Yes. I think I did."

"Think?" Rwyan urged him. *"Remember."*

He closed his eyes and sighed. "There were eyes," he said at last. "Great yellow eyes that urged I come to them. You two were there, and the Changed named Urt. The eyes summoned us all. I thought"— he shook his head—"thought they held answers, though I cannot say to what. I felt that did I fail their call, I must be damned."

"I had that dream," Rwyan said. "And Daviot. Urt, too. We *are* summoned, I believe."

Tezdal said, "By what? The gods?"

Rwyan shook her head. "Perhaps the gods have a hand in this. I know not, but I believe fate calls us."

I suspect my expression matched Tezdal's then. His was of plain confusion, laden with disbelief. He gestured that she explain.

She said, "Daviot's the better way with words than I—let him explain," and turned to me and said, "Daviot, do you tell him of the pattern?"

Almost, I shook my head and told her no; that this was all some phantasm born of despair. That she clutched at straws when we had better ready ourselves to die. That Tezdal's Way of Honor was the only escape from our plight.

But I could not: she fixed me with her blind gaze, and had I not known her talent was curtailed by Trebizar's magic, I'd have believed she englamoured me. I ducked my head and began to speak.

I told Tezdal of all my dreams, and those Rwyan had known. I told him all I knew of the dragons (little enough, that), and of Urt's dreams. I told him of the pattern. I told him of the crystal Urt had brought us, and all we'd learned from that stone.

And as I spoke, I came to a kind of belief. It was tainted with doubt (all the time there was a skeptical voice inside my skull, whispering in my ear that this was only phantasmagoria; the last, wild imaginings of folk condemned to inevitable death), but through that doubt I saw a spark of hope. I could not forget how vivid those dreams had been, and it seemed to me my words kindled the flame. I wondered if I went mad.

When I was done, Tezdal rose and brought the decanter to the table. He filled Rwyan's cup and mine, then his own. He drank deep and looked me in the eye.

"Do you believe this?" he asked.

I hesitated before I shrugged and said, "I cannot say you aye, only that it seems mightily strange." I could not, then, meet Rwyan's gaze.

He looked to her and asked the same question.

She nodded. "I do."

Tezdal emptied the cup. "Then tell me what it means."

Rwyan said, "I cannot give clear answer. I can only tell you I believe we none of us need die; that there's hope."

"Of what?" he demanded. "How?"

Rwyan smiled. "Of intervention. Of some power beyond our understanding that offers us escape. From death and from war—some hope of a future without this conflict that binds us all to its bloody cause. A hope of peace. Between your people and mine; between we Dhar and the Changed. Hope of a different world; perhaps a better world."

For a long time Tezdal stared at her. I had the feeling then that our future hung suspended on a fragile thread of belief in creatures of legend. Creatures likely long gone into the mists of time. Dead and forgotten by all save we Storymen.

Yet still there were the dreams; so vivid, so real, I felt the flame of my burgeoning hope surge fiercer. I felt, somehow, that to doubt was to betray that power that came to me in sleep, that I could not— nor should—turn my back on those great eyes that judged and offered hope.

I heard Rwyan say, "Daviot first sowed these seeds in my mind. I did not believe him then; I do now. I believe there *is* some pattern woven between we four. Between him and me, and you, and Urt. I believe we are summoned to change our world."

She took my hand as she spoke, and smiled at me, and I felt horribly ashamed that I had doubted her.

Tezdal said, "By dragons?"

Rwyan went on smiling as she shrugged. "Perhaps the gods work their will through dragons. I cannot say—I'd not assume to interpret such commands. But this I tell you—that I believe we've hope. And do we ignore what these dreams have told us, we betray a greater cause than any held by Ahn or Dhar or Changed."

Tezdal studied her face awhile. His own was a kaleidoscope of emotions. What mine showed, I cannot say: confusion, I suppose, or hope—for her voice was a clarion calling me to a victory in which I could hardly dare trust, but neither ignore.

Tezdal asked, "Then what shall I do?"

I saw the beginnings of belief on his face; I heard hope in his voice. I heard Rwyan say, "First, find some means to speak with Urt.

Delay Allanyn. Dream again—I believe the answer shall come. Stand ready when it does."

He studied her for long moments, intently as if he'd draw his answers from her sightless gaze. She faced him calm, her lovely face resolute. Then he ducked his head, that simple motion somehow become a formal admission, and said, "I shall. But best this promised answer come soon—I think neither Allanyn nor my brothers shall allow you too much more time."

Rwyan stood and took his hands. "Only believe, Tezdal, and perhaps we'll find the way to change this world."

He smiled, and gave us both a formal bow, and went out the door. I looked to Rwyan and asked her, "Do you truly believe all this?"

She said, "Yes," and kissed me. And asked, "Do you not?"

I could only sigh and shrug: I'd not her faith, then. I thought I'd spun out yarns of fancy, the weavings of a young man's imagination, and she caught in them, like a netted fish that swims hither and yon, not seeing the skeins that drift ever closer until finally they close and mesh the catch firm, until it dies.

I should have trusted her better. She was ever wiser than I.

No word had come from either Urt or Tezdal; but neither had we been summoned by the Raethe or Allanyn appeared to gloat. That last I considered a favorable sign that Tezdal had succeeded in delaying her, and therefore came to believe truly in Rwyan's prognostications. Or perhaps he had only endeavored to save the lives of two friends. Or perhaps he had taken the Way of Honor and was given whatever funerary rites were the Kho'rabi custom, of which none thought to inform two Dhar prisoners.

I had little appetite that night, either for the food served us or for Rwyan. I held her and we made love, but my mind was ever on the morrow and what it should likely bring. I felt lost.

And when the dream came, both stranger than before and clearer, it slung me further into confusion. It was as though some message came to me, but writ in language I must struggle to comprehend.

I sat atop some craggy peak, all jagged stone that thrust stark fingers at a darkened sky. Cloud hid the land below, and a fierce wind stabbed my naked skin. I looked about, thinking to find companions— Rwyan, Urt, and Tezdal—but there were none: I was alone.

Then thunder filled the air, and all around me settled vast forms, not quite distinguishable, but misty, impressions of wide wings and fangs and claws. I cowered under the observation of eyes that studied me with an alien passion. It was as if I stood under the gaze of gods, their interests greater than a mere man's, and born of other concerns, higher and unknowable.

I felt afraid: I knelt.

And into my mind came a question: *Why do you fear us?*

I answered, "Are you truly real?"

And the voice said, *We are real. You called us; now we call you. Shall you answer, or shall you die?*

I said, "I'd not die."

And the voice said, *Then have faith. You called us. We heard you then, and now we answer you. Believe!*

I said, "And do I? Shall you save us, all of us?"

And the voice said, *Those who believe, aye. They are chosen, and those we shall save.*

I asked, "Are you gods, then?"

And the voice belled laughter that blew me down, my hands raised to protect my ears, and said, *Not gods. But your salvation, do you believe.*

I said, "Give me a sign then."

And the voice said, *You are the sign, Daviot. And Rwyan; Urt and Tezdal. Call us, and we come. We are salvation.*

I said, "Then come. Take us out of this place."

And the voice said, *So be it. But shall you pay the price?*

I said, "What price?"

And the voice gave me back, *Life over death.*

I said, "Yes. Only save Rwyan, and whatever price you name I'll pay."

And the voice answered me, *Stand ready.*

The wings spread then, hiding the sky, and from all those glowing eyes I felt a promise, a pledge of absolute certainty, even as I was beaten down by the thunder and cowered beneath that terrible wind as my ears were dinned with shrieks of triumph, as if all the wolves in the world howled in unison.

I woke filled in a manner I cannot properly describe with confidence. It was like the cessation of an illness, the abatement of fever: when you fall asleep sweat-drenched and troubled and wake cool, knowing the sickness gone. I felt I had made a decision. The burgeoning dawn seemed somehow brighter. I smiled.

Beside me, Rwyan stirred. I stroked her cheek and her eyes opened. She "looked" at me and smiled. "You dreamed," she said, and it was not a question, but confirmation that we shared this thing.

I said, "Yes. They shall come soon, I think."

She nodded, understanding, and I sprang from the bed to wash and dress, that I be ready for—what? I could not say. Only that I felt —no! that I *knew*—the future must soon shift in its course.

It was anticlimax to see three gifted come in with our morning meal. I know not what I had expected—some explosion, perhaps, the roof of our chamber ripped away, and dragons come down to carry us off; Urt and Tezdal come storming in with drawn swords. To find only our usual guardians bearing bread and fruit and cheese, tea, was prosaic. Rwyan "saw" my expression and laughed (which utterly disconcerted our warders) and told me, "Trust." Which confused the Changed the more.

We ate and waited. Rwyan was far more composed than I: I found it hard.

Harder still when Urt came to us with solemn mien and shoulders slumped and said, "Do we walk awhile in the garden? I am asked to speak with you again."

Past him in the corridor, I saw three gifted Changed. Their faces were hard to read, but I thought I saw the flashings of triumph in their eyes. I feared then that the dream had come too late, and we were both of us condemned. But Rwyan said, "Yes, that should be pleasant," and took my hand, the pressure of her slim fingers a reminder to trust. And so I smiled and echoed her, and we went out into the open air.

It was obviously the design of the Raethe that Urt have one last chance to convince us Rwyan should give her knowledge willingly. He led us down the winding paths into the strange woodland, our golden-banded escort hanging back a few careful steps as if they'd afford him time and space to win us over.

In a tone designed to carry, he told us we had no hope but could only submit to the will of the Raethe. That the Great Coming was a foregone conclusion, and we no choice save between cooperation and its rewards, or the unpleasant alternative.

In whispers, he spoke of the dream he'd had. He shuddered as he told it, still not at all happy with the notion of a Changed and dragons communing. It was much like mine: reassurance offered, pledges given, and he no more able than I to say exactly what it meant. But still, for all that the likelihood of rescue seemed to diminish with each step we took, I felt oddly confident, my faith firmed by those oneiric promises. I smiled and whispered back, "Did you believe, Urt?"

He sighed and lowered his head, the gesture more submissive than confirming, and said, "I did. I felt not much choice. I felt . . . that did I refuse, I should betray my kind."

Rwyan laughed; confidently. My smile grew broader.

We walked, then, through a copse of tall beech trees. The ground beneath was bare, the earth hard and scattered with cobs. The trees were stately in the manner of beeches, fending sunlight through their boughs like duelists weaving traceries of light and shadow down in dancing patterns. I thought the same shadowplay worked over Urt's face: hope and disbelief mingling.

He loosed a gusty sigh and glanced at me. "It was easier in Durbrecht, Daviot," he said wearily. "I'd no dreams there; save freedom. Now—now I dream of dragons and a wider liberty. Can it be so?"

This copse was akin to some cathedral: I could only answer true. I said, "I've known those dreams, Urt, and last night I was given a promise. I cannot explain it properly, but I believe we've hope."

He said, "Tezdal said as much. He was set to the Way of Honor, but then you spoke with him and we compared our dreams, and he delayed. He promised to find you here. But . . ." He looked up as if he'd find an answer in the sky, through the wide-spread branches that scattered all the light of hope and doubt over his face. "But save Rwyan agree to give up all the secrets of Dhar magic willingly, Allanyn shall take her and use the crystals on her this night."

Suddenly the shadows seemed darker, like gathering storm. The breeze that rustled the beeches seemed harsher. I felt Rwyan's hand clench hard about my fingers.

"She's the ear of all the Raethe," Urt said, "and neither I nor any other could dissuade them. By sun's set, they agreed. Can I not persuade you by then . . ."

He shrugged. I looked up. The sun was westered: not far off its setting. I looked at Urt and saw no doubt in his eyes. There was only despair there, such as would match and meet what I'd felt before I'd accepted the dream's promise.

Rwyan said, "You told Tezdal?"

Urt nodded. "Everything; all of it."

She asked, "And he believed?"

Urt said, "He did. But even so—Allanyn will bring you to the crystals at sunset."

Rwyan said, "Have faith, Urt. Allanyn shall not have her way! Neither with us nor the world."

He looked at her with worried eyes. "I'd believe you, Rwyan, but how can it be?" His eyes flicked sideways in mute indication of our escort. "Three gifted watch us e'en now; and your magic is powerless here. How shall you escape Allanyn?"

There was a way: my promise to her. My newfound confidence faltered then. Rwyan "saw" my expression and said, "Fear not, Daviot. It shall not come to that."

In that moment I shared Urt's fear. Against the rock of my belief there washed fierce waves of doubt. The shadows of the beeches hung long across the ground as the sun moved ever closer to the west, closer to its setting. It seemed to me the orb moved with unnatural speed.

Rwyan said, "Urt, does Tezdal know of Allanyn's intent?"

He nodded, not speaking, and she asked him, "And does he know you walk with us here?"

Again he nodded. This time he said, "But what good that? What shall Tezdal do? What *can* he do?"

Rwyan smiled. "We shall see."

We walked awhile in silence then, our escort a discreet distance behind. I wondered if they were out of earshot or if their talent enabled them to hear all we said. If that, I knew us lost. I thought that did they call us back, then I should strike that blow I dreaded. Beyond the trees I heard a stream gurgling over stones. It sounded to me like a clepsydra, measuring out the moments left us. I looked to the east and saw the sky darkening; to the west the sun stood close on the treetops. I felt Rwyan's hand in mine, warm and dry. I conjured my last dream, reliving it vivid in my mind, that I might renew my threatened hope.

Then I gaped as I saw Tezdal come strolling through the wood. He was dressed in his Kho'rabi finery, but now he wore the long sword he named a kachen sheathed on his waist. His expression was dark: I thought him troubled by some inner turmoil.

Rwyan loosed her hand and murmured soft, "Stand ready."

I made some inarticulate sound in confirmation and watched as Tezdal approached our three guardians. His gait was somehow altered, so that I was minded of a stalking cat, its casual approach concealing its murderous intent. I was reminded of the Kho'rabi I had met in battle. I moved away from Rwyan, toward the three Changed.

They had halted politely as the Sky Lord came up. He offered them an arrogant bow and said, "Allanyn would see you in the crystal chamber." He gestured in our direction. "These you may leave in my charge."

The Changed glanced at one another, frowning. One said, "How so, my lord? Our orders are clear—to grant Urt until sunset to convince the mage. Can he not, then to bring her to Allanyn."

Tezdal's shoulders lifted in a shrug. "Do you question me?" he asked.

No: he did not ask, but demanded, challenging. In that moment he was entirely Kho'rabi. It took the Changed aback.

The speaker said, "I fail to understand, my lord."

I saw Tezdal's fingers drum irritably against his scabbard: a man accustomed to command, in no wise familiar with disagreement. He said, "What's to understand?"

The Changed said, "Forgive me, my lord, but our orders were explicit. We are not to leave these three alone."

Tezdal said, "Then I've no choice."

And drew his blade.

I saw what he intended. I thought he attempted an impossible task: these three were gifted. One, perhaps, he might slay, but even as that one died, the others would bring their magic against him and destroy him. Fleeting into my mind came the thought that perhaps that was his wish—that he chose this Way of Honor.

I had fought Kho'rabi and knew their deadly skills. I had seen none so skilled as Tezdal.

His blade sliced a bloody line across the Changed's belly. I saw a crimson cloud explode as the man doubled over, hands clamped to the dreadful cut. Tezdal spun full around, the long sword lifting to hack through the upraised wrists of a second victim. The mouth that had begun to shape a gramarye opened wider as the hands fell, and a horrible scream replaced the spell. Tezdal reversed the stroke—how could any man move so fast?—prepared to carve the third like some piece of kindling wood.

And he was flung back, hurled away by an occult wind that picked him up and threw him down as if he were no more than a feather. I saw the sword ripped from his hands. It spun high in the darkening air as he struck the ground with such awful force, I heard the gusting of the air punched from his lungs. I saw the blade turn, supported by magic as it ceased its spinning and came back toward him, hovering above his supine form preparatory to skewering him.

Had I owned the time to think then, I'd have blessed Keran and Cleton for all their lessons. I think Andyrt should have been proud of me.

I was running: I hurled myself up, as I had been taught, launching myself feet foremost into the air. My boots struck the gifted Changed square between the shoulders. He was thrown forward onto his face. His spell ended abruptly in a shrill exhalation that choked off as his mouth filled with dust and dropped beech cobs. The sword hanging above Tezdal wavered, twisting around, then fell careless across my friend's chest.

I rolled to my feet. The martial training of Mnemonikos and Kho'rabi knights was never so different: attack, and you are committed. I turned as I rose, my hands finding the Changed's chin even as my knees lodged against his spine. He grunted, and I felt his power gathering, a prickling on my skin. I pulled up and back, turning the jaw. I heard the horrid sound of cracking bone and felt the head come loose in my hands. I felt the life go out and my stomach churn. I wanted badly to vomit. Instead, I sprang away. I told myself I had no choice: that these slain folk would have slain me and Rwyan. All of us; but still I felt scant appetite for the killing.

I looked to the wounded sorcerer and saw her kneeling, weeping over the bloody stumps that ended her arms. She shaped a gramarye to quench the flow of spurting blood. All her attention was focused on that. I did not know what to do.

Tezdal rose. He shook his head as if to clear it of nightmares' memories and picked up his sword. He looked at the weeping Changed and came staggering toward her.

I said, "No!"

He paid me no attention; only raised the blade and cut off her head. It rolled away over the dry ground in a fountain of blood.

I forced my stomach not to empty itself. I heard Rwyan make a sound that was part scream and part cry of hope.

The first victim of Tezdal's attack knelt over a glutinous mass of spilled entrails. My Sky Lord comrade beheaded him with the calm efficiency of a slaughterman. Then he drew a patch of silk from his belt and wiped his sword. His face was an expressionless mask. I swallowed bile. I looked to where Rwyan stood. Her eyes were wide with disgust and horror, but there was also something more that I could not properly define. She clutched Urt's arm, and on his face I saw only amazement. I looked around, suddenly aware that twilight fell. Stars already freckled the eastern sky. The darkening of the clearing amongst the beeches matched the darkening of the ground. The sun hung red in the west; the soil lay red at my feet.

(Is it always so? Must we always find our truths in blood?)

Tezdal sheathed his cleaned sword and said, "Come! I've horses waiting past the wall."

Urt said, "Where can we go?"

Rwyan said, "Toward hope! Do as Tezdal says!"

I said nothing. I knew we were committed now, all of us. Did we remain, we had no hope at all. Allanyn should have her revenge on all of us, unthinking and blind as her ambition. I could only trust that whatever came to us in those oneiric sendings did not offer false hope but told us truth. I felt, still, that certainty that had come to me; but also the surety that now we were horridly dead, save we escaped this place. Our lives balanced on a knife's edge: I saw no choice save to trust in Tezdal and run. In those moments I did not think at all of the planned invasion or of what Ennas Day should bring to Dharbek, but only of our personal survival.

I said, "Urt, do you stay here, you're dead! Come with us!"

I took his hand and Rwyan's and ran after Tezdal.

I felt a tug, and then Urt was with us, leaving go my hand to run faster than I, going by Tezdal.

As he passed the Sky Lord he shouted, "Where past the wall?"

Tezdal yelled an answer I could not hear, and Urt loped ahead. I saw his canine ancestry then, as he ran, loose-limbed and fleet. But I heard him shout back, "After me, then. I know these trails."

Trails?

I had seen this woodland from the window of our prison. I had walked here: gardens, surely, woven by Changed magic into disregard of season, but no more than that. No more than some expression of sorcerers' vanity, or the vested power of Trebizar's crystals. I should have guessed better when we trod that grove of beeches. I should have known magic better.

We did not run through some garden: we fled through a forest. It was not possible, and yet the evidence of my eyes told me it was so. We quit the clearing, and beeches were replaced with majestic oaks. We splashed across the stream I'd heard and followed Urt through the willow curtains beyond. We ran across a meadow that could not have occupied so much space, the grass long—and leaving a clear trail for trackers, I thought; did those who must surely come after us have need for such mundane signs. We ran past stands of ash and hornbeam, and it became quite impossible to judge time, my chronological sense distorted by these weird dimensions.

Dusk fell, the sun offering a last defiance of encroaching night, layering the western sky with red and gold as if some vast furnace threw wide its gates. Urt slowed that we not lose sight of him. I felt my damaged leg begin to throb. I had not run so hard or so far in too long. I looked to Rwyan and saw her panting, her hair flung wild, her skirts gathered up to reveal long slender legs. She smiled at me and without speaking urged me on. I nodded. I thought we could not escape. Even did we reach the wall, even did we find the promised horses—where should we go? Where could we go? The valley ringed us with hilly walls. Even did we reach those mountains undetected—

and I could not see how that might be—we should still find all of Ur-Dharbek our prison. Either coast was too far, the Slammerkin was a barrier, the north an unknown country.

North.

Sheer startlement made me stumble as the voice spoke inside my head. It was an emotional compass, a disincarnate magnet that summoned the fibers of my nerves.

North!

It was an imperative: a clarion of promise, urgent. It was as soundless as the voices of my dreams, but so clear, so vivid, I turned my head, thinking to find the speaker running at my side. I pitched full length onto the dirt of the narrow trail. Rwyan cried out and halted, stooping to help me rise. I spat dirt, embarrassed and confused. She said, "You heard it," and it was not a question: I nodded.

"Then come!"

I grunted. My leg hurt badly now, twisted by the fall. I limped as I matched her pace. She took my hand, and it seemed strength flowed into me. I thought her magic was returned her, but likely it was only her determination. I wondered if I heard a bell ringing, an alarum, or if I heard only the pounding of my blood within my skull.

Then, through a line of yews, I saw the white barrier of the wall. Urt halted there; Tezdal shouted, gesturing, and they both began to search along the wall.

Tezdal had planned well: I marveled at his resourcefulness. A length of thick rope, knotted to afford firm handholds, hung down. He called, beckoning us.

Urt went first, limber to the wall's top, where he perched, reaching back to help Rwyan up. She joined him there, looked back a moment, and disappeared. Tezdal pushed me to the cord, touching his sword as he stared back, head cocked. I heard the bell clear now. I took the rope and began to climb. I thought my leg should fail me then: it seemed that fire burned my muscles. I moaned and gritted my teeth and willed myself to climb. I felt Urt's hand on my wrist, strong, hauling me up. He took my belt and manhandled me over, setting my hands on the rope on the farther side.

I dropped the last few feet and cried out as I struck the ground. Urt appeared beside me, then Tezdal, and they each took an arm and raised me to my feet, almost dragging me to where Rwyan stood with the reins of four restive horses in her hands.

Then they must shove me astride, for my leg could no longer support my weight. It was a relief to find the saddle.

North!

It seemed to echo in my mind like the ringing of the bell behind us. I drove heels against my horse's flanks and brought the bay to a gallop. Rwyan rode to my left, Tezdal on my right. Urt was a neck ahead. We rode as if all the Church's demons bayed at our heels. I thought no kinder creatures would follow us. I thought of Allanyn's feral eyes and decided confrontation with demons might well be the lesser torment.

The land was gentle here, like a park, grassy and undulating, with small hursts visible under the light of the moon. That orb was risen full, huge and butter-yellow. It minded me of the eyes of my dreams.

North!

And with that command, a sense of urgency. It was not articulate but entirely emotional. It was a promise I could not define but only accept. I knew, somehow, that we must gain distance from the building by the lake—from the aegis of the Raethe's strongest power— before the promise might be fulfilled. I hunched in my saddle, willing this stranger horse to run as I knew my old gray could. My hurt leg throbbed; I dismissed the pain. Far worse awaited me—awaited all of us—did we not make whatever rendezvous lay ahead.

I chanced a backward glance and saw the town across the lake lit bright. There was light from the Council building, too; and the moon's image shimmered on the water. I saw the skyboats glimmer redly, the fires of the Kho'rabi encamped below reflecting off the sanguine flanks of the great craft. I turned away: there was no point in looking back, now less than ever. Did Changed magic not somehow find a way to reach out and strike us down, then surely the Sky Lords must soon enough launch their little boats and quarter the night sky until they found us.

North!

It was our only hope.

The lights of farmhouses shone far off around us. Dogs barked, their keen ears doubtless alert to our desperation. The land rolled and folded. We galloped through streams and crossed, slower, rivers. We ran through fields of autumnal wheat and stands of trees. Our horses threatened to falter. We drove them hard; too hard. I felt slaver blow back against my face, and under my knees I could feel the bay's ribs heaving. His neck was wet with sweat. I knew he could not hold this pace much longer.

Urt shouted, gesturing back. I could not hear what he said, but there was no need: the sight of it was plain enough.

Low in the sky came a skyboat.

It was one of the little scout craft: a questing hound that darted this way and that, crossing our trail, returning to the scent. It followed us inexorable as doom.

I saw others, but none so close. They roamed the valley, but only this one seemed to find our path. I wondered how long before the Kho'rabi wizards felt sure of their prey and sent word to their fellows, and all those darting specks I saw should converge above us and send their magicks against us, and we be all destroyed.

Or would they only trap us? Come down and ring us with such might of magic or plain steel as must deny us all escape?

I thought that then I must deliver Rwyan my promise.

I thought of that gifted I had slain and saw my love's head turned loose in my hands the same way. I should do it: I had given her my word, and it were better than to leave her to Allanyn's revenge; but still I felt my belly recoil at the notion.

We rode on. Hooves drummed on hard-packed dirt. I thought the sound must echo against the sky, an aural beacon to our pursuers.

What need of that, to those who bound the aerial spirits to their cause? They could ask the elementals to sound the air, the vibrations of the ground, the flavor of the wind; all of it to their cause: to find us. I looked back and saw the little skyboat cease its questing. It ran straight now, after us; sure as a scented hound. I thought I saw the archers in the basket beneath. I felt my shoulders tense, anticipating the prick of arrows, the blast of magic.

I wondered how it should feel to die. I looked to Rwyan and saw her smile. She called out words I could not hear over the thunder of the hooves and the rush of the wind. I smiled back. I felt no hope at all and could not understand how she could; not now.

Surely we were doomed.

I saw the skyboat closing on us, arrowing after.

And then a shape descend out of the night.

It was a blackness against the stars, a swooping shadow across the face of the moon. I reined my mount to head-hung standstill and sat the heaving animal entirely oblivious of my comrades, of still-impending danger. I was Mnemonikos—and now I looked on what no other Rememberer had ever witnessed. I could not ignore it, even at cost of my life.

I looked on a dragon.

It came down so swift, I had only an impression of the angled leathery wings that spread impossibly wide as it broke its meteoric descent. A long tail lashed and plumed straight. Great limbs thrust out, much as do a cat's when that lesser creature looks to break a fall.

A massive head extended on a serpentine neck, the jaws opened to display fangs as long as Tezdal's sword; I had no doubt they should be as sharp. I glimpsed enormous eyes, yellow and unblinking.

It made no more sound than a swooping owl. It was as deadly — and if it were the owl, then the skyboat was the mouse.

There was a gaseous explosion as the dragon struck. For an instant it was outlined clear in the fireball of the skyboat's destruction. It fell through the wreckage, taloned hindfeet closing on the basket, large enough to encompass that float. The wings beat, lifting the massive body back up through the burning tatters of the ravaged supporting sack. I heard the screams of dying men. I saw the dragon rise, the forelimbs clutching now at the basket, the head descending to pluck at the Kho'rabi as if the awesome creature snatched tidbits from a platter. It shook its head as does a terrier worrying at a rat. Bits and pieces — basket and men all mingled — tumbled down. The dragon let fall its prey and beat its wings and hurtled toward me.

I was only dimly aware of Rwyan turning her horse to come back, to stand beside me as we both stared, awed, at this terrible spectacle.

Then our mounts screamed in naked terror and began to buck as the massive shape swooped low overhead.

I felt pain, and the night sky spun madly before my eyes. Then I felt myself lifted and saw three Rwyans kneeling close, all of them expressing a confusing mixture of concern and terror and amazement and hope. I closed my eyes, and when I opened them again, there was only one Rwyan, and she was asking if I were well.

I nodded and wished I'd not. I think I said yes, but my gaze was already moving past her to the battle in the sky above. I climbed to my feet, wincing as pain's daggers stabbed my leg. She came close, easing a shoulder beneath my arm, and I held her and leaned against her as we both watched legend unfold.

Urt came trotting back afoot. He was dirtied by his own fall. His eyes were wide, and his jaw hung open in unalloyed wonder. He said nothing, only stared. He radiated fear: I reached out and set an arm around him. His support was welcome, but mostly I sought to reassure him: he shook like an autumn leaf in a savage wind, hung by the most tenuous connection to the sanity of the tree.

I said, "Urt, they come to save us. Only that! They offer us no harm." I hoped I spoke true: what I saw in the sky was pure chaos.

He gave me back no answer but a moan. I drew him closer and felt his arm span my waist. He was very hot and trembled constantly.

Rwyan said, "Remember the dreams, Urt! Believe them! This is our salvation come."

He made a sound like a puppy's whimper. I thought that this must be how it had been for all those Changed we Truemen left behind in Ur-Dharbek as dragons' prey, that we might live free. I thought him then the bravest of us all, for he did not run but stood with us and fought the terror inherent in his blood; inherent in what we'd made him.

I heard hoofbeats and saw Tezdal come back, fighting his terrified mount. I wondered at his horsemanship, that he could still control the panicked animal. He snatched it to a stop and sprang down. He was no less amazed than we. I could not tell if he was so frightened, but he let go the reins and stared skyward as the roan stallion ran wild. He drew his sword, and I believed that he would fight the dragons if they attacked us.

Rwyan said, "They come to save us, Tezdal," and there was such confidence in her voice, he sheathed the blade.

Above us skyboats fell in blossoms of fire.

The night filled with those sparkling flowers as the balloons were burst by claws and fangs and lashing tails. My ears dinned with the howls of dying men and the savage calling of the dragons. Worst, somehow, was the shrieking of the elementals, for that sound lanced sharp into the deepest fibers of my being. It was the sound of creatures entrapped and resentful, now freed and glorying in the destruction of their jailers in a manner quite alien to the triumphant belling of the dragons. Theirs was the shouting of warriors come to honest battle. It was clean as the howling of wolves: they did not gloat, only announced their victory. The elementals made a different sound, and it grated on my nerves and set my teeth on edge. It told me it was wrong to bind such spirits to man's cause, or any other, save their own. I saw them burst loose and I *felt* their gratitude, that they were freed from bondage to unwilling cause. I saw (I cannot be absolutely sure, but I tell you what I believe) numerous of them join with the dragons to slay the Kho'rabi, like prisoners turning on their captors. I believe I saw bodies rent without attention of the dragons. It was as if vague forms wound around the falling Sky Lords and slew them as they fell; as if the very air plucked them apart. I think they took their revenge.

Then, I saw only the falling skyboats and the terrible culling of the dragons. The Kho'rabi wizards flung ineffectual magic at the sourian predators; and it was useful as blunt-tipped practice arrows against battle armor.

The dragons seemed not to notice. They shrugged it off and fell and clawed and bit, oblivious of anything save the need to pluck the skyboats from the sky.

Which they did with the calm and bloody efficiency of a wolf pack cutting deer from the herd. Cold as mathematics; indifferent to aught save the task in hand.

And we four stood watching, huddled fearful and patient under that stained and fire-filled sky. Watching our pursuers slain; wondering what our fate should be.

I held Rwyan, and I felt Urt's terror. I wondered how Tezdal could stand so calm to see his kin slain. I was not afraid. I had passed beyond fear: I felt only wonder then, and I stood awed in witness of what Truemen said could not be, but was.

And then the dragons came down to land before us.

As I had done in dreams, now we all knelt under the beat of those wings. No more oneiric but real; lifting great clouds of swirling grass and dust, heavy as thunder. Awesome as dream—or nightmare —come true, shaped out in flesh: *real!*

I looked into yellow eyes that took the moon's place: there was nothing else. I saw bloodied fangs, hung with remnants of flesh. I felt hot breath on my face. I saw talons settled in the dirt before me, like roots sunk in betwixt ground and sky. I saw wings hung all leathery, spread in promise or condemnation. I could not tell or know; only marvel. I saw, beyond the massive body, a tail switch restlessly, lofting clouds of grass. I saw a paw rise: a pink tongue lap absently at crimsoned claws.

I heard a voice say, "So, you are saved. Do you come with me, then? Or shall you wait here like frightened sheep until your hunters come?"

I only stared, dumbstruck. It was Rwyan who said, "Who are you? I'd have a name ere I go with you."

Laughter then, like any man's; but more, as if he found amusement in her courage past my understanding.

"Your hope," he said. "The answer to your . . . prayers? Surely to the calling of your dreams. Come now; or stay and die here. All of you."

I could not quite believe that Rwyan rose so readily and went to him—toward those awful, bloodstained fangs. But she paused and reached out to take my hand, and said again, "Who are you?"

And past the dragon's head I heard him answer, "I am Bellek. Now come with me."

I followed Rwyan. Urt and Tezdal came behind us. I think not even the Sky Lord was unafraid then.

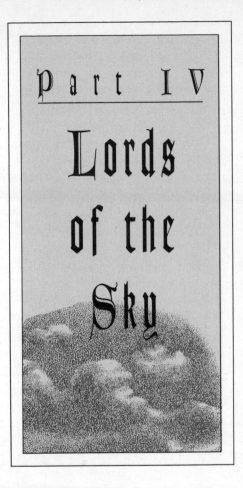

PART IV

Lords
of the
Sky

32

I halted, wary as the dragon's head descended closer. But it was only that the rider might dismount, clambering from the long neck to one great shoulder, springing from that to the ground. He grunted, though the distance was not so great, and straightened his back with a heartfelt sigh. The dragon turned its massive head a fraction, an eye observing him with an expression I could only interpret as concern.

He said, "By all the gods, I grow too old for this."

I stared at him. His hair was the white of snow lit by a cold moon, tied back in a tail that hung to his waist. His face was leathery as his mount's wings, as dark and seamed with wrinkles, like deep cuts in the flesh. He was shorter than I, about Urt's size, dressed like some wildman, some hermit come down off his mountain; which, of course, he was. He wore a shirt of patched hide, sewn crude and belted with woven hair, and breeks in no better condition, loose and patched and stained. A wolfskin jerkin was stretched taut by his broad shoulders. Hides bound in rough semblance of boots covered his feet. He smiled, exposing teeth that were startling for their pristine regularity.

"So, you are Rwyan." His eyes—I could not be certain of the color in the moonlight, but I thought them pale blue or perhaps gray —scanned us all, as if confirming our identities. "And you, Daviot. Then this must be the one called Urt, and this the Sky Lord."

Tezdal said, "I am Tezdal Kashijan," offering a deep, formal bow.

Bellek chuckled. "Tezdal shall do, Sky Lord. What ceremony we follow is theirs."

He gestured at the dragon crouched beside him like some watchful hound.

I leaned on Rwyan and Urt and marveled at all this. I asked, "How do you know our names?"

He laughed again. I wondered if I heard an edge of madness in the sound. He said, "Blood calls to blood, Daviot; and there's truth in dreams."

That sounded to me like oracular riddling, but Rwyan said, "I told you! It's the pattern."

Bellek shrugged. "What's in a name?" he asked. "The blood's in you and called us. Is that a pattern? Perhaps it is. But we can discuss that later—in some place your hunters shall not find us."

He hesitated then, head cocking toward the dragon, and nodded. "Aye, sweetling, I hear them. Soon, eh? Do you call them, and we'll be gone."

I felt then—you know those moments when it seems a voice whispers over your shoulder? Or from the corner of your eye you catch some movement? But when you tune your ear or turn your head, there's nothing there?—it was like that. I knew Bellek and the dragon spoke together, and almost I could hear what they said. I saw the dragon raise its head and loose an oddly soft hooting call that was answered from across the fields. Then the air grew loud with wingbeats, and more of the terrifying creatures landed about us.

They settled, monolithic and magnificent, bathed in pale moonlight like barbaric statuary. I choked on blown dust, blind a moment. I heard Urt moan softly and felt his shoulders hunch under my arm.

Bellek said, "They'll not harm you, Urt. Those days are long gone. But you must trust them and ride them."

His tone was kindly but tinged with impatience and a hint of contempt. It crossed my mind that it was the tone a sated predator—a wolf or an owl—might use, did predators speak to potential prey when their bellies were filled and they hunted no longer.

Urt shuddered and shook his head. It was difficult to discern that particular motion from the general shaking of his body.

I said, "Urt, you must! Trust him!"

Urt said, the words forced past chattering teeth, "I cannot! No—not dragons!"

Bellek said, "If he'll not mount, we must leave him here."

Tezdal said, "I do not go without Urt. Leave him, and you leave me."

Bellek said, "There are more of your kind coming, Sky Lord; and Changed sorcerers. You die if you stay. I think it should be slowly."

Tezdal said, "Then I shall die. I'll not leave Urt."

I broke from Rwyan's grip, wincing as my weight fell on my hurting leg. I looked into Urt's face; set hands on his vibrating shoulders. I said, "Urt, do you trust me?"

He moaned back, "Yes, but I cannot ride a dragon."

I thought it must take all his will to stand upright and speak; I admired him. I said, "You must. Do you not, then Allanyn shall take you and punish you in ways far worse than any fear you feel now. Worse! She'll have her way and bring the world to bloody war for only her ambition. Would you allow that?"

He said, "I'd not. But—" His eyes roved wild and white-rimmed over our encircling audience. "Dragons, Daviot? I cannot!"

I asked again, "Do you trust me, Urt?"

He nodded again and began to speak. I shifted my grip from his shoulders to his neck. I was afraid I'd do it wrong; that my hurting leg would refuse my weight, but it did not. I found the nerves there and squeezed, whispering, "Forgive me, Urt," as he started and fought me. It was too late. I saw his eyes jump wide, then glaze. For an instant they held an outrage that filled me with guilt. Then he fell loose from my hands. I fell down with him.

Rwyan and Bellek helped me to my feet. Her eyes were clouded with doubt and approval, all mixed. His were entirely approving. He said as I rose, soft in my ear, "You've the makings, Daviot."

Tezdal lifted Urt, and on his face I saw only disapproval.

I said, "Does he stay—do either of you stay—you'll die. I'd not see that. Do as Bellek says."

Tezdal's face shone angry in the moon's light. "Does he not have the right to choose his death? Is there no honor in Dharbek?"

Rwyan spoke for me: "We've larger concerns, Tezdal. I'd not see Urt die for fear of going with friends. I'd not see you die needlessly. Do not forget your vow!"

Her voice was forged steel, hard and unyielding. Tezdal stared at her. I thought he'd argue. Stay here to take his Way of Honor, Urt his squire; and both lost.

Rwyan said, "We've hope, Tezdal! Bellek offers us hope, and I hold you to that vow."

The Sky Lord's face was black as he nodded. "What shall I do?"

Rwyan looked to Bellek. He said, "You must all do what none save I have in too long—you must ride the dragons."

Leaning on Rwyan's shoulder, I stared at the beasts and wondered how.

Bellek said, "And soon. More of those little flying craft come after you; and horsemen. I cannot command so many dragons as to defeat them all—so you mount, or I leave you here."

Rwyan said, "We mount."

I said, "How?"

Bellek gusted that crazy chuckle again and beckoned to us.

"Set Urt on Kathanria," he said. "I'll show you how."

He gestured at the beast he had ridden, which raised a sky-consuming eye as if in inquiry of mention of her name. He spoke to her, and she lowered her great head against the ground as does a cat or a dog eager to be stroked, anxious to obey that it earn the approval of its . . . *master* is the wrong word. There is a relationship between species, between dogs and their owners; between cats and their owners. It seems to me a thing born of trust and mutual dependence—that one species gains from the other in equal measure.

Then, I knew only that this formidable creature laid down her head, stretching out her neck so that I saw a saddle set forward of her shoulders. It was a kind of bucket, high at cantle and back, with straps hanging loose and bags beside. It was not dissimilar to the saddle I'd long ago set on my gray mare, but far larger; in keeping with this mount's size.

We climbed up the splayed foreleg. The dragon stretched it like a ladder. Bellek went first, and Tezdal passed him Urt's loose body. The silver-haired man beckoned the Sky Lord up, and he climbed as if familiar with dragons. I stood with Rwyan by the massive forelimb. Kathanria lay still, but I could feel the heave of her ribs as she breathed and smell the dry-dust odor of her skin. I saw insects crawling there, but they paid me no heed. I thought I was likely too small to merit their attention.

Aided by Tezdal, Bellek stretched Urt's limp form behind the saddle. From the bags, he brought cords with which he bound Urt secure. I wondered how far we should travel, how long, and dreaded that Urt should wake and panic. I feared he might step over that line betwixt sanity and madness did he open his eyes to find himself in flight, across a dragon's back. I feared he would not forgive me.

Bellek clambered down. "He'll be safe enough," he promised. "Kathanria's a gentle lady."

I eyed the beast, which eyed me, unwinking, back, and wondered how so dreadful a creature might be described as "a gentle lady." I think that then my mind was so occupied with thought of pursuit and escape, the full realization of what *I* was about to do had not sunk in.

It was driven home by Bellek's next words: "So do I introduce you to your mounts?"

He did not await our response but waved us after him as he marched briskly toward another dragon.

Kathanria's hide was brown, the reddish hue of a deer. This beast was darker, mottled gray and black. Her eyes were tawny. I could not understand how I knew her name (or how, again, I knew she was female) before Bellek spoke.

"This is Anryäle," he said. "Rwyan, do you take her?"

Rwyan nodded and reached out to touch the dragon's snout, for all the world as if she stroked a beast of no more import than a horse. Anryäle blew a gusty exhalation, and I knew she took pleasure from the contact. I gaped as Rwyan followed Bellek's instructions: up the splayed forelimb to the shoulder, a foot set in the stirrup dangling there, that the leverage she needed to settle herself in the saddle. Bellek climbed after her, showing her straps and buckles that were swiftly fixed in place. Rwyan clutched the frontage of the saddle and looked down on Tezdal and me.

Bellek sprang down; winced, cursed volubly, and said, "You need do nothing. Only sit and try to contain your fear. If"—this with a grin at Rwyan, who was beaming wide as any child embarking on some great adventure long dreamed of and now come true—"you are afraid."

She said, "I'm not."

It seemed to me her voice came from high above.

Bellek turned to Tezdal: "You shall ride Peliane, Sky Lord; and know what flight is."

Tezdal nodded. His face was expressionless; I wondered if he truly felt no fear or only hid it well. I was suddenly torn between a desire to stay and take my chances on firm ground, and the knowledge that to do so was to hand myself to Allanyn. I told myself that Rwyan evinced no trepidation at this incredible venture, and so nor should I. It was not easy.

Peliane was black as Kho'rabi armor, save for streaks of dull yellow about her wide jaws and along her wings. Tezdal mounted her smoothly as he did a horse. I watched, favoring my hurting leg, as Bellek showed him where the straps fit, to hold him in the saddle.

Then it was my turn.

The crispness of advancing autumn chilled the night air, but I felt hot. My mouth felt very dry, and my stomach recalled its last meal. I told myself all this was foolishness; that were harm meant us, these beasts could easily have devoured us. I knew they meant us no harm. I knew they were our only hope—not only of escape, but of far more. Hope of fulfilled dreams; of what I'd dreamed so long ago in Durbrecht. Still I felt afraid.

Bellek said, "This is Deburah, Daviot. After Kathanria, she's the sweetest, swiftest lady in the castle."

I looked at Deburah. She met my gaze with a placid topaz eye. Her hide was blue as the moonlit ocean and sleek as a sea-washed pebble. It came to me that she was beautiful, in a terrible, awesome manner. I felt her pleasure at that thought. I was far too confused, too frightened, to wonder how either she or I could know that.

It was not easy to climb her leg—my own hurt as it had not done before—but I found the saddle and sat there as Bellek strapped me in. Belts passed over my shoulders and belly, holding me firm in the saddle; more held my legs; my feet rested in the buckets of the stirrups. The saddle was cut with handholds in the front: I locked my fingers there.

Bellek said, "Only sit firm, and leave all to Deburah. Trust her."

I nodded and forced out a gasping "Yes."

He laughed and slapped my thigh, which made me wince. Then he was gone, trotting back to Kathanria.

I clutched the saddle. I realized the dragon's—no! *Deburah's*—back was ridged, as if the spine sat high above the ribs, the belly. It was a comfortable seat. I was mounted just forward of the wings, which now lay flattened back against Deburah's flanks. I realized I could look forward past the neck and head and see where we should go, what lay below us. I felt suddenly calm: it was as though she spoke to me; not in words, but in emotion. I felt my fear dissipate, like poison bleeding from an infected wound. I felt suddenly happy: I smiled.

Then stared in naked wonder as she unfurled her wings.

Those great sails had looked large enough when I watched them from the ground. Now, as I felt her lungs inflate, her ribs lift me, the vast membranous canopies seemed impossibly huge. They spread proud across the sky. They covered the moon and the stars. They were angled, sharp and jagged, but nonetheless beautiful, worked by a musculature alien to my knowledge. It came back to me again that I was witness to sights many in my College would have sold their souls to see. I clutched the saddle tighter as I felt her legs rise and bunch, and into my mind came that almost-understood voice, and I knew we were about to fly.

From all around came a belling, anticipatory. I looked across to where my comrades sat their incredible mounts. I saw Rwyan astride Anryäle, her head tossed back as wild and eager as the dragon's. I saw Tezdal, on Peliane, grim. I saw Bellek raise an arm and level a finger at the heavens.

Deburah lifted her head. Her neck drew in and then thrust forward, upward. Her hindquarters straightened, propelling her into the sky as her wings beat down, smoother than any galley's oars; cleaner, so that jump and wingbeat carried us aloft.

Displaced air drummed thunder through the night. Dust rose in thick clouds below. We sprang toward the stars, the moon. My breath was snatched from my mouth. I felt my back rammed hard against the saddle. The binding straps dug against my belly and chest and thighs. I entirely forgot my hurt leg. How could I feel pain when I rode the sky? When I experienced such wonder?

We climbed.

Her wings were a constant windrush at my back; steady as her heart's beat: as sure. My face chilled; my hair blew wild. I yelled in pure joy. Fear and marvel became a single thing; and trust: I rode the sky.

Up and up; fast, until I was heady with the speed of it. Deburah's body was warm under me, so that I minded not at all the cooling of the air. It seemed her heat filled me, wrapped me comforting against the cold. I shouted out in joy and looked about, forward and back and down: dimensions shifted here. I saw the others group around. Bellek flew ahead; Rwyan flew to my right; Tezdal was on my left. I looked back and down and saw the plain of Trebizar grow smaller. I saw the Council building dwindle into insignificance. If riders chased us, I could not see them; nor they, now, hold hope of catching us. I saw the lake painted silver by the moon that seemed so close, I might reach out to touch it. I saw the city like some child's toy laid out by a puddle. I saw the shapes of the Kho'rabi skyboats lurking red beside the water. I saw the fleet darting shapes of the little scoutships that came after us, and then the winged shapes that opposed them.

They attacked singly, as if it were a matter of pride: only one dragon falling on one skyboat. They attacked and slew and howled their triumph into the night so that the valley filled up with their belling and the rocky walls threw back the echoes.

And when they had sent all the pursuing boats down in tatters of burning red, they wheeled, a terrible night-come squadron, and swept back to rend the larger air vessels.

I saw vast fire-flowers bloom, reflecting off the lake so that silver moonlight was replaced with bloody red. The Kho'rabi encampment lit with fire as burning gases and flaming fabric fell down over the tents and the men. Some drifted free over the town, and I saw fires start there. We were too far away that I might hear the screaming, and I was glad of that. But I heard the yammering of the elementals as they were liberated.

I thought it was not such a different sound to the howling of these other dragons: a sound of bloodthirsty triumph. I wondered if the dragons and the elementals were so different; or both creatures of an older world, forgotten by Truemen and now come again. And angered by the forgetting.

Then Trebizar was lost behind, and the mountains that ringed the valley rose ahead. I felt Deburah beat her magnificent wings stronger, climbing up the sky to crest the buttress and loft, wondrous, over.

I saw mountains that would take men on horseback days to climb rise before us. The peaks were craggy, sharper and higher than the southern compass. Snow shone white there. Cloud hung there, gray and forbidding.

And Deburah beat her wings and rose above it all: the mountains became foothills, insignificant. The air grew winter-cold, and it did not matter. I was somehow cocooned, as if her body warmed me. I looked down on daunting peaks and felt only confident. The sky grew gray and wet; I could see neither moon nor stars. I felt no fear, only trust in my steed, my sky-flier—my wondrous beautiful dragon. I *knew* she would loft above these heights and bring me safely down: such is the communication between dragons and their riders.

And then the peaks were gone and the air was clear again, all bright with moon's light and the twinkling of the stars that sparkled on my mount's hide like gleaming jewels.

I looked down onto a landscape I'd seen before, in dreams. High plains drifted below, spreading out across all the country north of Trebizar. Wild, they were, and empty of habitation: no little twinkling lights from farms or villages, but only a moonlit desolation of heathered heath and grassy moorland. I saw rivers silvered by the night, and ridged hills that ran all wild and withershins. Then great stands of timber that stretched out black to east and west, and northward ran toward such mountains as I had never seen or thought could be. Those hills that ringed Trebizar, the heights of Kellambek—they were mounds compared with these. These reached up from ground to sky like a granite curtain. The forests ran out against their lower slopes as if the trees lacked the strength to climb such ramparts. They shone as blue-black as Deburah's hide where the naked stone defied attempt to climb. Where they melded with the sky, I saw the gleaming white of permanent snow. I thought we could not cross them, that nothing could fly so high.

And into my mind there came a—I must use words such as I know, that you shall understand; so—a *voice*. It told me I need not fear, that this was only a little barrier to my mount, that we should ride above this petty thing to the wondrous land beyond.

It was as a dream, when words are unnecessary: understood in terms of emotion. I felt it in my soul. My disbelief evaporated. I felt no longer any doubt, nor any fear; only an absolute confidence, an utter trust. And as if in return, measure for measure, I felt Deburah's pleasure in my belief. I felt a melding, a union I had known only once before: when I knew I loved Rwyan.

Do you who listen to my tale remember that first time you fell in love? That moment of absolute certainty, when you understood, not knowing how or why, that your life was irrevocably bound to another's? That moment when it became impossible to imagine a future without your partner? When you *knew* that to separate from this being must diminish you, lessen your existence?

It was like that. In that breathy instant I knew myself bonded with Deburah. I'd have given my life for her; and knew that she would do the same—had already taken that chance, in the skies above Trebizar. I opened my mouth and shouted my joy into the wind.

That was the moment I became a Dragonmaster.

We rose, our wingbeats proud thunder in the night sky. We chased the stars. The air grew thin, and we grew heady, intoxicated with the pure joy of effort, of surmounting obstacles impossible to lesser creatures. Slow crawling men might find a way through those mountains, but only hard—through the passes, climbing up and halting, resting to climb again. We flew above them. They mattered nothing to us: the sky was ours to command. We were the Lords of the Sky. We looked the moon in its face and flaunted our wings at its cold observation. We spread our wings wide to catch the currents of air the land gave gifting off. We found the skystreams and rode them as fishermen do the slower tides of the ocean, glorious. We sailed the heavens. The mountains thrust up snow-tipped peaks to catch us; the moon loomed above. We soared over such crags as seemed to me like teeth designed to enfold the world. We saw the snow give way to bare rock, like blood bled off of dragons' fangs. Forests clung black and green to the farther sides, and then faltered against the climb that must bring them up to those hills that ran on and on as far we could see.

I thought there could not be so many mountains in all the world. We were come to those crags I knew from Durbrecht's teachings were called the Dragonsteeth, and that this was the Forgotten Country: Tartarus.

Home.

She spoke into my mind. I no longer wondered how.

She beat her wings and turned us eastward, then west, circling after Kathanria, who led our flight. I looked to Rwyan and to Tezdal. They sat their spiraling mounts like children set high and insecure on plowhorses. As I had long ago ridden Robus's old gelding, as excited as I was afraid. I wondered if they clutched their saddles hard as I did.

The sun teased the eastern sky: we'd flown the night away. It hinted red across the Fend. Was it still the Fend here? Where neither Ur-Dharbek nor Dharbek held sway, but only dragons: Did they name it different? I thought then that I'd gone into the past; or the future. I was wild with exhilaration. I looked about and saw riderless dragons winging high above, as if they'd be sure of our safe homecoming—why did I think of it as that?—before they landed.

Ahead, I saw peaks high enough that dawn was not yet come to the western slopes. That way the sky was still dark, stars lingering there, the moon reluctant to set. I looked down on rocky fangs that bit the sky, and Deburah swooped down after Kathanria.

Trust.

"I do," I replied.

We spread our wings and glided in to land.

We lowered our legs as the wind swung up to hold our wings.

We beat our wings to master the updraft.

We hooked our claws on the rock and settled.

We folded our wings and plucked a moment at a particularly irritating fragment of flesh or fabric that had earlier lodged between our teeth. It had been an interesting skirmish; better than hunting: more challenge. We hoped there should be more.

I sat awhile bemused, as Deburah picked at her teeth. I felt . . . I could scarcely define what I felt.

Amazed: yes, that's easy.

Bewildered: that, too.

What else?

Exultant. Proud. In love. (Not, I hasten to add, as with Rwyan, but in a different way that I cannot properly describe, though a Dragonmaster would understand.)

I unbuckled the straps that held me to the saddle and clambered down the leg she extended. I set a hand against that vast blue cheek. It was dry and warm. I said, "My thanks," and Deburah favored me with a sidelong glance of her tawny eye and went back to the picking of her teeth.

I limped across a yard that disgraced Durbrecht's courts—that should surely have made Kherbryn's small—to where Rwyan stood.

Her hair was blown out wild; but that was nothing to the excitement in her eyes. I could not then think of her as blind: it was as though the dragons gave her sight beyond her occult vision, to something more and greater. I took her hand.

She said, "Daviot," and shook her head, laughing.

I said, "Yes. I understand. I felt it too."

Tezdal joined us. He said, "Do we fetch Urt?"

Guilt then, that I could so easily overlook my good true comrade: I nodded, and we went to Kathanria, where Bellek was already loosing Urt from his fastenings.

He was not yet quite conscious. I was not certain whether from my grip on his nerves, or desire to refuse his situation. I helped him down and held him as he tottered, eyes peering slowly about, at first hooded, but then opening wide in naked wonder. I felt him shudder and held him tighter. He said, "Where are we?"

I looked to Bellek for the answer I thought I knew.

Bellek said, "In Tartarus. In the last Dragoncastle."

I stared about, amazed, on sights so antique they were forgotten by even the greatest Mnemonikos. For all that had transpired this wild, incredible night, still I could scarce believe the evidence of my own eyes. It was as though that flight had carried me back in time, to a past long lost.

We stood atop a mountain. Not the highest—vaster summits loomed all about—but still so great, it seemed we stood atop the world itself, the valley below dwindling insignificant, like a child's gouging from this wild landscape. As I've said, the yard was vast, in keeping with the size of the dragons that perched on the ledges raised up all around—and those not so large as the beasts that came down now. Their calling filled the morning. It sounded to me like the shouting of soldiers after battle, boasting of victory.

Bellek said, "Those are the bulls. They'll not be ridden, but they fight hard for their broods." He looked at us, his pale eyes intense, and added, "Steer clear of them until you know this place and your mounts better. The males are jealous of their status, and not always predictable."

Rwyan laughed. "Much as with men, eh?"

I looked to where the males landed. They were twice the size of the females and colored brighter, all reds and yellows, greens and blues, and though they were fewer in number than the females, they dominated with their sheer bulk. I saw one enormous creature come striding down the ramparts to where Deburah perched. He craned out his neck, rubbing his cheek against hers, and she ceased her preening to rub back. I felt a stab of jealousy.

And then found his enormous eyes locked on mine, lips drawing back from fangs that might have skewered me as he hissed.

Quite unthinking, I ducked my head in apology and said aloud, "Forgive me."

The lips closed slowly over the teeth and he returned his attention to Deburah. I felt dismissed; and very small.

Rwyan laughed and took my hand, and asked me, "Have I a rival?"

I shook my head and forced a nervous chuckle. "You understand?"

She gave me back, "How could I not? By the God, I felt"—she turned her face about, encompassing our surroundings, the vast shapes that stood there—"like a god."

Bellek smiled. "You bond. Your feet are on the road. Soon you'll be Dragonmasters."

In a small voice, Urt said, "I? A Dragonmaster?"

And Bellek clapped him on the shoulder with a force that belied the silver of his hair and the wrinkles on his face, and said, "Aye, my friend. You, too. The dreams don't lie."

I said, "Shall you tell us of these dreams? Shall you tell us how"—I gestured around—"all this? Why you saved us?"

"Of course." Bellek's teeth shone white in the early sun. "All of it, in time. There's no great mystery to it."

No great mystery? I stared at him; my jaw hung open, my eyes gaped wide. He laughed at me, and beckoned that we follow him across the yard.

Squadrons of cavalry might have exercised there, with room along the ramparts for archers and war engines. They were lit now by the rising sun, and I saw better than before that they were built on a monumental scale. It seemed to me we traversed a melding of natural stone and man-built structure, the two contiguous. I'd have remained, marveling, had Rwyan not tugged me after our rescuer host.

We passed beneath an arch clad thick in moss, into a wide corridor that dripped moisture from its roof to run along the edges and pool, in places, over the floor. I felt suddenly cold and grew aware how thin the air tasted. I shivered. I heard Rwyan's teeth begin to chatter.

Over his shoulder, Bellek called back, "Away from the dragons, you'll feel the cold. But there's a fire lit, and food."

I asked, "How's that? How can the dragons warm us?"

The Dragonmaster only laughed. "In time, Storyman. All in time."

We went on. What illumination there was came from slits cut deep through the rock, slanting the dawn light in narrow bands across our way, so that we walked from light to shadow and back again. Water splashed under my boots. I saw rats scurry in advance of our passage; the tunnel smelled of mold and decay and age.

We emerged into an atrium that had once been very grand. Now ivy and the roots of hardy trees wound around the colonnades. Creepers and boughs filled the space above, patterning the air as if we traversed a bower. Across the floor, stone was disrupted, divided and broken by the roots that drove down remorseless between the flags. Birds had nested here: I saw their droppings white on the floor, and the remnants of ancient nests overhead. I looked up and saw the circle where the sky should have shown clear all filled with entwining limbs, a tracery against the burgeoning blue. I looked at Rwyan, and she frowned her lack of understanding. I watched Bellek pause at a doorway and wondered if I understood better.

There had been doors hung here once. Magnificent doors, to judge by the remnants that lay scattered and rotting across the floor. From the jambs there still protruded hinges of long-blackened metal, distorted by the weight they had once supported, even as it fell down, decaying.

I suppose Bellek saw my expression, because he smiled, and shrugged, and said, "It was finer, once. A long time ago."

Beyond that rotten doorway, steps descended. They were worn away in smooth curves that spoke of many feet, much use. What light there was—there were no windows, not even those narrow embrasures I'd seen above—came from the moss and fungi that grew in fulgent clumps down the walls and roof. The air was damp and tasted of decay; more rats scurried away, at sound of our footsteps. Which were not loud, given the coating of the floor. I saw large beetles scuttle before us; and more crawling overhead. I wondered at the decrepitude of this Dragoncastle.

The stairs ended at another arch, beyond it another court, where rotten wood and winding roots wove a foot-tricking maze across the stone. This place seemed to occupy the mountain, but I could not imagine what hands had carved it out. A corridor then, brighter for the embrasures that let in the sun; worse for what the light revealed. Then a last descent down time-worn stairs to doors.

I found myself surprised to see them: I had begun to assume that no wood existed any longer in this decaying place, save what nature wound into the stone. But these were firm and black, banded with solid hinges of dark metal. And Bellek flung them open like some proud aeldor inviting guests into his sanctum.

Which I suppose he was and we were.

I could not help but gape: after what we'd passed through, this was magnificent.

It was a hall such as I'd not seen. Not in any place I'd been, not even Durbrecht. I thought not even Gahan—now his son and the ill-met regent—in Kherbryn could boast such a hall. As the yard where the dragons landed had been great, so was this chamber; and more.

It was vaulted high, with beams of stone like the ribs of some creature even larger than the dragons. My feet tapped out small steps on the floorstones, lost in the fading echoes of the far walls, which rose up tall as those beeches in Trebizar's gardens, as high and wide and overwhelming. The floor was marble, pure white under the thick dust. My boots left tracks there. The walls were black as darkest night, save for where the rising ribs of floor lofted white beneath their layering of cobwebs, as if all this chamber were fashioned of a single thing, mingling. It was as though we stepped into the belly of a beast entrapped in the stone of the mountain. High windows like dragons' eyes cut through on three sides, and as the sun rose higher, so light spread brilliant through the chamber, sparkling off the dust that filled the air. I went to one of those windows and looked out (what kept the glass so clean?) and gasped at what I saw. This chamber was cut from within some bulge of stone, jutting out over the panorama below so that I felt I hung suspended in the morning. I moved back to join the others, who followed Bellek across this wondrous hall.

I saw hearths filled with dead and ancient wood; and tables of carved oak set around with high-backed chairs of intricate design. Spiders' webs strung their backs, and dust lay thick over the surfaces of the tables. From the vaulted roof hung chandeliers that were likely gold beneath the verdigris that dulled their luster. It was not easy to tell, for webs spun them around, and fat spiders dangled, horrid in the light.

I felt Rwyan tighten her grip on my hand. I saw Tezdal frown, disgust naked on his face. Only Urt seemed undisturbed, and I thought that was likely because he felt himself safe underground, away from the dragons.

Bellek followed an old trail through the dust to the far side of the chamber.

He'd not lied about the fire: it burned in the hearth there. Smoldering down now into sparking embers, but lit up quick enough when he tossed on fresh logs from the stack beside. There was a table there, before the hearth, of some dark wood; round and set with five chairs, as if we were expected. Bellek ushered Rwyan to a somewhat dusty seat, and I helped Tezdal lower Urt to another. We took places either side. Only Rwyan seemed at ease.

I was pleased to see the table clean and that the chandelier above was empty of spiders. (I've no liking for spiders.) So I watched as Bellek filled five golden goblets from a decanter of matching gold and wondered if the tarnish would taint the taste.

He said, "Drink, and welcome to the Dragoncastle. I'll find you food."

He went out through a door beside the hearth, and I looked at my companions. They looked at me: none of us had answers to the questions our eyes asked. I sipped the wine and said, "It's good."

Tezdal said, "What is this place?"

Rwyan said, "A Dragoncastle, as Bellek told us."

I said, "It's old. I never thought to see a place so old as this."

Urt only sat silent and still, his body rigid; as if locked to the dusty chair. I should have comforted him or tried to, but I was caught up in such wonder at all I saw that I am ashamed to say I overlooked his predicament.

Bellek came back, laden with a platter of meat that he set down before us. He smiled and went away, returning with vegetables and bread; then brought us plates and knives. "Eat," he said. Suddenly I found myself mightily hungry.

The meat was venison, spit-roasted, so that the outer flesh was charred, the inner bloody. The vegetables were barely cooked, and the bread was coarse. I cared not at all: I set to with a will.

"You must forgive me." I looked up and saw that Bellek addressed himself to Rwyan. "I'm not much of a cook."

She licked a droplet of blood from her lips and asked him, "Are you alone here, then?"

For an instant his eyes grew bleak. Then he smiled and shrugged and ducked his head. "Save for the dragons, aye. And have been for a while—hence this disorder."

I said, "What of the other Dragoncastles?"

He answered me, "Empty of Dragonmasters."

I said, "You're truly the last?"

He only nodded in reply; there was a terrible sadness in the simple gesture.

I looked around and saw time's hand all about me. I felt the weight of ages in the stone. I saw it in his eyes. I asked, "How long?"

He looked at me and smiled, and once again I wondered if I saw the glint of madness there. He said, "I'm no Mnemonikos, Daviot. I lose track of the days, the years; but . . . a long time."

I said, "In Dharbek they believe the dragons dead and the Dragonmasters with them."

He said, "As you've seen, they are wrong," and laughed and filled our tarnished cups.

I asked him where the wine came from, the food.

He said, "Meat's easy—the dragons do my hunting. The rest?" He paused, grinning mischievously. "I've some few friends. Such as may reassure Urt."

I frowned, chastened by that reminder. I looked to Urt, who ate disconsolately, his head lowered toward his plate. He looked up at that, and I had seldom known his expression so easily read: it was one of hope and disbelief; and fear his hope should prove unfounded.

Bellek said, "There are Changed here, Urt. They've no fear of the dragons; no need to fear them."

Urt said, "Where?" His voice was strident with hope.

Bellek said, "In the valleys. They've farms there; they gift me a tithe of their produce."

Urt looked at him with wondering eyes. My own, I suspect, were wide with curiosity. I said, "How?"

The Dragonmaster laughed. I believe he enjoyed himself, spinning out all these tidbits of knowledge held so long to himself; now to be shared—but slowly—like long-hoarded treasures. He was more than a little crazed. Or saw the turnings of the world from a different vantage point from ours.

He said, "When the Truemen sorcerers created the Changed and left them behind in Ur-Dharbek, there were always some few who lived north of Trebizar. They learned early what I suspect that Raethe of yours knows now—that the dragons hunt men not as food, but for sport. Think on it! You've ridden dragons, you've seen them hunt." He gestured at the meat cooling on our platters. "Deer are nothing to them. By the Three, they take a deer easy as a terrier a rat. They take the aurochs—and few men would face such a beast! No, they hunted the men who came here because they enjoyed the sport, and because men challenged their supremacy. And for a while they hunted the

Changed of Ur-Dharbek for the same reason. But the Changed—forgive me, Urt—proved poorer sport than Truemen. I think it was likely that Truemen commanded magic earlier, and there's a . . . taste . . . to that; one the dragons enjoy."

He paused to drain his cup; refill it. I felt a horrid dread. I glanced at Rwyan. Bellek saw my look and the direction of my thoughts and said, "No fear there, Daviot. Anryäle's bonded with her now, and so she's safe."

I felt relieved; but no wiser.

I suppose my emotions showed, because Bellek continued: "In many ways the dragons are not so different to most animals. They guard their hunting grounds against intruders and oppose any threat to their welfare. Truemen *were* a threat, when they discovered the powers of the crystals and turned them against the dragons—"

He was interrupted by Rwyan, who said, "You know of the crystals' powers?"

He grinned again. "Am I not a Dragonmaster? *My* power came from the crystals. These hills are rich with them, and the dragons eat them."

"*Eat* them?" I gasped.

"As do birds swallow stones to assist their digestion," he said, "so do the dragons eat the crystals. And over the ages, that's changed them. They've a kind of magic now, and it rendered the easy pickings of Ur-Dharbek . . . less interesting. Until now. Dragons enjoy a challenge. They're like—what?—horses bred only to race or fight; like hunting dogs. But far more intelligent: prey that's too easy to take offers them no challenge."

Rwyan said, "The crystals drive Truemen mad, are we with them too long. In Trebizar, Allanyn and her followers were made mad by them, I think. What of the dragons then?"

Bellek said, "They're different. An older race that lives a different life. They do not go mad. Rather, it seems the crystals make them fonder of those special few who share communion with them."

He turned his seamed face slowly around, encompassing us all with his gaze; and said, "Like you."

I said, because none of my companions spoke, "Do you explain?"

Bellek said, "I'm not sure I can. But . . . you've the Storyman's talent, no? And Rwyan the mage's. I, that of the Dragonmaster—"

I interrupted him: "And Urt? Tezdal? What of them?"

He shrugged and said, "I cannot say. Only that my dragons told me I was no longer alone. That there were others like me, abroad. They've powers I cannot explain, Daviot. They dream; and I think their dreams span the whole world. I know only that they dreamed of you and knew you were come to Trebizar, and in danger."

I said, "That fails to explain it. I dreamed of dragons long before Trebizar."

He gave me back, "Perhaps that's how, or why. Perhaps it was because you *believed* in them. Perhaps because you gave your belief to Rwyan; and somehow, too, to Urt and Tezdal. Perhaps they found their talent in company with you—I don't know. Only that Kathanria and Anryäle and Peliane and Deburah found—do you not understand? By the Three, you've ridden them!—souls linked to theirs. And sought you out. And saved you!"

Rwyan said, "The pattern! Did I not tell you, Daviot?"

I nodded. There was much to digest here. I knew that I had been snatched from an untimely (in my opinion) arrival into the Pale Friend's embrace by creatures I had dared hope were not legendary. I had dreamed of dragons—but should that flesh them? I had told Rwyan of my dreams, and Urt—but should that make them part of the dream? How should Tezdal become a part of this fleshed fantasy?

I reached for the gilded jug and found it empty. Bellek chuckled and rose, shedding dust in a cloud behind him as he took the jug and carried it away.

Tezdal said, "I understand none of this."

Urt said, "Changed live here? Under the dragons' wings?"

Bellek returned with the filled jug in time to hear that question and said, "As I told you: in the valleys. The brave few, who came back when they saw the direction your Raethe took."

Urt lost a measure of his fear. He shaped a frown, and took the goblet Bellek offered him, and demanded, like me: "Do you explain?"

The Dragonmaster chuckled. "Are there not always a few who'll dare what others will not? Those who choose to take their chances and refuse the common belief?"

He looked us, all four, in the eyes, and said, chuckling, "Like you." But his words were directed largely at Urt.

I said nothing. I felt this was Urt's moment: that he stood at the edge of a precipice. The past was the solid ground behind, the future the leap over the rim. He could step back or take flight, as if on dragon's back. Or plummet groundward. I waited on his answer.

He said, "Tell me."

Bellek said, "They came north. I cannot tell you why, only that they did; and that they were brave. They came out of Ur-Dharbek to live in these mountains. And more came when they understood what Allanyn plans."

Rwyan said, "How could they know?"

Bellek said, "I cannot tell you. Am I honest, it did not much interest me; not at first. But more came—and settled; and built up the holdings that used to be here. And I'd no quarrel with that; nor my dragons." He laughed. "I think my dragons grew somewhat lonely by then. However—they settled in the valleys and made this land into some semblance of what it used to be. And I welcomed them: they're good folk."

Urt asked, "May I meet them?"

The Dragonmaster chuckled. "Why not? Certainly in time, but bide yours awhile, eh?"

I saw that Urt was greatly enthused by this: he smiled with genuine relief and said, "Soon, I hope. It should make me feel more easy."

Rwyan said, "But how do you know all this, Bellek? You tell us that you live lonely, yet you speak of Allanyn—the Raethe, and events south—that suggests intimate knowledge. Do you tell us how you know?"

Bellek's smile stretched his lips like skeins of skin across his teeth. I saw that he took enjoyment from his awareness of such mysteries. Like Rwyan, I wondered how he knew.

He said, "My dragons dream and see the world. And sometimes I fly them south to . . . observe. Mostly, they . . . feel . . . what transpires there, or have the knowledge of the elementals." He must have seen my jaw drop, for he smiled and said, "Men are newcomers to this world, set beside the dragons. They're an ancient race and closer to natural things. I know not the how of it, but that they commune with the elementals is certain."

He glanced at Tezdal then, as if the Sky Lord should understand this better, but Tezdal only shrugged and said, "The Attul-ki command the spirits, not we Kho'rabi."

I asked, "How do you control the dragons?"

And Bellek laughed and told me, "Dragons are not controlled, my friend. Best learn that early! They allow themselves to be ridden— the dams, at least—because they take pleasure in that union." His leathery face grew serious as he scanned us all. "You *ask* the dragons; you *suggest* a course. You do not—ever!—*command* a dragon. In a little while, when you know your bond-mates better, you'll understand."

"When shall that be?" I asked. The excitement of that flight filled me yet.

"Soon enough," Bellek said, and hid his face behind his goblet.

As wine and food took their toll, I began to feel greatly tired. I think there is a limit to the excitement a body can experience, and that when that limit is reached, it craves rest, for all the mind would have it otherwise. I yawned; I could not help myself.

Bellek laughed and said, "Aye, doubtless you are all weary. It was a long night, no? So—do I show you to your chambers, and we'll speak again when you've rested."

There were more questions: too many. I ducked my head. The notion of bed was immediately as tempting as the odor of the meal had been. I looked to Rwyan and saw the lids of her eyes drooped heavy over the blind orbs. She smiled and nodded her agreement. Urt looked as if he'd find some bolt hole to lie in secure until the world resumed a safer course. Only Tezdal seemed untired, but still he shrugged and grunted his agreement.

"Then do you follow me?"

Bellek rose and led us out through a door I'd not noticed, into a corridor that ran through the mountain's rock. There were no windows, but it was lit. I could not understand how.

Rwyan gestured at the glow. "You've the understanding of the crystals then, Bellek. Are you a sorcerer?"

He chuckled and returned her, "I'm a Dragonmaster, lady. Does that make me a sorcerer—then, aye. But not like you."

She said, "Magic shaped this place, no?"

And he chuckled again and said, "It did. In olden days, when magic was different. When the firstcome Dhar were different. Think you that talent remains always the same? Or that the crystals do not change? I tell you, no. The crystals shift in accord with those who use them; and those who use them shift in accord with the crystals' shaping."

He shrugged: a gesture of resignation. Rwyan said, "Whoever built this place commanded a mighty talent."

Bellek said, "Once, aye. Once the Dragonmasters were supreme. They built this place and all the other castles, where only dragons had nested before. Once, we were the Lords of the Sky. But we outlived our time and folk forgot us. That bleeds out power, forgetting."

I said, "What happened to the others?"

And he returned me simply, "They died."

He fell silent after that. It was as if the dull light of this dusty passage leached out his vitality, or his memories of what had once been. I asked him no more questions but only found Rwyan's hand and walked beside her in silence.

Bellek brought us to chambers along the way. Three, set at intervals down the corridor. Each had a door of black wood banded with golden hinges. Clean and uncorrupted by time: as if held in readiness. He ushered Rwyan and me into the first.

He said, "I trust you'll be comfortable here. Do you need me, I shall be in the hall. Am I not, I'd suggest you wait for me there—this is a large place, and somewhat mazeish. Also, do you wander outside, beware the bulls."

We entered the chamber. I was surprised to find it clean. There was no dust on the smooth stone floor, nor any webbing about the arching bands of stone that shaped the roof and walls. Wide windows of unsullied glass looked over the valley, and when I peered down, I saw a veil of distant smoke rising, as from farms or villages. There was a massive bed, set with clean linen, and a vast armoire. Behind a door of polished wood was a cubicle that held a bath and such other offices as I'd seen only in the grandest keeps.

Rwyan said, "There's magic here."

I surveyed the room and said, "At least it's clean."

She said, "That's magic at work. Bellek's more talent than he admits."

I said, "And yours?"

She closed her eyes, as if in thought, then smiled and told me, "Returned in full. There are no constraints any longer."

I said, "Save that we're now his . . . guests. Or his prisoners?"

She laughed and took my hands, "looking" up into my doubting eyes. "Daviot," she said, "he saved us. Were it not for him, we'd be dead now. That, or worse."

I said, "Yes; I'll not argue that. But now? Must we live here the rest of our lives, whilst all the world falls down in bloodshed? By Ennas Day, Allanyn claimed. I'd not stand idly by to witness that war."

She kissed me on the cheek. "Think you I forget that date? Or those dreams you spun in Durbrecht? I've not, but nor do I forget that now we have a future—thanks to Bellek and the dragons. Think on that."

I did, murmuring agreement even as my mind raced. I'd spoken then of riding dragons in defense of Dharbek. Might we now, Rwyan and I, make that dream flesh? The dragons had seemed only fancy once, and I the only Trueman who thought of them at all. Now I knew them for creatures of flesh and blood and bone—and more!—and so perhaps that other dream might be made reality. But not now in defense of Dharbek alone; rather, as instruments of peace betwixt my people and Tezdal's, betwixt Truemen and Changed. Excitement flared: I smiled as old hopes grew new flesh.

To Rwyan, I said, "I'd speak of this to Bellek."

I'd have found him there and then, but Rwyan held me and said, "Aye, but tomorrow, eh? Likely the dragons destroyed all those skyboats moored in Trebizar, and it must take the Sky Lords time to rebuild that navy. We've a breathing space, I think, and now I'm weary. Shall we sleep?"

I ducked my head. I was truly tired: we left our clothes scattered and found the bed.

I woke to an unfamiliar sound: the beat of rain against glass. I rose, careful not to disturb Rwyan, and padded barefoot to the windows. It looked to me that we'd slept the day away, or most of it, but it was hard to tell. We were close to the sky here and a long way north, and the darkness might have been only the clouds that now hid the peaks and hurled their watery burden at the land. The valley was lost in brume, but I stood a long while staring, thinking of such a downpour over the drought-parched fields of Dharbek. I pressed my face against the glass, unanswered questions flooding anew into my head.

Was all this truly the weaving of a pattern? If Rwyan was correct in that, then what might we four do?

I doubted not that we should learn to ride the dragons. But to what end? That Bellek have company in his lonely castle? I was not entirely sure but that we had exchanged one prison for another. Nor was I by any means certain Urt would agree to remain. He held that fear of dragons inherent in his blood under tight control, but could he bring himself, willingly, to ride the creatures? I thought perhaps he'd sooner find a place with those other Changed Bellek had spoken of.

And Tezdal? He had sworn to defend Rwyan—and held true to that vow. But now might he not consider Rwyan safe and look to rejoin his Kho'rabi brothers? Did he become a Dragonmaster, then might he not seek to ally dragons with skyboats, form such an armada as must surely be invincible? If not—likely Bellek could prevent it— then would Tezdal deem Rwyan delivered safe from harm and he freed to take his Way of Honor? That thought I liked not at all: I was vaguely surprised how fond I'd grown of the Sky Lord.

I started as a peal of thunder dinned over mountaintops suddenly revealed by the brilliance of lightning. I wondered if dragons flew in such weather. I wondered . . . the list was too long, and I turned away to find Rwyan stirring.

She tossed aside the sheets, deliciously immodest, and came to join me. "It's been so long," she said, "since I've seen rain."

I nodded and held her as great rolling drumbeats of thunder beat over the castle and lightning flung spearing tongues of pure fulgence at the peaks.

"This is a wild place," I said.

"A place fit for dragons," she returned, and laughed, and folded herself against me. "An old world that perhaps shall make a new."

I said, "I'd find that out. And ere Ennas Day."

She smiled agreement and cupped her hands about my neck, drawing my face down. Our kiss was fierce: a commitment.

"So," I declared when at last we tore our lips apart, "do we find Bellek and the others and set this dream to flight?"

But I must curb my impatience awhile.

In the days that followed we found Bellek a somewhat furtive host. Oh, he was friendly enough and gave us answers to the questions we hurled at him, like some bombard from those war-engines dead Gahan had ordered built. But there were always things left unexplained, or hints of doubt in answers that seemed honest and clear.

How old he was and how long he'd lived alone, he would not say. He gave us to understand that certain of the female dragons—my lovely Deburah, Kathanria, Anryäle, Peliane—had dreamed of us as long as we had dreamed, unwitting, of them. I think he could not explain this clearly, any more than an ordinary man (and Bellek was by no means ordinary, or any longer quite sane) can explain the substance of his night fancies. They, I gathered, rather than Bellek, had been the manufacturers of our rescue—it was they had sensed our presence in Trebizar and the danger we faced. Bellek had followed their instincts, when he brought them to us.

He showed us the lairs—natural caves dug deeper into the stone by the bull dragons—where the broods lived. Each bull lorded a harem of some five or six dams, which he guarded with ferocious jealousy, and each dam guarded her nest with no less enthusiasm.

The caves were warm and filled with the scent of the dragons, which was akin to leather drying in the sun, a hint of raw meat. I came close to soiling myself the first time Bellek led us in, past that same huge bull I'd seen caressing Deburah, his hide all yellow and black mottlings, not unlike the mountain cats that inhabit the forests of the massif.

He sat proud on the ledge before the cave, talons and teeth busy as he preened. He was vast, far larger than the dams, and as we approached, he fixed us with his yellow eyes and spread his wings and opened his jaws in rampant display of sword-blade teeth. He hissed. I felt his suspicion and halted as Bellek raised a warning hand. I heard Rwyan gasp in naked wonder, and from behind me Urt's small cry. I looked back and saw Tezdal clutch the Changed's shoulder. The Sky Lord did not flinch, only met the dragon's stare with his own.

Communication with dragons is not verbal, and their minds do not follow those tracks ours take. Bellek did not speak, but I found my head filled with . . . emotions, images—I can tell it no better. The Dragonmaster urged the bull to calm; he radiated a plea that we be granted entry to this magnificent place, that we might marvel at the bull's harem, which was irrevocable proof of his greatness. From the dragon came a sending of pleasure, of pride and agreement: we were allowed entry.

We walked under the shadows of his wings. His breath was hot and meaty. I looked into his eye and shaped a thought of obeisance: it was not difficult. I felt in return strength, permission. I understood his name was Taziel. I walked past and moved away from Rwyan as a spiritual tugging too powerful to ignore governed my steps. Rwyan seemed scarcely to notice: she was moving toward Anryäle even as I went to Deburah.

My—almost, I say, *love*—crouched upon her nest. She turned her head toward me, and I felt beckoned. I climbed the ragged stone that brought me to her perch and saw the egg she coddled. It lay upon a bed of branches and torn hides not unlike the nest of a bird. It was pure white, veined with a tracery of red, and high as my waist. I understood that I was allowed to touch it: I did and smiled as I felt the pulsing heartbeat within. It was slow and steady as a metronome, and I understood from Deburah that it should hatch within the year, and be a bull, and mighty as his father.

I felt awash with love. I touched Deburah's cheek, and she turned her head against my hand, almost pitching me from the nest. I stumbled against the leg she thrust out to catch me and leaned against her shoulder.

Into my mind came the thought: *Shall we fly soon? Shall we hunt?*

I answered, *Yes. Soon,* and got back such pleasure as makes the finest wine nothing. I left the cave dazed. Nor was Rwyan in better state. (That night we made love with a passion that left us both as weary as exhilarated: the communion of dragons and Dragonmasters heightens the senses.)

Bellek took us on to other caves. This mountain—this Dragon-castle!—was riddled with them. Peliane sat an empty nest in the first, and we others stood back as Tezdal went to her, and looked her in the eye, and bowed formally as if he attended some high-born lady in the courts of Ahn-feshang.

Then I saw something that we neither of us ever mentioned. I had never thought to see it, not since he told Rwyan and me of Retze's death. I saw Tezdal shed tears. They ran ignored down his cheeks, and from Peliane I felt an outpouring of sympathy and compassion. I watched as Tezdal stepped blindly toward her and raised his arms, as if he'd fling them about her neck. She ducked her massive head and swung it close, so that he stood leaning against her, his face pressed to her cheek.

Into my ear, Rwyan whispered, "Tezdal shall be with us, I think."

I only nodded and held her close. I thought my Sky Lord friend had found some other bond to fill that vacuum in his life. I thought he should put the Way of Honor behind him now. I hoped it should be so.

Of Urt I was far less sure.

I saw the sweat that beaded his face despite the cold that gripped the mountainside between the caves as we went to where Kathanria built her empty nest. (Dragons mate frequently but are seldom impregnated. Their gestation periods are counted in years, and the production of an egg is a rare and marvelous event. My Deburah was special in this, as in so many other ways.) He shuddered as we entered under the watchful eye of a bull striped bloody red and dark green. He looked about at the dams that studied us from their ledges. I thought he might turn and run, but then he made a sound that came from deep in his chest and stumbled over the bone-littered floor to climb toward Kathanria. He seemed not entirely willing but rather compelled by an emotion that overrode his fear. He seemed to me like some gamblers I'd known in Durbrecht—afraid of the losses their gaming might bring but incapable of resisting the temptation. He seemed almost to fight himself as he climbed the path to the dragon's nest.

Then Kathanria fixed him with her eye and raised a paw that swept him to her cheek, whether he be willing or not. And I heard Urt moan and saw him lie against her like a puppy finding its dam.

"Urt, too," I whispered into Rwyan's ear. "Soon, I think."

But should it be soon enough? Could we learn so much in time? I saw that fateful Ennas Day loom ever closer, a threatening reef in the sea of my ambition, and I could only curb my impatience and hope it should be in time.

We saw the winter out in the Dragoncastle. We saw such snows fall as I'd not ever seen, or imagined. We learned to saddle our bond-mates—even Urt, though he was slow to overcome his innate terror, for all Kathanria's sendings of comfort and confidence—and we learned to ask their cooperation. Ever that—to *ask;* never to command

—and that alone was hard enough for folk better accustomed to heeling horses into direction, with use of bridle and bit. I was minded of my gray mare (was she yet hale? I hoped she was) as I learned to *request* of Deburah that she go where I'd have her fly.

But what glory to sit aback a dragon and vaunt the heavens. To soar above the clouds that dusted the valleys with snow and see the high blue sky, the sun that rode its path from east to west, invisible to those below us.

And to hunt!

Oh, I came to understand the joy of that. To loft the sky on slow-beating wings, alert to those beating hearts below, the warmth of pulsing blood. To swoop over the forests, searching hungry. To find the one chosen and plummet, claws poised to snatch and slay. To fold our wings and drop, the air howling past us. To anticipate the evasions, avoid the crags and trees our quarry sought to hide in, and take it. Swift! A single pounce, and beat our wings to rise again, triumphant. I came to understand the challenge it must be to contest with sorcerers for mastery of the sky. I grew impatient to bring my Deburah south. I found a taste for bloody meat: I changed.

For better or for worse, I'll not say. I was carried on a flood of belief, of trust in Deburah and the attainment of all my hopes. I know that Urt and Tezdal came to share the dream and joined my loves and I in its shaping. I think we all changed then, that long winter in the Forgotten Country, and was that wrong, I give you Rwyan's answer: it was the pattern. Did we change, it was not for lust of power—though whatever gods exist know we came to own that commodity in full enough measure—but rather for desire of some calmer order in face of the chaos men bring.

The dragons changed my thinking. They were fleshed creatures and magical both. They ate those crystals that waste Truemen and drive Changed mad, but they suffered no such fate themselves. They held communion with those elemental spirits that the Attul-ki sought to control and master, to bend to their will; but the dragons knew them as cohabitors, as other, equal beings. The dragons are different. I think they are likely wiser than we men, True or Changed, Ahn or Dhar. And we who consort with them are likely made different by such proximity to them and those strange stones that even now I cannot pretend to understand.

We learned to ride the dragons. We explored the Dragoncastle, and that of itself could make a tale.

It was no keep, this place, but rather a town, a city, built into and about the mountain. Only great magic could have shaped those courts

and halls and yards, those cleft-spanning bridges, the winding corridors and the multitude of chambers, large and small. I questioned
Bellek on this, but he proved evasive and left us mostly to guess the
manner of the making and the numbers that must once have inhabited
the warren.

Memory of magic lingered still, side by side with ruin and decrepitude. A lightless passage all draped with spiders' webs and paved
with rats' droppings was likely to emerge onto a plaza large as any in
Durbrecht and clean as if new-swept, where neither wind nor rain nor
snow gained entry but was held off by the power that still lingered
there. Or a square all disrupted by roots and ivy, where birds left
reminders of their springtime nesting, would offer us a rotted door
beyond which lay pristine, dustless chambers. We found halls as great
as that in which we ate and balconies that wound vertiginous along
the mountain's flanks. There were manufactories filled with rusted
machinery I did not comprehend; others in which great wheels and
cogs turned silently, glistening with oil, untouched by time and entirely inexplicable. We saw armories filled with rusted weapons and
antique battle gear; rooms where dust and cobwebs hid the contents,
and rooms that might have been only recently vacated. There were
salons where tapestries hung rotted and gnawed by mice, alive with
insects; and others where the draperies were as bright as if the weaving were but yesterday finished.

I spent much time studying these, but all they told me was that
once men had ridden dragons and lived here happy, it seemed. I saw
no evidence of any children, but I thought little of that, then.

We investigated Bellek's kitchens, and Rwyan voiced her disapproval and used her own talent to restore all there to pristine cleanli-
ness. After, she and Urt and I (Tezdal had no knowledge at all of the
culinary arts) took over the preparation of our meals.

We met with the Changed who farmed the valleys. We gave them
meat that winter and took in return Bellek's tithe of their produce. It
was a fair exchange, and none of them feared the dragons, but rather
saw them as fellow inhabitants of this wild land. We spent days
amongst them. Urt was first amazed that they showed no fear of our
coming, and then entranced by the life they led, under the shadow of
the dragons' wings. They laughed at his doubts and told him they had
freedom here, from Truemen and war and Allanyn. He was surprised
they recognized her designs, and they no less that he'd not seen them.

Ere long, he came to wholehearted support of our cause.

•   •   •

Tezdal was harder to persuade.

The Sky Lord was come to the same communion with Peliane as I had with Deburah: he loved her. But he was not yet to be convinced he should bring her against his Kho'rabi brethren.

"You ask too much of me," he said. "You ask that I gainsay those vows that shaped me. I cannot expect that you understand what it is to be Kho'rabi, but you know that in my language that means 'the Dedicated,' and that is what we are—dedicated to the reconquest of our Homeland."

I opened my mouth to speak, but he raised a hand to halt me, and so dour was his dark face, I held my tongue. I had known him long enough now I might judge his moods, and for some while he had been sunk in melancholy introspection. Indeed, the only time I saw him happy was in company with Peliane. Oh, he remained civil—his manners were ever better than mine—and he acknowledged the debt he felt to Rwyan, the friendship that had grown between us, and between him and Urt. But a worm of doubt had been chewing at his soul since first we came to the Dragoncastle and he deemed Rwyan safe. I had endeavored to speak with him of such matters, and so had Rwyan, but he would not, or could not, and gave us only responses as evasive as Bellek's. This was the first time he showed any willingness to discuss it openly, and so I sat silent as he continued.

"You cannot understand," he said. "You Truemen Dhar came down into Kellambek with your magic and your swords, and you made my people slaves—those you did not slay. You brought your one god and mocked the Three—you took away my people's heritage and ground us down under your heel. But Attul gave us back our hope and showed us the way east, to the islands of Ahn-feshang; and then the Three gave us those gifts I've told you of, that we might take back what is rightfully ours. The Attul-ki show us the way now, and we Kho'rabi yearn for the reconquest—what you call the Great Coming.

"No, listen!" This to Rwyan, who had moved to speak but fell silent as I under the bleak intensity of his eyes. "I do not name you enemy. Not you two Dhar; nor you, Urt. But what you ask is too much! You'd have me ride Peliane against my own. You ask me to betray all that I've believed in. I am nothing save I be true to my beliefs, but you ask me to fight my brothers, my kin. You ask me to go against the wishes of the Three! You ask me to damn myself for your dream, and I cannot do that."

He closed his eyes, his head flung back so that his long plait hung down behind his chair. I saw his left hand finger the dagger at his waist and knew what he should likely say next.

I was right: he said, "Already I've betrayed my kin in aiding your escape from Trebizar. I could do no less in face of my pledge to you, Rwyan. But this—" He shook his head wearily. "No. Better that I take the Way of Honor now."

Rwyan said very softly, "Do you truly think that's the honorable course, Tezdal?"

His eyes sprang open. His head came forward. He stared at her, fierce as a bull dragon. "Yes."

I said, "I'd not see you open your belly, my friend."

He laughed. The sound rang wild about the empty hall. It seemed to me brother to the howling of the wind outside. I ached for him. I knew his decision was infinitely difficult.

He reached for the jug. I pushed it toward him, and he filled his cup; drank it off before he spoke again. "Would you deny your god?" he asked, rhetorical. "Would you ask me to deny the Three, all my beliefs, all my life has meant? Forgive me—I intend no disrespect, but you Truemen Dhar lack that honor that shapes us. I am Kho'rabi: my life has been lived for the single purpose. And now you'd ask me to deny it?"

Rwyan began to shape an answer, but to my amazement Urt set a hand upon her arm and motioned her to silence; and it was he who gave Tezdal the response.

"I was born Changed," he said. "I am the by-blow of Dhar magic: dragons' prey, a servant. In Dharbek I was nothing—invisible, a creature born of made things, born to serve unseen, unthanked. I was traded like an animal, as you'd no doubt trade a hound or a horse or a cow. I was nothing!

"Do you not think I dreamed of conquest then? Of my people rising to overthrow our masters? I'd not go back to that. No! Not ever! That was why I fled Karysvar and crossed the Slammerkin, to find the wild Changed and live free.

"But what did I find in Ur-Dharbek? That those who promise freedom dream of power! That Allanyn and her cohorts would join with you Kho'rabi to destroy the Truemen, to set themselves up where the Dhar stand now. Not make a better world—only shift the order of the old. I'd have no master, Tezdal, neither Trueman nor Changed. Only be myself, free.

"What think you the Great Coming shall mean? Surely bloodshed, when your battalions come down out of the sky and Allanyn brings my people south over the Slammerkin, and the Changed of Dharbek rise. And after? What then? Shall your Attul-ki and Allanyn parcel out their conquests? Or shall ambition vaunt itself again and Allanyn decide she'd not share with Sky Lords, or your Attul-ki decide to enslave my Changed people? Where shall those Dhar who still survive be then? As you Ahn were—slaves and outlaws, dreaming in their turn of reconquest? I've found honesty in Truemen—two sit before you now, exemplars!—and I've known cruelty. I've found the same in my own kind, and I tell you that we are none of us so different. Daviot saw that years ago and paid the price of his vision. Rwyan saw it, and now she's here—a Trueman mage, her life dedicated to defense of Dharbek. Until now! When she sees a truer future."

He broke off. He seemed to me almost embarrassed by his eloquence. He took up his cup and drank. I said nothing; neither Rwyan. I think we both knew Urt had said it all, and we could not put it better. I smiled at my old friend, but he was looking away at Tezdal still. His eyes were locked with the Sky Lord's, as if he'd burn the import of his belief into Tezdal's brain.

My Sky Lord friend sat silent awhile, his aquiline features impassive, a mask. I had no doubt he hid the turmoil within.

We waited, all of us.

Finally, Tezdal said, "A truer future, Urt? Tell me what that is, eh? Tell me what truth there can be in vows denied."

Urt still did not look at me, or at Rwyan, but only held Tezdal's gaze. He said, "A better world, my friend. A world of equals, not servants and their masters. Neither vanquished and oppressed; neither any who dream of conquest or liberation, but only live together in freedom."

"And how," Tezdal asked, "would you achieve this utopia?"

Urt said, "I think it shall not be easy. I think it shall cost us pain, and the payment of it be likely bloody. But I have come to Rwyan's belief, to Daviot's dream—I believe we might achieve it."

Tezdal lowered his eyes to his empty cup. Rwyan rose and filled it. The Sky Lord drank and brought a hand to his mouth, where a droplet of red wine sat upon his lip. He wiped it, fastidious, away. He studied his fingers.

Then he said, "Tell me."

His tone was carefully measured, his expression controlled. I saw he hid the anguish that consumed him, the pendulum swing betwixt despair and hope that Urt's justifying argument set in motion. I pitied him. I'd not dare say it aloud—he'd likely have found that an insult to his Kho'rabi honor—but I grieved for him in his torment, knowing that he, more than any of us, was caught in the dilemma of perceived betrayal. I thought, as I watched his bleak face, that if this pattern I'd described to comfort Rwyan, this pattern she now believed in and I almost could see, were true, then it was not unlike those spiders' webs that had decorated this hall before Rwyan brought her talent to their clearing. It was a great web of many strands, impossible to trace to ends or center, sources or conclusions. It was larger and far more complex than we caught in it could see, and poor Tezdal was like a fly landed there by none of his own design—only caught, the mandibles of decision's spider moving ever closer as he struggled to find a way, an honorable way, out.

I looked at his face and felt my soul bleed for him as I outlined the stratagem I'd wrought.

The wind tapped demanding knuckles at the windows as I
spoke. It was yet only midafternoon, but the sky was dark,
laden heavy with the promise of snow to come that night.
What little light the sun succeeded in thrusting through the
clouds fell in long slanting rays over the mountains. I spoke with all
the eloquence of my calling; and more, for I was impassioned by conviction. I saw it kindle a fire in the Sky Lord. He was, at first, still
doubtful, but then I saw his eyes narrow, and then widen, as the seed
Urt had planted took root and grew under the sun of my words. I
watched as his expression shifted, swift as those patterns of light and
shadow dancing over the snowfields and forests beyond the windows.
I saw him come to belief, to trust, and his hope minded me of the sun
in springtime, emerging from winter's gloom.

"Think you it might be done, truly?" he asked, not of me, but of
Rwyan.

She nodded and told him, "I believe it might. I believe that to fail
its attempting is to betray all our peoples."

Tezdal looked then at Urt, who lowered his head in solemn, silent agreement.

He turned to me, brows raised in question. I said, "Save we go on as we've done, in war unending, I see no other way."

He asked, "Even at the price you Dhar shall pay?"

"Weighted by the lives lost—those likely saved—that price seems small to me."

"It seems to me a very great price," he responded.

I shrugged and said, "We'd change our world, Tezdal. I think that price must always be high. But still worth the paying."

He hesitated. He filled his cup and drank again. It seemed he offered a toast. He set the goblet down and said, "I'm with you." And then, much softer, "May the Three forgive me."

"Hurrah!"

We all of us started as Bellek's voice came from a doorway. How long he'd stood there, silent and listening, I could only guess. I thought perhaps since first our conversation had begun, for he came to join us with so purposeful an expression, I must assume he knew all we had decided.

He glanced at the jug and took it from the table. "Such weighty decisions demand a weightier wine," he said, going to the kitchens. Calling back over his shoulder, "And you'll require my aid in this."

He came back with the jug replenished and filled all our cups. It was a rich, red vintage, smooth and heavy. I'd tasted nothing so fine.

"I'd wondered how long it should be," he said, "before you came to this."

I stared at him. "You knew?"

He chuckled. "I know your dreams," he said. "The dragons tell me. I was not certain—I could not be—but I suspected that such as you must sooner or later come to some decision. And that decision must go the one way or the other. You choose the course I thought you'd take."

Rwyan said, "And shall you aid us, Bellek?"

The Dragonmaster fixed her with his pale eyes. On his face I saw emotions chase like shadow and light over the mountains, one overlaying the other so swift, I could not read them clear. I thought I saw hope and confirmation balanced with some indefinable loss. He said, "It shall not be without a price."

I said, "Name it. Likely we'll pay."

Bellek chuckled again, and in the sound I heard the echoes of those mixed emotions that had just decorated his seamed features; also, that hint of madness. I wondered what the price should be.

He said, "That you become, truly, Dragonmasters."

I sensed behind his words some hidden meaning. I said, "Shall we achieve our aims if we are not?"

He shook his head. "No. Save you be utterly committed, you cannot take the dragons into battle."

Rwyan said, "Then I accept."

I found those pale eyes on mine. I glanced an instant at Rwyan, then ducked my head. "I accept."

"Good." He looked to Urt, to Tezdal, who both nodded and gave their word.

"Then," Bellek declared, "let us plan this thing. It shall not be easy, but"—his eyes twinkled as he surveyed us—"I think the dragons shall greatly enjoy it."

We fell then to talk of stratagems, of distances and objectives.

We each had in our possession information of great value, that should make the task easier; or so I hoped. Rwyan's was of that magic commanded by the Dhar sorcerers—of the Sentinels and the Border Cities, and what was owned by the mages of Kherbryn and Durbrecht, the other great cities. I could offer knowledge of the keeps of Dharbek, of the war-engines and the warbands, the mood of the people and the aeldors. Urt spoke of Ur-Dharbek—of Trebizar and the magic Allanyn and her followers possessed, the strength of the Changed armies. Tezdal told us of the Kho'rabi and the Attul-ki, of the preparations for the Great Conquest.

It grew late as we talked. The winter darkness outside gave way to that brief twilight the mountains know, and that to night. The wind fell away, seemingly satisfied its task was done. Great banks of moonlit cloud obscured the sky, and from them fell snow that drifted soft and silent, building on the ledges and the parapets of the Dragoncastle. We repaired to the kitchen, still talking as we assembled a hasty meal, continuing as we brought the food to the table, talking still as we ate.

There were no clocks here, neither clepsydras nor sundials (for what good they'd have done in this season) nor any other kind. It was as if time ceased here, and what divisions of the days and hours existed were imposed only by our urgency. I had seen none in Bellek until now; that I now perceived him quickened worried me in a manner I did not properly understand.

You know from this accounting of my life that I'd that teaching of my College that allowed me usually to interpret a body's language —the hints of eye and intonation, the movements of the hands and shoulders, those little oft-hidden signs that speak as loud as words.

Bellek remained a mystery. I believed I sensed excitement in him, but also a multitude of other emotions I could not explain. I trusted him — I had no doubt he should aid us as he promised — but there was something else, something he concealed. It was that that prompted me to follow him when he left us.

I followed Bellek across yards tracked thick with snow and passages where the trickling water froze and rats skidded on the ice. We came out into a night whirlwinded white and slipped and slid our way — he confident, I furtive as a nightcome thief — along the trailing walkways that brought us to the caves where the dragons lived.

It was cold. I wished I'd brought a cloak. I shivered, thinking that my drumming teeth must reveal my presence, but Bellek showed no sign, only paused before the cave, and then went in.

I came after. I halted at the entrance. The bull Taziel was inside the gaping arch, alert. His wings were furled; his fangs were exposed. He looked at me, and I sent out that silent message Bellek had taught us all.

Peace. I mean no harm. You are mighty and magnificent, and I humbly beg to admire your brood.

He granted me permission, and I went after Bellek into the cave.

I could no more ignore the sending I got from Deburah than I could my earlier curiosity. I should have thought of that before; should have known it. But I was then still newcome to that relationship, and like a lover slowly sensing out all those areas allowed and forbidden that lovers delicately find, I knew not how much this monstrous, majestic love of mine would tell.

She bade me welcome. I stroked her glossy cheek, her sinuous neck. I plucked a fragment — a hunk! — of troublesome meat from her teeth. She thanked me; I loved her as well, albeit differently, as I loved Rwyan. I asked her how her egg fared. (I'd know what Bellek did and why he came here so late, but there's a decorum to dragons as patterned as any formal aeldor's court. They live long, dragons, and to a slower beat of time: unhurried, save by hunger. There are always prices to be paid in dealing with dragons. It is, I think, a price worth the paying.)

She told me her egg fared well. I set my hand on it and felt the pride of the bull as I gloried in Deburah's triumph. I could feel the pulsing of the heart within. It required an effort to remind myself why I'd come here. I asked Deburah.

I cringed then, under the sadness I felt. I'd not known what it is to lose a bond-mate.

I looked across the cave and saw that Bellek knelt on a ledge. The relics of a nest lay there, and the shattered fragments of an egg. He touched them reverentially as I touched Deburah's; but his were in pieces, ours whole and pulsing vigorously with unborn life.

He looked on the past: I looked on the future.

I wondered why no dam sat there.

Deburah told me she'd died.

Of age, she said, ancient even more than Bellek, and even in her age produced an egg. I felt Deburah's pleasure at my arrival in Tartarus, and understood—albeit only vaguely then—that the laying was somehow linked to the presence of Dragonmasters, that I'd an inexplicable hand in her fecundity. I felt her sending as a comfort against Bellek's grief, her pride in *our* egg, though I scarce understand even now how that should be—that the dropping of a dragon's womb can somehow depend on the belief that a person, Changed or Trueman, gives. I felt a terrible sadness for Bellek's loss.

Then, I'd barely tasted the bonding of dragon and Dragonmaster, but still I felt Bellek's pain. It was a blade twisted in my soul. But still I did not understand the entirety of its meaning.

I made a sound. I did not know it until Bellek turned toward me. The width of the brood cave stood between us, but in the radiance of the walls I saw the tears that glistened on his cheeks, his filled eyes, all overrunning. That was such grief as I'd never seen.

For long moments we stared at one another. I knew embarrassment: I knew I intruded on private grief. Then he wiped a sleeve across his face and blew his nose. It was a thin, reedy sound amongst the shufflings and snortings of the dragons, but I heard it clear as scream of pain. I said, "I'm sorry."

The distance between us was too far he could hear me, the noises the dragons made too loud, but he did. And I heard him say, "No matter," and knew he referred not to my sympathy for his loss but to my apology for intruding. They were the same thing: he knew it. We spoke in words, but it was the minds of the dragons that carried our voices back and forth. I watched him rise, and sigh, and stretch his shoulders before he clambered down from the ledge and came toward me.

I stood waiting, leaning against Deburah. I felt afraid in a manner I cannot explain, as if I saw through mists my own future, I become Bellek, old and soul-weary, likely crazed. My sweetling told me I was not, and I stroked her cheek in gratitude.

Bellek halted before her ledge. He said, "You know something of it now. I told you there was a price."

I said, "You did not define it."

He said, "You did not ask I should. Had I?"

I shrugged. So close to Deburah, enfolded by her thoughts, I could only answer, "No. It should not have mattered."

He smiled. On Thannos Eve we Dhar don masks and revel for a night in honor of the Pale Friend, death. It's a festival of which the Church does not entirely approve, for it is redolent of the old ways. The masks depict grinning skulls or a lovely woman's face, each incarnation representing the Pale Friend counting her harvest. Bellek's face reminded me of those death's-heads.

Without preamble he said, "Aiylra was her name. She was beautiful; a queen."

His voice was low and husky, empty of inflection in that way men have when they contain anguish. Let us not disgrace ourselves with exhibition of weakling's pain. Or is it only that we cannot handle it in any other way, save that denial of it? I knew he hurt in ways I could not yet imagine: unthinking, I touched his shoulder. As men do, I thought; and turned my hand to hold him. He leaned against me and wept openly. I put my arms around him and felt him shudder. My shirt got wet.

Against my chest he said, brokenly now, "Oh, Daviot, she was so beautiful. She laid Kathanria, which is how I can ride that one. And Deburah; though"—proud laughter came now through his weeping; such as a father accords a beloved child—"though Deburah's like her dam—proud. She'd have only her one rider. She'd bond with only one master. She'd not let me mount her. Only you. Do you understand?"

I began to grasp it: I felt afraid and proud. I said, "I'm not sure."

Bellek said, "You love Rwyan, no? Whatever risks we take in the days to come, you'd live out your life with her and none other, no?"

I said, "Yes." And to Deburah, silently, *And you.*

"And should you lose her?" he asked me.

I said, "I did. But found her again; I think I should die, did I lose her now."

He said, "It's worse."

I asked, "How?" I could imagine nothing worse than losing Rwyan.

He pushed clear of my arms, rubbing again at his eyes. He looked very old. He looked weary as Tryman, in that tale that tells of how the giant held up the world for his penance. He said, "Dragons live longer than men; and those who dwell with dragons. That was the price. That, and love."

"What do you tell me?" I asked, half suspecting; fearful.

He said, "That you—all of you—must become true Dragonmasters if you're to win this war. That to become Dragonmasters you must bond yourselves, soul to soul, with your mounts."

I said, "I know that. You told us that: we agreed."

He said, "I did not tell you the whole of it."

I said, "I guessed as much. But even so, we accept."

He said, "Had I told you the whole of it, perhaps you'd not have agreed so readily."

I said, "Perhaps not. But the bargain was struck, and do we turn back now—what? The Great Coming? The rising of the Changed? Blood shed all over Dharbek? Can we but implement Rwyan's design, then we can change all that. We can build a better world. Surely that must be worth the price?"

He sighed then, and straightened his back, and looked me unblinking in the eye. "To become a Dragonmaster you must accept the curse of long life. Sometimes longer, even, than the dragons'." He laughed: again that hint of madness. "Does your bond-mate drop an egg, then that may prolong your life. And dragons live a very long time, Daviot; and they're demanding creatures—they'll not let you go easily. That's the bargain we strike, we Dragonmasters."

I said, "Still, I don't quite understand."

And he laughed, so loud the bull on watch outside stirred and turned his baleful eye back. I heard the scrape of claws on stone.

The Dragonmaster said, "Long life. To watch your loves, your friends, your comrades—all of them—die. To live on when they are gone. Glorious, aye; to live with dragons and ride the skies. Such glory! And such pain when it ends. When your bond-mate dies. Like Aiylra! Had she not birthed Kathanria and Deburah I'd have died ere now; or taken that Way of Honor Tezdal thinks of."

I saw a truth then. It was stark, as truth often is. I asked Bellek, "Is that what happened to the others? Your fellow Dragonmasters?"

He ducked his head and told me, "Aye. Their bond-mates died, in battle or age, and they'd no brood-kin to hold up their hopes. Or"— again he laughed that crazed laugh—"hold them here. Only I! And those threads that bind me to this tiresome life grow thin now. Aiylra's gone, and I am weary. Kathanria and Deburah held me, but they've new bond-mates now."

I said, "What shall you do?"

Bellek said, "Teach you to ride dragons in battle."

I said, "And then?"

He said, "Find peace. Go into the Pale Friend's arms. I'd welcome that embrace as you shall, in time."

I asked him then, "Is it so much pain?"

He lowered his head, and I saw fresh tears fall out of his eyes as he answered me, "Aye. Pain beyond your imagining. I think your Sky Lord friend's the better way. It should be better to put a blade in my belly than suffer this."

I said, frightened, "Then why don't you? Why haven't you?"

He said, "Because I had Deburah and Kathanria. Aiylra's laying, them; and mine. I'd have followed her into death, save there were no other Dragonmasters then, and I'd not leave my charges solitary. They are my children as much as his."

I followed the direction of his eyes toward the entrance of the cave, where the bull sat massive on his guardian's ledge, and understood what Bellek told me.

I felt my mouth go dry. I felt my bowels shrivel. I committed my life here, and Rwyan's; and carried Urt's and Tezdal's with me. I knew that then: I felt small and afraid. Like a boy standing on the beach as the airboat came closer and spread its malign shadow over me. Hoarse, I said, "I understand now."

Bellek said, "Do you accept it?"

I looked at Deburah and found no choice. I said, "Yes."

Bellek said, "You cannot tell your friends. Do that—do they disagree—and you'll fly no dragons against the armies that threaten."

I looked at him and asked, "Think you they'd disagree?"

He said, "It shall mean your lives here, in no other place; and they shall be very long lives. It shall mean you cannot return to Dharbek, but must take my place in the Dragoncastle."

I think I knew it even then, but still I must ask him, "Why?"

He said, "Because the dragons will not leave this place, and do you enter fully into the bonding, then nor shall you. You begin to feel those ties e'en now, I think. They shall grow stronger—glorious chains that bind you to the ending of your days."

I did begin to feel it. Already it was a painful notion to contemplate parting from Deburah. I said, "That, I can accept. I think the others would, too."

Bellek coughed laughter. "It's not so easy," he said. "Shall Tezdal agree to never more walk the earth of Ahn-feshang? Shall Rwyan give up her sorcerous friends? Urt not go back to Ur-Dharbek?"

Doubt clogged my throat, sour. I swallowed. "Why can I not put it to them?"

He turned his face away at that, and when I saw it again, it was composed. "Because they might disagree. Not Rwyan, I think; at least, not so long as you remain. But Urt and Tezdal . . . ?" He took hold of my hands. I winced at the force of his urgent grip. "You must take my place! You four can bring new life to Tartarus; you can make the dragons great again. But you must pay that price!"

I weighed it in my head. I sensed Deburah waiting for my decision. I wonder, had I not already taken the first strides along that road that binds Dragonmaster to dragon, if I'd have chosen different. But I had, and so I can never be sure. Was it I made that decision? Or was it that I'd see that dream I shared with Rwyan fulfilled? Or was it Deburah made up my mind? I know not; and likely never shall.

I do know that I answered Bellek's grip then and said, "So be it. I'll not tell them."

He said, "Not even Rwyan?"

I shook my head. I felt a dreadful guilt as I told him, "Not even Rwyan."

I felt such intoxicating pleasure then as makes the headiest wine akin to tepid water. I felt . . . this is not easy to describe, but a promise of glorious days to come, of long happiness, shared lives, pleasure. I was sent stumbling forward as Deburah craned her great head down to nudge my back. Bellek caught me, else I'd have fallen, and on his face I saw reflected the satisfaction I felt from my lovely dragon.

I said, "My word on it," and silently, inside my skull, where the deepest and most hidden of our thoughts reside, *Forgive me, Rwyan.*

There are some bargains as rest heavy on the soul. For each bright shining promise, there exists a dark shadow. Bellek had extracted from me an agreement I was not certain I should have given: I committed my love and my friends to a future in which they had no say. But had I not, then surely our agreed aims could never have been accomplished.

I told myself I had no other choice as I walked with Bellek back along those snow-clad ledges that brought us to the castle.

I had no other choice.

It did not help me much. I thought Rwyan must surely read the guilt I felt inscribed upon my face. My mouth went dry, and when we found the empty hall and stood before the banked fire with snow coming vaporous off our clothes and hair, I found the wine jug and drank deep.

"Remember," Bellek said, likely not aware he insulted me, "that do you say aught of this, no dragons shall fly."

I nodded and set down my cup. There are some bargains as sit heavy on the soul.

Rwyan was asleep when I came in. That magic she'd set about the chamber brought gentle light from the walls and ceiling, and perhaps it was that stirred her. Perhaps it was only my presence, the small sounds I made, or her own curiosity. I confess that I'd hoped she would remain asleep, and I be able to slink silent to our bed and not need give answer to questions I'd sooner not now face, but wait for morning and the prevarications of a rested mind.

But I had no other choice: she woke, and raised herself against the pillows, and pushed tumbled hair from her face, and fixed her sleepy, blind eyes on me. I saw them grow alert: I felt afraid. I'd sooner dare the jaws of a bull dragon than this.

She said, "You were long with Bellek."

Inevitably, a question hung between us. I ducked my head: I'd not then much wish to meet her eyes. In that moment I regretted the promise I'd given the Dragonmaster; I thought of breaking it. I knew I could not, else her dream be damned at its birthing.

I said, "Aye. He had things to speak of."

She said, "What things?"

I shrugged. "Let me wash first. It was cold out there."

She said, "In the brood cave?"

How much did she know? I said, "Yes," and hid myself within the alcove, toweling my hair dry, washing: delaying.

At last I must emerge and face her, this woman I loved deeper even than what I felt for Deburah. And likely tell her lies. I think I've not felt sorrier than that in all my life.

And in a way she made it no easier for me — love's fond cruelty — for what she did was fling her magic at the hearth so that the fire flared brighter to warm me better, and hold back the bed's coverings that I climb in beside her, and then fold her arms around me to warm me with her own body's heat. And all I could do was crawl guilty in and lie against her, as she told me I was cold and asked if I'd have her warm me ale or wine. And I could only shake my head and ask she keep her arms around me and trust me.

And then the worst: she said, "I do."

I could only extemporize then.

Or was it prevarication?

I said, "Bellek's bond-mate died."

She stiffened. I felt her shudder, knowing she experienced the same shared horror I'd known; that she felt the growth of the bonding no less than I.

She said, low, "That must be . . ." And shook her head, her sunset hair curtaining my face until she flung it loose and finished: "Poor, poor man. And you were there. You shared his grief."

Against her breasts I mumbled, "Yes. He wept . . . He . . ."

Almost, I told her all of it, but she kissed me then, soft, and said, "Some of that I felt. It was like a dream, but I think Anryäle sent it me. I think she'd not lose me. . . . I think I begin to understand what it is to bond with dragons."

I asked, "Do you? Truly?"

If she'd told me no then, I'd likely have broken trust with Bellek and told her everything, but she did not. Instead, she kissed me again and said, "There are sometimes things revealed in grief that are private and should not be shared. Did you promise him as much?"

I said, hoarse and hollow against her breasts, "Yes."

And she said, "Does your promise gainsay our purpose?"

I said, "No. My promise ensures it. But—"

She set her fingers gentle against my lips and told me, "Then I trust your promise. Bellek asked you hold it secret, no?"

I said, "Yes."

She said, "Then honor your word."

I said, "But you don't know what it was. You should."

She said, "No," and laughed, rising over me in the bed to straddle me and pin me down with her soft thighs and arms against my shoulders. "Shall I not trust you, Daviot? Shall I not believe the man I love is capable of promises I can trust? What should that make me?"

I said, "I don't know. But this promise concerns not only you and I but also Urt and Tezdal."

She lowered her face to mine and kissed me soft and long and said, "Do you tell them, shall it threaten our purpose?"

I said, "Perhaps it should."

She asked, "Shall it harm them?"

I said against her lips, "I think not."

"But it might? Or should it turn them away from this new world we'd build?"

I moved my mouth from hers. I pushed her hair away that I might see her face clear. I looked into her green eyes. Blind—aye!— but clear with total purpose, with such certitude as gave me no choice but to nod my head and say, "It might."

She said, "And should it be a better world if they turn from it? Should we change anything?"

I could only say, "I think not. I think it should be much the same —all war unending."

"Then honor your promise to Bellek," she said. "Honor that greater obligation. I'll not ask what the Dragonmaster told you; say nothing to them."

I asked, "Is that fair?"

I was startled how well she could mimic my voice. She said, "All war unending," and it was as if I spoke to myself. She smiled.

"Daviot; Daviot. Shall we stand by and watch our world go down in war and blood? Shall we do nothing, save contest with our finer conscience? Spend all our time wondering what's right and what's wrong? Shall we take this path, or that? Or shall we—when we see a way—take it? Do you believe that what we plan is wrong?"

I shook my head. It was a pleasant sensation: it brought my lips against her breasts.

She rose, so that I could not any longer, and faced me square, "looking" deep into my eyes. She said, "Then to do other than what we believe is right must be wrong, no?"

I said, "Yes."

I felt horribly tired, and at the same time lustful. I wanted Rwyan badly, and I wanted sleep no less. I felt guilty, and she persuaded me I was innocent. She held true to her belief; I doubted mine.

I said, as I'd said to Bellek earlier, "I'll not tell them."

She said, "Good. I think that shall be for the best. I think we'll build a better world."

Then she bent down to kiss me, and sunk me into her, and I lay back as she moved on me, and I almost forgot my weariness. Because I loved her, and loved Deburah, and knew that we, all of us, built fresh eggs, and dragons should once more ride the skies, become again the Lords of the Sky, and the one thing was the other, all mingled, and I was no longer sure whether I lay with Rwyan or Deburah, and cared not which, only that they both loved me, and I them, and we were together.

35

Winter's fist still gripped the mountains of Tartarus as we readied to fly south.

Bellek would ride with Urt on Kathanria, and all swathed in furs against the chill, we climbed astride our bonded steeds. I buckled myself in place on Deburah's back and felt her eagerness. My blood quickened. I felt the lust to hunt. I was no longer entirely myself, but a gestalt creation—dragon and rider bound in such union as only Dragonmasters can ever know. I looked to where Rwyan sat Anryäle, and on her face I saw the same excitement I knew must infuse my features. I had not seen so many dragons gathered in one place before. Our castle was augmented by the others, so that there was not a perch or ledge or tower did not seat a dragon, and more beat restless wings against the snow-laden sky, anxious to go south, to the hunting.

Bellek raised an arm, like some ancient general readying his troops.

Before it came down, the bulls were lofting. I felt their battle-hunger, wild in my blood. Then Deburah spread her magnificent wings and hurled us skyward. I shrieked my joy, which small cry was quite lost amid the belling of the dragons.

Up we went, the loftiest peaks as nothing to us; up to where the clouds ended and the sun shone. Up higher than any bird could dare; up and up to the true domain of the dragons, up to the great panoply of unsullied blue that covered all the world. Then south, beating high above the Dragonsteeth Mountains and the empty moorlands of Ur-Dharbek that came after. I saw those hills that ringed Trebizar draw steadily closer as the morning gave way to afternoon.

I grew afraid we came too late: it was already spring here. I told myself it was not yet Ennas Day.

Crops sprouted in the fields below, the cattle grazed on verdant grass. I thought on how that magic the wild Changed commanded could do all this, of what a fruitful land this unknown country was; and then that it must surely be enough for anyone. I thought it likely was for the ordinary Changed who lived their ordinary lives here, and that it was Allanyn and her ilk who'd bring these peaceful folk down over the Slammerkin in war. And then that had we Truemen not treated the Changed so poorly, they'd not go to war.

A memory of Pele and Maerk flashed through my mind: confirmation that understanding was possible, that Changed and Trueman might live together in peace and love.

But not easily. Surely not without this lesson we'd deliver. Surely not without we impose our design on the world. Not for the first time, I wondered if what we did was right. If we looked to overturn some natural order that defined men in strata, master and servant, friend and foe. I pushed the thought aside: I was committed now. There was no turning back: we'd tear down that we might erect a better society from the wreckage of the old.

And Deburah's enthusiasm filled me. She sensed the magic ahead, and it sharpened her appetite. She'd contest with these upstart creatures for mastery of the skies. As would the bulls: I felt their battle-lust as a heady tide that denied all doubt. They'd only fight now and turn on any who turned back. I gave myself up to it: better that than wonder if what we did was right.

I looked around and saw the sky all filled with dragons, dread squadrons come out of legend to fall upon a younger world.

They were superb! They were incarnate glory. Their wings hid the afternoon sun; their fangs shone bright. They were winged wrath; and I was with them: one with them. I forgot all else as we rose over Trebizar's footling hills and swept down toward the skyboats.

There were more now. Where a score or so had hung moored beside the shining lake, there were now hundreds. They sat like blood-filled slugs above the land, and spread below them were the pavilions of the Sky Lords, all bright banners in the sun.

Men came out as we approached. They looked like ants swarming from myriad close-packed nests, all gleaming black armor, with useless swords and ineffectual bows raised against us. I saw a handful of the little skyboats climb to meet us and felt the surge of the bulls' contempt as they—forerunners of our dread army—beat their wings and turned to attack.

The Sky Lords were brave. Let no man ever say different, for those few tiny boats came hard against us, and the Kho'rabi wizards flung their magic at us, and the warriors in the baskets, though they were so few, strung bows and hurled javelins at creatures that must surely have terrified them.

But they were not enough, and the elementals the Kho'rabi wizards held in bondage did no more than their masters forced them to. I heard their joyous laughter as the bulls dove, talons spread wide, jaws all agape. I saw the little skyboats erupt incandescent, like crimson flowers blossoming against the blue of that springtime afternoon. I heard the belling triumph of the bulls and the wild laughter of the elementals as they were freed of occult shackles. I saw more than a few Kho'rabi taken from the air by invisible hands and rent apart. But not so many as the bulls slew.

And then we were closing on the greater skyboats, all of us; all our terrible battalions.

The Kho'rabi boats were moored, grounded. Neither the warriors nor the Kho'rabi wizards were readied for our attack. I doubt it should have been different had they been. Perhaps longer, but not different: they were not accustomed to fighting dragons. How could they be?

We came on.

I gave up all thought, all doubt: I was one with Deburah as she slavered hunger. We chose a skyboat and beat our wings hard, to catch height. The prey lay below us: we furled our wings and dropped. Our limbs thrust out, talons spread wide. Elementals screamed encouragement, howling to be freed. We fell out of the sky. We struck. Our talons burst the skyboat's skin, and fire gusted around us. Elementals drove the flames away. We fell down through the ruptured canopy and hooked our claws in the basket beneath. There were men there. I supposed they thought to loft the airboat. We lowered our head even as we spread our wings wide to avoid the ground. And ducked our head to pluck the men out. Bite them. Sweet taste of warm blood! And drop them; to select another. Fore- and hindlimbs clutching; tearing. Beating wings sending ragged flags of burning hide in tatters around us. Until there was nothing left living there, and we rose to find fresh prey.

From the elementals: gratitude that we set them free.

That part of me that still looked out from behind my own eyes saw a Kho'rabi running below us. He was armored but without his obscuring helmet, so that I saw his face as he looked up. He held a sword that was the sister of Tezdal's, and he raised it even as Deburah's talons closed on him. Never doubt the courage of the Kho'rabi: he swung his blade even as he was lifted up and carried to her—to *our!*—jaws. I did not hear him scream, but I think he did. Surely his mouth sprang wide and his eyes were huge as those fangs closed on him and severed him. I watched the two pieces fall down onto the bloody, burning ground.

I laughed.

We gained height and saw our sister, Kathanria, tearing at a skyboat. We flew to join her. I saw Bellek's face lit as I'd not seen it before. I wondered if it was vomit that stained Urt's furs. But no time for that: this was battle, and we'd win it. We sank our talons into the skin of the sky's usurper and rent it asunder. Men fell out of the basket, and we quested after them in sisterly rivalry. We claimed more. And ours the Kho'rabi wizard: that taste sweeter for the impotent magic he flung against us as our jaws closed on him. Fool! To think his weakling magic should be of use against us, who own the skies!

We went on.

There were no more skyboats left, only burning wreckage, but we could still pluck tents and the little fleeing figures of men. Like tidbits after a feast, taken almost lazily. Not hunger anymore, but only the gratification of sated appetite: to be taken because they were there.

Then Bellek's call. We rose to meet it, circling the blue sky over Trebizar.

Under us the lake was lit by the flames of the burning skyboats, red upon the blue. Like the darkening of the grass where men's blood had fallen.

Trebizar? The Council? Allanyn?

His voice was lost under the thunder of the dragons' wings, the triumphant howling of the bulls. I heard it only through Deburah's sending. Just as I returned my answer: *Aye! Best that we end it swift.*

Rwyan's agreement was immediate, the others' slower and less certain. From Urt I heard a heartsick plea that we delay; at least avoid such slaughter as we'd wrought on the Kho'rabi, not butcher his Changed kind as we had the Sky Lords.

And from Tezdal . . . I could not be sure. Sorrow? Commitment? A disgust directed inward? I gave it not much thought: I was filled up with Deburah and knew only triumph and the satisfaction of the hunt. I lusted for more; and better: against harder quarry. Aloud, my inadequate voice carried on Deburah's sending, I said, "Only Allanyn, and those who'd oppose us. Let none others be slain."

That, Bellek returned me, *shall be difficult. The bulls have the taste now, and shall be hard to control.*

I gave him back, *Only do your best.* And to Urt, *It should be better ended here and now, lest Allanyn flee. You need not take part.*

What I felt then, from Urt, sent out by Kathanria, was a dreadful mixture of emotions, akin to what I'd felt from Tezdal. Inside my head I heard my old Changed friend say, *No. Are we to do this, then I've a part I cannot ignore. Allanyn must be mine, lest my people say it was Truemen alone delivered this fury.*

Brave Urt! That was courage indeed, and common sense; but still I ached for the pain I heard inside his words.

So be it. This from Bellek, and without further ado we swept across the lake, toward the Council building.

We left the Kho'rabi behind, decimated and confused, a milling mass of warriors unable, I suspected, to properly comprehend what had happened, the nature of the terrible airborne wrath brought against them. Certainly, they made no move to follow but only watched as we descended on the oval of the Council building. I saw some fall to their knees with hands upraised: I wondered if they believed this was some deliverance of Vachyn, some divine expression of disapproval.

Then I had no more time for wondering, but only action: we fell upon that strange white structure, and the harder part began.

The bulls landed first. They came down and set to tearing away the roof and walls. The rage that possessed them as they sensed hostile magic was formidable. As a dog bred solely for combat knows only the lust to destroy when it scents blood, so did the bull dragons react: the afternoon was not much longer aged before the Raethe's building had no roof, nor many standing walls. As Deburah circled above, I looked down on a complex of halls and chambers and corridors all strewn with rubble, and the little fleeing figures of the Changed councilors.

Some tried to reach the lake shore: they failed.

We descended, Deburah and I, and I loosed my buckles and slid from the saddle, only dimly aware of the others landing and dismounting around me.

Take care.

That from Deburah, her wondrous head ducking down from the jagged ramparts of a wall to nudge me. I rubbed her cheek and drew the ancient sword Bellek had given me and told her, "Yes. I think I'll not be very long."

I recognized this hall, for all it was now roofless and littered. It was that chamber where Rwyan and I had first been brought to face Allanyn. I saw the corpse of Geran, ruptured by broken stone. There were other faces I remembered, felled by masonry or the bulls' rage. Across the now-open area I saw Allanyn.

Her beautiful face was a dreadful sight. It was contorted with a horrid fury that absolutely overcame her inborn fear of dragons. Were the bulls incarnate power, then she was incarnate rage. She stood beneath the shelter of an arch, the way beyond blocked by rubble. She wore a gown of crimson, dusty now and speckled with the blood of the slain. Her lips were peeled back from her white teeth: I saw her gums and could not help but think of a mountain cat brought to bay.

She screamed, "What have you done? Do you think to live after this?"

And as she spoke, her hands formed sigils in the reeking air, shaping magic.

Uselessly, I raised my sword.

Urt shouted, "We'd bring peace to the world. Shall you listen?"

Allanyn's answer was a bolt of power. I'd never seen such occult strength. Save perhaps when I'd witnessed the magic of the Sentinels, which I knew was a thing combined of many sorcerers, drawing on the power of a crystal. I thought to die then, at the beginning. But Rwyan raised her hands and met the blast with a countering gramarye that deflected Allanyn's magic and sent it, like flood water held by a barrage, around us.

She gestured again, and Allanyn was flung back, a ragdoll thrown against the fallen stone behind her. Disheveled, faced with the inherent terror of our dragons, still the gifted Changed was defiant. She said, "So. This communion with dragons appears to make you strong; but I'll contest you to the end."

Urt raised a commanding hand. "We'd not fight you, Allanyn, save you force us to it. But you shall hear us out!" His voice was clear and loud; it held a plea and a promise.

Allanyn's response was no less impressive.

She picked herself up from the rubble and smoothed her gown. She looked up, eyes casting slowly around the ravaged walls where our dragons perched. All fear seemed drained out of her now: she surveyed those terrifying faces with only contempt.

Greater still was the contempt she turned on Urt. "Tell me then, traitor." Her voice was a challenge. "Tell me how you shall bring peace when all you offer is fear. Shall we bow our heads to you now? Swear fealty to your dragons?"

Urt ignored the disdain in her voice. "We'd end this dream of war that can only bring suffering to all our people. Must we use the dragons, then so be it, for we've no better answer. But better that fear awhile than what you'd bring. We'd make a lasting peace—a new world, without Truemen masters or Changed servants, neither Sky Lords in lust of conquest or Dhar in fear of invasion. We'd build a new order, in which all have a place and a part. And when that's wrought, the dragons shall return to Tartarus. So—shall you join us in that? Shall you seek not to shed your people's blood but only aid them?"

Allanyn brushed red hair from her face. "So you find your true calling, Urt. A lapdog to these Truemen! Think you you can win? Shall you turn over so many lifetimes of suffering? Shall your dragons make the Changed forget the oppression of Truemen? Shall you persuade the Ahn to forget that the Dhar drove them from their Homeland?"

Urt said, "No. Those things are writ in blood; they were done—right or wrong—and cannot be forgotten. But what you intend is no different. Only a new oppression. What we'd build is a new world."

Allanyn laughed at that.

Urt gestured at we who stood silent beside him. "I am Changed," he said. "Rwyan is a sorcerer of Dharbek. You know Daviot for a Storyman. Tezdal is Kho'rabi. We—all of us—are joined in this purpose. Can you not take that as pledge of union and join us? It should be better so."

Allanyn snarled and flung fresh magic at us. Rwyan dismissed it with a gesture that was almost casual.

She did not this time throw the Changed mage down, but rather seemed to bind her with occult chains that leached out Allanyn's own power. Allanyn stood a moment shaken, an expression of disbelief on her lovely, ugly face. Then she drew a dagger from the folds of her gown and sprang, cat-quick, at Rwyan.

I leaped forward, but Tezdal was far swifter: his was the sword that struck the blow aside. Allanyn's blade went spinning up, striking the broken stones of the wall, then tumbling bright in the sun down to the stained marble of the hall's floor. It lay there like a defeated dream.

Tezdal held back the downstroke of his blade. He turned to Urt and said, " 'Lest my people say it was Truemen alone delivered this fury'?"

Urt closed his eyes and nodded. I knew he'd no taste for this: of all of us, I think he was the gentlest. But still he drew his sword—I'd not then noticed he'd left it sheathed—and brought it up high above his head.

He said, "I'd sooner it not be this way."

Allanyn spat and returned him, "Traitor! Trueman's lapdog!"

He was not expert: he'd no training in swordwork. His blow did not take off Allanyn's head as he'd intended, but only drive an awful cut between her slim shoulder and her slender neck.

Allanyn screamed and fell down. Blood rose in a ghastly fountain that sprayed us all. Urt cut again, and she was silent. I felt a dreadful calm and hoped I was not become inured to bloodshed. I looked to my friend and saw him stoop, mouth wide as he spewed.

It was Tezdal who held him then, and took the antique sword from his hands, and told him, "It was a thing needing to be done. You'd no other choice."

I heard Urt groan, "No? Are you sure?"

It was Rwyan who answered. She stood speckled with Allanyn's blood, her hair blown wild. She was, I thought, like some goddess of war or justice, come out of the past like the dragons that watched our drama. She said, "Allanyn would have made a worse world, Urt. What you did was for all the Changed who'd live free."

Leaning back within the compass of Tezdal's arms, he turned to face her. He wiped vomit from his mouth. "Are you sure?"

And she said, "Yes. Allanyn owned your Raethe, and she'd lead your people into a war that none of us, neither Changed nor Dhar nor Ahn, could ever win."

I started as I heard hands clapping slow (and mocking?) applause, but it was only Bellek. He said, "That Council exists no longer. Those not slain here were taken by the dragons. I think there are not many Changed left with that power."

Urt said, "What of the town? Are the folk there safe?"

Bellek said, "Aye. Some flee, but the dragons have not attacked them." Then he laughed and added, "Yet, at least."

We mounted and crossed the lake, bringing utter panic. The streets of the town were filled with terrified Changed, those not hiding inside the houses cowering beneath the beating of our wings as we came down to land. I felt disgusted by the pride I felt as I strode down the wide avenues, Deburah strutting behind me, her wings brushing the verandas, her talons gouging ruts from the streets. I felt like some god then, potent in my ability to dispense death or life, knowing that I need only give my lovely mate a word to see all around me destroyed.

Power corrupts. It's a heady brew that is hard to resist: I pride myself that I did, for it was a difficult temptation as I watched them cower and felt Deburah's contempt. But resist it I did, and we found Ayl and a few brave others. They held swords, and I think they'd have fought us had Urt not been with us. Certainly, their expressions were grim—they looked to me like men readying to die.

As it was, our former jailer saw my Changed comrade come marching down that fear-struck street with a dragon in tow and stared wide-eyed and gape-mouthed, until Urt called out, "Ayl! I need a sound man here."

Then Ayl dropped his sword and fell to his knees and asked what Urt would have him do.

He was terrified. He would not look at the dragons, and he shuddered and trembled as Urt spoke to him.

I waited in the street as Urt told him, "Allanyn's dead; and most of the sorcerers—there shall be no more thought of war. The Sky Lords' airboats are destroyed, and all of Allanyn's dreams. Tell the people that, Ayl. Tell them we open the gates of a new world. Tell them to forget the war." He gestured at the dragons at his back, those circling overhead. "Tell them no harm shall come from these creatures, save the war goes on. Tell them that any attempt to cross the Slammerkin shall be met by these."

Kathanria sensed his mood and raised her head supportive. Her jaws gaped wide, displaying those terrible fangs, and she loosed a ferocious cry. I saw folk dart back through doorways. But Ayl, for all he was shuddering with fear, remained.

Urt said, "There's a new order coming, Ayl. A new and better world. We Changed shall be no longer servants; neither subject to the gifted. We shall be free and deal as equals with the Truemen and the Sky Lords. This I promise you. Tell the people this."

Ayl nodded. I could not help but wonder if it should be so easy. Not even when Rwyan brought Anryäle up alongside Deburah, and found my hand, and told me, "It begins now, Daviot. That peace we dreamed of."

Even then, that first battle won, that first step so forcibly taken, I wondered if it could be so.

We had denied Allanyn's dream of conquest, aye. But what of the rest? What of Jareth's dreams? What of the Sky Lords', Tezdal's kin? Could we truly force peace on the world?

I was not sure, but I knew I was committed to that road. I knew that I could not turn back; not now, not with bloodied hands. I knew that only success could cleanse that stain.

We had provisions of the frightened town and took flight. There was nothing more we could immediately do in Trebizar, nor in Ur-Dharbek, save trust that Allanyn's bellicose dream was dead with her, and that such good souls as Ayl should bring some order to the chaos we left behind. Later we could return, but now—now we'd new battles to fight, fresh conquests awaiting us. And those to be won before the Sky Lords launched their armada, before Ennas Day. I hoped we came timely, that what we left behind, all we had wrought in Trebizar, not be for nothing.

As the sun went down and the fires of our coming lit the sky, we flew to those hills that ringed the valley. Our dragons roosted there, calling amongst themselves as we five made camp and laid our plans for the morrow.

Neither Urt nor Tezdal offered much comment but remained largely silent. They had both seen their own kind slain this day: I wondered how I should feel when we brought our dragons against my own people. I thought that night, as I held Rwyan in my arms and tried to sleep, that I should find out soon enough. It was not a pleasant anticipation. It was made worse by Tezdal's lonely figure, not sleeping but only sitting staring into the flames.

The dragons belled in the dawn. They took pleasure of this warmer weather, and I felt their eagerness to fly again, to drive southward to the combat promised there. Their lust enthused me, so that I forgot my doubts (or a part of me forgot them) and I found myself suddenly as eager. I saddled Deburah and mounted with alacrity, lifting her skyward even as the forerunner bulls beat their massive wings and climbed toward the rising sun. We circled once in dread reminder over Trebizar, and then turned away in the direction of the Slammerkin.

We reached that strait by noon.

I had never seen the Slammerkin, nor the Border Cities, and I was startled by the size of both. The dividing waterway was vast, far wider than the Treppanek, and I wondered how any Changed succeeded the crossing. I supposed only the most determined—like Urt—could hope to bridge that great expanse. And the Border Cities—they were each of them near large as Durbrecht, like vast fortresses spread all along the southern shore. I felt a pang of alarm then, thinking of the sorcerers in those sunlit towers and the magicks they could throw at us.

From Deburah, then, I got a sense of calm, of tremendous confidence, an absolute certainty that we should cross this barrier unscathed. That no mortal magic could harm me so long as I sat her back. I hoped she was right: I had no choice but to trust her.

I watched the cities come rapidly closer. Even had they not already sensed our approach, they must surely see us now—we filled the sky. Squadrons of dragons spread to either side, and more behind. The land and then the water below us was shadowed under our passing.

They did see us, but no occult blasts were sent against us: as Rwyan had promised, we took them by surprise, and our passing was so swift, the sorcerers there had no time to link and draw on the crystals' power. We were come and gone fleet as the shadow of a wind-driven cloud on a summer afternoon. We left the Border Cities behind us, our destination Kherbryn.

That was another proposition entirely: Kherbryn was a citadel, fortified even stronger than Durbrecht; and warned of our approach.

We were met with magic and, as we closed, those bolts Gahan's war-engines threw. I saw a bull—a magnificent silver-skinned creature—turned from his path by occult power. It spun him in the bright afternoon light, holding him like a cork tossed on contrary tides, even as he beat his wings and fought to free himself. Before he could, he was struck by a gleaming shaft. His wing was pierced, close to the shoulder. Through Deburah I heard him shriek, less in pain than in rage and wounded pride. I had not seen dragon's blood before: it is red, like yours and mine. It spread along his ribs as he attempted to gain height, but then a second shaft took him full in the chest and killed him. I felt that as I'd never felt a death before. I knew what it was to see a friend die; I knew what it was to put a sword in a man and feel his life spent. But this . . . I'd not felt this, ever: I shared the outrage of the dragons.

And even as the great body tumbled from the sky, the horror began.

The bulls came down like those demons the Church threatens. Even as Deburah—as *we*, for there was no longer, not then, any difference between us—followed them, I saw two bulls plummet like stooping falcons on the engine that had flung the bolt. One caught it in his hindpaws and lifted it, the soldier-mechanics falling from it like insects shed from a raised carcass. He beat his wings and carried the engine high above the walls. I saw a luckless soldier clinging to the machine, and then falling down as the bull loosed his hold and let the engine drop into the streets below. The other, meanwhile, was landed on the ramparts—I had seen this before, in a dream; but then it had been Kho'rabi knights the dragon snatched and tore and chewed, not Dhar warriors, not soldiers of the Lord Protector's warband.

Then I was too close to observe anything more than what Deburah did. What *we*, locked in our gestalt identity of dragon and Dragonmaster, did. And that was terrible enough: a bull was slain— our wrath must be delivered in full measure, these upstart creatures taught a lesson.

We swooped low over the ramparts of Kherbryn, slaying as we went. Not pausing but driving on, talons and jaws slashing and snapping, our tail a sweep that dashed men down, screaming, to the stones below. We left only ravaged bodies in our wake. The war-engines were too heavy for us—we left those to the bulls, who left them wrecked. We took the men; like a fox in a chicken coop. We knew only the venting of our fury, and when there were no more left on the walls, we swooped over the city, all of us. Rwyan was there, and one with the dragons' anger; and Tezdal, and Urt, with Bellek fearsome on Kathanria.

And when it was done, when Deburah sat in the yard before the Lord Protector's great palace, and dragons sat like the God's judgment upon the walls and more hung in the sky above, I climbed from the saddle and became, a little, myself again. Enough that I looked around, and felt my stomach churn, and fell to my knees, and emptied my belly, as Urt had done in Trebizar. And when I rose, telling Deburah that I could not properly explain why the slaughter should upset me so, I saw Rwyan's leathers all discolored with vomit, and her face so pale, I thought she must faint.

She leaned against Anryäle, who radiated the same satisfaction as Deburah, and wiped her mouth, and said, albeit thickly, "We did not think it should be easy, eh?"

I shook my head, and spat, and answered her, "No. But neither like this."

Tezdal said, "This is war. In whatever cause, it is still war, and war is a bloody thing. When we go east, it shall likely be worse."

I thought there might be some measure of pride in his voice, or even satisfaction, but I offered him no response, because just then I caught sight of a bull across the yard. He was digging claws between his teeth to dislodge something caught there, and when it came loose, I saw that it was the head of a man, trapped between the fangs by the column of the spine the bull had torn from the body. There was a helmet still locked in place, and from it hung that slender length of linked bones. It fell loose and rolled across the flagstones. I had thought my belly quite emptied, but I managed to vomit again at that.

It was Urt who helped me up, and his face was drawn as Rwyan's. He said soft in my ear, "This is not easy, Daviot."

I said, "No," and heard my voice come thick. "I never thought . . ."

"Nor I," he said. "But we can do it. We must, now. Now more than ever. Or it means nothing, any of it."

I felt his hand firm on my shoulder and remembered the touch, from Durbrecht. I spat again and ducked my head and told him, "Yes. For all the world."

He smiled, and it was not dissimilar to that expression I'd seen on Bellek's face when he told me of Aiylra's demise. It was not dissimilar to the smile of the Pale Friend.

I said, "Then let us do it. But I think it must be hard to fight our way down those long corridors. The palace must be filled with warriors intent on defending Taerl and Jareth both. We could scarce dare hope to win through. Not without terrible carnage."

Bellek said, "It should not take long to destroy it—the bulls would welcome it. Or we could send the dragons out to scour the streets until our quarry comes to us."

I said, "I'd see no more blood spilled, can we avoid it."

Bellek looked, I thought, disappointed. His pale eyes glistened in the afternoon sun, and there was an excitement expressed in his stance; like the restless flexing of the bulls. I wondered then, even when my blood knew it, how close Dragonmaster grew to dragon, and how much humanity was left after that bonding was complete.

I said, "Do we send heralds in and ask that the Lord Protector and the regent attend us?"

And Bellek laughed and called a bull forward who—before any of us had opportunity to disagree—rose on his hindlimbs and tore the door that barred our passage from its hinges.

Wood lay in splinters before us as a Changed servant came out, the yellow rag of submission waving on a pole that trembled in his shaking hands. In the hallway behind him I saw a squad of crossbow men.

Rwyan moved to speak, but I sprang before her: I'd not see my love slain now.

I shouted, "We'd speak with the Lord Protector, Taerl; and with the regent, Jareth. There need not be more bloodshed."

The frightened Changed sprang back, and a moment later a commur appeared. His plaid was immaculate, his armor polished. He'd not seen battle yet, but still his sword was steady in his hand, and his voice was firm as the steel. At his back the archers held their crossbows leveled on my chest. I felt a great desire to be elsewhere.

The commur demanded, "Who are you to ask this?"

I could not see his face behind his helmet, only his eyes, but they were indignant. I studied him a moment and saw that his plaid was not Kherbryn's but that of Mardbrecht: Jareth's man.

I heard Bellek say, "Let the dragons have him."

And Rwyan, "No! We come to parley, not to slay."

I said again, "We'd speak with the Lord Protector."

The commur eyed me past the bars of his helm. I saw his gaze move on to the awful beasts surrounding me, to those upon the walls and those in the sky above. It is difficult to read the body language of an armored man, but under his pauldrons I thought I saw his shoulders droop a fraction. I said, "We need fight no more. But do you choose it, then these dragons will tear Kherbryn apart. Do you doubt they can do that?"

His eyes gave me answer first, and then his voice: "No. Do you wait here?"

I said, "Awhile."

He ducked his head and turned away. The archers remained. I could see their faces clear. I could see the terror there. I applauded their courage, for none ran or lowered their weapons.

We waited in that yard baked hot by the magic of the Attul-ki, and I had time to see what that had wrought. I saw dead plants and dried fountains, wilted vines and withered trees. There was an aura of despair, of sun-dried hope; flagstones were cracked, weeds climbing up, even they yellow and enervated. The dragons luxuriated in the heat. I shed my furs and still felt sweat mask my body.

Then horns sounded and a herald appeared. His hair was lank, and droplets of perspiration trickled down his face. His tabard was stained, but his voice was loud: "The regent Jareth grants you audience. Do you follow me?"

I said—it seemed I was for the moment appointed spokesman—"No. Do you bring the Lord Protector Taerl and the regent here."

I did not envy him. He swallowed hard and stared harder at the dragons, then ducked his head and said, "I shall convey your message."

I said, "Do that. And also, that if they fail to appear before"—I glanced up and found a bull perched atop the wreckage of a pergola—"before the sun touches that dragon's head, I shall send him and all his kin to find them."

Power corrupts: I enjoyed the paling of the herald's face. I heard Bellek chuckling as the luckless fellow went scuttling away. I was still aware of the crossbows aimed at my chest. I did my best not to stare at them.

Then Taerl and Jareth appeared.

The Lord Protector, for all he was not that much younger than I, seemed an innocent child. He wore a soldier's armor, but not easily. He seemed clumsy in the steel, and the sword belted on his waist seemed somehow an embarrassment, awkward and more likely to trip him than be drawn. He carried his helm under his arm, so I could see his face clear. It was a young bland face, unlined for all it was creased in worry. His hair was fair and long, as I'd heard Gahan's was, and his eyes were large and blue, opening in naked wonder as he surveyed the dragons. I liked that: that he showed not terror, but wonder.

Jareth was a different matter. He was tall and thin, wide-shoul-dered under armor more resplendent than the Lord Protector's, all gleaming silver plate and gold-etched rococo. He wore such a helm as aeldors wear, but grander: crested with a rolling comb and decora-tions at the temples in resemblance of eagles' wings. It had a visor shaped in facsimile of a lion's snarling face, lifted up so that I could see his own arrogant visage. That held no wonder but only spiteful anger, as if he found our dragonish intrusion tiresome. His nose was thin, the nostrils flaring as he scented the air—which, I must admit, was noisome with the stench of spilled blood and dragons' breath (and be I honest, the emptying of their bowels). But still I thought he had no right to assume that arrogance. I looked at his eyes and found them cold and dismissive. I liked him not at all.

From Deburah I felt a surge of anger: she felt my distaste and sent it back, augmented by her own. I felt a great desire to draw my blade and cut this strutting charlatan down.

Rwyan said (aware of that unspoken conversation betwixt drag-ons and Dragonmasters), "Easy, Daviot! No more bloodshed, eh?"

I said silently, knowing it should be sent back to her, *No; save he force us to it*.

I looked at his arrogant face and almost I hoped he should.

He said, "I am Jareth, regent of Dharbek. What do you ask of me?"

I said, "Nothing. I'd speak with the Lord Protector of Dharbek."

Jareth's nostrils flared afresh at that, and I saw clear the outrage burning in his eyes. I held his gaze and prayed he'd not be so foolish as to order his archers open fire, not unleash the slaughter that should inevitably follow. Taerl seemed embarrassed. He shifted inside his armor and dragged his gaze from the dragons to me. I looked past him and saw that the archers were now augmented with sorcerers. There were nine of them.

Inside my head Rwyan told me, *They are Adepts, Daviot. I doubt I can defeat them all.*

I gave her back, *All well, you'll not need to. But ward yourself.*

And you, she asked. *Shall you survive?*

I looked at the sorcerers and the archers and wondered if I should. But I had no choice anymore; no other way to go than forward. So I looked the Lord Protector in the eye and told him, "I'd speak with you, Lord Taerl; with you alone. About the future."

Jareth said, "I speak for the Lord Protector. Have you demands, put them to me."

I sent a message to Deburah then, and she came strutting forward across the yard, letting her wings loft idly and her jaws drop wide. She halted at my back, looking over my head. She spread her wings, and the regent sprang back.

Power corrupts, but its usage can be most enjoyable. Certainly, I enjoyed the sight of Jareth sprawling, armored buttocks over head, across the flags as I took Taerl's arm—I think that had I not, he would have stood marveling at the dragons until we quit Kherbryn—and took him a little way aside.

I heard someone shout an order then, and Taerl turned and raised a placatory hand and called, "No harm! Hold your fire!"

That was the moment I decided he might be a suitable successor to his father.

I decided!

And who was I to pick and choose from the nobility of Dharbek who should rule and who should not? But then again, why should I not? I thought Jareth was not fit, and I knew from all my wanderings that I was not alone in that notion. I knew that good decent folk— aeldors like Sarun, and more besides—shared that feeling. So why should I not express it?

Especially when I had dragons to enforce my opinion.

I told the Lord Protector of our design; all of it. All we planned and all we'd do. Rwyan came to join me, and then Urt and Tezdal. Bellek stayed back, more accustomed now to communion with the dragons than with Truemen. And as well he did, for Jareth must have sensed the drift of our talk and looked to protect his own interests.

I cannot be sure.

All I know for sure is that I heard Bellek shout and Deburah shrill a warning, and I looked back in time to see crossbow bolts glitter in the sun as they hurtled toward us.

I had no thought for Taerl then: only for Rwyan—I threw myself at her bodily, driving her down onto the flagstones of the yard. She screamed, and as we fell I smelled the vomit that discolored her leathers. I had no thought but that bolts might hit her, and I could protect her with my body.

I did not see Tezdal fling the Lord Protector down, nor Urt cover Taerl's body with his own.

I did see Deburah and Kathanria snarl and take Jareth between their jaws. And then Anryäle and Peliane contest the prey. I did see the archers loose useless bolts that only bounced off the hard hides of the dragons. I did see Jareth's ravaged body torn in pieces, and the archers die under the talons and the fangs of the vengeful dragons. I did hear Bellek laugh.

Then it was over. There was only a horrid smearing of blood and mangled flesh strewn across the palace yard, sad relicts of ambitious men. None others looked to oppose us further, but only stood, awed.

Urt and Tezdal helped the Lord Protector Taerl to his feet. He was shaken. His face was white as he surveyed the yard. He said, "What would you have me do?"

I said, "Build a new world. It's begun in Ur-Dharbek now, and soon we shall carry it to Ahn-feshang."

Taerl said, "Tell me."

And through all the slaughter, I found hope.

36

Taerl offered no resistance to our suggestions; indeed, he offered some of his own, which told me two things about him. That he could adapt so swiftly to such dramatically changed circumstances told me he *was* his father's son; that he accepted so readily told me he was not overly happy with his position. He seemed to welcome our suggestion (which, in light of the creatures stalking Kherbryn's walls, was not really a suggestion at all) that from henceforth the Lord Protector should govern under advisement of a Council of Aeldors, together with the chosen representatives of the sorcerers and the Mnemonikos. He was somewhat taken aback by our suggestion (our demand!) that the Changed of Dharbek be no longer indentured servants but enjoy the rights and privileges of free Truemen. But as that long night paled toward dawn and we told him what we knew and all we'd learned—and what might be the outcome did he refuse—he agreed those bonds should be struck away. His advisers were less ready to accept, but the word of the Lord Protector and the unspoken threat of dragonish retribution brought them around, to lip service at the least. I knew there must be factions within Taerl's court, those who'd argue our design in the cities and the holds, but such dissent was not an immediate concern. For now it was enough that Taerl heeded us and smoothed our way. I knew there should be difficulties later as surely as I knew my mouth was dry from talking and my belly began to rumble; but it was begun. There should be much work for we new Dragonmasters in the days to come, but the first steps were taken and our world shoved in a new direction. For now we could do no more—save that one last thing that should likely prove the hardest of all.

That we discussed as food was brought, and we fell on it like the dragons on prey. There was no thought of etiquette: there was no time for such niceties.

Taerl perhaps lacked the stern fiber of his sire and surely the ambition, but he had all Gahan's wisdom. He it was broached that final matter. He said, "Do we instigate all we've agreed, then well and good—I think it shall likely make Dharbek a happier land. But what of the Sky Lords?"

The sun was risen now, though it had no right to climb so high so early in the year. The chamber was already hot, even with opened windows, through which we heard the calling of the dragons. I feared they might grow hungry and set to hunting the streets.

Bellek had the same thought, for he wiped a careless hand across his mouth and pushed back his chair. "We know what we shall do," he said, rising, "and these are details you discuss. I'll leave you to them and take the flock ahunting."

I nodded my grateful agreement, but it was to Urt the silver-haired Dragonmaster turned and asked, "May I ride Kathanria?"

Urt (who was already somewhat uncomfortable in this assembly) was taken aback. "You ask my permission?" he said.

Bellek nodded gravely and returned him, "She's yours now, my friend. I can ride her only by your leave."

Urt frowned and said, "You have it."

I thought he'd sooner go with Bellek, but he made no move, and I watched the ancient Dragonmaster offer him a formal bow and walk away. I could not interpret Bellek's expression, but I thought it strange.

As he left, Rwyan called, "You'll choose your hunting ground with care, eh, Bellek?"

He laughed and told her, "Aye, lady. I'd not tear down what you've built. Not now."

His laughter seemed to hang in the hot room. But I'd no time to muse on that: Taerl had asked a most pertinent question.

I glanced at Tezdal, who sat silent and somber, and said, "When we Dhar first came down into Kellambek, we slew the Ahn or made them slaves. That was wrong."

Taerl nodded. "Hindsight would suggest it so. But are we guilty of our fathers' sins?"

I said, "Do we not right them, yes."

Taerl nodded again and allowed me the point: "So what do you . . . suggest?"

I said, "We drove the Ahn from their homeland, and it was that began the Comings. Save we make reparation, the Comings shall continue."

From amongst the dignitaries assembled along the table, a man said, "With such allies as your dragons, we can defeat the Sky Lords." I noticed he wore Mardbrecht's colors.

I saw Tezdal stiffen, and Rwyan's hand drop to his wrist, where his own gripped his swordhilt. Quickly, I said, "With our dragons we could ravage all Dharbek. But we'd sooner not. We'd sooner see peace—an end to the Comings; an end to war."

Taerl raised a hand before the man could speak again. "I'd put my seal on that," he said. And then demonstrated a fine quickness of wit. "Should that not be a great monument to us all, my lords? That we be the architects of such a peace? Think on it! The Great Coming defeat—" He bit back the word, giving Tezdal an apologetic smile. "No longer a threat; neither any Comings. Daviot's College should mark our names for that, I think, and tell such tales of us as must live on down the years."

I smiled. I could not, because the sun was bright, be certain, but I thought the Lord Protector winked at me then. He said, "So tell us how this peace shall be won."

I said, "We must give back the Sky Lords' homeland."

I had expected outrage at that, and it came. Voices rose in dissent, screaming that we Dhar had bought that land with blood; that to return it to the Ahn should betray our forefathers. I feared Tezdal would take offense and draw his sword.

Taerl impressed me again then. He took his wine cup and hammered it so hard against the table, the gold was bent. I saw a gem fall loose, unnoticed as the wine that stained the Lord Protector's sleeve. When he had silence, he said, "We shall hear Daviot out. Do you stay silent, and only listen. Or would you contest the argument with his dragons?"

He'd not the voice of an orator. Rather it was somewhat soft, but he affected so imperious a manner that he stilled them.

I murmured thanks and said, "Blood has been spilled down longer ages than any here can count. Ahn blood was spilled first, when we Dhar took the land. Then our fathers gave their lives against the Sky Lords, against the Comings. The right and the wrong of it both lie in the past—the future is ours to decide. Shall we perpetuate ancient wrongs? Or look to set them right? I think there is only one way to achieve that aim; and save we do, the Comings shall not end, but go on and on and on."

The same dissenter muttered, "Save you take your dragons and destroy them. As any true Dhar would."

It was Rwyan who answered, putting in plain words what I began to know, and (I think, then) feared: "We are no longer true Dhar, neither Daviot nor I. Nor is Urt any longer only a Changed servant gone wild. Nor Tezdal now only a Sky Lord. We are Dragonmasters now, and not like you. We are become different—we see this world through the eyes of our dragons, and they do not look out through the eyes of Truemen or Changed or Sky Lords. They see it different, and so do we. And we shall make it different! And you shall not prevent us! *You cannot!*"

She had not moved from her seat. Neither had she bathed nor changed her soiled clothing. She had run fingers carelessly through her hair, but no more than that. Her cheeks were dirty; blood dried brown on her shirt, and speckles clung to her cheeks. Her tan was paled by the weeks passed in the winter-bound Dragoncastle. Her blind eyes blazed fierce as emeralds held to fire, but the fire there came from within. I felt my love for her blaze even higher. I saw that Taerl watched her with awestruck eyes. That did not surprise me: she was magnificent, impressive. I *was* surprised by the expression on Tezdal's face: it was one of pure devotion.

Someone said, "Do you threaten us, lady?"

And Rwyan smiled like some messenger sent by the Pale Friend and lowered her head once, a single gesture of confirmation that required no words to drive home its import.

Someone else said, "This is too much."

I thought then we perhaps went too far. This was a delicate path we trod and better not sown with anger's dissent but weeded clean from the start. So I asked, "Too much?" And pointed to the windows. "Is this heat too much? How are Kherbryn's granaries? Or Durbrecht's? Or those anywhere in Dharbek now? Are they filled? Are the cisterns and the reservoirs filled? Or do the streams run dry and the cattle die in the fields? Are the people hungry or fed well? Listen —I'm a fisherman's son"—someone muttered, "I'm not surprised," but

I ignored so cheap a sally—"and some time ago I went home. The catches were poor then—how are they now? Does Dharbek prosper, or suffer famine? And drought?"

A voice I recognized now said, "You could end that."

It belonged to a plump-cheeked man of middling years. His hair sat lank with sweat about a round visage that suggested he suffered no great deprivation. I fixed him with my eyes and saw his drop as I said, "Yes, we could. We could likely take our dragons east to Ahn-feshang and destroy the skyboats readying for the Great Coming as easily as we destroyed those moored in Ur-Dharbek. Likely we could tear down the holds and cities of the Sky Lords as easily as we could Kherbryn. *But we will not!* Can you not understand this? *We will not!* It's as my lady Rwyan says—we are Dragonmasters. We shall not perpetuate old hatreds, but deliver a new order. Do you accept it or not, still it shall come."

Silence then, heavy and hot. The voice that broke it was Taerl's: "How shall you do this?"

I said, "We shall go to the islands of Ahn-feshang and present to the Attul-ki the same terms—that they lift this gramarye destroying Dharbek and give up their dream of conquest."

Taerl spun his dented goblet between his hands and said, "And in return they have back Kellambek?"

I shook my head. I said, "No. In return, they have the right to settle in Kellambek. To live and work alongside those Dhar and those Changed who live here now. Just as any Dhar or any Changed shall have the right to live in Ahn-feshang, do they wish."

"That," Taerl said, "shall not be easy, I think."

I said, "No, it shall not be. Old hatreds fester like poisoned wounds and sully new flesh. But it might be done. And there shall be dragons in the skies above all the lands, to hold the peace."

Taerl said, "Hold it? Or enforce it?"

I shrugged. "It must depend on men," I said, "in the end. But must we Dragonmasters enforce it, then we shall. Think you that shall be worse than the cycles of war?"

The Lord Protector looked me in the eye. Then turned to Rwyan; and then to Tezdal. To the Sky Lord he said, "Can this be done? Would your people accept it?"

Tezdal said, "As well as yours. There will be some who . . . argue . . . but do you give us back our Homeland, then—yes, I believe we might win this peace."

Taerl studied him for long moments and then laughed, shaking his head. "By the God," he said, "my father would not believe this! Look at me!" He rose, kicking back his chair to turn, arms spread wide to encompass us all. I thought he was perhaps a little drunk, or tired by the long night's talking. "The Lord Protector of Dharbek in earnest discussion of peace with the Sky Lords and the wild Changed. I heed a Sky Lord! And a Changed servant gone from his master across the Slammerkin. I listen to the words of a Storyman. And"—this with a not-entirely-steady bow in Rwyan's direction—"a rebel mage. Is this not a wonder, my lords?"

I heard a voice then mutter, "Not from you, boy," but when I looked down the table, I could not find the speaker. I thought it was likely that fat noble in Mardbrecht's plaid, but I could not be sure. I watched as Taerl crossed to the windows and looked out over the ravaged yards of his palace. He set his elbows on the sill and said wonderingly, "They are all gone. Just as your friend—Bellek?—promised."

The voice that had muttered before said, louder now, "Then we might slay them. All of them! Why not, Lord Taerl? Cut off the dragon's head now, and when the other comes back—slay him, or buy him off."

I saw the speaker now: it was indeed that plump supporter of Jareth. He rose from his chair in his enthusiasm. I saw that his belly was fleshed round as his cheeks. I saw also that Rwyan could no longer hold Tezdal back. I saw rage suffuse the Sky Lord's face. I still could not believe anyone could draw a blade so swift.

It rose, lit bright by the sun that now spanned the room, glittering as Tezdal strode down the length of that long table. The nobility of Kherbryn cowered before him. Not one moved to halt him. The fat man shrieked: I was minded of pigs at gelding time. He raised both arms above his head and went tumbling over his turned chair as he sought to flee.

"Halt!"

This, to my surprise, came from Taerl.

To my much greater surprise, Tezdal did halt. He stood over the quivering figure with lifted sword and naked rage in his eyes. I saw a pool of urine spread out from between the fat man's thighs. It stank.

Taerl said, "I'd offer my apologies to you, Tezdal Kashijan, for the insult Gaerth of Mardbrecht gave." He turned to we others and said, "I offer my apologies to you all."

I watched as Gaerth scrabbled back. Tezdal let him go. He left a wet trail behind. I smelled feces. I wondered what the Lord Protector would do next.

He called the commur who stood guarding the doors forward and said, "Execute this traitor."

I saw that the commur wore Kherbryn's plaid; but still he hesitated.

Taerl said, "Do you take my order, or do you join him?"

There was a long silence.

This was akin to bonding with dragons: it was an instant of decision, in which future power becomes decided. I applauded Taerl: he saw the way and took it.

But I was not sure he should succeed until the commur sank his blade into Gaerth's heart and the fat man died.

Then I truly thought we might succeed.

We lingered seven days in Kherbryn, but I saw no more of the place than I'd already seen from astride Deburah. We were cloistered in Taerl's palace, locked in discussion, evolving stratagems, composing messages. Sorcerers came and went, deferring to Rwyan as if she were now mistress of their College, their magic sending word of all that had passed and all that was to be down that occult web that connected the holds and keeps. Mnemonikos came, recorders of what we did, and eyed me as if I were some strangeling marvel. I knew some of them from Durbrecht, but it was as if lifetimes stood between us now, and they were strangers. Or—more correctly, I suppose—I was, for I could no longer pretend I was not different. It was as Rwyan had said: communion with the dragons made us something other than Truemen.

Urt spoke with his Changed fellows and through them sent word in addition to what his kind would hear as aeldors spoke and faceless servitors stood silent by. That should not be for much longer, I thought, for as the word was spread, it must become common knowledge that the Changed were more, and better, than Truemen took them for, and did all go well as we intended, they should find a place beside Truemen in Dharbek. We made it plain that no harm should come them, no retribution, on pain of transgressors answering to our dragons. I suggested that our new-found council grant a place to the Changed—Lan, I said, would likely make a sound representative.

And there were other suggestions—that aeldors such as Sarun and Yanydd have seats; I mentioned Cleton's name.

In all of this Taerl proved himself far more than the ninny of popular suspicion. I thought he'd likely lived too long beneath the umbra of his father's reputation, for he constantly demonstrated a quickness of wit, a ready grasp of this fluid situation, that impressed me. I thought that we should leave Dharbek in good hands when we quit our tenure. I had no doubt that we should, eventually. I was altered, I saw the world through different eyes: I missed Deburah when she hunted with Bellek as fervently as I knew I'd miss Rwyan, were we parted again; could I not "speak" with her, I felt an absence in my life, and when she returned, I felt a happiness I'd known before only with Rwyan. I knew we could not remain in Dharbek, not even after our intended journey across the ocean. I knew we must go back to the Dragoncastle and live there, for that was the natural abode of the dragons, and they'd not be happy elsewhere. I felt this as a wordless pressure in my blood, a soul-deep certainty that I could understand no better than I could deny it: it was a given fact and irrevocable. I began, albeit vaguely, to understand why Bellek had remained in that lonely place so long.

But I still did not know *how* long he'd been there; nor would he say, but only smile and change the subject when I tried to probe him.

But then that was the least of my concerns: we'd a future to build, a new world to fashion, and that occupied the larger part of my days and nights. It is no small thing to make a revolution.

Provisioned by the Lord Protector and clad in the fresh clothing he supplied us, we set out for Ahn-feshang on the morning of the eighth day.

It was early in the morning and the year, barely past dawn and barely Ennas Day, but the sun stood hot and heavy in a sky devoid of cloud, its blue silvered by the implacable heat. The weight of the Sky Lords' magic lay hard on Kherbryn and all of Dharbek, and as I mounted Deburah, I was aware of the hope we carried with us and the terrible burden of responsibility we gave ourselves. We had dictated terms—now we must make good our promises or be forever cursed.

But as I locked myself to the saddle of my beautiful, wondrous sky-riding steed, I felt only heady excitement. I lusted to fly again, to be adragonback. I'd been too long grounded, and as I turned to wave at my companions, I saw they, too, felt that urgency. Even Urt was smiling and answered my wave with a reckless hand. I caught Rwyan's eye and saw her teeth flash white in the sun. Bellek was beaming as if his dreams came true. Tezdal nodded and grinned, but I thought him far less elated than we others. I said, knowing Deburah would communicate it past the thunder of the wings, "We make peace, my friend. We do this for all the people of our world, yours and mine and Urt's. All of them!"

I heard back, *Yes*, but nothing more; and I was too eager to be gone that I felt the need to question him further or wonder at his reticence.

Then, I knew only the thunder of myriad dragons' wings rising to beat the sky. To climb above Kherbryn as folk stared in naked wonder at the impossible squadrons that circled over the city. I wondered if the Ahn had felt such wonder as I saw on the rapidly disappearing faces of those Dhar, when Attul led them eastward into their exodus.

But that was a brief thought: those faces were too soon gone as Deburah spread her magnificent wings and climbed toward the sun. And Kherbryn was left behind in moments, and we were winging east over parched farmlands to the coast.

Sea under us then, which was disconcerting—to find no secure land beneath, but only the argent blue of the Fend; ahead, the Sentinels.

No contest from them: Taerl had sent firm word we should not be interrupted in our passing, and we crossed them without disturbance. We were high enough I could not discern individual faces, but I saw —for the first time—the great white towers that held the crystals. And I felt their magic like a prickling against my skin. It was akin to what I'd felt in Trebizar: a sense of terrible power, not unlike that dread the Sky Lords' airboats delivered.

The dragons felt it: stronger even than we who rode them, and I "heard" the calling of the bulls, that they be allowed to go down and rend the towers, pluck out the crystals and all who used them. Bellek, echoed by us all, bade them no, that this was not suitable prey. At least, not yet. I told Deburah we'd a greater duty, and reluctant as the rest, she winged onward, so that soon the Sentinels were lost behind us.

We flew above the Kheryn-Veyhn now.

We Dhar had no name for the sea other than "the eastern ocean," for we'd no use for any name: our world extended no farther. This was the sea the Sky Lords crossed to bring the fylie of the Kho'rabi against us; it was unknown. Tezdal had crossed it in that skyboat that Rwyan's magic had brought down, but that (so he had told us) had been a hard journey, even with the Kho'rabi wizards whipping the elementals onward in service of their vessels. For us, it was easy, up where the air is thin, and only dragons can fly, and the sad worldly magic of humble men has no power.

I saw elementals then, like fleeting visions glimpsed from the corners of my eyes. I could not quite believe them, but Deburah told me they were there and helped us on our way, because she and all her kin were closer to them than human folk, who looked only to govern them and control them, not live with them in equality.

Except, I was gratified to "hear," *for Dragonmasters.*

I did not properly understand, but I wanted to learn and accepted for now that explanation. More urgently, I wanted to reach Ahn-feshang and set in place the final part of our design.

For which I must wait: not even dragons can fly that ocean without halt. The elementals can, but they are not entirely of this world—they live in the spaces between, while dragons, for all their innate magic, are entirely physical beings: they must rest.

Which they did, to my consternation.

The sun was setting behind us. The sky there was red and burnished gold, like the dying flames of a forge. Ahead was a blue darkness pricked by stars and the indifferent face of the newly filled moon. The air, despite that aura of warmth Deburah afforded me and the fur-lined leathers Taerl had given me, was chill enough I began to feel it needling my skin. I heard Bellek call that we should go down and rest for the night; and wondered where and how. Deburah showed me as we swooped seaward.

I had not known dragons can swim: I found out then.

They've not much liking for it, but they can—are they forced to it —sail the waves as readily as they command the sky.

We came down onto a darkly moonwashed sea filled with rolling billows. It was not a very great swell—I'd ridden far greater waves in my father's boat—but even through Deburah's calm and confident sendings, I felt afraid as we settled on that ocean. I had never been so far from shore.

She spread her wings as we landed, just as she did when we swooped on prey, and broke our fall gently, so that only a little salt water splashed my boots. Then she furled her wings and began to paddle, and it was a fond memory of nights afloat in my father's boat, rocked by the Fend's currents. *No fear, Daviot,* she told me. *Only awhile resting.* And I trusted her—how could I not? She was my Deburah, and I knew she'd give her life for mine, and I the same—and looked about to find the others paddling toward me.

A strange alfresco dinner, that. Deburah and Anryäle and Peliane and Kathanria swam, gently dozing, as we riders passed food and ale between us. The other dragons floated easy on the swell, most with heads tucked under wings like sleeping swans, and only the outrider bulls alert. Cold food, yes; but warm in its wonder—that we *could* eat in such manner, like drowsy fishermen riding such boats as only legend knew.

Had I a regret, it was that I could not hold Rwyan but only remain apart from her, buckled to my saddle even as I slept. But that slumber was in the cradle of the sea, and I was not unfamiliar with that: I slept very well.

And woke startled to the beat of dragons' wings as Bellek shouted us awake and we took flight.

It was not yet dawn. The sky was opalescent: that thin gray that presages the sun's rising. On land there should have been birds chorusing the new morning. Here there was only a brightness in the east and the gray roll of waves against Deburah's flanks. I gasped and clutched the saddle as she rose.

In moments we were in the sky again, climbing up to meet the rising sun, winging onward toward Ahn-feshang.

Night was come before we reached the islands.

I saw them first as jagged outlines lit by the moon. They minded me of the Dragonsteeth, but sea-washed. They seemed all sharp and rugged, without smooth places where men might live, limned by the breaking surf that bathed the shores, and inland all obdurate peaks and wooded valleys that must surely defy habitation or farming. Each island was dominated by vast peaks that painted the night sky with a faint red glow, as if the earth gusted hot breath against the night.

Then I heard Bellek call, asking where we should best descend to deliver our message.

And Tezdal answer, "Ahn-khem, where the High Ones of the Attul-ki build their dozijan."

I asked, "Shall it be safe?"

And got back negative laughter as Tezdal advised me, "I doubt any of this enterprise shall be safe, my friend. Think you we'll find a better welcome here than in Kherbryn?"

Rwyan said, "Perhaps we should wait."

"For what?" Tezdal demanded, and even though it was Peliane sent me his voice and Deburah translated the words, still I heard an echo of wild desperation. "To give my people time to gather? To oppose us harder, that more die? No! We do this now or not at all."

There was a terrible finality to his tone, as if he reached a decision and would not grant himself time to think on it, but implement it before dissuasion gain a hold. Nor did he allow us time, but drove Peliane on in a furious beating of her sable wings, so that even the bulls were outpaced and we could only follow after.

Over wave-washed beaches we swept, a vast red-mouthed mountain rising dreadly magnificent above us. Across tilled fields and wooded valleys; I saw the lights of scattered villages, and rivers tumbling down steep slopes to find the sea. And then I cried aloud in unalloyed wonder as I saw the skyboats hung about the mountain. They drifted on mooring lines all down the slopes. They seemed to me like piglets clamoring for the sow's teats. There were hundreds; or when I thought of all those red-lipped crags, likely thousands.

I had not believed so many could exist. I had not thought so many hides could be found and sewn together. I thought that so much wicker and wood as made the baskets beneath must denude the slopes of all these hills. I marveled, and Deburah sent that unspoken message to Peliane, so that Tezdal gave back answer.

"The skyboats take in the breath of Byr and ride Vachyn's winds. These you see are readying to fly."

I'd no more faith in Byr or Vachyn or Dach than I felt in the One God. I thought, from all Tezdal had told me, that what I saw was a magnificent human construction. A vast enterprise that satisfied an entirely human dream, fueled by priestly ambition. But I could not help but marvel at that ambition and the labor of its construction.

Then I must marvel anew at the entirely physical prowess of the dragons.

As the squadrons fell, Deburah's lust to join her kin swept heady through me. I gave her her will, and we dropped down to where the skyboats hung and joined in the ravaging.

It was a liberation. I was a fisherman's son from Whitefish village, and the skyboats were the nightmares of my childhood: it was that child's triumph to see them rent by the claws and fangs of my dragon. No less, I felt—through Deburah—the desire for freedom of the elementals bound to service of those boats. And as we ripped the bloodred cylinders apart and rode the gaseous blasts escaping them, so we freed the aerial spirits from their bondage. They laughed as they flew clear, and I felt ethereal hands brush my face in gratitude. Some, like soft silken figures spun out of moon's light, coldly kissed my lips or darted thankful, insubstantial fingers through my hair. Mostly I felt Deburah's pleasure in the destruction of malign magic.

Then guilt as we winged skyward, no prey left any longer below, only wreckage that lit the flanks of the red-mouthed mountain with a brighter, more immediate glow. I saw Tezdal riding Peliane, who had not descended, held aloft by the Sky Lord's will and torn for that between her desire to please him and the lust she shared with the other dragons. I felt her sadness and his, and his was a soul-deep wound of hope and confusion.

I brought Deburah higher, to join Peliane, and sent out: *I think it could not be otherwise, my friend. I doubt we could have stopped the bulls.*

No, he answered me, *likely not.*

We end a war, I said, *and build a peace. And there were not many of your folk slain.*

He gave me back, *No. Only their dream.*

Which we'll make good, I said. *The Ahn shall find a place in Kellambek again, and all men live equal.*

He answered me, *Likely so,* and closed his mind, so that I knew only Peliane's concern for the awful sadness in him. I thought on how I'd felt when we descended on Kherbryn and had no answer for that, but only pity.

Then Rwyan came up on Anryäle and told me Bellek took the squadrons to Ahn-zel and Ahn-wa—wherever the hot-breathed mountains fed life into the skyboats, to destroy them on the ground, before they had a chance to fly—and suggested we go down to the dozijan to give our terms to the Attul-ki.

It was a little after dawn; long enough after that the sun struck bright lances of golden light around the edges of the red-lipped mountain, like rays of hope flung against the fading night. The peak blushed, no longer entirely from its summit, but now also from the fires burning down its slopes, that glowing matched by all those other places where the armada of the Sky Lords was destroyed.

The dozijan was built upon a ledge of the mountain. It was a splendid and forbidding structure, standing high above the town below, the two connected by a winding road. Both town and temple were lit well with lanterns—none there could have ignored the clamor of our coming, or what we did—but the bulk of their structures stood still in shadow. I saw that the dozijan was a place of wood and stone, the walls and bases all dark granite, the upper levels swooping curves of timber and outflung balconies, with overhanging roofs and narrow windows. There was a high stone wall set with a massive gate that we ignored.

We landed in the pebbled courtyard, Rwyan and Tezdal and I. Those dragons Bellek had left with us settled where they could—on towers and spires and walls—so that all the dozijan was ringed with grim dragonish shapes.

And the Attul-ki came out to meet us.

They were dressed in robes of crimson and black, decorated with arcane sigils in gold and silver weavings. They bore no arms, and if the dragons awed them, they hid it well. They faced us as if we were what we were—intruders, invaders of their holy place. There were perhaps fifty of them, likely as similar of visage to me as any Dhar would seem to them, save for the obvious leader. He was taller, and his hair was a silver that glittered in the morning's sun as it came up over the buildings behind. I wondered if he'd planned it so: I could not imagine any folk so self-possessed they would wait indoors whilst dragons landed all around and glowered down, their breath a susurration that drowned the birds' song and filled the yard with the memory of digested meat. But these did and only stood in silent ranks as that impressive figure strode out in front.

His tilted eyes dismissed me with contempt, lingered an instant on Rwyan, and fixed on Tezdal.

Tezdal bowed deep. I saw his face lorn then. He would not meet that gaze but only said, "Dhazi, forgive me."

He had tutored us enough in the language of the Ahn that past winter that I was able to somewhat follow what they said. The emotions in their words, the dragons gave me, and the rest Tezdal told me later. Then, I watched as the Dhazi studied him, as I'd long ago seen tutors in Durbrecht study some biological specimen. I was reminded of Ardyon: almost, I bent my knee.

The Dhazi said, "Do you betray your people and your gods, gijan? Do you renege those vows you made, that you come here with these land-stealers to defeat the Conquest? Do you forget that you are Kho'rabi?"

Tezdal fell to his knees. He lowered his head to the pebbles of the yard and wailed a heart-forsaken cry.

"Traitor, you," the Dhazi said. "Blooded Kho'rabi, you. But you come with Dhar to break the dream of the people and gainsay the dictate of the Three. Apostate for that—damned by the Three and all the Kho'rabi. Were you fit, I'd tell you take the Way of Honor; but you're not! Better you live out your miserable life in remembrance of disgrace and die outcast and alone. The Three be praised the lady Retze does not see this."

I did not understand all he said, but I found its import in the ice-cold tone and the steel-hard glimmer of his unforgiving eyes; and I saw what I'd not ever thought to witness: Tezdal groveling in guilt and self-abasement. I was embarrassed for my friend, and terribly angry. I hated that hard priest as I'd not found it in myself to hate anyone, save Allanyn, so fierce before. I thought him bound to a view he would not change. I felt in him a surety of belief that allowed no other opinion. I heard the dragons stir as they received the tide of my dislike. Their wings rose like banners in the morning sun, and their displeasure filled the yard with a threatening whisper that was further emphasized by the irritated gnashing of their fangs and the scrape of their talons on stone and wood. I watched Tezdal bow his head—that hard, proud man bow his head! My friend, who should not need to subjugate himself thus!

In carefully rehearsed Ahn I said, "We come to talk of peace. The Ahn come back to Kellambek."

I heard the Dhazi say, "We shall come back. Oh, yes! *We shall come back!* We shall come back with your flayed skins for sails; and the bones of this sad traitor set afront our skyboats in all his disgrace."

That was too much: Tezdal was my friend and looked, like us, to build a better world. I drew my sword in warning. A foolish move that, to threaten with plain steel such sorcerers as these. I heard Rwyan shout and saw the Dhazi smile dismissively as he raised a casual hand. I was flung back, as if a giant fist came hard against my chest. My head spun, aching, and I think that had Rwyan not sent her own magic to my aid, I should have died there. As it was, I tumbled down beside Tezdal, fighting for my breath. Through eyes awash with tears of pain, I saw the Dhazi level a condemnatory finger. I moaned in rage and agony and knew I could not avoid his cantrip.

But the dragons were swifter and, perhaps, angrier.

It was Peliane who took him and clutched him a moment in her talons. Not long; but I heard him scream as he saw her jaws gape wide, and the fangs there, before they closed and cut him asunder like butchered meat, and he fell down all bloody and in pieces. And then the others fell on the Attul-ki and slew them, so that soon there was nothing left in the yard of the dozijan except bloody wreckage strewn across the pebbles, and Tezdal weeping, and the dragons gone wild to tear up the roofs and the walls and leave only devastation behind.

And all the while Tezdal kneeling and wailing, as if his life were stolen and all his hope gone.

There were no soldiers in the dozijan, no Kho'rabi knights to oppose us and give their lives to the slaughter—the Attul-ki were too confident of their power that they should guard themselves with warriors. What need, in a land that saw them as gifted by the Three, themselves like gods, omnipotent? But there were Kho'rabi in the town below, and they were coming fast in defense of the priests. "The Dedicated," they named themselves, and that they were, for they evinced no fear at the sight of what sat atop the walls of the dozijan, and flew above the place, and tore it apart. They only advanced, perhaps seven fylie, black-armored and hurrying, intent only on joining in battle with such invaders as they could never have seen and likely never even dreamed. But still they came determinedly on.

I stood aghast in the yard, my spirit divided between nausea and the savage triumph of the dragons. Rwyan stood beside me, and we both had a hand to Tezdal's shoulders as he crouched and wept, the both of us knowing it should do no good, not now, to speak with him. There were no words that fit.

It was Deburah told me the Kho'rabi came, just as Anryäle

warned Rwyan and Peliane Tezdal. He paid his dragon no heed, but Rwyan and I bent close then and spoke into his ears, and then he raised a face all run with tears and said, "As you love me, let there be no more killing."

Rwyan said, "That was never our intention; only peace."

Tezdal said, "Then let it end! I cannot bear this guilt!"

I thought it should be hard to halt the dragons and certain that they would fall on the Kho'rabi were we threatened. I looked for Deburah and found her lifting up a section of roof, the timbers spilling like splinters from her rending claws. I called her down, not sure she'd respond, and felt surprise that she came so swift to my summons.

Peliane and Anryäle landed with her, and I felt their concern for Tezdal like a surge of heady anger. They'd rise up and fall on the advancing column—they'd swoop all the skies of Ahn-feshang in bloody destruction—but Rwyan bade them be calm and take us away and bring the others with us, and—reluctant—they agreed.

We lifted Tezdal to his feet and helped him mount Peliane. I buckled him in place. He sat slumped, his eyes tight-closed, though tears came trickling out from under the shut lids. I mounted Deburah, and Rwyan climbed astride Anryäle. We winged into the brightness of the morning before the Kho'rabi reached the gates of the dozijan, and I was bemused that all the dragons followed us; as if we took Bellek's place as leaders.

We gained height, and for the first time I saw the magic that filled the Sky Lords' dread airboats. It gusted from those mountains like pus from an opened boil, as if the earth blew poison into the air. They were raw caverns, those hills, the stone of their peaks melted off into the savage fires below, great gaping maws all filled with flame and molten stuff that spewed out in great liquid bubbles and wafts of noxious gas. I felt about them as I did about the crystals that empowered Dhar magic—they had their own life and corrupted men.

The dragons, no less, were unhappy around those holes, and so we took them away to find Bellek and Urt and decide our next move.

Which we could not until Tezdal woke from his stupor.

He sat Peliane's saddle like a tranced man. His eyes were closed and he gave her no commands, only slumped, swaying with the motion of her wingbeats as we went north. She followed Deburah and Anryäle, her sendings a wash of concern for her bond-mate. They were no smaller than my own.

We found Bellek winging back to join us, glorying in the destruction he'd wrought. His seamed face was lit with joy, as if he'd found some climax to his life and should not find better. I felt the message he sent: *All's done! There are no more skyboats — the armada is destroyed! There shall be no more Comings.*

I felt a measure of relief at that, but also a sadness, for I thought some part of his humanity was gone away; and I feared some part of mine must follow, for I had known that glorious sharing in the naked power of the dragons and wondered if I should go down that same path.

I "heard" Rwyan ask, *What of Tezdal?*

And Bellek answer, *He'll do his duty. Wait.*

I could not be certain what followed then — a transportation of messages between the dragons that I'd not yet the subtlety of control to properly understand. I knew only that Bellek communicated with the dragons and Tezdal woke as if from drunken sleep.

He raised his head and wiped his eyes, and Peliane's proud head rose higher, and he said, *The dozijan of Ahn-khem is not the only stronghold.*

Bellek said, *No. But the others shall not oppose us.*

Tezdal said, *Then the Attul-ki are gone?*

Bellek said, *Many of them. Some live still, but there shall be no great magicks sent against us. Neither the Great Coming sent against Dharbek. That dream is ended.*

There was a long silence as we circled over Ahn-khem. It was a sorry silence, for all we'd done what we planned to do; or most of it. I wondered why I felt no sense of success or triumph, but only empty, a chagrin that scattered ashes on my soul.

Then Tezdal said, *The Khe'anjiwha resides in his citadel, at Khejimar. Best we go there to present our terms.*

His voice was brittle, like a wire drawn too tight.

Rwyan said, *Then do we go there, and settle this matter?*

And as he'd done before, as we approached his homeland and his honor's heart, Tezdal drove Peliane onward in a great rush of wingbeats, as if he'd outfly his destiny. Or hurry to meet it. I knew not which, only that I must ride Deburah after him and be with him, for I think I loved him no less than she, or Rwyan, or Urt. I surely know that I felt afraid of what I heard in his voice and saw in his eyes.

We came to Khejimar as the sun sank westward. It was Kherbryn built in wood, only the walls that surrounded the city and the Khe'anjiwha's palace showing any stone. It was a vast sprawling place, the half spread up the sides of a precipitous valley, the rest layering down in wide terraces to the banks of the river that gushed through floodgates and mill-races to the broad stream below. It was all stone-walled, intricate lines of blue and red bricks rising in com-

plex folds about the wooden houses inside to meet the dark gray granite of the palace. That stood aloof over the city, all towers and curving
arches. I saw gardens and wide streets, fountains fed by the spilling
river water. Mostly I saw wide eyes and gaping mouths as we swept
in, adragonback, out of the sun.

There were archers on the ramparts, and they loosed shafts at us.
Dragons fell upon the bowmen. Deburah laughed at them, and I
laughed at them. How could arrows hurt us? We were the Lords of
the Sky: we imposed our will on pain of death.

Power corrupts: I must remember that. What we did, we did in honest
desire for peace; or so I hoped. But I could not deny that feeling: it
was too wild, too exciting. It was too powerful as we came down over
the ramparts of Khejimar, the taste of the slain Attul-ki yet strong in
our mouths, to deliver our terms to the Khe'anjiwha.

They came out to meet us: the Great Lord of all Ahn-feshang,
with his retinue behind him. He seemed of Tezdal's age and wore
armor, so that I could not properly read his eyes or face, and around
him stood several hundred Kho'rabi knights with swords drawn ready
and axes lifted. Behind them were a score of the black-robed sorcerers
of the Attul-ki; and behind them, pike-bearers and archers. More
along the battlements—those the dragons had not taken in revenge of
the shafts fired.

It was not so large a yard as Bellek's Dragoncastle, which was to
our advantage, for it meant that the dragons settling all about dominated the beetle-armored Kho'rabi. And there were riven bodies
strewn in bloody pieces about the ramparts that made our point to
horrid excess. But still I thought that these were folk not easily given
to defeat, but more likely to fight unto death, in honor of their dream.
In honor only.

I must admire such courage: our dragons stood all around us, and
likely word had come of what we'd done to the Attul-ki and the
dozijan, but still the Khe'anjiwha faced us in full battle armor, with his
palace guard behind, and seemed entirely prepared to defy us.

I looked to Deburah, standing at my back, and knew her readiness to fight. From Kathanria I felt Bellek's eagerness: *End it now! Slay
them!*

From Urt: *No! Save we must.*

From Rwyan: *We came to speak of peace. Shall we not do that? Hold
back, until we've no other choice.*

From Tezdal only dismay and horror.

Aloud, I said to him, "You must act the spokesman, my friend,
for we've not such command of your language."

He nodded. His face was a mask held in place by effort of will. A pulse throbbed on his temple. He fell to his knees, bowing until his forehead touched the flags. For long moments he remained thus, then the Khe'anjiwha barked an order, for all the world as if it was he who commanded here and not we Dragonmasters. Tezdal rose.

The Khe'anjiwha spoke again, and a man came forward to unlatch his helm, remove the casque, and step back. I had surmised correctly: he was no older than Tezdal, perhaps even a little younger. His face was handsome in the Ahnish way, all planes and angles, with black eyes that studied Tezdal and we others with a mixture of interest and annoyance. Certainly there was no fear there. His hair was oiled and bound back from his face, and there seemed no softness about him. I feared this should prove harder bargaining than with Taerl.

He said, in a voice no softer than his expression, "So those rumors were true—you did not die."

Tezdal swallowed and would have fallen again to his knees had the Khe'anjiwha not motioned he remain standing. He shook his head and said, "No, Great Lord, my boat was destroyed, but this woman"—he gestured at Rwyan—"saved me."

The Khe'anjiwha favored Rwyan with a lingering inspection. "The Dhar mage," he said, "yes. And this is the one named Daviot?"

I met his gaze and answered him as best I could in his own language, "I am Daviot, Great Lord."

I had the pleasure of seeing his eyes narrow at that. He said, "You speak the tongue of Ahn-feshang?"

I ducked my head and told him, "Tezdal has tutored me, Great Lord. Are we to build a new world, I think we must all learn new languages."

He said, "Your accent is atrocious. But it intrigues me that you'd understand our tongue. Are you not come to impose yours on us?"

I shook my head. "No, Great Lord. We do not come to conquer—no more than we've conquered Dharbek or Ur-Dharbek. We come to speak of peace."

He laughed then, and I realized that I understood these people hardly at all. There was genuine amusement in his laughter, and the hardness quit his face a moment as he threw back his head, guffawing like any common soldier. Behind him, his retinue sent back polite echoes.

He swept a gauntleted hand in the direction of the dragons and said, "You come astride these creatures across the Kheryn-veyhn to ravage my armada, to sunder the dozijan of the Attul-ki and slaughter my priests, and you tell me you come peaceful?"

I found it hard to understand all this, and Tezdal must interpret for me. When he had, I said, "Great Lord, forgive me, but your language is not yet easy to my tongue. Might Tezdal speak for us? He is one of our number, and one with our enterprise."

The Khe'anjiwha studied me in silence. Then he looked at Tezdal again, and his eyes grew again cold. He said, "Tezdal Kashijan does not exist. Tezdal Kashijan died when his skyboat fell. His death led his wife down the Way of Honor. More—when word came from our allies that a Kho'rabi knight chose to live as friend to the Dhar, Tezdal Kashijan's father took the Way, and his mother, for they could neither live with such dishonor."

I heard Tezdal wail then, and when I turned, he was on his knees, his hands locked about his head. Urt went to him and knelt beside him, holding him. I saw the dragons stir restless and felt their growing anger. I feared new slaughter should commence, and all our dreams fall down in bloody ruin. I went to Tezdal's side and bent my knee that I might speak soft and urgent in his ear.

I said, "Tezdal, listen to me! I am sorry, but set your grief aside for now. *You must!* Lest the dragons take offense, and the Khe'anjiwha be slain, and all we've planned collapse. You must play your part, or none of this has any meaning."

He said, "You do not understand."

I said, "No, but I'd learn. I'd learn about you Ahn and know you well as I do my own people. What else has this been for? Do you fail us now, then all the lives spent are wasted and we are only traitors to our dream. Shall you let that happen?"

He said again, "You do not understand. I *am* a traitor."

Rwyan drew closer then and dropped to her knees before Tezdal and set her hands upon his cheeks, lifting his fallen face so that she "looked" directly into his eyes as she said, "Tezdal, I'll not hear you name yourself thus. Do you heed me, for this hangs on a knife's edge now. Do we not understand one another, then it shall surely come to fighting. The dragons will attack, and your people will fight. And those Attul-ki will look to destroy me first, for we are all sorcerers, and I shall be the first target of their power."

He shook his head and answered, "No," and it was a cry from the depths of a lost soul.

Rwyan said, "Then make this Great Lord of yours understand what we intend, that there be no further bloodshed."

Tezdal closed his eyes and groaned. Rwyan bent closer, touching her lips to his, and whispered something I could not hear, nor ever asked what. I saw Tezdal sigh, and wipe his moistened cheeks, and climb wearily to his feet. In faltering Ahn (she'd never my facility with language) Rwyan said, "Great Lord, as Daviot tells you—we've not such understanding of your tongue that we are able to clearly explain —we need Tezdal as spokesman. Shall you allow that?"

The Khe'anjiwha met her blind green gaze and then let his own travel past to survey the dragons. A fatalistic smile played upon his thin lips. "Have I a choice?"

Rwyan said, "Yes, Great Lord. Do you refuse to listen, then we shall go away."

Now those proud features displayed surprise, that rapidly swallowed by disbelief. "What do you tell me, lady? That you'd come here to wreck my people's dream and go away? That you'd defeat all the might of Ahn-feshang and not take the spoils? You'd go away? No more than that? No tribute paid, no lands taken? Only go away?"

Tezdal translated this, and I answered for us all, "Yes. We do not come to conquer; only to speak of peace."

The Khe'anjiwha frowned, for the first time disconcerted. Then he said slowly, "This is not easy."

I said, "No. Peace is always harder than war. War is simple: slay your enemy. It is much harder to name him friend and learn to live with him. But it may be done."

The Khe'anjiwha stroked his shaven chin. His skin was very smooth. I was minded of my stubble and my doubtlessly unkempt appearance. Also, my stomach began to complain: we had not eaten in a long time.

The Khe'anjiwha granted me a small smile and turned to confer with his retinue. Then he said, "Tezdal Kashijan is dead, but I shall allow this gijan to speak on your behalf."

I did not know what that term meant, but it was redolent of contempt. Tezdal shuddered like a hound cowed by a ferocious master. The dragons, in subtler ways than mine, understood, and began to shift angrily, readying to attack.

I looked to Bellek and said, "Hold them back!"

And Bellek chuckled and answered me, "They're yours now, Daviot. Yours and Rwyan's, and Urt's and Tezdal's. You hold them back."

And we did. We bade them be still, for we spoke with men, who lacked the knowledge of dragons and saw only their own desires, not the greater concerns of the world and the places between, and could not think as dragons do. And somewhat to my surprise, they obeyed us and settled. So that we might—through the gijan, Tezdal—deliver our terms to the Khe'anjiwha and tell him what we'd do, and how the new world should be ordered under the wing shadows of the new Lords of the Sky.

We spoke with the Great Lord of Ahn-feshang, the Khe'anjiwha, in that courtyard with our dragons perched all around like harbingers of dreadful retribution, and he listened to us.

We told him—through Tezdal—what we'd done in Ur-Dharbek and in Dharbek. He was not easy of convincing, but the dragons stood emblems of our power, and he was pragmatic in defeat. We sat in his Council chamber, with dragons menacing on the balconies outside, their great-jawed, fanged faces peering in to remind him of our wrath. And he listened. I suppose he had little other choice, save the reaving of his land; and already that dream he'd shared with Tezdal was gone: the skyboats and the braver of the Attul-ki were gone, and so he'd not much more hope of the Conquest.

So perhaps only because of that, he listened, and we told him of our peace, and of the consequences did he argue it. As we did, the dragons filled the paneled chamber with their meaty breath and watched, alert, for sign of danger. And the Khe'anjiwha knew that, and knew that we could slay him, and all his armies, surely as the Lord Protector Taerl had known that irrevocable fact.

We slew his dream; but we gave him another in its place. Just as we'd slain Allanyn's dream and given Urt's people another. Just as we'd slain Jareth and shown Taerl a new vision.

And he listened—for which I was thankful, for I'd had enough of bloodshed and would not see more could I avoid it.

So . . .

We quit the islands of Ahn-feshang in hope, winging back to Dharbek with promises. Though our own were paramount: that there should be no more war, but only our demands met. All of these forced true by the dragons, lest we bring them again against those who'd oppose we newcome Dragonmasters.

None argued with us.

How could they?

We owned the skies: neither Dhar magic nor Ahn's could defeat us. We could rend the Sky Lords' boats from the air and loose their enslaved elementals. We could tear apart the Sentinels and, after, ravage every city and keep in Dharbek: we dictated our terms.

Was I corrupted by power? Were we all?

I think Rwyan was not. I think she only pursued our dream in honest belief. I think that Urt was not, for he'd only see a better world made for his Changed kind. Tezdal was not, I am sure.

Bellek?

Perhaps he was. Or gone so long into Dragonmastery that he no longer cared. Nor any longer saw the world through human eyes, but only from that different view. It no longer matters, nor did much then, for we were only bent on the achievement of our goal and had no time for fine philosophical musings. Those should come later, when the Great Peace was secured.

For now, we'd much to do. As I'd feared, there were some few amongst the aeldors of Dharbek and the Kho'rabi of Ahn-feshang who would not accept, and we brought the dragons against them. I had hoped the bloodshed ended with our coming, but we spilled more as we destroyed those rebels. And when that last fighting was done, we must travel the land awhile in reminder, so that any who still harbored notions of conquest or vengeance might look to the skies and know their thoughts were better left unspoken.

We were the watchmen of the skies, and ambassadors betwixt the three lands. We even carried Taerl to Ur-Dharbek and to Ahn-feshang. The Lord Protector was besotted with the dragons as I'd once heard he loved horses. I think that had he not that greater duty, he'd have asked us to take him with us and he endeavor to become a Dragonmaster, but he must satisfy himself with those rides we allowed. How young he looked as he climbed astride Deburah, his face all lit with wonder as she spread her wings and launched herself into the heavens! He had no fear at all but whooped with glee as we flew.

Certainly it impressed the Khe'anjiwha that the Lord Protector of Dharbek should come to him and promise him a welcome in Kellambek. They got on well together, those two; like warriors met in the aftermath of battle, respectful of one another. Or like two young men lonely in their power, each finding in the other an equal with whom he might share a little of that solitude. It did our cause no little good that they were able to meet as friends.

In Ur-Dharbek, too, Taerl acquitted himself admirably. He met with the new-formed Raethe, and they spoke lengthily together, and I began to hope that we should not much longer need to patrol the skies but leave the world to run itself again. Though that should not be quite yet, for our plan was grand whilst the arguments and envies and rivalries of men are mostly petty and require much debating ere agreement is reached. We'd brought the world to peace and held it there, but it were better we leave the folk who should live in it after us to settle their differences than entirely force them to our will.

"Let them firm out the details of it," Rwyan said, "so that they can, after, believe it was as much their doing as ours and not resent what we impose."

That was wisdom, and it largely worked, and I felt happy. Rwyan, too; and Urt. Tezdal and Bellek, however, became increasingly withdrawn, as if they felt their roles in this drama were played out and would exeunt, like mummers whose parts are ended.

In those busy months I was too occupied with all those affairs of state to notice much how reserved they grew. Or when I did, to speak with them as I should have done: another charge laid against me.

Also, as that first year of peace aged to a second, I felt the growing *difference* in me. I must more and more force myself to patience as I sat with Taerl and the Khe'anjiwha, with the Changed Councilfolk, the priests of the Attul-ki and those of my own land. I found it ever harder to spend—*to waste!*—so much time on the ground but would mount Deburah and taste the heady joy of dragonflight again. I realized I missed those fierce mountains that bordered Tartarus as I'd not missed any place before, not even my home. And with that realization came the knowledge that I had no longer any home but that Dragoncastle; that I'd return there—where Deburah's egg lay. And even did she tell me it was safe and I'd no need for concern, still I'd know for myself. Touch it and be sure: I felt it was as much mine as hers or the bull's that seeded her.

The bonding of Dragonmaster and dragon is a powerful thing, seductive. It gets inside your blood and holds you firmer than any chains men have ever forged.

I knew that, or sensed it, and consequently should have known better what Bellek felt and likely might do.

I remember walking with Rwyan, that second year, in those fabulous gardens of Trebizar. The Council building lay in ruins behind us, and Taerl was with Urt and Tezdal in the town, deep in discussion with the Changed and those Kho'rabi stranded in Ur-Dharbek by our destruction of their skyboats. It was Taerl's intention (and his idea, not ours) to offer them ships, that they might go south to Kellambek or home across the ocean. Bellek had taken the dragons off hunting. It was a hot summer's day, and it was a comforting feeling to know that ordinary summer now held sway in Dharbek and that the magic of the Attul-ki should no longer stifle the land. I heard birds singing. Rwyan leaned close against me. The sun was warm on our faces, and she'd tied a scarf about her hair, so that she minded me of a beautiful fisherwoman.

I thought on how different this place now seemed and how it was no longer tainted with Allanyn's crystal-born madness. I asked, "Should we hunt out the crystals? Destroy them all?"

Rwyan laughed and shook her head, which sent tendrils of sun-bleached red against my face because I was trying to kiss her neck as she spoke. I sneezed. Her hair had tickled my nostrils, and the air was heavy with pollen.

She said, "I doubt we could. The crystals are part of this land, like those fire mountains of Ahn-feshang. Could we stopper them? And if we did, what should it do to those islands?"

I frowned. I thought such a task impossible; and that were it possible, it should seal up that molten breath like a brewer bunging his casks too early—to see them explode as the sealed-in fermentation grew too powerful for its confines. I thought those islands must explode: I said as much.

And Rwyan nodded and said, "No more can we destroy the crystals. Would you tear up all Tartarus, all of Ur-Dharbek, to find them?"

I said, "But might it happen again—that seduction—should we not seek to find them and destroy them?"

Rwyan said, "Can you halt hate, Daviot? Can you excise envy from men's minds? Can you end greed?"

I said, "No."

She said, "No more, nor better, can you find all the crystals. Nor perhaps should you. We've done what we've done. By the God, we've ended a war that not even you, Mnemonikos, can trace down all its years. Is that not enough? I think we've done our part, only to bring that about."

I said, "But the crystals—"

And was silenced by her finger on my lips. She said, "Are power. Lessened somewhat, now; and perhaps a lesson learned. We've taught the world a different way; let those who come after us learn to use the crystals better. But let them make their own decisions!"

I said, "But we decided. We found our power and forced our will on the world. And spilled blood in the forcing."

She said, "Because we followed that dream. We only chased what we thought right. Perhaps, after we are gone, there shall be others with a different dream; and they'll pursue it no less fierce than we."

I said, "But is that right?"

And Rwyan smiled and turned her face to me, so that I was met by her blind gaze; and then she took my face in her hands. "I think it so. I've done what I've done because I saw no other way, and I do not feel guilty. I regret the blood we shed, aye. But—do I remember this aright?—'you cannot cook a fish without gutting it first, lest after you fall sick.' That's what we've done, Daviot: we've gutted the world's fish and presented it for the eating. Would you have it otherwise?"

I looked at her and shook my head: "No."

She said, "Good," and kissed me again, harder.

We were walking hand in hand when the dragons came, like thunder out of the northern sky.

We both stopped silent in our tracks, a tocsin ringing loud in our souls. My grip on Rwyan's hand tightened, and hers no less on mine. We turned to the north and saw them coming fast and low from the hills. I felt a fear of what message they brought.

And then it was delivered.

Deburah and Anryäle landed before us in a great skirling of dust from the sun-dried ground. Kathanria winged restless overhead. I felt their emotions, but they were so flustered I could not immediately comprehend what they told us: only that they were mightily disturbed and brought bad news. I felt a leaden weight descend on my soul and was utterly confused.

Rwyan interpreted better. She went to Anryäle and stroked the mottled cheeks of her dragon. I felt Deburah nudge me, and staggered, and turned to find her lustrous eyes fixed hard on mine. I swear, could dragons cry, she'd have been weeping then.

I said, "What's amiss?"

And Rwyan answered me, "Bellek! He's gone."

I said, "What? How mean you, gone? Gone where? Lost?"

Rwyan and Deburah both answered me, and from above, Kathanria: *No, not lost. Gone: dead.*

I was astride Deburah's saddle before I knew it: sometimes action runs faster than thought. Rwyan was not much slower, and we climbed into the sky as if the hounds of all the gods I could not believe in were snapping at our heels.

We winged furiously north. To where Bellek had taken the dragons to hunt. And then farther north still, over those southern foothills of the Dragonsteeth Mountains to the Dragoncastle.

The ramparts were filled with dragons. I think all the broods were there, and all filling the sky with their belling. My head rang with it. It echoed off the mountain walls and drove me to cover my ears for the promise it sounded. It was a sad sound, and as Deburah landed in the yard, I felt a new weight of dread fill my soul.

Her emotions were a turmoil I could not properly understand: only that Bellek was dead.

He had told us nothing of that valley. Perhaps because he knew he would go there, once he was confident his dragons had new masters, and was, perhaps, afraid that it should deter us from that inheritance. I think it would not have: I think that bonding is too strong.

It was high amongst the peaks to the north and west, where crags fell down in jagged lines like dragons' fangs on a line that let in the morning sun and saw its eventide setting. No trees grew there, nor any water ran, and the topmost hills were yet blanched with snow. It was a still place, the only sound the keening of the wind. It was filled with bones, more bones than I'd ever seen, all white and stark, no flesh on them. Or not on most of them: amongst the tangles of ribs and wingbones and skulls lay a little fragment that wore Bellek's gear.

I saw that clear as we landed, because Deburah showed it me and I felt her grief.

I sat her back—this was so precipitous a place, I had no hope of climbing down there, and I knew she'd not descend. At least, not until it was her time; and that I'd no sooner think on than Rwyan's demise. This was the last resting place of all the world's dragons, and none felt happy to be here before their time. So I sat astride my saddle and heard all the dragons bell their mourning at the falling sun and, when they were done, asked Deburah what had happened.

She told me: *We came north to hunt. Bellek was on Kathanria, but he sent us off alone after we came here. He told us he'd spend a while with Aiylra, in remembrance. We hunted. Then we felt him die and came here, and he was gone.*

I told her: *He wanted it so. He chose his way.*

And then, because I felt her fear, that I'd never thought to feel from any dragon: *He left us behind. We'll not forsake you.*

Her pleasure overcame remorse at Bellek's chosen death. I looked down at the broken pieces of that strange man and surmised he'd flung himself off the heights to join his lost Aiylra in the bones below.

I think he's happy now, I told my Deburah.

And she asked me: *And you'll not leave?*

Aloud, I said, "No!" And heard my exclamation echoed by Rwyan.

I felt the happiness of the dragons then, and it filled me, replacing what sadness I felt for Bellek. Which, am I honest, was not much: I thought he'd lived out his span and picked his end, and that I should deny no man.

That second year became a third, and the world's ways shifted. The Changed of Dharbek were proclaimed free citizens. Those Attul-ki not slain by the dragons reversed their magic, so that Dharbek blossomed. Under escort of our dragons, skyboats crossed the Fend for the first time in peace, to deliver Ahn back to the shores of Kellambek. Those Changed who would cross the Slammerkin went over free, knowing they might return if they would. The Khe'anjiwha ceded lands in Ahn-feshang to those few (very few!) brave Dhar or Changed who'd find a new country.

Of course there were disputes, but when the sorcerers sent word, we came with our dragons, and none would argue with them.

We saw the Changed freed and Ahn find homes in Kellambek. Taerl presided over a Council similar to that governing Ur-Dharbek. In Ahn-feshang the Khe'anjiwha and the Attul-ki now held less power and spoke with the Dhar about the future, as if that were now a thing shared between equals. Our world seemed set fair on the course we'd given it.

And we Dragonmasters hungered for our castle and the high, wild mountains of Tartarus. Our dragons were bored; sated with battles and eager to go home.

I shared that feeling. I could no longer deny it: Dharbek was no longer my home, but only those tall mountains where the dragons lived, and I (was I cursed by Bellek? Were we all?) felt at ease.

I spoke of it with Rwyan, and she agreed; and so we went back.

Tezdal and Urt came with us. They felt the call no less than we, and like us felt separated from the worlds of men now. Urt had been offered a seat in the Raethe; begged to take it when he refused, and still refused.

"It would not feel right," he told me one bright and windy autumn day as we walked the ramparts and watched the wind chase clouds across the sky. "I am a Dragonmaster now, and did I sit in Council and argue and folk agree with me, how should I know them honest and not merely afraid of Kathanria?"

I nodded. I'd the same feeling and had given Taerl similar answer when he asked much the same of me.

"Nor," Urt went on, "are my people even now entirely at ease with dragons."

"Blood's memory dies hard," I said.

"And so they are neither at ease with me," he murmured. Then laughed, "Nor I with them. I am different, Daviot."

I said, "We all of us are. This is our home now, I think."

"Yes." He crossed to a crenellation, leaning out to stare down the vertiginous mountainside into the valley. The Changed village was a cluster of minuscule buildings, like tiny pebbles dropped beside the slender thread of the river. It had grown now, as more of Urt's people ventured north—those whose blood did not hold such innate fear of the dragons. Absently, he said, "We should hunt soon and lay them up meat for the winter. Also, their ale is near ready for drinking."

I moved to join him, setting a hand companionable on his shoulder as I leaned past him. "And Lysra should have that blanket finished, eh?" I murmured.

For all they are long distanced from their animal progenitors, still the Changed own some of their ancestors' characteristics. They do not blush, for instance; but did they, I think Urt should have then. Lysra was the daughter of Prym and Valla, who supplied our ale. South of our mountains she'd have been married, for she was a comely woman. But there were not so many men here, and she had so far rejected those suitors who contested her hand. For Urt, however, she found only smiles and on learning of our return had set to weaving such a blanket as decorates a marriage bed. It was a hint he could hardly ignore. Also, it was obvious to all of us save Urt that she loved him.

He said, "She is very beautiful, no?"

I said, "Yes, she is lovely."

He said, "Do you think I should . . ."

I waited, but he was suddenly embarrassed, so that I could only laugh and slap his shoulder and tell him, "I think you should. She waits for you, and it should be good company for Rwyan to have another woman about this place."

He nodded solemnly, his eyes fixed firm on the village. "I shall," he said. "Tomorrow I shall go down there and ask her."

"She'll tell you yes," I said. "And when you've set the date, I'll go south to beg some good Kellambek wine off Taerl, that we may celebrate in suitable manner. Doubtless he'll want to attend the feasting. Or even volunteer you his palace for the ceremony. Likely he'll invite the Khe'anjiwha, and all the—"

"Enough!" Urt stepped back, his face so paled I began to chuckle. "It shall be no more than the village and we Dragonmasters. No pomp, Daviot, I beg you."

I forced my face to gravity. "The Lord Protector will likely be most disappointed. Insulted, even."

Urt frowned. "Well, perhaps Taerl might attend."

"And the Raethe," I said. "It should not be diplomatic to leave them out."

Urt's frown grew deeper. "Think you so?" he asked.

I nodded, stifling laughter. "Nor—does he wish it—the Khe'anjiwha. Or, of course, the Church. And the Mnemonikos. And the—"

Urt's fist caught me lightly on the ear, and I could no longer stifle my mirth. I said, "It shall be no more, nor any less, than you wish, my friend."

"Simple, then," he said, his relief expressed in a broad smile. "I've enough of pomp and ceremony to last me all my days."

I said, "May they be long and happy. Now—do we go break this momentous news to Rwyan and Tezdal? And begin our celebrating?"

"Modestly," he said. "I've not your Storyman's capacity for drink, and I'd not go to Lysra in my cups."

"Modestly then," I agreed. "But go to her I think you should. Else I've a feeling that when that blanket's done, she'll climb the mountain to deliver it."

Laughing together, we went inside.

But Tezdal . . . he'd lost more than any of us. What had we lost that was not outweighed by what we gained? I'd my two loves and the dream I'd so long ago shared with Rwyan come true. She'd Anryäle and me and the satisfaction of a world at peace. Urt had Lysra, and Kathanria. But Tezdal—he'd only Peliane and cold, old wounds that poisoned from within. His wife was dead, and his parents, and for those deaths he held himself accountable. In the eyes of his people he was still gijan—outcast. None of us could properly understand that, or the dreadful burden it laid on his soul.

I tried. I swear I did my best, but it was a thing beyond my comprehension. I remember the day we spoke of it.

It was a wild windswept day, when stormclouds built above the eastern peaks and threatened snow, the sky sullen as a poisoned wound overhead. There was cloud in the valley below thick enough that the village was hidden and the dragons had retreated to their caverns. Deburah's egg was not far off hatching. Urt was wed. (Taerl *did* attend, but—somewhat to the alarm of the new-formed conclave of advisers—alone. Indeed, had he not taken Urt's hands and begged to be a guest, he'd not have come. But the Lord Protector snatched at every chance he could grasp to ride adragonback, and his entreaties were so fervent, Urt could only smile and laugh and agree. And thanks to Taerl we'd barrels of fine wine and sweetmeats, and the new-wed couple such marriage gifts as should make an aeldor blush for envy.) Ayl and Lan and a few others had been granted (reluctantly on Urt's part, but Lysra was delighted) permission to attend and overcame their terror to ride the skies. We had celebrated the wedding, and Lysra moved into the Dragoncastle. We had returned Taerl to his duties and settled back to our own. They were not so many now.

Throughout the celebrations Tezdal had smiled and laughed and drunk his fill or more. I had sensed a desperation behind his revelry: he was by nature a sober man and lately had been taciturn, even solitary. So when all was quiet again and I noticed him donning a fur-lined cloak, I took my own and followed him. Much as I'd once followed Bellek.

He climbed to the highest reaches of the Dragoncastle, where the ramparts stood tall and the view ran out all around as if it should never end. The wind battered my face as I joined him, and I wished I'd thought to don gloves. He stood looking to the east. He doubtless heard my approach—I think that brave Kho'rabi did not miss such things—but he did not turn until I touched his shoulder. Then, I could not be sure whether it was the wind or grief that watered his eyes.

I said, "Shall you tell me?"

I saw his lips curve in a smile, but it held no humor.

"Tell you what?" he asked.

I must bend closer to catch the words, lest the wind carry them away. I said, "What ails you, friend."

"What ails me?" His smile was rictal. "Life ails me, Daviot. I'd give it up."

I set my hand firmer on his shoulder, for fear he might fling himself away into the emptiness beneath us. I said, "Is it so hard?"

He turned his face away a moment. When he looked at me again, his eyes burned. "I am gijan. You cannot know what that means."

I shook my head. I moved to embrace him, but he waved me off, and I could only stand and hear him out. We must both shout over the wailing of the wind.

He said, "I have no name."

I said, "You are Tezdal Kashijan. You are a Dragonmaster; and my true friend."

He said, "I am a Dragonmaster, yes. You call me Tezdal, but I no longer own that name. I am gijan. I have no right to friendship."

I opened my mouth to speak, but he put his hand there, silencing me. "Only listen, eh?"

I nodded, and he unclamped his fingers.

He said, "You will not understand this: you cannot. You are Dhar, and though we are friends, we are still different. Different as we Dragonmasters are become to—" He waved a desperate hand, encompassing all the land below us, all the world around. "I was born and raised Kho'rabi. I took vows—you know this. And that I betrayed those vows."

I said, ignoring his plea for silence, "In service of another. In service of this peace we've won."

I wondered then how any man could smile so; or how a voice be so bereft of life.

"Yes. Is it not strange? As if the Three use me for their dice. But heed me, Daviot. I was born Kho'rabi—Dedicated—and all my life lived to that end."

I think I sensed then where this conversation led, and again I ignored his imperative to say, "And have you not achieved that end? The Ahn come back to Kellambek now; and that was your doing, as much as mine or Rwyan's."

Perhaps I should not have spoken her name. Certainly I saw pain flood his face at the mention.

He said, "Retze slew herself for my disgrace; and then my parents. Now I am gijan—the clan Kashijan exists no longer because of me." He saw my incomprehension and barked his awful laugh again. "No," he said, and I heard the terrible weariness in his voice. "You do not understand. How should you? Only we Ahn understand that. Listen! I offer you a choice—Rwyan or Deburah. One you must forgo. Which?"

I said, "I'd not make that choice. I do not think I could."

He said, "I did."

I saw the direction he took and gave him back, "But you'd lost your memory. You were dying; Rwyan saved you."

He said, "And then I got back my memory and knew who I was and what I had been."

I said, "I saw Sky Lords speak with Changed and said nothing of it. I learned the Changed communicated. I think I guessed they planned rebellion, but I said nothing. Are you steeped deeper in guilt than I?"

He said, "Are your parents alive? Is Rwyan dead?"

I had no answer for that.

He said, "It is different for me, Daviot. I knew what I was when I came to that grove in Trebizar and slew Allanyn's people. I knew I betrayed my own people when I brought you horses and set you free. When I came with you."

I said—*No!* I shrieked—"Because you'd given your word to Rwyan! Because you are an honorable man."

"Yes." He ducked his head. "And now my honor shows me only one way to efface my shame."

I said, "You've no shame, Tezdal."

He said, "Were I Dhar or Changed, likely I'd agree. *But I am not!* I was Kho'rabi, and now I am gijan. All those I loved are dead because of what I did. The clan Kashijan is disbanded for what I did."

I said, helplessly now, "You forged peace. You gave your people back their homeland."

I watched his lips stretch over his teeth. Inside his cloak he shrugged. "Perhaps for that the Three will forgive me. But I cannot."

I said, "What of the future? What of us?"

He said, "I think the future's settled now. And you?" He turned away, resting his hands on the battlements, his head lowered. "Urt's his Lysra now; and you, Rwyan. Are you not happy?"

I said, "Yes. Save you—Tezdal!" I hunted, desperate, for such words as might dissuade him from the course I knew he took. "Might you not find another wife?"

He shook his head. He said, "In all my life I've loved only two women. One was Retze; the other is . . . not mine to have."

I should have known it!

But I had not, and so I said, lowly, "Rwyan?"

His laughter disputed the wind's howling. "Could you not see it?" he asked.

I shook my head.

"She does," he said. "She knows it and loves you. And she'll not leave you."

I had no words for this. Only a numbing dread of what might follow. I had been as blind as any man in love; and as much stupid.

"So." Tezdal turned from his contemplation of the ramparts' stone to face me. "Shall we fight for her? Shall you slay me, or I slay you? Might that secure me her love?"

I said, "Tezdal, I'd not fight you."

He said, "Nor I you. Nor should it win me more than her hate. So . . ."

I said, "What of Peliane?"

He said, "Dragons live after their masters. How else are we here? Bellek's gone, no? She'll mourn me awhile, but she's you and Rwyan and Urt now. And likely there shall be other Dragonmasters found ere long, now that we've forged our Great Peace. Do I betray her, Daviot? If so, then it's only one more betrayal to my account. *And I cannot live longer with this pain!* I tell you true—I cannot."

He shed his cloak then, and I saw what he wore beneath: the blades of a Kho'rabi knight. The kachen and the dagger, and I knew with a ghastly surety what he intended and what he'd ask of me. I staggered back, shaking my head.

He said, "I'd take the Way of Honor, Daviot. Even though I am gijan and so undeserving. Did you know the Khe'anjiwha favored me? Gijan—we few!—are usually crucified. Upside down, Daviot. Had you not needed me to interpret, I'd long ago have hung head down on a tree, with all who passed spitting on my face. Or worse. Listen to me!" This because I backed away, and shook my head, and pushed out my hands to reject the duty he gave me. "Listen to me! I shall die. Like Bellek, do you not prove your friendship. But I should sooner do this with what honor's left me. As if I were still Kho'rabi. Perhaps that shall placate the Three, and they grant my soul peace."

"*No!*"

I did not recognize my own voice. It sounded like the wind's wailing. It sounded like the mourning of the dragons. I did not know it came out from between my lips. Inside my head I felt the dragons stir; and Rwyan and Urt.

I staggered back until cold stone denied me further retreat. But Tezdal advanced still, and still his hands held out the burden of friendship's duty.

He said, "As you love me, friend."

His eyes allowed no other choice: I took the blade and asked him, "What must I do?"

He said, "This should be done with Attul-ki attending. Or at least Kho'rabi knights. But . . . you wait until I've opened the Way, and then use the sword on my neck."

I said, "Is there truly no other way?"

And he shook his head. "No. Neither would I ask this of any other. Only of my truest friend."

He clasped my hand, and there was such longing in his eyes, I could only nod through my tears and slide the sword from its sheath as he knelt and loosed the fastenings of his tunic and shirt and slipped the garments off, so that his torso was bared to the wind and the cold. And his neck to the sword I held. It shone in the failing light. It rested heavy in my hands: heavy as the weight on my soul.

I said, "I am not sure I can do this, Tezdal."

He said, "As you love me, you can."

And then, before I might argue further or throw down the sword and run away, he drew his dagger and sank the blade deep into his belly. He made no sound as he cut, but I saw the agony on his face as his lips contorted in denial of the pain. And in his eyes a terrible relief as he found his Way of Honor.

So I did what he asked of me. I raised his sword and brought it down against his neck. I'd never held so fine a blade before, nor one so sharp: it took off his head in one clean cut.

I fell to my knees, weeping as his skull went bouncing over the bloodstained flags.

I knew only pain until I felt hands touch my face and looked up into Rwyan's blind eyes. I saw grief there, and then more on Urt's face, and Lysra's. And then I was aware of dragons perched all around. I could not speak; only clutch at Rwyan's knees and weep.

She asked me, "Did he demand this of you?"

I nodded against her gown, and she knelt beside me and put her arms about me and held me close and said, "Oh, Daviot! My poor, poor Daviot. How he must have trusted you."

I said, "That I'd slay him?"

She said, "That he trusted you with his honor. That he'd have you perform this awful service."

I said, "I killed him, Rwyan."

She said, "He slew himself, my love. Because it was the only way for him. What you did was friendship's duty, and I think there's likely no greater love than that."

We wrapped Tezdal in his cloak, and Urt brought a canvas that we might sew the sundered parts safe together, and we saddled our dragons and fastened Tezdal's body to Peliane, and flew to the valley of the dead, and spilled him down there. Down where Bellek and all the other Dragonmasters lay, and all the centuries-long-dead dragons.

Ours keened their mourning, and Peliane's was loudest of all. I felt that like a knife in my heart, sharp as that swift blade Tezdal had sunk into his belly. I think it hurt me not much worse than what he'd had me do or what I felt for his loss. I had lost a beloved friend: she had lost her bond-mate. I could, in a way, comprehend why he chose that course: she could not. For nine days she battered the Dragoncastle with her keening, and I believe she might have flown out looking herself to die had Deburah's egg not hatched.

Death and life run in cycles, no? One dies, one is born: life continues, and pain abates. Mine did, albeit slower than Peliane's. She found a new reason to live.

Dragons are proud and magnificent and, in their own way, loving, but they do not love as Truemen or Changed. An egg is a triumph for all the brood, and its tending shared between them all. Sometimes the mother will have nothing to do with the hatchling—it is the laying that's important—and so Deburah was perfectly content to leave the tending of the bull she bore to Peliane. She was proud, yes; and so was I, for I could not help but feel that the mewling babe that cracked his shell with such force, it shattered all at once and he came out screaming to be fed, was mine as much as hers or the bull's that had seeded her. But she let Peliane attend the infant, and even I, when I went to stroke his glossy blue head and admire his needle-sharp baby's teeth (carefully, for young dragons are not overly particular whom they bite), must first pass Peliane's inspection. And admire his growing wings under her watchful eyes, and not come close until she allowed.

Thus was Peliane saved from her grief.

And Rwyan saved me from mine in long conversations that at last convinced me I'd not done wrong but only service to a friend who'd have it no other way.

I accepted that, but I tell you—I still cannot properly understand that code by which the Kho'rabi lived, nor much respect so harsh a servitude. I accept that it was Tezdal's way and that I did no less than duty by him, but I was forced to that just as he was forced to our duty by that vow he gave to Rwyan. And I still wonder if we were, any of us, right.

Coda

We had none of us fully realized the weight of time that burdened Bellek. I had suspected it, but that was only guessing, for he'd never set it out clear. I am convinced he meant it so, in care of his charges, and for fear we should reject that inheritance, did we see it in all its long entirety.

Dragons live longer than men: ages longer. And Dragonmasters share that longevity. Even now, as newcome masters find their bonding and the halls of the Dragoncastle fill up again with life, we do not understand it: only that it is, and that it is a choice a Dragonmaster must make. We did not, not truly, but I think that we'd still have chosen that road had Bellek pointed us toward its invisible, timeless ending. Could we have denied that love?

I've told them, the newcome Dragonmasters, and they accept it. Taerl's son chose it; and the daughter of Ahn-feshang's last Khe'anjiwha chose it. Cleton's grandson came north when he had the dream and shrugged acceptance when I warned him. The dreams of dragons are hard to deny. They choose it, and laugh when I warn them of the years, and tell me they can bear the weight.

I think they will: the world is changed now, and they no longer fear the dragons; not even the Changed, whose children come to laugh and sport amongst the claws and take their knocks with the hatchlings.

The love of dragons is a heady seduction.

I think it is a better world now.

I hope it is, for otherwise my life was all wasted.

But I cannot believe that so, even as I think on the blood that paints my hands. Were it so, then Rwyan was wrong, and that I'll not believe.

No!

But I ramble somewhat. So:

We set Tezdal to rest in the valley of bones and mourned him. Peliane tended Deburah's hatchling—and now Kaja is the mightiest bull in all the Dragoncastles, a splendid creature, and a seeder of numerous dams. There are more dragons now; it is as if a balance were restored.

Urt and Lysra bred seven children, all of them hale and decent as their parents. Two chose to go south and found places in the Raethe of Ur-Dharbek. The others remained here, and their descendants tend me now with a respect I find ofttimes embarrassing. One is a Dragonmaster.

My Changed comrade is dead, and I shall talk of that no more than I'll speak of Rwyan's passing. That's too much pain to set in words. I outlived them all, and I wish I'd not. I'd sooner have gone with them.

But . . .

. . . It was not unhappy. We all of us lived long past our natural span, and I was happy with Rwyan.

I was happy as I'd not believed could be possible.

Good years, those; all of them. A gift, I suppose, for we had more time than ordinary folk are granted to be together. But still, in time she died, and some time after Anryäle followed her. Kathanria is dead, but Peliane lives on, and Deburah, though both are old now and fly less often. I've lived on because Rwyan set that duty on me, no less than Tezdal bound me to his strange honor, and I'd not betray my loved ones again.

We changed our world, but we could not change the accretion of the years, when bones grow brittle and blood flows slower down the veins. I think that perhaps that's the only god: time. The ager who takes us all.

But I had long years with the woman I loved, and did we have no children, still there are Urt's offspring; and I've known friends and rode the skies on dragon's back, and known the love of dragons.

And that is something of a life, no?

I'll not complain.

I'll accept my guilt and let the Pale Friend take me and judge me. And do I face the One God or the Three, then I shall tell them that what I did was done in honest belief of trust and friendship and the chasing of a dream. And if they should tell me that it was a dream I sowed in Rwyan's soul and she was wrong, then I shall spit in their faces and deny them. For I'll not deny her; ever!

And I think that Deburah would join me then, and Anryäle, and all the others. And must it be so, then we'll deny the gods as we denied the men who'd know only strife, and fly against them as we flew against the Sky Lords and the ignorance of Truemen.

But that is yet to come.

First, I must meet with the Pale Friend.

Does she permit it, I'll saddle Deburah one last time and fly her to that valley where the bones are, and does the Pale Friend meet me there, I'll take her hand and go with her. That shall be a great journey, no?

An Acknowledgment

Lords of the Sky is not entirely my own work.

Originally, the book was a lot more words (wordier?), but my editor got to work and suggested where I might cut the manuscript, to tighten it up and keep the narrative flowing without excess verbiage. No less, she pointed out where the psychology of my characters went astray and how to bring them back in line. I believe she made the book better, and for that I owe her.

So—thank you, Janna E. Silverstein; long may you edit.

Angus Wells
Nottingham, 1993.